GW00645303

Fortune's Lament

A NOVEL

Book Three of the Anthems of al-Andalus Series

JOHN D. CRESSLER

MILFORD HOUSE

an imprint of Sunbury Press, Inc.
Mechanicsburg, PA USA

MILFORD HOUSE

an imprint of Sunbury Press, Inc.
Mechanicsburg, PA USA

NOTE: This is a work of fiction. Names, characters, places and incidents are the product of the author's imagination or are used fictitiously, and any resemblance to actual persons, living or dead, business establishments, events or locales is entirely coincidental.

Copyright © 2018 by John D. Cressler.
Cover copyright © 2018 by Sunbury Press.

Sunbury Press supports copyright. Copyright fuels creativity, encourages diverse voices, promotes free speech, and creates a vibrant culture. Thank you for buying an authorized edition of this book and for complying with copyright laws by not reproducing, scanning, or distributing any part of it in any form without permission. You are supporting writers and allowing Sunbury Press to continue to publish books for every reader. For information contact Sunbury Press, Inc., Subsidiary Rights Dept., 50-A W. Main St., Mechanicsburg, PA 17011 USA or legal@sunburypress.com.

For information about special discounts for bulk purchases, please contact Sunbury Press Orders Dept. at (855) 338-8359 or orders@sunburypress.com.

To request one of our authors for speaking engagements or book signings, please contact Sunbury Press Publicity Dept. at publicity@sunburypress.com.

ISBN: 978-1-62006-372-9 (Trade Paperback)

SECOND MILFORD HOUSE PRESS EDITION: June 2018

Product of the United States of America
0 1 1 2 3 5 8 13 21 34 55

Set in Bookman Old Style
Designed by Crystal Devine
Cover by Lawrence Knorr
Edited by Jennifer Cappello

Continue the Enlightenment!

Books by John D. Cressler

Historical Fiction

Anthems of al-Andalus Series

Emeralds of the Alhambra

Shadows in the Shining City

Fortune's Lament

Non-fiction: General Audience

Reinventing Teenagers:
The Gentle Art of Instilling Character in Our Young People

Silicon Earth:
Introduction to the Microelectronics and Nanotechnology Revolution

Silicon Earth:
Introduction to Microelectronics and Nanotechnology – 2nd Edition

Non-fiction: Technical

Silicon-Germanium Heterojunction
Bipolar Transistors

Silicon Heterostructure Handbook:
Materials, Fabrication, Devices, Circuits and Applications of SiGe and Si
Strained-Layer Epitaxy

Extreme Environment Electronics

For more information on any of these books, please visit:
http://johndcressler.com

Anthems of al-Andalus Series
Historical Novels Set in Medieval Muslim Spain

Emeralds of the Alhambra (2013)

Emeralds of the Alhambra is a love story set in the resplendent Alhambra Palace in Granada, Spain, during the Castilian Civil War (1367-1369 C.E.), a time when Muslims took up their swords to fight alongside Christians. *Emeralds* tells the story of William Chandon, a Christian knight captured and brought to the Alhambra to be used by the Muslim sultan as a political pawn, and the Sufi Muslim princess Layla al-Khatib, daughter of the sultan's chief counsellor. As Chandon's influence at court grows, he becomes trapped between his forbidden love for Layla and his Christian heritage, the demands of chivalry and political expediency. Chandon and Layla must make choices between love and honor, war and peace, life and death, choices which ultimately will seal Granada's fate as the last surviving stronghold of Islamic Spain.

Shadows in the Shining City (2014)

The Golden Age of Islamic Spain was during the tenth century, a time when the benevolent Muslim caliphs ruled Iberia from Córdoba, the site of the iconic Great Mosque of Córdoba and home to the Royal Library, one of the largest collections of ancient books ever assembled. Tenth-century Córdoba was the richest, most populous, and most cultured city in the western world. Under the tolerant Muslim caliphs, the pinnacle of *convivencia* was attained, that unique period of Spanish history when Muslims, Jews and Christians lived together in relative harmony and peace. Multicultural Córdoba was an enlightened city that treasured its books, celebrated art and literature, advanced science and medicine, and its myriad accomplishments were envied by both the west and the east alike.

Shadows in the Shining City is a prequel to *Emeralds of the Alhambra*, and immerses the reader in Islamic Spain's Golden Age. *Shadows* tells the story of the forbidden love between Rayhana Abi Amir, a Muslim princess of the royal court, and Zafir Saffar, a freed slave. Young love blossoms in 975 C.E. in Madinat al-Zahra, the Shining City, Caliph al-Hakam II's magnificent royal palace located just outside of Córdoba. Their love story is set against the backdrop of the epic rise to power of Rayhana's ruthless father, Ibn Abi Amir, a man history will come to both celebrate and revile for the role he plays in the collapse of Islamic Spain.

A Note on Reading Order for My Novels:

As might be expected since these novels are part of a series, there are important connections between events and principal characters in all of the books contained in the Anthems of al-Andalus Series. That said, each novel is designed to be read by itself, independent of the others. The books are not written in chronological order, focusing instead on seminal events during the 800-year history of Muslim Spain. *Emeralds* is set in Granada in 1367 C.E., during the pivotal Castilian Civil War. *Shadows,* a prequel to *Emeralds*, is set in Córdoba in 975 C.E., at the height of the Golden Age of the Umayyad Caliphate. *Fortune's Lament* is set in Granada in 1488 C.E., at the beginning of King Ferdinand and Queen Isabella's final conquest of the Kingdom of Granada, an event that will mark the end of Muslim Spain.

Emeralds and *Fortune's Lament* are fairly closely coupled (e.g., Layla appears in both books, and what happens to her after *Emeralds* is told in *Fortune's Lament*). *Shadows* and *Emeralds* are only weakly coupled, which is logical, given the much longer time lapse between them. (But you *do* learn how the al-Khatib family comes to Granada, and where my emerald eyes come from!)

Interested readers thus have two viable reading options: 1) read the books in the order they were written—*Emeralds* first, then *Shadows*, and then *Fortune's Lament*; or 2) read the books chronologically—*Shadows* first, then *Emeralds*, then *Fortune's Lament*. Either path is just fine, though you will likely (hopefully!) notice a maturation in my writing chops with each successive novel. Want to start the series with *Fortune's Lament*? No worries. Go for it!

There will be (at least) a fourth novel in the series, a sequel to *Fortune's Lament*. Stay tuned!

Praise for John D. Cressler's
Fortune's Lament

"In his latest spellbinding volume, *Fortune's Lament*, Cressler throws us into the cacophony of the decline of Islamic Spain and the conquest of Granada. His compelling descriptions of horrendous religious battles between the Moors and Christians, often orchestrated by strong and cunning women, are startling. The familiar explorer, Columbus, is seen in a different context as he campaigns for the queen's favors. Fearless warriors, quick to fight to the death on a bloody battlefield, were often not willing to fight off the field for love. Cressler's tender, almost reluctant, portrayal of Yusuf and Danah's 'Great Love' was authentic, poignant and mystical. I was fortunate enough to experience my own 'Great Love' in this lifetime and yes, it transcends even (his) death."
—*Valerie Jackson, "In Conversation," NPR's WABE, Atlanta*

"*Fortune's Lament* is an enthralling tale from start to finish. In this third book in the Anthems of al-Andalus Series, Cressler has truly hit a stride with his narrative craft. Like *Emeralds* and *Shadows*, *Fortune's Lament* is richly layered with political, architectural and military detail, and presents a textured portrayal of the messy and stubborn yet ubiquitous combination of religious ideology and political power that has made and broken many an empire. Wrapped up in yet another deliciously satisfying love story, *Fortune's Lament* provides readers with an intimate view of the complex geo-political panorama surrounding the fall of the last Muslim stronghold in Iberia and the rise of Catholic Spain on the world stage. Cressler accurately situates the most well-known of Isabella and Ferdinand's pursuits— Columbus's voyage—within the horror wrought on Jews and Muslims in the Catholic Monarch's quest for political and religious unity. We all know how the story ends, but Cressler's moving portrayal builds the hope that perhaps, somehow, with the compassion and tolerance the novel evokes in us, things just might turn out differently."
—*Julia Baumgardt, Assistant Professor of Spanish,*
Marian University, Indianapolis

"The Kingdom of Granada is approaching its end. Beset by internal conflict and pressure from their enemies, the future appears bleak for the Moors. Extensively researched and beautifully written, Cressler's novel leads us into an exotic world

of love, ghosts, intrigue, and betrayal. A must-read for all lovers of historical fiction."
—*Joan Fallon, author of the Al-Andalus Series, Málaga, Spain*

"*Fortune's Lament,* Cressler's third historical novel of al-Andalus, soars to new heights as a compelling tale that leaves nothing wanting: provocative prose that delights the imagination, intrigue on multiple levels, vivid scenes both tender and terrifying, and Great Love that spans generations. Cressler invites each reader into a fifteenth-century drama that cannot help but challenge contemporary perceptions and responses to the personal, family, national and global complexities of our time. May the promised sequel be in our hands and hearts with little delay!"
— *Catherine Crosby, co-founder of the Neshama Interfaith Center, Atlanta*

"American novelist John D. Cressler realizes a European dream. '*Nie Wieder Krieg*,' (German for 'Never war again') is a painting the German artist Käthe Kollwitz created after she found out that her son, a soldier, had been killed in the First World War. Only a few decades later, the horror of the Second World War was upon us. In many ways, the European Union was created to prevent future wars. Peace became a realizable dream, enhancing civilization our core business. Today, sadly, tensions are rising once again, often spurred on by ignorance, nationalism, and religious conflict. With lovely, poetic prose, Cressler uses his historical fiction to bring alive, in vivid detail, medieval Muslim Spain, whose lessons in peaceful coexistence and multiculturalism are still very relevant 1,000 years later. Using a beautiful love story set during the final collapse of Muslim Spain, *Fortune's Lament* reminds us all of what truly matters most in the end, and that our dream of peace remains within our reach."
— *Hugo Vercauteren, screenwriter and creative producer, Mortsel, Belgium*

"As in the first two volumes of the Anthems of al-Andalus Series, this third entry, *Fortune's Lament*, weaves together an intriguing tale of love, war, technology, and medicine in medieval Spain, with a touch of mysticism to add to the mix. We are transported back in time to bear witness to a world and a set of peoples that most of us do not know very well at all, but should. This volume continues to prime the imagination in a wonderful and quite captivating way, especially as we see this fictionalized world place us on the cusp of the global landscape that we know today."
—*Jacqueline Jones Royster, Dean of the Ivan Allen College of Liberal Arts, Georgia Tech*

"Cressler's *Fortune's Lament* brings to life the glory of Islamic Spain in dramatic and vivid prose, and his work shows the value of extensive research. His fascination with Andalusia under Muslim rule is apparent, and his historical novels do justice to the epic sweep of this period of history. The lesson his storytelling leaves with us is the importance of coexistence and the richness that multiculturalism brings to our world—one that is perhaps even more relevant in our day."

—*Christopher Thornton, Zayed University, Dubai, United Arab Emirates*

"*Fortune's Lament* is set in Granada at the end of the Middle Ages, during the encroaching reign of Ferdinand and Isabella. Cressler expertly uses the rich history of this period as scaffolding to build a beautiful tale of love and intrigue. The story grabbed my heart while provoking me to think more deeply about the value of religious pluralism."

—*Reverend Thomas Kenny, S.J., Cristo Rey Atlanta Jesuit High School*

"Cressler has an amazing ability to transport the reader to another time and place with his use of descriptive language (one can smell, see, taste, hear and feel the scene) coupled with his scholarly dive into this rich history. This has been proven before with *Emeralds of the Alhambra* and *Shadows in the Shining City*, and now no less in *Fortune's Lament*. The weaving together of love stories, tales of power and conquest, of the horrors of war and the ways in which religion can be used for political gain, juxtaposed with stories of divine mystical love produces a novel which will grab the reader from its opening chapter. In addition to being a page-turner, Cressler offers us an expanded and more nuanced understanding of history that can serve us as members of one human family: especially as diverse cultures and religions still struggle to live, understand and love together. There is much to engage the reader, and much to ponder here."

—*Marian Monahan, co-founder of the Neshama Interfaith Center, Atlanta*

Early Reader Reviews

"Granada in the fifteenth century was wracked by bloody religious battles; court jealousies, cunning, and intrigue; ominous religious persecution; personal suffering, guilt and forgiveness. Yet love thrives! *Fortune's Lament* conjures Layla and William from *Emeralds of the Alhambra* through jinns and magical realism to show how Great Love endures for an eternity, transcends religious differences, and transforms and embraces Hakim Danah and her betrothed. Yet we have one more ever-present love in *Fortune's Lament*: Nature, the verdant earth and her magical skies, the scents and beauty deliciously described in wondrous detail throughout. This book uplifts the soul."

—*Denise Black*

"*Fortune's Lament* is a page-turner that constantly surprises. It is all there—a love story, great battle strategies, palace intrigue. I am not sure when I have learned so much while being so greatly entertained."

—*Trish Byers*

"I found myself turning page after page without realizing the passing time. *Fortune's Lament* was equally thrilling, thought provoking, emotive, and historically interesting. The history is brought alive through champions of honor, dignity, and love, and the story told in a manner that resonates with today's society, moving the reader to pursue Great Love in his or her own life."

—*Angela Como*

"Historical fiction at its best leaves you wanting to learn more about people, cultures, places, and events. *Fortune's Lament* succeeds."

—*Douglas R. Davis*

"An epic tale of love and war with bigger than life characters. *Fortune's Lament* is a fast-paced visual panorama of unconditional love and the harsh realities of war. A thrilling page-turner that leaves you emotionally exhausted."

—*Dennis Day*

"It's all here, yet I want more. Political intrigue, parallel love stories, inspiring quests for knowledge, and damnable acts of subterfuge spurred me through the fascinating history of late fifteenth-century Spain depicted in *Fortune's Lament*, the third novel of the Anthems of al-Andalus Series. Cressler clearly loves his subjects and has ignited my curiosity in the integral lessons of the fall of Muslim Spain and the emergence of European colonialism. Can differing faiths coexist—even thrive—in peace? How often must we forget the tragedies of history? And most of all, what is that mystery called Great Love?"

—*Howard Holden*

"Another masterfully written tale by Cressler. The history is rich, the romance intense, the intrigue suspenseful, and the action compelling. I loved it and I think you will too!"

—*Tom Jablonski*

"*Fortune's Lament* is a reader's delight! Cressler has done it again in the third book of the Anthems of al-Andalus Series. While Queen Isabella plots and schemes to achieve the downfall of the Moors in late fifteenth-century Granada, the Spanish Inquisition endeavors to root out all Christian non-believers in Spain, Columbus seeks the favor of the Spanish crown to support his voyage to the 'ends of the earth', and love blossoms between a Moorish knight and a young woman who seeks to become the first female physician in Granada. A page-tuner par excellence will keep the reader entranced until the wee hours of the night. History, political intrigue, religion, architecture, and adventure concoct a savory stew that will have readers salivating until the final denouement. Highly recommended!"

—*Roger A. Meyer, MD*

"With its evocative, often beautiful prose and key insights into the history of the time, Cressler's latest book is an exceptional work of historical fiction. He skillfully weaves the separate story threads into an intriguing tale that appeals to readers who enjoy complex stories, strong characters, and enlightening history come to life."

—*Barbara Nalbone*

"*Fortune's Lament* is a treat for lovers of historical fiction. In this exciting third novel, Cressler weaves a masterful story set in fifteenth-century Spain, during the turbulent times of Queen Isabella and King Ferdinand, when conquest and desire to cleanse Iberia of Muslims and Jews takes precedence. Caught in this sweeping landscape of war and peace, Danah is an endearing protagonist, a young woman who is aspiring to become a physician while struggling with love and self-discovery in a society dominated by men. I was quickly swept into the story and could not put the book down. A masterfully crafted novel of love and intrigue that once more emphasizes Cressler's enthusiastic belief in the goodness of humankind."

—*Acar Nazli*

"*Fortune's Lament* invites readers into a time and place in history which continues to impact us profoundly today: the beginnings of the Spanish Inquisition and ongoing hostilities between the Christian and Muslim worlds. We enter into the lush world of the Alhambra and the court of Ferdinand and Isabella, getting a glimpse of Muslim, Jewish and Christian worldviews while being entertained by engaging characters and their stories, both historical and fictional. It is a fast, entertaining read that will leave you pondering what might have been done differently, and what we should be doing differently in today's world so that history doesn't continue to repeat itself."

—*Patty Smith*

"*Fortune's Lament* takes us back to Spain in the late 1400s and unfolds a story filled with history and love. It tells of choices we all have to make in our lives. We meet historical and fictional characters, woven together in a way that helps us see our time through their eyes. Ultimately, the story makes it obvious that only love can transcend our differences. Only love can make it possible for us to live together as Allah/Yehovah/God intended."

—*Bud Treanor*

"My favorite book so far in the Anthems of al-Andalus Series, *Fortune's Lament* weaves together a series of intertwining narratives with one in particular at the forefront. We follow a young Muslim woman as she defies social norms to become the first female doctor in her community, embarking on a quest for truth along the way that ends in her finding Great Love. Though set in medieval Spain, this story evokes emotions and teaches lessons that transcend both time and space."

—*Lara Tucci*

"I felt like I was dropped into fifteenth-century Spain, experiencing a full range of emotional twists and turns as the mystery of true love unfolds amidst the harsh realities of war. A truly remarkable novel that explores the power of Great Love."

—*George Tzintzarov*

For my Maria:

One body, one heart, one soul.
Our Great Love is for eternity.

I believe.

"Seldom has so much love been lavished on a land. Like a man wooing a woman, the Arabs courted, cossetted, adored and adorned Spain with orchards, gardens, fountains and pools, cities and palaces, and century after century sang her praises in unforgettable verse. The pleasures and sorrows of their days. Love, friendship, revelry. The flora and fauna. The beautiful women. Horses and war. And the water. Oh, the water. The courtship lasted almost 800 years; the suitor was rejected in the end, and we are left with the love letters."

Cola Franzen
Poems of Arab Andalusia, 1989

Contents

Map 1. The Iberian peninsula in 1488 C.E., showing the borders of the Kingdom of Granada, Castile, and Aragon.

Map 2. Blowup of the Kingdom of Granada, showing major towns and battles within the story.

Map 3. The city of Granada.

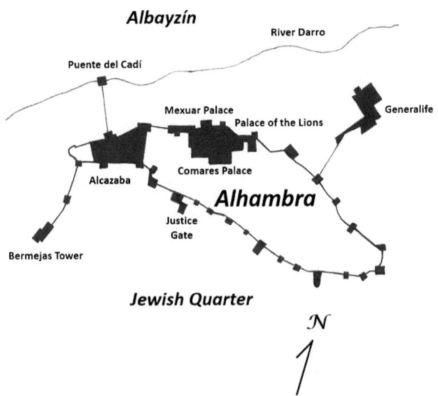

Map 4. The Alhambra Palace.

Characters

Abd al-Salam - Sufi master and friend of the Amiriya family

Aben Comixa* - grand vizier of Boabdil

Abu al-Haytham - high elder of the Abencerraje clan

Abrabanel* *(Don Isaac Abrabanel)* - a Jew; financier and legal counsellor to Isabel and Fernando

Ali al-Attar* - military vizier of Sultan Abu l-Hasan

al-Zaghal* *(Muhammad al-Zaghal)* - Sultan Abu l-Hasan's brother

Battal *(Battal Amiriya)* - an elder of the Abencerraje clan and father of Danah

Boabdil* *(Abu Abd Allah, his given name, and later, Muhammad XII; also known to the Christians as El Rey Chico—the boy king)* - son of Sultan Abu l-Hasan

Cárdenas* *(Alonso de Cárdenas)* - master of the Order of Santiago and Christian general

Colón* *(Cristóbal Colón—Christopher Columbus)* - mariner and discoverer of the Americas

Danah *(Danah Amiriya)* - Battal and Mayya Amiriya's daughter

David *(David al-Adani)* - Jewish royal physician

Duke* *(Enrique de Guzmán, Duke of Medina-Sidonia)* - Christian general and patriarch of one of Castile's leading noble families

Ezar *(Ezar al-Mufaddal)* - chief physician of the Atfal Hospital

Fatima* - Sultan Abu l-Hasan's wife; mother of Boabdil

Faynan - wife of Umar al-Makki

Fernando* - king of Aragon, married to Isabel

Great Captain* *(Gonzalo de Córdoba)* - Christian general and commander of the Queen's Guard

Isabel* - queen of Castile, married to Fernando

Layla - heroine of *Emeralds of the Alhambra*

Malik - suitor of Danah

Mendoza* *(Cardinal Mendoza)* - chancellor of Castile

Miriam *(Miriam al-Adani)* - wife of David al-Adani

Mayya *(Mayya Amiriya)* - wife of Battal Amiriya

Ponce de León* *(Rodrigo Ponce de León, Marquess of Cádiz)* - Christian general and patriarch of one of Castile's leading noble families

Santangel* *(Luis de Santangel)* - finance minister of Fernando and Isabel

Seneor* *(Abraham Seneor)* - a Jew; chief tax collector of Castile and court rabbi

Sultan* *(Sultan Abu l-Hasan Ali; Muley Hacén to the Christians)* - sultan of the kingdom of Granada and father of Boabdil

Talavera* *(Hernán de Talavera)* - monk of the Order of St. Jerome; confessor and confidante of Queen Isabel

Torquemada* *(Tomás de Torquemada)* - grand inquisitor

Umar *(Umar al-Makki)* - Yusef al-Makki's brother and nephew of Ali al-Attar; a knight and cavalry commander under al-Zaghal

Venegas* *(Abu l-Qasim Venegas)* - grand vizier of Sultan Abu l-Hasan

Yusef *(Yusef al-Makki)* - knight and cavalry commander under al-Zaghal; nephew of Ali al-Attar

Zoraya* *(Isabel de Solis)* - slave, concubine, then wife of Sultan Abu l-Hasan

* Historical characters

A Note to Readers:

Substantive back matter is contained in this book, including: my personal reflections, historical footnotes, a pronunciation guide, photographs, fact vs. fiction, a bibliography, and discussion questions for book groups.

Muslim, Jewish, and Christian terms that may be unfamiliar to the reader are included in a glossary. Such words are italicized when they first appear, but not afterward.

— *ONE* —

Qasida in the Rhyme of Nūn

Now we are far apart
One from the other
My heart has dried up
But my tears keep falling.

In losing you my days
Have turned black.
When I was with you
Even my nights were white.

It's as though we never spent
That night together
With no third presence
Save our two selves made one,

A night our lucky star
Caused even gossips
Who would spy on us
To turn away their eyes.

We were two secrets
Held by the heart of darkness
Until the tongue of dawn
Threatened to denounce us.

Ibn Zaydūn
(d. 1070 C.E. — Córdoba)

1

Sutures and Smoke

IN THE BERMEJAS HOSPITAL WITHIN THE JEWISH QUARTER, GRANADA, **6 JANUARY 1488.**

"It is time, Danah."

His tone is gentle and kind, but firm. She locks her extraordinary emeralds on him, uncertain still. He nods his encouragement. You can see the girl's determination, but also the shadow of her fear. She wills a deep breath, holds it, exhales, then lifts the curved sliver of metal and begins to thread the catgut. He sees that her hand is steady as a rock, which pleases him.

She had been an eager learner from the first day Abd al-Salam, the best-known Sufi master in the city, brought her to him for training. His first female student. A young Muslim woman from a powerful family, her heart was set upon becoming a physician. Scandalous, of course, in Granadine society. Predictably, her father, Battal Amiriya, an elder of the clan of the *Abencerrajes*, strongly disapproved of the medical arts as an acceptable pursuit for any woman, much less his daughter.

Abd al-Salam interceded on her behalf to arrange the tutelage. Even as a friend of the Amiriya family it required the Sufi's formidable powers of diplomacy to sway her parents. In the end he triumphed, but with little margin to spare. The arrangement? She would train under the royal physician himself, *Hakim* David al-Adani, and would work only at the Bermejas Hospital, a twenty-minute walk from their home. Only three days a week. And never on Fridays, of course. Her designated escort to and from? Yasin, the family gardener, who, when told, was mildly resentful about the extra duty added to his long list of daily chores. Her parents pushed forward a last-minute demand that she never be allowed to treat male patients, but this was simply unacceptable, an affront to all that David stood for as a physician. There was no place in the medical arts for such arbitrary boundaries. So he, a Jew, flatly refused. In the end, Abd al-Salam prevailed with her parents, but only by a hair.

Why the Bermejas Hospital? Because in the Jewish Quarter she would not be seen by either the ruling Nasrids within the Alhambra proper or members of her own Abencerraje clan, who dominated the Muslim Quarter of the city, the *Albayzín*. Out of sight, out of mind. There was a good distance between the Jewish Quarter, on the south side of the city, and both the Alhambra and the Albayzín to the north. These words were never spoken, but the inference to be made was obvious to all.

She was old to begin a medical apprenticeship, but Abd al-Salam insisted that her gifts warranted the opportunity. The Sufi master called her 'a rare treasure,' and swore that he would not be disappointed. He and Abd al-Salam have been friends for years; there was an element of implicit trust. Still, David remained skeptical, only reluctantly agreeing to the unusual arrangement after consulting his wife's wisdom in such matters. "As you know better than any, the power to heal is a great gift from Yehovah. All are called to *tikkun olam*, David. Do not deny the girl the opportunity to serve. She knocks. Open the door for her."

A simple handshake between the two men sealed her fate.

He smiled as he recalled meeting her for the first time. Slight, but with an oddly confident stance, as if belying some hidden strength of will. No makeup or perfume; quite unusual for a young Granadine woman from a prominent family. Her demeanor was stiff, her manners coiffed and polished, almost overly polite. Eyes cast downward in deference; her parents' doing, no doubt. Her expression never deviated from serious, not once; not even a hint of a smile to brighten her features. One-word answers, simple nods. But that unshakable resolve, that will of iron—not something she intended to project, exactly, but it clung to her like a stubborn shadow nonetheless. David felt inclined to tease a smile from her but resisted the impulse. Why scare the poor girl on the first day? Even at that first brief meeting he could discern a hidden agenda; a quest. And those eyes, dear Lord, those remarkable green eyes! Brilliant cut-and-polished emeralds.

She arrived all folded and pressed and tucked into her elaborate *hijab*, formal and proper. Part of the arrangement. After all, she, an unmarried young woman, would be working in the vicinity of the royal physician, a Jew, and his patients, some of whom were inevitably male.

Her demeanor shifted on day two. Still serious, but no more eyes on the floor. By the third visit she conquered her fears and began to speak. There was, and still is, a defiance about the girl, as if she had something to prove to herself and to the world. Determined, that much was sure. Their conversations remained formal, technical, though from time to time she surprised him with a bit of candor or slipped in a playful jab. The ice was thawing.

But to this day, she has not indulged him with a single smile. Not one. At this, his own amused smile widens, his fondness for his new charge more than obvious.

She finishes and looks up, silently lifts her work for his inspection.

His expression fades to serious as he examines the needle and suture arrangement. He nods approvingly. "Good." He lifts his palm to the patient and raises his eyebrows expectantly.

She hesitates, looks down.

"Danah, it is time."

She will not meet his eyes.

"As you know—" The timbre of his voice shifts to indicate a quotation is coming. He enjoys sprinkling his teaching moments with ancient wisdom. "'What we have to learn, we learn by doing.'"

"Aristotle." She doesn't even have to search for the answer.

The royal physician smiles. *Clever girl.*

She never ceases to amaze him; the brightest of any student he has ever taught, and there have been more than a few good ones. Curious about everything and refreshingly quick when learning new medical techniques, she is not afraid to get her hands dirty, thank goodness. She reads faster than he does and is already working her way through his substantial library. On each visit she removes a codex to take back with her to her home in the Albayzín. While he completes paperwork at his desk she peruses the shelves with a studious expression until she settles on a victim and removes it. Her head turns, silently requesting his permission. He shrugs and nods *yes*; or sometimes says, "He is difficult to understand, but be my guest if you think you are up to the task." This always produces a wicked smirk, and a hardening of her determination—his intent, of course.

Only Yehovah knows how late the girl reads at night. David started by having her spend time with the important medical encyclopedias—selected volumes from the *Hippocratic Corpus*, Galen of Pergamon, Abu al-Qasim, Ibn Sina, Ibn al-Khatib. She can now recite long passages from memory. She boldly proclaimed Ibn al-Khatib the ablest of the lot. She found Galen derivative and overrated; sentiments he secretly shares. He scolded her, of course. "Refrain from judging, Danah. There is something to be learned from all of the teachers who came before us." Predictably, she unleashed that adorable, little girl frown as she readied her retort. He could see the barb coalesce in her mouth, but in the end, she thought better of it and acquiesced with a shrug.

Then on to Ibn Rushd and Ibn Arabi, even his beloved Maimonides. None of those for the faint of heart! She is presently working her way through Ibn Khaldun's theory of history. She has begun to blossom with a newfound confidence, as if her excitement over this new knowledge she is acquiring is impossible to constrain. These days she rattles on and on during their time together, talking with those dancing hands, relating what she is currently reading, peppering him with questions on all manner of topics, medicine to philosophy to science; some he can answer, many he cannot. She never hesitates to disagree with the opinions of the dead authors whose logic she finds flimsy or flawed. Usually respectfully, or at least some close approximation. Yes, a remarkable young woman. As a student, she is a breath of fresh air. As her teacher, he often feels that he learns as much from her as she from him.

Still, not a single smile, though she clearly is in heaven. He patiently waits for the day, knowing it will turn a new page between them.

She adds, with a twist of sarcasm, "I do not believe Aristotle ever had to sew a wound like this."

He has to fight back a smile. "Perhaps not, Danah, but your time has come."

She looks uncertainly at the patient. The wound is ugly, but not life threatening. An ill-timed reach by a young apprentice. The freshly honed blade of the master silk-cutter made a hand-length slice down the boy's forearm. To the bone, but neat, and no major vessels to deal with. An ideal case for reducing his lessons to practice. The boy has been drugged and sleeps. The bleeding has stopped, and the two of them have already methodically cleaned and treated the cut for infection, the real worry in a wound like this. All that is left is to suture and bind it. Her task.

Her decision is made with a curt nod, and concentration slides onto her face. Her emeralds sparkle as she leans forward and surveys the wound. She punctures the edge of the parted olive skin with the needle and pulls it to the knot, then immediately moves to the opposite flap.

He tilts his head, pleased, and discreetly follows her work. As she snugs the first stitch to close the end of the wound, he says, "Good."

She touches the needle to her intended location for her second stitch and pauses without looking up, giving her teacher time to level an opinion.

He says, "Not quite so close. The wound must be able to expel fluid for the first few days."

A tick of her head and the needle slides out, then enters the skin.

"Perfect."

She methodically works her way to the end of the wound, ties off the knot, reaches for the scissors, clips the catgut, then examines her work. Satisfied, she proudly proclaims, "Done." Not a trace remaining of her initial hesitancy.

He lifts a metal probe from the table, steps beside her, and leans down; checks the tension of a stitch, then another, and then tests the knot. "Excellent work, my dear. Neat and precise. The boy will have a fine scar to impress the maidens, but otherwise, good as new."

She unleashes a radiant smile.

All he can do is helplessly widen his eyes.

The rare gift she grants him is quite disarming. Her face is instantly transformed, as if a *jinn* snapped his fingers and ladled magic upon her plain features. What was ordinary just a moment prior is suddenly extraordinary. A beautiful girl.

She playfully teases, "'What we have to learn, we learn by doing.'"

He nods, still mesmerized by her transformation. "You are going to make a fine physician, Danah."

"Thank you, Hakim al-Adani." She is still smiling.

"No, Danah." He shakes his head disapprovingly as he scolds her with his finger. "I told you, I am only a simple physician. David will do just fine. Please."

"Certainly, Hakim al-Adani."

He mock-frowns.

She laughs loudly, a surprisingly husky, throaty thing. Another first. Her laughter is contagious, too boisterous to come from a young woman of such slight stature and prim manners.

He can't help himself and laughs with her.

THAT SAME DAY, IN THE *VEGA DE GRANADA*, FOUR *ARAB MILES* TO THE SOUTHWEST OF THE CITY'S ELVIRA GATE, ALONG THE ROAD TO ALHAMA.

The morning is crisp, the sun's rays angular and sharp. The sky is an effervescent azure, a crystalline blue so piercing that an apology for such an unabashed celebration of splendor might be in order. Cold, but not unpleasant, with a refreshing moistness in the air; almost no wind. The master pruner and his crew work their way down the long rows of grapevines making precise cuts of the dormant runners where they join the central trunk. He knows his craft and expertly shapes the vine to enhance the coming year's harvest. The man working just behind him uses a flat spade to neaten the edges of the irrigation channel to precise dimensions. Water is essential to the Vega de Granada's culinary treasures.

As the pruner leans down and extends his hooked blade to make his next cut, he hesitates, lifts his head, looks left to the horizon, then right. He rises, rubs his complaining hip. Puzzled, he cups his ear and detects a faint but persistent rumble in the distance, unnatural on such a clear winter's day. He turns to make eye contact with his companion behind him, then the rest of his crew, who are also now standing and listening. Their eyes slowly track to the road angling across the low rise a stone's throw to their rear. The rumble grows louder, then louder still, finally rising to a rolling thunder.

The blue and gold standard shows first, the *Nasrid* colors of Sultan Abu l-Hasan. Granada's royal cavalry. The helmeted heads of the two commanders crest the hill first, then the bannermen, then the cavalry proper emerges. Four columns of twenty-five riders fold over the hill. The horses canter in perfect time, their lines clean and precise, a fine testament to their rigorous training. The cavalry kicks up a smoky haze of fine dust along the road, the nostrils of their Andalusian stallions producing cadenced jets of fog.

As they approach, the two commanders raise gauntleted hands in greeting. The master pruner returns the favor as he squints, then smiles with his recognition: the two al-Makki brothers, Yusef and Umar, the finest cavalry commanders of the realm. They serve under their uncle, Prince Ali al-Attar, the Sultan Abu l-Hasan's military *vizier*. Handsome young cavaliers, feared on the battlefield, these two brothers are known throughout the kingdom, and even to the Christians, by their nickname—*Saqr*, Falcons. They dive from the sky like lightning when least expected, raining death and destruction upon the enemy. Their daring cavalry tactics have carried many a battle against the Christians. The cohort bends left at the edge of the vineyard, moving southwest along the road to Alhama.

The younger brother, Umar, turns to the older with a twinkle in his eye, and shouts to rise above the thunder, "Shall we race,

Brother? Around the orchard." He points ahead of them. "Then back to the crossroads beyond; three sides of a square. No more than a half mile, surely."

He is answered with a smile. Yusef says, "The men would enjoy seeing you lose again, Brother."

A hearty laugh. "If only, sir. The loser squires for the rest of the week. Deal?"

"Done." Yusef turns to his adjutant. "Ahmad, hold steady at canter and we will rejoin you at the crossroads beyond the orchard."

An amused smile. "Certainly, my lord."

With a crinkle of flexing leather, Yusef leans forward in his saddle and begins to whisper to his stallion, *Nasr*. Victory. The horse's ear pivots to greet him, and when the instructions cease, the Andalusian's crest arches into a downward C, the lovely lines of his haunches coiling, spring-like. Without looking back to his brother, Yusef shouts, "Hyah, Nasr, HYAH!"

Umar's face steels with concentration as he kicks to the chase. The collective shout of a hundred voices cheers them on.

As the two brothers reach the edge of the orchard they break hard right and vanish, Yusef still in the lead, though just barely. Umar has the faster mount, but only by a hair, and Yusef is the better rider. These two race with reckless abandon, the outcome far from certain. The cavalry canters on as if nothing happened, but smiles begin to sprout along the columns. The Falcons are famous for such antics. Bets will be made.

The vineyard workers watch until the patrol fades into the distance, then resume their pruning.

The city sleeps under a sickle moon. The Nasrid royal guardsmen pace the walls of the Alhambra high above the city, stopping periodically to stamp the numbness from their toes. Down by the river's edge a dog yaps once, twice, then yelps as it is struck by its annoyed master, triggering a mare's unsettled neigh from the nearby stables. The silence crawls back in.

The Amiriya family lives in one of the finer *carmen* homes of the Albayzín, a stone's throw north of the River Darro and convenient to the largest *hammam* in the city. Not palatial, but well beyond comfortable. The family, a clutch of servants, even a gardener and a stableman—all fruits befitting an elder of Granada's Abencerraje clan.

A dull crimson glow leaks from the stoked brazier that pumps heat into her lamp-lit room, beating back the chill of the elaborate ceramic tilework lacing the walls. Danah lies on her side, head pinioned to her fist, the codex splayed and pulled tight to her. She has been racing down the pages for over an hour now. The second book of Ibn Khaldun's *Kitābu l-'ibar*. She is shocked to find the study of history so completely riveting. Her lids are finally beginning their inevitable droop, and her pace slows, then stops, as her eyes fold closed.

Her dark-olive skin is a wonderful contrast to the bleached cotton of her nightgown. As are those eyes. She was teased mercilessly about her emeralds as a young girl, either by boys inept in the arts of flirtation, or else by jealous girls who longed for her exotic look. She pretended to shrug off the bite of the barbs and jabs, of course, as all children do, but the cruelty of youth can produce deep and lasting wounds; calloused over, perhaps, but inevitably buried within where they are prone to fester and erupt unexpectedly.

She secretly fancies the rarity of her cut jewels, though she would never admit it. She has never seen anyone with eyes like her own. Her wavy chestnut-brown curls, thick and lustrous, stretch to the small of her back. Luxurious hair like this requires work, obviously, and extended time during her daily visits to the hammam. Her long tresses are the one vanity she permits herself. As barter, she shuns both makeup and perfume—to her mother's displeasure. "How do you expect to show the young men you are interested, Danah, if you do not care about your appearance and your scent?"

That she is attractive would not be disputed. But beautiful? Hardly. Not in a city celebrated for its extraordinary women. Then again, there is that remarkable smile. When it comes, it produces an uncanny transformation of her features, the unanticipated blossoming of some rare orchid hidden deep inside her, clenched tightly, lest it be glimpsed by the world. When she smiles it is as if her face is suddenly lit from within by a thousand candles. Then a dusting of dimples insist themselves upon her cheeks; but only a hint, as if some ancient bloodline begs for expression but in the end is denied. Still, the hint adds marvelously to the whole.

A smile like that conjures memories of the raven-haired beauties of ancient lore, the sirens of a timeless Bedouin world in the Arabian deserts, about whom long poems were fashioned and dedicated, then recited from memory deep into the night beneath a diamond-studded sky.

A smile like that commands double-takes from men, both young and old. From the young, a pounding of the heart, a sweet gnaw in the gut, the raw, unsettled ache of longing; from the old, the admiring lift of an eyebrow followed by an appreciative nod.

With the ease of her smile, however, her face returns to its normal serious pose, and the men, both young and old, are left wondering what exactly was so captivating about her. Her beauty is fleeting; here, then gone. More than once this has produced a confused shaking of heads. But these occasions are rare, for she willfully refuses to indulge the world with her exquisite smile. She tells herself that her refusal is simply self-protection against unwanted advances, but the truth is that she is insecure about her looks, the timeless bane of many a young woman.

Unlike the other Granadine maidens of marriageable age, Danah does not clamor for the attention of dashing young knights, of whom there are many, of course. Indifference might be the best word to describe her attitude with respect to the world of young men. At those public festivals and gatherings that bring the two sexes into close proximity, she skillfully melts into the background to avoid notice, content to observe the strange gyrations and avoid participation. Without that smile, her looks are plain enough to accomplish this disappearing act with ease. She sees; she judges. She secretly despises the ridiculous swoons and giggles and fawning of the pretty young maidens, and ruthlessly condemns the preening knights as they prance about, teasing and flirting.

Truth be told, those young knights she *has* met she finds tedious and uninteresting, obsessed with swordplay, horses, and firearms, pursuits boring to someone of her intelligence and aspirations. Inevitably, these meetings are her mother's doing, arranged with a single goal in mind: her marriage to someone who will reflect favorably on their family and elevate their social status. When these potential suitors learn of Danah's dream to become a physician, and to spite her mother she makes sure that they do, she is reminded that a wife's place is in the home with her children. Without fail, this unleashes an angry retort from Danah; at its worst, a firestorm of fury. Even the most confident young knights lose their swagger and wither under her unforgiving gaze and sharp tongue. No use denying it—the girl has a temper. The manners her parents have so carefully honed can revert to rudeness in the presence of such foolish bravado. The bolder among the would-be suitors spread ugly rumors about her, or call her names, as scorned young men are wont to do. As might be expected, her mother, hands on hips and lips pursed, chastises her for such antics. "Shame on you! Hold your tongue, girl. How will you ever find a good husband, Danah? Tell me how? How?!"

She refuses to play the game, tells herself that love is a strange and frivolous thing, something beneath her, something subordinate to her true calling as a physician. It is a tidy and convenient attitude to be sure, at least most of the time. More than once, though, in the quiet confines of her room as she stares into the mirror, she has felt a tinge of jealousy over the maidens who seem to so effortlessly master the rules of the game, who possess the knack of attracting handsome young men to their sides as if moths to a flame. There is a gentle tug of curiosity, an unsettled flutter in her gut. Just for a second, only a second, she indulges the fantasy—*I wonder what it would be like to be kissed by a handsome young knight?*

These rare moments testify to the universe's enduring dance, the relentless pull of female to male, male to female, nature's inexorable drive to complete life's circle. Her fantasies are fleeting, however. To settle herself and neaten her life, Danah grinds such distractions under her heel, chides herself for such foolishness, then reminds herself of her quest—to study, to practice, to learn, to discover the joy of serving, to master the gift of healing. To become a physician. Hakim Amiriya.

Rather than dwell on young, foolish suitors, she much prefers to devote her energy instead to more engaging topics: Ibn Khaldun, Ibn al-Khatib, Ibn Rushd, Ibn Arabi, Maimonides. Still, she knows she is old to be unmarried, and at the very least should be betrothed by now, a fact her mother harps on with annoying frequency these days. Danah frowns her displeasure at the mere broaching of the subject, then retreats to the safety of her room and her books as quickly as decorum permits. She finds respite in her work at the hospital, though only three days a week. She secretly longs for seven. She has found her calling; a dream from her early childhood marvelously come true.

Her breathing changes, and a moment later the prop under her head buckles and she starts, realizing that this long day is done. She yawns, gently closes the codex and sets it on her bedside table, cuts the flame of the lamp to a blue nub, then crawls under the covers, pulling them up to her chin like a little girl. She is asleep by the count of ten. She will wake naturally at first light. Always has.

The room is still, peaceful, her breathing even and relaxed. The jinn's hour approaches. Danah's pupils flick back and forth in tandem beneath her lids. The lamp flame sputters and pops, rises in height as if by magic, then settles. Brilliant gold sparks alight in the still air like magical fireflies as they begin to shimmer and dance.

Danah sits up.

An old woman writes at a low-slung table in the corner of her room. Long white hair. She rapidly scratches with her reed upon the polished paper, oblivious to Danah's presence. Without looking up she lifts her hand, touches the reed to the ink pot and continues writing.

"I am dreaming."

The reed stops.

"You are not real."

The old woman lifts her head, turns to her.

Danah gasps when she sees the old woman's eyes. *Her* eyes.

The old woman smiles. There is kindness there, affection, but deep sadness, too. There is something about the woman's features, something vaguely familiar, but Danah cannot quite place it. She repeats. "You are not real." Recognition struggles to focus but remains just beyond reach. *The smile. Something about the smile.*

The woman sets her reed down, looks up at Danah once more, smiles again, then says, "When I was a little girl, the children at court mercilessly taunted me for the birth-stamp you and I share. You, too, have felt that sting, dear one, I am certain of it. Tell me, my cherished girl, do they still call us . . . green-eyed devil?" She impishly smiles.

Danah's eyes spontaneously fill, the hurt inflicted by her childhood tormentors surprisingly lasting and deep. She answers the old woman with a strained whisper. "Yes."

The old woman nods at the shared recognition, then continues. "As a grown woman, I was called many ugly things besides this, by many different people, both here in the Maghreb and in my beloved Granada, from which I was banished. Unholy temptress. Satan's curse. Sufi harlot. But one name hurt more than all of these together." She hesitates, then croaks, "traitor's spawn." The old woman suffers to utter the words.

Danah hugs herself with her arms, shakes her head side to side. "You are not real. This is a dream."

The old woman sniffs away the pain, then continues. "Know in your heart, dear one, that the tales told about my father are lies. It is time for you to discover the truth." The old woman stops and locks eyes with Danah. "What should you call me, my cherished girl? You know me by legend. I am the 'Emeralds of the

12

Alhambra.' I am Layla, your great-great-great-great *tetta*, the last al-Khatib. Perhaps Tetta Layla would be best. Yes, call me Tetta Layla." She offers a warm smile. "Though we no longer share a name, your blood is my blood, your eyes are my eyes. The Great Love I once knew, you too shall know." Her emeralds burn into Danah's. "Come, dear one, I will tell you my story, that you may know your own. Neither time nor distance can separate you from me, my beloved girl. Come to your tetta." She opens her arms.

Danah wakes with a gasp and sits up, panting. Her heart is pounding. She throws the covers back and raises the lamp flame to chase away the jinn. She turns and stares at the empty corner of the room as her breathing calms. Her eyes track to the window. Still dark. She takes a deep breath, holds it, exhales through pursed lips. She never recalls her dreams, never; but this one stands alive in her waking memory. She can see the old woman with the crystalline emerald eyes. She whispers, "Tetta Layla."

"Brother? Would you mind fetching my meal? Not too much of the lamb stew." A teasing smile. "But perhaps an extra piece of bread. Oh, and do not forget my mint tea. A little less honey this time. And do bring a cloth to wipe my face."

He is answered by an elaborate, hand-sweeping mock of a bow. "Certainly, Brother. For you, anything." Yusef turns, grumbling under his breath, angry with himself for permitting Umar to cut inside on the final turn. A stupid mistake. Their troops find it all quite entertaining, of course, and while none would dare to speak openly to either commander about how the race was actually won, hidden smiles and elbow nudges abound. *Umar beat Yusef!* A rare event. Much silver has changed hands this day.

Umar beams as he watches Yusef depart. Younger brothers always relish triumphs over their older siblings, of course, but the relationship between these two is different. Orphaned at a young age, they have grown up side by side, every step of the way under the watchful eye of their widower uncle, Granada's most famous knight, Prince Ali al-Attar, military vizier to the sultan. Their uncle has seen to their education, insisted it be classical in form. First, the arts, literature, mathematics, philosophy, poetry, calligraphy, chess; then, the *Quran* and the *Hadith*. Next, horses. Only then, swords, daggers, pikes, crossbows, firearms, and cannons. Finally, battle tactics and the nuanced elements of command. Gentlemen of court, to be sure, but with a lethal edge. Just like their uncle.

13

Chiseled, handsome young men, feared by their enemies, respected by their troops, and, inevitably, adored by the eligible young maidens of the city. Even some that are not so eligible. Umar relishes the attention; Yusef sees it as an annoying distraction. Alas, to the collective wistful sigh of the city's fair maidens, Umar, considered by all the more handsome of the two, is now spoken for, married just six months prior to Faynan, the beautiful elder daughter of the Emir of Guadix. Still, as the brothers ride through Granada's narrow streets, shutters are opened, heads turn. The two are dogged by furtive feminine glances, hushed whispers behind open palms, quick giggles, even a bit of blushing.

These two are competitive, yes, as might be expected, but Umar has great admiration and respect for his elder brother.

Yusef is the better rider and a more capable field commander; a gifted strategist and leader. Candid and well-spoken in front of his superiors. But when given a choice he prefers solitude to crowds, drawing his energy from the quiet. There is a seriousness about him, bending at times toward a pensive melancholy. He is stiff, uncomfortable even, around women, and prefers the company of the knights under his command. He is not one given to easy smiles. A thinker, content to spend an evening alone, reading. The elder Falcon tends toward cautiousness while in command, sometimes to a fault, but his valor and steadfastness on the field of battle, when his men's fate hangs in the balance, is widely celebrated. Knights clamor to serve under him.

Umar is gregarious and fun-loving, playful, content being the center of attention. He enjoys the game of flirtation with women, both young and old. On the battlefield he has a daring edge to him, a casual willingness to entertain risk in exchange for a quick victory, and sometimes that daring is required to carry the day when the outcome depends on it.

The Falcon brothers make a formidable team. Umar loves Yusef as only the younger of two orphaned brothers can—more than life itself.

It is early afternoon and the day remains glorious. Warmer now, and quite comfortable without a cloak. Translucent wisps of alabaster clouds creep in from the west. They have reached their destination, and the cavalry has dismounted for the midday meal. When finished, they will ride out to provide security while the test is conducted.

Their uncle's orders were clear. "We have procured, at great expense, a new black powder recipe. Said to have come from the great Hasan al-Rammah of Damascus himself, but not one found

14

in his treatise. He calls it 'pelleted black powder,' evidently an innovation from the East. You dampen the ground mixture of sulfur, charcoal, and saltpeter using a special naphtha distillate, form the paste into mill cake, then press it through a special sieve to make small, uniformly sized pellets. The pellets are then dried and bagged. Just before use, you grind the pellets; coarse grit for cannons, fine grit for firearms. The pelleted powder withstands moisture and is supposed to be twice as potent as ordinary black powder." The old man's bushy white eyebrows lifted dramatically as he raised two fingers. "Twice, boys, twice." The nephews nodded in tandem. "Certainly much better than what the Castilians have gotten from the French. A batch of pelleted powder is being made as we speak. Verify the claims in secrecy, and if accurate, bring me a plan for how the sultan's army can best utilize it against the Christians."

Yusef had chosen the spot for the test. A fallow field with a low rise on one end. Far enough from Granada or any of the major towns in the Vega so that secrecy could be guaranteed. The cavalry would take up stations around the field against any prying eyes. The two massive bronze cannons and their carriage mounts, beastly things weighing over two-thousand pounds each, were disassembled from their batteries on the Bulwark of the Alhambra's Alcazaba and brought along a different route the day before via heavy wagon. Six horses to pull each monster, and even then the progress was painfully slow. Two additional wagons were loaded with the pieces of the carriage mounts. The gun crews trailed behind.

The trip for both the royal cavalry and the cannons proved uneventful. As far as any Christian spy might tell, the royal cavalry was just out on a routine patrol in the Vega, as a wagon convoy with an armed escort made its way toward Alhama.

Near the end of their evening meal, Danah's mother, Mayya, dismisses the servants and settles into a conspiratorial smile. "Danah, your father has a surprise for you."

Danah's shoulders slacken as her expression wilts. Her eyes drift to her plate. She is smart enough to know where this is going.

"Tell her, darling." Mayya beams her enthusiasm and waves him forward. "Tell her, Battal."

Battal finishes chewing, wipes his mouth, and clears his throat. "Yes. I spoke with Imam al-Yanni this morning. There is a new teacher at the *madrasa* he thinks you should meet. His name is Qatan al-Faraj. Bright and ambitious, from a well-respected Abencerraje family."

Her mother adds, "And handsome."

Danah has not stopped frowning at her plate.

Mayya's smile is glued in place. "He is more . . . mature . . . than the young knights you have so conveniently driven away with your quick tongue. He will not scare so easily." So smug. "We have invited him to dinner on Friday. So that you two can meet and talk."

A sad headshake. "No, Mama, please. No. Not again."

Mayya's stubborn cheer instantly evaporates. "I am sick of the way you treat your suitors, young lady! Sick to death. Sick! It is time for you to marry, Danah. Past time!"

Her father chimes in, but more subdued. "Yes, Danah, it is time."

Danah's eyes still have not left her plate. She speaks to her largely untouched food, "Hakim al-Adani says I will make a fine physician, *Baba*. That is all that I desire; all that I have ever desired. I will marry later, when the time is right. After my training is complete."

Her father's voice grows stern now, with an unforgiving edge. "What a fool I was to listen to Abd al-Salam." He scoffs, "These crazy ideas of yours . . ." His cheeks have flushed dark. "Shame on me for indulging you!" He is fuming now. "Danah, if you wish to continue your medical studies at the Bermejas Hospital, you *will* meet suitable men that your mother and I approve of, and you *will* be nice to them, and you *will* give them a chance for your hand. This lack of a betrothal shames our family. If you cannot choose, we *will* choose for you. Understood?"

She refuses to meet his eyes but, in the end, limply nods her acceptance.

The room grows silent, the air tense and oppressive. Danah pushes food around with her fork as her parents sustain their harsh stares. Finally, a tandem of heavy sighs and the *tink* of utensils against ceramic resumes. The standoff stretches to minutes.

Danah looks up. "Baba?"

He frowns, then offers a curt reply. "Yes, Danah?"

"What do you know of the al-Khatib family? They used to live in the Alhambra. Many years ago."

Battal glances at his wife, who first looks puzzled, then wary. She hides in her plate.

He shifts on his pillow, eyes his daughter. "The al-Khatibs? Not much. Old man al-Khatib served as grand vizier to Sultan

Muhammad V. He was originally from Loja, I believe. A friend of the Nasrids." The last word has an unwelcome edge to it. "But that was over a hundred years ago, at least."

"I have read his work, Baba. Lisan al-Din ibn al-Khatib. Hakim al-Adani let me borrow his medical encyclopedia. Brilliant stuff."

A weary sigh. "I see."

"He saved the city from the Black Death."

"Mm."

"What happened to him?"

Battal pauses to formulate his answer. "A fall from grace. He shared state secrets with the Marinid court in Fez; something to do with a treaty between Granada and the Christians of Castile. He was not executed, but instead was banished from court to the Maghreb. He died in Fez some years later, a lackey to the Marinid sultan. Or so the story goes." He studies her. "Why do you ask?"

"Did he have a daughter?"

Mayya looks up now, concern etched on her face.

Battal sighs once more, heavier this time. "I believe he did."

"What was her name?"

He hesitates. "I do not recall."

Danah can tell that he is lying. She answers her own question. "Layla al-Khatib." She turns to her mother for confirmation. "Mama?" Mayya remains mute. "Mama, she had eyes like mine." Louder, "Eyes like mine, Mama!"

Shock is splashed across her mother's face.

Danah looks back to her father and continues, "She was known to the royal court as the 'Emeralds of the Alhambra,' Baba."

Silence.

Danah gives up and stares into space. She slowly whispers, "She came to me in a dream . . ." Her heart is racing. "She told me to call her . . ." Her voice cracks under the unexpected weight of emotion. She begins again, her voice quavering, "She told me to call her Tetta Layla."

Battal's mouth falls open as his eyes widen, but words do not come.

Mayya gasps, "Dear Allah!"

Later that evening in the quiet of her room, Danah sits on her floor pillow in her bedclothes, legs crossed, eyes closed, palms cupped and turned upward in her lap to receive Allah's Grace. A single slender taper in a silver candleholder is set before her, its brilliant flame steady and sharp, standing watch against the darkness. She breathes in and out, slowly, nose to mouth, in and out.

In her mind's eye she follows patches of brilliant color as they stride in one by one from the blackness of infinity. The colors approach and stand before her, bid her welcome, then slowly fade —first violet, then indigo, then blue, then green, then yellow, then orange, and finally red. The colors of the rainbow. The sequence repeats, a circle of light, a ring of truth, an infinite progression testifying to Allah's presence in all things.

She practices the Sufi meditation form called the *Muraqaba of Light* that Abd al-Salam taught her. He told her it was intended for beginners interested in the Sufi Way, and she could lean upon it for comfort in times of uncertainty and strife. Sufi meditation forms, of which there are many, are intended to invite the seeker to begin to watch over the movements of their hearts, to acquire an understanding of its capricious whims and deepest desires, its wistful longings and its hurts. What began as a challenging exercise for her—what young person is used to sitting in silent stillness for twenty minutes?—is now a welcome salve when she is tense.

In and out, in and out, the colors file past her for ten more minutes. She slowly opens her eyes. The candle flame flickers its recognition. She inhales deeply, then exhales. She quietly recites the Words of Completion her Sufi mentor has taught her:

> *Within and without—Allah is here.*
> *Allah has turned all things to Him.*
> *Within and without—Allah is here.*
> *The seeker must seek truth within.*
> *Within and without—Allah is here.*
> *The heart yearns for its maker.*
> *Within and without—Allah is here.*
> *Allah is light, behold the truth.*
> *Within and without—Allah is here.*
> *Amen.*

The two bronze cannons stand side by side on their massive wooden carriages, their respective gun crews at attention beside their pieces: artillery officer, swabber, powderman, shotman, and primer.

Umar turns to Yusef. "Which cannon will use the pelleted powder, Brother?"

"I do not know. We will let our eyes decide."

Umar nods. "Excellent."

"I have instructed each artillery officer to fire for maximum distance, at a forty-five degree elevation. Single charge." He points. The sharp edge of the field is half a mile out, marked by a narrow road, then pear orchards beyond.

"Perfect."

Yusef turns to the gun crews. "Gentlemen, let us begin. Ready the first cannon."

The officer nods and barks at his crew, "Charge cannon!"

The swabber dips his poled sponge into the water bucket, runs it down the length of the barrel, then removes it. The powderman inserts the oblong cotton powder bag into the end of the barrel, and the swabber uses the other end of the rammer, this end dry, to run the powder tight to the breech of the bombard. The shotman hefts the iron shot to the end of the barrel and inserts it. The iron ball slowly but audibly rolls to the breech, coming to rest against the powder bag. The swabber plunges once more to ensure the charge and shot are tightly packed. The swabber shouts, "Charge ready, sir!"

The officer shouts, "Elevation!" The swabber and powderman insert wooden wedges into the slots on either side of the gun carriage, then step aside. The shotman and the primer pound them into place with wooden hammers, stopping when the angle on the guide registers forty-five degrees. "Elevation ready, sir!"

The officer barks, "Primer!" and the three men stand back as the primer inserts an iron pick into the touch hole to puncture the bag. In and out, in and out. He removes the pick and fills the hole using his powder horn, then steps back, and shouts, "Gun primed, sir!"

A timekeeper watches, mouths his cadence. This entire process takes precisely thirty-two seconds. The gun crew stands at attention while the officer looks to Yusef and Umar, and announces, "Ready to fire, my lords!"

Yusef nods.

The officer turns and shouts, "Stand clear!" The gun crew brings their hands to their ears as the officer lifts the smoldering rope and presses it to the touch hole. A quick sizzle, an expectant pause, then a bright flash and percussive *BOOM!* The gun carriage jumps away from the eruption of sound and flame. The blast is startling in its sheer violence, causing all but the gun crews to recoil and duck. The jerk of the convulsion travels through the ground to those within fifty paces, shimmying up their legs to jiggle their guts. The cannon belches a choking, billowy cloud of ivory-gray smoke, the aggressively acrid, sulfuric smell causing eyes to tear up and burn.

Umar shouts, "Spotter!"

The man is a stone's throw away along the rise, standing in his saddle. There is a long pause, then "There, my lord!" He points at the billow of dust about halfway to the edge of the field. The ball hits and bounces twice before coming to rest.

Yusef and Umar nod appreciatively to each other. "Second cannon."

The gun crew snaps into action and is ready to fire in precisely thirty-one seconds. Competition between the sultan's gun crews is fierce. In this new world of artillery, the time between shots has been rightly recognized as the fine line delineating victory and defeat. Words of unabashed pride will be spoken that evening around the campfires about that single second. Challenges and bets will be laid.

The second artillery officer shouts, "Stand clear!" He presses the smoldering rope to the touch hole. A tooth-rattling *BOOM!* The sound has a slightly different pitch than the previous shot, more guttural somehow, and the smoke cloud is tighter, more confined.

Umar barks, "Spotter."

Nothing.

Louder, "Spotter!"

Still nothing.

Umar's impatience edges into his voice, "Well, man?!"

"My lord, the shot did not land."

Umar is incredulous. "What?"

"I did not see it strike the ground, my lord."

Puzzled looks are exchanged among the gun crews, and as the smoke begins to clear, eyes track to the horizon.

Yusef says, "That is because it landed in the orchard. Beyond the edge of the field."

The shocked silence is broken by Umar's loud laughter. "Over twice as far, Brother. Twice! Just as Uncle said."

"Yes, more than twice." He turns to his adjutant. "Ahmad, take some riders and find the exact spot where it fell. I would like to know how far into the orchard it went."

"Certainly, my lord."

"And Ahmad?"

"Yes, my lord?"

"Make sure no one witnessed the test. When you are satisfied, round up the rest of the men. We ride for the city."

Ahmad's quick hand motions launch a cadre of cavalry.

Umar is beaming. "Uncle is going to be very pleased, Brother!"

Yusef smiles. "He will indeed." He whistles. "He will indeed." He falls silent as he begins his analysis. His expression grows serious as he commences his elaborate calculations of strategy. Umar knows not to intrude. Two minutes later, Yusef speaks. "This changes everything, Umar. I have some ideas. Come, let us ride for the Alhambra. We must speak with Uncle."

Betrayer and Betrayed

The Alhambra is alive with a thousand different sights and sounds of water—a muted rush through channels set beneath cobbled streets; the bright, pearly tinkle of sun-sparkled drops striking marble; the hearty spatter of thin jets arcing into pools crammed with the syncopated kisses of iridescent fish; ruby bougainvillea blossoms carelessly floating atop brimming paper-thin alabaster bowls set within decorative wall niches; the comforting hiss of the hammam's steamy hot breath as it strains skyward, only to surrender as an engorged plop upon the scorch of the polished stone floor; the liquid-slip down miniature staircases, a staggered alternation of dribbled stillness and panicked rush; breezed ripples neatly carved into glass-topped pools wafting trails of vapor under the greedy glare of the haughty morning sun. The palace is lacquered in a comforting aquatic murmur; a symphony of gurgles and drips, of splashes and sighs.

To desert peoples, a cupped hand dipped into cool, dark water, then lifted to drip its essence upon parched desert sands begets the entire meaning of existence; its purpose and its song. Water defines life and death, beginning and ending. They are born into this world bathed in the warm, salty gush from their mother's womb. Their eyes fill with tears as they taste life's sorrows and joys. With their bejeweled daggers they will bleed any who dare betray the clan. Under the dome of their tents they quicken their wives in a fevered spurt. And when their days are done? Their bodies are wrapped in linen shrouds and buried, returning their precious water back to the source from whence it came.

To desert peoples, water is at once a source of strength and of power, an emblem of pride, a repository of cherished traditions. Water is the dividing line between rich and poor, fertile and barren, even good and bad; a primal division understood by all at a depth far beyond the reach of words.

Each of the three religions sharing *al-Andalus* sprung from the desert. No wonder, then, that water is essential to their rituals and their rites: *Ablution, Baptism, Shabbat.* Water is life-giving, holy; water is everything.

The architects of the Alhambra understood this, of course, when they scattered a thousand different sights and sounds of flowing water among the glorious halls and sculpted gardens.

Water is as integral to the Alhambra as the sun is to day, as the moon is to night.

The last, and finest, of the Nasrid additions to the Alhambra was the Palace of the Lions, completed in the 1360s under Sultan Muhammad V. With its magnificent fountain set in the fabled courtyard, a circle of carved lions spouting jets of water, the Lion Palace serves as the private domain of the sultan, his royal harem, his closest advisors, and on special occasions is also used for lavish parties, concerts, and poetry recitals. The Hall of the Two Sisters within the Lion Palace, named for the massive twin marble flagstones on its floor, is a masterpiece of both Islamic art and architecture. The Two Sisters contain some of the Alhambra's finest examples of decorative arabesque wall art, highlighted by Ibn Zamrak's embedded poetry chiseled in elegant *Kufic* calligraphy, the stunning Mirador of Lindaraja, and the magnificent honeycombed *mocárabes* ceiling assembled from over five thousand hand-carved prismatic blocks. The concave ceiling has the appearance of a massive stalactite sculpture, an homage to the Cave of Hira where the Prophet Muhammad received the revelations of Allah via the angel Jibril, Gabriel to the Christians.

The remarkable ceiling set high above the marble floor magically lifts and amplifies whatever sound is offered to it, playfully teasing and stretching the imprisoned chords and spoken syllables to produce an uncanny reverberating harmony that almost defies logic. The woven layers of sound can grow so dense and rich as to shock the uninitiated ear, and even those who frequent the hall can be moved to tears listening to a poem beneath the canopy of the Two Sisters that seemed merely ordinary when recited elsewhere. Ibn Zamrak himself, the most celebrated of the Alhambra's many poets, described the ceiling as a 'celestial vault,' a recital venue without peer.

The Two Sisters play a similar game with light. The stained glass windows ringing the top of the tower invite chariots of color to break upon the honeycomb, first bending and folding the kaleidoscopic menagerie with its prisms, then flinging the light beams in a shivering cascade onto the vast space below. The effect is to give life to the walled landscape of arabesque, the lines of Zamrak's poetry magically leaping from their plaster prisons, begging to be spoken aloud. Legend has it that for one seated on the floor staring up into the dim of the mesmerizing cavern, the light shifts imperceptibly from sunrise to sunset, second by second, such that no single view is ever repeated. A metaphor for the infinite nature of time and the endless layers of love emanating from Allah.

The evocative scenes forever imprisoned within the Two Sisters are justifiably famous. Just the previous night, under the dancing shadows tossed upward into the celestial vault by the standing floor lamps, the pleasing gurgle of the floor fountain was joined by the tender sighs of lovemaking. What began as endearingly timid kissing and touching, led soon enough to entwined nakedness upon the pillowed divan, the contortions heaving and twisting as the sounds grew urgent. The sultan's newest slave-concubine proved to be an expert in the feminine arts of persuasion. She had her way with her royal lover, and then some, in the end subjecting him to that most pleasurable of tortures. At the crescendo of her masterful performance, and to her great satisfaction, she wrenched from him a loud, anguished plea, a cry so taut with sweet agony that it filled the magical space then roamed freely for what seemed like minutes. The floor lamps dimmed in awe. The Two Sisters have jealously guarded such secrets for a great many sultans.

The evening grows late. Those of court favored with quarters in the Alhambra's *alcázar* have retired to the privacy of their rooms. Within the Hall of the Two Sisters, Sultan Abu l-Hasan is joined by his only brother, Muhammad al-Zaghal. The two recline on divans covered with the finest Granadine silk under the honeycomb high above, the floor fountain between them. Hot mint tea rests on a tiny table beside each man, the tendrils of steam wriggling for freedom. Four heavily-armed, red-robed royal bodyguards stand expressionless at attention outside the tall wooden entrance doors, the only movement their rhythmic pulses of breath-fog. A clear, cold night. The braziers pump hard to heat the compact space.

The brothers sit in silence, their eyes closed, listening to a master coax a lovely tune from his ivory-inlaid guitar. Contented smiles have settled onto both men's faces. The weeping chords join the fountain's song, then hand-in-hand drift like mist up into the heavens. When the last chord is struck, it lives on for many seconds more, then fades into oblivion, leaving only the sustained murmur of a bubbling brook.

The Hall of the Two Sisters is Sultan Abu l-Hasan's favorite space for enjoying performances of all kinds; music, poetry, and those of a decidedly more feminine leaning. The sultan opens his eyes. "Glorious, as always."

"There is no place in the world with finer sound, Brother."

The silence is comfortable.

"Zoraya is exquisite."

Al-Zaghal smiles. "Indeed. A most extraordinary maiden in a city of beautiful maidens. I thought you might enjoy her."

"Where have you been hiding the girl? The finest of my royal concubines pale in comparison. Those blond curls—dear Lord!" He whistles. "Extraordinary." He beams. "Caliph Abd al-Rahman III of the Umayyads had his Zahra. Sultan Abu l-Hasan of the Nasrids now has his Zoraya." He muses, "Some of the things she does . . ."

Al-Zaghal's smile widens. "She is well-schooled in the arts of love, Brother."

The sultan nods appreciatively. "She will do nicely." He replays some of the previous night's antics in his mind, ending in a ragged, wistful sigh. "If only Fatima could have learned such tricks, my life would be charmed."

Al-Zaghal chuckles. "That is why sultans have concubines, and not just wives. Fatima is too highborn for that much fun. Her place is to bear you sons. And nag."

They share a laugh. "Yes, I suppose that is true. Tell me about Zoraya."

"Her Christian name is Isabel de Solis. The youngest daughter of a Castilian noble, the Mayor of Martos, who is known to Isabel and Fernando's court. I captured her on a raid near Jaén. How could something that beautiful not catch my eye? I assumed she would command a fine ransom when I took her." He shrugs. "Her father refused to pay a single dinar. It seems she is the black sheep of the family. The father banished her to the convent for some youthful . . . adventures. Evidently, a dalliance with a stable boy that scandalized the family. I liberated her, you see." He smiles. "With no ransom, I decided to just keep her as my slave. She had quite a temper those first few weeks; in need of some discipline, I am afraid." He laughs at the recollection. "A spirited girl, that one."

"Spirited . . . yes."

Al-Zaghal continues, "I sent her to the palace in Baza to learn some obedience, and how to properly bathe. She took to it well. While she was there, I made sure she received a proper education in the arts of love." He winks. "Especially those subtle skills perfected in the East. I am told the Persian concubines saw to it personally." They share a smile. "I was surprised when she asked to convert to the faith, but evidently she no longer wants to claim her Christianity. Just as well." He muses. "She is a smart one,

Brother, and ambitious. I suspect she converted just to gain favor at court. That, and to add mystique to her many charms. The girl aims to be irresistible to you." His expression grows serious. "My advice would be to enjoy her ample gifts, but do not take her into your confidence. My guess is that she might use what you say against you if given half a chance. Think of her as a beautiful dagger; lovely to look at and pleasing to handle, but with an edge that will draw blood if pressed."

"I will remember that, Brother."

"Zoraya is my gift to my sultan."

Sultan Abu l-Hasan nods his acceptance. "And she is a fitting gift. I am indebted, Brother." He stares into space as he whispers, "Zoraya." *Princess.* "Zoraya."

"I just do not understand it, Miriam. She has been moping all week. She completes her lessons, yes, but the light in her eyes has gone out. Not a single smile. And she has stopped asking questions. I have to pull hard just to get one word answers to my queries." He shakes his head. "And she has not even bothered to ask to borrow a book all week. Not once. Can you imagine?" David widens his eyes incredulously.

"My, that *does* sound serious." Her sarcasm flies past him. "David, have you asked what is troubling her?"

He just stares blankly at his wife. The obvious always seems to elude the royal physician. A tepid response is all he can muster, "Well . . . no. But . . ."

She widens her eyes, then raises her hands helplessly and dramatically shrugs.

"But what would I say?"

An exasperated sigh. Miriam says, "Perhaps, 'Danah, I have noticed that something is troubling you. Would you like to talk about it?'"

"But I cannot say that!"

"Why?"

He stammers, "I just . . . cannot." He blurts out, "Dear Lord, she is a woman, how am I supposed to do that?"

His wife smirks her disapproval.

Then, sheepishly, "Would you ask her? She will talk to you. Please, Miriam?"

She answers with an amused smile. "You do realize that you are a foolish man? Yes, I will talk with her."

David breathes a sigh of relief. "Thank you, Wife."

Miriam's smile bends coy. "I expect favors for this, Husband."

"Again?" She scowls. "But that is the third night this week."

Fath, the head eunuch of the royal harem, looks pained. "Yes, Sultana."

"Al-Zaghal and his cursed gifts. She is nothing but a Christian whore!"

The eunuch gently corrects her. "I believe she is a convert, Sultana."

"So they say . . . I am not sure I believe it. And how dare she call herself 'princess'?" She growls. "How many of the other concubines have shared his bed since she joined the harem?"

An awkward hesitation. "None, Sultana."

"Where did she meet him tonight?"

The eunuch cringes. "The Hall of the Two Sisters, Sultana. Always the Two Sisters."

"I see . . ." Fatima's energy evaporates. "It has been years since he made love to me there."

The eunuch's expression is apologetic. "His exclusive preference of Zoraya is most unusual, Sultana. But I am sure that this is temporary. As you know, his appetite for his concubines is fickle. He will tire of her soon enough and return to you."

"He had better, Fath! I am the mother of his son and heir, for Allah's sake. Mark my words, Boabdil will rule as sultan of Granada. Boabdil *will* rule!"

"Of course, Sultana."

"Fath, I want you to find out everything you can about the Christian whore. Everything. And be discreet. I want to know the instant she leaves the harem, for any reason." Her expression twists sinister. "If you can find a way to get eyes into the Two Sisters, there will be gold for you. Much gold, Fath. I want to know what sins those two are committing. The Christian whore has placed a spell upon him, that much is clear. And I am sure Supreme *Mullah* Abd Allah would be interested to know such details. Very sure."

The eunuch bows. "Your wish is my command, Sultana."

Miriam slips into the room and leans against the wall to watch the girl work.

Danah sits cross-legged, her back to the door. The woman she is tending is ancient, a bed of bones laid out upon the floor mattress. The old woman's eyes are closed, her breathing labored and wheezy. It is apparent to Miriam that this woman will not be leaving the hospital; she has come to die.

Danah folds the sheet down and begins to bathe the old woman. She dips her cloth into the warm water, squeezes it out, carefully wipes down one arm, then the other. Another dip and squeeze and she begins to gently clean her face. Danah leans close. "All will be well, dear one. Shhh . . . all will be well. Rest easy, Yehovah is coming for you soon, Banat. Shhh . . ." There is great tenderness in the girl's words. She begins to softly hum a song from her childhood.

Miriam smiles. "You are going to be a wonderful physician, Danah."

The girl jumps.

"I am sorry. I did not mean to startle you."

Danah turns. "Miriam. It is always good to see you. I was lost in thought and did not hear you enter." The girl's tone is oddly lifeless.

Miriam studies her face, sees that David is right. The girl's fiery eyes are shadowed, the usual animation vacant. Miriam sits. "Tell me about her."

Danah looks back to the old woman. "Her name is Banat. She fell and broke her hip a week ago. She was in a great deal of pain, and then she began to have difficulty breathing. Her family could no longer properly care for her, so they brought her here. Hakim al-Adani . . . David . . . said that there was no point in trying to set the bone, since it would never heal. We have been giving her an elixir to ease the pain and to help her sleep. I am just trying to make her comfortable until her time to pass arrives." She affectionately caresses the old woman's white hair. "She has not said a word, but there are times when she opens her eyes. You can see the kindness of her heart, Miriam, and her weariness from life's long journey." The girl's tone has brightened with each word. "She is ready. The family comes twice a day to sit with her and pray."

"Your kindness in these final hours is a great gift to her, and to her family, Danah."

Danah looks at Miriam. "But I am the one who receives the gift, Miriam. She honors me by allowing me to care for her. Tending to her needs fills my heart with joy."

"Yes, I can see that. That is why you will make a fine physician. I am sure that Allah smiles as He watches you work."

As the silence settles in, Danah resumes bathing the old woman.

Miriam studies her. "David is concerned about you."

Danah's hand stops, but she does not look up.

"He believes that something is troubling you."

She resumes her bathing, dips the cloth, squeezes it out, starts on the old woman's shoulders. "I have a great many things on my mind these days." Her spirit has again died.

"Yes." Miriam helpfully adds, "Your parents . . ."

Danah looks up. Tears are close. She blurts out, "They have told me that if I wish to continue my studies, I must . . ." She can't quite get it out. "I must . . . become betrothed."

"I assumed as much." Miriam smiles to lighten the mood. "You are a beautiful girl, Danah. I am sure there are many young men in the Albayzín who would fight for a chance to hold your hand and whisper tender words of love into your ear."

Danah dabs her eyes as she frowns.

"And to be fair to your parents, you are of age."

Danah's face contorts. "Yes . . . I know." Pensive silence. "My parents selected a teacher from the madrasa they thought would be *ideal* for me, and they made me entertain him." A sharp edge clings to her words. "The man was so *old*, Miriam. *Ancient!* Like all the other suitors my mother has arranged, when I told him I was studying at the Bermejas Hospital so that I could become a physician, he scoffed and informed me that that was not a proper role for an Abencerraje wife, and that I should consider something more suitable, like learning to cook and clean, perhaps to sew. And learning to care for children, of course." She grimaces. "It seems that all I am good for is breeding. Like a cow!"

Miriam cannot hold back her smile. "And how did you respond?"

From beneath her smoldering emeralds, a torrent of words gush. "I told him his brain was the size of pomegranate seed and that he had much to learn before he would be worthy of any woman, much less me."

Miriam laughs. "I see. And how did he take that?"

"He called me a green-eyed devil in need of a good whipping, then he stormed out. But not before giving my parents an ear-full on what an impudent daughter they had raised. Mama was furious."

"And your father?"

"I could tell he did not really think the man suited me. Too old, and too rigid. But in the end he supported Mama."

"And when was this?"

She sighs. "Friday. They both reminded me that without a betrothal I would not be continuing my studies with David."

29

"Have you talked to Abd al-Salam about this? Perhaps he could intercede on your behalf."

"No, that is impossible. He is visiting the Sufi madrasa in Málaga."

"I see."

"Besides, my father already said he was a fool for allowing Abd al-Salam to convince him to allow me to train at the Bermejas."

"Ah."

Danah looks down. "I am not sure what to do, Miriam. I can only imagine who they will choose next. I feel trapped." She lifts her hands to the room. "This is my calling. I can feel in my heart that I am meant to be a physician. And that Allah desires this as well. I want to serve, Miriam. I have no objection to marrying, truly. But when the time is right. And to someone my age." Her tone stiffens. "I will only marry for love, Miriam. To a man who understands and respects me and my need to serve others. Is that so much to ask?" The girl's plea is desperate. Tears begin to leak from her emeralds.

Miriam touches her arm. "No, my dear, it is not. Perhaps you can meet your parents halfway."

Danah's eyes rise from her lap, her expression skeptical. She sniffs. "What do you mean?"

"Tell your parents that you have thought long and hard since Friday's events, and that you agree to a betrothal, but that you must first find someone worthy of your hand and your family; someone your own age who respects you and understands your need to serve others. Your parents love you, Danah. They will understand this. Tell them that you want Abd al-Salam to be the one to select a suitable match for you. Tell them you will respect his decision and agree to be betrothed to the one he chooses for you."

"But Baba is angry with him."

"Despite what he may say, Abd al-Salam is respected by the Abencerraje elders. That matters a great deal to your father."

"But Abd al-Salam may be in Málaga for some time."

A devilish smile. "Precisely."

Danah's eyebrows lift, then, thankfully, a hint of a smile. Another sniff and an encouraging nod.

"Your parents will write to Abd al-Salam on your behalf with their request. David will also write to him and explain the situation." She smiles. "Do not worry, I will help him craft the words. Abd al-Salam knows better than anyone that Allah planted this desire to be a physician within you. Serving others is the Sufi

Way, after all. He will agree to their request to find a suitable match for you. But this will take time."

Danah smiles and nods. "I see . . . yes . . ."

"Surely Abd al-Salam can locate a fine boy your age in Málaga who is also studying the medical arts. Someone that would suit you. Sad to say, I am sure he will first have to complete his own training before marrying. He can come to Granada to meet you and ask for your hand. That will satisfy your parents. But the wedding will not occur until after both of you are physicians. Proper matches do take time, you know."

Danah's smile finally blossoms, igniting her face. "Yes . . . they do take time. Thank you, Miriam, thank you!"

A bright, metallic *ping*, pause, *ping-ping,* long pause, *PING.* One might naturally assume a blacksmith hard at work upon his anvil.

But then the shout, "YOU DOG!"

A teasing tone answers, "Your skills are slipping, Brother. I am worried for you."

No response. Then a rapid-fire, *ping-ping-ping-ping-PING.*

Silence.

The two stand together, tense with strain, swords crossed and locked, but Umar's dagger is within an inch of burying itself beneath his brother's ribs. Both men are shirtless, their rippled torsos slick with sweat. That these two duel with steel and not wood is remarkable enough, but truth be told, their mastery of the art protects them. At least most of the time. Each man bears scars inscribed by his sibling.

They remain motionless, their expressions deadly serious.

Umar is the first to smile. He cannot contain himself and begins to laugh, then steps back and gives in, doubling over as his laughter grows. This is followed by a chorus of cackles and hoots from the ring of their troops surrounding them. He stands. "My victory, Yusef!" He slaps his chest defiantly. "Mine!" The pride of the younger brother is unmistakable.

Yusef's face remains frozen. Finally, a hint of a smile. He relaxes his posture and beams. "You were lucky!"

Umar is incredulous. "Lucky? Did you say *lucky?!*"

"One more time, Brother."

Umar crows, "I fear for your safety, sir!"

"One more time, Brother."

A rowdy cheer from the troops. Bets are hastily laid.

The Falcon brothers readjust their grips and level their weapons as their smiles vanish and they begin to slowly circle each other. They slink like stalking tigers, their movements fluid and precise, their swords and daggers living extensions of their arms.

Umar charges as quick as a lightning strike, forcing Yusef into an orderly retreat under the whir of gleaming steel. *Ping-ping*, parry, turn, *ping*, slash down, parry, spin, *PING!* Their swords and daggers locked, they jump back from each other and begin to circle anew. The lethal dance of master swordsmen.

She whispers into the darkness, "Tell me your thoughts, Battal."

It is late, but neither can sleep. He is on his back, eyes open, staring up into the void hugging the coffered ceiling. She has been tossing from side to side and finally gives up.

He sighs. "My thoughts? I was wishing that we had had a boy, not a girl. So much simpler."

Mayya titters, rolls onto her side and snuggles up against him. "What do you make of her proposal?"

Silence.

"I find myself wondering how she came up with such an idea."

"Perhaps she finally saw that we were serious."

"Perhaps. In any case, what she proposes is a reasonable path forward."

She lifts her head. "Reasonable? Why should Abd al-Salam be the one to choose for her? We are her parents, we know her better than anyone. For Allah's sake, Battal, what can a Sufi possibly know about match-making?"

"Very little, I would guess. But do not forget that all we have accomplished to date has been to alienate her and make enemies of half of the eligible bachelors of the Albayzín. It is time to try a different approach, Mayya. Abd al-Salam is respected in both Granada and Málaga, by both the Abencerrajes and the Nasrids. Walking the tightrope between the two clans is no small feat, even for a Sufi."

She scoffs, "Yes, and he is the one who cajoled us into indulging this silly dream of hers. The girl's prospects are spoiled, Battal. A physician?! Jews are physicians, Battal, not daughters of clan elders. I say she is too smart and too strong-willed for her own good. No decent man will have her now."

Silence.

Battal muses, "The royal physician says Danah is the most-talented student he has ever taught."

She absorbs his words. "Al-Adani told you this?"

"He did. He said that he has never before had such a bright and capable student." He measures his words. "He said he believes she has a calling from Allah to serve as a healer."

An incredulous, "A calling to serve as a healer?"

"Yes. Service is the Sufi Way. It is an honorable life, Mayya."

She replies, "It is a life that will spoil her chances to marry well."

"Perhaps not. It simply requires the right young man. Someone who understands her. Someone who shares her calling." He turns to her, pulls her tight. "Danah's happiness is important, Mayya. She is our only child."

Nothing. Finally, a barely audible reply. "Yes."

A comfortable silence settles in as they contemplate their daughter.

Battal chuckles.

"What?"

"Do you remember the time she cut up all your sheets to bandage the baker's son after he fell from the wall?" He chuckles again.

Mayya smiles. "She could not have been more than seven years old. Crazy girl."

"Gifted girl. Mayya, it is time we recognized that Danah has her own path to walk, a path different than the one we imagined for her. This quest of hers to be a healer comes from deep within, perhaps even from Allah. It would be wrong for us to stand in the way."

Silence.

He continues, "I am confident that Abd al-Salam will select a young man of the appropriate rank within the clan; a young man with promise. The elders will give their blessing. And, just as importantly, he will be a young man also with a vocation in the medical arts. This will please Danah. Who knows, perhaps there will even be love. And being from Málaga, he will be unknown to the gossip mongers of the Albayzín—a decided advantage. We do have her word she will betroth whomever he chooses. Our Danah could be married within a year, *inshallah*." Allah willing.

"And babies soon afterwards, inshallah." The excitement in her voice is impossible to mask.

"I will write to Abd al-Salam tomorrow."

A long pause. "Fine, but please be specific about the type of young man we require for our Danah. And I insist on meeting him before any betrothal is considered. He will have no choice but to climb to the Zafarraya Pass and make the journey to Granada to meet us."

"Of course, my love."

"And I want information on his family."

"Of course, my love. I will make discreet inquiries with the elders in Málaga once we know his name." He pulls her tighter with each acknowledgement.

"And their lineage back to the Maghreb."

"Of course, my love." Tighter still.

They settle back into a comfortable silence.

"Battal?"

"Yes, Wife?"

"Danah's fascination with Layla al-Khatib. It worries me."

Battal exhales his weariness. "Yes. The history she seeks is dangerous to our standing in the clan. We must ensure that the answers elude her."

"Where is she getting these crazy notions?"

"Dreams, or so she says."

"I say jinn."

"Perhaps you are right. We must be subtle in discouraging her. There are times when I feel like the girl sees right through me."

"Yes, the both of us."

Possessed

Sultan Abu l-Hasan and al-Zaghal walk side by side as they exit the Hall of the Kings, their gaits matched. Two royal bodyguards follow at a discreet distance, expressions blank, but eyes alert and darting.

The brothers are dark and handsome, close-cropped beards and penetrating almond eyes. Easy enough to see the family resemblance. Abu l-Hasan is the elder, of course, and looks it. His beard is flecked with gray, though they differ in age by only two years. The stresses of the sultanate.

Both men are dressed in formal court attire, multiple layers of flowing silk robes embroidered with elaborate patterns of gold and blue thread; Nasrid colors. The sultan favors robes of brown, tan and turmeric; the brother, his signature all-black. Both men don turbans that flow down to join their robes. Swords fashioned from Damascus steel hang in jeweled scabbards at their hips. Ancient swords such as these were named hundreds of years ago, passed down along dynastic lines. The brothers' needle daggers are tucked beneath their waist sashes. There is no mistaking that these two are Nasrid royalty.

As they exit the Lion Palace and enter the fine, narrow Hall of the Mocárabes, they turn right, then left into the short tunnel leading to the Court of the Myrtles. They exit into bright sunshine. Royal guardsmen stand at attention in the corners of the courtyard, hands resting on their sword hilts, eyes fixed to the ground; the proper posture in the presence of the sultan.

The brothers stop to admire the massive shimmering pool. The orange fish instinctively rise to greet them, then swarm to beg for food, a thousand ravenous mouths opening and closing as one. The lovely, textured spice of the sunken myrtle hedges roams freely about the courtyard. Above, the dazzlingly quick swifts dive and dart in hectic play as they race in circles about the courtyard at frightening speeds, their giddy, metallic squeaks piercing, almost deafening.

Al-Zaghal says, "You saw Zoraya last night, sire?" Informality is permissible in private, but never in public.

A long pause. "I did." A deep breath, followed by an exaggerated exhale.

Al-Zaghal chuckles.

"I am putty in her hands, Brother. She grows bold. Deliciously bold. And so beguiling. She has some very interesting ideas about the Christian kingdoms and the new king and queen. A bright girl, that one."

"Your newfound attentions have not escaped the notice of the royal harem, sire. Or Fatima."

The sultan sighs. "No, I expect not."

"I would suggest indulging some of the other concubines with your affections. And perhaps your wife. To keep the peace, sire."

"Perhaps you are right." There is something odd about the sultan's tone.

Al-Zaghal turns his head to study his sibling. "Remember, sire, Zoraya is a beautiful dagger."

"So you told me." A menacing edge surfaces, commanding attention.

Al-Zaghal does not press. He knows his brother's famously unpredictable temper better than anyone. He shifts back to the meeting at hand. "The Vizier Council awaits, sire. There is much to discuss. The new ambassador to Castile will join us. Amir al-Yasa."

"Mm . . . the Falcon brothers are coming?" The hard edge has vanished as suddenly as it appeared.

"Yes, sire. Ali al-Attar has important news on the pelleted black powder. It seems that Yusef has some ideas he would like to offer for your consideration."

Sultan Abu l-Hasan nods. "Good. Very capable for such a young man."

"Indeed. He and Umar are invaluable to the kingdom. Boabdil will be joining us as well, sire."

The sultan grimaces. "Is that really necessary?"

"He is your son, sire. Fatima prevailed upon Venegas to include him."

The sultan opens his mouth for a barbed retort, then thinks better of it and simply grunts. "Very well. Make sure he keeps his mouth shut."

"Of course, sire." He lifts his hand toward the Hall of the Ambassadors towering above them to their right. "Shall we, sire?"

Sultan Abu l-Hasan nods, and the two continue on.

The absence of patients requiring surgery over the past week has slowed Danah's training in incisions and suturing. Instead, the royal physician has had her focus on the more mundane aspects of the medical arts: the proper setting of broken bones, the treatment of the various ailments of digestion, how to best deal with boils and infections, the distillation of elixirs, the preparation of rubs and powdered medicines, the best techniques for bandaging. Routine, for the most part, but important skills to master nonetheless.

A soft knock. David's eyes rise from his paperwork. "Come." He is surprised to see her so soon. "Finished already?"

"Yes."

"Did he survive?" He chases this with a smile. Thankfully, the old Danah is back and he is free to tease.

"Barely." A playful roll of her eyes. "A bit of a whiner, that one. He survived the setting of the bone, but just by a hair."

David laughs.

"I bandaged it with splints between heavy felt, and immobilized the wrist as well as the forearm. Wrapped tightly with linen soaked in cerate to keep him from moving the bone."

More serious now, ever the teacher. "How many parts oil to resin?"

"One oil to two resin. Inflexible when dry."

"Good. Which splints?"

"The thin elm shakes."

"How many?"

She involuntarily snorts. "Four, of course. Two on either side of the fracture. As you taught me."

He nods, pleased. He has never had to repeat an instruction with this one. "And?"

"And I gave him a supply of powdered bone, and told him absolutely no lifting of any kind with that arm. He will return in a month to remove the bandages and begin heat treatments and massage at the hammam. Then motion exercises."

"Excellent, Danah."

"What is next?"

"Sit and relax. You have been on your feet all day, and we have no new patients. Sit, Danah, and let us talk." He lifts his palm to the floor pillow. "Sit."

She reluctantly settles onto the floor pillow.

He offers a warm smile. "You never told me how you came to be so possessed."

A puzzled look. "Possessed?"

"Possessed by the medical arts. Female physicians are rare, you know, and those few that do exist are inevitably Jewish, never Muslim."

"I have wanted to be a physician since I was a little girl."

"To be honest, Danah, when Abd al-Salam approached me and stated your case, I was skeptical. He pressed, as only Abd al-Salam can do, but I remained uncertain." He chuckles over the memory. "In the end, it was Miriam that swayed me. She felt that any young woman with a calling to serve as a healer should be granted an opportunity to use her gifts. We Jews call that tikkun olam, 'healing the world.' Each of us bears a responsibility to transform the world, to make it a better place."

She nods as she smiles. "You cannot begin to know how happy you have made me, David. I am learning so much."

"Your future as a physician is very bright, Danah." A flowering of fatherly pride.

She beams.

"How did you come to know a Sufi master?"

Danah replies, "I first met Abd al-Salam after my father was elected elder of the clan, almost two years ago. The Abencerrajes have close ties with the Sufi madrasa, and Abd al-Salam is often consulted on important decisions."

"I see. He and I have known each other for many years. The Sufis have a special love for healing and care of the ill and downtrodden. Abd al-Salam often sends his disciples to assist me as a part of their training. He always says that caring for the needs of others is the best way to turn our focus away from our selfish concerns. The first step along the Sufi Way."

"Yes. He and my father became friends. He often visited us, usually for dinner. My parents would sometimes tell him stories about my clumsy attempts at healing."

David is intrigued. "Like what?"

"Well, when I was younger I used to use our pets to practice tying bandages. You should have seen our cat when I was finished with him."

They both laugh.

"Before I began my studies with you, I came to love frequenting the spice and herb markets to learn about herbal remedies and medicinal plants from the purveyors themselves. When they saw that I was serious about their craft, they began to tell me fascinating stories of magical cures and elixirs from the East. Sometimes they even gave me tips on where to find the best local plants and how best to use them."

"Such knowledge is not easy to come by, Danah. It will serve you well."

"I keep my collection of medicinal plants and herbs in my room. Mama hates it, but Baba indulges me. My parents belittle my passion for medicine, especially Mama. But Abd al-Salam would listen intently to their stories of my antics, asking a question here and there." Her voice grows serious. "I will never forget the day he brought a copy of Hippocrates' *On Ancient Medicine*. After receiving permission from Baba, he asked me to read it. He said he wanted to know my opinion of the medical knowledge of the ancient Greeks."

"An excellent choice. I consider that particular volume one of the finest in the *Hippocratic Corpus*."

She gushes, "I had never read anything like it, David. I felt like Hippocrates was speaking directly to me, opening up the world for the very first time. Suddenly I understood all that I felt inside me, all that I desired to be and do. I devoured the book in three days. This greatly pleased Abd al-Salam. Whenever he would come to visit, when he finished with my parents, the two of us would talk about medicine—various ailments and their cures, how the best healers practice their art, why we become ill in the first place. Everything." A wistful sigh escapes her.

"You miss him."

"Yes. He is an amazing man."

"Indeed he is."

"When he asked me if I would be interested in studying to become a physician, I could not believe it. My prayers were answered. It took some time for him to convince Baba, but in the end he prevailed."

"I am glad he did." David laughs.

She is amused. "What?"

"You were so shy and stiff those first few visits. I was not quite sure what to make of you, Danah. I wanted to tease a smile from you, but feared I might scare you to death."

She laughs. "You were scary! I was afraid I would say the wrong thing, or ask a stupid question, or make some silly mistake, and then my studies would end before they ever began."

"I have never had such a capable student as you, Danah. As Hippocrates said, medicine is an art, a craft to be learned, and success in healing depends on the firsthand experiences of the physician. That acquired knowledge must be passed on. The best physicians still follow the path laid down by Hippocrates, nearly two thousand years later. Teacher and pupil. You and I."

They share a warm smile.

She says, "Abd al-Salam taught me the Hippocratic Oath."

David nods appreciatively. "'I will teach my art without reward, and I will impart all my acquirements, instructions, whatever I know, to my pupils, who shall bind and tie themselves by a professional oath, and to none else.'"

Danah adds, "'With regard to healing the sick, I will devise and order for them the best diet and care, according to my judgment and means, and I will ensure that they suffer no hurt or damage.'"

"'I will comport myself and use my knowledge in a godly manner.'"

They both laugh, delighted by their conjoined knowledge.

"When the time is right, Danah, you will be asked to swear that ancient oath."

She cannot hide her excitement. "It will be the happiest day of my life."

"Be patient. That time will come soon enough."

"How did you come to be a physician?"

"Well, it was easier for me than for you, Danah. You see, I come from a long line of royal physicians. We Jews have served the sultans of Granada all the way back to the time of Samuel ibn Naghrillah, nearly five centuries ago. A great man, Yehovah rest his soul. Much like you, while still a young boy I became fascinated with medicinal plants and their use in the treatment of various maladies. As the eldest it was natural for my father to direct me toward the family profession. I studied under royal physician Hananel Abd al-Wahid, and when he passed, Yehovah bless his soul, the sultan appointed me royal physician. In addition to my duties at the Bermejas Hospital, I attend to the royal family and the court officials in the Alhambra, and ensure that all of the city's hospitals are functioning smoothly. For me, though, I very much like being both a physician and a teacher." A warm smile. "My calling."

She returns his smile. "Yes, your calling."

They are both pleased at this exchange of stories, new ground broken between the two of them.

David changes the subject. "I was thinking . . ."

"Yes?" Always that endearing eagerness.

"I have to visit the Atfal Hospital on Wednesday. A new patient the chief physician wants me to examine."

"The orphan's hospital."

"Yes. Would you like to accompany me?"

She beams. "That would be glorious, David!"

He loves to study her face when she smiles. Such a remarkable transformation. "Good. Wednesday then." He hesitates. "I might suggest that you keep this to yourself. As you know, your parents are sensitive about where you are permitted to practice what you learn. The Atfal is at the edge of the Jewish Quarter, so it should be safe from the eyes of the Abencerrajes." He winks.

She nods. "It will be our secret."

"Good. We are done for the day. You are free to choose a book, though I might suggest something on the maladies of the mind."

"Maladies of the mind?"

"Yes. Our patient at the Atfal. Abu al-Qasim's *Kitab al-Tasrif* has a chapter in one of his volumes. I forget which."

"I will be ready for Wednesday." She rises and begins to peruse the shelves for the encyclopedia in question.

"I know you will, Danah." He drifts back to his paperwork.

When she locates the thirty volumes of the massive *Kitab al-Tasrif,* she removes the guide book and begins to peruse the listing of its contents. Without turning from the shelf, she says, "David, have you ever heard of Layla al-Khatib?"

He lifts a single eyebrow but continues his work. "As a matter of fact, I have, yes. Layla al-Khatib was the original founder of the Atfal Hospital. She was known in the city as the 'Emeralds of the Alhambra.' Why do you ask?"

"I had a vivid dream about her."

"Mmm . . ."

She pulls a book from the shelf, opens it, begins to examine the contents. "She spoke to me." Her tone is nonchalant.

He looks up now, but she continues to explore the codex. "I see. We know so little about dreams, Danah."

"Layla had my eyes, David."

"Yes, I expect so, given her nickname. The depth of your green is very rare, you know. I have never seen the like."

She re-shelves the book and turns. "David, I believe we are blood-kin."

He stares, puzzled, then frowns. "That does not seem likely, Danah. The Abencerrajes were still in the Maghreb when Layla al-Khatib lived in Granada. That was during Sultan Muhammad V's reign. The late 1360s. She would have died long ago."

"I am not sure how, but I know that we are related." She muses. "My parents were very evasive when I asked about her. I could tell they were hiding something. What else do you know about her?"

"Hmmm. Well, let me see. One of my ancestors served Sultan Muhammad V during the Castilian Civil War. A royal physician named Salamun al-Harani. He was a close friend of Layla's father, Lisan al-Din ibn al-Khatib, whom you have already discovered."

"Ibn al-Khatib saved the city from the Black Death."

"Indeed. Salamun helped implement his plans for fighting the contagion. A horrible time, but Granada was largely spared. To my mind, Ibn al-Khatib's medical encyclopedia is the finest available, at least after Abu al-Qasim."

She nods vigorously. "Yes, I completely agree."

"Legend has it that Layla lived in the Alhambra. The Comares Palace, I believe. She evidently fell in love with a captive Christian knight. Supposedly he saved the life of the sultan and became a favorite of the royal court, though I do not know the details. In any case, he converted to Islam and they married. He was known to court as Shahab . . . Shahab . . ." He searches. "Chantel? Chandos? I forget. He died defending Granada when the army of Enrique of Trastámara invaded the kingdom at the end of the Castilian Civil War. As I recall, his actions were decisive in our victory. He died outside Jaén, with Salamun and Layla at his side. Or so the story goes. War is cruel."

"Yes . . ."

More silence.

She asks, "How long were they married?"

"I am not sure, but it could not have been long."

"Did they have a child?"

He shrugs. "I do not know."

"Baba said that Ibn al-Khatib betrayed the sultan and was banished to the Maghreb."

"That is the legend, yes. Ibn al-Khatib was Sultan Muhammad's grand vizier. I do not know the details, but Ibn Zamrak was evidently instrumental in uncovering the treason."

"The poet?"

"Yes."

"I see . . ."

"Ibn al-Khatib and Layla left Granada for the Maghreb, banished for life. He died under unusual circumstances in Fez. Some say he was murdered."

"What happened to Layla?"

"No one knows for sure."

"Is it possible that she ever came in contact with the Abencerrajes?"

"I have no idea. But Fez is a long way from Algiers. Many things are possible, Danah, but that does not mean they really happened."

The silence stretches out.

"She founded the Atfal Hospital?"

"She did, yes. As I recall, the same year her husband was killed, though I would have to verify that. Back then the Atfal was an extension of the Maristan Hospital, which during that period housed the outcasts of Granada. The Sufis were closely connected to both. Abd al-Salam may be able to tell us more. In any case, Layla started a Sufi madrasa for girls at the Atfal, though it no longer exists. She was evidently quite a woman."

Pride wriggles into Danah's expression. Her eyes sparkle like cut jewels. "Yes, quite a woman."

David smiles. "If you are related, that might explain a great deal, you know."

Danah fires off that husky laugh.

"We can ask about her on Wednesday when we visit the Atfal. Who knows, they may still have some records from that time."

"That would be wonderful, David."

"Did you locate that volume?"

"Yes. Number eighteen in the canon." She turns and pulls it from the shelf. "Chapter twelve—*On the Treatment of Infirmities of the Brain.*

"Good. Wednesday, then?"

Her smile lights her face. "Wednesday." She does not move. Her smile grows limp then vanishes. "Thank you for writing Abd al-Salam, David. Finishing my training means everything to me." Her eyes well up. "You and Miriam have been so kind. And you are such a wonderful teacher. I will never be able to properly thank you."

Warm, fatherly pride emanates from him. "Think nothing of it. You have a gift to give our world, my dear. Miriam helped craft the letter, of course, but I am certain that Abd al-Salam will help us. You will see." His turn to grow serious. "I hope you know, Danah, that it will take a very special young man to deserve you," he says quietly to the daughter he never had.

She blushes and lowers her eyes.

"Not to worry, my dear, the three of us will help you find him."

She looks up. "Thank you, David. I will see you on Wednesday. I am going to stop by and check on Banat on my way out. I will give instructions to the night nurse."

"Of course, Danah. I expected nothing less."

"Sire, perhaps it would be prudent for Granada to renew its payment of tribute to Queen Isabel." The man's tone is tentative, his pitch high and grating, almost a whine. Amir al-Yasa, the new ambassador to Castile, is greeted by silence, and interpreting it wrongly, he pushes on. "I am confident that our gold would prevent many problems with the Christians from ever surfacing, sire. After all, they have been at war with Portugal for three years now, and I have good information that their coffers are nearly bare. Fernando and Isabel desperately need gold, sire, if they are to press for victory." He hesitates, eyes darting nervously around the room. "Perhaps . . . ." Suddenly self-conscious and sensing his peril, his words begin to hobble. "Perhaps we can . . . leverage that . . . somehow . . ." he ends awkwardly.

Sultan Abu l-Hasan remains silent and expressionless on his divan, as if he has not heard the man. The sultan's lids slowly fold closed.

Al-Zaghal turns to study his brother, sighs, then looks back to Ambassador al-Yasa. The storm approaches.

The first sign of trouble is a darkening of the sultan's face. The lobes of his ears poking from beneath his turban begin to glow like coals in a hearth. His jaw muscles bulge as he clenches his teeth and balls his hands into fists. Quivering with rage, his eyes pop open and he screams, "NEVER! Granada is DONE with paying tribute to CHRISTIANS!" Flecks of spittle escape with his shouts; venom from the viper. "I will NEVER send another DINAR to those INFIDELS! And NEVER TO A WOMAN! Do I make myself CLEAR, AMBASSADOR?! NEVER!" His withering fury sucks the air from the hall.

In fairness, the ambassador to Castile is new to the Vizier Council. Still, the man surely has heard the stories and should have known better. He cowers, muttering, "Forgive me, sire, forgive me."

Strained silence envelops the regal space. A single drop of water landing upon the tiled floor would prove deafening.

The Vizier Council has witnessed such outbursts many times, though that does not ease the tension. Those present shift uncomfortably on their pillows as their eyes remain glued to the safety of their laps.

The Hall of the Ambassadors serves as the royal throne room of the Kingdom of Granada, and was designed explicitly to both impress and intimidate official visitors to court with its splendor. Its magnificent arabesque walls are adorned with rolling scrolls of embedded calligraphy and poetry, and a massive, yawning marquetry set two stories above; a stunning wooden ceiling, the Seven Heavens of Islam, constructed from thousands of hand-carved and painted cedar puzzle pieces. A breathtaking work of wooden art. The Hall of the Ambassadors was famous when constructed centuries earlier, and that fame has only grown with each renovation, the latest under Muhammad V, one hundred and twenty-five years earlier. While few Christians have ever entered this sublime royal space, the Hall of the Ambassadors is known by reputation throughout Europe, and as far to the east as Persia. To the Christian north, it represents a galling emblem of Moorish wealth and power, a testament to the annoying Islamic foothold clinging desperately to the skirts of Christian Iberia.

Normally the sultan's Vizier Council would convene in either the Hall of the Kings within the Lion Palace or the royal hammam. Instead, because of the presence of the new ambassador and the invitation issued to the Falcon brothers, Grand Vizier Abu l-Qasim Venegas chose the Comares Palace. More formal. Decorum trumps all other considerations within the political machine that is the Alhambra.

Sultan Abu l-Hasan reclines on his white divan in the central niche beneath the pixilated starburst thrown by the sunlit panels of stained glass. Pairs of royal guardsmen flank all entrances to the hall, their white robes and Granadine blue sashes lending a studied formality to the space. Four royal bodyguards stand stiff at attention behind the sultan, lost in the kaleidoscope of spilled color. They are dressed in solid red, their identity unmistakable. By intent. These knights are so still they could be asleep, their eyes vacant, seemingly unseeing, their open palms resting casually upon the hilts of their broadswords. But this is a practiced deception. In truth, the royal bodyguards are trained killers, the most feared swordsmen in the kingdom. Despite appearances, they stand cocked and ready to visit deadly retribution upon anyone who dares threaten the sultan.

To the front of the sultan are gathered the members of the Vizier Council and the guests, circled upon silk floor pillows. To the sultan's left is Grand Vizier Venegas, the second-most powerful man at court; Royal Treasurer Tawd ibn al-Kamil; the sultan's new ambassador to Castile, Amir al-Yasa; then Boabdil, the sultan's son and heir. To the sultan's right is his brother, al-Zaghal, commander of Granada's armies; Military Vizier Prince Ali al-Attar; then the Falcon brothers—first, Yusef, as elder, then Umar, who closes the circle.

Before Ambassador al-Yasa misspoke and unleashed the firestorm, all had been smooth sailing, Venegas briskly leading them through a variety of benign topics during the first half hour of their meeting: the state of tax collections and the treasury; the silk trade and new export opportunities; a few interesting cases from the law courts; the final tally from the Vega's bountiful harvest; the standard religious demands from Supreme Mullah Abd Allah and his troublesome imams; planned military maneuvers; the inevitable attempts to induce friction at court incited by the elders of the Abencerrajes. Normal matters.

Then, on to Isabel and Fernando. Always a delicate subject with the sultan. Castile's war with Portugal, waged on both land and sea, has stretched to over three years now. The new king and queen, suitably occupied, had largely ignored Granada since unifying Castile and Aragon with their marriage, but rumor had it that the war was drawing to a close, producing an unsettling air of uncertainty in Granada. Recent border incidents further complicated matters.

In fairness, Rodrigo Ponce de León, the Marquess of Cádiz, started the trouble without the full knowledge of the new king and queen, leading an expeditionary force against Garciago in a surprise raid. Between the garrisoned troops and the townsfolk, almost four hundred Muslims were killed. Al-Zaghal retaliated with a daring dawn attack on the much larger Cieza, north of Murcia, routing the well-defended town and taking over two thousand Christians captive. A few were ransomed, but most were sold into slavery. Point made.

To add insult to injury, the sultan then sent a letter to the new queen refusing payment of Granada's annual tribute to Castile, ending a practice begun over two centuries earlier. To date, no formal response had been received, but the border had remained on high alert.

Venegas waded into the dark water, successfully, until the ambassador unwisely decided to open his mouth.

Venegas, always the brave one, breaks the silence. "Sire, if I may. We have all heard the rumors about King Fernando and Queen Isabel." There is nothing tentative about Venegas.

The sultan's color has ebbed, the bulge rimming his jawline smoothed out once again. No doubt Venegas held for encouraging cues before commencing. The sultan turns and scowls at his grand vizier, but remains silent.

Venegas scoffs, "Second cousins." He whistles. "Can you imagine? One has to wonder about the sanity of the House of Trastámara. And then the papal dispensation approving the nuptial between two cousins, secured after a hefty bribe from their family friend, the bishop of Segovia, turned out to be a forgery. Ahhh . . . sweet incest! Alas, the coveted title of 'bastard' was granted to the spawn of their wedding night." A mischievous smile. "They say she is quite the minx in bed, you know. In the end, of course, that devil Rodrigo Borgia was able to secure the dispensation from the man he named pope." He rolls his eyes. "The lengths the Christians go to for their children!" A wry smile. "I am told, however, that Sixtus IV made those two promise to never share a bed again . . ." The man's timing is impeccable. "Evidently the pope feared the new abominations the kissing cousins might produce if they grew too fond of each other." He laughs loudly.

He is answered by quiet chuckles and a refreshing breeze of levity. Even the sultan manages a hint of a smile. The storm has passed. Venegas, the consummate tactician. Venegas sifts the expressions of the group one by one. Satisfied, he continues. "Sire, Fernando and Isabel aim to drive us from al-Andalus once and for all. There is no mistaking their ambitions. While I wholeheartedly agree that we should not renew payments of tribute, what the ambassador was trying to suggest is that trouble is surely coming once they settle matters with Portugal. My spies indicate that a treaty between Castile and Portugal is presently under discussion. Once there is peace between them, it will only be a question of time, sire, before Castile turns its attention to Granada. You can be certain that they have not forgotten Cieza. It would thus be prudent to search for some creative means to blunt their efforts, preferably before they commence." He muses. "A peace treaty between Castile and Granada would be ideal, though I do not foresee that possibility just now. So a distraction, perhaps. Maybe even another show of force." He smiles as he rubs his hands together. "Or at the very least a shrewd placement of bribes so that we might learn of their plans well in advance." His eyes again circle the room, widening just slightly when he reaches the ambassador. The man weakly nods his appreciation. Venegas knows he has gained a favor by sparing the man, a card to be played at the appropriate time. No action by Venegas is ever without an agenda.

"What does my military vizier have to say?" The sultan's voice is level and calm.

Ali al-Attar is gray and grizzled, the oldest man present by at least two decades. A formidable knight and battlefield commander still, he is a man of unquestioned honor and valor; a legend in his own time. His very presence on the field of battle garners the respect of his troops, and fear from his enemies. He clears his throat. "I agree with Venegas, sire." The man's voice is as raspy as sandpaper. "Ponce de León easily captured Garciago. Its defenses were much too weak. Now is the time to fortify our borders and strengthen our castles, sire. Granada, Málaga, Almería, and Guadix alone are reasonably ready for attack, but they cannot save the kingdom by themselves. Loja's defenses are modest at best, sire, as are many of the border towns. The siege walls of Baza and Íllora are pathetic. Even Ronda is weak. None will withstand concentrated cannon fire. Our border garrisons must be augmented with troops, and provisions laid in. We must be ready when they come, sire, as surely they will. It is imperative that we not be surprised again."

Al-Zaghal joins in. "I agree. Surprise must be avoided at all costs. We should establish signal fires on the peaks at the border, as in the days of old, sire. We must know the moment any Christian force, small or large, crosses into the kingdom. No sneaking over our border like at Garciago. Quick, decisive action, in force, is Granada's best defense, sire. They will surely probe us again by raiding another of our border towns. If that outcome is favorable, they may then commit an invasion army. The Christians must be crushed mercilessly when the raiding parties come. I say we kill every knight and infantryman they send, even the squires and cooks and whores, and make slaves of those that surrender. No ransom. None. We can use this to sow fear among them. We must make the infidels question the wisdom of invading, sire. We must clearly show them that it will cost them too high a price."

Boabdil blurts out, "I will happily command a cavalry unit, Uncle."

Al-Zaghal turns to his nephew and frowns. *So dashing, but such a slow learner.*

The sultan pivots to scowl at his son. The room tenses once more, but the explosion does not come. Instead, a simple, though unequivocal, "Quiet, boy." He stares his son down until the young man lowers his gaze and surrenders. It is plain enough that the relationship between sultan and son is strained.

Ali al-Attar ignores the father-son skirmish and replies to al-Zaghal. "Violating the rules of war would work against us, Muhammad. We will require ransom for our own knights, just as they will. And it is barbaric to kill those not on the field of battle. Granada must fight with honor, as she always has."

Al-Zaghal dismissively shakes his head, as if al-Attar represents a relic from a dying age. "Now that Castile is allied with Aragon, Ali, they are far stronger and better armed than us. They have far more cannons. If given half a chance, the Christians will put the Vega to the torch, lay siege to Granada, blast our walls to rubble, and starve us into surrender. We need new tactics if we intend to survive."

Ali al-Attar chides, "As I recall, Muhammad, Granada was heavily outnumbered when we defeated Enrique of Trastámara at Jaén a century ago. Granadine bravery bought us lasting peace and prosperity. We fought with honor then, and won."

Al-Zaghal answers, "The old ways will not save us this time. We need new tactics, some advantage."

Venegas steps in to marshal the conversation. "New tactics, yes. Sire, Ali has invited the Falcon brothers to tell us about their latest experiences with the pelleted black powder. Perhaps we might hear from them?"

The sultan's expression brightens. "Yes, good. Yusef, Umar, I am pleased that you have joined us."

The brothers bow deferentially. Yusef says, "You honor us by inviting us, sire."

Ali al-Attar shakes his finger at al-Zaghal. "You will have your tactics, Muhammad. Tell them, Yusef." The old man's pride in his nephews shines like a beacon.

Yusef clears his throat. "Sire, we have carefully tested the pelleted black powder. Uncle had the mixture carefully prepared using the secret recipe of Hasan al-Rammah of Damascus." He pauses to build suspense. "With the same charge, sire, the new powder can fire an iron ball over twice as far."

The sultan is incredulous. "Twice as far?"

"Twice, sire."

Ali al-Attar smiles as he echoes, "Twice as far as the powder the Christians are using."

Al-Zaghal is rapt. He muses. "That would mean if they try to lay siege to our cities, we can hold their cannons at bay with our own."

Umar responds for his brother. "Correct, sir. It will give us a decided advantage in siege defense. Should it ever be required."

The sultan replies, "Excellent news."

Al-Zaghal asks, "Can the bronze of our cannons withstand the added force of the new charge?"

Yusef answers, "That is unclear at present, sir. I agree that this must be carefully tested. We have used only half-charges thus far, and all seemed well." He hesitates. "However . . ." He now has everyone's attention. "I think the new powder also provides us a unique opportunity. Potentially, a new tactic."

Al-Zaghal smiles greedily. "Do tell."

"The cannons the Spanish possess are mostly French bronze, unrivaled in quality. They have a range better than our own cannons, and of course, they have many more than us. But with their weak powder, they are forced to use massive charges in their guns to achieve sufficient range. Thus, the bronze at the breech is very thick, and the barrels must be long, making them so heavy they cannot be moved without at least a dozen horses, and then only very slowly. Because they cannot keep pace with a mobile attack force, they can only use their cannons during sieges to destroy castle walls and battlements, never on the field of battle." All eyes are glued to him. "Just suppose, however, that we produced much smaller, wheeled cannons, ones light enough to easily move. With our new powder they would still have enough firepower to be useful at close range. If we constructed a proper *limber* to match, I believe such a cannon could be pulled, and pulled quickly, by a single horse, or perhaps a pair."

Umar excitedly blurts out, "We would then have artillery on the field of battle, sire! These cannons would not need to fire only solid shot, but instead, grapeshot. Against their infantry, archers and pikemen. We will sow death by the bucketful!"

Yusef adds, "I have made some calculations, sire, and even some drawings. With your permission, I would suggest that we cast a prototype cannon and construct the limber and test it. We will not know until we try." He sheepishly smiles. "Though I think our chances of success are excellent."

Umar blurts, "It *will* work. Yusef is always right!"

Laughter.

Al-Zaghal is beaming. "Excellent work, Yusef. Most excellent! This could give us the edge we need against their superior numbers, sire."

"See to it, Yusef, and keep us informed." The sultan turns to the royal treasurer. "Tawd, provide him whatever he needs."

The man ticks his head deferentially. "Certainly, sire."

The sultan continues, "In addition to these new cannons, I want the borders of the kingdom bristling with freshly fortified castles, secure garrisons, and ample provisions. And signal fires on all the border peaks. Our armies must be ready to fight when the campaign season commences. The Vega *must* be secure. Tawd, open the treasury for Granada's defense. If it runs dry, I will levy more taxes. Granada's future hangs in the balance. We must act, and act now."

Ali al-Attar says, "I will pay a personal visit to the border castles and make an assessment of exactly what needs to be done."

The sultan replies, "An excellent idea, Ali."

Al-Zaghal says, "The kissing cousins will be forced to think hard before considering an invasion, sire. Very hard indeed."

The sultan's disposition has grown sunny and bright. "Precisely."

Even the poor ambassador has grown cheery.

IN MÁLAGA, SIX DAYS LATER.

The man looks positively ancient, his forehead a plowed field, his eyebrows an explosion of teased cotton. A giant crow has planted its feet beside his bloodshot sky-blue eyes. Too much reading. His face and neck are studies in sag. His unkempt beard scraggles halfway down his chest, the color of wood smoke, a few stubborn streaks of unlikely black clinging for dear life. He wears the plain gray robes and turban of a Sufi master. There is a disheveled air about him that he seems completely oblivious to, as if he has been so lost in thought or prayer that he forgot to have his robes laundered or visit the hammam.

But there is something about the man's eyes that demands a careful accounting. They are watery with age but sparkling with intelligence and a deep sense of contented satisfaction with his place in this world. Warmth also, and a playful, mischievous twinkle, as if he is in on some private joke and is fighting to suppress a smile; or perhaps has a prank up his sleeve he is about to unleash on some unsuspecting soul. There are layers of wisdom, too, cultivated by a life of study, service, and prayer, but tempered with the profound kindness such pursuits engender. The man has a grandfatherly benevolence that lends comfort to all those he meets.

He lifts the parchment letter, retracts his head, and squints to bring the signature into focus. From the royal physician:

> *Dearest Abd al-Salam—Greetings, old friend. I trust you are behaving yourself for once. I am not certain Málaga can . . .*

The drape of wrinkles lifts into a smile. He quickly follows the neat Arabic script, right to left, right to left, his eyes widening with surprise as he nears the middle of the page. Finished, the letter slowly folds to his knees as he stares into space. He whispers, "Lovely Danah, my gifted girl. *Barakah Allah.*" May Allah bless you. "The Compassionate and Merciful One has great plans for you, dear child, great plans indeed." He chuckles to himself. "I have never played matchmaker, O Lord. Help me find a path for Danah that pleases You . . . and her."

His back straightens as he draws his arthritic, age-mottled hands to his lap and cups them into a triangle, ready to receive Allah's Grace and blessings. His mind and heart meld as he closes his eyes and narrows his focus to the sacred breath of life. Twenty minutes later, he begins to quietly chant the *Dhikr*, the remembrance, the invocation of the ninety-nine names of Allah.

Al-Rahman - The Compassionate.
Al-Rahim - The Merciful.
Al-Malik - The Sovereign Lord, Our King.
Al-Quddus - The Holy, the Pure, the Perfect . . .

Westerlies

Two hours past sunrise, on the open ocean to the southwest of Lisbon, Portugal.

The acrid reek of unwashed bodies is pervasive, chased by an unmistakable whiff of stale urine and loose bowels. The stink hangs thick in the air, almost visible; ripe and invasive, eye watering. The organic fetor of rotting fish mixed with oiled leather, oak, a hint of gunpowder, salt, wax, broken wind, lye, sodden hemp, days-old rancid stew. Given its lack of ventilation, the hold is the worst, of course—especially given their cargo—though the sleeping quarters are not far behind. The one respite is the cool, steady breeze, sweet and saline. Alas, there are no portholes on this small *caravel*. Those who can stay aloft in the fresh air do so, and in decent weather most of the crew will choose to sleep above deck under a heavy blanket on the hard planks rather than brave the stench in their swaying hammocks.

As the tiny room slowly rolls from one side to the other, the oak timbers of the hull groan and creak their protest at the constant torture inflicted by the three-foot swells. The hanging lamp swings lazily back and forth, back and forth, a drowsy metronome.

Even with a crew of twenty, the work on a caravel is remarkably quiet, the sailors going about their tasks with resigned determination. They are close to port now; they can feel it in their bones. The only sounds to be heard: the occasional bark of an order to cinch the slack from newly laid rigging, a cursed imperative to recheck a knot, the taut slap of the canvas *lateen* whipping in the cool wind.

Toscanelli's nautical map lies splayed before him on his writing table, a secret Florentine treasure passed on before the astronomer's death. Those who have heard the rumors of its existence could be counted on two hands. That it lies open in the captain's quarters of this particular Portuguese caravel is a tribute to a lasting friendship and a shared quest—a westward water route to the East Indies.

Few would call the man handsome. He tends instead toward nondescript, though on a good day, perhaps 'agreeable' would be more apt. Of medium height, with strong limbs, his eyes a translucent blue and slightly bulging; but he is intelligent, determined. A large aquiline nose, pale complexion, a scatter of freckles, his red beard and hair running quickly now to cotton white.

The man hunches over the map, dividers in one hand, quill in the other. He widens the divider set to five nautical miles, looks to the sheet of figures, then dips the quill and records a number in tiny script along the edge of the map.

Gridlines of *latitude* and *longitude* cut across the parchment. Below the Strait of Gibraltar, the coastline of the Maghreb first bulges westward, then southward to Dakar and the wilds of West Africa. At the very beginning of the eastward bend of the coastline lies the port of Elmina and its imposing castle, São Jorge da Mina. Guinea, the land of gold and slaves, jealously guarded by the Portuguese.

What makes this map so remarkable is what lies due west of the Canary Islands—the East Indies, home of the cherished spices worth their weight in gold throughout Europe: cinnamon, cassia, cloves, cardamom, ginger, pepper, saffron, nutmeg, turmeric. Gifts from heaven to estates and courts, castles and cathedrals, knights and noblemen, merchants and clerics; anyone with ready gold. Such spices are a godsend for curing the incurably bland— diets marked by crude stews and porridges, boiled root vegetables dulled by the dirt that birthed them, bloody spits of grilled meats, rehydrated moldy fruits.

Toscanelli's choice of longitude for the East Indies is highly unusual, the result of his painstaking calculations of the diameter of the Earth, informed conjecture on the size and shape of *Cathay* and *Cipangu*, his opinion on the hotly-debated longitudinal span of Eurasia, and more than a tad of wishful thinking. The intriguing result? According to Toscanelli, only eighty-five degrees of longitude separate the Canary Islands from the East Indies, far less than Ptolemy's ancient calculations that scholars and mariners alike still embrace as unassailable fact. Eighty-five degrees. A tough sail, to be sure, but reachable for a skilled navigator with detailed knowledge of the Atlantic *westerlies.*

Conventional wisdom mandates that no viable western water route to the East Indies exists, the distance simply being too great to reach under sail. Three months to landfall is the common understanding, perhaps as long as four. And that assumes fair winds. A caravel can only carry a month's supply of fresh water and food for a standard crew complement. Once stores are exhausted, death by thirst or starvation or worse awaits. And, of course, the inevitable horrors of scurvy before the end comes. Veteran mariners view the idea of a westward route through uncharted waters to be a fool's errand, a voyage of no return. Suicide. None have ever been bold enough, or crazy enough, to attempt it.

Even a Florentine of Toscanelli's notoriety dared not state his claims publicly. Still, all would agree that a viable westward water route to the Indies, should it ever be found, would fundamentally alter Europe's balance of power. And wealth. Lands could be claimed for king and country, souls won for Christendom, fortunes secured. Given the daunting odds against a successful westward passage, the finest mariners sailing under Portuguese colors are instead intent on finding an eastward water route around Africa. All but one.

The caravel is two weeks out from Elmina on the return voyage to Lisbon, its hold laden with gold, ivory tusks, and three-dozen African slaves.

The captain chose a most unusual route for his return, unprecedented really. He first sailed northwest for the Cabo Verde Islands, as usual, then, instead of sailing northeast for the safe harbor of the Canary Islands, he headed due north toward the distant Azores, finally veering back to the northeast at thirty-five degrees latitude, and on to Lisbon. His westward route added four days to the journey, and considerable risk, but if asked he will blame it on persistent coastal storms off Tantan. The reason for his detour? To take soundings of the Atlantic westerlies, the western trade winds, both strength and direction, during all hours of the day and night, so that he can add them to Toscanelli's secret map. He has a plan.

Aw uck. The man lifts his head, the dividers still glued to his thumb and forefinger. *Aw uck. Aw uck.* The awkward, throaty squawk of a gull. Companions join the fanfare, *Aw uck-aw uck-aw uck, aw uck-aw uck-aw uck.*

A faint, "Land ho! Land ho!"

A moment later, a crisp *tap-tap.*

His eyes flick nervously to the door. He lays his dividers down, lifts his log and places it on top of the Indies. Hidden treasure. "Come."

The door creaks open. "Captain Colón." The second mate's face confirms the good news. Two weeks is a long time to be on a laden caravel from equatorial Africa during winter. "Land sighted, two points to starboard. Portugal, sir. God save the King!" he says excitedly to Christopher Columbus.

55

"Excellent, Martim. Steer for Lisbon. And see to the slaves. I want them presentable when we make port."

"Aye-aye, sir."

"I am afraid your calculations are in error, sir." A quick sniff, then a haughty smile. The king's counsellor exudes a dismissive, courtly arrogance. King John II watches blankly from his throne.

Colón flushes, then scowls. "My calculations are most certainly *not* in error!" His tone is challenging, well beyond permissible protocol for a royal audience.

The counsellor's smile evaporates. Several of the attendants anxiously glance at the king as they begin to look uncomfortable.

Realizing his mistake, Colón stops himself, bows his head as he opens his hands in submission, and attempts to adjust his tone. "Forgive me. My calculations are correct, my lord. Eighty-five degrees longitude, no more. And I have now mapped the westerlies. From the Canaries, I can reach the Indies within a month. I am certain of it."

"I have had the royal geographers check and recheck your numbers, sir." That dismissive tone. "I must tell you that they do not agree with you. They insist the real distance is thrice what you claim. At least. Perhaps you would care to show them your figures on the westerlies?" His eyes narrow into a challenge.

Colón ignores the request. "I have based my calculations on those of Toscanelli, my lord. Perhaps you have heard of him?" An ill-considered dose of sarcasm. The Florentine astronomer is famous; of course they have heard of him.

The counsellor flicks his wrist, waving away the thought. "Toscanelli, God rest his soul, was well known for harboring strange ideas about longitude, sir. I can assure you that we have examined his writings at length. We judge them to be in error."

Sensing defeat, Colón turns to appeal directly to the king, another serious breach of protocol. "Majesty, I will claim the Indies for Portugal. I only require three caravels. Three. Think of the opportunities, majesty!"

The silence is sharp-edged, crystalline.

The king sighs. "Claiming the Indies for Portugal would be a great thing indeed, Captain Colón, but your demands strike me as excessive." The king's tone is soft and steady; reasonable. "To be named 'Great Admiral of the Ocean,' to be appointed governor of all lands discovered, and then awarded one-tenth of all revenue generated from those lands?" He widens his eyes incredulously. "Even so, at my request the royal geographers have carefully studied your proposal. As I am sure you know, they have spent years determining the westward distance to the Indies. These are men, Captain Colón, who have spent their entire lives navigating the esoteric arts of geometry and astronomy. I can assure you that your proposal has been given due consideration." Another sigh, this one betraying a weary edge. "Their opinion is that the Indies are far beyond the reach of a caravel. Even with good knowledge of the westerlies one would—"

"But, majesty, I . . ."

Interrupting the king? Decidedly unwise. The room visibly stiffens. Even the king frowns. "Even with good knowledge of the westerlies one would run out of stores long before reaching landfall." His tone has shifted to curt. "A fool's errand, I am afraid. In any case, I have received word that Captain Dias has successfully rounded the tip of Africa. Portugal will soon have a viable eastward water route to the Indies."

"I heard the rumor, yes, but . . ."

The king lifts a finger to silence him. "The matter is closed. You are free, of course, to seek another sponsor. Perhaps Genoa or Venice would be interested." The king glances at his counsellor, who does not miss such cues. The audience is ended.

The counsellor clears his throat. "I am afraid the king has urgent matters to attend to. We thank you for your time, Captain Colón." The man's wry, satisfied smile serves as an exclamation point. He has no patience with these upstart foreigners.

Options exhausted, Colón has no choice but to bow and retreat, heavy frown glued to his face. An eternity for an audience, now nothing. He has already received letters from Genoa, Venice and England, all of whom have rejected his proposal.

Scars

The Jewish Quarter spans nearly one-third of the land bounded by Granada's massive outer defensive walls. An impossibly dense maze of narrow, cobbled alleys, bending and folding, twisting and turning, first bifurcating then unexpectedly rejoining. To the uninitiated, a confused tangle of canyons, the alleys just wide enough to pass a cart or fit two horses side by side. But despite the congestion, or perhaps because of it, there is great verve here, the close proximity of souls and families and livelihoods producing a warm coziness, an air of familiarity and friendliness, of shared lives and traditions, of gossip and laughter and stories; a place swaddled in a celebration of the sheer joy of living.

This is one of the oldest parts of the city, the heart and soul of Granada's *medina*, the haphazard construction built from a legacy of laying down floor upon floor, joining wall to wall, room to room, family to family. Decade after decade, century after century. In the medina one adds; one never subtracts. High above the western edge of the Jewish Quarter stands the imposing Bermejas Tower, a *barbican* linked by an elevated walkway to the southwestern tip of the Alhambra, and a formidable citadel in its own right.

In between the Jewish Quarter and the River Darro lies the famous Alcaicería, Granada's legendary silk market, principal source of the kingdom's wealth and the sultan's taxes. Granadine silk is universally recognized as the finest in the western world, and no small share of Granada's glory lies in her endless orchards of mulberry trees, which stretch from the hills surrounding the city up into the high reaches of the Alpurrajas Mountains.

David and Danah walk side by side, matching the modest pace of the traffic as they traverse the slope down through the Jewish Quarter. The narrow alleys are crowded in the morning market hours, and they are forced to twist and dodge as they move through the throngs.

Empty geranium boxes adorn shuttered windows, and laundry lines crisscross high above, many already draped with freshly washed clothes hung out to dry. Bougainvillea vines climb like youngsters toward the open sky; sleeping still, but with buds swollen tight with promise. Even against the brisk chill of an early spring morning, the coming bounty beckons.

David greets those he passes with a simple nod, a kind word, or an easy smile. He is known here, after all. She walks in silence, observing. She has never been in this part of the Jewish Quarter. Her shrouded head pivots right and left, up and down, back and forth as she absorbs the scene, a tethered ball batted about. He occasionally steals a glance to check on her, and smiles.

One final turn and the street broadens out into a plaza, unusual in this part of the medina. The edges of the plaza are lined with carts and tables selling all manner of goods. The air is alive with enticing aromas; freshly baked bread from the communal ovens, skewers of lamb sizzling on charcoal braziers, simmering stews, a heady mélange of exotic spices and herbs. The scene is bustling with activity—the hawking of wares; the inevitable haggling over prices; the playful chant of barkers; whispered gossip behind palms, quick to be answered by a rolling of eyes or sharp giggles; yapping dogs; hearty cackles chasing bawdy jokes, then back-slaps and playful elbowing; the lifted hands and widened eyes of a tall tale teller; the impish glee of young children at play as they flit about among the towering adults; the muted strum of a guitar playfully answered by a fiddle's steely whine, then sporadic clapping. Everyone here contributes their smiles to the intimate celebration of life.

At the far end of the plaza is a two-story, whitewashed building with keyhole jalousie windows, a low-angled terra-cotta tiled roof, and an ornate red ochre and white Umayyad horseshoe arch bounding the oaken entrance door. The structure stands apart from the others on the plaza, a rich cousin among paupers. David touches her shoulder and they stop. He lifts his palm. "Behold, Danah, the Atfal Hospital."

A satisfied smile lights her face as she studies the façade, a masterpiece of polychrome arabesque stucco set over Granada's famous ceramic tilework—here, a tight weaving of thin ribbons; blue, rust, gold, green, and black. Just above the door arch is decorative Arabic script. Without prompting, she quietly announces,

> *The Atfal Hospital—A gift of Sultan Muhammad V to the forgotten ones of Granada. May the most Compassionate One grant you refuge and peace. Dedicated in loving memory to Shahab Chandon, loyal knight of Granada. There is no victor but Allah.*

David says, "Of course . . . Chandon. Shahab Chandon."

"Tetta Layla's husband."

"Indeed. The Atfal is smaller than the Bermejas. In Layla's day it served the physically and mentally deformed, both Jewish and Muslim. Today, it exclusively serves the orphaned children of the city. Those not claimed by extended family, for whatever reason."

"How many are there?"

"Two dozen, perhaps three."

She nods, but there is a lingering wariness. As an only child, she knows almost nothing about little children. Never once has she held a baby in her arms or changed a diaper.

"Why was the women's madrasa closed?"

"I am not sure." He smiles. "I would suggest you ask the chief physician yourself. Hakim Ezar al-Mufaddal. A good man, and a dear friend. You will like him." He again lifts his palm. "Shall we?" They brave the crowded plaza and begin to weave their way toward the entrance.

MOCLÍN, ON THE NORTHWESTERN RIM OF THE MOUNTAINS RINGING THE VEGA DE GRANADA.

A surprise visit by Prince Ali al-Attar, the sultan's military vizier. The old man is trailed by a sizable entourage; his adjutant, two bodyguards, the castle commander and his second, then two dozen of the garrison officers and staff. The hosts are understandably nervous. The inspection has followed a predictable path: the fresh repairs to the city walls, the armory, the garrison, cisterns and siege provisions. So far, so good. A grunt here, a nod there, two minor compliments, no significant complaints.

Last is the signal fire atop the limestone promontory on the western edge of the castle mount. The squared pyre stands half the height of a man, each thigh-sized log notched and fitted upon the next to ensure stability. The interior cavity is filled with layers of kindling and shredded rags. The top is covered with a fitted leather tarp to ensure the wood remains dry. Three ceramic amphora rest against the pyre.

The old man limps around the structure, casting a critical eye upon the construction. After completing the circle, he stops and rests his hand on the pyre, tests it by shaking it, then checks the cinch of the ropes holding the tarp.

"Too small." The pronouncement is raspy, impatient. "This is the last high peak before the plain, Commander al-Fihri. It is vital that the watchtower of the Alhambra be able to easily see your signal fire. Day or night."

"We have the means to produce smoke, my lord." He lifts his hand to the amphorae. "Two are filled with oil in case the weather is wet, one with bitumen-soaked sawdust. It will produce a thick black smoke visible for many miles."

"Mmmm . . ." The old man turns to face the valley and steps forward to the edge, stopping uncomfortably close to the sheer cliff. The wind is spirited; cool, but not unpleasant. The sky is a piercing robin's egg blue, heralding the coming of a glorious day. The only sound is the flutter and snap of the old man's robes.

A spectacular view of the plush Granadine Vega unfolds before him—massive, verdant rectangles of finger-high spring wheat troweled upon gently rolling hills. Green's green apogee. Pastures carpeted in thick grass, contented cattle lazily chewing and swishing their tails; fallow fields thick with blooming clover cut by wide swatches of glorious red poppies that go on and on; neat runs of trellised vineyards alive with pale green shoots; dark-brown squares of rich loam combed into precise rows, the tender sprouts just breaking the surface; cherry orchards exploding in puffs of glorious pink; endless stretches dotted with tufts of shimmery, silver-hued green—olives. The Vega's abundance spreads as far as the eye can see. There is a pleasing suggestion of freshly turned earth upon the wind, chased by composted manure and the homey scent of livestock. A rich, organic wholesomeness. Hundreds of specks dot the fields, laborers hard at work already fussing over the coming spring bounty.

Ali al-Attar lifts his arm and points southeast. "There, Commander." A squint of the eyes reveals a tiny dab of white set upon a faint red ochre smudge, the backdrop of the majestic snow-capped Sierra Nevada rising high behind. "Fourteen miles to the Alhambra. Rest assured, King Fernando and his army will pass this way. It is imperative that I know the instant the infidels advance. The kingdom's fate depends upon it."

"Understood, my lord."

"Double the height of the pyre, and add a second amphora of bitumen."

"Certainly, my lord. You may depend upon Moclín, my lord, we will be ready."

The old man grunts his approval, then turns to his adjutant. "Iyad, we make next for Íllora. And send a rider to my nephews. Have them join us at Montefrío for dinner two days hence."

"Consider it done, my lord." Hand signals set the group in motion.

"How long has she been in your care?" David's tone is a mixture of professional interest and concern. They have left the chief physician's office and entered the long hallway leading to the wards, the two men in front, Danah a step behind.

Ezar stops, his impossibly bushy eyebrows first lifting in puzzlement, then furrowing with concentration. He raises his hand and slowly begins to count on his fingers.

Danah wrestles a smile. She already likes this man.

The other hand rises. *Six.* "Six days now." His face brightens with his answer, then dims. "But no improvement at all. None."

David frowns. "Is she eating?"

"No, nothing."

"Drinking?"

"Very little. A sip of water here and there, but we basically have to force it on her." He sighs. "She is wasting away. No will to live. That is why I sent for you, David. She is physically fine, not a single cut, no blow to the head, no broken bones. Nothing. She acts like a caged animal. You can see the terror in her eyes when I enter the room, as if I aim to harm her, not help her. And she has not spoken a single word since she arrived. Not one. Perhaps she is mute? Or mute and deaf." He lifts his hands, helpless. "I have never had a case like it."

Danah, who to this point has been all eyes and ears, finally speaks up. "I have a question."

Ezar widens his eyes dramatically as he settles his gaze upon her. The man seems to live for exaggeration; he looks as if he just witnessed a miracle. His eyes twinkle as his face brightens. Even though they met only ten minutes ago, you can already see his fondness for her growing. After all, he has six children of his own, all girls, the oldest nearly her age. "Praise the Lord, she speaks!"

David chuckles.

"Yes, Emeralds, and what is your question?"

Already a pet name for her. Uncharacteristically, she is charmed; a favorite uncle she never had. Her grin is spontaneous. Those bushy eyebrows just will not quit! Frizzy black woolly worms crouched over his eyes. She clears her throat. "You said her parents were murdered. Do you know what happened?"

His smile relaxes as the sad story set before them returns. "Alas, we know very little, I am afraid. The official word was a

62

border raid by rogue Christian mercenaries. A small village near Campotéjar. Razed to the ground. The Falcon brothers found her."

"Falcon brothers?" She has no clue.

The woolly worms arch their backs. His barrel chest puffs out; his teacherly pose, for which his own girls tease him. Mercilessly. "You have never heard of Granada's famous Falcon brothers, Emeralds?"

She shakes her head.

An incredulous, "Never?"

She awkwardly shrugs, uncomfortable with ignorance of any kind.

He beams, always ready to preach. "Yusef and Umar al-Makki. The Falcon brothers. Nephews of Prince Ali al-Attar, military vizier to the sultan. The most famous cavalry commanders of the realm, young lady. And favorites of the sultan."

"Knights . . ." Her tone is dismissive.

"Knights?" He scoffs. "Oh, much more than that, Emeralds. Princes of court, yes, but well educated and pious. Very intelligent young men. And gallant! As versed in literature and chess as they are skilled with a broadsword and a crossbow."

Danah nods but is clearly still skeptical.

David says, "What exactly did the Falcon brothers find?"

Ezar's smile fades. "Well, their cavalry patrol saw smoke and rushed to the defense of the village. What they found was shocking, even for Christian mercenaries. All of the adult villagers, almost two dozen, were murdered. Rounded up, hands tied behind their backs, forced to kneel, then decapitated. Men and women. And their heads were missing, David. Trophies of war, evidently." He shakes his head. "Awful stuff."

Danah grimaces. "Dear Allah . . ."

David says, "Barbarians."

"The cavalry found the girl wandering aimlessly near the village. They assumed she was away on an errand when the raiders arrived. Or perhaps ran and hid before she was seen." He shrugs. "I am afraid that is all we know. She was unresponsive when they found her, but otherwise unharmed. The Falcons sent her directly to the Atfal. Six days ago."

David asks, "Surely there were other children found in the village?"

"Oddly, none. The assumption is that the raiders took them all back to Castile as slaves. Only Yehovah knows."

David considers the facts, then says, "If she did witness the murders that might explain her condition. Extreme trauma can induce many odd symptoms."

"Perhaps. But if she was close enough to see what happened, I cannot imagine that they would not have found her. And if so, why would they not have taken her with the other children?"

No response. There are no easy answers.

Ezar smiles to inject some levity. "Shall we?"

They resume their walk, but all three are silent now, contemplating the many possibilities.

They stop in front of a closed door. The entrance to the main ward is at the end of the hallway, ten paces farther on. He whispers, "We have kept her in a room by herself. For now. I thought the other children might scare her. Ready?"

David and Danah nod.

Ezar lifts the door latch. They ease into the room, standing side by side. Ezar gently closes the door behind them with a single crisp, *snap*. The space is compact. A lone floor mattress against the far wall and a low-slung writing desk. A small jalousie window looks onto the courtyard.

The girl lies prostrate on the bed, arms by her side, a blanket pulled tightly across her, leaving only her head exposed. As if a parent tucked her in after a nightmare. The girl's eyes are open but staring at the ceiling, as though she did not hear them enter.

Danah studies her. *Thirteen years old, perhaps fourteen.* The girl is petite, with long, straight brown hair. She registers the swell of breasts under the covers. *She has either had her first bleeding moon, or is close to it.* A dusting of freckles cross her pale cheeks. Danah's heart melts. *Just a girl. And so pretty.*

Ezar takes one step forward and stops, clears his throat.

The girl's head slowly rolls toward the sound. Her eyes lag behind the movement, but when they finally rest upon Ezar, you can see the terror jump into them. She slides away from him, tries to disappear into the wall. A pathetic whimper is all that escapes her lips.

Ezar tries to soothe her. "There, there, darling. Shhh . . . No one is going to hurt you. There, there. Shhh . . ."

A more desperate whimper.

"I have brought two people to see you. Both are famous physicians. David and Emeralds. They are here to help you, darling. Shhh . . ."

After 'famous physicians,' Danah spontaneously smiles. The girl's eyes track to the brightness and remain there, fixed. Danah's smile relaxes, but the girl does not break eye contact.

Both David and Ezar follow the connection and remain frozen.

Danah weighs the facts laid before her, sifts them against Abu al-Qasim's treatise on infirmities of the brain. *Pretty girl approaching womanhood. Mute and unresponsive. Vacant eyes. Terrified, with no will to live.* Danah's eyes fold closed as she engages her rare empathetic gift. She beckons Allah's healing Grace. *Come to me, O Lord. Come. Help me to feel what weighs upon this girl's heart. Help me, O Lord, to take away her pain. Help me, Allah . . . Help me, Allah . . . Help me, Allah . . . Come, O Lord . . .*

The room stills as the agony focuses to a sharpened point, an additional presence in the room. Danah groans as recognition dawns. *The Christian raiders found her hiding place.*

As if by silent cue, the girl's frightened eyes well up, brim, then tears break free and slide down her cheeks.

Danah gasps as if she has taken the pain into herself. Her eyes open, then fill, as she intuits the awful truth. *This girl was raped. Then discarded as worthless trash, unfit for transport back to Castile, even as a slave.*

Confused, Ezar attempts to step forward, but David touches his arm and whispers, "Give them space."

Danah wipes the tears from her own eyes, sniffs, then another smile reignites her face, this one forced. She reaches up and slowly removes her head scarf, drops it to the floor, not even debating whether or not to break the cultural taboo of revealing her uncovered hair to the two men watching the scene unfold. She tilts her head back and shakes her mass of chestnut-brown curls to free them. Danah smiles once more, then begins to ease toward the bed. The girl's eyes remain glued to her, wary. Danah stops and stands motionless, silently counts to twenty. As she sits, the girl flinches but does not break her stare.

Two minutes pass. David and Ezar stand like statues, eyes wide with awe.

Danah lifts her hand and ever so slowly touches the girl's cheek, thumbs the tears away. The girl does not resist. Danah leans forward and begins to breathe words into the girl's ear. The two men strain to hear but cannot make out what she is saying. Only a breathy, warbled whisper. This goes on for over a minute, to no response. Danah stops, gently strokes the girl's hair, then begins anew. The girl's lower lip begins to quiver. Her shoulders begin to shake as her chest heaves. She bursts into tears. Danah pulls the covers down, slides her arms underneath the girl, and hugs her tightly. The girl begins to wail. Danah pulls her closer still.

Danah turns to David and Ezar and flicks her head toward the door. Ezar does not register the signal, but David does. He touches the other man's arm and they retreat from the room. The door snaps shut behind them.

They can hear that the girl is sobbing uncontrollably now.

Ezar is incredulous. "What just happened, David?"

"You have witnessed a healing, my friend. Or at least the beginnings of one. Some healings do not require a bone to be set or a wound to be sutured. Compassion, a kind heart, and some gentle words. And, of course, Yehovah's Grace."

"It was almost as if Emeralds physically felt the girl's pain . . ."

"Yes. She possesses amazing powers of intuition and empathy."

"But what did she say to the girl?"

"Only Yehovah knows."

Ezar nods in amazement. "Dear Lord, Emeralds has the gift."

David smiles, his face filling with pride. "She does indeed."

"She must help me nurse the girl back to health, David. Please, lend her to me, just for a while. Her studies can wait. Her calling is here at the Atfal, at least for now." He temples his hands. "Share her with me, David, please. I am willing to beg."

"Of course, my friend, of course."

MONTEFRÍO, TWENTY-FIVE MILES NORTHWEST OF GRANADA.

The old man winces. "How many?"

The three of them are gathered around a campfire.

Yusef answers. "Twenty-two, Uncle. Including eight women. All beheaded. A village south of Campotéjar. Razed to the ground. All of the animals were taken."

The old man scowls as he considers this unexpected news. "Sounds like the work of those barbarians you faced at Mata Bejid."

Yusef looks down to hide his anguish.

Umar studies his brother with a concerned expression. He softly answers for Yusef. "Unlikely, Uncle. That was three years ago."

"Mm." Sometimes the old inadvertently forget the pain that can be inflicted on the young by certain words. Ali al-Attar continues, "A bold move to be sure, but why? A reprisal for our attack on Cieza? Or perhaps the test of our border defenses has commenced?" He coughs wetly into his hand. "Both unlikely, I think. Fernando would be a fool to attack us before he and Isabel settle their business with Portugal. Why start a second war before the first is over?"

Umar says, "We assumed it was rogue mercenaries, not knights of Castile or Aragon."

"Perhaps. Or cleverly made to look like that." He shakes his head. "And they took the children?"

Yusef finally looks up, seemingly himself once more. "They did, Uncle. We have no idea how many, but they were gone when we arrived. All but one. A young girl. We found her wandering not far from the village."

"So she witnessed the attack?"

"Unclear. We were not able to get a single word out of her. My guess is that she hid herself when they came. What she saw must have been so terrible that it struck her dumb."

"No doubt."

Yusef adds, "We sent her to Granada for care."

Ali al-Attar nods. "The Atfal?"

"Yes. She is an orphan of Granada now. Hakim al-Mufaddal will see to her. Perhaps he can find a way to restore her speech so we can learn more about what actually happened."

The old man grunts his approval. "They surely realize that the taking of our children is not something Granada will tolerate."

Umar grows excited. "Let us track them, Uncle. The trail is still fresh. Yusef and I could take a dozen riders, rescue the children, kill the infidels, and be back by week's end."

"Mmm . . ." The old man strokes his chin.

Yusef replies, "I believe that that is what they want us to do. This attack was far too brutal to make sense. Mercenaries would have looted the village and taken the livestock, then quickly retreated to safety in Castile. Why burn the village? And why behead the adults and take the children? There was nothing for them to gain by doing so, and much to lose." He muses. "No, I suspect they did what they did because they wanted us to follow them back into Castile. So they committed acts too grievous to leave unanswered. They wanted us to give chase. My guess is that they plan to ambush us once we cross into Castile, then make it look as if Granada made an unprovoked attack upon Christian lands."

Umar counters, "If they were trying to set a trap, then why use mercenaries? Untrustworthy and unpredictable."

"That they were mercenaries is only an assumption, Brother. I just find it hard to believe that knights of Castile would stoop to that level of barbarism. All Christian knights are bound by a code of honor, just as we are."

Umar replies, "That did not prevent what happened at Mata Bejid, Yusef."

Yusef stiffens. "Those were foreigners, Umar. They did not even speak Castilian."

"Foreigners, yes. But Christians nonetheless."

The old man adds, "One reason to use mercenaries is that the whole incident could be disavowed if it did not play to their liking. We will need more information to know for sure."

The three men fall silent.

Ali al-Attar coughs once more, clears his throat. "We will leave it be. For now. But I want you to triple our border patrols from Loja to Montejícar. We must make our presence known. If any of our cavalry happen to engage the Christians, mercenaries, or knights, under no circumstances are they to pursue them into Castile."

The brothers reply as one. "Understood."

The old man changes the subject. "Tell me about the cannons."

Yusef smiles. "The limber is nearly ready, Uncle. I designed it to be pulled by two horses. The first cannon should be cast any day now. If all goes well, it will soon be ready for mounting on the limber. Then a field trial."

Umar's face grows animated. "We aim to ride for Granada tomorrow morning, Uncle, to check on the progress."

"Excellent. Make sure no one sees your creation when it is ready for testing. Surprise is key."

Umar replies, "All movements will be made under the cover of night, Uncle. We will send word as soon as there is news."

"Good. I have a few more weeks of inspections, then I will head back to the city. Make sure you check with al-Mufaddal to see if the girl has recovered enough to tell us what happened. We need information."

Yusef nods. "Understood. We will ride for the city at daybreak. Come, Umar, let us settle the men and rest." The two young men rise.

Ali al-Attar offers a rare smile. "May Allah protect my boys."

They reply in unison. "Allah's blessings be upon you, Uncle." Yusef lifts the old man's hand, kisses the back of it, then touches it to his forehead. Umar repeats the action. Much love. And much respect.

Late that evening. Yusef and Umar sit on either side of their campfire, a stone's throw outside Montefrío's outer walls. A moonless night, the landscape opaque as calligrapher's ink. Their troops have settled into their tents, and the camp is quiet. The air is cool and moist but pleasant enough. There will be dewfall by morning. The cavalry's cooking fires have settled into glowing embers, stoked just enough for easy revival at first light and a hot breakfast before they ride for Granada.

The brothers' conversation about the best path and pace of their coming ride has concluded. Umar wants to pass through the towns along the way to make their reassuring presence felt; Yusef prefers to incorporate drills and training. In the end they settle on a mix of both. They will ride via Tocón, Brácana, and Pinos Puente, with battle maneuvers around Sierra Elvira.

Silence settles in. The brilliant canopy of stars pulses with latent energy, commanding introspection. Both men stare into the mesmerizing coals, lost in their own thoughts. Yusef lifts a stick and begins to poke and tease the bed of crimson back to life. He quietly says, "You will hold Faynan in your arms tomorrow night." An odd tinge of wistfulness clings to his words.

Umar looks up, puzzled. Yusef rarely speaks about his new wife. The trickle of new flame casts dancing shadows upon Yusef's face, making his expression unreadable. "I will, yes." He smiles. "I aim to dream about it all night, Brother."

No response.

Finally, Yusef softly says, "You love her." There is hint of resignation in his voice.

Umar is confused by his brother's tone. "I do. More than life itself."

Yusef sighs. "Yes . . ."

Strained silence.

Umar tries to lighten the mood. "Perhaps it is time for you to marry, Yusef. Why should I have all the fun?" He smiles again.

"No." Yusef's tone stiffens. "Marriage is not my calling." Before Umar can reply, Yusef says, "It is late, Brother, and I need sleep." He rises. "I will see you at first light."

Umar frowns as he watches Yusef disappear into the dark.

"And how is our patient, Emeralds?" Ezar's expression is worthy of the Greek theater.

It is their final meeting of the day before she leaves to march back uphill to the Bermejas Hospital to meet her escort.

"As well as can be expected . . . Frizzles." Danah chases her words with a playful grin. Two can play that game.

His mouth falls open, aghast.

She arches her right eyebrow for punctuation.

His shoulders shake as he begins to chuckle, then laugh loudly, finally doubling over, hands on knees, as he roars. She rewards him with a smile, and the two begin to laugh together.

As he recovers, he says, "Frizzles? FRIZZLES?! I love it! If only my own girls were half as clever." He mock-frowns as he looks skyward and attempts to tame his woolly worms with his thick fingers. "I do try to keep the beasties in check, you know. Well played, young lady, well played!"

Their mutual affection brightens the room. As the air settles, they move back to the more serious topic at hand. He says, "Is she eating?"

"Not much, but enough to sustain her. And she is taking in plenty of water now."

"Out of the woods, then. Good. Maybe try and ply her with some delectable sweets. We need to get some weight back on her bones. Any words yet?"

"Alas, precious few. Her name is Samra. She turned thirteen in December. She had two brothers, both older. Taken by the raiders." Danah lowers her voice. "She was raped by five men." Her voice hardens. "Five. Four held her down while the other had his way. Then each had a turn."

Ezar grimaces. "Horrible. Any information on who the raiders were or why they did what they did?"

"Nothing of use. We must give her time. My sense is that the story will eventually come out. In the meantime, I think we should continue with only female attendants if I am not here. For obvious reasons—men terrify her. Even you."

"Agreed."

"I have been meaning to ask you . . ." She hesitates.

A beseeching furrow. "Ask me what?"

"About the founder of the Atfal Hospital. Layla al-Khatib."

"Ahhh . . . the Emeralds of the Alhambra. You two share some things in common, you know."

She answers with a smile.

"I know the standard legends, of course. Why?"

She grows serious. "I dreamed about her. It was so real I felt like I could reach out and touch her. She told me that we were related by blood."

"Intriguing. Dreams are funny things, Emeralds. Not always to be trusted. Jinn enjoy such games."

"I understand. That is why I want to learn more. Do you think her father was really a traitor?"

He considers this. "Hard to say. He did many great things for Granada, of course. Saved the city from the plague. And he left us his medical encyclopedia, treasure that it is. But supposedly there was good evidence of his betrayal of the kingdom to the Marinid sultan in Fez. Evidence provided by Zamrak the poet. Interestingly enough, Zamrak was al-Khatib's protégé."

Her eyes widen at this new information.

"It is true. Ibn al-Khatib discovered him in a madrasa in the Albayzín, brought him to court, and taught him everything he knew, then saw that he was appointed secretary to Sultan Muhammad V and lauded as court poet. As I am sure you know, his poetry adorns practically every building in the Alhambra. So unless there was good evidence, I cannot imagine why Zamrak would betray his mentor." He shrugs. "But who really can know? It has been so long."

"Yes, ages. Does the hospital have any records or artifacts from that time which I might examine? Anything at all related to Layla?"

He considers this. "As a matter of fact, we do. We have patient records dating back to that period, various accounting documents, bills of sale, discharge papers. Boring stuff, mostly. But there *is* something that may interest you. A small wooden box. Remarkably, it was hidden inside a wall, evidently plastered in for safe keeping. It was found only ten years ago during some new construction I had commissioned for the ward. The box bore her name. Precious little inside, I am afraid, given her important role in founding the Atfal—some letters, a few trinkets, two old books. It has been many years since I looked at it, but given that it contains the only surviving artifacts of our founder, we keep it under lock and key. Would you like to see it?"

She beams. "That would be wonderful. May I take it home with me this evening?"

He looks skeptical. Rules exist to be obeyed. "I am afraid it is not supposed to leave the hospital . . ."

"Please, Frizzles? I promise to return it safely on Wednesday. I will guard it with my life. Please?" She flashes her very best disarming smile. How exactly is one supposed to say 'no' to such a face? He is putty in the hands of comely young women. His defenselessness against his own daughters' wishes and whims is the stuff of family lore. He gives up and shrugs. "Of course, Emeralds. Your word is golden at the Atfal. Perhaps you can do a final check on Samra while I go and retrieve it? Meet me in my office when you are finished. I will find a bag to discreetly carry it in, and you can open it when you get home."

She is glowing. "Thank you, Frizzles."

He walks away shaking his head, chuckling to himself.

With a sharp giggle, she roughly pushes him backward onto the floor pillows and straddles him, her hands pinning his shoulders, her knees locking his arms to his sides so that he may only see, not touch, her magnificent breasts.

He happily plays the captive. He begs her, of course—what man wouldn't? "Please, Zoraya, be fair. Just one touch."

She smiles that sultry smile of hers and replies, "Soon enough, my sultan, soon enough. But first you must obey me."

His voice is clenched with desire. "Command me, my lady."

A smoky whisper, "Lie still. Your eyes are not to leave mine. If they do you will suffer. Obey me, my sultan, and I will reward you."

His voice tightens with anticipation. "Your wish is my command, my lady."

She locks her eyes to his with a wicked smile and grinds those glorious hips upon him. So close, but so far. Beads of sweat dot his forehead. She stops to study him, almost as if she is calculating, then leans down, curtaining his face with her blond curls. He tries to kiss her, but she pulls back just beyond reach. It is clear that she aims to torture him. Again. For an instant his eyes leave hers. She strikes like a viper, nipping his lower lip hard enough to draw blood. She laughs as he winces, then she kisses away the blood and in a single motion buries her tongue in his mouth and impales herself upon him. He gasps, then moans. He tries to tilt his pelvis to get her to move on him, but she refuses, her exquisite curves an alabaster statue worthy of the ancient Greeks.

She sits up straight, mock-scolds him with her finger. "Obey me, my sultan."

He nods his helpless submission.

With another wicked smile, and without moving her hips, a fluid wave of muscular contraction runs along the length of him, some magician's trick she plays with her body. He draws a sharp breath and clenches his teeth to endure the sweet agony, then releases a heavy exhale. "Dear Lord, woman . . ." He is answered by a satisfied smile. She licks her lips seductively and promptly begins again. This time he cannot stifle his groan.

"Isabel is the one you should fear, my sultan."

They lie naked, entwined still, he on his back, she on her side, her leg scissored across him and head fitted neatly into the notch of his shoulder. She idly twists her finger into his chest hair. It has become their way, to lie and talk about matters of state under the great honeycombed ceiling of the Hall of the Two Sisters.

"Isabel? No, Fernando is the one to fear, my love. A capable knight and commander. He leads the combined armies of Castile and Aragon. A young man, it is true, but my sources tell me he handled himself well against the Portuguese king and his army. Once a truce between Castile and Portugal has been signed, they will turn their attention to us. Fernando dreams of the riches of fair Granada. He craves our gold to fill his treasury."

"That is true, my sultan, he does crave your gold. But Isabel's motivations are different. She lusts for power and dynasty. Her greatest desire is to unify all of Iberia under her Castilian banner. She is far more ambitious."

"Mmm . . ."

"She has already maneuvered to win the battle for the crown of Castile, my sultan. King Enrique's daughter, little Juana, was the true heir to Castile. My father said there was proof. The queen's coup, tenuous at first, will become complete if there is a truce with Portugal. They will trouble Castile no more. Trust me, she will shrewdly marry her daughters to princes scattered across Europe. She aims to govern the world with her progeny." She pauses to let him absorb this. "And remember, my sultan, Fernando is merely Isabel's consort, no more. His titles are tied to Aragon alone, not Castile."

He frowns. "But they are king and queen."

"In name only. There are documents that bear this out."

He looks incredulous.

"It is true. She insisted upon them when they wed, my sultan. Isabel retains sole control of the Castilian crown. My father told me."

"But she is just a woman!"

"A formidable woman." Her tone hardens. "You would do well never to underestimate her, my sultan."

Silence.

Zoraya continues, "Isabel is dangerous for her ambitions, my sultan, but perhaps even more so because of her piety. She is a Christian monarch in her heart, one who rules by God's intent, and she aims to reclaim Granada for Christendom and cast the *Moors* into the sea. She sees it as a holy quest, a duty God has placed upon her soul."

He is dubious. "Granada is no threat to her. Aside from an occasional border skirmish, a semblance of peace exists between us."

"It is the Ottomans who are the real threat in Isabel's mind. Europe quakes in fear of Mehmed II's *jihad*. First, Constantinople, then half of Greece, Anatolia, Albania, and most of the Balkans. Now Otranto, on the Italian peninsula. The Turks have sworn to capture both Vienna and Rome. Father says that Isabel fears that the Ottomans will soon come calling and use Granada as a beachhead to sack Iberia and claim her birthright in the name of Islam."

"Nonsense. Sultan Mehmed does not even see fit to answer my letters. Let the Turks have Rome and Vienna. They would never venture this far west."

"I agree, my sultan, but perception, as you well know, often trumps facts. I tell you, Isabel will not rest until Granada flies a Castilian banner. She has papal support, of course, but also the backing of the nobles in both Castile and Aragon. Fernando will command her army against us, but rest assured, it is Isabel and her ambitions that will frame the rules of conquest."

"Mmm . . . Perhaps you are right. I will give it thought."

"Of course I am right, my sultan." With a sly smile her hand slides from his chest toward his groin.

Crescent Moon

Danah sits cross-legged on her floor mattress, the wooden box before her. Her heart is pounding. She picked at her dinner, then pushed it away, complaining of a stomachache, and asked to be excused. Her mother seemed skeptical, but after feeling her head for fever, she reluctantly agreed, though she insisted Danah take hot mint tea with her and promise to go straight to sleep. "You are working too hard, Danah. No reading tonight!" After a perfunctory promise, Danah slipped off to her room and the waiting treasure.

The box is polished cedar, aged to a warm copper hue; as long and wide as wrist to elbow, and half as deep. Silver corner bindings with a fine spiderweb of scrollwork; the work of a skilled jeweler. It is tarnished now into a dingy, gray-tan patina and locked by an ornate silver latch. An elegant, expensive box. In fine Arabic script, inlaid with lapis lazuli, she reads,

Treasures of the Heart
Layla al-Khatib
Beloved Wife of William Chandon

She touches the inlay, runs her finger over her tetta's name. *William must have been his Christian name.* She studies the latch mechanism. Unusual, but obvious. *Why would she need to hide this in a wall?* The lock opens with a metallic snap. With bated breath, she slowly folds back the lid and surveys the contents.

She gingerly lifts a small bundle of papers. The collection is tied together with an emerald ribbon knotted into a bow. She lays the bundle on the bed beside her. *Later.*

She lifts a single chess piece carved from ivory—the grand vizier. She tilts an eyebrow, lays it down. *Her father?*

Next is a gold brooch, with a massive cut ruby surrounded by gold. *Expensive. Beautiful.* She lays it down.

She lifts a tiny glass vial, holds it close. Inside is a lock of wispy blond hair tied with a silk thread. *So they did have a child.* She smiles, pleased with the possibilities.

She stares at the next object before she lifts it. A palm-sized rectangle of silver plate, not much thicker than heavy foil. Tarnished. She frowns, puzzled. *What on earth?* She carefully picks it up by its edges. Mirror-like still, but covered in brownish smudges. She tilts it to catch the light and suddenly gasps as a ghost emerges. She narrows her eyes, studies the image. A young man sitting in front of a bookcase, beaming. Very faint. She tilts it to find the best light. *Handsome.* He holds a piece of paper in front of him. She squints as she tries to make out the Arabic script. She slowly whispers, "Rayhana: my beautiful wife, my beloved, my heart and soul. I believe." *Rayhana?* She gently lays the silver foil beside the letters.

Next is a single sheet of parchment. Old and delicate. Calligraphy, but, oddly, the words are Castilian.

Face that lights my face—

She stops. She knows this poem. Rumi, from the *Masnavi*. She reads aloud:

"Face that lights my face, you spin
Intelligence into these particles

I am. Your wind shivers my tree.
My mouth tastes sweet with your name

In it. You make my dance daring enough
To finish. No more timidity! Let

Fruit fall and wind turn my roots up
In the air, done with patient waiting."

A love poem.

Two books are all that remain—one small, one large. She lifts the small codex. The leather binding crackles as she opens it. A Quran. Beautiful calligraphy; red Arabic script with blue and gold arabesque ornamentation. *Exquisite.* She turns to the front corner to check for an inscription. She reads:

To Layla and her Young Knight. May Allah's Grace and Peace rest upon your holy union. Let your Great Love light the midnight sky. May your years together be many, may each moment be filled with bliss, and may your children be as numerous as the stars in the heavens.
Salamun

Her eyes are wide; her heart pounds. *It was a wedding gift from the royal physician.*

She lays the Quran beside the rest of the treasure-trove and raises the large volume with two hands. *Fine leather binding. Looks ancient.* She tilts it to read the spine. "The *Ambrosian Iliad*. Homer." She has heard of the *Iliad* but has never read it. The binding cracks painfully as she slowly opens it. *Beautiful color illustrations.* She turns to the inside cover. Filled with compact, neat calligraphy. She reads:

> *Zafir Saffar gives this* mahr *to his beloved, Rayhana Abi Amir, in the royal gardens of Madinat al-Zahra, the glorious evening of Eid, 29 September 976. Let the Great Love begin.*
>
> *Zafir and Rayhana al-Khatib, married, 22 January 977. Arrived in Loja, 13 February 977. The first of the al-Khatibs. Daughters: Rayya, Rebekah, Durr*
> *Sons: Samuel, Razin*

She stops. *Rayhana. 977?! Dear Allah! Madinat al-Zahra, the legendary Umayyad palace of Córdoba.* Every Granadine child knows the story of the shining city, the 'ornament of the world.' She frowns. *But why would they come to Loja? It could not have been more than a sleepy village back then. And why would they change their names?*

No dates of birth or death. The entries after this are simpler, a listing.

> *Samuel al-Khatib married Fatima al-Qadir, 12 July 1004.*
> *Isa al-Khatib married Idlal al-Karim, 2 May 1027.*
> *Bakr al-Khatib married Najma al-Wadud, 11 October 1058.*

She stops again, looks back to the top of the page, nods. *The wedding dates of the first sons. The al-Khatib lineage.* She quickly scans the list, counting—one, two, three, four . . . nineteen entries. She reads the last entry at the bottom of the page.

> *Lisan al-Din ibn al-Khatib married Danah al-Basir, 21 June 1342.*

The most famous al-Khatib of all. Grand Vizier Ibn al-Khatib from Loja. She smiles. *And his wife and I shared a name.* She turns the page, reads aloud:

Layla al-Khatib of Granada married William Chandon of Brittany, 26 September 1368. The Great Love continues.
Son: Shahab

She frowns. The list ends with Tetta Layla. She turns the page. Nothing. *Who did her son marry?* She chews her cheek as she puzzles over this. She nods. *Of course! She was forced to hide the box when she and her father were exiled. For some reason, she was forbidden from taking her treasures with her to the Maghreb. Or perhaps she was afraid they would be taken from her if they were found. Or perhaps the contents contained incriminating evidence of some sort.* She sighs, frustrated by the opaqueness of it all. She whispers, "But there *was* a son . . . Shahab Chandon."

She stretches into a Y and yawns loudly. She returns the items to the box; all but the bundle of papers. She rises, changes into her bedclothes, cleans her teeth, turns down all but her bed lamp, then slides under the covers and onto her side. For a long moment she simply stares at the bundle, excited, but also nervous about what she may learn within those pages. She pulls the bow. She unfolds the first sheet of paper, rolls onto her back, holding it above her. Castilian.

My darling Layla:

No date. She turns the page over, sees his name. *William.* She turns back and begins to read.

I write from my tent outside Jaén, on the eve of battle. The walls of Castillo de Santa Catalina are visible from the ridgeline. A thousand Christian campfires dot the horizon.

She looks up and quickly calculates. *They were married in September of 1368. The battle of Jaen was in July of 1369. They were married only ten months. Dear Lord . . .*
She returns to the letter.

Tomorrow is Granada's day of reckoning. Though we are balanced on the edge of a dagger, I am confident my plan has a good chance to succeed. All we need is a bit of luck. I know you wanted me to stay, Layla, to run from this fight.

But the man you love is a knight of Granada, and I am duty bound. I fight for Granada, for her children. Do not worry, my love, Barq is at my side, and Musa and Yazdan stand with me. All will be well.

I try with all my might to stop thinking of you, my love. I cannot. My heart is filled with the great gift of our last night together in your secret hiding place in the Generalife. You said we would conceive our baby, Layla, as we lay together under the stars. God willing, may it be so, my love, may it be so. No matter what happens tomorrow, I will live on in your heart for eternity, and in the child our love has conceived. The Great Love we have been given is from God, and of God, and will endure forever. I will always love you, Layla, I will ALWAYS love you!

Your William

He never saw his son. Dear Allah, he never saw his son. She gulps air to steady herself between forceful exhales. *How Tetta Layla must have suffered, her heart broken into a thousand pieces. Oh, dear Allah, how my Tetta must have suffered . . .* Heaving breaths now. "Dear Tetta, I am so sorry, so very sorry. Tetta . . . dear Tetta . . ."

For reasons she cannot fathom, her eyes slowly fill, as if a flood overwhelms her from within. Her chin begins to quiver and her shoulders convulse. Tears leak from her at first, then gush as if from a riven dam. She turns back onto her side and curls into a fetal position as she begins to sob uncontrollably.

It is some time before the storm passes. A great release from a great many hurts. Cathartic, but exhausting. She wipes her eyes as she sniffles, her ragged gasps damping out as she tries to calm herself. She lifts the letter and holds it to her heart, then closes her eyes. She begins to imagine the two lovers; talking, laughing, walking, playing, kissing. Such a short time together. She imagines their secret hiding place in the Generalife. The child.

A hushed whisper, "I want to know Great Love, Tetta. I want to know Great Love . . ." Her breathing steadies as she drifts off.

The Albayzín sleeps. Her room is a soft twilight, peaceful and still. The jinn's hour steps near. Danah's breathing is steady and relaxed. As if on cue, her pupils begin to dance beneath her lids. Then a delicate twitch of her cheek, a flick of her index finger, a soft groan as her leg stretches the covers. The lamp flame flickers and pops, magically lengthens, then settles. A shower of brilliant gold sparks shimmer into the corner of the room, hover in midair.

Danah sits up.

Tetta Layla is cross-legged on a floor pillow, her hands folded in her lap, eyes closed.

"I am dreaming."

The old woman's eyes slowly open. Watery emeralds. She raises her eyes to Danah and smiles. "I have been waiting for you, dear girl."

"I am here, Tetta, I am here." She hesitates. "I found your cedar box. The one you hid at the Atfal Hospital."

Layla smiles. "Of course you did, child. William gave me that box. The treasures of my heart. They were waiting for you all these years. They are yours now."

Danah opens her mouth to say something, then stops.

"Go ahead, dear, say it."

"I am so very sorry, Tetta. Ten months with William; only ten months. So little time, so precious little time."

Layla fights back her tears. She can only nod as she bites her lip.

"What happened to little Shahab, Tetta?"

No answer.

"How did I come to be, Tetta? What is my connection back to you, and to Shahab?"

Layla stares into space, as if struggling to recollect. There is pain buried near the surface; so much pain.

"I am Abencerraje, Tetta. Amiriya, not al-Khatib. I want to know my lineage, Tetta. Help me claim my history. Help me, Tetta."

Silence.

Layla begins, "My father and I lived in a suite in the Comares Palace at the time. William was wounded in the first battle of Jaén, then brought back to the city as a political pawn. Father had him placed in a room directly across from me." She smiles. "He was a famous knight, you know, the most dashing cavalry commander in Brittany." She stops, stares into space. "And, dear Lord, was the man handsome!" She laughs, pulling a smile from Danah. "The sultan commanded me to teach him Arabic, and to learn English from him. I wanted no part, of course, and even fought Baba tooth and nail over it. You see, by that point I was working at the Maristan Hospital as a part of my Sufi training. I had no time or use for men." A broad smile. "Just like you, dear girl." She laughs as Danah blushes.

"Did you fall in love the first time you met?"

Layla gives a quick chortle. "We fought bitterly the first time we met. I lost my temper over his use of the word 'honor.' I insulted the poor fellow." She widens her eyes. "He was four years my senior, you know, and a famous knight. Quite unbecoming of me."

Danah smiles.

"If only father had known where it would all lead . . ." She releases a sly smile. "Secret midnight rendezvous by the Comares reflecting pool. Remember, he was a Christian prisoner and I was a princess of the royal court. Quite scandalous! As you will discover yourself, matters of the heart are rarely simple things, dear girl. Our first kiss was in the Courtyard of the Myrtles. Under a rare winter's snow." She sighs as she recollects. "I remember it like it was yesterday. It was the first time we exchanged words of love." She brightens. "William was a wonderful man, with such a kind heart. He saved me from being ravaged by a scoundrel, you know. He even saved the sultan's life. After that he was favored at court and things got much easier for us. He was appointed military vice-vizier. Quite an honor, though I knew even then that it would eventually lead him to battle. He converted to Islam and asked Baba for my hand." Her smile twists devilish. "We made love while we were still betrothed. Under the stars in my childhood hiding place in the gardens of the Generalife."

Danah's look of utter shock is comical.

Layla laughs. "It was my idea, you see. Ours was a Great Love, dear girl, a blessing bestowed upon us by Allah. A special kind of love. A rare kind of love. It was that night under the stars that he and I first experienced *tawhid* together, the mystical union with Allah that all Sufis seek. No Layla, no William, only Layla *and* William. One body, one heart, one soul. A month later we were married. We were so happy. So very happy . . ." She falls silent.

Danah whispers, "Then Jaén."

"Then Jaén." Layla's words become weighted with lead. "I had a dream that he had been injured during the battle. Against Baba's wishes I rode for the battlefield. I was at William's side as he passed from this world into Allah's embrace. Before he left me I told him we had conceived a child, and that our Great Love would live on." Layla dabs a tear, her words drowning in that ancient grief. She forces a smile. "Without little Shahab I do not think I would have survived the agony." She conjures her son's face. "A spitting image of his father, you know. Same blond hair, same smile. But, praise Allah, our emerald eyes."

Danah smiles.

She continues, "Such a beautiful boy. Caring for him gave me the strength to live. Within the year I had founded the Atfal Hospital. And then the women's madrasa. I learned to find happiness in my work."

Danah gently asks, "Did you ever remarry?"

"Remarry?" She frowns. "Oh, there were suitors anxious to take William's place . . ." Her expression grows serious as she stares into space. "One in particular. Zamrak . . ." Her anger coils around the name.

"The poet of the Alhambra."

Layla looks back at Danah, studies her, then smiles warmly. "Your fate is to experience Great Love too, dear girl. It is why I have crossed time and space to come to you."

"Abd al-Salam is searching for the one I am to marry, Tetta."

No answer.

Anxious now, Danah, asks, "Tetta Layla?"

The old woman says, "There is a deep chasm separating you from your Great Love, child. You must build a bridge within your heart . . . then close your eyes and cross it."

Danah's eyes widen. "Will I know my Great Love when I meet him, Tetta?"

She is answered by more silence. It is as if the old woman is weighing whether Danah is ready to hear the truth.

More urgently: "Will I know him when I meet him, Tetta?"

Nothing. Finally, she says, "Trust your heart, child. And look for the crescent moon."

"Excuse me?"

Gold sparks begin to shimmer into the corner. Layla grows ghost-like, ethereal.

"Tetta, how will I recognize my Great Love?" Danah's tone grows frantic. "How? Tetta, tell me! TETTA!"

Layla's words fade into the stillness as her body dissolves. "Look for the crescent moon, dear one. The crescent moon."

Danah pleads, "Tetta, do not leave me. Please, Tetta. Please!"

Only gold sparkles remain, hovering in the air. They wink out one by one, and the room is once again still.

Danah wakes with a gasp. She sits up, heart pounding. She stares at the empty corner of the room as her breathing steadies. She whispers, "Look for the crescent moon . . ."

Auto-da-Fé

THE CASTILIAN ROYAL PALACE IN CÓRDOBA.

"A letter has arrived from Toledo, my queen. It seems that Inquisitor de Morillo has pronounced judgment on the false *conversos* of the city and called an *auto-da-fé* to make public their penance." Hernán de Talavera, a priest of the Order of St. Jerome, is Isabel's confidante and confessor, one of the few who enjoys ready access to the queen. He is tall and thin, robed in the plain black of a common monk. Neatly trimmed beard and tonsured hair. A handsome man, though a tinge of gaunt stubbornly clings to his features, a consequence of his ascetic leanings. Intelligent. Quite shrewd in picking his way through the delicate dealings of the Castilian court. He would not still be here if he were not. Though not given to jollity, the man has kind eyes, a gentle voice, and manners. He is an excellent listener.

Isabel looks troubled by the news, though she has been expecting word. She remains silent.

"Shall I read the letter, my queen? It is signed by the official court notary, and bears the seal of Inquisitor de Morillo."

"Very well. Read it." Her tone is curt.

Talavera reaches beneath his robe and retrieves the letter, breaks the seal and unfolds it. He clears his throat and begins.

> *May it please her royal majesty, the true and righteous Queen of Castile—Sunday, 12 February, was clear but bitterly cold. Inquisitor Miguel de Morillo convened the auto-da-fé at sunrise. All of the reconciled accused of the city's seven parishes were forced to march in procession. There were about 750 in number, men and women.*

She interrupts. "Surely there were not that many."

Talavera raises his eyes. "It would seem that there were, my queen. Toledo has a rich Jewish heritage." He resumes.

> *The men were all together, wearing nothing on their heads or feet. They bore unlit candles in their hands. The women also marched in a group, without any head covering, their*

faces and feet bare like those of the men, and with the same unlit candles.

Isabel grunts.

Talavera stops.

Without looking up she flicks her wrist to bid him continue.

In the group of men were many of prominence and high standing in the city. In the terrible cold, they suffered. A very large crowd turned out to watch their dishonor and disgrace. The accused went along sobbing and howling, and pulling at their hair, more for the dishonor they received than for their offenses against God. In this way they went in tribulation through all the city, along the path where the procession of Corpus Christi goes, until they arrived finally at the cathedral. At the entrance to the cathedral were two chaplains, who made the sign of the cross in ashes on the forehead of each of the accused, saying, "Receive the sign of the cross, which you denied, and being deceived, lost." Then they went through the church until they arrived at a scaffolding put up by the new door, and on it were the official inquisitors, standing in judgment. Nearby was another scaffolding from where the Inquisitor de Morillo said Mass and preached to them about sinfulness and salvation. After this, a notary rose and began to call out each one of the accused by name. Each person, when called, raised his candle and said, "Here." Then the notary read aloud publicly all the ways each man was accused of Judaizing. Next, the same thing was done with the women. When all this was over, Inquisitor de Morillo announced publicly to them their penance. The accused were ordered to go in procession for six Fridays, scourging their naked backs with cords of hemp, going without covering on their feet or their heads. They were to fast from all food and drink on each of the six Fridays. And they were ordered to never, for as long as they lived, hold public office. Those that held such offices were told to resign them. And the accused were never to work again as moneychangers, shopkeepers, spice sellers, or hold any official position whatsoever. They should never again wear silk, nor clothes that were colored, nor any gold, silver, pearls, jewels, or perfume. And they were told that henceforth they were unworthy to serve as witnesses in court. They were then ordered to pay a tax on their sins, within seven days, equal to thirty percent of their worth. If they could not pay that tax in gold, their holdings would be liquidated to do so. Inquisitor de Morillo then ordered that if they relapsed into the same error once more, and did again what had been attributed to them, they would be condemned and would . . .

Talavera halts.

The queen snaps, "Read it!" Sometimes it is preferable to pull the scab from a festering wound with one quick jerk.

Talavera clears his throat.

Inquisitor de Morillo then ordered that if they relapsed into the same error once more, and did again what had been attributed to them, they would be condemned and would burn at the stake. When the pronouncement of their penance was finished, about two o'clock, they were dismissed, and the auto-da-fé concluded.

Talavera slowly folds the letter, returns it to his robe, and with his thumb and forefinger begins to rub his eyes. A profound weariness settles upon his bones. Under his breath, he lets slip, "Dear Lord, help us."

The queen turns on him. "What, Hernán? Do I detect sympathy for the false conversos of Toledo?"

"Not sympathy, my queen, just surprise. So many. And so harshly treated, even the women."

"Harsh, but necessary, Hernán. You understand that these false conversos are Christian in name only. They are Jews that hide in plain sight." Her voice is rising as she speaks. "They celebrate Mass, taking the Holy Eucharist upon their tongues as pious Christians, then light their menorahs and celebrate Shabbat behind closed doors." She stops to gather herself. She muses, "The king strongly supports imposing an Inquisition in Aragon as well as Castile."

Talavera smirks. "No doubt. But where the king sees only the gold to be had for fitting out his army, you have a higher calling, my queen."

She eyes him, but does not speak. Finally, she says, "As you know, Hernán, we have the pope's approval for our actions."

"Our dear weak pope, Sixtus IV, bless his soul. He gave his *reluctant* approval. But yes. Ceding authority to a foreign crown for an Inquisition is unprecedented. It warrants special prudence, my queen."

They fall silent.

He continues, "I am told the common folk have taken to calling the false conversos '*marranos*'—swine."

"So I have heard. These . . . marranos . . . have been a stain upon Castile for long enough. Let us not forget the *moriscos* living among us either. Even a baptized Moor is suspect, Hernán. Can a Moor truly ever forget his roots? Both are painful affronts to our Lord and Savior."

They join eyes. The monk sighs. "I fear where this may all end once it is begun, my queen. Burned at the stake for a second offense? Is there to be no mercy?"

"The crown cannot tolerate Jews masquerading as Christians, especially when so many hold high office. It is a scourge against God. They must be rooted out and dealt with swiftly, with no mercy." She pauses. "God has ordained me for this task, Hernán. I intend to restore purity to the realm that God has seen fit to grant me."

A deferential nod. "I understand, my queen, but I fear that those who are innocent may also be swept up in the Inquisition's wide net. There is such a thing as a true conversion, you know."

"Of course. And those who are true to the faith need not worry."

"Perhaps. I have heard rumors, though, about Inquisitor de Morillo's tactics that give me—"

Isabel lifts a hand to silence him. "You will write to the Inquisitor de Morillo and express my commendation and strong support for his fine work."

The monk's hesitation is long enough to draw her glare. "Of course, my queen." His disapproval has been registered.

"Thank you, Hernán." Her tone softens. She changes the subject. "Have the Marquess of Cádiz and the Duke of Medina-Sidonia arrived yet?"

"Late last night, my queen."

"Good."

The monk offers a wry smile. "I brought each entourage into Córdoba by separate gates, and we have settled them into rooms at opposite ends of the palace. For the safety of the court."

This produces a shadow of a smile. "Mark my words, Hernán, those two will be allies soon enough."

"It will be a welcome change, my queen. Their petty bickering has gone on long enough."

She nods her agreement. "I will meet with the Royal Council tomorrow morning in the throne room. Invite our guests, but do not show them in until I call for them. And find the king—I believe he has gone hunting. Inform him that his presence is required."

The monk hesitates. "The king will not wish to have his hunting interrupted."

Her tone stiffens, "Inform King Fernando that his presence is required at court."

"I will see to it, my queen." He turns to leave.

"And, Hernán?"

"Yes, my queen?"

"I am in need of . . . *confession*." Her odd inflection lingers in the air.

He studies her for clues.

She signals retreat by looking away, quite uncharacteristic for her. The queen's private confession is normally reserved for Saturdays, to ensure her heart is pure for the *Eucharist* of Sunday Mass. "After *Vespers*, if that is convenient."

"Of course, my queen. Our Lord will be pleased to hear your sins and absolve you."

A simple nod without looking back.

The monk makes a sweeping bow, then retires, sifting the exchange for hints.

The royal palace of Isabel and Fernando lords over the deep green of the River Guadalquivir, no more than an arrow shot from the Great Mosque of the Umayyads. That ancient forest of red ochre and white-striped horseshoe arches bears silent witness now to Christian Masses, the breathtaking mosaic and gold *mihrab* boarded over almost two and a half centuries ago.

What was once the Moorish alcázar of the Arab caliphs, with its lovely gardens, hammams, flowing water, and fountains, is now one of the southern royal palaces of the king and queen of Castile and Aragon. The formidable towers and walls still bear the unmistakable stamp of Almohad crenellations, a Moorish trademark, though most of the elaborate arabesque wall decorations of the palace have been stripped away, replaced by sterile whitewash, now hung with ornate tapestries, sundry coats of arms, oil paintings, and crucifixes.

The queen and king sit side by side in regal attire, their thrones three steps up from the audience. An elaborate gold-trimmed crimson velvet tapestry drapes the wall behind them, the queen's coat of arms prominently displayed in the center—eagle and crown set above a chessboard shield of lions and castles interspersed with the red-and-yellow insignia of the House of

Trastámara, the shared ancestral heritage of these second cousins.

Both king and queen wear their crowns. Isabel is dressed in a flowing, floor-length hunter green robe with white inner-sleeves, its gold-laced piping and trim studded with jewels, the look a perfect complement to her fair skin. Her only jewelry is a small gold cross hanging from a necklace. A sheer mantilla is draped upon her wavy, strawberry-blond locks. She studies the men in silence, her steely blue-gray eyes alive and bright. She is a comely woman, shapely and buxom, her features youthful still for a woman having borne four children. She projects a stern countenance by intent, but a closer look reveals the unmistakable hint of a vulnerable femininity, of a latent sensuality; something she tries to mask, but which clings to her like the inviting dark swell of a perfectly ripe plum.

The king favors crimson robes at court. His pearl-studded cape is trimmed with ermine, a dense study of woven gold and blue silk, in the Moorish style. He wears a massive gold pectoral cross. Of modest height, but strong and well-proportioned, he is a keen sportsman; his prowess with horses and in the jousting arena are now legendary. Fernando is a consummate swordsman, a proven battlefield tactician, and an able leader. Confident. Dark, straight shoulder-length hair, fair complexion, like his cousin. He is celebrated for his wit and charm, his easy smile and boisterous laugh, though truth be told he is more comfortable with his troops than at court. Fernando is a handsome man by any reckoning. Even without his noble rank he would garner the attention, and favors, of the more adventuresome maidens at court.

This morning, where the queen's expression is unreadable, the king looks mildly perturbed. He slouches in his throne, annoyed by the interruption of life's finer pleasures. He is impatient to be quickly done with this meeting and be back to the hunt in the game-laden foothills of the Sierra Morena.

Before them, standing, bedecked in the requisite formality of such audiences, are the members of the queen's Royal Council: Hernán de Talavera, the queen's confessor and confidante; then Alonso de Cárdenas, minister of war and Master of the *Order of Santiago*; Luis de Santangel, finance minister; Cardinal Pedro González Mendoza, chancellor of the realm, the highest-ranking cleric in Castile; and finally, the dashing Gonzalo de Córdoba, the Great Captain, Fernando's second-in-command and brilliant battlefield commander, head of the queen's personal guard and Isabel's close friend since childhood. He is the only member of the Royal Council fluent in Arabic.

She offers the men a surprisingly warm smile, which sets the chamber at ease. "Gentlemen. I am grateful for your presence and good counsel."

The five men offer a formal bow in unison.

"There are several important matters requiring our attention."

The king sighs loudly enough to be heard, then sits up.

Isabel ignores him. "I am delighted to tell you that Cardinal Mendoza has made substantial progress toward a treaty with Portugal." She lifts her palm to him. "Cardinal, if you please?"

The cardinal clears his throat. "As you know, after the stalemate at the Battle of Toro, the queen sent three separate delegations to Alcáçovas to discuss terms of peace with the King of Portugal. The Duke of Alba and I have served as principal negotiators for the queen. I am pleased to tell you that Portugal is finally willing to recognize Queen Isabel as the legitimate ruler of Castile, thereby ending the war."

Talavera says, "Wonderful news, my queen."

Alonso de Cárdenas, the minister of war, interjects, "At what price?"

The cardinal turns to the Master of the Order of Santiago. "Castile will cede the disputed Atlantic territories to Portugal."

A gruff, "Which territories?"

"Cape Verde, Madeira, the Azores, Guinea, and all undiscovered territories south of Guinea."

Cárdenas frowns. "But those are ALL of the disputed territories, Cardinal Mendoza."

"We will retain control of the Canary Islands."

Luis de Santangel, the finance minister, adds, "The gold we require is not in the Canary Islands, sir, it is in Guinea."

Cárdenas scoffs, "Nor are ivory and slaves."

Queen Isabel says, "Gentlemen, securing Castile and legitimizing my rule has always been the principal goal of this war. The Atlantic territories can wait. As I am sure you are aware, Portugal has twice the number of caravels as Castile."

King Fernando adds, "And they are better armed and faster under sail. Defeating Portugal on the ocean is wishful thinking at best, at least for now."

Isabel nods deferentially to her husband. "Indeed. This treaty will ensure that Portugal recognizes my reign as Castile's legitimate queen. Princess Juana will retire to a convent and make no more claims upon my throne. Portugal will never again make an incursion into Castile, for any reason. Our western border will be secure in perpetuity, so that we may then confidently turn to other matters at hand."

"The Moors." Gonzalo de Córdoba states the obvious.

The queen remains expressionless.

The silence is deafening.

Cárdenas turns to Cardinal Mendoza. "Will gold be sent to Portugal to settle the treaty?"

Cardinal Mendoza hesitates. "Well, yes . . ."

The queen interjects, "To secure peace with Portugal, Princess Isabel, our eldest, will be wed to Prince Afonso, the son of King John II. The gold will serve as her dowry."

Cárdenas frowns. "How much gold?"

The queen answers, "Just over 100,000 *doblas*."

Cárdenas widens his eyes in disbelief. "Dear God! Why so much?"

Cardinal Mendoza says, "Those were Portugal's estimated expenses for the war."

Cárdenas rolls his eyes, "I could conquer Portugal, France, *and* England for that sum, sir."

The finance minister looks pained. "But, your majesty, such a sum will bankrupt the treasury."

Isabel replies, "Yes, very nearly. But it will buy us a lasting peace with Portugal, gentlemen." She looks from man to man. "The king and I have a plan to restore our solvency. As you know, while my half-brother Enrique ruled as king, he foolishly sold off most of the royal estates at prices far below their value."

All eyes are on the queen.

"The crown will repossess those lands and rents. Those that have not been granted as a reward for services will be restored to the crown without compensation. However, there will be no revocation of gifts made to churches, hospitals, or the poor. Those that were sold at a price far below their true value will be bought back for the same sum."

Santangel interjects, "With such a large dowry leaving the treasury, majesty, where will we find the gold to buy back estates?"

The queen answers, "It has been arranged, Luis. Abraham Seneor and Don Isaac Abrabanel, whom you all know, have kindly agreed to lend us any amount of gold we require over the short term. At very modest interest."

Cárdenas frowns, "Jewish gold, majesty?" There is a bitter edge to his tone.

Her voice hardens. "Yes, Alonso, Jewish gold." She continues, "The king and I also plan to bring all mints under royal charge, and put an end to this wholesale minting of gold and silver coins that my half-brother foolishly permitted. In addition, taxation of commerce in my realm will be standardized. This rampant practice by the local lords and barons of adding their own arbitrary tariffs for goods passing through their lands will end. Today. In short, the crown will control the money supply."

More silence. A daring plan. A brilliant plan.

Santangel casts a sober eye. "The noble families will balk, majesty. They have grown accustomed to having their own way."

"Indeed they will, Luis, but those days are over. To help ensure their compliance I am greatly expanding the role of the *Santa Hermandad*."

Eyes widen. The Hermandad is a brotherhood of well-armed vigilantes that patrol and protect the thousands of pilgrims that make the journey to Santiago de Compostela each year. Their casual brutality and swift, cruel justice to any who dare mettle with penitent pilgrims is legendary.

"The Santa Hermandad will grow a hundred-fold and will soon patrol the streets of all the towns and villages of Castile. They will maintain peace and order by any means necessary, and they will answer only to the queen. Any lords or barons who dare challenge their authority will find their lands confiscated by the crown." She studies the room. "I assure you, gentlemen, the noble families *will* come into line."

Murmurs. Bold moves, these.

She continues, "Cardinal Mendoza, as chancellor, has already issued the necessary decrees and is working to ensure their legality if challenged. The reclamation of the royal estates has already commenced, and the first elements of the Santa Hermandad are on their way to the major provincial towns as we speak. Recruiting is also well underway."

The minister of war frowns. "These are all worthy plans, majesty, but the army must be refitted, and the troops paid."

"Indeed, Alonso. That leads me to the next topic. As you know, based upon the testimony of Father Alonso de Hojeda, the Dominican friar from Sevilla, we now know that a large number of false conversos are practicing as Christians within the realm. Cardinal Mendoza has confirmed this claim."

The cardinal offers a solemn nod.

"Judaizing conversos are an affront to our Lord and Savior, and are a threat to the integrity of the crown and Christendom. They will be forcibly rooted out and punished. The king and I have received authority from Pope Sixtus IV to convene a Holy Inquisition to do just that. As Father Talavera knows, the first auto-da-fé was held in Toledo." She pauses. "Seven hundred fifty conversos were found guilty of Judaizing."

Somber nods circle the room. They knew this was coming, but so many? Talavera studies the floor.

"We will cleanse Castile of false conversos, gentlemen. Those found guilty will be required to forfeit thirty percent of their family's wealth to the Inquisition. As penance. I intend for the crown to receive its fair share."

Shocked silence.

The king claps his hands and rubs them together. "As far as I know the gold of marranos will buy just as many pikes and cannons as Castilian gold." Fernando has supported this unprecedented move from the first moment he caught wind of it.

The queen continues, "These supplemental . . . resources . . . will be tapped while we are waiting for my other financial reforms to bear fruit. Alonso, you may commence with refitting the army."

Cárdenas offers an appreciative nod. A shrewd play—two birds with one stone.

"There is one final matter to deal with, gentlemen." The queen motions to Talavera, who bows, then withdraws. "I have asked the Marquess of Cádiz and the Duke of Medina-Sidonia to join us. They arrived late last night."

Uneasy eyes circle the room. This is news. Even the king looks surprised. Rodrigo Ponce de León, Marquess of Cádiz, and Enrique de Guzmán, Duke of Medina-Sidonia. Two of Castile's most important families, well known to all of Iberia. Bitter rivals would be too kind a characterization. Each hails from the noblest of noble Castilian families; each wears his pride on his sleeves like a badge of honor; and each possesses substantial private armies and the skill to wield them. Their armies are formidable—armies which, though nominally placed in service of the crown, answer only to the marquess and the duke. Both men are, however, steadfast supporters of Queen Isabel.

The two are heard before they are seen. A collection of squeaks and dinks and heavy clanks spills down the hallway in front of them. Santangel rolls his eyes. The queen actually smiles. Not surprisingly, the two are dressed in full battle armor, reveling in their glory as knights of Christ. A moment later, Talavera leads the two men in, all gleaming plate armor, scarlet silk capes pinned to their shoulders, red-on-white crusader's crosses painted on their chest plates, fine leather boots and gloves, ornate broadswords fixed in bejeweled scabbards. Thankfully, no helmets or gauntlets.

Ponce de León, ruddy and famously hot-headed, with his legendary red hair and beard; Guzmán, dark-olive complexion and flowing black hair. Two dashing knight-commanders of the realm.

And bitter rivals for the queen's favor. Each ignores the other, dramatically drops to his knees in unison with the other in a metallic crush, and they bow their heads in submission, eyes glued to the floor.

"Majesty, you beckoned."

"Majesty, you beckoned."

The queen manages to bury her smile. She makes them wait just long enough to remind them of their station. "Rise, gentle knights, my most vigilant defenders."

Ponce de León and Guzmán struggle to rise under the weight of their armor. Talavera and the Great Captain are clearly amused.

She begins, "I have summoned you both to receive a special mission. A task. A quest that is vital to the survival of Castile." She offers a warm smile.

In unison they bark, "Command us, majesty."

She addresses the gathering. "As you all know, the Ottoman Sultan Mehmed II is again on the move. In short order he has recently captured Serbia, Anatolia, Thessaly, Amasra, Wallachia, Negroponte, Albania, and much of Greece. After a brief pause, he has sailed for the Italian peninsula, and has now captured Otranto, in the Kingdom of Naples. Over half of Otranto's 22,000 citizens were put to the sword, the rest sold into slavery. Gentlemen, the Turks aim to devour Rome and the Papal States, the very heart of Christendom."

Shocked expressions circle the room.

"Castile and Aragon will send armaments and as many troops as we can muster to support the King of Naples. He is, after all, my husband's cousin. I am certain that the rest of Europe will do likewise. The Ottomans must be stopped, and stopped now."

Nods of approval.

Ponce de León blurts out, "Majesty, my sword stands ready to travel to Naples to slay the Ottomans!"

"A worthy desire, Don Rodrigo, but the greater fear lies far closer to home. Gentlemen, the king and I have recently learned that Sultan Muley Hacén of Granada has sent a letter to the Ottoman sultan requesting his support in a war against Castile."

Alarming news.

"If the Turks can land on the Italian peninsula, they can most assuredly land at Málaga."

Silence hovers in the chamber.

"I have decided that there is only one prudent course of action." A long pause. "The battle that the Christian kings of old began must now be completed. Granada must fall, gentlemen,

93

and the Alhambra razed. The Moors must be vanquished then expunged from Iberia, once and for all."

The minister of war blurts out, "Dear God, do you know what you are saying, majesty?!"

She turns to Cárdenas and silences him with her steely glare.

Cárdenas continues, more carefully, "Granada is ringed by hundreds of impregnable castles, majesty, with watchtowers on every pass through the mountains. Their armies are easily the equal of our own, especially after the toll taken by our war with Portugal. And almost certainly they will supplement their ranks with Berber cavalry from the Maghreb if we attack."

"I understand the difficulties, but consider what conquering Granada would mean for all of Christendom. Think of it, gentlemen, an Iberia free of the Moors! This was the dream of my Visigoth ancestor Pelayo almost 800 years ago. I am destined to complete his quest."

She exchanges a furtive glance with the Great Captain. His eyes sparkle over his slight smile. This is not the first time he has heard of her daring plan.

The king weighs in. "A worthy goal, I agree, and given the Ottoman ambitions of late, an imperative goal for the survival of our kingdoms. That said, we need time, and ample preparation before any serious invasion of Granada can be attempted."

The Great Captain says, "I concur, majesty."

Agreement begins to circle the room.

The queen continues. "To buy us the time we need to refit the army and fortify our border castles, I propose that we offer to extend a new peace treaty to Sultan Muley Hacén."

Santangel scoffs. "Majesty, the Moor has already announced that he will no longer pay the yearly tribute he owes Castile. He has insulted the crown. He has insulted *you*, majesty!"

"I understand, Luis. That is precisely why he will accept my offer of a treaty of peace between us. War is never good for commerce, and Granada thrives on commerce. He sees us as weak, and certainly not a serious threat. I say, let him feel strong. I have not responded to the brazen insult he offered me, and he knows that our war with Portugal has strained our resources. No doubt his spies will soon report the dowry payment as well." She pauses. "I want him to see us as weak. A treaty will buy us the time we need. Granada will relax. Meanwhile, gold will once again begin to flow into the treasury. This will allow us to refit the army for invasion."

The king says, "We will need twice as many heavy cannons as we presently possess. Cannons will prove decisive. Granada's castles are the most formidable in the world, impregnable unless we can breach their walls."

The room is coming round; she can see it in their faces.

The queen says, "Which brings me to the marquess and the duke."

"Majesty."

"Majesty."

"Gentlemen, from this day hence, the Marquess of Cádiz and the Duke of Medina-Sidonia will be allies. No more bickering. No more fighting. No more raiding of each other's lands. Your armies will be put under the direct command of King Fernando, and together we will ready ourselves for war against Granada. Together we will vanquish the Moors. We will fight for the honor of Christ Our Savior and His Mother Mary. But we will fight under one Castilian banner, with one united army. Do I make myself clear?"

Silence. The two men's heads bow.

"You do, majesty," comes the meek reply.

"Of course, majesty." Meeker still.

"Very well. One more thing. I have learned that Christian mercenaries have attacked a small village south of Campotéjar, just inside the border of the Kingdom of Granada. The villagers were all beheaded, and the children brought as slaves back to Castile." She stares down both knights. "I do not approve." The room tenses. "I DO NOT APPROVE!" She has colored a deep scarlet. Rarely does the queen raise her voice.

The Marquess of Cádiz kneels and lowers his eyes. "Forgive me, majesty. I had hoped to draw the Moors into battle so that I might ambush them. As retribution for the massacre at Cieza." He sighs. "Alas, they did not take the bait."

The queen steadies herself, then sniffs. "Let us not forget that we are Christians, Don Rodrigo, not barbarians. The children will be given to good homes. I want them educated and raised as pious Christians."

"Certainly, majesty, I will see to it personally."

"Regardless of your motives, Don Rodrigo, all incursions into the Kingdom of Granada will cease from this moment. The borderlands must return to peace if we are to gain the time we need to make ready for war. No actions will be taken against the Moors without the direct permission of the king and queen. Is that understood?"

"Yes, majesty."

She turns to the Duke of Medina-Sidonia.

"Yes, majesty."

"Very well. We will not speak of this incident again. In the meantime, gentlemen, let us prepare for war."

He sits in his vestments behind the densely woven grill of the confessional. He hears the door open. He marks his place in his Bible, closes it, rests it on his lap. She closes the door. He is curious still about that odd inflection in her voice. He watches her kneel.

She takes a deep breath, holds it, then exhales. Her eyes avoid the grill. She joins her hands together in prayer, the tips of her index fingers just touching her chin.

He studies her for clues. She seems unusually nervous. After all, she goes to confession at least once a week. Her expression is troubled, but also vulnerable, tender. She looks as if she is close to crying. He lifts a single eyebrow, intrigued.

She bows her head in submission. The posture of the penitent. Silence.

He begins the sacrament. "May God's Grace and peace be upon your soul. Trust in the mercy of God, my queen. What is it that you desire of your Lord and Savior?"

A slight hesitation, then, "I seek forgiveness for my sins." Her voice is hushed and taut, strained with emotion.

"You may trust in the Lord's mercy, my queen. Let us begin. *In nomine Patris, et Filii, et Spiritus Sancti. Amen.*"

She makes the sign of the cross as he intones the ancient words. "Amen."

"You may tell the Lord God what is troubling your heart, my queen."

The silence stretches out.

"I have had impure thoughts," she says, just above a whisper.

So. "I see. Impure in what manner, my queen?"

Her voice begins to quaver. "I have lusted in my heart."

He lifts both eyebrows now. New territory for the two of them. He composes himself. "My queen, the lustful desires between a husband and a wife are common. Such feelings are quite natural, and nothing to be ashamed of." He muses. "It has been some time now since Princess Maria's birth. Perhaps it is time to consider another child. I am sure the king would welcome this."

"The king avoids my bed." Hurt seeps into her words. "He has no desire for me. None."

"I see . . ."

She blurts out, suddenly angry, "God love him, and I do, but we both know that my husband is a philanderer. For God's sake, he keeps a mistress in Zaragoza and has the nerve to entertain dalliances at court behind my back." She flushes. "Does he think I have no spies?!"

Talavera takes a deep breath, holds it, releases. "I understand your frustration, my queen. Please continue."

The silence stretches.

"The lust I have felt in my heart is not for my husband, the king." The anger has vanished; shame now clings to her words.

He opens his mouth, frowns. "Oh." It is a rare occasion indeed when Talavera is at a loss for words. "Tell me more, my queen."

"I have had . . . feelings of lust . . . for . . ." She stops.

"Yes, my queen? Go on."

"For Gonzalo de Córdoba."

Dear Lord! The Great Captain. Fernando's second-in-command. Champion of the Queen's Guard. A close friend of the queen since childhood. Dear Lord. His heart is racing. "I see." He fights for control. "Your lustful feelings have remained locked in the silence of your heart?"

"Yes," she responds in nothing more than a whisper.

"And does Gonzalo know of your feelings?"

The silence stretches. "I do not think so."

The priest offers a sigh of relief. *Thank God!* "Good. My queen, these lustful feelings must remain forever a secret between us. They must remain sealed within the silence of the confessional. Think of the scandal, and the harm it would do to your children, not to mention Castile, should it ever become known."

Her tone is limp, resigned. "That is why I suffer so. I am tormented."

Silence.

"My queen, Gonzalo must leave court, at least for the time being. We must think of a mission that requires his presence. Perhaps . . . perhaps he is needed to help refit and organize your army. Or perhaps he can visit Ponce de León and de Guzmán to arrange the transfer of their armies to the command of the king. We must think of a mission for him . . ." He ponders this. "I will give it my full attention . . ."

She fills the silence with a meek, "Thank you."

"In the meantime, we must entice the king to return to your bed. A fifth child would be a great blessing for the crown, my queen. And it would help heal the rift grown between you two."

"That would be most welcomed."

More silence as he races through the chess match of implications. This problem requires a deft touch, to be sure, but he is a master of such subtleties. *Thank God she did not act on her desires.* Satisfied, he says, "The Lord God has heard your heavy heart, my queen, and your remorse, and seeks to cleanse you."

She bows. "I am heartily sorry for my sins and my offense."

"Your Lord and Savior stands ready to forgive you, my queen. For your penance, spend one hour before the Holy Presence contemplating the importance of your virtue. You must pray for strength, my queen. In addition, you will say an *Ave Maria* just before bed so that your dreams may remain pure while you sleep. You must beg God, my queen, to free you from these thoughts and the dangerous stain they have cast on your heart and soul. You must beg God, my queen."

She nods. "I will beg." Resignation.

"You may now approach our Lord and Savior for His forgiveness."

She whispers, "O my God, I am heartily sorry for having offended Thee, and I detest all my sins, not only because of Thy just punishments, but most of all because I have offended Thee, my God, who art all good and deserving of all my love. I firmly resolve, with the help of Thy Grace, to sin no more and to avoid the near occasion of sin."

"Good." Finally, the words of absolution.

> *Deus, Pater misericordiárum,*
> God, the Father of mercies,

> *resurrectiónem Fílii sui mundum sibi reconciliávit et Spíritum qui per mortem et Sanctum effúdit in remissiónem peccatórum,*
> through the death and resurrection of his Son has reconciled the world to himself and sent the Holy Spirit among us for the forgiveness of sins,

> *per ministérium Ecclésiæ indulgéntiam tibi tríbuat et pacem.*
> through the ministry of the Church may God give you pardon and peace.

> *Et ego te absolvo a peccatis tuis in nomine Patris, et Fílii, et Spiritus Sancti. Amen.*
> I absolve you from your sins in the name of the Father, and of the Son, and of the Holy Spirit. Amen.

She makes the sign of the cross. "Amen. Thank you, Hernán. I feel better already."

"Bless you, my queen. Your soul is pure as snow. Do not fear; we shall conquer this challenge together. All will be well."

Turn of Fate

"Thank you, Yasin, I will see you this afternoon."

The gardener of the Amiriya family bows. "My lady." The wisp of breath-fog trailing his words marks the crispness of the early spring morning. Yasin is Danah's designated escort through the maze of streets and alleys linking her family's carmen in the Albayzín with the Jewish Quarter.

She watches him until he disappears around the corner.

Her eyes rise over her right shoulder to the Bermejas Tower to fix her bearings, then she sets off at a brisk pace into an alley for the Atfal Hospital, the downhill trek through the fevered crush of the Jewish medina something she has come to relish.

There is a metallic groan as Danah pushes open the heavy outer door of the Atfal. She passes under the red ochre and white-striped Umayyad arch and into the anteroom, turns, two-hands the door to close it, and is answered by a heavy thud. She is surprised to see that no one is manning the entrance to the hospital. She walks down the hallway to Frizzle's office. The door is cracked, and with an impish grin she eases it open without knocking, her rehearsed, well-crafted barb ready to sling at her new mentor and friend. Her grin relaxes. Empty. She furrows her eyebrows. *Odd. He said he would be here this morning to meet me.* She shrugs, turns, walks two doors down to the temporary office he has given her, steps in and closes the door. A satisfied sigh. Tiny, but all her own. She lays her book down on the low-slung desk and removes her woolen wrap, hangs it, then takes off her gloves. She has brought a copy of Ibn Zamrak's poetry to read to Samra.

The girl is improving with each passing day. Eating more, even gaining some of her weight back. Danah is able to coax out short answers to her questions without too much difficulty, though not yet any sort of real conversation. She does allow Danah to help bathe her and dress her, and she loves to be read to; a child still in many ways. Danah's immediate goal is to ready Samra for a move into a room with girls her own age; perhaps by month's end if all goes well.

She arms into the robe Ezar has gifted her, a lovely cobalt silk, the colors of a physician. Danah's pride and joy. When she takes her final vows a scarlet *Staff of Asclepius* will be embroidered on each sleeve.

She stops by the linen closet and gathers new bed sheets and fresh clothes. For the girl's bath, she selects several plush towels, some perfumed soap, and a ceramic wash basin. The stack is tall enough to fill her arms. She places the book on top of the pile, then bends and lifts, resting her chin on the volume of poetry to keep it from sliding off. She slowly wends her way down the hallway, hoping to meet someone who will help her, but no one is to be seen. She arrives finally at Samra's room, feels for the door latch, then rotates and backs her way into the room. As she turns to greet Samra with a smile and a kind word, she screams, dropping the entire load. There is a heavy, percussive crush as the basin meets the floor and shatters. The poor book of poetry slides helplessly across the room, coming to rest at the feet of two armed knights.

She locates Samra, who cowers against the wall, terror-stricken, bedsheets pulled tight to her chin. It takes Danah only an instant to discover her rage. She flushes dark, then bellows, "WHAT IS THE MEANING OF THIS?!" Instinctively, she moves between the two knights and the girl. The men step back. She turns and locks eyes with her charge. "Shhhh, Samra. All will be well. I am here now, Samra, all will be well. Shhhh . . ." The girl's expression does not change—sheer panic. Danah turns on the two knights, livid. "You have frightened my patient. What do you have to say for yourselves? WELL?!" Her emeralds burn. A tigress defending her cub.

The two knights are dressed in fine tan and brown robes with sky-blue and gold piping. Leather riding breeches, white turbans. The knight to her left wears a gold and sky-blue sash; the one to the right a red and gold sash. Bejeweled daggers tuck into their wide belts; soft leather boots and gauntlets. Granadine broadswords hang at their sides. Princely attire. The two are young and deeply tanned, with close-cropped beards. Neither man looks particularly flustered.

She repeats, less forcefully, "Well?"

The knight to her left speaks first. "Forgive us, my lady, we were sent by our uncle, Prince Ali al-Attar, military vizier of Sultan Abu l-Hasan. We were instructed to see what we might learn from the girl about the Christian mercenaries that massacred her village outside Campotéjar."

Incredulously, "How did you get in here?" She scoffs, "Hakim al-Muffadal would never have granted you entry."

The knight continues undeterred. "On the contrary, my lady, Hakim al-Muffadal welcomed us and brought us to this room."

She looks intensely skeptical. "Then where is he?"

The knight shrugs, "He was summoned. Evidently an accident with one of the boys. He said he would return shortly and told us to wait for him here."

Stalemate.

Danah frowns her disapproval. "And you are?"

"My apologies, my lady. I am Yusef al-Makki." He lifts his palm. "My brother, Umar al-Makki." Both men formally bow. "We rescued the girl and sent her to Hakim al-Muffadal for care."

The gears whir for only an instant before she makes the connection. *So. The Falcon brothers.* She suddenly feels off kilter, struggles to steady her breathing. Her tone softens. "I see."

Umar kneels and picks up the book, scans the title. "Zamrak. Excellent choice, my lady." His eyes bore into her as he recites from memory,

> *How much pleasure there is here for the eyes!*
> *In this place the soul will find idyllic reveries.*

She simply stares at him, dumbfounded. *Does he mean me?* He continues.

> *The dreamer will be accompanied by the five Pleiades*
> *And will wake to the gentle morning breeze.*
> *An incomparable cupola shines with beauties*
> *Both hidden and open to the gaze.*
> *Seduced, Gemini holds out her hand to you and the moon*
> *Comes with her to converse.*

He topples her with a disarming smile. The man is distractingly handsome. She feels woozy.

"From the Hall of the Two Sisters, the finest room in the Court of the Lions, my lady. One of my favorite poems. Zamrak had a rare talent, may Allah rest his soul. Fortunately, much of his best work is captured for eternity on the walls of the glorious Alhambra." Again, that disarming smile. "If I might say, my lady, his verses pale in comparison to your beautiful eyes."

Danah blushes a deep crimson.

The silence is deafening.

Yusef frowns at Umar and says, "Forgive my brother's boldness, my lady. He means no harm. Our apologies for startling you. We were only after information that can help us locate the mercenaries and punish them."

She remains silent.

He continues, "May I inquire as to your name, my lady?"

She weighs his request. "I am Danah Amiriya."

"It is my pleasure to meet you, Miss Amiriya." Yusef bows once more. "I see that you are wearing the colors of a physician . . ."

She looks down at her cobalt robe. "Yes. I am studying under Hakim David al-Adani, the royal physician. At the Bermejas Hospital."

Yusef replies, "How pleasing to hear, my lady. The city can certainly use more physicians like Hakim al-Adani. He is a gifted healer."

She is suddenly self-conscious, and her nervousness somehow compels her to keep volunteering information. "I am working temporarily for Hakim al-Mufaddal. That is why I am at the Atfal Hospital." She lifts her hand to the girl. "Samra is my patient."

Umar asks, "You are Jewish, then?"

"No. I live in the Albayzín." A long pause. "My father is Battal Amiriya, an elder of the Abencerrajes."

"Ahhh . . ." The two brothers exchange a knowing glance. Bitter rivals of the Nasrids.

The silence turns awkward.

Danah begins to recover her nerve. "Surely you both are aware that weapons are not allowed in the Atfal. Hakim al-Muffadal should have told you." She sighs. "I suggest that we wait for him in the hallway."

Yusef replies, "Certainly, my lady."

Danah turns, sits down on Samra's bed, leans in and begins to whisper into her ear. The girl nods once, twice, three times as she warily eyes the two knights. Danah continues to whisper as she rubs Samra's arm.

With her back still to them, Umar turns to Yusef, gives an exaggerated, approving nod, points at his brother as he grins, then winks. Yusef frowns his response.

Danah eases Samra away from the wall and helps her sit in a more relaxed posture. "All is well." Her voice is hushed, soothing. "I will return very shortly, Samra; you have my word." The girl's eyes cling to her, but the terror in them has eased.

Danah turns back to them. "Shall we?" She has regained her composure. She leads them back out into the hallway, and after glancing at Samra, she eases the door closed.

Umar hands the volume of verse to her with an amused smile.

Yusef says, "Forgive our intrusion, my lady, we truly meant no harm."

"I understand. Please, I am not a princess of court. You may call me Danah."

Umar beams. "Then you must call us by our first names. After all, we are not so different in age."

A sober nod. "Very well."

Yusef says, "Would you like some help cleaning up the mess we caused you, Danah?"

"I think it would be better for Samra if I did it myself. She does not do well around men."

Yusef looks puzzled. "She is terrified of us. Why does she refuse to speak? She is safe now."

Danah hesitates, considering whether to tell the man the truth. Decision made, she says, "Samra was raped. Four knights held her down while the other had his way. Each had his turn. She was deeply scarred, especially her mind."

Yusef is visibly wounded by this awful news. "Dear Allah! That such a horrible thing should happen to a maiden of Granada."

Umar suddenly looks dangerous. He growls, "Rest assured, the Christians will answer for their crimes." His hand instinctively moves to his sword hilt.

Danah shakes her head vigorously. "No!" Her tone turns derisive as she flushes with anger. "You knights are all alike. No. NO!" She grows uncomfortably loud. "Revenge accomplishes nothing, other than to stroke your own false pride. It certainly does not help me heal Samra! How will we ever find lasting peace if all you can think of is to answer violence with yet more violence? How? Tell me how?!" The tigress has returned. "WELL?!"

Umar looks stung, opens his mouth to retort, but thinks better of it.

It is Yusef's turn for an amused smile. Umar is not used to being put in his place, especially by a woman. He looks back at Danah and considers her words. He gently says, "She is right, Brother."

This clearly surprises her.

Yusef continues, "Will Samra fully recover from her wounds?"

She ponders this. Her emeralds rise to meet Yusef, who returns her gaze. "I believe she will, yes. She has responded well to my care thus far. She is eating again and has spoken a few words to me. It will take time, of course, and Allah's Grace. She is an orphan now, so my hope is that she will learn to fit in with the other girls her age at the Atfal so that she might enjoy some semblance of a normal life. I will not rest until Samra is fully healed, of that you can be certain." She hesitates, unsure why exactly she feels the need to open herself to this stranger. "Since I was a little girl I have felt within my heart a calling to be a physician. I believe it is Allah's Will that I serve His people as a healer. If I can ease the suffering of one person, just one, my life will have had meaning."

Yusef stares at her intently. Unexpectedly, his voice thickens with emotion. "You are a rare gift to our world, Danah." He swallows hard. "You will make a fine physician, of that I am *most* certain."

Without thinking, she unleashes a dazzling smile.

Mesmerized by the transformation, his eyes remain glued to her. His heart begins to race.

His brother cocks an approving eyebrow. As he turns and sees Yusef's shocked look, he grins. He has never before seen his brother so taken with a woman.

Danah registers Yusef's odd expression with surprise. As her smile relaxes, the silence inflates.

Yusef's knees have inexplicably grown weak. His turn to feel woozy. His eyes sink helplessly to the floor. He has to muster all his courage just to open his mouth and speak to the tiles. "It would be helpful to know . . . what, uhhh . . . Samra remembers about the . . . uhhh, mercenaries." He wills his eyes up. "Perhaps I could . . ." He clears his throat. Twice. "Perhaps I could stop by the hospital to check on her."

Umar's grin widens.

Yusef adds, lamely, "With your permission . . . of course." He swallows hard.

Danah's confusion is etched upon her face. She is not quite sure what to make of this turn of events. Uncertain what to do next, she opens her mouth to reply, then slowly closes it. Words escape her.

Umar is watching this transpire with great amusement.

Without warning, Yusef slips the leather gauntlet from his right hand, steps forward, and before she can react, lifts Danah's hand, bends, and kisses it.

She is flabbergasted.

Yusef does not let go of her hand, and she does not resist. Her heart is pounding now. He steps closer still, buries himself in her shimmering emeralds, searching for something deep within her, longing for something he cannot name. She meets his gaze, and she can feel his emptiness, his hurt. His need. She finds herself inexplicably drawn to this man.

Who can know why things happen as they do? A chance meeting that changes everything; a specific word spoken at the very instant it most needs to be heard; a single look amidst a thousand looks that magically melts an anguished soul; the one key that opens the lock set fast upon another's heart. Who can explain such things? Who can know the turn of fate? Who can know if such a divine moment is fortune's laud or fortune's lament?

Gently, Umar says, "We should be going, Brother. The sultan and al-Zaghal are expecting us."

Yusef's eyes refuse to leave her face. All he can manage is a whisper. "Yes . . ."

Danah's pulse is throbbing so loudly in her ears that she is not sure what he just said.

Umar playfully nudges his brother. "Yusef. We must go."

After a drawn-out moment that actually seems to pain him, Yusef reluctantly nods, then releases her hand, which floats for a moment more as if suspended by magic, then slowly folds to her side. The spell broken, the flow of time resumes its normal pace. The brothers bow formally, turn, and slowly walk down the hall toward the front entrance.

Danah's eyes track the two knights until they turn the corner and disappear. She is pale as a bleached cotton sheet. As her heart calms, a wisp of a smile sprouts, lingers for an instant, then vanishes. Amazed at what just occurred, she takes a deep breath, holds it, and forcefully exhales. She shakes her head to clear it, then opens the door to check on Samra.

"But how could you allow them into the Atfal with their weapons?" There is a hard edge to her tone.

Ezar lifts his hands in self-defense. "They are the Falcon brothers, Emeralds. Knights of the Alhambra. Not to mention Nasrid princes and favorites of the sultan. What was I supposed to do?"

A dismissive grunt. "You could have told them to leave their swords and daggers in your office." Her hands are on her hips; rarely a good sign.

The physician looks wounded by her words. "It was they who saved the girl, after all. And they had orders from the military vizier to question her."

The barrage continues. "But to leave them alone with Samra? In her room?!" The bite of anger. "She was terrified when I arrived, Ezar, terrified."

He can only muster a resigned sigh. "You are right, of course. I was not thinking. Forgive me. It was an emergency, Danah. Hasan fell on the edge of the pool and hurt himself. They came for me, and I rushed to help. It all happened so quickly I did not think things through. I should not have left them in her room."

Danah's voice softens. "How is Hasan?" It is impossible to be mad at the man for long.

"Alas, a broken arm. That boy has been trouble from day one."

"A clean break?"

"Thankfully, yes. He will mend soon enough. And Samra?" His turn to express concern.

"Much better, praise Allah. I was able to calm her, though it took some effort. She will be fine."

"I am relieved to hear that."

She lowers her eyes. "I am sorry that I lost my temper." Her tone has returned to normal. She looks up. "Samra is my first patient, Frizzles."

This elicits a warm smile. "She is indeed. And I would expect nothing less from any able physician. You were right to defend her, my dear."

The tension between them evaporates.

He continues, "I assume the brothers were unable to obtain any useful information? I told them as much when they arrived, but they insisted on seeing her."

Her expression takes on an odd, pinched look. Softly, "No, they got nothing." She averts her eyes and strives for nonchalant as she mutters, "Yusef said he would come again to check on her."

His woolly worms flick to life, arch their backs over his twinkling ebony eyes. "Yusef said? Yusef? Since when has Danah Amiriya been on a first-name basis with a Nasrid prince?"

She blushes, shrugs like a little girl. A helpless, "He insisted."

A slow, dramatic nod. He smiles, "He insisted? I see. *He insisted.* Of course! What a Falcon wishes, a Falcon shall have!" He will milk this for all that it is worth. "You must tell me more, Emeralds."

Her blush deepens.

"Come, let us have some mint tea and talk. Come, girl!"

"How long does Ali al-Attar think it will take?" Al-Zaghal is pacing as he speaks, his black robes swishing with each step. The man is obviously anxious. Sultan Abu l-Hasan and Grand Vizier Venegas recline on their divans in the third chamber of the Hall of the Kings within the Lion Palace. The mood is somber.

Yusef answers, "He said at least six months for Montefrío, my lord, perhaps even longer for Íllora and Loja. Their outer walls are weak and in disrepair, and their cisterns leak like sieves. Montefrío does not even have a functional signal fire. And no watchtower. Each town will require skilled stone masons and large cadre of laborers, perhaps even a new quarry. And none of the three cities have ample siege rations. Uncle says they must be ready to hold for six months when the Castilians invade."

"As I feared," replies a frowning al-Zaghal. He stops and turns. "Sire, we must commence with these repairs to the border towns immediately. As you know, those castles are the final line of defense protecting the Vega. Without our bread and fruit basket, the city will starve. We can send masons from Granada and Alhama, with slaves from around the kingdom to support them. And part of the spring wheat harvest should go to laying in stores."

The sultan softly says, "Agreed. Venegas will see to it."

A curt nod from the grand vizier.

Al-Zaghal turns back to the Falcon brothers. "And what of Moclín?"

"Fortunately, Moclín is in much better shape, my lord, though they do need rations and some minor modifications. The commander of the *alcazaba* is to be commended."

"At last some good news. Fernando will be forced to pass Moclín when he attacks from Córdoba. I imagine most of the castles along the border between us and Castile are in poor shape. I am afraid we have much work to do, and it must be done quickly."

"Indeed, my lord."

Al-Zaghal turns to the sultan and grand vizier. "We are likely to require an increase in taxes to pay for all this before we are done, sire."

The sultan nods.

Venegas answers, "And they shall be levied in short order, Muhammad. I will inform the royal treasurer to draw up the papers."

"Good."

The sultan strokes his beard, contemplating the news. "Tell me, Yusef, do you think our border castles can withstand a six month siege?"

Yusef weighs this carefully. "I do not, sire." Candor has always been his gift. "The Castilians possess heavy cannons. There will be no need for them to build siege engines. They will first survey the walls to find the weakest point, then they will concentrate their cannon fire there. When the wall is breached, it will simply be a test of will and strength of numbers. King Fernando will have far more troops on attack than our castles are capable of holding in defense. We cannot hope for any of the border castles to hold off a siege of six months, sire. Málaga, Almería, and Alhama, perhaps. The others? No."

Al-Zaghal says, "I agree. We cannot win a protracted castle-by-castle siege against Fernando. We must meet the Christians on the open field of battle, where our strength in cavalry can be best deployed to our advantage. It will require cunning to get them to engage us."

Yusef says, "That is true, sire. Our forces will be more mobile in a pitched battle, a decided advantage, and our cavalry is superior to theirs. But King Fernando knows this as well as us."

Umar says, "In addition to our cavalry, we will also soon have horse-drawn light cannons, sire. The Christians will not be able to match that."

The sultan responds, "Yes, and that is good, a tactical advantage we will need. Has the first cannon been completed?"

Yusef answers, "We just visited the forges. The prototype has been cast, but it has not yet been joined to its carriage. It needs to be assembled and then test-fired. If that goes well, then production can commence."

"Excellent." The sultan exchanges a glance with al-Zaghal. "Yusef and Umar, you are my most trusted commanders. My brother has a plan that requires your immediate assistance."

The brothers bow. A tandem, "We live to serve Granada, sire."

The sultan lifts a hand to al-Zaghal to begin.

"I believe that Málaga will prove to be the key to the defense of the kingdom. Its port is the linchpin of Granada's trade. Even if Fernando manages to capture our border castles and seal off the Vega, we can still receive food and materials through Málaga. At least enough to keep us from starving. Málaga also presents an ideal harbor to land a supporting army from the Ottomans or the Egyptian *mamluks*, should we manage to convince them to send assistance. Alas, no such luck as yet, but one never knows; perhaps they will respond favorably when we are attacked. A safe harbor will be key in any case. Fernando is not stupid. He will aim to cut Málaga off as soon as possible to deny us this option. Therefore, the city must be defended at all costs."

Umar says, "My lord, Málaga is better defended than even Granada. The fortifications of the Alcazaba are the best in the kingdom, and the Gibralfaro Castle is impregnable."

Al-Zaghal replies, "Before there were heavy cannons, yes. Now? Unlikely. Because of this, the sultan has recruited one thousand cavalry and three thousand infantry mercenaries, at great expense, to anchor Málaga's defenses. Berbers from the Maghreb. Ferocious warriors to a man, we have been assured that these Berbers will fight to the death in defense of Islam against the infidel. Their army is presently en route by ship. They will be placed under the direct command of Hamete Zeli."

Yusef replies, "A good choice, my lord. I have seen Zeli fight. He is a skilled battlefield commander and an able leader."

"Indeed." Al-Zaghal continues, "Understandably, the *emir* in Málaga is very nervous about housing a Berber army within his city walls. I want you and Umar to ride tomorrow for Málaga with a squadron of royal cavalry. As the sultan's personal representatives, your presence will set the city at ease. While you are there you will inspect the fortifications, draw up defensive plans and contingencies, and discreetly help Hamete Zeli organize his new troops and prepare for war. Before you leave, I want Málaga ready to withstand a Christian siege. Understood?"

The doleful look on the elder Falcon's face produces a double-take from al-Zaghal. "Is there a problem, Yusef?"

Yusef recovers instantly. "No, my lord. We will be ready to ride at sunrise for Málaga."

Umar eyes his brother, then asks, "But what about the new cannon, my lord?"

"There is no time to test it now, but we dare not delay production. I will send word to the forges to produce a dozen more, with carriages, enough to field a mobile battery. You can test them all when you return from Málaga, and then we can begin full production."

Yusef opens his mouth to disagree but then closes it. He is not fond of risk taking, though he is confident in his design. "Very well, my lord."

"Good. It is settled, then. *As-salamu alaykum.*" May Allah's peace, mercy, and blessing be upon you. "The only victor is Allah."

They answer, "*Wa-alaikum salaam.*" And peace be upon you. "The only victor is Allah." The Nasrid motto.

"Danah?"

Nothing.

"*Danah?*"

Still nothing.

She is standing at the window, staring out at the courtyard fountain, chin propped on her two fists, elbows forming a neat triangle with the sill.

David frowns, steps to her side and touches her shoulder. "Danah?"

She jumps like a spooked cat.

"Forgive me, I did not mean to startle you. Did you not hear me call you?"

"I am sorry, David, no. I was lost in thought."

He studies her face. "Are you unwell, my dear?"

She tries to force a smile but does not succeed. "No, no. I was just thinking."

David continues to scrutinize her troubled expression. "I see. Well, Yasin is here. It is time for you to head home."

"Yes, of course. Let me get my things."

"It was the girl that made you hesitate with al-Zaghal."

No response.

Umar smiles. "Let me see, what was her name? Dhuna? Daja? Dhayl? Danah?" His smile widens. "Yes, I believe it was Danah." His tone is playful. "Danah with the captivating emerald eyes. And that ravishing smile."

Yusef grunts. He has been uncommunicative all day. One-word answers, resentful scowls when questioned, curt commands barked at subordinates.

The hour grows late, their preparations for tomorrow's ride finally complete. The soft trickle of the floor fountain is the only sound to be heard. The flicker of the oil lamp throws dancing shadows across the arabesque walls. It is the kind of light that beckons feelings buried deep within.

Undeterred, Umar continues, "She has a temper, truth be told, and soon to be a physician, may Allah help us all. And, of course, there is the minor fact that she is Abencerraje, our sultan's sworn enemy." He whistles. "It would be complicated, that much is true. Still . . . I like her. She suits you, Brother." He smiles, hoping to break open Yusef's shell. "I could tell you were taken with her."

Yusef looks up and sneers. "She is a distraction I can ill afford, Umar."

As Umar registers the pain etched into his brother's face, his smile slips away.

"I am a knight-commander of Granada, and our army relies upon my sound judgement on the field of battle. Granada herself depends upon me. If my thoughts lie elsewhere, if my concern for

110

another weighs heavily upon my heart, then I risk endangering our men with poor decisions." Yusef's voice is strained with emotion. "That I cannot do."

Umar frowns. He softly says, "No, Brother, you are wrong. Your decisions will be better with a woman in your life, not worse. You will have something to hold on to, something to live for. You will understand for the first time what is truly worth fighting for—worth dying for. You will be a better commander, Yusef, not worse. It has been so for me. Faynan grounds me like I have never been grounded. She is my heart and soul, reason enough for living."

Yusef does not answer. The man is suffering. His voice stills to a whisper, weaving among the shadows. "When you and Faynan married . . ." His words are heavy as lead. "I was secretly envious. Envious of what I did not have. Of what I would never have." A pained sigh.

Umar touches his brother's arm with great tenderness. "Yusef . . ."

"I saw the love between you two, and . . ." His words trail off. He tries again. "I tell myself that I do not need love, that a knight-commander cannot afford love, but . . ." His words are absorbed by the fountain's soft gurgle.

Umar gives him space. He has never witnessed his brother this vulnerable—or so truthful about his deepest feelings. He gently says, "Yusef, I can name a dozen beautiful maidens at court that would jump into your arms if you would but offer them an encouraging word. Yet, you never have; not once."

The sway and dance of the shadows calls.

"No . . . not once." Nothing but the soft dribble of the floor fountain.

They sit is silence for several minutes. Finally, Yusef shakes his head in anguish. "After Mata Bejid, my heart—"

"Mata Bejid was three years ago, Yusef."

He does not seem to hear. "After what happened at Mata Bejid . . ." He is unable to continue. He hisses, "So much horror, so much needless death." He croaks, "They were innocent children, Umar."

"I know," the younger brother replies tenderly.

"And I failed to protect them."

"Yusef . . ."

"The things I had my men do afterward in the name of revenge . . . what *I* did . . . there can be no forgiveness for that. None." A rattling sigh; tears are close. "My heart, it . . ." Yusef falls silent as his eyes helplessly sink to the floor.

"Your heart what, Yusef?"

"After Mata Bejid, something inside me died, Umar." Barely a whisper. "My heart turned to stone. Stone. I do not deserve love. I will never deserve love. Never."

"That is just not true." Umar studies his brother. "Time heals all things, Yusef. Even what happened at Mata Bejid. Everyone deserves love, Brother."

Yusef looks up, his eyes full and glistening in the lamplight. "Something happened to me today at the Atfal, Umar, something I never expected." His face is a portrait of pained bewilderment. "I felt something today that . . ."

"What did you feel, Yusef?"

His voice begins to quaver. "I felt the need to hold a woman tightly in my arms, to give my heart to her. To be held by her. To love her and be loved by her." He grimaces. "What a fool I am."

Umar lovingly touches his brother's arm. "Love can heal your wounded heart, Yusef. It can heal you of this pain . . . if you let it."

No response.

Umar continues, "The Sufis say that we can only find our completion in Allah by loving another. Allah calls to you, Brother. Love finally calls to you. What happened today with Danah is a sign that you must let go of Mata Bejid. I am sure of it. You must answer Allah's call, Yusef. You *must*."

Yusef sadly shakes his head. "Clearly that will never happen. We ride for Málaga tomorrow."

The silence is immense.

"You must write to her, Yusef."

Yusef looks up, confused.

"Write to Danah."

He wilts. "I would not know what to say."

"Just tell her the truth. That is all. Open your heart to her and tell her what you felt when you looked deeply into her eyes. And then tell her that you must be away for several months in Málaga, but that you wish to call upon her when you return. That is all you need do."

Yusef looks terrified at the thought.

"Write to Danah, Yusef. Right now, before you sleep. If this is meant to be, it will be. I will see that it is delivered. You must write to her."

Yusef whispers, "The thought of what that path may bring frightens me, Umar . . . more than any peril I have ever faced in battle."

Umar smiles. "Love is like that, Yusef."

"What if she does not want to see me again? What then?"

"Write the letter, Brother."

Yusef's head sags as he slowly nods his resigned agreement.

Umar stands. "I must spend time with Faynan before we leave. I will meet you an hour before sunrise outside the Justice Gate." A warm, loving smile. "Bring the letter, Yusef."

She sits cross-legged on her floor mattress, heart racing. She stares at the letter resting in her lap as if it were a viper coiled to strike. A courier from the palace delivered it to her mid-morning at the Atfal. It is late afternoon now, and she is back at home, and still its seal remains unbroken. She lifts it for the hundredth time, examines the seal, lays it down again. The letter might as well contain some sorcerer's curse that will instantly turn her to stone if read. Paralyzed, she helplessly stares at the thing.

The courier said only, "Tidings from the Alhambra, my lady," then turned and left. She was so shocked that she did not ask from whom. The ring seal pushed into red wax tells it all, of course. A tethered falcon. But what words lie within?

She is nervous, excited, cautious, confused, petrified; she senses somehow that the letter contains her future, the unfolding of the whole of her life, and to dare to read the words will seal her fate forever.

Minutes pass.

Enough! She picks it up once more, but this time she decisively breaks the seal with her thumbnail. Her heart pounds in her chest as she opens the letter. She takes a deep breath, exhales. Her fingers are trembling. Her emeralds settle on the first words, "My Lady," which have been crudely scratched out and replaced with "Danah." This produces a flick of a smile. She begins to slowly track right to left, right to left, as she eases down the page. Her expression subtly shifts as she reads his words—first wary, then puzzled, then pleased, then sad; then something more, something deeper, something very tender. An odd tingle gnaws along the inward curve of her spine. She is consumed by an unsettled flutter in her gut, an anxious tilt; then a strange heaviness in her chest, as if the world is somehow pressing in upon her. It is a feeling she has never felt, a feeling both exhilarating and terrifying all in the same instant. As she comes to his signature her eyes fill, then brim. A neat tear rolls down each cheek. Her eyes lift from his words, and she stares into space. She whispers, "Yusef . . ."

Her eyes move back to the top of the letter, and she reads it once more, her pace slowing to savor his awkward scrawl. She smiles, then frowns, then exhales her bewilderment through pursed lips. "Dear Lord."

Just as she finishes, there comes a soft knock on her door. "Danah?" Her mother's voice. "Danah?"

She sniffs, wipes her eyes, folds the letter, and slides it beneath her. "Yes, Mama?"

"May we come in?" Her father.

She gathers herself. "Certainly, Baba."

The door opens. Her parents stand before her, all smiles. Danah is puzzled. *What on earth?*

Her mother says, "We have news, Danah. Wonderful news!"

"News?"

"Yes, Danah." Her father. "We have received a letter from Málaga. From Abd al-Salam."

Danah straightens her back as her eyes widen, her heart racing once again. "I see. I trust Abd al-Salam is well?"

Her mother is beaming. "He has found a young man for you, my darling. His name is Malik al-Karim. The boy is only a year older than you, and training to be a physician in the royal hospital in Málaga!" She can't suppress her excitement. "Abd al-Salam says he is a pious young man with a good heart." She beams. "Dark and handsome. His family traces its lineage back to the Maghreb. Near Algiers, just like us. Can you believe it?!" She is incendiary with glee.

Her baba chimes in, "His father is a *qadi* in the law courts. A widower. Abd al-Salam says the al-Karim family is well-respected in Málaga."

Her father's voice grows odd; tinny and muted to her ears. Danah blinks and shakes her head to clear her lightheadedness. "I am sorry . . . what did you just say?"

He studies her. More slowly, "His father is a qadi in the law courts, and well-respected." He pauses. "It is an excellent match, Danah. Just what you asked for. I will write to Abd-al-Salam and the boy's father this evening to arrange matters."

"I see."

Her father playfully glances at his wife. "Mama is insisting that the young man and his father make the long journey to Granada to meet us, but that is just a formality. Abd al-Salam says he needs to complete his studies before marrying, but I do not see why a betrothal cannot be concluded by the end of the summer."

"I see. By the end of summer . . ."

Her mother adds, "Of course, your baba will make some discreet inquiries with his contacts in Málaga. Just to be sure. But this is a perfect match, Danah, a perfect match!" Her enthusiasm is irrepressible.

It takes every bone in Danah's body to force a smile. "This is excellent news. It does sound like a perfect match. Thank you both."

Her father has resumed studying her, but her mother is beaming ear to ear.

Danah rubs her temples. "I am sorry, I must be working too hard. I feel a bit weak."

Her mother says, "Rest, my darling. This will be an exciting time for you. For all of us! You will be married and starting a family by this time next year, inshallah."

"Yes . . ."

Her father says, "I will go begin my letters."

"You rest, dear."

"Thank you, Mama, I will."

She is alone. Her world collapses in upon her, a cage with no bars, but suffocating all the same. She turns pale and grows listless, numb. She eases down onto her mattress and curls into a fetal position, begins to gently rock herself like a little girl. She whispers her desperate plea, "Tetta Layla . . . Tetta Layla . . ."

— *TWO* —

Absence

Every night I scan
The heavens with my eyes
Seeking the star
That you are contemplating.

I question travelers
From the four corners of the earth
Hoping to meet one
Who has breathed your fragrance.

When the wind blows
I make sure it blows in my face:
The breeze might bring me
News of you.

I wander over roads
Without aim, without purpose:
Perhaps a song
Will sound your name.

Secretly I study
Every face I see
Hoping against hope
To glimpse a trace of your beauty.

Abu Bakr al-Turtushi
(d. 1126 C.E. — Tortosa)

Eye for an Eye

THE HALL OF THE KINGS WITHIN THE LION PALACE OF THE ALHAMBRA.

"My lord." The royal bodyguard manning the door bows deferentially to al-Zaghal.

"Please tell the sultan I have arrived. He is expecting me."

An awkward hesitation. "I am afraid he is not here, my lord."

"We were to meet." Al-Zaghal frowns. "I have important news. Where is he?"

A long pause. "In the Hall of the Two Sisters, my lord."

Al-Zaghal's frown deepens.

The bodyguard lowers his voice. "He is with the girl, my lord."

Zoraya. He shakes his head. He has long since regretted his decision to give the girl to his brother. She holds far too much sway over him.

"Was she there all night?"

"Yes, my lord. Their breakfast was delivered an hour ago."

Brazen and rash. Even a sultan must abide by the time-honored rules of court. Concubines may entertain wherever required, but they sleep in the royal harem. Period. The entire Alhambra will be privy to this new development by noon, likely sooner. The Lion Palace leaks gossip like a sieve. No doubt the fireworks within the harem have already commenced. "Very well." An angry swish of black silk as al-Zaghal abruptly pivots and marches the forty paces to the entrance to the Two Sisters. By the time he arrives his jaw is clenched tight, muscles bulging. *This foolishness has gone far enough.*

A pair of royal bodyguards flank the massive wooden door of the Two Sisters. A tandem, "My lord," followed by bows.

"I must see the sultan." Icicles dangle from his words.

The senior of the two bodyguards clears his throat. "I am sorry, my lord, the sultan gave strict orders not to be disturbed." Pained hesitation; the royal bodyguards have great respect for al-Zaghal. "By anyone, my lord, for any reason. The sultan was explicit. I am sorry, my lord."

As al-Zaghal's ebony eyes begin to smolder, his grimace bends toward menacing. The air grows dense.

A muted giggle is just discernible. This is answered by a guttural laugh, then another giggle.

Al-Zaghal curses.

"I am sorry, my lord. Truly." Their opinion of the situation is more than obvious.

Al-Zaghal hisses, "When the sultan emerges from his—tryst, inform him that an urgent matter of state requires his immediate attention. I will be with Grand Vizier Venegas." Without waiting for a reply he turns and marches out of the Lion Palace, the black folds of his long robe struggling to keep pace.

The bodyguards exchange uneasy glances.

The rapping at the door is insistent, sharp enough to cause Venegas to wince. He looks up from his writing, grimacing. The angry knocking repeats. Venegas hates to be interrupted when he is honing his calligraphy for an official document. He sighs and lays his reed down. "Yes?"

"We need to talk."

Venegas frowns. *Al-Zaghal. What now?* "Certainly. A moment, please." The grand vizier seals his ink pot, blows on the polished paper to ensure that the ink is dry, then lifts a book and lays it upon the document. He rises from his low-slung desk and makes his way to the door. The grand vizier's suite is the largest of the apartments surrounding the Courtyard of the Lindaraja; spacious for a confirmed bachelor, spare in furnishings but wall to wall with books, and with the added pleasure of jalousie windows looking over the glorious garden and fountain.

Al-Zaghal hears the first locking latch slide open, then a second, a third. Venegas likes his privacy. That, or he fears assassins. The Alhambra has certainly endured its fair share over the centuries.

The heavy door creaks open. Venegas smiles, "Muhammad. How delightful to see you." Not a hint of sarcasm. He lifts a hand. "Please, come in. Should I send for mint tea? Perhaps some sweetcakes?"

"No." Curt.

Venegas inwardly smiles. *Always so serious.* They settle onto adjoining floor pillows. "What seems to be the matter?"

Al-Zaghal scowls. "Guess."

"Let me see . . . our darling Zoraya?"

Al-Zaghal grunts. "My brother has gone too far this time. She spent last night with him in the Two Sisters."

A pained sigh. "I see. I was afraid of that. Fatima will roast the poor girl alive. I am sure the eunuchs are already fussing about trying to extinguish the inferno within the royal harem."

"Indeed."

"I warned your brother, Muhammad. He should know better than to test the mettle of the sultana and her minions. Wife or not, she is much too capable to toy with, even for him. Especially for him. Nothing good can come of this dalliance."

"My brother is a fool. He cares more about having that nymph make love to him than ruling his kingdom."

A hint of a smile from Venegas, but he then lifts his finger and wags it. "Careful, Muhammad. As we both know all too well, your brother has a ferocious temper. Do us both a favor and try not to unleash it."

Al-Zaghal scoffs. "Let him rave." To steady himself he takes a deep breath, holds it, then exhales. "We must both try to talk some sense into him, Venegas. He needs to be reminded that he is the sultan. He should banish his plaything immediately and return to Fatima. Hopefully before he has done irreparable harm to the kingdom."

"No argument there, but easier said than done."

"What a mistake I made by bringing her to Granada. I should have known better."

Venegas offers no salve.

Al-Zaghal continues, "That Christian whore needs to be sent back to Castile where she belongs. Let her father deal with her."

"Mm."

They fall silent as they consider the conundrum.

Al-Zaghal finally gives up and says, "I have important news. From Castile."

Venegas lifts an eyebrow. "Do tell." The grand vizier temples his fingers under the tip of his nose as his lids close to thin slits. His calculating pose.

Al-Zaghal says, "It seems that the Duke of Medina-Sidonia and the Marquess of Cádiz have parleyed."

Venegas slowly nods as he absorbs this. "My, my, that *is* news. And quite unexpected." He mulls over the possibilities. "A trusted spy ferried the news, I assume?"

"Yes, and well placed at court in Córdoba. He does not make mistakes."

"I see. Very good."

"What do you make of it?"

Venegas replies, "Well, I cannot say that I ever would have imagined those two sitting down to parley of their own accord.

There is far too much bad blood between their families. My guess is that this was the doing of the king and queen." Venegas looks up and locks eyes with al-Zaghal. "There can only be one reason for this development, Muhammad. Castile is preparing to make war upon Granada."

Al-Zaghal nods his concurrence. "Yes, just as we feared. Both men have formidable armies, that much is sure. And both are capable commanders. Join them together and suddenly Castile's battlefield capabilities in the south have grown five-fold."

"Or more."

"Or more."

Venegas adds, "And suppose they decided to place this new conjoined army under the direct command of Fernando, whom we both know is himself a capable tactician, with the duke and the marquess as his generals."

"Precisely my fear. A scenario that does not bode well for us."

"No, it does not. We must hasten our preparations, Muhammad. When you knocked I was in the middle of crafting the new provision to raise taxes on the merchants and landholders of the kingdom. Sad to say, with the expenditures to repair Montefrío, Íllora, and Loja, and the ridiculous sum required to secure the Berber mercenaries for Málaga's defense, the treasury is nearly depleted. Not that it was especially flush to begin with."

"They will grumble mightily, especially the Abencerrajes."

Venegas replies, "They will not grumble, they will howl. And then proceed to sow seeds of discord in the city. No doubt the Supreme Mullah will choose to side with them, fool that he is. Still, it is imperative that we be ready when Castile strikes, as surely they will. We need gold." He muses. "I would suggest that we not allow this news of the parley to spread beyond the Vizier Council, at least for now. Who knows, if the Supreme Mullah and his Abencerraje lackeys work themselves into a frenzy over the new taxes, I may need this news to sober them up."

"Agreed. It is imperative that the kingdom's defenses be ready when Castile strikes." He widens his eyes for emphasis. "We must act quickly."

"Tell me why I should not have you whipped?" The sultana reclines on her plush divan casually sipping mint tea. Her tone is even, matter of fact, her expression a blank slate. But this is a ruse; Fatima is livid. She is a consummate actress, after all, able to instantly bury or expose whatever emotion best suits her needs. Fath, the head eunuch of the royal harem, stands beside her, all prissy and proper in his flowing purple robes, his face painted up and decorated. His expression is more telling, his disapproving pout unmistakable. Concubines that disturb the order of the royal harem are generally disposed of quickly. Though Fath recommended against it, Fatima insisted the girl be brought before her. This is their first meeting.

Zoraya stands in front of them in clothes meant for entertaining in the bedroom—sheer silk robe, virginal white, of course; not quite transparent, but not far from it. Her nipples strain provocatively against the silk, impossible to ignore. A veil curtains her face, her lovely almond eyes all that is offered. It is remarkable how obscuring a treasure builds anticipation to possess it. Her rich, blond curls spill down onto her shoulders. A choker of giant pearls circles her neck, with matching gold and pearl earrings. Both expensive, both the property of the royal harem. Her scent is unmistakable; the royal perfume—enticing citrus spice with an ethereal hint of musk. The recipe is centuries old and jealously guarded. Evocative of feminine charms and the promise of waiting pleasures. As intended.

The girl was summoned as soon as she walked up the stairs of the royal harem and removed her cloak. By intent, she was afforded no opportunity to change her clothes.

"I have done nothing but what was commanded of me, Sultana." Her gaze is lowered, but a hint of defiance clings to her words.

No shift in the sultana's mask, but her eyes are ablaze. Fath's pout settles into a thin frown. His response is impatient. "You will remove your veil when speaking to the sultana."

Zoraya reaches up and unpins her veil, folds it back from her face. Lovely olive complexion, sultry, full lips, pronounced cheekbones. Smoky eyeshadow over long eyelashes, but no other obvious makeup; anything more would only subtract. A prominent beauty mark perfectly placed on her left cheek. There is no arguing that the girl is exquisite. Not classical features exactly; more exotic somehow, and all-the-more compelling for it. Beautiful and luscious, yet somehow innocent and vulnerable. The seductive virgin, a heady combination lethal to even the most steadfast and pious of men. It is easy to see why the sultan is captivated.

Fatima studies the girl. "Take off your clothes."

She looks confused. "Excuse me?"

"I *said,* take off your clothes." She intends to shame the girl.

Zoraya hesitates.

121

Fath raises his voice. "You heard the sultana. Take off your clothes."

She pauses just long enough to register her resentment, then slowly unties her sheer robe and allows it to slide to the floor. Zoraya's eyes have hardened, but otherwise there is no emotion discernible. A figure that was seductive while obscured behind silk, blossoms into something truly extraordinary; fruit ripened to perfection. Her body is flawless—full, beautiful breasts; lovely, sweeping curves.

To the sultana's chagrin, not a hint of embarrassment or self-consciousness. Evidently the girl is quite comfortable with herself. Useful information to be filed away for later use. Fatima's eyes track to the girl's belly. Just below her navel an elaborate decoration of henna art unfolds downward, ending in her precisely manicured pubic hair. Henna is for brides, and then only for the hands and feet. The girl surely knows that what she has done is forbidden. Fatima remains silent to heighten the tension. Most concubines would have been in tears long before now. Fatima is curious to test the girl's mettle. After all, she will need to break her soon enough.

After correctly assessing that there will be no easy victory with this one, Fatima sniffs dismissively. "Turn around."

Again Zoraya hesitates.

The sultana twirls her finger in the air. More forcefully, "I *said*, turn around."

Zoraya slowly pivots in a circle. More glorious curves.

Fatima scoffs. "What he sees in you I shall never know. There are a dozen concubines in the harem more beautiful and shapely. Tell me, Zoraya, what evil spell have you cast upon my husband?"

"Evil spell, Sultana? I have cast no spell." She pauses, then adds, "It seems that the sultan simply prefers my company." She, too, is prepared to draw blood.

Fath furrows his eyebrows as he frowns. "Mind your tongue."

A hint of a smirk from Fatima. After all, she does relish a challenge. She will enjoy breaking this girl. "You are aware that *concubines* do not spend the night outside the harem. For any reason." She twists the word tightly to remind the girl of her station.

Zoraya locks eyes with Fatima. "Of course, Sultana. I told the sultan as much. But he commanded me to stay the night. Who was I to argue? He is my sultan; his wish is my command."

Fatima tries to stare the girl down, but Zoraya refuses to give in and look away. Without breaking eye contact, Fatima flicks her wrist dismissively. "Fath, remove this Christian whore from my sight."

"Certainly, Sultana." He steps forward and begins to shoo her out. "Put your clothes on and return to your quarters. At once. Go."

Zoraya continues to stare at Fatima for an additional moment, registering a last act of defiance, then turns and walks naked to the door and is gone. Halfway down the hall she unleashes a cunning smile.

Fatima continues to stare at the silk robe laying crumpled on the floor. "This one is trouble, Fath. Brazen and recalcitrant."

"I agree, Sultana. Shall I arrange for her to disappear?"

No response. Fatima stares into space, calculating.

He eagerly clasps his hands together. "Then how about a poison? Something slow and disfiguring. I know just the one. It would take a month for her face to melt into awfulness. Then oozing lesions covering that lovely body, followed by insanity. Trust me, before she expires she will rue the day she crossed you, Sultana."

Fatima sighs. "No. With my husband so smitten, there would be hell to pay. He is many things, Fath, but stupid he is not."

"I understand, Sultana."

"No, Fath, we must be cleverer than that. We must let the girl sow her own demise. Have you had any success getting eyes into the Two Sisters?"

"Not as yet, Sultana." Fath brightens. "However, if she begins to regularly spend the night in the Two Sisters, there *may* be a way. I have made some inquiries. It seems there is a window—"

Fatima lifts a hand. "Stop. It is better that I do not know the details. Just bring me information that would be of interest to the Supreme Mullah and the elders of the Abencerrajes. Something that would force my husband to disavow her."

"I will see to it personally, Sultana."

"*Then* we will find out what she thinks of your poison. I would enjoy watching the girl suffer for her insolence."

"It shall be so, Sultana."

"Good. By the way, I assume there is no risk of a child?"

"Impossible, Sultana. The preventative is administered in her food each day. Undetectable." A sinister smile. "Sad to say, Zoraya is infertile."

"Excellent. Bring me some information, Fath. Something I can use to flay this Christian whore. I want to see some real fear in those defiant eyes."

"It shall be so, Sultana."

"In the meantime, we must find a suitable replacement. See to it. Someone blond, and with Zoraya's exotic look."

"I will see to it, Sultana." He bows and withdraws.

It is long past midnight. The Alhambra sleeps. The Lion Palace is alive with the soothing sounds of flowing water, lending an aquatic tranquility that wends its way through the maze of rooms and halls, working its liquid magic upon all within. It is said that there is no more restful sleep to be had in the entire world.

The moon is full, the sky cloudless. In answer to the cascade of moonbeams, the Alhambra begins to pulse with otherworldly energy, releasing its famous effervescent glow, an ethereal bleached-bone aura that clings to the walls, commanding the intricate calligraphic poetry to rise from its stucco prison and begin to dance. The aura hovers over the fountains to count the silvery drops of pearly tinkle one by one; tiptoes across polished white marble floors in slippered feet; dips a finger into the mirrored pools to raise an orgy of concentric ripples. The Alhambra comes alive by moonlight, the shimmering aura wily and gamesome. Legend has it that the original architects constructed the palace to be viewed by full moon from a floor pillow in the center of the courtyard; a view both startling in its spectacle and heartrending for its sheer beauty.

The Two Sisters was built for such lunar performances, its upper tier of windows angled to woo the moonlight and lead it inward by the hand, only to break it against the honeycombed mocárabes ceiling and spill it marvelously downward upon the waiting guests far below. To maximize the effect, all of the standing oil lamps have been extinguished. Artificial light of any kind would subtract from the sublime experience to come.

Zoraya and the sultan lie together on the floor mattress, naked and glistening under a sheen of sweat, limbs still twined together. They both stare expectantly up into the cavernous mocárabes heaven. This will be her first time to witness the magic of the Two Sisters by full moon. Though they cannot see the golden orb as yet, a beam of eerie pale has just been chalked in from the window to the opposite wall, seemingly solid enough to climb. Instantly, the entire space within the hall begins to luminesce. She gasps. He smiles, satisfied. They snuggle closer together. He has been excited to give her this rare gift.

Their lovemaking continues to evolve. She still has her way with him, of course, teasing then torturing, revealing then withholding, punishing then rewarding. She delights in making him beg, by extracting groans and soft curses through clenched teeth, seemingly at will. Though trained in the eastern arts, she has shown a serious knack for innovation, for invention, for pushing the limits. She has grown bolder, more daring. He is putty in her hands, to be sure, a plaything to bend and twist as it suits her whims. He is a most willing accomplice. The seductive virgin no more. No, Zoraya is now a gifted and exciting lover, at the top of her game. There is not a concubine in any harem in the kingdom that could match her formidable skills. And she knows this.

There is a surprising new twist to their lovemaking, however, one that, interestingly enough, has grown even more captivating to the sultan. She has begun allowing her own pleasure to be the center of his attention. First, subtly coaxing him. Then, directing him. Now, commanding him. He loves watching her as those lovely almond eyes defocus into oblivion as ecstasy contorts her face and has its way with her features. A clenching of her jaw as her breasts heave forward, a quick shiver, then finally a cry of pleasure so intense that it reverberates within the Two Sisters for a dozen heartbeats. It is a sight to behold, ridiculously intoxicating to any man, even a sultan.

An objective observer might logically wonder how much of this was an act on her part, an exaggeration meant to ensnare, a calculated manipulation of the weaknesses of the more gullible sex. Who can know such things for certain? Regardless, one undeniable fact remains: He is hopelessly smitten.

It is late afternoon, and the shadows thrown by the pillars lining the Courtyard of the Lions are lengthening in an especially pleasing manner, evocative of a palm-lined oasis in the Syrian desert at sunset.

Fatima has come to him, not the other way around. She is not foolish enough to pretend that this meeting would have transpired any other way. Venegas arranged it, as usual. She insisted there was an important matter to discuss but would not divulge what exactly was so pressing.

The sultan reclines on his divan in the Hall of the Abencerrajes within the Lion Palace, a book open on his lap. When she is announced and shown in, he sighs as he dismisses his bodyguards with the flick of his wrist, marks his page and closes the book. There is always an agenda with his wife. There is only one question to ask. What is she up to now?

"Fatima." He tries his best to adopt a friendly tone.

"Husband." A carefully chosen word. Her tone is warm, inviting. She slowly removes her over-robe, lays it across the foot of his divan. Her white silk robe is low-cut and clingy, the spill of dark curls offering a lovely contrast. Not a hint of the matronly about her.

He studies her. No use denying that she is a beautiful woman. She was stunning in her youth; her beauty clings to her still in an effortless way. Her curves have grown a bit fuller, true, her skin a little looser, yes, but in an especially satisfying way; that uncanny manner by which youthful beauty deepens pleasingly with age, burnishing angular and pert to soft and curvy. He stiffens as he admires her.

Still, she has over twenty years on Zoraya.

She understands her body, of course, knows well how to wield it as a weapon. But she is also aware that she can no longer simply rely on her youthful allure to impose her will upon men. No, much more subtle tactics are required, and if anything, her skills at seduction have become more finely honed and formidable with age. A fake pout upon demand; a coy, seductive smile at the perfect moment; a well-timed laugh—not too loud, not too soft; the angle she permits her shoulder to dip as she turns; instant tears, when tears will serve; a calculated parting of her robe as she bends forward, innocently revealing the heavy swell of her breasts, the deep rose of her areolae; the suggestive tease of her bare thigh sliding beneath silk; helpless cries of pleasure, exactly timed to elicit the strongest possible response; the angle she holds her dainty foot with her carefully painted nails. The list is endless. Subtle, oh so subtle, this art of seduction.

Her perfume is intoxicating, of course. He does not invite her to sit. Much too dangerous. Instead he says, "You are well, I trust?"

A lovely smile. "I am, thank you. It is good to see you, Husband. It has been far too long."

He ignores this and says, "Venegas sent word that you had an urgent matter to discuss?"

"I do, yes. It concerns our son."

His perturbed sigh is spontaneous. "Yes?"

"I wanted to express my gratitude to you and your brother for giving Boabdil a cavalry command."

The sultan lifts his eyebrows. *Fatima, grateful?*

She continues, "I have never seen him happier, Ali." The use of his given name is intentional. "He so wants to help defend the kingdom. And to please you." Her words are uncharacteristically tender. Ever the dutiful mother.

The sultan stammers, "Yes, well, it was my brother's idea. The boy has much to learn about command."

A warm, loving smile. "But you have given him a chance to prove that he has what it takes to become a sultan."

"As I said, he has much to learn." He suddenly feels uneasy.

"Thank you, Husband." So warm and loving.

He nods. He is again limp. His eyes drift back to his book. He longs for an end to this encounter.

"I miss you, Husband." Soft and vulnerable, raw emotion clings to her words.

Surprised, he looks up to study her but offers no response. He instinctively senses danger. He has been burned by her so many times.

"I so miss those evenings we used to spend in the Two Sisters together; reading poetry to each other, talking about all manner of things. Watching the moon rise." A long pause. She whispers, "Making love." Magically, her youthfulness has returned to light her features. The sultana is suddenly a young virgin once again. She steps closer, licks her lips provocatively. "I ache for you, Ali." She lays her hand upon his to make her intention plain.

It has been years since he has seen her this vulnerable and needy. He is afraid to move a muscle.

"You remember those days, Ali. The fire between us. Dear Lord, what a great lover you were. You could bring me to the brink of bliss just by looking at me with those hungry eyes. The intensity of the pleasure still makes me blush." And she does.

His heart is pounding.

"It could be so again, Ali." She steps closer still, allows her thigh to brush his arm. She lifts her hand and slides it onto his shoulder, traces a tiny circle with her finger. "I yearn to share your bed again." She is breathless with desire. "I want you inside me, Ali." So vulnerable and needy, so seductive.

The silence stretches out. She patiently waits for her spell to work its magic and unravel his will. Her charms have never failed her before. Not once.

Instead, his eyes grow steely. "You are my wife, Fatima. You gave me a son and heir. For that I am grateful. I do remember those days, yes. But they are long past."

She is stunned. She lifts her hand from his shoulder.

Emboldened, he feels the impulse to draw blood, to punish her for her years of insolence and nagging. Rarely does such an excellent opportunity present itself. He suddenly wants to wound her, to maim her, to break her legs. After all their years together he understands his screaming is not the answer. No, he needs something subtler; something so cruel it will slice any woman her age to the bone. Calmly delivered but razor sharp and able to butcher her limb from limb. Something that even she, for all her strength and cunning, is not immune to.

Zoraya has fed him such words, and instructed him on how and when to use them. He inwardly smiles as he draws his word-dagger. "How could I possibly invite you into my bed? You are old, Fatima. Sad to say, your beauty has faded, and you have grown fat. I need someone young and beautiful, someone eager to please me. Someone who actually understands the art of lovemaking." A matter-of-fact, measured cadence, designed to inflict maximal damage. Delivered just as Zoraya told him.

Fatima recoils as if branded by a glowing iron, and for an instant, only an instant, the terrible pain clouds her eyes as the blade sinks deeper into her flesh. She quickly turns her face away to hide it, wills the tears from welling up.

When she turns back to him, her face is a hardened mask, her battle armor latched tight. She seethes, a menacing black thunderhead dropped into a cloudless sky. "You are a fool, Ali, if you think that your Christian whore can make you happy. Do not delude yourself that bedding a child will bring back your youth." She morphs into a pit viper as she hisses, "You are a pathetic excuse for a sultan, a pathetic excuse for a father, and a pathetic excuse for a husband." He simply stares at her, expressionless, just as Zoraya coached him. "And most definitely a pathetic excuse for a lover. You always thought you were so good in bed." She scoffs. "I faked my climaxes, Ali. *Every. Single. One.* After you left me I had to touch myself just to find some satisfaction. No doubt your young whore does exactly the same thing."

His face is chiseled granite.

She sniffs, dismissively. "Sinful man. I fear for your soul, Ali. Rest assured, Allah stands ready to judge you. You *will* be punished."

He continues to study her, then calmly says, "Leave me, Fatima. I may vomit if I have to endure your face any longer." He opens his book and pretends to read, clearly done with her.

She smolders as she stares, nostrils flaring. "Do not think you can be rid of me so easily, Ali. The Christian whore may have seduced her way into your bed with some devil's spell, but never forget that I am the mother of your child and heir. Boabdil *will* sit on your throne one day, with or without your permission. Mark my words, fool. *Mark my words.*"

128

He does not even acknowledge her last barrage. "Guards!" The two bodyguards instantly appear. "Please escort my wife back to the royal harem." He flicks his wrist to be rid of her.

She fumes for a moment more, then lifts her robe and tucks it under her arm, turns and leaves.

He looks back up to follow her out. A thin smile settles onto his face. A rare victory. *Zoraya was right. Zoraya is always right.*

The first irate shout is as abrupt as a cannon shot on a still morning at first light. "HOW DARE YOU!" The booming voice flattens the tranquility of the Lion Palace like a battle-axe crushing an almond. Those within earshot, and there are many, instinctively recoil.

The eyes of the royal bodyguards sprinkled throughout the court turn toward the Hall of the Kings. The elegant calm that defines the Alhambra is instantly shattered.

"MIND YOUR OWN BUSINESS!"

The guards' hands instinctively slide to the hilts of their swords but then relax as the author of the vitriol becomes obvious. This is clearly not the first time they have heard such a tirade.

There is a muted response, the words too faint to be understood, then a cascade of screamed insults, ending with, "DAMN YOU, YOU MISERABLE SWINE!" Another muted response, this one a little louder, the tone more insistent. The only words that can be made out are, ". . . for the good of the kingdom." The statement is answered by yet another barrage of bellowing, even more violent. "I AM THE SULTAN! IT IS *MY* BUSINESS!" There is an expectant pause, then, "DAMN YOUR MEDDLING, BROTHER! I HAVE HAD *ENOUGH* OF YOUR INSUBORDINATION! I WILL ENTERTAIN WHOMEVER I WISH, WHENEVER I WISH, AND FOR HOW LONG I WISH! *UNDERSTOOD*?!"

The ensuing stillness is not comforting.

Suddenly the door to the Hall of the Kings flies open and al-Zaghal exits, his pained grimace deeply etched on his face. He is still muttering to himself as he marches around the corner and into the tunnel leading to the Comares Palace, his black robes swishing. The royal bodyguards lower their eyes as he passes, then exchange anxious looks. The sultan's ill temper never bodes well for those assigned to duty in the Lion Palace.

The sultan and Zoraya are together in the Two Sisters every evening now. He is addicted to her, certainly, but his feelings for her are changing, growing warmer and more loving by the day. She basks in his attention, relishes his gifts of jewelry and gold, and miraculously, seems to become even more desirable by the hour, though that hardly seems possible.

Their evenings together are predictably filled with adventure, but when their bodies are finally spent, they drift off to sleep spooned together, he protectively enfolding her. As their eyelids begin their inevitable droop, he whispers tender words of love into her ear. She smiles to herself, responds in kind, then curls tighter within his arms. Success.

By the standards of court decorum, they sleep in unfashionably late, long past sunrise, and the sultan, always a sound sleeper, often as not awakes to her caresses, a well-placed kiss here, a delicious arc of the tongue there. He stretches as he groans, and they are at it again. Afterwards, they refresh themselves with basins of rose-scented water then proceed to enjoy the sumptuous breakfast sent over from the royal kitchens and spread regally upon a low-slung table by doting eunuchs. It has become their habit to talk over their meal, often for an hour or more. Their conversations range far and wide, but there is no denying that her preference is always for matters of state.

By mid-morning, when the Alhambra is all hustle and bustle in full administrative stride, their trysts end and the sultan's bodyguards escort her across the courtyard and up the stairs and into the safety of the royal harem. The eyes of those in the Lion Palace track her movements; some lustful, some resentful. Fatima's eunuchs still frown when Zoraya arrives back in the royal harem, registering their disapproval of her egregious rule-breaking. But they have been given strict orders, from Fath himself: "Do not question her. She is free to come and go as the sultan commands, no matter the time of day or night."

Zoraya's head is always held high. She will lock her dismissive eyes on any who dares challenge her, then offer up a withering glare or a whispered curse. After all, she is the favored one, the sultan's new love, the First Concubine. After she enters her private quarters and closes the door, the jealous gossip within the royal harem ignites and races through the complex like wildfire.

"My brother received some interesting news from Castile."

She looks up. "I assume more of the same old rumblings?" Despite her intense curiosity over court politics, her face is a picture of nonchalance. She does not pry; she only invites.

He finishes chewing. "Yes, but with a twist. It seems that the Duke of Medina-Sidonia and the Marquess of Cádiz have parleyed."

Her eyes narrow slightly as she reaches for a grape, pops it into her mouth. Another. "How could your brother possibly know that?"

"It seems he has a well-placed spy in the king's court in Córdoba."

She nods, filing this tidbit away. "A parley between those two is hard to imagine given their long-standing feud."

"That is exactly what I said. He and Venegas insisted that Fernando and Isabel had arranged it. I told him to check his source again for confirmation."

"A wise move. One cannot be too sure about such things."

"No. Venegas thinks that Fernando and Isabel aim to use their combined armies to invade Granada. My brother concurs. They feel strongly that war is coming much sooner than we anticipated."

She considers this. "I am not sure I agree."

He looks up from his plate. "Why?"

"Well, Castile's war with Portugal is not yet settled. And if the rumors are to be trusted, and I am confident they are, the ridiculous dowry Isabel has paid to Portugal to wed her child to Prince Afonso will bankrupt Castile, or at least nearly so. They have no means to ready an army to attack us, even with Ponce de León and Guzmán reconciled. No, I say we have at least a year still before our troubles commence. Perhaps longer."

He muses. "Ample time to finish preparing our defenses."

"Yes, ample time. Just to be sure, we could delay it further still by making a surprise attack on one of the Christian border towns. Remind Castile who exactly they will be forced to reckon with should they be foolish enough to attempt it."

"Mm."

"Make a strategic strike, in and out. But deep enough in Christian territory to send a clear message that Granada is not to be toyed with. Isabel is vulnerable to a surprise attack. Who knows, perhaps she might be forced to offer a truce to ensure her border remains peaceful in the interim. Either way, it buys us time."

"Perhaps you are right." He falls silent as he looks back to his plate and picks at his food.

She studies him. "What is troubling you, my sultan?" Soft as a down pillow.

"My brother. I let my damned temper get the best of me again. We had words."

She meekly lowers her eyes. "Over me." Not a question.

"He thinks you hold too much sway over me."

She looks up, tears welled up and prepared to spill. On command. "I cannot bear the thought that I might cause you difficulties, my love. You must send me away. Banish me." By all appearances, she is a portrait of sincerity.

He reaches for her hand, squeezes it. "Never. I will exile him before I exile you. I told him to mind his own business."

She wills the tears down her cheeks. "I do not deserve you, my sultan."

"Of course you do. We were made for each other, Zoraya." He smiles to reassure her.

She dabs her eyes with her napkin. "You need your brother. You must promise me you will make peace with him."

He frowns. "I am the sultan. Let him make peace with me."

"I understand, and I agree. But he is your most trusted counsellor. And do not forget that he commands your army and has the support of your generals and troops. You will need him in this coming war."

The sultan stares at her as he continues to chew. "I suppose you are right."

Zoraya unleashes her most enchanting smile. "Promise me."

He cannot suppress a smile. "Very well, you minx. I promise."

"Thank you, my love." She is now playfully seductive as they fall into a comfortable silence.

"I have a surprise for you, my sultan." A coy smile, unusual for Zoraya.

He is intrigued. "Tell me, my darling."

She looks down, uncharacteristically tentative.

Zoraya, shy? Concern colors his face. "What is it, Zoraya?"

She counts silently for maximum effect. *One-two-three-four-five.* "I am with child." Barely a whisper. She looks up, eyes again full. "I have never been happier."

His joy is instantaneous. "A child? Dear Allah, what a blessing. What a blessing!" He laughs loudly, then rises and grabs her, pulls her to her feet then spins her in the air until they both are laughing. "You have made me very happy, Zoraya, very happy indeed." He lays his hand upon her flat belly. "A boy. It is a boy! I can tell." He laughs. "When? Tell me when will I hold my son?"

A radiant smile. "Patience, my love. I have missed only one bleeding moon. Winter."

He is beaming. "Winter. Excellent. *Excellent!*"

Tears are streaming down her cheeks. "I want so much to give you an heir, my love."

He is beaming. "Yes, Zoraya, an heir." His smile relaxes. "An heir . . . Then, praise Allah, no more need for Boabdil."

She is beautiful even when crying. She sniffles. "No more need for Boabdil." She holds for maximum effect. "Or Fatima."

They lock eyes.

She opens her mouth to speak but then refrains.

"What?"

"It was a crazy thought, forgive me." More sniffles.

"Tell me, my darling."

"I was only thinking . . . if you married me, we would have more than just our nights together. We could go anywhere we want, at any time. And we could raise our son together, as a real family."

He widens his eyes at this new possibility. It is obvious that the thought has never occurred to him.

"Imagine, my love. If I was your wife, and not simply your concubine, the court would no longer have anything to gossip about. And all of your brother's worries about my influence would have no merit. None at all."

"Yes . . ."

"You are permitted four wives by law. I would simply be your Second Wife. Who could possibly object? I am fertile, and you are simply extending your royal bloodline, for the good of Granada and her people."

She can see that he is warming to the idea. But suddenly, he frowns. "Fatima would make your life miserable, Zoraya."

She clearly wants to say something but again hesitates. She waits for his invitation.

"Tell me."

"Fatima would indeed make my life unbearable. But only if she was still residing in the Alhambra."

"What do you mean? Fatima is of noble blood, Zoraya, albeit not Nasrid. She has many friends in many places within Granada, and close ties to some of the oldest clans in the kingdom. Not to mention the ear of the Supreme Mullah and his cronies. No, I dare not divorce her; there would be hell to pay."

Zoraya shakes her head. "No, my sultan, not divorce. No, I agree, she must always remain your First Wife." A sly smile. "But her quarters in the royal harem are so very cramped. Perhaps she would enjoy life in a large carmen in the Albayzín. She could live in luxury and have all the servants she desires. Surely that would finally make the old crone happy." She maintains her look of pure innocence.

He slowly nods. "Yes, I see. Out of sight, out of mind." He brightens. "And perhaps Boabdil could join her, keep her company."

"Precisely. I am sure there would be more than enough room in their carmen for the two of them." An angelic smile.

He strokes his chin. "Yes . . . plenty of room."

"Think of how much more peaceful life at court would be, my love. You would be promoting the tranquility of the Alhambra. And I would so enjoy caring for the royal harem."

He is nodding. "Yes . . . yes . . ."

She leans into him, eases her hand beneath his robe, cups him. She whispers, "The palace would be ours to enjoy, my love."

"Yes . . ." His voice has grown husky with lust.

Suitor

"You should seem pleased that he has traveled all the way from Málaga to meet you." She waggles a scolding finger as she widens her eyes for emphasis. "But not *too* pleased." Mayya smiles as she absently picks a piece of lint from Danah's gown, smooths a wrinkle, tucks a wandering curl back beneath her silk head scarf. "After all, your father is an elder of the Abencerrajes. Malik must prove himself worthy of your hand."

This produces a grimace. Danah nervously tugs at her newly purchased finery. Her mother's doing. She clearly is uncomfortable under the weight of all this formality.

"Do not be anxious, dear. Baba and Malik's father will do all the talking. You and Malik are simply here to formally meet each other. Polite nods and smiles. Words will come later." Mayya smiles. "I am certain he will be handsome."

A roll of the eyes that Mayya fortunately misses.

"There is no arguing that he has a fine family lineage. And thankfully, from what your father has learned, his family has no sympathy for the Nasrids."

"How long will they be in Granada?"

"Long enough that all of the details of the betrothal can be formalized. Perhaps a week."

"So long." Danah sighs. "I do not intend to miss my days at the hospital, Mama." A wisp of defiance.

Her mother purses her lips disapprovingly. "Making a good first impression is so important, Danah. Please cooperate." A thought occurs to her. "Perhaps later in the week you can show Malik the hospital and introduce him to Hakim al-Adani. I am sure he would enjoy that."

Danah's shoulders sag.

"For today, it will only be a formal meeting, and small talk between the two fathers. Relax, Danah."

"And if I decide I do not like him?" There is an edge to her tone.

Mayya frowns. "Danah. Remember our agreement. This is Abd al-Salam's choice for you. You must trust his Sufi wisdom, dear." A convenient about-face.

Danah averts her eyes.

"You must be friendly, Danah."

135

"Yes, Mama." Resignation.

"And stop pulling at your clothes."

"Yes, Mama."

"And remember to smile!"

"Yes, Mama."

Mayya's eyes fill as she reaches up to touch her daughter's cheek. Their eyes join. "You are so beautiful, Danah. My baby girl is all grown up and soon to be married. I am so happy for you."

Danah softens. "Mama."

Mayya wipes her eyes, then smiles. "Well then. They are waiting for us. Shall we?"

Danah takes a deep breath, exhales.

The three men rise as Danah follows her mother into the room. By tradition, Danah's eyes are cast downward in submission. Despite her pleas, her mother was insistent upon this formality. Mayya lifts a palm to her daughter, and with a bright face, says, "May I present our cherished daughter, Danah."

Danah formally bows without lifting her gaze.

Battal is beaming with fatherly pride. She looks lovely in her new finery. A deft touch of makeup to complement her eyes, and a pleasing hint of orange spice perfume. Her mother's doing. "Danah, may I present Bashir al-Karim and his son Malik from Málaga."

She looks up.

Malik's eyes grow gigantic as he beholds her emeralds. Both visitors return her bow.

Bashir says, "We are honored to make your acquaintance, Danah." It is not the son's place to speak to her as yet, but Malik is clearly pleased by what he sees. Bashir continues, "Abd al-Salam speaks very fondly of you, my dear." He is beaming.

A polite dip of the head, but no smile.

Mayya, watching her daughter closely, grimaces. A missed opportunity to enchant.

Battal says, "Shall we sit and have some tea?"

As they settle onto divans, a servant arrives on cue with hot mint tea and a lavish assortment of sweets and nuts.

Battal continues, "I trust your journey was not too difficult?"

Bashir answers, "No, not at all. We traveled via Vélez-Málaga, and then up through the Zafarraya Pass to the Vega. I have clients in Alhama, so we spent two days there. I so enjoy the hammam at the hot springs just outside the city. Have you been there?"

"I have, yes. Glorious."

"Indeed. Then on to Granada. I had forgotten how lovely the Vega is this time of year. All red poppies and waves of golden wheat." He smiles, reaches for a sweet. "It has been almost six years since I was in Granada, you know. I had forgotten how big the city has grown. And so prosperous! The markets are positively brimming with people and wares."

Battal answers, "We are fortunate. The silk trade is booming, and the Vega is bountiful as ever."

"The breadbasket of the kingdom." He smiles. "While we are here I intend to renew some old business acquaintances, and visit the law courts and Sharia library. I have a cousin who teaches at the madrasa, you know."

Without moving her head Danah cuts her eyes to discreetly steal a look at Malik, who is intently following the conversation. Dark-olive skin, penetrating amber eyes. A bright, engaging face. Handsome. Malik, perhaps sensing her gaze, turns his head. As she quickly looks back to her father, Malik smiles.

Battal says, "Excellent. And what of Málaga?"

Bashir spreads his hands. "Well, it has been eventful of late."

"Oh? How so?"

"A Berber army has arrived from the Maghreb. A thousand cavalry and three times as many footmen. Supposedly fanatical Berber warriors hired by Sultan Abu l-Hasan for the defense of the city. Must have cost a fortune."

"No doubt." Battal knows the precise amount. The Abencerrajes are grumbling mightily; they will bear the brunt of the tax burden.

"The Berbers have been settled just beyond the city walls. A knight-commander named Hamete Zeli has been placed in charge of the city's defenses." He shrugs. "Evidently the sultan fears for our safety, though it is not especially evident why. Castile has its own problems with Portugal. Still, I suppose one cannot be too sure when it comes to the ambitions of the Christians."

"No, indeed."

"One thing is clear. Having so many Berber horsemen camped at our gates has made people nervous."

"Yes, I imagine so."

Bashir continues, "Oh, and the Falcon brothers arrived."

Danah's eyes retreat to the safety of her lap.

"Yes, I had heard rumors that they had been sent by Prince al-Zaghal."

"They have been tasked with overseeing the shoring up of the city's fortifications, and consulting with Zeli on plans for the defense of the city. It is all quite unsettling."

"To be sure. Abd al-Salam is in good health?"

A broad smile. "He is. The man is simply ageless!"

Danah looks up, but her expression is blank. Her mother tries to get her daughter's attention to encourage her to smile, but is unsuccessful.

"I tease him that he must have Sufi jinn guarding his health."

Battal chuckles. "Did he say when he intends to return to Granada?"

"As you know, he is overseeing the implementation of a new plan of study for the incoming cohort of students. The Sufi madrasa is a popular place these days. *Long* waiting list." He measures with his hands. "I believe he is to return to Granada by the spring, assuming all goes well."

"That is good to hear. He is sorely missed."

A comfortable silence passes.

Bashir brightens. "Battal, perhaps Malik and Danah would enjoy some time by themselves in your garden? They must find our conversation very tedious." He smiles warmly, expectant.

Battal looks surprised. A breach of protocol for a first meeting. He recovers quickly, returns the smile. "I think that is an excellent idea." He turns. "Danah?"

The girl looks petrified at this unanticipated request.

Mayya purses her lips disapprovingly as she sees her daughter's face. She quickly says, "Yes, Danah. You can show Malik my prized pomegranate. The finest in the Albayzín, Malik."

Danah still looks uncertain.

Malik smiles and says, "I would *love* to see it." He turns to her. "Danah, I would be honored if you would show me." Another breach of protocol to speak directly to his intended at their first meeting.

A long pause, then a resigned, "Of course." Danah's expression is brittle and tense. She rises and lifts her palm. "This way."

The eyes of the three adults silently track their exit, then a ring of smiles. Bashir says, "Danah is lovely. And a budding physician, no less. You both must be very proud. I hear great things about her from Abd al-Salam, Battal. He says she has a rare gift for healing. Very rare."

"Yes, so it would seem. Hakim al-Adani says she is the best pupil he has ever had."

"How wonderful to hear. I can tell you that Malik speaks of nothing but his training in surgery at the Royal Hospital. The boy has found his calling. He has been very anxious to meet Danah. I am sure those two will have much in common."

"He seems to be a fine young man." Battal glances at Mayya, who nods her assent. "Shall we discuss the details of a betrothal, Bashir?"

A giant smile. "The pleasure would be mine, Battal."

"What a marvelous garden." Malik nods approvingly as he surveys the scene.

Granadine carmens are celebrated for their interior peristyle courtyard gardens, and the Amiriya home offers a fine example. Intended to both delight the senses and provide a secluded, meditative refuge. Completely hidden within the interior of the home and sealed off from prying eyes.

The space is quartered by a narrow path paved in elaborate patterns of vertically set black-and-white river stones—a Granadine specialty. In one quadrant are two compact white marble fountains connected by a thin, rectangular reflecting pool. Hand-length iridescent orange fish lazily mill about in the dark water. The two adjacent quadrants are carefully manicured, the narrow raised L-shaped brick-lined flower beds laid out in three terraces covered with close-cropped grass. Fragrant blooming roses are set within the beds; unruly masses of leadwort and limonium spill over the edges. Wisteria vines streaming hundreds of grape clusters strain skyward then rest their palms upon the second-story roof with a satisfied sigh. Bougainvillea awash in ruby blossoms. In the pea-pebbled quadrant opposite the water feature, four orange trees, a pair of lemons, and her mother's famous pomegranate, positively loaded with thumbnail-sized fruit. Narrow irrigation troughs set in a pleasing geometric pattern wend their way between the trees. A clutch of sculptures are tastefully sprinkled throughout the garden, and stone benches have been strategically placed beside the water feature. The placid sounds of moving water blanket the garden in an organic, soothing hush. The sense of peacefulness is tangible. By intent.

"That is the largest pomegranate tree I have ever seen!"

A long pause before she answers. "Mama's pride and joy." Though still anxious, Danah has recovered her footing.

He steps to the tree to finger the fruit. "I cannot believe how much fruit the tree has set."

"Mama pampers it like a growing child."

He laughs.

"At harvest time she hosts a party for our neighbors to enjoy fresh-squeezed juice sweetened with honey then ladled over chipped ice brought down from the Sierra Nevada."

"How delightful!" He turns back to her. "Where is your room?"

She is taken aback by his impertinent request, and pauses to consider whether to answer him. She points. "There. I have the best view of the garden."

He backtracks. "Forgive me, Danah. I have a bad habit of just saying what is on my mind."

She absorbs this, then says, "As do I. Though it often gets me into trouble."

He beams. "Me too!"

Silence settles in as they survey each other.

"Your eyes . . ."

Danah's gaze sinks as she blushes. "Since I was a little girl I have been teased for them."

"You have the most beautiful eyes I have ever seen."

She looks up to determine if he is mocking her. The answer is obvious. A soft, "Thank you."

Unexpectedly, he chuckles. "All this formality in match-making." He whistles. "So stiff and uncomfortable. I asked father if I could wear my physician's robes to meet you."

Remarkably, Danah smiles. "So did I!"

His heart skips a beat at the transformation of her face, then begins to pound in his chest. He opens his mouth to say something clever, but closes it, suddenly unnerved. As her smile fades, the weight of the air presses in upon him. He turns and steps to the pool to compose himself, pretends to study the fish.

An amused expression settles on her face as she patiently waits. She is finding that she enjoys turning the table on men. As he pivots to face her again, her amusement vanishes as quickly as it came. He says, "Abd al-Salam told me that you are under the tutelage of Hakim al-Adani. His skills as a healer are legendary in Málaga."

She steps forward to join him by the pool. Finally a comfortable subject. "I am extremely fortunate to serve under David. He is the best teacher I could ever hope for. You would not believe his library!" Her hands begin to lift and dance as the words rush from her mouth. "He lets me borrow any book I want. At the hospital, he teaches me everything, from setting bones to sewing wounds, from procuring herbs to mixing elixirs. He challenges me, which I have come to realize I *do* need, but he also defers to my judgment when the situation calls for it. I have my own patient now. A young girl named Samra." Her excitement over her chosen profession is contagious.

"That sounds so wonderful, Danah! I work under Hakim Abu Idris at the Royal Hospital. Do you know of him?"

"I am sorry, no."

"He is a demanding teacher, and he can be a taskmaster at times; but he is incredibly skilled, especially in surgical techniques. He is a sworn disciple of Hakim al-Qasim of Umayyad Córdoba. The royal physician to Caliph al-Hakam II of Madinat al-Zahra. It is amazing that Hakim al-Qasim lived nearly five hundred years ago. Do you know his work?"

She nods. "Of course. His *Kitab al-Tasrif* is remarkable."

Malik is impressed. "Surgery is my calling, Danah. A gift from Allah." Malik smiles warmly. "Hakim Idris says it will not be long before I am ready to begin to practice on my own. A year, perhaps less. There is a new hospital that has just been built in Málaga. The al-Mulk." He hesitates, now endearingly self-conscious. "There will be a need for several new physicians." His tone has changed, his words suddenly leaden. "I am sure that someone with your excellent training would be a most welcomed addition to the staff." He swallows hard, examines his toes.

"I see." Her amused expression returns, but in truth, his words please her.

"There you two are!" Mayya is beaming. "Danah, it is time for Malik and his father to leave." She steps back into the hallway to give them space.

The spell is broken. "Yes, Mama. Coming."

They turn and face each other. A line in the sand between them has been crossed.

"I have enjoyed talking with you, Danah."

"As have I, Malik." The truth.

"I will be counting the moments until we meet again." His expression is expectant, hopeful for an acknowledgment, an encouraging word, something.

She nods, but no more.

As he reluctantly gives up and turns to leave, she says, "Perhaps you would be interested in seeing the Bermejas Hospital on Wednesday. I will be working. I could introduce you to Hakim al-Adani, if you like."

"I would *love* that, Danah!"

She rewards him with another smile. "Good. Then we shall plan on it. Come just after noon prayers."

"Excellent!"

"Danah?!" From the hallway, more insistent now.

"Coming, Mama."

They are standing close, so close. Hands joined, breathing quick and shallow, eyes glued to each other.

"From the first moment I saw you, Danah, all I wanted was to take you in my arms and hold you, to kiss you. I have dreamed of you, Danah. Dear Lord, night and day I have dreamed of you."

She is breathless. All she can manage is to helplessly whisper his name. "Yusef."

He devours her with his eyes. He narrows the distance between them. She does not retreat. He bends his knees to even their heights, reaches their locked hands around the small of her back, pulls her hard against him. In tandem they release weighted sighs. Electric-blue sparks begin to twizzle and dance upon their bodies, the lightning bolts teasing and fraying their nerves. "Danah. My Danah."

She is defenseless. She aches for him. "Yusef." Breathless. Never once has she felt the desire to kiss a man. Suddenly she would trade everything she owns for this kiss. Out of nowhere Rumi's verse jumps into her mind. "There is some kiss we want with our whole lives, the touch of spirit upon the body." *Please let him kiss me. Please.* "Yusef." *Please.*

Her eyes fold closed as her lips part in anticipation.

She jerks awake, entwined in her blanket, heart pounding. Her face is flushed, her nightgown damp with sweat. First confusion, then recognition that she is in her room. An embarrassed, "Dear Lord." She waits for her breathing to calm, then begins to untangle herself. She throws back her covers, takes a deep breath, frees it. *So real.* She shakes her head, incredulous. *So real.* Another breath, another weary exhale.

In the Dark of Night

"You should have seen me, Mother! I split my cavalry into two squadrons so we could converge on the wagon train in a pincher maneuver. My squadron made a direct assault on their front, the other hidden behind the ridge until the last minute. Splitting my command was a daring move, but all went according to plan. And the timing, Mother! You should have seen it!" He is as breathless with excitement as a young boy after his first taste of mock battle. "Just as my squadron made our run at the lead wagon, my second squadron broke from behind the ridge and fell upon their rearguard. A complete surprise! If it had been King Fernando's real army we would have easily routed them, I am sure of it!" He puffs up. "I would have captured a king!"

The sultana beams her approval. "Excellent, Boabdil. Learning the ways of command will serve you well. Did your Uncle al-Zaghal witness it?"

"He did, yes. He signaled his approval."

"And the men under your command respected your decisions?"

"They did, Mother. It was as if I have been their commander for years." He is beaming. "They are so well trained. So disciplined."

"And afterward . . . did you thank your uncle for giving you your command?"

"Yes, Mother, just like you said."

"Excellent." She is clearly pleased. "Boabdil, you have one immediate goal." Her expression turns serious as she raises a single finger. "Only one."

"And that is?"

"You must become indispensable on the field of battle, a key commander in Granada's army. With the Falcon brothers safely sequestered in Málaga, this is your chance to shine." Her sudden smile is calculated to encourage him. "When your uncle has a difficult task to accomplish, you must be the commander he thinks of to carry it out, Boabdil. You must be firmly entrenched within al-Zaghal's inner circle before the Falcons return."

"I understand, Mother. It shall be so, you will see."

Fatima replies, "I believe in you, Boabdil. This is an important first step on your journey to the sultanate. You must first become

143

a famous knight-commander of the realm. Then you must win glory in battle defending the kingdom when Castile finally attacks. If you are seen as an able leader capable of defending Granada from the Christian hordes, the elders of the city and the mullahs will rally behind you when the proper time comes. Sultan Boabdil."

His cheerful expression collapses. "I will do my part, but you know Father will never permit me to rule."

She answers him with a cunning smile. "Leave your father to me, Boabdil. Think of it as a chess match. Getting your father to grant you a cavalry command was only my first move. A simple jump of my knight into an open space on the board. Seemingly innocuous, but vitally important. You must make the most of it."

He nods, "I will, Mother."

A warm smile. "Yes, I know you will." She continues to size him up. "Come, let us sit and share some tea." She motions to the matching divans. They settle into a comfortable silence as she pours for him.

Boabdil is a striking young man. Medium height and build, wrapped in exquisite cream-colored robes with ornate gold piping and trim, and a matching cloak and turban. Profoundly expensive attire, even for the Alhambra. He tucks his priceless bejeweled dagger into his waist sash in the Bedouin style, a show of pride for his ancestral roots that stretch all the way back to ancient Damascus. Dark-olive skin, close-cropped beard, ebony eyes, sculpted features, firm jaw. A dashing prince of court. Though the sultan would never admit it, you can easily see the father in the son. He looks every bit the part of a Nasrid sultan's heir.

The young man is too eager to please, though, and given to speaking before he considers his words, often at times when his opinion has not been sought. A serious vice his mother has tried hard to break him of. With little success, sad to say. He also tends toward a youthful impulsiveness in his decision making, another vice. Thankfully, he does not possess his father's explosive temper, leaning more toward his mother's silent cunning, a preference for conducting business in the shadows by whisper. He shares her gifts but lacks her skills, something she is trying desperately to remedy.

Like most young men his age, he dreams of winning glory through valiant combat; he believes that war is the place where dreams are made and unmade. He exudes confidence, projects a high opinion of his prowess, and yearns to test himself. Truth be told, however, he harbors the same insecurities all young men do and carefully obscures them with his bravado. Given the ever-present cadre of court sycophants on the loose, it is difficult for a prince of his rank to have any real friends. Too risky. Which is unfortunate, since it forces him to rely solely on his mother for advice and counsel. Or perhaps that is her doing?

Not surprisingly, he is fashionable with the ladies of court, many of whom, despite the priggish rigors of decorum regarding the intermingling of young men and women, prowl about hoping to raise their stature, to gain favor, and knowing that this is best accomplished with their clothes off. To be sure, he has deflowered his fair share of adventuresome maidens. Fortunately, no bastard children share his looks. Yet. His mother scolds him for such foolhardy behavior, of course, and maneuvers behind his back to ensure that none of these ambitious young maidens manage to capture her son's heart. If in doubt, they are quietly exiled from court, or else their families are threatened. Boabdil is puzzled when they disappear, or when they inexplicably lose interest in him, but he simply shrugs and moves on to his next conquest. It goes without saying that when the time is right, Fatima will ensure that a comely young virgin of her choosing will make her way into his path and succumb to his charms. But first things first.

As a prince of Granada, Boabdil has received training in the arts of weaponry since he was a young boy, has become quite proficient with sword and dagger, and is an expert at handling a horse. But then again, winning sparring matches with wooden weapons is a far cry from cleaving an arm with a broadsword in the fevered heat of combat; from driving a lance through the chain-mailed chest of a mounted knight swinging a battle-axe at your head.

Like most of the nobles at court he shuns the new match-lock black-powder *arquebuses* making their way around Europe. Difficult to load, unreliable in firing, and inevitably belching thick clouds of smoke that obscure the field of battle. Delivering a mortal wound to an adversary via a lead ball fired from a hundred paces? Bordering on cowardly. No, Boabdil subscribes to the still-prevalent view that honor in battle mandates close-quarter combat, knight against knight, where one's courage and skill with a blade determines life or death. Only when victorious in such a bout can a knight secure the honor so desperately craved.

Who can say for sure why the sultan so dislikes his only son and heir? Certainly Boabdil has his distracting qualities, but then again, most young people do, and that is what education and training are for, to erase such faults. Perhaps an heir coming of age and constantly in the wings is a reminder to the sultan of his own mortality, that his days in this world are numbered; that he is not immortal after all. Certainly, Fatima's constant scheming to advance their son's position at court does not help matters. In response, the sultan tries his best to thwart her plans at every turn, to deny his heir a proper reckoning. Just as a matter of principle. As of late, courtesy of Zoraya's clever counsel, he feels he finally possesses the verbal weaponry to hold the sultana at bay. Or so he thinks.

So why did the sultan agree to the cavalry command for Boabdil? Truth be told, it was his brother's doing. After those two made amends, al-Zaghal suggested an overture of peace to Fatima, to make up for Zoraya and the mayhem the girl has caused within the royal harem. In a weak moment, he agreed. Perhaps it was his feeling of imperviousness to his wife's scheming that there was suddenly less to be fearful of with her. Fool.

Boabdil sips his tea, and without looking up, says, "The gossip at court is all about Zoraya." A simple statement of fact.

Fatima's eyes are smoldering, but her expression is blank, her voice even, smooth as silk. "Yes, well, I fear that the sun is about to set on the Christian whore's influence at court."

Boabdil looks up. "I see." He knows his mother and her skills. "An unfortunate accident, perhaps? A sudden illness? Maybe a morsel of bad food?"

She responds with a sly smile. "Oh, just a feeling I have."

He chuckles. "Well, for me, the sooner we are rid of her, the better. They say she has charmed jinn into casting an evil spell upon Father."

Her face is unreadable. "Perhaps."

"They also say she is more skilled at lovemaking than any concubine in the kingdom. That no man can withstand her charms." He pauses as he conjures her face. "To be sure, she is incredibly beautiful . . . but there must be more than that to hold Father's attention so firmly. It makes one wonder . . ." He stares into space, stiffening as he savors some lewd fantasy.

Fatima's smile evaporates. "Mark my words, Boabdil, Zoraya's days are numbered." When he does not respond, she turns, scowling. "Boabdil!"

His image of her vanishes into thin air. He shakes his head to calm his lust. "I say, good riddance."

"Yes. Good riddance."

As silence settles back in, Fatima studies him. "I intend to make secret contact with the elders of the Abencerrajes, to solicit their help with our cause." Bold words, even for her.

His expression is a caricature of shock.

His mother frowns. The boy simply refuses to learn to master his emotions.

"The Abencerrajes?! Our sworn enemies? There was good cause to banish them from the Alhambra, Mother."

"Perhaps. But that was such a long time ago." She demurs. "A chess match, son. *A chess match.* Do not worry, my overture will be discrete. If what I have just learned is true, the Abencerrajes will have a part to play in our path to checkmate your father. My intuition tells me that it is not a small part, either."

Boabdil frowns. "I see. Care to share your plans with me, Mother?" Annoyance has crept behind his words, another fault.

An exasperated sigh. "In due time, my son, in due time."

"Your man actually saw her do that?" Fatima is incredulous.

"Indeed, Sultana. He was quite emphatic."

"Dear Lord . . ."

"Spilling the sultan's seed in such a manner is unnatural, Sultana. Unholy."

She can't shake the visual image. She shudders. "How obscene. No wonder the whore has him under her spell." She hisses, *"Christian devil."* She looks up. "You are absolutely sure, Fath?"

"I am positive, Sultana. I arranged for the broken pane in the upper window to be replaced with a piece that could be silently removed with a thin blade." The eunuch is clearly proud of his endeavors. "My man lay deathly still on the outside edge of the cupola until the cover of night, and when they were distracted by each other, he removed the pane and slipped a small mirror—"

Fatima lifts her hand to stop him. "Please, Fath, I do not need to know the details."

"He could see everything they did, Sultana, and hear every word they spoke. You know how the Two Sisters amplifies sound." The eunuch smiles. "It seems that our Zoraya has learned quite a few pleasure tricks from Persia. My man could not believe how loud the sultan's cries were."

Fatima frowns. "Enough."

Fath recoils. "My apologies, Sultana."

She waves a hand dismissively as she looks away, but Fath catches a glimpse of the gaping wound the sultan inflicted upon her. He has no clue as to what exactly transpired between the two of them, of course, but even so, he has rarely seen her in pain, and this puzzles him. He pauses as he considers the possibilities, then continues, "That is not all, Sultana."

She looks back. "There is more?"

"Indeed. I saved the best for last." A wry smile from the eunuch. "It seems your husband is divulging state secrets to the girl. And she is clearly attempting to influence matters of state. Which he permits."

Fatima allows herself the barest hint of a smile. "Ahhhh . . . Now *that*, Fath, is what I want to hear. Tell me more."

"Well, for one, he has clearly informed her about the parley in Córdoba that al-Zaghal's spy reported."

Her smile widens. "How interesting."

"And it seems that she is advocating that the sultan order a preemptive attack on Castile. An unprovoked surprise attack by Granada."

"My, my, the vixen is bold. Where?"

"Zahara."

She frowns. "But that castle is deep in Christian territory, and well defended. She may end up precipitating war before Granada is ready."

"She evidently knows the layout of the place from her former life. She claims to have visited it many times. She believes an attack will send a stern message to Fernando and Isabel to respect our borders. He whispers, "An objective observer, Sultana, might interpret her words as treason."

Fatima actually smiles. "Indeed they might, Fath, indeed they might. What else?"

Fath licks his lips. "Many things, Sultana. Our troop strengths in various regions, pending trade agreements, the cost of the Berber mercenary army he sent to Málaga, the balance of Granada's treasury." He reaches into his robe and removes a palm-sized scroll. I had him write down everything he heard, word for word. Three nights' worth of fodder. It is all here."

"My spellbound husband is an imbecile. You have done excellent work, Fath. Fifty gold dinars will be delivered to your room by first light."

Fath bows. "You are kind, Sultana. I live to serve you."

"This is plenty with which to approach Supreme Mullah Abd Allah. Given the sexual perversions and the betrayal of state secrets, I have all I need to strangle my stupid husband with his own foolish pride. I am afraid the condemnation of the Supreme Council will be thunderous, with the mullahs and imams close behind." She rubs her hands together in delighted expectation. "And wait until the elders of the Abencerrajes get wind of these juicy morsels. They will call for his head. Mark my words, Fath, my husband the sultan will soon be cowering in the Generalife, and his unholy plaything will be long gone from the Alhambra."

Fath licks his lips. "It shall be so, Sultana."

Fatima turns and locks her eyes on him. "Your spy. He is now a liability I can ill afford, Fath. Do you understand?"

The eunuch nods. "It has already been arranged, Sultana. I had his dinner specially prepared. He will not wake tomorrow morning."

"Good. See that his family is well cared for."

Fath nods.

"I will complete my letter to the Supreme Mullah before I retire. I want it delivered first thing in the morning, while our two lovers are still engaged in their abominable couplings."

"It shall be so, Sultana."

JUST BEFORE MIDNIGHT, THREE DAYS LATER.

The city sleeps. A waning gibbous moon methodically scales the star-studded canopy. There is a slight breeze, the pleasing cool a welcome respite after the warm, cloudless day. The dull yellow flicker of the oil lamps hung at regular intervals along the street spills an uneven, dingy hue upon the cobbles, lending an eerie twilight. Each intersecting alley of the impossibly dense maze of the Albayzín is a cavernous yawn of black.

No more than a stone's throw from the River Darro a cloaked head eases from the shadows from one of a thousand such dark alleys, surveys the street—first left, then right—then retreats into nothingness. After a count of five, a wraith darts across the cobbles and disappears into the opposite alley. A slash of black, then gone.

Five minutes later the wraith arrives at his destination, a nondescript door on a nondescript alley. A heavily-armed guard dressed in black robes stands like a statue flanking the door, all but hidden. The wraith whispers the code word. The guard nods, turns and opens the door. The wraith disappears into a deeper shade of darkness, and the door is closed behind him.

Once inside the small anteroom, the wraith whispers a second code word to the guard manning the only door in the room. The guard turns and taps twice on the door, is answered by the slide of a metal latch, followed by a sharp snap. The door opens. This room is candlelit. The wraith folds back the cloak from his head. An old man with a flowing white beard—an elder of the Abencerrajes. He disappears inside and the door is relocked.

The seven men sit in silence on floor pillows circled tightly around a large candelabra. The ribbons of flame atop the twelve lit tapers dip and juke in response to an unseen draft, but the room is crammed with a pulsing warm glow. It is a compact space, unadorned, without a single window, and only the one door. Each man is dressed in identical black robes and turbans. Four of the seven are old. Ancient would be more accurate. Close-cropped, totally gray beards, weepy eyes undercut by heavy bags, an assortment of age spots. Two are younger; one late middle-aged, one middle-aged—the baby. The seventh, the elder among elders, sitting opposite the door, could pass for Methuselah. Long, flowing, cotton-white beard. Wizardly, but not of the kindly sort. His penetrating eyes are intense orbs of smoldering ebony. His face has been hewed into hills and valleys, his right cheek hillock sporting a noticeable sag. With each labored exhale, the sag twitches with a life of its own, a tic distracting enough to require a deliberate act to avoid staring at it.

The wizard breaks the silence. "*As-salamu alaykum wa rahmatullahi wa barakaatuhu.*" May Allah's peace, mercy, and blessing be upon you. His voice is deep and raspy, but surprisingly strong. The voice of an impassioned leader on an urgent quest.

The six respond softly, "*Wa alaykumu s-salam wa rahmatullahi wa barakatuh.*" May the peace, mercy, and blessings of Allah be with you, too.

"*Alhamdulillah.*" Praise be to Allah.

The six respond, "Alhamdulillah."

The wizard continues, "Thank you, gentlemen, for coming out so late at night." He stops to cough into his palm. Wet and unhealthy. "I am afraid that there are urgent matters that require the full attention of the Council of Elders."

Sober nods. Clandestine meetings of the elders of the Abencerrajes are nothing new.

After the previous Abencerraje-dominated Supreme Council was murdered by the treacherous Nasrid Sultan Abu Nasr Sa'd nearly thirty years back, the clan was evicted en masse from the Alhambra. Banished in a political coup. They were ruthlessly persecuted throughout the city in those early years, and to survive they melted into the nooks and crannies of the Albayzín, forswore their allegiance to the clan in order to make peace. Or so they said. Publicly, the Abencerrajes all but disappeared from view. Privately, however, they began to assemble influence by any means possible, slowly but surely, without attracting undue attention. Shadow deals were made, handshakes behind closed doors, gold pressed into palms, virgin daughters promised and delivered.

This rebirth of the Abencerrajes progressed by fits and starts, with triumphs then setbacks, but after thirty years they have once again become a force to be reckoned with, especially within the lair of the Albayzín, their new power base. They have also grown rich from their influence peddling, and presently dominate most of the merchant guilds of the city, especially those of the all-important silk trade. They are a capable people, after all, well-educated, bright, ambitious, and possessing that all-important singular goal: to take back what rightfully belongs to them—the Alhambra herself.

They have managed to assemble a respectable number of cohorts of the City Guard that owe them secret allegiance, and supporters have been sprinkled throughout the sultan's army, many now in positions of leadership. Politically, they aim to reach a majority on the Supreme Council. When they do, they will be ready to flex their muscles and reclaim their rightful place in dictating what happens within the city and the kingdom. For now, however, they bide their time, continue to grow their influence, and wait for the right opportunity to make their presence felt.

The response of the Nasrids to this stealthy accretion of power? Weak, laughably ignorant to the rising danger. They assume that once the clan was decapitated and scattered, it would always remain so. A minor annoyance, certainly, but one to easily brush aside and trample should the need present itself. Fools.

"You have no doubt heard the latest rumors regarding our *beloved sultan* and his *dalliance* with the *Christian whore*." He tortures the words.

Affirmative, nodding frowns.

"The Supreme Mullah informed me this morning of some new, and quite interesting, information."

A half-dozen pairs of eyebrows expectantly lift.

"One might even say, damning information . . ." He allows his words to trail off into an expectant pause. A skilled orator. "It seems that the whore has placed some sort of evil spell upon *our* sultan." He twists the word enough to hurt it. "They have taken to engaging in unnatural sexual acts."

There is a collective furrowing of brows, but no one has the audacity to ask what those acts might actually entail. Predictably, their imaginations run wild. Hard swallows abound. Though none of the elders have met Zoraya, they have heard plenty about how beautiful and desirable she is.

"While such sexual . . . transgressions . . . might be forgiven, it seems clear now that *our* sultan is also sharing state secrets with the whore. And he is taking her advice on decisions that affect all of Granada. That, my friends, is treason."

"Where did this information come from?" The old man to his left seems skeptical.

The wizard's eyes widen. "He would only say that the source is highly trustworthy." A long pause. "I have my suspicions." He does not volunteer anything more. A sinister smile struggles onto his face. "But there is more. Much more." The air tenses as his eyes circle from elder to elder. "The sultana has approached me. Very discreetly, of course, by a third party. Fatima and I have now met in private."

Murmurs. This *is* a surprise.

His smile wriggles haughty. "I must say . . . it was an interesting conversation. It seems the sultana wishes to ally with our cause."

Grumbles now, followed by a sprouting of frowns and dubious head shaking.

The old man to his right snorts. "Ridiculous. Why would she possibly want to do that? *We* are the ones banished from the Alhambra." He sniffs. "I smell a trap."

The middle-aged man interjects, "How could we possibly trust anything that conniving woman says?"

The wizard lifts his hands to calm them. "Please. Let us remember that she is not Nasrid. We all know she is bright. And ruthlessly ambitious. And she certainly has no qualms about opposing the sultan, even publicly. She could be *most* useful to us."

They do not seem convinced.

The wizard continues, "It seems the sultana has a singular goal; a goal that our sultan violently opposes." Another wet cough into his palm. "Fatima aims to have Boabdil succeed his father. A reasonable desire. He is the sultan's only heir, after all." He holds for emphasis. "But she is not content to wait until the sultan passes from old age. It seems she is willing to make an alliance with us to ensure this transition in power comes to pass sooner rather than later."

A clutch of more murmurs, then silence settles in as they mull this over.

The wizard says, "Gentlemen, this may be the opportunity we have been waiting for. The kingdom is unsettled. Everyone agrees that the Christians will soon come calling to demand a reckoning. The Alhambra's eyes are clearly not focused on the Albayzín."

The man to his right joins in. "These new taxes they have imposed—" He flicks his wrist as if swatting at an annoying fly. "They are strangling the guilds! Already they are crushing my profits. If that fool Venegas taxes us any higher, it will break me. Life under the Christians would be preferable to this!"

Murmurs of assent.

"Something must give. And soon!"

The wizard nods his concurrence. "Yes, something must give. The sultana has suggested that I meet with Boabdil and the three of us settle on a course of action that suits both of our ends."

His eyes circle the room.

The old man to his right mutters, "A dangerous game to cast our lot with those two. She will never voluntarily cede power to us if she is successful in winning the sultanate."

The wizard turns and studies the man with knit brows. "No argument. If we are clever, however, by then we will control the Alhambra. In my opinion, the reward justifies the risk. Think of the possibilities."

"Mmm . . ."

He continues, "I would request the Council of Elders' permission to engage this path. Discreetly, of course, and cautiously."

Eyes lock on the wizard.

"All in favor?"

Every hand lifts, though two are noticeably slower than the rest.

"Very well. When I have news, we will meet again. You will hear from me by the usual channels."

Sober nods.

"Good. Let us close by celebrating the Dhikr."

Backs straighten, upturned palms settle into laps, eyes fold closed.

The wizard softly intones, "*Al-Rahman—*"

The circle answers, "The Compassionate."

"*Al-Rahim—*"

"The Merciful."

153

"*Al-Malik—*"
"The Sovereign Lord, Our King."
"*Al-Quddus—*"
"The Holy, the Pure, the Perfect."

"*What?*" Fatima's face instantly flushes with fury. "WHAT?!"

Fath's shoulders grow limp as his eyes retreat to the floor. A scolded puppy. "It seems she is with child, Sultana." No more than a whisper.

"Impossible! That is what you said, Fath. *Impossible!* You said that the remedy was administered each day in her food. Undetectable, you said. Zoraya is infertile, you said!"

He cannot bring himself to look up. "I did say those things, Sultana. It seems I was mistaken."

"It seems I was mistaken." A whine, chased by a derisive sneer.

He winces under her mocking. "She tricked me, though I am not quite sure how. I have failed you, Sultana."

Her eyes are still bulging. "Yes, Fath, you HAVE failed me! YOU HAVE!" She is livid.

He mutters. "Forgive me, Sultana."

She ignores his plea. She takes a deep breath to steady herself, attempts to exhale her anger. "Do you understand what this means, Fath?"

Silence. He knows perfectly well what this means.

"If it is a male child, Boabdil is no longer the sultan's only heir." She worriedly chews her cheek. "How did you learn of this?"

"She let it slip to the chambermaid that was bathing her." He shakes his head, confused. "Or perhaps it was intentional."

"Of course it was intentional, you fool. This fits the whore's ambitions perfectly. I am certain it was her plan from the first moment she laid eyes on my husband. I can hear it now." She sneers, "*The sultan's favorite concubine carries his son. A new addition to the royal bloodline. How joyful!*" A derisive hiss. "She is immune now to any threat. Sad to say, she has secured her place at court."

The eunuch finally looks up, shamefaced. "Now that the Supreme Mullah has your letter as evidence, Sultana, surely the sultan will have to banish Zoraya from the city. After all, she has incited him to commit treason."

"No, Fath. A potential heir changes everything. There are those at court who will rally around him." She curses under her breath. "Do we know how far along she is?"

"The chambermaid said only a slight thickening, but her breasts were noticeably fuller. Less than three months, I would guess."

Fatima mulls this over. "Still vulnerable, then, to a natural ending." The calm of calculation steadies her breathing. "There must be some way to expunge this bastard child before it sees the light of day. Think, Fath, think!"

"I have been doing nothing else, Sultana. Unfortunately, Zoraya no longer sleeps in the harem. And she eats and drinks only when she is in the sultan's company. As a matter of standard protocol, he has all of their food and drink sampled by the royal tasters. So an abortive elixir is no option."

She considers this. "No . . ."

"She clearly recognizes the danger she is in."

"But why reveal this so soon? Whatever else she may be, the whore is no fool. She knows she is not safe until the child is born. She will sequester herself; under his protection, of course."

"The only option I can see, Sultana, is to do her violence. I could arrange for her to drown in her bath. Or perhaps slip and fall from the balcony and break her neck. But this would be difficult to hide, and I am afraid the repercussions for you would be extreme. Still . . ."

Fatima frowns. "Violence is no option." She curses again. "You must come up with a better plan, Fath. Something clever, less direct. Do not rest until you have a plan for me. We must act quickly, while there is still time."

"You may depend upon it, Sultana."

"Leave me. I must think." She dismisses him with a flick of her wrist. Her anxiety is uncharacteristically written upon her face.

Angst

"The arrangement of the wards is not unlike that of our Royal Hospital, though I dare say the Bermejas is better equipped and staffed."

This time, Malik is wearing a surgeon's robe, turmeric with brown piping. As with Danah, he is still missing the crimson Staff of Asclepius to be embroidered on each sleeve upon taking his final vows.

Needless to say, Danah was anxious before he arrived, but like before, their conversation quickly turned easy and unforced as it began to weave its way into the medical arts. She is wearing her cobalt physician's robe, a perfect foil to his colors. Truth be told, they make a handsome couple—a fact not lost on Malik. His eyes cling to her, as discreetly as he can manage.

David was still on business in the Alhambra when Malik arrived, so Danah introduced him to several of the hospital staff then began a tour of the facilities. She paraded him through the various wards, the surgical theater, their large collection of medical instruments, and finally, the room dedicated to medicinals, where herbal treatments are prepared and stored, and various elixirs are mixed or distilled, then bottled.

As they slowly walk, she points, she describes unusual cases, she lists the techniques she has had the opportunity to learn, the skills she has yet to master, her animated hands adorably lifting and dancing in time to her words. She is clearly in her element. He takes it all in, asking polite questions as they stroll. He steals as many opportunities as he can to study her face without her noticing. Inevitably, she finally catches him at his work and smiles awkwardly while blushing. Her young suitor is clearly smitten.

When Malik had arrived just after noon prayers, she was already two hours into David's list of medicinal preparations. Replenishing their supply of surgical antiseptics is her assignment for the day; tedious but important. With each new concoction she readies, she transcribes the entry from David's medicinal journal into her own. Proportions, order of addition, the expected hues of the various colors of the components, other nuances that might be easily missed. She endures these mundane tasks while secretly hoping a challenging case will find its way to her before she leaves. Her time is still split between the Atfal and the Bermejas. On Thursday morning she will be back with Samra and Ezar.

The week has been reasonably quiet at the Bermejas: the normal collection of stomach ailments; a bloody stool; one serious poisoning from spoiled lamb; a middle-aged woman's bleeding moon that will not relent; two broken limbs, one a clean break, the other an ugly compound fracture; a clutch of children down with sundry fevers; some ugly boils and buboes that required lancing and draining; an old man's abscessed tooth; a wicked mule kick that broke a farmer's ribs; a troubled childbirth that ended up requiring emergency surgery—the highlight of her week thus far. Both mother and child survived. Her awe for David's skills is boundless.

Banat, the old woman in her charge, has since passed into the arms of Allah. Danah cried like a baby the morning she checked on Banat and discovered her cold and stiff. David indulged her hysterical shower of tears, then quietly reminded her of the great gift of dignity she had given Barat in her passing. When Danah calmed, they jointly prepared her body and consoled the family when they arrived. In the end, it was an excellent learning experience. David knew this, of course, when he assigned her to care for such a hopeless case. "Death is a natural part of living, Danah, just as night follows day. As a physician you must always remember this." He widened his eyes for emphasis. "We are not miracle workers. Our patients sometimes die despite our valiant efforts." Danah had nodded soberly as she dabbed her tears.

"There are no female medical apprentices at the Royal Hospital."

"Mm."

He is watching her pour a viscous ruby liquid from a dark flask into a large beaker. Wine vinegar concentrated by boiling. Her eyes concentrate on the measuring lines etched into the glass.

"It must feel strange to care for men."

Nothing. She stares intently at the gradations as the fluid in the beaker slowly rises.

"To wash their bodies and touch their bare skin. Does it bother you?"

Finished, she rises and turns to him as she considers this.

"It was difficult at first, yes. But now?" She shrugs. "No. I am a physician, Malik." A self-conscious smile. "Or soon will be, inshallah. My vocation is healing. David says that medicine knows no bounds, not for age or sex or color of a person's skin. Or even religion. It is the oath we physicians swear to abide by. Why should it be any different for me, as a woman?"

A warm smile. "Well said, Danah. My thoughts exactly."

She turns and lifts another flask, checks its label, then kneels to place her eyes level with the next gradation on the beaker. She begins to pour the golden liquid. Naphtha thinned with olive oil, then infused with yarrow root. Where the thin stream breaks the surface, a burst of bright orange.

"Have you been given your own *matula* yet?"

She nods. "I have, yes. David had the glass-blower make it especially for me. He favors a flared conical shape, which is different from what many physicians use."

"Interesting. How many of Ibn Sina's twenty-one colors have you identified?"

"Less than half. Still, it is truly amazing what the sight and smell of urine can tell us about disease."

"Indeed. You said you have a patient under your direct care?"

"I do. Samra. A young girl."

"What ails her?"

Danah hesitates, then opts for the truth. "She was raped by Christian marauders, then discarded as trash."

Malik winces. "Dear Lord."

"Not surprisingly, her mind was injured by the trauma. I am seeing to her recovery. She has made progress, though she still has a long journey ahead of her. It took over a month before Ezar or David could enter her room without inducing panic. That has changed, thankfully."

"Poor girl. May I meet her?"

"Certainly. She is in the Atfal Hospital. Not far. Perhaps we can meet again tomorrow morning? David permits me to split my time between the two hospitals." She flashes that glorious smile.

"That would be wonderful, Danah! I so love seeing where you practice your art."

"You really *must* meet Hakim Ezar al-Mufaddal. He is chief physician at the Atfal. And a dear friend. So funny! He has these beastly eyebrows that have a life of their own." Her husky laugh fills the room.

Charmed by the profound mismatch between what he expected her laugh to be and its reality, he can't help himself and begins to laugh with her. "Any friend of yours, Danah, is a friend of mine."

Their eyes join; they linger.

She finally breaks the trance. "Watching me prepare medicinals must be incredibly boring." She lifts another flask, checks its label.

"Not in the very least. I so enjoy our time together. It is always a gift to witness a skilled physician at work."

She sees that he means it, which pleases her. She turns, lifts the flask, reads the label. "Distilled autumn mandrake." She pulls the cork, sniffs, wriggles her nose. "What a fascinating aroma." A sly smile. "Care for a smell?"

He shrugs, leans forward, then suddenly jerks back. "Gahhh! What a terrible stink!"

She laughs wildly.

"Youuuu!" He playfully scolds her with his finger.

"I am sorry, Malik, I could not resist." She has settled to a husky chuckle.

Truth be told, he is charmed by her flirting. "I intend to return the favor, my lady. Something when you least expect it. Just wait!"

Their smiles linger on each other.

She takes a deep breath, returns to her task. "Thankfully, the last ingredient." Back to business. "Then we can meet with Hakim al-Adani. He should be back from the Alhambra by now." She kneels, begins to pour. "He is personally caring for the sultan's new wife. She is with child."

"Yes, I had heard."

She rises, recorks the mandrake. She lifts a glass rod, stirs the beaker well, then pours the elixir into an empty flask, inserts a cork, then labels and dates it. "Done. Shall we?"

He lifts his palm as he smiles. "Please, after you." Safely behind her, he is free to let his eyes drift admiringly from her head scarf to her heels. Her robe cannot quite hide the fetching sway of her curvaceous hips.

"Hakim al-Adani, it is a tremendous honor." Malik bows deeply.

His deference pleases Danah.

"I am delighted to meet you, Malik. Abd al-Salam speaks very highly of you. Is Hakim Idris managing to behave himself these days?"

Malik smiles. "He is, sir, yes. He is a fine teacher."

"His surgical technique is among the best in the kingdom. I know he can be brusque at times, and he works his students very hard, but there is much you can learn from him, Malik."

"Indeed there is, sir. I consider myself very fortunate."

"How much longer is your training to last?"

"Less than a year, inshallah. Hakim Idris has indicated that I will be offered a position at the new al-Mulk Hospital that is presently being constructed."

"Good. That sounds like a fine opportunity for a young physician."

"Indeed." An awkward pause. "My hope is that Danah will consider joining me there, sir. As a physician."

"Ahh . . ." David seems caught off guard by this news. "I see. Of course. Yes. Right." He dims, brightens momentarily, dims again.

Danah's eyes well up. The fatherly protectiveness of her mentor means the world to her.

David clears his throat, stares intently at Malik. "Danah is as fine a student as I have ever known. Her gift of healing comes from Yehovah, to be savored by our world. She is a rare jewel to be treasured, Malik."

Danah examines her toes.

Malik beams. "I could not agree with you more, sir."

He studies Malik, sees that the young man is sincere. "Excellent. Abd al-Salam is a dear friend. I see that he has chosen well."

"Thank you, sir."

Danah reaches desperately for a safer subject. "And how is the Alhambra's most famous expectant mother?" A running joke between the two of them.

David finally relents and smiles. "Zoraya is doing well. Five months along, or nearly so." He chuckles. "She insists it is a boy. I tell her the sex is impossible to know, but she presses me constantly to officially declare it." He waggles his finger at both of them. "Never let royal wives cajole such a pronouncement from you, no matter how persistent they are!"

Danah and Malik both laugh.

David shakes his head incredulously. "You should see her bodyguards. Massive black Africans; four of them. And sporting broadswords as tall as you, Danah. They set up camp just outside the room where I examined her. The sultan paced back and forth in the hallway like a caged animal. You would think he was a young father anxiously awaiting his first child."

Comfortable silence.

David claps his hands together enthusiastically. Eyes wide, he announces, "I have a treat for you both. A difficult surgical case that should be arriving any moment. Prince Abul-Jalil. A qadi in the Alhambra law courts. Though only middle-aged, he is nearly blind from a bad case of waterfall disease. Without his sight, his usefulness to the sultan will end. I have been requested to surgically repair his clouded eyes and hopefully give him his sight back. Eyes are as delicate a surgery as there is. You both can assist me."

The young couple beam their approval.

"There you are."

Danah stares into the bubbling fountain, lost in thought. She sits on a stone bench beside the pool in their garden. Abu al-Qasim's treatise on the maladies of the eye lays open on her lap, but remarkably enough, unnoticed. For the first time in a long while her thoughts are not on medicine.

"Danah?"

She finally registers the voice and looks up, confused. "Yes, Baba?"

"You were a thousand miles away, darling." His tone is gentle, fatherly.

She shakes her head. "I am sorry, Baba. There is much on my mind these days."

He sits beside her. "Yes, I expect so."

They admire the fountain's pearly tinkle in silence.

He turns to face her, affectionately wraps her hands within his. "Mama told me that Malik visited you at the hospital today."

"He did, yes."

Her father lifts his eyebrows. "A good visit?"

She considers this and nods. "It was, yes. We have much in common. And our conversations are easy. I introduced him to David, who approves. We both assisted him in a delicate surgery of the eye, which was a remarkable feat. I am not sure I will ever have his skill as a surgeon."

Battal smiles. "Of course you will, Danah."

She suddenly looks pained.

"What, darling?"

After a long pause she says, "Malik told me that he has been promised a position in the new hospital being built in Málaga. The al-Mulk."

"Yes, his father mentioned it. It sounds like an excellent place to begin a career."

"Yes." She hesitates. "He said that he was confident I would be offered a position there as well. To practice as a physician by his side."

"I see." He carefully weighs his next words. "Malik is an excellent match, Danah. The young man is clearly taken with you. Two practicing physicians in the same family. Imagine!" His expression runs to serious. "I was a fool to be so reluctant in permitting you to follow your life's calling, Danah. I see that now." He stops. "I am proud of you and all that you have accomplished." His words thicken with emotion. "Very proud."

Her eyes well up. "Málaga is so far away, Baba."

He nods. "It is, yes." Now he smiles. "But to visit my grandchildren? Well, I would make that journey very often. Very often indeed!"

Her gaze sinks to her lap. "Baba?"

"Yes, darling?"

"How did you know that Mama was the one for you?"

He chuckles. "Dear Lord, I was smitten with the woman! After I laid eyes upon her that first time, I could think of nothing else but her." He conjures a memory, grows more serious. "When I was with her, Danah, I felt . . ." He searches for the right words. "I felt like my life was finally complete. That I would be a better man with her at my side." He smiles. "And when she finally permitted me to kiss her? Well!" He whistles. "My heart was pounding so hard I thought it would explode! I will never forget that kiss." He reaches out to lift her chin. "It will be like that for you, Danah. You will see."

Nothing.

He softly says, "Your mother and I are waiting for your word, darling. To formalize the betrothal."

She turns to stare into the fountain. "I know."

They sit in silence for a moment longer, then Battal rises and leaves.

She cradles the infant in her arms, her gown slipped down off her shoulder to expose her engorged breast. A beautiful baby boy. He roots for her, impatiently, finds her nipple, then loses it. Annoyed, he opens his eyes wide to protest. Brilliant emeralds stare up at her. A motherly smile. "Silly boy." She reaches down to guide him home before he can squawk. He latches on hard enough to make her wince, closes his eyes, and begins to contentedly suckle-sigh. She can feel her warm milk flowing from her body into his. She cups her baby boy's tiny head, strokes the silky wisp of chestnut-brown hair. She is so incredibly happy it brings tears of joy to her eyes.

The door opens and she looks up. She smiles. "Yusef!"

He comes to her, kisses her. "My love. And how is our little knight?" He touches his son's pulsating cheek.

"Greedy with my breasts." She smiles. "Like his baba."

Yusef laughs loudly.

She wakes with a start, gasping for air. *So real. Dear Lord, so real. Have mercy on me.* He has come to her every night since Malik arrived, though she prays with all her might for a dreamless sleep. Tears begin to leak from her as she desperately whispers, "Come to me, Tetta Layla. I need you. Come to me. Please." She pleads, "Why will you not come to me, Tetta? I need your guidance. *Please.*"

Málaga

"Hold up, Brother, let me catch my breath." Umar is doubled over, hands on his knees.

Yusef turns back to chide him. "You grow soft, Brother. Too much riding, not enough walking." He stops.

As Umar catches up, they turn to survey the city laid out in all its glory before them. A fine, clear morning. They arrived at the city gates the previous evening, and after delivering the official communiques and paying their respects to Emir Abul-Hawari al-Khuldi, governor of the city, they billeted their cavalry in the garrison, then settled into their quarters within the Alcazaba and had a late meal.

They left at first light, alone, to scale the steep incline to the legendary mountaintop Gibralfaro Castle, one of the largest and most formidable fortresses in the kingdom. A difficult climb even for two fit young knights. They are to meet with Hamete Zeli, the knight-commander now in charge of the defense of the city.

Umar wipes his brow. "Dear Lord. I had forgotten that Gibralfaro is high enough to touch the clouds. We should have taken horses."

"No, slow is good. This will allow us to better gauge the condition of their defenses, and to understand what the Christians will have to face when the time comes. We must memorize the sightlines and the possible angles of attack if we aim to form a proper defense."

Umar looks down the near-vertical slope to the sea. "It is hard to imagine more impenetrable defenses."

"Heavy cannons change everything, Umar. Even walls this thick will collapse under concentrated fire."

"Tell me how Fernando is going to move his heavy cannons up this mountain?" He indicates the impressive slope. "By magic?"

Yusef frowns. "Never underestimate your enemy, Brother. The Christians will find a way. Depend upon it."

They fall silent as they take in the view. The air is moist and sweet. A pleasant saline tang kisses the gentle sea breeze. A nightingale lights on the battlement a short distance below them and unleashes an impossibly dense barrage of bright whistles, trills, and gurgles.

Umar smiles. "I had forgotten how lovely Málaga is. It is good to be back."

Yusef grunts.

Umar turns to study his brother. *The girl.*

Yusef meets his brother's stare but does not respond. He returns to the panorama laid before him.

The stunning cobalt blue of the Mediterranean stretches to the horizon to their left. It is difficult to discern where the sea ends and the sky begins. The Mediterranean is placid, dotted by sailing vessels making their way to and from the port. Málaga is an ancient city, founded by the Phoenicians nearly three millennia ago. The city's lifeblood has always been commerce. As the principal export hub of the Nasrid kingdom, it receives dozens of vessels daily from all the major ports of the western world: Venice, Genoa, Athens, Beirut, Benghazi, Antalya, Algiers, Alexandria; even London, Paris, Hamburg, and Rotterdam. Trade is brisk and lucrative. Granada's exports are prized, and they include: raw silk, cotton, a myriad of textiles—banners to carpets to prayer mats to all manner of clothing sporting a thousand different hues; silver and gold filigree, olive oil, saffron, leatherwork, ceramics, precious stones, spices, wine, paper, dyes, iron, copper, alum, animals, books . . . the list is endless.

The city is cradled on three sides by imposing saw-toothed mountains that ring the city then fall into the sea, a formidable natural barrier to land attack. The city is bounded on the north by the Gibralfaro Mountain, one of the southernmost peaks of the rugged Axarquía Mountains that divide the coast from the Granadine plateau; on the west by the Guadalhorce River; and on the south by the larger Guadalmedina River, which empties into the sea just beyond the city. Between the imposing city walls and the mountains lie thousands of hectares of incredibly fertile farmland. The land is a verdant patchwork of fields and farms and orchards, sprinkled with country villas for the wealthy. In the spirit of the Granadine Vega, though in miniature.

Málaga has historically been vulnerable to attack by sea, a problem finally remedied by the Almohad Berbers almost three centuries back. Approaching vessels are forced to lower their sails and drop anchor, then patiently wait their turn to enter the six arched ingresses in the fifty-foot high, ten-foot thick harbor wall that stretches an arrow-shot out into the sea. When the time comes, the harbor-master uses signal flags to direct each merchant vessel to its assigned entryway, which must then either row or be towed in through the wall. Once inside, the vessels make their way to the wharf, cast lines, unload their wares, then load new cargo and provisions. If the city is threatened, heavy iron gates can be lowered to seal the harbor entries. Two crenellated fortresses at each end of the wall guard the approach, their battlements bristling with cannons capable of making quick work of any vessel of ill intent. The harbor enjoys an excellent reputation with merchants around the Mediterranean, and the city has prospered wildly as a result.

From the wharf, the land rises to a terraced, oblong knob, then turns and climbs steeply up the Gibralfaro Mountain. Clinging to the knob, and lording over the city, is Málaga's famous Alcazaba, the emir's palace and garrison. The Alcazaba has an impressive inner wall surrounding the palace proper, a concoction of elaborate architectural surprises, water features, and lavish decorations. Not unlike the Alhambra herself, though alas, considered by all a poor impersonation of the original masterpiece. An even more massive tower-studded outer wall encircles the entire complex. The open space between the two walls enables the rapid movement of both infantry and cavalry to any point on the outer wall that is under attack. The Alcazaba has never been captured by force of arms.

The Gibralfaro Castle was constructed upon Phoenician ruins in 929 by Umayyad Caliph Abd al-Rahman III of Córdoba, then expanded and strengthened by the Nasrid Sultan Yusef I of Granada in the early 1300s. One of the unusual features of Málaga's impressive fortifications is that the Alcazaba and the Gibralfaro Castle, though separated both laterally and vertically by almost a quarter mile, are actually connected via a *coracha*. Added by Sultan Yusef I, the coracha consists of a pair of impressive turreted walls separated by fifty paces. The paired walls break from the upper end of the Alcazaba then charge uphill to link to the castle high above. This enables troops and cavalry to quickly move between the two fortresses as required to thwart an attack on either. The linked Alcazaba and Gibralfaro Castle essentially form a single gigantic fortress, one of the largest and most impressive found in Europe. The thin strip of land between the walls is terraced as it makes its way up the mountain, allowing ideal shelter for billeted troops. It is on the eastern parapet of this unusual coracha that Yusef and Umar stand, three-quarters of the way up the summit.

Umar points west, just beyond the Puerta de Granada, the gate by which they entered the city. "The tree line is much too close to the outer walls. See?"

Yusef turns and assesses. "Agreed. In many places. The western approach to the mountain has a much gentler slope and is clearly more vulnerable than the seaward side. This is where Fernando will launch his attack. The entire slope leading up to the castle should be cleared of trees to improve firing lines. And perhaps some spiked earthen moats added at the base of the castle walls." He too raises his finger to point. "See that low rise? Behind it would be an ideal place for a Christian cannon battery. Close enough to hammer the Gibralfaro's outer walls, yet out of the direct sight of our gunners."

"Then we should cut the top off the hill."

"Correct. There is much to be done." This will not be a short stay. Yusef turns and looks upward to their destination. "Not much farther. Shall we?"

Umar affectionately slaps his brother's shoulder. "We shall, sir. Al-Zaghal was right, Málaga needs us, Brother. Let us see to it."

A sober nod from Yusef as they resume their climb.

"Commander Zeli." Yusef and Umar bow respectfully. They are his equals in rank, though he has twenty years on them. Hamete Zeli is a respected veteran knight-commander who has proven his mettle many times on the battlefield.

Zeli returns the courtesy. "Welcome to the Gibralfaro. Falcons are always a welcome sight on my watch." A warm smile.

Yusef continues, "The sultan and al-Zaghal send their best regards."

"I trust they are in good health?"

"Indeed, excellent health."

"And your uncle?"

"He is fine, thank you."

"Please, sit. You must be tired from the climb. I will send for tea." Zeli catches the eye of his servant, who turns and departs. The three are now alone. They settle onto floor pillows. "It is good to see you again, Yusef, though I must say, I had no advance warning of your arrival. I should have come to greet you properly at the city gates."

"We thought it best to travel without fanfare."

"I see. Well, know that you are most welcome in Málaga, sir. I assume you brought cavalry?"

"Yes, but only a squadron as escort. They are billeted in the Alcazaba's garrison."

"Good. I will see that they want for nothing."

Yusef replies, "Thank you. We have been assigned a special task by the sultan, Hamete."

"I suspected as much. Long ride for a courtesy call." He smiles.

Umar says, "We are to help you survey the city and come up with a plan for its defense. That, and to advise you on how best to deploy the Berber army when the time comes."

"Excellent. I can certainly use your experienced eyes."

Yusef adds, "Hamete, there is good reason to believe that the Christians will invade the kingdom. If they do, they will be forced to attack Málaga before converging on Granada. To cut off our supply line and source of income."

"Yes. It is what I would do. How soon?"

"Difficult to know. Six months? A year? Perhaps longer. The Castilians must settle their business with Portugal first, then refit their army. In any case, you must be ready. The kingdom will not fall as long as Málaga holds. Preparations have already begun on refortifying the castles guarding the perimeter of the Vega, filling cisterns, laying in stores, sharpening swords."

Zeli takes a deep breath, exhales. "So it comes to war, then. As I am sure you have already seen, there is much work to be done here before we can repel an army the size Fernando is likely to bring."

The Falcons nod their concurrence.

"While the Alcazaba and Gibralfaro are reasonably sound, the garrison troops are green and unbloodied. They need some serious training, perhaps some maneuvers in the wilds of the Axarquía to toughen them up."

"Agreed. My cavalry officers can assist with their training."

"Good."

Umar asks, "How many cannons do you possess?"

"Seventeen for the Gibralfaro, six for the Alcazaba. Another dozen guarding the harbor. Nothing on the southern and western walls of the city."

Yusef frowns. "I see."

Zeli continues, "The gun crews are adequate, but rusty. The city walls on the western side are especially weak and in need of repair. And the tree line is far too close for my taste." He lifts his hands, helplessly. "There is much to be done, gentlemen, but no easy means to do it. I need money, Yusef, and more critically, dedicated workers at my call."

Yusef says, "You shall have both. The sultan has issued a decree instructing Emir al-Khuldi to provide the gold you need, and the power to raise taxes on exports to help the treasury bear the burden. He is also to hire a thousand laborers to put at your disposal, and however many slaves he has in hand."

Zeli brightens. "You bring excellent news, sir!"

"It will be a start at least. We must make haste."

"Indeed."

Umar says, "Tell us about the Berber army."

Zeli smirks. "An odd lot. They speak some strange desert dialect. Quite different from Andalusi, and hard to understand."

Yusef replies, "No doubt."

Umar chimes in, "Are they as fearsome as the rumors?"

Zeli nods appreciatively. "They are indeed, Umar. If Fernando chooses to attack us, they will prove to be a stout backbone. They take an oath to die before retreating, you know. Fanatical warriors." He chuckles. "I would lay good odds that they would march on Córdoba itself this very day if I but gave the word. These Berbers live for jihad. Their greatest desire in life is to kill Christian infidels and defend the faith."

Umar asks, "How many?"

"A thousand horsemen and three thousand infantry, give or take. Their officers are quite capable. And needless to say, the army has battle experience. Expert riders to a man, and very proficient with their weapons. The horsemen can let loose their bows at full gallop. Their drills are quite unique, an impressive sight to behold."

Umar smiles. "I would like to see that."

"You will."

Yusef asks, "Where are they billeted?"

"In the valley to our west. I thought it best to keep them outside the walls until the city grows used to the idea of their presence."

"Good. We must ready Málaga for siege without inducing fear or panic. When the time is right we will ease the Berbers into the castle a company at a time. Between the castle grounds and the coracha, we will need to ready space for them to billet."

"Their camp is spare. I have already made some preliminary calculations. There should be adequate room, I think."

"Excellent. When Fernando lays siege to the city, he will be forced to take the Gibralfaro first. The Berbers will anchor our line and lend us a lethal counterattacking force."

"My thoughts exactly. After our tea, I will introduce you to the Gibralfaro and her ramparts." He smiles. "She is a thing of beauty, gentlemen. Then we will set to work." Zeli beams. "You bring such good tidings. I am glad you both have come."

Umar answers for them. "As are we, sir, as are we."

The brothers have moved into spartan quarters within the castle keep of the Gibralfaro. The real work is here, at least for now. They get on well with Zeli, finding easy agreement on most matters. The emir bristled at the sultan's financial demands, but in the end relented. Gold was released, and workers were hired. He then promptly raised the export taxes on raw silk and silk textiles, Granadine specialties, to ensure that his treasury remained solvent and that his resentment of Nasrid edicts was registered.

Their first focus has been to clear the trees from the western slope of the mountain and dig dry moats in front of the castle walls. Slow and tedious work, but progressing.

Official mail parcels depart the Alcazaba every third day for the Alhambra, a seventy-five mile journey by armed escort, with brief stops in Vélez-Málaga and Alhama. Umar writes to Faynan each evening prior. A quick recap of their progress on the city defenses, tender words of love, then some bawdy line about what he misses most about her. Just to make her laugh. He often smiles as he writes, sometimes chuckling with amusement. More than once he has teared up as he signs his name and presses his ring to the hot red wax.

He does not open her letters until the day is done and evening prayers are completed. Faynan's letters are much longer, and he reads them with a bright smile pinned to his face. News from Granada; the convolved machinations of courtly life; juicy gossip, especially the rumors surrounding the sultan and Zoraya; the latest book she is reading; the people she is meeting. She ends with heartfelt words of love, of course, and her heartache over his extended absence. He cackles when she boldly chooses to return a bawdy tease.

During these moments, Yusef reads, brow pinched with concentration, trying his best to ignore his brother. Unsuccessfully. Occasionally Umar will share a tidbit of news, or the latest gossip, but mostly he keeps her words to himself. He is sensitive to his brother's anguish.

This night, when Umar finishes Faynan's letter, he sighs contentedly and says, "There are times, Brother, when I wonder what I did to deserve such an incredible woman."

Yusef grunts but does not look up from his page.

Umar turns and contemplates his brother. His heart melts. "I wish the same for you, Yusef. That you find the love that I have found."

Yusef slowly closes his book but does not raise his eyes. He softly says, "I think of her day and night." Wistful.

"Love is a beautiful thing, Yusef."

He looks up. "No. She tortures me, Umar. Day and night, she tortures me." Pain settles onto his face.

A kind smile. "Yes. I know."

"Our time in Málaga will be measured in months, not weeks. Perhaps longer." He is listless, resigned.

"Danah has your letter, Yusef. She will wait for you."

"Who am I to hope for that? Perhaps she read my words and was offended. Perhaps she never even bothered to open my letter. Perhaps . . ." He stops.

"Then write to her again, Yusef. Let her know your feelings. Tell her how much you miss her. Faynan will see that she gets it. Perhaps Danah will write back with an encouraging word."

Yusef shakes his head. "I have made my feelings known, Umar."

"Brother, you are so incredibly stubborn."

Yusef does not reply but simply reopens his book and begins to read.

Umar rolls his eyes, then utters a sigh of resignation.

Exile

"Please try and see the positive, Fatima." Grand Vizier Venegas' tone is soft and reasonable. Always the diplomat.

She is speechless. Stunned. Pale as a cotton sheet.

"You will be free of the tedious drudgery of running the royal harem." He frowns as he says it. Even coming from him this sounds lame. "I have secured one of the finest carmens in the Albayzín for you—Dar al-Horra. Very spacious, with fountains and a garden, and with a great view of the palace. Breezy during the summer months."

"I see." Her words are devoid of life. "I cannot believe he actually married the whore, Venegas." It is more than obvious that she did not anticipate Zoraya's masterstroke. A rare mistake indeed. "When?"

A long pause. "Yesterday."

"And he actually managed to find a mullah that would officiate such an unholy marriage, knowing everything that has happened? You have seen the charges."

"He did. A minor one, but legal nonetheless. Gold was exchanged, clearly, but mostly it was because of the child, Fatima."

A listless frown. "Of course. Maintaining the Nasrid dynasty is all that really matters."

Silence settles in.

"How soon?" She struggles to find the energy to speak.

He sighs. "By end of the week, I am afraid. You can take the harem eunuchs and chambermaids with you. All but Fath."

"How gracious of her." The sultana's words are venomous.

"Zoraya intends to leave Fath in charge of the harem."

"And deprive me of his services. Logical." Her words are dead.

"I am sorry, Fatima." You can tell he means it.

She lifts her head to lock her eyes on him. "I cannot believe you are doing this to me, Venegas. I thought you were a friend."

"Please, Fatima, our friendship is not in question. I have done, and will do, everything in my power to help you. But you know as well as I do that when your husband sets his mind to something it is impossible to sway him."

"But this was not his idea. It was hers."

"I know." His words are gentle. "Since Zoraya came, he has changed. I simply cannot fathom the control the girl exerts over him. It is as if she has cast a spell upon him. Al-Zaghal is livid with his brother. Called him a fool to his face."

"You know the danger she poses to the kingdom, Venegas. My stupid husband heeds her words, even before those of the Vizier Council. She will destroy Granada."

"I understand the danger, Fatima, I do. I will do everything I can to thwart her and try to talk some sense into the sultan. With war coming, this is no time for foolish games. Lives are at stake. And now he insists that we all dance upon a dagger's edge."

Only her eyes have come back to life. They begin to smolder with hate. She muses, "His wife of twenty-four years replaced by a Christian whore in just twenty-four hours . . . Who would have thought?" She shrugs, helpless. A resigned sigh.

He opens his mouth to reply but chooses not to.

"I see now that I underestimated the whore. Clever girl. First seducing him with her sex tricks, then outfoxing Fath to conceive his child. Now marriage." She hangs her head and shakes it, incredulous. "This last move, I did not anticipate. To my peril." She looks up. "And Boabdil?"

Another sigh, this one heavier. "I am afraid he must leave the Alhambra also, Fatima." It clearly hurts him to say it. "At least for now. I think it would be best if he lives with you in the Albayzín. He must not do anything rash, Fatima, or tempt the sultan to banish him to the Maghreb. He must tread very lightly."

A sad smile as she shakes her head side to side. "Of course."

Fath reclines upon a divan, his hot mint tea resting upon a side table within easy reach, his writing board settled on his lap. It has been a long day, and his letter to Fatima must still be written. Invisible ink, of course, to be smuggled out with the morning laundry to the Jewish Quarter and then on its way to her carmen in the Albayzín. News from the previous day usually reaches her by mid-morning. Fath relishes his new role as the sultana's eyes and ears within the Alhambra. It lends him an importance he has always sought.

Fath's days since Fatima's banishment have been busy. The initial explosion at court due to the sultan's scandalous marriage to Zoraya, then his banishment of Fatima and Boabdil to the Albayzín. The initial response was a *How-dare-he!* outrage, finally settling into a simmering stew of disapproval. Needless to say, the

Abencerrajes and their minions fanned the flames at every opportunity, of which there were many. Even the generally tolerant Granadine citizenry shook their fists at their leader's dubious actions.

While the sultan stands condemned in the court of popular opinion, Zoraya knows that time is on their side. The Alhambra's gossips are predictably fickle, after all, with new and juicy morsels a cheap daily commodity. Six more months would be all she needs to tame the crowds. Six short months. New dynastic heirs can work miracles in the court of popular opinion.

The arrival early in the week of a pair of harem eunuchs and matching chambermaids from the finishing school in Ronda produced a flurry of whispers within the Lion Palace. The second lot in as many weeks, and more on the way. In Fath's view, competent, but green. Still, he relishes the chance to teach, to bend the new servants to suit his needs. Proper training does take time and energy, but it is satisfying work, something he enjoys.

Zoraya has occupied the harem and is now officially in charge. She moved into Fatima's old suite, of course, after every single trace of her predecessor was expunged and the place was thoroughly scrubbed and whitewashed. Her first edict was to expel all of the sultan's concubines. Fath's objections were dutifully leveled—tradition, protocol, common sense—but then, quietly, though firmly, disregarded. To a one, the sultan's sizable collection of ripe young beauties is gone. Without the royal concubines the harem seems strangely empty, with the predictable result that there is too little to do for the new eunuchs and maids. When Fath raised this point after the second set of eunuchs arrived, Zoraya waved him off, insisting that she required a full complement of harem staff. For what, exactly, she declined to say. She made it quite clear that it was not his place to press her.

Four heavily-armed black African eunuch bodyguards now mark Zoraya's every step within the palace. They are mute. Or more correctly, tongueless. They embody an exotic, and it must be said, imposing, new presence at court, a striking contrast to the blond-haired, light-skinned northern European royal bodyguards historically favored by Nasrid royalty. The Africans arrived via Egypt and were supposedly trained in Persia, though no one seems to be able to verify this. Evidently, Zoraya insisted upon personal bodyguards for the heir-to-be, and she made sure that no expense was spared.

Predictably, Zoraya is rarely to be found within the confines of the harem, which suits Fath just fine. She prefers to spend her time in her husband's presence, and returns reluctantly, as if the place bears some ancient curse or lingering stink. Only when her husband leaves the Alhambra on matters of state does she slither back in, and is always careful to post her Africans in strategic locations. Her attire has been carefully crafted, at great expense, to prominently display her swelling belly, to leave no doubt as to the coming gift she will present to the Nasrid kingdom. An heir, no less. She trumpets this as fact, though clearly it is impossible to be certain as to the sex of the child. Six months and counting. Time will surely tell.

Fath lifts his tea, savors the aroma of fine mint, blows to cool it, takes a sip. Another. This brings a satisfied smile. Fath's new life is actually to his liking. He angles the paper, lifts his reed pen and dips it into the ink pot, beginning his letter to Fatima.

> *Dear Sultana. I trust that you have settled in and are comfortable. You are sorely missed. The new parcel of harem staff seem capable enough, though inexperienced. I am afraid they will require some serious retraining.*

He lifts his reed, blows on the paper. The words slowly vanish, black then gray then smoke then gone. A jinn's playful phantasm. He dips his reed once more and continues.

> *I will send a letter to Ronda and remind them of our special requirements. This is Granada after all. I must say, Zoraya's African bodyguards are an unsettling presence at court. It seems their tongues were cut out to preclude any gossip. My guess is that they are illiterate as well.*

He repeats the process.

> *Venegas came to see me this morning. He sends his best. An interesting development has arisen. He said that the Vizier Council will meet—*

Fath's head jerks back. He stares into space, a puzzled expression on his effeminate, painted face. His forehead instantly beads with sweat. His reed slides from his fingers and clinks on the floor. He lifts his hand to his chest to check his heartbeat. A confused frown, still uncertain what exactly he is feeling. He lifts his fingers to his neck to take his pulse but notices that his arm has grown leaden. His frown deepens with concern. He turns his head and stares pathetically at his cup of tea, the thread of steam innocently spiraling upward a hand's length before it disappears.

His color darkens as his eyes widen with raw terror. He swallows hard, wrestles the air for a breath, and gulps it down like a starving man. He struggles to open his mouth to call for help. Nothing. Panic grips him. His face is now a deepening shade of crimson, his lips running to purple. He tries mightily to move— just lift a hand, just move a foot—but he is frozen in place, a fly helplessly trapped in amber. All he can do is groan; an awful, throaty croak. His eyes begin to bulge as frothy drool escapes his contorted lips. He groans again, more subdued this time. Another groan, softer still. His left eye twitches once, twice, then a long, slow exhale. He does not fight for another breath.

He sits, staring into space, a portrait of abject terror. His eyes are fixed and dilated, opened wide, so wide, the whites now glowing with an unnatural golden hue. A trickle of blood slips from his left nostril, crosses his pursed lips, meanders down his chin, slowly drips onto his fine robes. The spatter wicks into the white silk, a crimson amoeba growing with a life all its own. His trademark perfume, so ethereal and costly, is joined by a whiff of fecal reek.

Matchmaker

Umar and Yusef are both mid-bow when he interrupts them.

"You both know I have no use for such formalities. Come closer! Come!" His hands wave wildly, motioning them forward.

They can't help but smile. Abd al-Salam has known them since they were young boys.

"Closer! Let me look at you both." Hands on hips, he dramatically leans back, lifts his chin, and squints to size them up. "Still handsome, I see. Dear Lord, how the women of Málaga must swoon when you two pass! There are beautiful creatures on every corner, are there not?" A deep belly laugh and a twinkle in his eyes.

Umar playfully replies, "I am a married man, sir. I have eyes only for Faynan." He lifts his hand to his brother. "This rogue, on the other hand, lives to make the maidens blush!"

Yusef smirks at Umar.

Abd al-Salam chuckles. "Yes, yes, no doubt, no doubt. They say it is the quiet ones you have to watch." He winks at Umar. "I had heard rumors that a pair of falcons had slipped through the gates." He clasps his hands together. "It is good to see you boys. Good, indeed! Come, let us sit." He motions to the floor pillows. "Come." The brothers settle and politely wait for the old man to creak himself down. Grunts and groans and a final loud sigh as he plops into the waiting pillow. The young men exchange smiles. "Would you two like hot tea? Some sweetmeats?"

Yusef answers for them. "Thank you, no, we can only stay a few moments. We are expected in the Alcazaba for a meeting with the emir."

"Ahhh. Matters of state."

"It has been too long, Abd al-Salam."

"Indeed it has, Yusef, indeed it has." A warm smile. "And how is that wily old uncle of yours? Up to no good, I am sure!"

Yusef replies, "He is well, thank you. These days he is out inspecting the border castles."

Umar smiles. "And scolding the knight-commanders for their soft ways."

Abd al-Salam chuckles. "Yes, I expect so. The famous scowl of Ali al-Attar. I have seen it a thousand times! More!"

Umar smiles. "You look to be in excellent health, sir."

The old man's watery eyes sparkle like diamonds. "Alas, Umar, I am old as the marble upon which you sit. But still alive by some strange miracle, praise be to Allah."

The brothers smile.

Umar asks, "Things are progressing on schedule at the madrasa? We have heard that you are completely changing the students' program of study. A bold move, sir."

Abd al-Salam's eyes widen as he frowns. "These young stags! They have grown up with too much luxury, too isolated from the sufferings of the world. They live to carouse and chase the young maidens. All they really desire from the madrasa is to leverage what we so painstakingly teach them to obtain positions of power and wealth. And, of course, the trappings that flow from those positions." He shakes his head. "Sad to say." He brightens as he opens his hands. "So I decided to go back to basics. To shake things up a bit. This new cohort will have to reckon with a renewed focus on service to the poorest of the poor. And *real* Sufi prayer. Dear Allah, these boys cannot even sit in silence for more than five minutes without fidgeting! How are they going to learn the Sufi Way?!" He chuckles. "They will curse my name, but they will learn, and learn well!"

Umar teases him. "You had better watch your back, sir!"

Abd al-Salam puts on a stern expression as he puffs himself up. "These young stags are no match for this old Sufi!" He begins to rock with laughter. Yusef and Umar join in. "Rumor has it that you are here to organize the city's defenses." His smile runs away. "Is there to be war, then?"

Yusef replies, "I am afraid so. Once Castile settles with Portugal, we expect that Fernando and Isabel will turn their greedy eyes upon Granada. It is only a matter of time, and we must be ready. The Christians surely know that Málaga has to fall before Granada can be cut off and taken. They will come. And when they do, they will bring their heavy cannons with them. Málaga must be ready to stand firm."

The old man sadly nods. "I was afraid of that. All is still quiet on the borders, yes?"

Umar replies, "Sad to say, not especially. A raiding party of Christian mercenaries just razed a small village near Campotéjar. It was a daring move intended to provoke us. They beheaded the townsfolk. Men and women both. And they took the children as slaves back to Castile."

"Dear Lord! No survivors?"

Yusef answers, "One. A young girl." He stops. "She was raped and left for dead."

"Oh my, how awful." The old man sadly shakes his head. "Attacking innocent children. What is the world coming to?"

Umar continues, "We brought her to the Atfal Hospital to be cared for."

"Good, good. Hakim al-Mufaddal is an able physician."

Yusef says, "Indeed. He has a female assistant who is looking after the girl. An apprentice working with Hakim al-Adani."

"Ahh. You must mean Danah. Danah Amiriya."

Yusef visibly stiffens.

Abd al-Salam continues, "Lovely girl. You surely noticed her exquisite emerald eyes. Brilliant mind, that one. And a voracious reader. She has a very bright future ahead of her."

Umar answers for them. "Yes, that is her. An impressive young woman. Strong-willed, has a mind of her own." He cuts his eyes to Yusef to tease, but Yusef avoids him.

Abd al-Salam beams. "Indeed. Pray for a world with more strong-willed young women, Umar. I am certain she has a calling to the Sufi Way. I have already taught her some classical Sufi meditation forms. She is a quick study." He smiles as he recollects her. "If only the young men in the madras had Danah's dedication to serve. She aims to be Hakim Amiriya, an admirable quest for a young woman from an affluent family. I managed to convince her father to allow an apprenticeship under Hakim al-Adani." He chuckles. "No small feat, I can tell you! David raves about her; thinks she is the most capable student he has ever taught." He muses. "She must be splitting her time between the Bermejas and the Atfal."

Umar replies, "Yes, she told us as much."

The old man's eyes sparkle. "She is to be married, you know."

Yusef's head jerks back as if slapped, shock stenciled onto his face. His gaze slowly sinks to his lap as his shoulders sag.

Umar frowns. "Are you certain of this, Abd al-Salam?"

"Quite certain. Her parents were pressuring her, you see. They insisted that she must be betrothed if she is to continue her studies under David. She is past age, you know. The parents asked me to locate a proper young man who would suit her tastes. Someone her own age, smart, and of good character, and with an Abencerraje heritage. And importantly, someone engaged in the medical arts." He chuckles. "No small task. Truth be told, it was Hakim al-Adani and his lovely wife Miriam's doing, though her parents have no knowledge of their role." The old man beams. "I must confess I have never played matchmaker before, but I am pleased to say that I proved up to the challenge! The young man's name in Malik al-Karim. A third-year student studying under

Hakim Idris at the Royal Hospital. He says the boy will make a fine surgeon and has a bright career in front of him. Malik's father is a qadi in the law courts. A widower, sad to say, but well respected. They left for Granada a week back to finalize the betrothal. They will not marry until after both have sworn their oaths as hakims. Malik will then bring her back to Málaga. At my urging, Hakim Idris is prepared to offer them both a posting in the new al-Mulk Hospital."

Umar is still frowning. "I see."

Yusef looks up, his face ashen. "It is time for us to leave. The emir is expecting us."

The old man studies Yusef with concern. "You look like you have seen a ghost, Yusef. Are you well, my boy?"

Yusef does not meet the old Sufi's eyes. He mutters, "Just a touch of nausea, sir. Probably something I ate in the Gibralfaro."

"I hope it is nothing. Promise me you two will visit me regularly while you are here. I must catch up on news from Granada. I hear some disturbing rumors about our sultan."

Umar speaks for them both. "We will visit, sir. Depend upon it."

"Good, good." The old man reaches forward to affectionately clasp hands with them both. "It was such a delight to see you again. Such a delight!"

Yusef and Umar rise.

"Forgive me for not walking you to the door. It will take my creaky bones ten minutes to rise off this pillow. I may as well enjoy some meditation while I am here."

Umar forces a smile. "We will come again soon, sir. Good day." The brothers turn and leave.

Umar has to firmly grasp Yusef's shoulders from behind to stop him. "Stop, Brother! Please."

Yusef turns to face him down. His expression is strained, angry.

"Yusef." Gentler. "I am so sorry."

Yusef sneers. "Sorry? *Sorry?!* Umar, *you* were the one who encouraged me to write to her. You!" He sneers, "*Open your heart to her and tell her what you felt when you looked deeply into her eyes.*" He shakes his head with disgust. "Dear Allah! What a fool I am. Loving a girl betrothed to another. I am a stupid fool! Stupid. *Stupid!*"

Umar locks both of Yusef's shoulders with his hands, looks into his eyes. "You must fight for her, Yusef. Fight! Write her another letter and declare your love. This is only a betrothal. They will not marry until both have completed their training. You have time. Fight for her, Yusef!"

Yusef shakes his head violently. "No! NO!"

"Since when did an al-Makki *ever* retreat on the battlefield in the face of long odds?"

Yusef balls his fists as he flushes with fury at the insult.

"Yusef, why should it be any different with Danah? Fight for the one you love! Fight!"

Yusef's eyes fill. "No, Umar! NO! I have said my piece. She knows my feelings. I have wasted too much time on this girl. Be damned! BE DAMNED!" He turns and storms off toward the palace.

He goes about his work as if nothing has happened, but his melancholy is palpable, a presence that dogs his every step. Umar fusses over him, tries to cheer him up, to no avail. Curt nods, one-word replies, grunts of acknowledgment. There is work to be done, after all, and Yusef throws himself into it with abandon, rising before dawn, working until sunset. Late in the evenings, after prayer, he leaves their room to walk the ramparts alone. He slowly paces, arms tucked behind his back. He stops from time to time to stare up and lose himself in the sea of pulsing diamonds. His eyes trace the broad brush of milk that stretches horizon to horizon. He does not return to their room until he is sure that Umar will be asleep.

On the fourth night after they visited Abd al-Salam, on his way back to his room, he stops beside the door to the empty office of Hamete Zeli's adjutant and steps inside. He closes the door and lights a candle, then locates writing implements. He sits on a pillow at the low-slung desk. He closes his eyes and conjures her face: that incredible smile; the long, dark tresses he has never once seen but so aches to run his fingers through. For the thousandth time he imagines holding her, kissing her, making love to her.

His eyes open. He reaches for the ink pot then lifts the reed. Without a pause he proceeds to spill his heart onto the paper. He bleeds his love for her, his desire for her, his dreams for their life together, their children, their children's children. Everything.

When he is done, he stares for a long while at the testament his heartache has produced. He slowly lifts the paper, holds its edge to the candle flame, and eyes full, numbly watches the fire consume his profession. The flame licks at his fingertips. He grimaces with the searing burn, finally releases the black ash, and shakes the sting from his fingers.

He stares into space for a full minute, then brushes the ash aside, withdraws a fresh sheet of paper, lays it flat in front of him. He lifts his reed, dips it into the inkpot, and begins.

Dear Danah:

> *I trust that my letter finds you in good health, and that your training at the Atfal continues to be fruitful. Please convey my best wishes to Hakim al-Mufaddal and to Samra. There is much to be done in Málaga, and it is clear now that my brother and I will be here for many months more.*
> *Danah. I have spent much time reflecting on the words I wrote to you in my last letter. I am honor-bound to inform you that the feelings I expressed to you were misguided and false. The chasm separating our stations in life is much too wide to ever bridge. You are a physician, I am a knight. You give life, I take it. You are Abencerraje, I am Nasrid. You must marry someone who shares your dedication to healing and the medical arts. If my hasty declaration of love caused you any undue anxiety, I sincerely apologize. I wish you nothing but a happy life.*

> *Yusef*

He sets the reed down, blows on the ink to dry it, and rereads his words. His eyes fill before he reaches the end. He carefully folds the paper, flattens it. He lifts the candle and the stick of sealing wax, positions it over the fold, then tilts the candle to let the wax kiss the flame. The viscous red blob plops onto the paper. He presses his ring to the wax.

Matters between them have largely returned to normal. They work, they talk, they eat, they sleep, they spar with their swords and daggers until their bodies glisten with sweat.

It is early evening, and they sit across from each other in silence finishing their meal. Umar, always the quick eater, pushes his plate aside and grabs the day's mail pouch to sift through the official communiques. And to retrieve Faynan's letter, of course.

"I wrote to her." Yusef's tone is matter of fact. He does not look up from his plate.

Umar stops and stares intently at his brother. "You did?" He is incredulous.

"Yes."

"Why did you not tell me?"

Yusef shrugs.

"When?"

"Three days back."

The silence stretches out.

"What did you say to her?" Wary.

"I told her the truth, Umar."

"I see. Well." Umar brightens. "Excellent. Excellent, Yusef! I am sure she will write back. I am positive she will write back!"

"I would not blame her for choosing a physician over me."

Umar frowns. "No. She will choose you, Brother. You forget that I saw the look that you two shared. I saw it, Yusef. Your love is meant to be."

"Time will tell."

Umar continues to study his brother before returning to the parcel. He finds Faynan's letter and sets it aside, begins to thumb through the boring legal documents. He halts. "Interesting." He lifts a formal-looking letter with an affixed royal seal.

Yusef looks up. "What?"

He holds the letter up to examine the seal. "From al-Zaghal. His personal imprint. Below the seal it says: *From Prince Muhammad al-Zaghal of the Alhambra—Under Penalty of Death, for None but the Eyes of Yusef and Umar al-Makki.*"

"Let me see."

Umar hands his brother the letter, and Yusef examines it. "Interesting indeed." He says, "Shall I?"

"Please."

Yusef breaks the seal, unfolds the letter, and begins to read. He stops. "Al-Zaghal has secret news from the Alhambra that we must know." His eyes dance from right to left as they race down the page. He mutters, "Dear Lord."

"What?"

Yusef raises a hand as he continues to read. "Unbelievable." When he finishes, he looks at his brother and shakes his head sadly. "What can the man be thinking? There are days when I question our sultan's sanity."

"What?!"

"The sultan has decided to launch a surprise attack on Castile. To teach the Christians a lesson regarding Granada's ability to defend herself."

"But that makes no sense. A preemptive strike? What if it triggers the Christian invasion before we are prepared? Dear Lord. Where?"

Yusef replies, "Zahara. Northwest of Ronda."

"Zahara?! Zahara is deep in the mountains and is heavily fortified. Not to mention, well into Christian territory."

"Indeed. And garrisoned by the Order of Santiago."

"Who are led by Alonso de Cárdenas."

"The same. A formidable general. And part of Fernando's inner circle of command. Al-Zaghal says that evidently Zoraya claims to have personal knowledge of how to penetrate Zahara's defenses."

Umar is shocked. "Zoraya? Zoraya?!"

"Zoraya. Al-Zaghal believes that she is behind this dangerous farce. He is beside himself. He says he tried to reason with the sultan, to dissuade him from this foolhardy path. To no avail. This was sent two days ago. The cavalry will have already left Granada. They are to join forces with Ronda's garrison, and then attack Zahara under cover of night."

Umar says, "If we leave tonight we should be able to beat them to Ronda."

"No." Yusef slaps the letter against his wrist. "Al-Zaghal insists that we remain here. It seems the sultan has appointed Boabdil to command the force. He has declared that the time has come for his son to prove his mettle in battle."

"That may be, but he is also likely to get many fine knights killed in the process."

"Indeed."

"Al-Zaghal believes Zoraya wants Boabdil to lead the attack so that he will be placed in harm's way. No doubt to ensure that the child in her womb is the sole heir of the sultan."

Umar shakes his head. "Uncle Ali would *not* stand for this nonsense! Surely he was consulted."

"Al-Zaghal says he was not."

"The sultan's military vizier not consulted on a battle plan?!" Umar is flabbergasted. "Since when?"

"Since Zoraya came to power and began to give orders to the sultan. The man is a blind fool, Allah forgive me. Uncle has not yet returned to the Alhambra from his inspections. Al-Zaghal has sent riders to locate him, but Boabdil's cavalry will be long gone when he arrives."

"Dear Lord."

"Al-Zaghal says we are to remain here unless summoned. In the event of a disaster. He says to pray for Boabdil's courage and leadership. And that the Christians may be drunk and asleep."

"Allah help us."

The Letter

A courier with an armed escort strides up just as Danah and Malik are leaving the Atfal Hospital on their way to meet David at the Bermejas. Another lesson in surgery is planned for the afternoon. David has promised to teach them a new technique for repairing bleeding vessels.

As she closes the door and turns, the courier steps forward and bows. "Miss Amiriya. A letter for you."

With Malik standing right beside her, she panics, touching her chest and giving her finest impression of innocent confusion. "For me? Are you certain?"

The courier frowns at the unintended insult—of course he is certain. "Hakim al-Adani informed me that you were here. A letter for you from Prince Yusef al-Makki arrived from Málaga this morning."

Helpless to prevent the inevitable, she silently curses the deep blush that rises to her cheeks.

Malik furls his brow in bewilderment as his eyes bounce between the courier and Danah.

"I see. Very well." She reaches forward, snatches the letter, and buries it in the pocket of her robe without examining the seal.

The two men bow in unison and vanish into the crowd.

Danah appears to study the busy scene in the square as she focuses on projecting nonchalance.

"Al-Makki. The Falcon brothers." Deliberately casual, but Malik is obviously perplexed by this new connection to his intended. *The unwed Falcon brother.* Jealousy in a smitten young man is never more than an arm's length away. "My father said that he had received word of their arrival in the city. You know Yusef al-Makki?"

She turns to face Malik. "Know him? No." Emphatic, but there is an odd inflection in her tone that does not escape his notice.

"I see."

She hesitates. "I mean. Not really. He and his brother came to the Atfal to check on Samra. After she became my patient. You see, they brought Samra to the Atfal after they found her in the village. They stopped in later to check on her and to see if she had any information on the Christian marauders. They met with Ezar." Another awkward hesitation. "I was in the Bermejas that day. Working with Hakim al-Adani. David." She silently curses herself.

Somehow she had neglected to tell him this story when he met Samra, which troubles him even more. "I see. And did she?"

"Did she what?"

"Did she have any information on her attackers?"

Danah shakes her head impatiently. "No. Well, nothing of consequence."

Tense silence.

Malik chews his cheek. "Should you open it? I mean, it must be important official business to warrant an armed escort from the Alhambra." A tinge of resentment dogs his words.

"It can wait." Her answer is perfunctory. "David expects us. We should hurry." Without waiting for an answer, she turns and starts walking.

Malik frowns, then follows. Jealousy leans in close to rest a sharpened claw upon his shoulder.

Not another word between them about it, though, truth be told, Danah is not herself for the rest of the afternoon. Stiff and formal; pensive; one-word answers. Malik does not appear to notice the change, or if he does, does not let on. David does notice, and later passes this information on to Miriam.

She shakes her head with disgust. *I lied to him. No use denying it. I lied to my future husband. I lied! What was I thinking?!* "Forgive me my sins, O Lord."

After they parted, she returned home and was instantly cornered by her mother, who wanted to hear every detail of every minute. As usual. Her mother, predictably, and not without some serious impatience in her tone, slipped in the fact that they were all waiting on her to give the word to finalize the betrothal. "Sand is slipping through the hourglass, Danah. Bashir has said that they will not be able stay in Granada much longer." She purses her lips as she glares at her daughter. "Malik is a perfect match for you. Remember your promise, young lady."

After enduring the interrogation and reluctantly offering some tidbits of their surgery together, Danah made a lame excuse of a headache, then retreated to the safety of her room.

She sits on the bed, door locked, staring at the letter, afraid to touch it. Heart pounding.

Her dreams of Yusef have been relentless. The man torments her nights. That she could have such wanton sexual desires, and act upon them, is shocking to her still. And titillating, of course. Her dreams of him are so incredibly real, they defy all logic. Their vivid, flesh-filled, phantasmal contortions have long since intruded into her waking hours, the ache of longing a distraction she has come to resent.

A quick hiss, "Enough!" She picks up the letter, breaks the seal, takes a deep breath, and holds it to steady herself as she begins to read. Her face is a whirlwind of contrasts that even a veteran stage actor would be hard-pressed to mimic. Excited concentration mixed with anxious frustration, then a wistful hint of a smile, then a troubled stiffening, then complete and unadulterated shock as her mouth falls open, aghast. She is forced to stop as her eyes fill and she can no longer read his words through the liquid blur. She releases her breath as she dabs her tears, then continues, lower lip quivering. Her countenance deflates as if her soul has just been punctured by a dagger. A weary, crushing sadness slithers in and curls around her bones. As she finishes, her eyes refill, and two neat tears slip down her cheeks. Blinded, she helplessly whispers, "Chasm." She stares into space for almost a minute, numb to the core, before the sadness morphs into a deep hurt, then a smoldering anger. She sneers. *"Chasm!"* Her swimming emeralds combust with her fury, brilliant green embers lifted with bare hands from a white-hot furnace. "Be damned!" She has not cursed a day in her life. Her scorn becomes a living thing. She crushes the letter in her fist and throws it to the floor. "BE DAMNED!"

She looks happy. She does.

He is beyond ecstatic.

The betrothal ceremony, the *khitba*, is a simple affair. Bashir and Malik stand side by side, facing Battal and Mayya. Danah is behind her parents, by tradition, and veiled. The father and son bow in unison and are answered by bows from her parents. Malik's father offers a formal prayer on the sanctity of marriage. Malik steps forward one step, states his full name, then makes a formal request to Battal and Mayya for permission to ask Danah for her hand in marriage. They agree to his request and offer their own prayer on the sanctity of marriage. Danah now steps forward. Her father lifts her veil. She raises her eyes to the young man to whom she will agree to give herself.

Malik says, "Danah Amiriya. With the blessing and guidance of Allah, and with our families as witnesses, I betroth myself to you, and desire with all my heart that we be joined as husband and wife." His lower lip begins to tremble. "My heart will always belong to you, Danah."

Mayya dabs her eyes and sniffles.

Danah quietly replies, "Malik al-Karim, with the blessing and guidance of Allah, and with our families as witnesses, I betroth myself to you, and desire with all my heart that we be joined as husband and wife." Together they recite a prayer on the sanctity of marriage.

The parents erupt with applause and laughter, then hugs and back-slaps all around. The glee in the room is heartfelt and boisterous.

He? Bursting with joy.

She? She looks happy. She does.

As the room calms, Bashir says, "I do apologize, Battal, but Malik and I must leave for Málaga. I had not planned to be in the city for this length of time, and I am afraid I have urgent cases in the court that are pressing. I have received a summons this morning from the emir himself to come at once."

"We understand. Of course. We will celebrate properly at the wedding."

Bashir turns to the young couple. "Perhaps you two would like a few moments in the garden? It will be some months before you see each other again." He looks for Battal's agreement, and the proud father of the bride-to-be nods. Another breach of protocol, but a minor one. They *are* betrothed after all.

Malik's eagerness is endearing. "We would, thank you." He turns expectantly to Danah.

She reaches for that smile but does not quite get there. "Of course." Amused looks follow the young couple out.

Malik's father says, "I shall be in touch by letter, Battal. I will inform you as soon as I know the date of Malik's oath ceremony."

"Yes. And we will do the same."

Mayya is beaming. "We are hopeful for a spring marriage."

"As am I. Imagine, two hakims in one family! What a blessing." A wistful sigh. "If only his mother were here to see this. These two are an excellent match, a most excellent match. I see love in their future, and great happiness, praise be to Allah."

Mayya can't stop herself. "And many children, inshallah."

Bashir beams. "Yes, and many children. That would be such a gift to us all."

They are standing side by side, facing the fountain, eyes glued to the cascade of pearls. Their relationship is formalized, their future carved in stone, but an endearing shyness stands between them.

"I have so enjoyed meeting you, Danah. And to work beside you under Hakim al-Adani's guidance . . . what a gift!"

"Yes, for me too."

"You are a talented healer and will make a fine physician, Danah. I will be honored to serve beside you at the al-Mulk Hospital." He steels his nerves and reaches for her hand. By tradition there should be no physical contact between the two, even as betrothed. Still, she does not resist his overture and allows him to twine his fingers into hers. They turn to face each other.

"You are kind, Malik. I will be honored to serve beside you."

Silence.

"I plan to study twice as hard as before so that Hakim Abu Idris will see that I am ready for my oath by springtime."

"Yes. Springtime."

He tightens his grip and whispers, "I will miss you so, Danah." His voice is suddenly laden with emotion.

"And I, you, Malik." Polite, no more.

"I already miss you." His lower lip quivers just perceptibly. It is beyond obvious that the young man is deliriously taken with her. How could she not be pleased?

He reaches for her other hand, which she permits, then he leans toward her, his expression hesitant but intent.

She suddenly realizes he wants to kiss her, and she panics, turning her head to thwart him.

He recoils as if slapped, flushes with embarrassment, then mutters, "Forgive me, Danah. We are only betrothed. I had no right. Forgive me, please. It is just that—" His wounded gaze retreats to the ground. "Forgive me."

When she looks back at him and sees his anguish, her heart softens. She gently says, "Malik."

He timidly looks up.

"You may kiss me."

His face relights. He looks over his shoulder to make sure they are still alone. He leans toward her, tentative, so endearingly tentative.

Her eyes fold closed.

His lips brush hers, barely, separate, touch once more, then separate again. A simple thing, but sweet.

He gushes, "Thank you. That memory will see me through these difficult months to come."

He is answered by the wisp of a smile.

"I will write to you each week." A boyish laugh. "Each day!"

Finally, a real smile. "That would be nice."

189

"Think of me, Danah. Please think of me."

"Of course I will, Malik." Another smile.

"Excellent. Excellent! You have made me so happy, Danah!"

She can't help but laugh.

"I am sure your parents must be pacing by now. We better go."

"Yes, of course."

He releases her hands and turns; she follows.

A flash of electric blue lost within a murky haze, and suddenly he is standing before her, blocking her path. She gasps. His intrusion is outrageous, but she is helpless to make him disappear. It is her dream of their first kiss, a vastly different affair than what she just experienced with Malik. He pulls her tight against him, enfolds her in his embrace, and kisses her long and deep and hard. As her organs melt, a delicious tingle races like lightning down her spine. She aches for him. When their wet lips finally part, all she can manage is a breathless, "*Yusef.*" He whispers, "*Danah, my love. I want you. I need you.*" As suddenly as he appeared, he vanishes. She is unsteady on her feet, has to shake her head to clear it. She hurries to catch up before Malik notices her lagging, all the while hating herself, despising herself.

That night she does not dream of him. He is gone. Vanished. She does not dream of him again. Not once. At night, when she sets her book aside and closes her eyes, both anxious and more than a little curious about what strange antics may transpire before dawn, a black nothingness slays her. Her sleep is a toneless void. She wakes rested, always a little surprised that he has not come to her. As the days pass, she sometimes wonders whether her nocturnal encounters ever really happened.

But she does not stop thinking about him. How could she? She conjures his face, and there he is, standing before her. In her weak moments, within the privacy of her room late at night, she brings him forth, lets him kiss her, caress her. And then feels profoundly guilty for it. *How unfair to my intended. How wretched. How despicable I am.* She hates herself for her weakness, curses him for tormenting her.

Her studies continue as before, more pleasant now with supportive parents. She is with David at the Bermejas every day but Thursdays, when she walks down to the Atfal to visit Ezar and assist him. Samra continues to recover, and thankfully, is living now with the other girls her age. Danah has her own cadre of patients at the Bermejas, has begun to conduct simple surgeries by herself, and mixes her own herbal concoctions for specific ailments. Her life moves on, her repertoire of surgical techniques and healing skills growing with each passing day. By any reckoning, Danah will make a formidable hakim.

Malik's letters begin to arrive. She dutifully answers them and tries to envision their life together in Málaga—and almost can. She crams each day with as much activity as she can possibly manage. But in those rare, quiet moments when she is not practicing new techniques, brewing new elixirs, studying ancient medical treatises, or reading some difficult codex for pleasure, a lingering uneasiness plagues her; a vague sense of dissatisfaction, a queasy insecurity, a deep loneliness she cannot quite shake or explain. She stops pleading to Tetta Layla to visit her for counsel, resigned that her begging will forever remain unanswered.

"I am happy for you." Ezar fusses over his surgical tools. Their cleaning and organization of the Aftal's instruments is long overdue.

"Thank you." Danah polishes each piece with a cloth, then hands them to him one by one to place in the cabinet.

"Malik seems like a fine young man."

"He is."

He finds her lack of just-betrothed enthusiasm odd. "Husband-and-wife hakims. Who ever heard of such a thing?!" He smiles.

Silence.

Ezar frowns. He turns, "You *are* satisfied with Abd al-Salam's choice?"

She does not look up from her work. "Of course."

Ezar sighs. The girl is so listless, so uncommunicative. "I will miss you, my dear."

She looks up. "And I will miss you, Ezar." She is earnest. "Málaga is so far away." Now despondent. "But there will be no marriage before next fall. Perhaps longer. We must both take our oaths before any date can be set." Her words are wilting before they leave her mouth.

"Mmm." This is not what David told him. Spring. He gives up and decides to change the subject. "I have not heard from the Falcon brothers since they left for Málaga."

Her hands freeze. She tries to frame a casual response but cannot quite get there.

He continues, "I am actually a little surprised they have not sent word to check on Samra's progress. Their need for information seemed an urgent matter. I think we both agree that she is well enough now to be interviewed."

She buries her eyes in her work.

Puzzled, he turns and decides to tease a smile from her, a chore he both relishes and is quite good at. His woolly worms arch their backs. "Emeralds, I would guess that an eligible young bachelor like Yusef al-Makki would be very disheartened to hear of your betrothal." There is a mischievous twinkle in his eyes.

Her expression darkens. She scoffs, "Yusef al-Makki." Her nostrils flare. "The man is as shallow as every other knight I have had the misfortune of meeting." Pure derision. "Life is too short for his foolishness. I sincerely hope he never sets foot in Granada again." Her venom is bracing.

Ezar recoils. "I see." His puzzlement doubles, quadruples.

She will not meet his eyes.

Gently, "I was only teasing, Emeralds."

The silence pushes the air from the room.

He refocuses on the task at hand, determined now to have a conversation with David and Miriam. "Let us do the bone saws next, my dear."

"Very well."

Miriam slips into the ward unnoticed and leans against the wall to watch her work.

David told her about Danah's new patient. A farm boy from the Vega; fourteen. A mishandled wheat sickle by a co-worker in the fields. A wicked puncture clean through the boy's calf. Deep and dangerously close to the major nerves and blood vessels running along the bone. David thought it would be safest to open up the wound to clean it thoroughly, else infection would be nearly impossible to prevent. Her most delicate surgery to date. He assisted, but she did the lion's share. Almost two hours and fifty-seven catgut stitches later, she finished. Infection is the real worry, but also nerve damage. She will be crushed if the young man is left with a limp.

After greeting him, she sits on his bed and asks him how he feels.

A shrug. "Fine." A timid young man. "Sore."

She nods, then turns and folds back the covers to expose his calf. She carefully removes the bandages, begins to intently study the wound. Significant swelling along the incisions, but the color is good all the way to his toes. Enough drainage to color the bandages, but no sign of pus. She leans close and lets her nose test for any hint of infection. Nothing. She nods, clearly pleased.

His expression as he watches her work betrays his age. Anxious self-consciousness at being examined by a female physician, mixed with the giddy elation of being so close to an attractive young woman.

Miriam smiles.

Danah lifts a metal probe and begins to test the stitches. She lightly pokes him just below the wound. "Can you feel this?"

"Yes."

"Here?"

"Yes."

"How about here?"

"Yes."

"And this?"

She brushes her finger along the bottom of his foot.

"Tickles." He offers a shy smile.

"Excellent. The nerves seem intact. And thankfully, no sign of infection. Your surgeon must be very skilled indeed." She looks up and smiles.

He blushes and helplessly nods. He watches her intently as she re-bandages his leg, completely smitten.

"There. You are healing nicely, Amir."

"When will I be able to leave the hospital, Hakim Amiriya?"

She chuckles. "Call me Danah. I have not yet taken my oath. Two more days should be safe. But you will have to visit every other day for a week so I can change your bandages and check you."

"Of course, Danah. Thank you." An ounce of boyish bravado. He will relish coming back just to see her face and hope against hope for another smile.

"You are welcome, Amir. You will be just fine. She lifts her finger to mock-scold him. "Though I would suggest a little more distance next time between you and your sickle-wielding friend."

The boy laughs, then blushes again.

Danah rises, says goodbye, turns for the door. As she sees Miriam, her countenance instantly brightens. "Miriam! David did not tell me you were coming today. You should have said something."

She loves this girl like a daughter. "I so enjoy watching you work. You have a rare gift, dear girl."

"You are kind. Come, let us talk while I put my supplies away. I miss you, Miriam."

Miriam gives her a hug, and the two walk together down the hallway, turn right, then left, then enter the storage room for medical supplies. As Danah begins her work Miriam chatters on about the juicy gossip in the Jewish Quarter and David's latest antics. Their relationship has grown so comfortable.

Danah carefully discards the spent bandage, thoroughly washes her hands, then begins to return the extra supplies and ointments to their appropriate bins. She works with a casual confidence, clearly knows where everything belongs. She talks about her recent cases, especially the surgeries.

As Danah rises on her tiptoes to reach a high cabinet, Miriam says, "Have you heard from Malik?"

Danah hesitates for just long enough to be noticeable. "Yes. He writes to me every other day."

"How sweet. The young man adores you, you know."

Danah closes the cabinet door and turns to face Miriam. "I owe a great debt to you and David and Abd al-Salam. I am happy."

Miriam studies her. Something behind the girl's eyes does not jive with her words. "I am glad to hear that, Danah. David says Malik has real promise as a surgeon."

"Yes." But the answer is too bland.

"Your parents must be pleased."

Danah rolls her eyes. "Elated. All Mama talks about is me starting a family. I think she would be happy with a dozen grandchildren." She shakes her head. "I have no desire for a baby. At least not now."

Miriam tries to smile but does not quite make it. "Mm." Miriam and David are childless, still an open wound for Miriam after all these years.

Danah sees her friend's expression and instantly realizes her error. "I am so sorry, Miriam. How thoughtless of me."

Miriam waves her off. "No, no. Your mother should be excited about grandchildren. And you, my dear, about starting a family. I am happy for you. So, when can we expect a wedding feast?"

Danah chooses her words carefully. "Malik is pushing hard for the spring. And Baba and Mama as well."

"I see. And you?"

No answer. Danah turns away and begins to replace the bandages in their proper boxes.

The silence grows awkward.

Gently, Miriam begins, "I spoke with Ezar yesterday."

"Oh?" Danah is suddenly wary.

"He relayed a conversation you and he had. He is worried about you."

A long pause, then finally, "I see." She is fussing about in the cabinet to avoid turning.

"Tell me about Yusef al-Makki."

Nothing. She refuses to face Miriam.

"Danah? Talk to me." Soft and motherly. "Please." She reaches out and touches the girl's shoulder. "Please."

Danah turns to face Miriam with full eyes. Her gaze sinks. "What?"

"It is nothing, really."

"Talk to me, Danah."

She looks up, distraught. "You remember my story about how Yusef and I met?"

"Of course. You said he and his brother came to interview Samra. They startled you and you broke a ceramic bowl. You lost your temper. Poor boys." She smiles to lighten the mood, but Danah will have no part.

"Yes. What I did not tell you is that something else happened between the two of us."

Miriam's eyes widen. "Something else?"

"Yes. At the end of our conversation, I was telling him about my calling to be a hakim. Yusef suddenly got very emotional. It was baffling, Miriam." She furls her brow, still puzzled by it all. "Then, without any warning, he took my hand and kissed it. I was shocked. We locked eyes for what seemed like an eternity." She shakes her head. "Something happened in that instant. I am not sure what exactly, but I know I have never felt it before. Never once." She searches for the right words. "I felt drawn to him, Miriam, powerfully drawn." She hesitates. "I was sure he felt the same." Tears are close.

Oh my. "I see. Go on."

"The next day he was sent to Málaga with his brother."

"Yes, I recall."

"He had a letter delivered to me before he left."

"A letter." Now Miriam is wary.

"He professed his love for me, Miriam." Barely a whisper.

Dear Lord. "And?"

"He said that he had never before felt what he felt for me at that moment when he looked into my eyes. That it took every ounce of his strength to not take me in his arms and kiss me. He said that when he came back from Málaga he would ask my father's permission to formally call on me."

"Oh my."

"That night, my parents informed me of Abd-al-Salam's choice."

"Dear Lord." *What have I done?*

"I felt trapped, Miriam." Tears are flowing now.

"You should have come to me, Danah. I could have spoken with your parents. With Abd al-Salam."

"I promised my parents that I would abide by his choice. I promised. *I promised.*"

"I understand, but—"

Danah is crying now. "Malik is a nice young man, Miriam. I like him. I do. He is a perfect match for me. Perfect."

"Yes, but—"

Danah's anger unexpectedly flares through her tears, and she blurts out the truth. "Yusef wrote to me from Málaga. He said it was all a mistake. That he was honor-bound to tell me that the words he wrote to me were misguided and false. False! FALSE! And that there was a *chasm* between us that was too wide to cross. A chasm!" Unadulterated fury and a wilting sadness all in the same instant. "I was crushed, Miriam. Am crushed."

"How odd. Something must have happened, Danah."

She sniffs. "Like what?"

"I am not sure. Something." She ponders the possibilities but comes up empty. "And after the second letter you gave in and betrothed yourself to Malik."

The girl's spirit is completely deflated. "Yes." She sniffles.

"Dear Lord." Miriam's brow is knit with worry. *Poor Malik.*

Tense silence.

"He comes to me in my dreams." A whimper.

Miriam frowns. "Who comes to you in your dreams?"

"Yusef."

"Yusef comes to you in your dreams?" Miriam is incredulous.

"Yes. At least he did. He came every single night that Malik was here." She lowers her voice. "Shocking dreams, Miriam. So lifelike. So real." She blushes a deep scarlet. "So sinful."

"Dear Lord." Miriam chews her cheek. "And now that you are betrothed?"

"The dreams have stopped. He has not come to me since the betrothal. Not once." Wistfulness clings to her words.

Miriam studies her. "But you cannot stop thinking about him."

Danah breaks into a heaving sob. "No. I feel horrible! Evil!"

Miriam folds her arms around her. "There, there. Shhhh. There, there, Danah. Shhhh." Miriam stares, worry lines etched deeply into her face.

Truce

The Castilian royal palace in Córdoba.

The queen sits at her writing desk, staring out the window. A thin, satisfied smile is set upon her lips. Below her in the courtyard, Juana and Maria, her two youngest, scamper hand-in-hand behind a bush and crouch down, all giggles. Her only son, Juan, her second born, sits on a stone bench and counts to ten, palms glued to his eyes. A game of hide-and-seek.

Laid before her is the latest report from Inquisitor de Morillo on the spoils reaped of the auto-da-fé in Salamanca. Necessary reading, but bracing. 550 conversos were charged with Judaizing. Though the Inquisition has been in operation for less than six months, the gold garnered from the harsh penance imposed upon the accused has been truly impressive. Even after the Inquisition's take for itself and Rome, the Castilian treasury, though not yet flush, is no longer reeling from the settlement with the Portuguese crown. Refitting of the army is finally underway. Orders for French heavy cannons, the best in the world, have just been placed.

A quiet knock—tap, tap-tap, tap. Their secret signal.

Her smile relaxes but her gaze remains fixed on her children. Juan is now dramatically exploring every nook except where he knows they are hiding. He relishes gaming with his sisters. The girls have clamped their hands to their mouths to squelch their peals of laughter. "You may come in, Hernán."

Friar de Talavera enters and bows to her back. "You sent for me, my queen?"

Isabel reluctantly breaks her gaze and turns in her seat. "Please sit, Hernán." She indicates the chair beside her desk before turning back toward her progeny.

As he crosses the room he indulges his curiosity and follows her sightline to the courtyard. "Your children are adorable, my queen."

This produces a spontaneous smile. "Yes, they are."

He sits. "And so precocious. Just yesterday Juan asked me why Isabel had to leave for Portugal to marry Prince Afonso."

The queen purses her lips. "And you said?"

Talavera shrugs. "The truth. To cement the Treaty of Alcáçovas and secure lasting peace between Castile and Portugal. How is Isabel adjusting to her fate?"

"My daughter understands her duty."

"It is a big step, to be sure, and she is barely a woman. Not just the marriage bed, but a new country. And to wed the enemy of her mother." He sighs. "A challenge for anyone."

"As I said, Isabel understands her duty."

There is an edge to the queen's tone that he registers, and he knows instinctively not to press her further. He opts to change the subject. "I am pleased to tell you that the children's new tutors should arrive by Friday."

"Excellent. I want all three to be versed in French, German, and Latin. Reading, writing, and speaking. And literature."

"Of course. The tutors come highly recommended. From the University of Paris."

She wrinkles her nose, nods her acquiescence. She has no love for the French, but her desire for the very best teachers for her children takes precedence. She turns and locks her eyes on the friar. "Inform the tutors that they are to work the children hard. I am determined that each will sit on a major European throne, Hernán. They must be ready when the opportunity presents itself. Mastery of foreign languages is key."

He nods but does not speak. *Why did she send for me?*

She looks down to the report and says, "Another auto-de-fé in Salamanca."

He sighs. *Ahhh . . . of course.* "I heard, yes. Another trove of those found wanting have been condemned." His sarcasm is unmistakable. There are very few at court who would be bold enough to attempt such a thing in the queen's presence.

She frowns but chooses to ignore his impertinence. "All told, 554 Judaizing conversos have been identified. And nearly 13,000 doblas in penance."

"I see. Inquisitor de Morrillo is nothing if not efficient."

"I understand your concerns, Hernán, but there is no arguing that marranos have infiltrated Castile and its power structure. He pulls a single thread and the whole cloth unravels. Every stone must be turned. They must be dealt with, and dealt with harshly."

"You have no doubt heard that the Inquisitor is now allowing accusations of our citizens to be made anonymously. The accused have no recourse to challenge the charge levied. That strikes me as a recipe for fraud, my queen, for easy revenge upon an enemy by the unscrupulous among us."

"I have heard. He explained that his intent was to make the *Edict of Grace* more appealing and effective. The more who step forward of their own accord the better. It makes the whole process so much easier. And no need for the instruments of torture. His methods will give the marranos second thoughts about not availing themselves of the opportunity to confess of their own free will."

He does not respond. He understands he walks a fine line between his role as her confidante and advisor and his own conscience. He opts to change the subject. "I understand the king has gone to check on the progress of the army in Arcos de la Frontera."

"Yes. My husband left this morning."

My husband. That is refreshingly new. Good.

She adds. "I will miss him." She seems surprised to say it.

Excellent.

Isabel looks back out the window. "Gonzalo de Córdoba is well?" She strives for nonchalance but does not quite get there.

He hesitates. A delicate matter. "The Great Captain is very well, my queen."

"That is pleasing to hear."

"To be sure, he is very busy these days."

Her gaze returns to her children. Softly, she says, "I never properly thanked you for your . . . help, Hernán."

"I live to serve you, my queen." He means it.

"My lustful imaginings could have done my family, and Castile, great harm. I see that now. How foolish of me. It shall never happen again." You could slice the contrition with a knife.

His lack of response amplifies the truth of her words.

"Sending Gonzalo to serve as liaison between the Duke of Medina-Sidonia and the Marquess of Cádiz in the readying of our invasion force was a shrewd move."

And not trivial to execute. "You are kind, my queen."

Silence settles in, but she clearly has more to say. As usual, he is intrigued.

"I am pleased to tell you that my heart is whole once more, Hernán. My husband is . . . well . . . Fernando is once again . . ."

"Attentive." He finishes the sentence for her.

She turns to face him and smiles. "Yes. Very attentive."

"His affections for you are genuine, my queen. Getting the king to return to your bed was a simple matter."

She smirks. "Banishing his favorite maidens from court did not hurt."

He tips his head. "Once I properly explained the situation, the king saw that he was in the wrong." *Threatened might be a better word.* "His confession was heartfelt. He knows he hurt you."

"He did."

"If I might say, my queen, another child would suit you well. Castile will rejoice."

Her cheeks blossom into pink roses. She looks half her age. "We are enjoying our time together. The way he dotes on me reminds me of our first year married." Her blush endearingly deepens. She looks away. "He promised that he would return within a fortnight."

"Excellent to hear, my queen." *Hopefully Arcos de la Frontera is devoid of buxom young maidens with a penchant for adventure.* He registers a mental note to make some discreet inquiries.

Zahara sleeps.

A Christian fortress deep in the mountains sixteen miles northwest of Ronda, Zahara is strategically placed to serve as watchdog for Moorish intentions in southern Castile. Zahara is one of the many towns garrisoned by the Order of Santiago, a military-religious order of knights founded in 1160 for protecting pilgrims on their way to the Shrine of Santiago de Compostela in Galacia. It has since evolved into a broader mission of defending Spanish Christendom against the Moors, and they command nearly two dozen castles along the contested border between Castile and the Kingdom of Granada. Their swords, and devotion, are sworn to the queen. The Order is commanded by Alonso de Cárdenas, who serves on Queen Isabel's Royal Council and is presently in Córdoba at her behest.

The castle guarding the town clings to a knife-edge rocky ridge climbing from north to south, leveling out enough for the castle keep and tower, then ending in a sheer cliff. The town lies a hundred feet below, nestled into the slight eastern bend in the ridgeline. The fortifications of both the castle and the towered walls of the town are of classical Nasrid construction, formidable by any measure.

Not a star in the sky. The landscape viewed from high above on the castle walls is murky, a dim twilight, sightlines unsettlingly short. An eerie landscape; ethereal and ghostlike. To those standing watch, scrub bushes on the plain become crossbowmen; boulders, mounted knights. Hard stares to the right or left of the object in question are required to form sound judgements.

The heavy clouds race to the east. The smell of rain clings desperately to the darkened clouds, the drops swollen and heavy but afraid to let go lest they disappear forever into the parched earth. The brisk, moist wind is cool, biting. The citadel sentries stop their pacing and look up, curse the troubled sky, pull their cloaks tight to their necks. Rain is coming.

Suddenly the clouds rip apart and the landscape flares into focus with a daylight clarity. The bone-white orb responsible for changing night into day is waning gibbous, only two days past full. Bright and high overhead; a defender's moon, not an attacker's. The sentries stop and lazily scan the suddenly visible plateau, but their hearts are not in it. After all, what is there to fear? This castle belongs to the invincible Order of Santiago. No Moor would be foolish enough to dare challenge its might.

One. Two. Three. Four. Five. Six. The rip tightens then vanishes, erasing the landscape.

As soon as darkness descends, two shadows dart from the cover of a large boulder and race to the base of the cliff, then disappear in the scrub. A moment later, the two emerge and split apart, widening the distance between them to thirty paces. They wait at the base of the cliff, melded with the rocks. No climbing tools except coiled rope and grappling hooks lashed to their backs. No weapons except the needle daggers tucked under their sashes. Each is dressed in solid black, their faces and hands smudged dark with soot. Mountaineers from the village of Pampaneira in the Alpujarras Mountains southeast of Granada. The cliff before them is nothing—child's play.

A stone's throw from the base of the cliff, three dozen knights crouch low, scattered amidst the brush and boulders, waiting for their signal to move. More mountaineers. Invisible in their black, twenty of the knights are armed with broadswords and maces, ready to crush skulls and wreak havoc. The rest are Alpujarran crossbowmen, their skill with their weapons legendary in both Moorish and Christian lands.

Ten minutes later the first drop falls. Then another. The rolling hush of the approaching rain blows in from the west and settles upon the castle. The sentries on the ramparts collectively sigh their dismay and lower their gazes so that their *morions* can better deflect the rain. The steady patter of raindrops on plate armor muffles all sounds to a muted whisper.

The two climbers begin to spider up the sheer wall.

201

"Captain Colón, it is a pleasure to meet you. I am Abraham Seneor, Chief Tax Collector of Castile and court rabbi." He raises his palm to the man standing to his right. "This is Don Isaac Abrabanel, court financier and legal counsellor to Queen Isabel and King Fernando."

Colón nods, but does not bow, an affront to court protocol that is not lost on these two. "I have been waiting for an audience for almost two months. I had hoped to meet with the queen." His tone is gruff, impatient.

Seneor's expression is passive, unreadable, though there is cause to be offended. A foolhardy move on Colón's part. These two are known to all at court and have a path to the queen's ear. The old Jew continues unabated, "My apologies for the delay. As you can imagine, Queen Isabel has many requests for audiences." A deliberate pause. "Some more important than others." Touché. "We understand that you seek the queen's backing for a westward voyage to the East Indies. Three caravels."

"Yes." He is curt, as if these two are wasting his time.

Abrabanel adds, "We understand that you made a similar request of the King John of Portugal."

Colón visibly stiffens. He hesitates, then finally blurts out, "The Portuguese court has no vision. None whatsoever." The man's contempt is palpable. "They will regret their error."

Seneor and Abrabanel exchange a quick glance, a silent conversation of numerous words. These two have known each other for many years.

Abrabanel lifts his palms and says, "Please, Captain Colón, tell us of your plan."

"I will prove to the world that a westward voyage can reach the East Indies."

The sleepy eyes of the two Jews sparkle.

Seneor nods approvingly. "An interesting proposal, Captain Colón. As you can understand, we will need to confer with Queen Isabel on the matter."

"I see." He seems surprised by the obvious. "Very well then." Colón is at a loss. "Then my fate is in your hands. You know how to reach me." Too brusque. Captain Colón awkwardly bows, then turns and marches for the door.

The two men continue to stare at the door, pensive, then retire to their chairs to talk.

Seneor begins. "Well? What do you think of our captain?"

Abrabanel answers, "Interesting man. Though painfully lacking in social graces."

Seneor mockingly lifts a scolding finger. "You are too kind, Don Isaac. The man is offensive and rude."

Abrabanel nods. "No argument. And I will grant that the whiff of arrogance clinging to him is unmistakable. But he is ambitious and clearly determined. 'Pushy' and 'rude' were the words I believe my source in the Portuguese court used. No wonder they expelled him." They both chuckle. "You have to admit though, Abraham, it *is* an interesting proposal. A daring proposition. A very risky investment to be sure. And expensive. Three caravels, crew, and provisions. And he wants half of the world's wealth and titles to match if he succeeds!" He whistles. "I am not sure what to make of him."

"Nor I."

The comfortable silence affords them more room for musing.

Abrabanel continues, "Do you think he is right about the distance? From all that I have read, eighty-five degrees seems much too close for a viable westward route."

Seneor replies, "I have no idea if he is right or not. Clearly King John thinks not. And there are good nautical minds in the Portuguese court."

Abrabanel counters, "True. But they do have an eastward route around Africa now, courtesy of Captain Dias, and thus no real incentive to look westward any more. In his favor, Colón does have Toscanelli's map. Or so he claims. And the secret westerly soundings, which are his alone. Assuming he is to be believed."

"Still . . ."

Abrabanel sighs. "If he is right, Castile could rule the world."

"Indeed."

They fall silent.

Seneor says, "I had Daniel look into Captain Colón's background. Just in case Queen Isabel decides to invest in him."

"You mean in case *we* decide to invest in him."

Seneor laughs. "Precisely."

"And?"

"Colón hails from Genoa. But he did not become a caravel captain until arriving in Lisbon. Married a Portuguese nobleman's daughter, who gave him a son. Her father set him up with the vessel. She is dead now, though. The boy travels with him."

"I see."

Seneor continues, "Colón ran slaves, gold, and ivory from Africa for Portugal until he was spurned by the court. He left angry and came directly to Córdoba, seeking an audience with the queen." He smiles. "I thought it prudent to make him wait. Two months seemed about right to remind him of his place at court.

And certainly no direct meeting with the queen. He did try to dangle his wares to Portugal first, after all." His smile widens.

Abrabanel laughs. "If your friends will not sponsor you, try their enemies."

Seneor chuckles. "It seems he has already found a Castilian woman to share his bed and tend to his son."

"Quick work for such an offensive man."

"A twenty-year-old orphan named Beatriz Enríquez de Arana."

"Ah. Half his age, or nearly so. A young Castilian mistress from the streets of Córdoba for a Portuguese captain out of favor at court."

Seneor says, "Mm . . . I am not sure I approve." Mock frown. "He seems to have devoted his entire life to finding a western route to the East Indies. An obsession, really."

"But why?"

"Who knows?"

"Everyone thinks a western route to the Indies is a fool's errand."

Seneor says, "That is actually an advantage for us. Not a single person but him believes it can be done. But what if he is right? Think of the profit, Abraham." He whistles.

"Yes. And the shift in Europe's balance of power."

Seneor continues, "Interestingly, Daniel could find almost nothing about his family roots in Genoa. None. Apparently, no living relatives, and not a trace of any document in the town hall or the cathedral archives. Quite odd, actually. It seems our captain has gone to great lengths to obscure his origins."

Abrabanel replies, "Interesting. Any speculation?"

"My guess is that he buried a Jewish heritage in Genoa."

Abrabanel lifts his eyebrows. "Converso?"

"Only a guess. But if true, hiding that fact would clearly be advantageous for winning royal favor in the courts of Europe."

"Especially in Portugal and Castile, now that the cursed Inquisition is upon us. Can we confirm that he is actually converso?"

Seneor replies, "I am not sure, but I intend to try."

"Mmm. Perhaps we should just ask him? After all, he may be a distant cousin of ours. We Jews are all related, you know." A giant smile.

Seneor chuckles. "Perhaps, old friend. Let me do some more exploring first. In the meantime, the queen should know about this opportunity."

"Trust me, she will care little for such distractions. She lives and breathes the destruction of Granada."

"Yes. And surprising as it may seem, she now lives and breathes the Inquisition."

Abrabanel muses. "Perhaps Santangel might be a better person to approach. After all, as finance minister he surely already guesses that a protracted war with the Moors is likely to bankrupt Castile. He will relish any opportunity, even at long odds, for solvency. Especially if we agree to front the gold."

"Agreed." Seneor smiles. "If the queen does find it in her heart to meet with our captain, she will not be as forgiving of his lack of manners."

"No, she will not. That should be fun to watch."

They both laugh.

As suddenly as it began, the choking downpour shuts off. An hour of chilling, beastly rain, then nothing.

One. Two. Three. Four. Five. Six. The sky tears open again, and the town and castle instantly draw breath, the glint of sharp angles in brick and stone and the spires of Nasrid crenellations glowing under the moon's greedy leer. Tendrils of lazy fog cling stubbornly to the ramparts high above.

Silence.

How odd that the four sentries normally stationed above the town's main gate at night are absent. Even in such dismal weather there is no justification for leaving their posts, if only for a minute to don dry clothing or secure a cup of hot tea. How odd.

The clouds coagulate, and the scene once again blackens.

A resonant *thunk*, dull and heavy, ruins the quiet. A loud mechanical *double-thunk* chases the first, though slightly higher in pitch. Now the metallic *clank-clank-clank-clank-clank* of a chain and ratchet unspooling, then the protracted, raspy sliding of iron against iron. One set of reinforcing bars is released with a loud *clink*, a long pause, then a second. A final, decisive *clonk*, then nothing.

The vertical slit in the gate shyly groans open a foot. A dark form slips through and waves a signal lantern blackened on three sides. Once back and forth, then once up and down, then the flame is extinguished. The form disappears back into the split in the gate.

The stillness tenses.

It begins as a gentle rumble that could easily be mistaken for distant thunder. Perhaps a new storm approaches? Suddenly the gate swings open wide, a yawning cavern cut into the wall. The shadowed movement of a dozen knights as they take up defensive positions on either side of the gate. Six crossbowmen ease onto the wall-walk, level their weapons on the town. The mountaineers clearly aim to see that the gate remains open.

The rumble grows steadily louder.

A warning bell begins to sound. *Clang-clang-clang-clang.* Pause. *Clang-clang-clang-clang.* Pause. *Clang—* The bell's cry abruptly ceases. A second bell jumps in to take its place. *Clang-clang-clang-clang.* A third joins. A fourth.

A skirmish breaks out just inside the gate. Bright *pings* of steel on steel. Castilian curses and shouts are answered by guttural challenges in Andalusi Arabic. Crossbows from above are loosed, chased by an awful mix of sighs and groans as the bolts thrump themselves deep in tender flesh. The agonized scream from a severed arm followed by the heavy wet crunch of studded mace on bone. Pieces of brain and skull splatter against the wall. The fray calms, the gate remains open.

The heavy rumble draws closer. The origin is now painfully obvious—cavalry at full gallop.

The town awakens, breathless, into a living nightmare. *Clang-clang-clang-clang.* Lamps in the city are frantically lit with shaky fingers. Panic rushes through the streets and into homes and beds. Utter confusion, harsh shouts, terrified whimpers, the hasty corralling of little ones by their petrified mothers, desperate pleading. *Clang-clang-clang-clang.*

The garrison stumbles to full alert. "To arms! TO ARMS!" Knights leap from their beds, hearts pounding. Chain mail and hammered plate armor are first picked up—"No time for armor! No time for armor!"—then dropped. The partially clad knights grab their killing tools and begin to stagger through the doorway into the courtyard. "TO ARMS! KNIGHTS OF THE ORDER! TO ARMS, I SAY!" A cacophony of screamed commands as knights rush about in the mayhem wondering what exactly is happening.

The roaring thunder is upon them. To his credit, Boabdil leads the charge, as is fitting for a Nasrid prince and knight-commander. As he makes the final turn and sees the gate yawning wide, beckoning, he raises his broadsword and issues the first battle command of his life. "Long live Granada! Long live al-Andalus! Death to the infidels! *Allahu Akbar!*" God is Greatest! "Allahu Akbar!"

He is answered by a hundred voices. "ALLAHU AKBAR! ALLAHU AKBAR!"

The Moorish battle cry strikes terror into the heart of the town. The shrill screams of women and children mix with the frantic mustering of some sort of defense. "TO ARMS DAMN YOU! TO ARMS I SAY!" *Clang-clang-clang-clang.*

The cavalry does not slow; it crashes full force through the gate, spilling into the town, swords slicing down and maces swinging wide, blood and gore spewing in their wake. The cavalry splits into a many-headed hydra as it races down the narrow alleys toward the castle gate, which is also magically yawning wide.

Zahara will not just fall this dreary night—she will be gutted and pillaged. The women and children will be treated as booty and sold into slavery. There will be no ransom for the captured knights, a serious breach of tradition. Those of the Order of Santiago who survive the onslaught will be destined for Ronda's dark dungeons. Christian Zahara is no more.

Message delivered.

ON A PLATEAU JUST EAST OF ARCOS DE LA FRONTERA, ONE-HUNDRED TWENTY-FIVE MILES TO THE SOUTHWEST OF CÓRDOBA.

"Ready to fire, my lord!" French-accented Castilian. The artillery officer signals with his raised hand.

Gonzalo de Córdoba, the Great Captain, looks dashing in his battle regalia. The Great Captain; Enrique de Guzmán, Duke of Medina-Sidonia; and Rodrigo Ponce de León, Marquess of Cádiz, sit in full armor atop their stallions, fifty paces from the French gun crew, eyes glued to the target—a stone wall three-hundred paces out. Twenty-feet wide, ten-feet high, and three-feet thick, constructed of limestone ashlar and quick-lime mortar. The stuff of Moorish castle walls.

The Great Captain is about to give the signal to fire when his adjutant says, "My lord. To the north."

The Great Captain turns to his left. In the distance a squadron of cavalry spill over the ridgeline, chased by a dust cloud. He squints. The Castilian battle flag pops and snaps in the breeze. "The king." He turns to the duke and marquess. "We will await his arrival."

Ten minutes later the squadron rumbles to a halt, and King Fernando walks his mount forward to join his three generals.

All three men bow in their saddles.

The king is all smiles. He lives for the battlefield. "Gonzalo. All is progressing with the refitting of my army?"

"It is, majesty."

"Excellent. Don Rodrigo, Don Enrique, it is good to see you two side-by-side and working together. Very good indeed."

They both nod, pleased by the compliment. Though they are sworn to the queen, they have come to respect her husband's tactical skills on the battlefield.

The Great Captain says, "Majesty. We did not expect you until tomorrow."

"I decided to take leave of the queen a day early. Tired of sitting."

"I trust the queen is in good health?"

"Indeed she is. And smiling again, thank God! Amazing how little it takes to make a woman happy." The king winks.

The Great Captain does not acknowledge the innuendo. He lifts his palm to the massive bronze cannon and the gun crew. "I was readying a test firing of our new cannon."

"Excellent! Perfect timing."

The eyes of the gun crew are on the Great Captain, awaiting word. He turns and nods to his imported artillery officer, and with his command voice shouts, "You may proceed, sir!" He turns back to the king and says, "This should be interesting, majesty. Keep your eyes fixed on the target." He points to the distant wall. "And be sure to cover your ears and tighten your reins."

The French officer shouts, "Stand clear! Prepare for discharge!" Everyone clamps his hands over his ears. "Firing!" The officer lifts the smoldering rope, blows it to a crimson ember, steps forward to the polished bronze behemoth, and presses it to the touch hole. An expectant, smoky sizzle, then a brilliant flash and convulsive, bone-crushing *BOOM!* The enormous cannon anchored to its house-sized carriage impossibly jumps backward three feet as it vomits a ten-foot jet of fire, then is instantly obscured by a billowing, gray-ivory cloud of acrid, sulfury smoke. A dragon belching flame from its cavernous lair. Those standing close to the cannon not experienced enough to hold their breath double over, choking and coughing on the acrid smoke.

The king and his three generals wince with the concussive shock. The eyes of their mounts grow white with terror. Several of the stallions in the squadron rear and whinny. Reins are instinctively jerked to hold the horses in place. Coincident with the explosion, a streaky dark blur whizzes in a soft arc toward the target. The stone wall explodes in a cloud of dust and debris. They continue to stare, mouths open in shock, as the dust begins to settle, eager to behold the cannon's capabilities. The damage is stubborn to come into focus, then there it is—a four-foot-wide jagged puncture wound, drilled clean through the center of the wall.

King Fernando raises up in his saddle in disbelief. "Dear God!"

The Great Captain is beaming. "As I assured you, majesty. Far more powerful than our stone-flinging bombards. Even the Alhambra will not be able to resist these new French cannons."

Fernando is beaming, and the duke and the marquess join in. "How thick was the wall?"

"Three feet of limestone ashlar, majesty."

"Bravo. Bravo, Gonzalo! How many of the cannons do we have?"

"For the moment, only two, majesty. But eleven more are being forged in France as we speak."

"When can we expect them?"

"Three months, perhaps four. They come with their own trained gun crews. For a hefty price, of course."

The king shrugs. He cares little for such details. "How many iron balls?"

"I have ordered five-hundred, majesty, and black powder to match."

"Make it a thousand."

"Of course, majesty."

"How many draft horses to move them?"

"A dozen Galiceños, majesty. The French estimate that we should be able to make a little less than three miles a day. On hard, level ground. Moving them through the mountains will be a serious challenge, of course, as will wet weather. But I have some ideas."

"I need five miles a day, Gonzalo." He holds up his hand and spreads his fingers, pumps it to hammer the message home. "Five. And three through the mountain passes. With rain." He folds back two fingers and shakes his hand. "Three. With rain. My cannons must be mobile if I am to keep the Moors guessing where we will next strike."

"And you shall have it, majesty." The Great Captain relishes a challenge.

"Good."

"I have more to show you." He flicks his head to the ridge. "Come, majesty." He turns his mount and kicks it to a canter up the slope. The king, the duke, and the marquess follow.

The Great Captain stops at the top of the rise. The king and his two new generals slow, then walk their mounts up beside him.

The duke and marquess are both smiling. They know what waits. As the plateau comes into view the king rises in his stirrups.

Awed silence.

Laid before them on the plain below, stretching nearly a mile from side to side, is the core of Castile's newly-fitted army. At present, thirty-seven thousand strong and counting—three thousand mounted knights in full plate armor, thirteen thousand light cavalry, three thousand archers, one thousand crossbowmen, eleven thousand infantry, three thousand pikemen, and three thousand knights from the church-sponsored Orders of Santiago, Calatrava, and Alcantara, each commanded by bishop-knights. The king and queen are hoping for an invasion force fifty thousand strong, twice the size that fought Portugal to a stalemate.

The army is rehearsing a large-scale tactical maneuver of its combined forces. Three massive rectangles of archers lie anchored to the far right. Behind them is a line of the stone bombards and their crews, and finally the supply wagons—the army's rearguard. In front of the archers, seven tightly-packed squares of infantry, each two thousand strong, each under its own regimental battle standard, marches forward in a staggered half-mile wide line to engage the imaginary enemy. Columns of light cavalry move forward on either side of the infantry battalions then join at their front to form a thrusting cavalry phalanx. The mounted knights flash and sparkle in the bright sun as their mounts canter down the flanks.

It is an awesome sight to behold. The four men admire the scene in silence for several minutes.

The king finally gushes, "By God, it is a sight to warm a king's blood!"

The Great Captain replies, "Indeed, majesty. The queen will be pleased at our progress."

"She will be, yes, very pleased. When can I expect my army to be ready?"

"Within two months I should think, perhaps three, but certainly before the last cannons arrive. We are presently thirty-seven thousand strong, and I remain hopeful for a full fifty thousand when all the promised allotments arrive, majesty. I am expecting three thousand cavalry, and two thousand each of infantry and archers from Ponferrada any day now."

The king replies, "Galicia."

The Great Captain nods. "Yes, majesty. Don Bartolome Gómez is in command."

"A good man in a fight."

"And double those numbers are promised by Salamanca."

The king nods.

The duke says, "You can see the knights of Medina-Sidonia on the right flank, majesty." He raises his hand and points. The man's demeanor betrays the pride in his private army, but something has changed. The satisfaction of being a prized cog in a larger machine, a vital part of a noble quest. The dizzying jubilation of the coming conquest of Granada. He aims to vanquish the Moors for his queen and church.

The marquess chimes in, "And the knights of Cádiz command the left flank, majesty." He, too, points. His manner registers the same sentiment. There is no detectable tension between the two rivals. The queen's mandate appears to have taken root.

The Great Captain adds, "The knights of Cádiz and Medina-Sidonia ride under the Castilian battle flag, majesty. The two forces are working splendidly together."

The king replies, "Excellent. The queen will be extremely pleased to hear that, gentlemen. The noble knights of Medina-Sidonia and Cádiz will anchor my right and left flanks. Together you will be my pincers when the time comes to crush the Moors." He illustrates the maneuver with his arms, then laughs.

"Majesty." The duke bows in his saddle.

"Majesty." The marquess follows suit.

The massive oak door to the Great Hall opens, and her Royal Council begins to file into the audience chamber. Even for her regular meeting with her advisors she dresses in regal formality, complete with crown and scepter. Her Bible lies closed upon the table beside her. She averages an hour per day of scripture reading and prayer, often more. The queen is a model of piety and devotion.

One by one the men enter, bow, and take up their stations in a semicircle before her throne. She studies each with her penetrating blue-gray eyes, her expression unreadable, as usual. Hernán de Talavera, her confessor and close advisor; Alonso de Cárdenas, her minister of war; Luis de Santangel, her finance minister; and Cardinal Mendoza, chancellor of the realm. Missing are the king and the Great Captain.

"Gentlemen. What news of my realm?" Her eyes move to the cardinal.

He clears his throat and says, "I am pleased to inform you, majesty, that the Treaty of Alcáçovas has been officially signed by all parties. A state of peace now exists between Castile and Portugal."

"Finally. And my daughter's dowry?" She turns to her finance minister.

Santangel answers, "The first half of Princess Isabel's dowry has been safely delivered to Lisbon, majesty."

"Good."

The cardinal continues, "Her marriage to Prince Afonso will proceed as planned as soon as arrangements can be made, majesty. I am pushing for a wedding in Córdoba in November, though the Portuguese seem to think Lisbon would be a far better choice."

The queen purses her lips. "My daughter will be wed in Córdoba, or not at all. King Fernando and I are in agreement on this. It is not negotiable."

A sober nod from the cardinal. "I will convey that to the Portuguese, majesty. I do not foresee a problem. After all, tradition is on our side."

"Good." She turns to her minister of war, "And what news of the army, Alonso?"

Cárdenas answers, "A rider arrived this morning, majesty. A letter from the Great Captain."

Talavera studies the queen, sees that her pupils dilate ever so slightly. Too subtle a response for any but his practiced eye to notice.

The minister of war presses on. "Progressing on schedule, I am pleased to convey. Nearly forty thousand strong at present. And the first two of the French cannons have arrived, majesty. Gonzalo is confident that by winter we will possess the fire power to breach any Moorish castle."

The queen nods, clearly pleased. "Excellent news." She hesitates, then asks, "I assume the king arrived safely at Arcos de la Frontera?"

"He did, majesty, two days ago."

Without thinking, she frowns her disappointment, an uncharacteristic betrayal of emotion which instantly vanishes.

Talavera sighs inwardly. *And no love letter to his newly-enamored wife. The man is impossibly dense. It takes so little to please women, even a queen.*

She forces a deliberate coy smile to mask her emotions. A skillful recovery. "The duke and the marquess are behaving themselves?"

Cárdenas answers with a chuckle. "It seems that they are, majesty. Gonzalo says they are model citizens."

"Good. Send word to the Great Captain that his queen personally commends him for his fine efforts."

Talavera's eyes have not left her face. He thinks he detects a slight rise of color to her cheeks but is not positive.

"Certainly, majesty."

The queen turns to the cardinal. "And is the new treaty with the Moors ready to send? Now that peace with Portugal is formalized, Granada will be watching our next move very closely."

Cardinal Mendoza replies, "Indeed. It is ready for your signature, majesty."

"Have it brought to me then. And see that our envoy to Granada makes arrangements for safe passage to the Alhambra to request a formal truce with Muley Hacén. The sultan must be made to believe that Castile cowers before him, its army sick of war and its treasury laid bare. You will lead the treaty delegation yourself." A statement of fact.

The cardinal blanches at the prospect. A resigned, "Of course, majesty."

"Majesty? If I may?" The minister of war.

She turns. "Yes, Alonso?"

"My contacts, though limited to be sure, say that the Moors have begun fortifying their border castles, especially between Castile and the Granadine Vega, and laying in weapons and stores. And we have just received word from Genoese merchants that even Málaga is being readied for siege."

"Not surprising, I suppose. After all, the Moors are not stupid. That is why this new treaty will help us. We must put their minds at ease, and stroke their egos while we put the finishing touches on our army. Time, Alonso, we must buy time."

"Agreed, majesty. I have also heard some interesting rumors coming from the Moorish court."

"Oh? What kinds of rumors?"

"Third-hand, to be sure, but interesting if true."

She waves him on impatiently.

"Evidently there is friction between Sultan Muley Hacén and his son and heir, Boabdil."

"Friction? What kind?"

"Rumors suggest that there is a growing faction of merchants within Granada that favors establishing closer ties with Castile. To broaden commerce, among other things. They are evidently drowning in the sultan's taxes. Supposedly Boabdil favors this as well. Or so the rumor has it."

"Interesting. If true, it would stand him in marked contrast with his insufferable father." She considers the implications of this possibility.

"It seemed surprising enough to be of interest, majesty."

"Indeed. Thank you, Alonso. See if your contacts can learn more. Discreetly, of course."

"I will, majesty."

"Good. We will swallow our pride and send this new treaty to the Moors, and in the meantime ready ourselves for conquest. Is there anything else, Alonso?"

"No, majesty, that was all."

Isabel's eyes circle the room. "Anyone else?"

Santangel lifts a finger. "Majesty, if I may?"

"I trust my treasury stands in good stead, Luis?" An uncharacteristically playful tone.

The finance minister smiles. "It does, majesty. And growing healthier by the day, praise God. Actually, another matter has unexpectedly presented itself. An opportunity, really."

"Go on." She is curious now.

"It seems that Abraham Seneor and Don Isaac Abrabanel have recently met with a Portuguese captain of Genoese origin. One Cristóbal Colón."

Cárdenas grimaces. *These Jews wield far too much influence at court.*

"And?"

"Majesty, he seems convinced that he can reach the East Indies via a westward voyage."

Cárdenas scoffs. "Dear God, man, the whole world knows that is a fool's errand!"

The queen raises a hand to quiet him. "Go on."

Santangel casts the minister of war an annoyed glance. "Sometimes, Alonso, the whole world is wrong." He turns back to the queen. "Colón claims his calculations prove otherwise, majesty. He claims to possess Toscanelli's map. And evidently, he has secret soundings of the westerlies, which he took on his last return from Africa. If he is correct, majesty, and I freely admit it is a big if, then a western spice route could enrich Castile a hundred-fold, a thousand-fold, perhaps more. Majesty, such a discovery would compensate ten-to-one for our loss of Africa and the Atlantic territories to Portugal. The possibilities are endless."

The queen touches her index finger to her nose as she thinks. "We are the first to hear of his plan?"

"No. He made his case to both Genoa and Venice. He even sent his brother to England to plead on his behalf. All turned him down."

"I would guess he has also propositioned Portugal?"

"He has, majesty, just before he came to Córdoba. Evidently, with Diaz's new eastward route around Africa now in hand, Portugal showed no interest."

Talavera replies, "That, or perhaps his mariners sifted the man's calculations and found them wanting."

The finance minister concedes with a nod. "Perhaps."

Isabel muses, then says, "And what does this Captain Colón require of me?"

"Three caravels, majesty, plus crew and stores."

A thin smile. "And?"

"And he wishes to be appointed "Great Admiral of the Ocean," to be made governor of any and all lands he discovers. All that, and to be given one-tenth of all revenue collected from any discovered lands."

Cárdenas is aghast. "My God! Did he not want to be made pope too?!"

The queen actually laughs. "This Colón is certainly a bold one."

Santangel says, "So it would seem, majesty. Forgetting his impossible requests for titles, a modest investment would seem worth considering."

She shakes her head. "Well, certainly worth considering, but all of Castile's gold is spoken for until the Moors are expelled from my realm. Do this, instead. Put Colón on a royal stipend. Nothing lavish, just enough to keep him from wandering off."

"I will see to it, majesty."

"And then have Colón's calculations carefully checked by my geographers and astronomers. I want to hear their opinions before I commit to anything."

Santangel nods. "He has requested to meet with you, majesty."

"He will wait. Thank you all for coming." The audience is over. As Isabel rises, they all kneel.

A frantic pounding on the door to the hall draws their eyes. The queen frowns. "How impertinent." She sits back down.

Cárdenas says, "Majesty?"

She nods. The minister of war's hand drops to the hilt of his broadsword as he moves to the door. He whispers a query, listens, then whispers again. The heavy door cracks open. An urgent flurry of hushed words from outside. Cárdenas nods, nods, frowns, nods. He asks a question, nods, another, then painfully grimaces as he sadly shakes his head. All they hear are his last words. "Very well." He closes the door.

All eyes are on him. He soberly says, "Bad news, majesty. Shocking news, I am afraid."

"Speak, Alonso."

"Word from Zahara. A surprise attack by the Moors during the dead of night. It seems they have—" He takes a deep breath to check his growing anger. "It seems the *Moors* have captured the town and the castle."

Bewildered expressions circle the room.

The queen is incredulous. "Captured Zahara? But Zahara is garrisoned by the Order of Santiago."

"It was. Zahara has fallen, majesty. Two-thirds of my knights fell in defense of the town."

The queen gasps.

"There is more, majesty. Evidently there will be no ransom for my captured knights. The women and children will be taken to Málaga and sold as slaves, and the knights imprisoned."

"Dear Lord, how barbaric!"

Shocked silence settles on the hall.

Cárdenas begins to purple with rage as he weighs these sad events. "Damn the Moors! DAMN THEM! They will pay, majesty! I will ride to the army today, and we will march on the Alhambra before the sun sets! By God, we will burn the place to the ground! Mark my words. WE WILL BURN THE DAMN PLACE TO THE GROUND!"

Talavera barks, "Hold your tongue, man! You forget you are in the presence of the queen."

Cárdenas glares at her confessor, seething with fury, but steadies himself.

The silence grows heavy.

Isabel is pale, stricken. "I assure you that we will indeed put Granada to the torch, Alonso." Her words are quietly tendered, but her tone is steely, determined. "You will indeed have vengeance for Zahara. But not today. The army needs time. Castile needs time. The treaty will be delivered to the Alhambra by Cardinal Mendoza as planned. We will not answer this outrageous attack upon Castile until the time is right. Our impotence will convince the sultan that Castile has no stomach for war."

Cárdenas is staring at the floor.

"Alonso?" Her voice is steady and firm.

The man slowly looks up, his face strained with emotion.

"Understood?"

"I understand, majesty."

"Send word to King Fernando and the Great Captain and inform them of the news. Tell them to double their efforts to ready the army, but to otherwise not engage our enemy." She lifts a finger to her chin. "No, wait. Tell them to disperse the regiments. They will have to train as separate units for the time being. Moorish spies will surely be roaming the borderlands. Arcos de la Frontera is far too close. If the Moors discover our invasion force, they will see that the truce is a ruse. We need time, gentlemen. Inform Gonzalo to set up staging areas for each regiment at least a hundred miles from the border, and a hundred miles from each other. They must not look like an army. He will visit each in turn while they continue their training."

"Very well, majesty."

As she rises once more, her counsellors kneel.

Disquiet

A warm greeting can be heard in the adjacent room. Eyes turn. A wizened old man shuffles forward, his limp pronounced. An expectant hush settles in as heads bow in deference. He looks positively ancient—watery almond eyes, face a field of sagging creases and deep wrinkles. A stern countenance, no nonsense; a weather-beaten scholar, not a doting grandfather. An unkempt, flowing white beard waterfalls down his expensive black robe, all pressed and formal, offering an ironic contrast. An ivory-tinted embroidered prayer shawl drapes across his shoulders; a black *kippah* floats upon his wild tease of cotton fluff. Conversations die away as those gathered track the old man's progress with bated breath.

The home of David and Miriam al-Adani is one of the largest in the Jewish Quarter, and located in the desirable neighborhood at the top of the hill adjacent to the Alhambra, a stone's throw from the shadow cast by the Bermejas Tower, and close to the hospital. Befitting the sultan's royal physician.

A dozen adults and a bevy of children and young people are crammed around the table. Ezar; his wife, Rebekah; and their six girls; two close neighbors and their nearly-grown children; a young hakim, David's first apprentice; the apprentice's wife and their three little boys; and two merchants and their wives, one with two girls and boy, the other with a swaddled baby.

The old man stops at the head of the table, silently turns to face the far window and squints. The room's eyes follow his as he studies the setting sun. The brilliant orange orb is diffracted in the wavy glass, unleashing an amoeba, which slowly fingers down the pane. The creature stops at an obstacle, ponderous, then gives up and begins to shrink, fading, fading, until it suddenly winks out, leaking its lifeblood into the air above the distant ring of mountains surrounding the Vega. The old man nods, satisfied, and turns back to the table, upon which stand two tall lit tapers that flicker and bend, producing a magical shimmer in the dying twilight. In front of him on the table rests a round challah loaf. Beside it is a water pitcher inside a matching basin, a small white cloth, and a silver goblet filled with red wine.

The door to the kitchen opens. Miriam. Behind her, the glistening, aproned wives look up from their fussing over an assortment of dishes. Miriam looks tired and slightly frazzled after the long day of preparation, but she is joyful and welcoming. She smiles and nods to her guests, then joins eyes with her husband. That knowing glance, quick enough to be easily missed, speaks volumes of the special love the two share.

A rich mélange of wonderful smells, some savory, some sweet, drifts into the room—leg of lamb marinated in olive oil, red wine, crushed salt, fresh rosemary and oregano, then grilled to perfection; a slow-cooked stew of braised kid and root vegetables, its rich brown gravy a minor miracle; loaves of hot bread just pulled from the oven; a warmed compote of candied oranges and lemons and cherries; roasted honey-almonds and salted pistachios; boiled beets with sautéed pearl onions; sliced eggplant basted with olive oil then coated in almori and grilled; sautéed chard tossed with toasted pine nuts and salt; the peppery, fresh-cut grass and herbs of fine olive oil; cinnamon, nutmeg, cumin, ginger, and cloves; an olfactory tapestry of spices woven into the fresh-baked pies—cherry, apple, apricot, plum; an assortment of honey-drizzled sweetmeats, puff pastries, dried fruit, fritters, and nougats; fresh-squeezed pomegranate juice infused with honeycomb.

Heads spontaneously tilt back as eyes close and nostrils flare with deep inhalations of the delectable menagerie of aromas. A mouthwatering epiphany. Smiles of anticipation circle the room, and not a few stomach rumbles.

At the far end of the table lies a large platter with sliced apples drizzled with honey, dried dates, pomegranates, and a whole fish with the head intact.

Miriam says, "We are ready."

Rabbi Zachariah al-Zuhri nods, then struggles to lift his open palms to the Lord as his eyes fold closed. The room stills. "*Tizku Leshanim Rabbot.*" May you merit many years.

The gathering solemnly replies in unison, "*Ne'imot VeTovot.*" Pleasant and good ones.

The cantor steps forward, lifts a three-foot long, spiraled *shofar* high in the air, and purses his lips. Smiles decorate the faces of the adults as they see their young children grow wide-eyed and open-mouthed. Even the young people forget their self-consciousness and are grinning ear-to-ear. Clearly, a much-anticipated event is ready to commence.

A long, pure steady note, brassy and loud, jolts the room. The cantor knows his business. Now three broken notes, a quick train of nine pulses, another long blast, then three broken sounds and nine more pulses. Then nothing.

The rabbi opens his eyes. Defying all expectations, with a mischievous twinkle in his eye he unexpectedly cracks a broad smile and exclaims. "*Shanah Tovah Umetukah!*" A good and sweet year!

The refrain is thunderous. "Shanah Tovah Umetukah!"

The room erupts with bright laughter, pumping handshakes, and hugs. The feast of Rosh Hashanah, the Jewish New Year.

Rabbi al-Zhuri stops to clear his throat, then continues.

> *And to this day it is said, on the mountain of the Lord it will be provided.*
>
> *The angel of the Lord called to Abraham from heaven a second time and said, "I swear by myself, declares the Lord, that because you have done this and have not withheld your son, your only son, I will surely bless you and make your descendants as numerous as the stars in the sky and as the sand on the seashore. Your descendants will take possession of the cities of their enemies, and through your offspring all nations on earth will be blessed, because you have obeyed me.*

He stops, re-rolls the Torah scroll, hands it to the cantor, then casts his eyes about the room. "The Holy Word of Yehovah, our Lord."

All reply, "Amen."

The rabbi smiles. "Brothers and sisters, let us thank the Lord for his great gifts. Let us break bread together and celebrate the coming of a blessed new year!"

"Amen!"

The shofar anthem sounds once more.

David exclaims, "Welcome friends! Our home is your home. Our food is your food. Our blessings are your blessings. Shanah Tovah Umetukah!"

"Shanah Tovah Umetukah!"

As Miriam and the wives disappear back into the kitchen, eyes follow them out and an expectant hush settles in. Suddenly, the door springs open with dramatic flair, and the steaming dishes are paraded in one by one with great fanfare. The room erupts with swooning exclamations of "oohs!" and "ahhs!" and cackles of delight.

A playful smile. "David, what do you make of the gossip swirling around the Alhambra these days?" The younger of the two merchants.

The men have adjourned to the sitting room for conversation as the women clean. The children have been unleashed upon the courtyard for semi-orchestrated mayhem. Piercing squeals are answered by riotous laughter. Sated, the men loosen their belts, pleased to be among friends and grateful for the health of their families and the many promises of the coming new year.

Trade in the Nasrid kingdom is better than ever. Jews occupy important roles in virtually all aspects of Granadine commerce—finance, of course, but also manufacturing and import-export. Fine jewelry and filigree, leatherwork, ceramics, wine, the famous Granadine silk of the Alpurrajas Mountains, either spun into cloth and folded into bolts, finished as clothing, or even woven into elaborate tapestries. And the Vega's endless assortment of artisanal foodstuffs, of course, grains, fruits, vegetables, spices. The list of highly-prized goods produced for export in the kingdom is nearly endless.

David puts on his best puzzled look. "Gossip? I have heard no gossip, Jacob. I am afraid the royal court is as dull as ever." They all laugh. A dramatic delayed smile before he continues, "Well, our sultan is smitten, there is no doubt of that. A young stud once more. His concubine-bride insists that the child she carries is male." He chuckles. "Time will tell." He lifts his hands helplessly. "Our poor sultan. Such a dilemma. A man by any reckoning past his prime, fawned over by a beautiful young lover half his age who is said to be the most seductive maiden in all of al-Andalus. *And*, if the gossip is to be believed, well-versed in the Persian arts of love. Whatever those might be." A sheepish smile.

Ezar whistles, "My, my, that *is* quite a dilemma! I almost feel sorry for the poor fellow. I hope the man's heart is strong." Bawdy laughter.

The young man presses on, "Is Zoraya as beautiful as they say?" He winks at the young hakim, who blushes.

The rabbi clears his throat and lifts a scolding finger, "Jacob, you would do well to remember what happened to King David after he stole a glance of the beautiful Bathsheba as she was bathing." More laughter. "Perhaps you have never heard the story, sir? It does not end well."

Jacob winks at Ezar. "Certainly, not for Uriah the Hittite."

The rabbi chortles. "Nor for King David, sir!"

Laughter.

221

Ezar turns to David. "What of the sultana? I cannot imagine a woman of her ambition and capabilities easily tolerating an upstart Second Wife."

David's smile relaxes. "Indeed, no. Fatima is now living in the Albayzín. Banished might be more accurate. Zoraya's doing, no doubt, though no one seems to know for sure. Somehow Zoraya managed to wrestle control of the harem from her as well. No small feat. Supposedly all of the sultan's favorite concubines have magically disappeared." Rowdy laughter. "They say the place is crawling with eunuchs with nothing to do."

Ezar asks, "Where in the Albayzín is Fatima staying?"

"Her new prison, I mean carmen, is at the highest point on the ridge. Dar al-Horra. They say it is lavish, and with the best view of the Alhambra that gold can buy."

The older merchant says, "So that Fatima is reminded constantly of what she has lost. A thumb in the eye."

"Precisely, Daniel."

Ezar says, "And the heir?"

David replies, "Boabdil? Him, too. The two of them were banished together."

"I cannot imagine this will end well if Zoraya produces a son to challenge Boabdil's legitimacy as heir."

David grimaces. "No, nor I. It would not be hard for me to imagine that Fatima and Boabdil will attempt some sort of mischief to undercut Zoraya's hold on the sultan." He muses. "Given the right circumstances, perhaps even an attempt to overthrow her husband and place Boabdil on the throne." Smiles die away. "Why not? It is no secret that the sultan and Supreme Mullah Abd Allah are enemies. And the mullah, not the sultan, has the support of the Supreme Council and the Masters of the Guilds. As we all know, Granada's power, and its gold, lies in the guilds, not the treasury. What if Fatima decides to join forces with them against the sultan?"

Daniel states the obvious. "But the sultan has al-Zaghal and Ali al-Attar and the army."

"True. At least for now."

Daniel continues, "The grumbling in the guilds over the sultan's new taxes is louder than I have ever heard. Especially in the Alcaiceria. *Granada's silk market.* And let us not forget that silk drives over a third of our exports."

Rabbi al-Zhuri says, "Any such rebellion would be a disaster for Granada. And hence, for us. Especially now that the Christians are once again rattling their swords. Fernando and Isabel must be licking their chops now that peace with Portugal is finally secured. Contested rule and a divided court would be an invitation to the Christians to come calling."

Murmurs of assent circle the room.

David says, "Speaking of Castile. There are some disturbing rumors coming out of Córdoba these days. Oblique references I have heard at court, mostly, nothing confirmed. But I have heard them now more than once." Eyes settle on him. "It appears that the queen has initiated what she is calling an 'Inquisition.' With papal backing, of course."

Rabbi al-Zhuri frowns. "Yes. I have heard those rumors."

Jacob says, "And what does this Inquisition seek to learn?"

"Evidently, it is intended to root out Christian converts that still practice their Judaism in private. It seems the queen wants to help them see the errors of their ways. 'False converts' the queen calls them. The Castilians call them . . . *marranos.*" Swine.

Grumbles. The word is an obscenity to Jews.

Daniel says, "Surely there are not many such hidden Jews in Castile. After all, practicing Jews are tolerated, if not embraced."

David replies, "That is not what the rumors say. They are being rounded up by the hundreds in all the cities."

Daniel looks puzzled. "But that makes no sense."

Rabbi al-Zhuri snorts. "Gold, man! The accused must ransom their souls with gold. A proper penance for their sins. Meanwhile, Isabel lines her pockets and Castile's treasury grows rich."

Nods of understanding. And concern.

The rabbi continues, "I fear that it is but a short step from punishing these so-called false converts to the open persecution of practicing Jews. The lives of Jews in Castile have been on tenuous ground for centuries." Nods of assent. "Let us not forget the pogroms of 1391. Or the thousands of forced baptisms that resulted. That, Daniel, is where these false converts came from that Isabel's Inquisition seeks. As you all know, our brothers and sisters in Castile, to this day, must don those cursed yellow stars."

Stunned silence at the painful reminders.

Daniel says, "Surely Granada is safe from such horrors. The Nasrids treat us well. The *jizya* tax, yes, but we are free to own land and trade as we wish. For goodness' sake, the guilds depend upon us for their financing!" He lifts his hand to David. "And let us not forget that a Jew cares for the health of the sultan himself, *and* the royal family. And we Jews run their hospitals!" He lifts a hand to Ezar, who ticks his head in acknowledgment.

Jacob chimes in, "There has been peace on our border with Castile for over a hundred years."

Ezar shakes his head sadly. "Times change, gentlemen."

Rabbi al-Zhuri softly says, "From all that I hear, Isabel aims to rid Granada of the Moors, to complete what her forebears began centuries back."

Jacob replies, "But Granada will resist. Granada is strong!"

Ezar says, "Jacob, the Kingdom of Granada is a hundred-fifty miles long and half as wide. We are a speck of sand compared to a unified Castile and Aragon. Prosperous, yes, and well-defended, but that will mean little to a determined queen at the head of an army intent on . . . crusade."

The men collectively wince at the use of the dreaded word.

David responds, "So imagine the worst. Suppose Granada falls to Castile and the Moors are expelled. We Jews would be far too valuable to dispense with. They would need us to help run the kingdom."

Rabbi al-Zhuri says, "Now there, I agree. Life will be more difficult, but in the end the Christians will discover that they need us. We must find a way to equate our presence in their midst to gold in the hands of the queen. That will be our saving grace. If Granada should fall, we Jews will bow our heads in submission, just as we have always done, then politely ensure they recognize that we are indispensable to their own prosperity. Which we are."

Ezar opens his mouth to disagree but then closes it.

David says, "I suggest that when the time comes we—"

"You suggest that we *what*, when the time comes, Husband?" Eyes turn to the doorway. Miriam, hands on hips, a scolding frown. She shakes her head disapprovingly. "Such serious men. And all this scary talk." Their eyes search the floor like children called out, even the rabbi. Miriam unexpectedly laughs. "It is Rosh Hashanah, gentlemen, a time for joy and celebration, not a time to talk of gloom and doom. Shanah Tovah Umetukah!"

Rabbi al-Zhuri replies, "You are right, my dear. Forgive us our wanton ways." His eyes are twinkling once again. "Shanah Tovah Umetukah."

The others join him, "Shanah Tovah Umetukah."

Satisfied, Miriam says, "We ladies are joining the children in the courtyard. Perhaps you men would care to join your lovely wives for some dancing?" A coy smile, and before they can answer, she turns with a swish and is gone.

David chuckles. "Whatever you say, darling." The others laugh. "My friends, shall we do our duty?"

Rabbi al-Zhuri struggles to rise. "I get the first dance with the prettiest girl!"

A riot of laughter.

He is folded tightly around her, spoon cupping spoon, his knees behind her knees, his toes touching her toes. He has lifted her long curls up onto the pillow they share, exposing the dark, downy nape of her neck. He has playfully insisted for many years now that this exact spot is by far the most seductive part of her body.

In a single movement he casually slides her nightgown upward with his thumb and begins to absently feather the tips of his fingers across the generous sway of her hip.

"David?" Barely a whisper.

"Yes, my love?"

"Do you really think Castile will invade?"

He does not answer. His fingers stop momentarily, then resume their soft, swaying dance along her curves. She shivers.

"Ezar seems to think so."

"And Rabbi al-Zhuri?"

"He says that even if the Christians somehow managed to conquer Granada, we Jews would be far too valuable to treat poorly."

Miriam mulls this over. "What do you think?"

"I think Christians need hakims just as much as Moors." His fingers begin to work their way down her thigh.

She ignores him. "This Inquisition sounds horrible."

"Mmm." He gently kisses the nape of her neck.

Her lids droop for an instant, then she abruptly flips over onto her back.

He raises up on an elbow, sees her concern. "This Inquisition will never touch us, Miriam."

She looks away.

"What is really bothering you, darling?"

She looks back. "Danah."

"Ahh."

"I know we did the right thing by finding her a match, but I still feel terrible."

"Look. Yusef was right when he said there is a giant chasm between the two of them. That relationship was never meant to be."

"I still find myself wondering what changed Yusef's mind."

"Who knows? Abd al-Salam has done well. Malik is a fine young man. And those two will be able to practice as husband-and-wife hakims. What a wonderful gift to the world."

"I know, but—"

"Miriam." He shakes his head. "You worry too much."

"I care deeply for her, David. I want her to be happy."

"As do I. She *will* be happy."

"But what if we stepped in the way of what Yehovah really intended for her?"

"Then Yehovah will find a way to set it right. Danah is back to her normal self, Miriam. Malik writes to her; she writes back. She seems content with her betrothal. Life moves on. I am sure she has put Yusef's letter behind her."

"Perhaps." She considers this. "But true love cannot be denied, David."

"Of that, I am quite positive." Without taking his eyes from hers, he uses his thumb and forefinger to slowly unbutton the top of her gown. She smiles at his boyish glee. He folds back her gown and leans down to kiss her breast.

"But . . ." She begins, as he teases her with his tongue. His fingers begin to explore. "True love . . ." Her toes curl as her knees rise off the bed. A soft, tortured moan escapes her. She begins to squirm, kicks back the covers. "Cannot be . . ." Her words trail off. Her eyes fold closed as she welcomes the approaching ecstasy.

There is truth in what David says—Danah *is* back to her normal self.

Ezar looks up from his writing, his woolly worms arched and gamesome. He mouths some barb to tease her. She is hunched over a marble mortar and pestle, grinding away. Without looking up she offers her retort. He chuckles, fires back. She laughs this time, which grows quickly into shoulder shaking tremors. She turns and looks back at him, rewards him with a brilliant smile.

As she opens the door, Samra runs and wraps her arms around her. Danah spontaneously cackles her surprise, then returns the hug, clearly overjoyed by the girl's sheer delight at seeing her. Samra bubbles over with childlike exuberance, her rapid-fire story filled with wide-eyed drama and exaggerated hand motions. As Danah smiles and nods, nods and smiles, the two walk hand-in-hand down the hallway, less physician and patient than two good friends. A sight to warm the soul.

She kneels on her prayer rug just before sunrise, facing southeast. Her elbows are raised, and her palms are level with her shoulders, fingers together. She leans forward, touching her nose, her forehead, and her palms to the carpet at the same instant. She whispers, "*Subhana rabbi al-acla wa-bi-hamdih.*" Glory to the Lord, the Most-High, the Most Praiseworthy. Again. A third time. Then, "Allahu Akbar." She rises back onto her knees, continuing her *salah*, a comforting touchstone to begin her day.

Her hands are stretched shoulder-wide, as if indicating the measure of something. David smirks and shakes his head *no*, offers his opinion. She smiles at her patient, nods *yes*, widens the gap by half a foot. He shakes his head *no* again, more vigorously this time. Her smile widens. A half foot more. He gives up and shrugs, turns back to his work. Her hands move back to their original dimension as she winks at her patient, who laughs loudly. David turns back with a mock-frown, but Danah's expression is completely blank. Except that those glorious emeralds are blazing.

Her mother is insistent. As usual. Danah shrugs off the query, a portrait of nonchalance. Her mother grasps her shoulders and nods as she queries once again, coaxing an answer as only a mother can. Danah cannot help cracking a coy smile, which her mother amplifies with her own. Her father looks up from his book at the spectacle, confused. As usual. On cue, mother and daughter burst out laughing.

The life of a betrothed young hakim goes on. And yet . . .
And yet, while comforting certainties and reasonable decisions ply the waking hours, seeds of doubt and wanton desires are the playthings of the night.
Her days are busy, by intent, and so are her evenings. She reads into the jinn's hour as the Albayzín sleeps, determined to find solace, and distraction, in her histories and her medical treatises. Slowly, pleasingly, the squiggles, dots, and dashes begin to work their magic, blurring her focus, easing her cares, until her world grays into a carefree oblivion. She wakes at dawn after a dreamless night as she usually does, refreshed, once again reassured, certain of her life's agreed-upon trajectory.
Most nights.

This night she is restless, tense, and cannot understand precisely why. After all, she is deep in Ibn al-Khatib's bold prescription for dealing with the plague threatening the kingdom in 1348. Riveting stuff—the man's radical view of contagion spared Granada. The Supreme Council fought him, but in the end, he prevailed, saving the city. She stops and frowns, realizing she has reached the end of the page without having comprehended a word. With a deep sigh she marks her place and closes the codex. She stares into space as her mind begins to wander. Dangerous waters, these. She finds that her eyes are inexorably drawn to her dresser. Hidden within, beneath her clothes, is a small box where she keeps her most valuable keepsakes. A jinn whispers to her now, a siren's call, pulling her forward against her will. Her heart begins to race. In self-defense she desperately re-opens her book, tries to read. She fidgets and fusses, then finally gives up. She has clearly been here before.

She eyes the dresser with a looming sense of dread. She knows what monster lurks there, the danger it represents. She does. Of course she does. She stares. Helpless to resist, she jerks herself off her mattress, and in one quick motion opens the drawer, retrieves the box, and lies back down. She turns on her side, pulls her knees up. She simply stares at the thing, afraid to move. She makes a tentative motion in its direction, then recoils as if she suddenly sees an adder coiled and ready to strike. She takes a deep breath, tries again. As she slowly lifts the lid, a shimmery blue glow flashes out from the crack and licks at her fingertips. Her heart is pounding. Pounding.

She lifts the letter out with bated breath, carefully unfolds it. She licks her lips and begins to whisper his words to her. She savors his declaration, slowly, so slowly. Her eyes well up as she makes her way down the page. The tears begin to leak from her, but she forces herself to the very end. Her hands, still cradling Yusef's profession of love, slowly sink to the mattress as she rocks herself to sleep, desperately pleading, "Tetta Layla. Tetta Layla. Tetta Layla."

MEANWHILE, IN MÁLAGA.

Yusef walks with his brother; Hamete Zeli; and the Berber commander, Sayf al-Milla. A dozen of the battalion officers trail a short distance behind. The daunting, four-foot thick, fifty-foot high outer walls of the Gibralfaro Castle tower above them. The group stands just beyond the freshly-constructed second outer ashlar and mortar wall; only a third the height, but filled with earth and intended to shield the base of the main wall from direct cannon fire. The space between the two walls is just wide enough to permit cavalry to pass. The stubby battlements of this outer wall offer ample protection for crouching archers. There is a deep earthen moat just beyond, impressively riddled with thousands of two-foot-long sharpened iron spikes, ingeniously hidden from view until the attackers stand at the lip of the moat. These wicked things are called 'gut-wrenchers,' and are intended to give pause to the attacking infantry, just long enough for the crossbowmen to take good aim.

Yusef is patiently explaining their defensive strategy. Hamete interrupts with a question. Yusef turns, points to the closest hill, northeast of where they are standing, and replies. He then sweeps his hand to the left along the downward slope, then turns back to the castle and points up at the cannon-studded rampart. Umar chimes in. Hamete nods, appreciatively, asks a second question. Yusef answers with a wolfish grin. Zeli and Umar both laugh. Even the stern Berber cracks a hint of a smile.

As the door opens, Yusef and Umar enter the mess hall. The battalion commander barks his troops to attention, and his men drop their spoons and hastily rise. The room grows instantly silent. Yusef lifts a hand and smiles, tells them to enjoy their meals. The men relax back onto their benches, but their eyes do not leave the Falcon brothers as they slowly walk from one end of the room to the other. The two stop and offer kind words here, affectionate shoulder slaps there, nods of recognition, teasing barbs, inquiries about family, loved ones. They know these men who are sworn to die in their service. From behind them, a query about their enemy and the battle to come. Yusef turns and thoughtfully considers the man's words, then answers truthfully, stilling the room. He is revered for his candor. To break the tension, one of the bolder knights tenders a bawdy joke. A long, awkward pause follows, then the brothers simultaneously laugh. The room erupts with cackles and whistles of delight. They resume their walk. Adoring eyes collectively follow the brothers until they reach the far end of the hall. The respect and the trust of the troops for these two is palpable. The rumor in the garrison persists: that Málaga is invincible as long as the Falcons are within its walls. When the door closes, a hundred conversations stir at once.

Hamete Zeli finishes reading aloud the official communique from the Alhambra, then re-rolls it. Despite their fears, it seems that Boabdil was successful in capturing Zahara after all. Total surprise was achieved, and minimal casualties were sustained. Defying all odds, Boabdil seems to have performed well in his first engagement. Zeli expresses his incredulity at this unexpected turn of events and shakes his head in dismay. Umar shrugs, replies. Always looking on the bright side of things. Yusef frowns, reminding them of the possible consequences of such an unprovoked attack, and especially the implications of denying ransom to the knights of the Order of Santiago. Zeli and Umar soberly nod their agreement.

They slowly walk from the sparring ground, side-by-side, broadsword in one hand, small, heart-shaped leather shield in the other. They are both dripping with sweat, muscles swelled tight with the exertion, their chiseled, shirtless bodies glistening in the morning sun. Their expressions are taut, serious, as they mentally review their successes and their failures. Umar grins at the ground, ready to tease. Without looking up he mouths a brotherly insult. Yusef absently nods, fires back dismissively. Umar offers a disparaging appraisal of Yusef's new move that he easily parried then turned to his advantage. Yusef sneers his response. Umar knocks shoulders with his brother, chides him playfully. Yusef attempts a smile, which does not quite coalesce. He hates being bested.

The life of a tethered Falcon goes on. And yet . . .
And yet, while comforting certainties and reasonable decisions ply the waking hours, seeds of doubt and wanton desires are the playthings of the night.

Yusef wakes with a start, confused by his surroundings. He sits up and scans the dimly-lit room, puzzled, wondering who would dare rearrange his quarters in the Alhambra without his permission. He grimaces as he recalls where he is, lies back, stares at the ceiling.
She comes to him at night, steps right into his dreams. He holds her, kisses her, makes love to her, yes; but there is more, so much more. His dreams of her are filled with their life together. Endless talks of blessings and Allah's Grace and love and prayer; of laughter, their home, their children, their future lives together. He is as close to being truly happy as he has ever been. Then he wakes, and remembers. And he cries. He resents her for her cruel intrusions, but he cannot bear the thought of these beautiful dreams of her ever ending.
As he stares into the darkness he pictures her lying in her bed, so lovely as she sleeps, those glorious curls framing her face. Only eighty miles separating the two of them, though it might as

well be a million. He scans the window. Dark, but moonlit. Whatever time it is he knows that sleep will not return. He rises, puts on his breeches and boots, swings a cloak over his shoulders, then dons his broadsword and dagger and slips out of their room, careful not to wake Umar.

He climbs the stairs to the eastern rampart, exchanges a few words with the sentry, then moves to an open stretch of wall where he can be alone. The cool, saline breeze is pleasing. Broken rows of white-tipped waves relentlessly march to the shore. He cups his ears, can just discern the cadenced hush of the surf. A dab of gray touches the horizon—an hour to sunrise. The endless, moon-kissed ocean, an infinity of infinities.

He whispers her name. "Danah." His shoulders sag with the weight of it all, wondering what he could have done differently, should have done differently. His eyes well up as the hurt digs its claws in deep. "My Danah."

Almost against his will, he summons her, drags her forth from his tortuous dream, even though he knows that in the end he will be punished mercilessly for this weakness. He pulls her against him. She lays her head on his shoulder.

"My angel, my love." He breathes in her hair, his favorite scent in the world, kisses the top of her head.

She nestles against him. "My beloved."

They silently stare at the horizon, content to be together, until the brightening gray purples then gushes a boisterous pink. As the rippling sliver of burnt orange breaks the plane of day, she vanishes. And he cries.

The courtier announces the delegation. "Honored guests. Supreme Mullah Abd Allah. Supreme Council. Grand Imams. Masters of the Guilds. Behold the glory that is the Alhambra." Their eyes involuntarily follow his lifting hand.

The gray-bearded clerics all wear long, black robes and black turbans, and seem quite content to project a stern and disapproving manner. The elders and guildsmen are a mixture of middle-aged and old men, most of substantial girth. To a one they are dressed in the finest Moorish attire, as befitting their high station—gold-trimmed silks, blues and reds and greens, with fancy embroidery and coordinated turbans.

As is customary, they have been received in the famed Hall of the Ambassadors within the Comares Palace, the official throne room of the Alhambra.

The journey to arrive at this precise spot is nothing less than a major ordeal. By design. Scrutinized and questioned first at the Pomegranate Gate down in the city proper, then the steep climb up the road to the palace, ending at the Justice Gate, the formal entrance to the Alhambra. As the menacing crossbowmen pace the ramparts above them, papers are checked and rechecked, more questions are asked. An armed escort is assigned once inside the Alhambra, and then after a long wait, a formal enrollment on the visitor register just outside the entrance to the Mexuar Palace. They wait for a royal courtier to escort them into the Courtyard of the Mexuar, then more waiting. A second courtier arrives to lead them into the Comares Palace, around the giant pool of the Courtyard of the Myrtles and into the legendary Hall of the Ambassadors. Here, they are finally announced, although the sultan is nowhere to be seen. It goes without saying that few are permitted this journey, and it has taken days to arrange the visit, even for the leaders of the city. To their intense resentment. There is no love lost between the sultan and this delegation.

Still, few have beheld this remarkable miracle of light and space. Despite their grim countenances, most of the men cannot refrain from looking up to admire the magnificent marquetry ceiling towering high above them. A fascinating depiction of the Seven Heavens of Islam. And the impossibly elaborate stucco walls covered with fantastic arabesque images, sprinkled at strategic points with artistically rendered poetry and Quranic sayings etched for eternity to enjoy. The entire interior of the hall is a masterpiece of symbolic ornamentation.

The silence is deafening, and as they wait, the delegation begins to fidget in their discomfort. Again, intentional.

An iron bell is struck somewhere in the distance. From a door to their right, Grand Vizier Venegas, then the sultan, then al-Zaghal emerge. They are dressed in formal courtly attire and are flanked by a dozen heavily-armed royal bodyguards in solid red robes, each with a single golden sash. Once in view, the sultan stops.

The courtier lifts his hands and proclaims, "His Royal Highness, Sultan Abu l-Hasan, son of Abu Nasr Sa'd, ruler of al-Andalus, twenty-first sultan of Granada, elder of the Nasrid clan, defender of the faith." A pause of impeccable length, then, "The only victor is Allah!"

The delegation dutifully responds, "The only victor is Allah." The delegation bows. Deep enough to satisfy protocol, but no more.

Without casting an eye in the direction of the visitors, the three men move towards the throne. The sultan sits, then Venegas and al-Zaghal recline on silk divans to his right and left. All three are expressionless. The royal bodyguards melt into the walls between the stained-glass windows behind the sultan. Their eyes are alert, their palms resting on the hilts of their Granadine broadswords. The most feared swordsmen in the kingdom.

The sultan suddenly smiles. "Gentlemen. It is always such a pleasure!" The bald-faced lie is lost on no one. "Sit. Please." Venegas ticks his head, and a dozen attendants burst from the shadows with silk pillows. The men settle themselves. Next, golden platters bearing hot tea, delectable sweetmeats, and a variety of candied nuts and fruits are brought forth. The Supreme Mullah waves them off with an annoyed grimace, and the delegation follows suit, though several seem reluctant to do so.

A hint of an amused smile from Venegas. He so enjoys the bluster and nuance of political machinations. This is the delegation's third visit in as many months. Always the same outrage, always the same demands. A fourth visit so soon can only mean that they have gotten wind of Zahara. He begins to size up their adversaries one by one. Only a few merit his attention.

Sultan Abu l-Hasan begins as if he has no cares in the world. "Supreme Mullah, to what do I owe the pleasure?"

This is one that does merit attention. The man's ebony eyes smolder. "As I have voiced several times now to no avail, I have serious concerns, sire. The Assembly of Clerics has serious concerns. The Supreme Council and the Masters of the Guilds have serious concerns, sire."

"Concerns?" A practiced nonchalance. "And what might those be?"

The Supreme Mullah counts on his fingers. "The unprecedented expulsion of your wife and heir from court is not acceptable. Your shameless dalliances with this . . . this . . ."

The sultan raises a finger. "Her name is Zoraya, Supreme Mullah."

"Sire, the city is still in shock that you would stoop to marry this Christian . . . *concubine*." It is clear that the cleric would prefer a different word. "We are appalled. It is simply not acceptable."

"And as you well know, Supreme Mullah, Zoraya is a convert to the faith, and our marriage is completely legitimate." The sultan's tone hardens. "*Completely legitimate!*"

Al-Zaghal cuts his eyes to his brother to cautiously assess his temperament.

The sultan studies the cleric. "You should be pleased, Supreme Mullah." He turns to the rest of the delegation. "You all should be pleased. I am happy to tell you that Zoraya is with child. A new heir to the Nasrid throne, praise be to Allah." His tone has nearly returned to normal. His brother relaxes.

Venegas watches the delegation's response closely. They already know she is with child. He sighs. Even in her banishment, Fatima is plying her trade with rigorous efficiency.

A standoff. These charges are nothing new.

The supreme elder, Dulaf al-Qawi, says, "Sire, it has come to our attention that Granada's army has attacked and captured Zahara. We were not informed in advance."

Venegas' amused smile returns. *Ahh. The heart of the matter.*

The sultan hesitates, puzzled by how they know this already. He says, "Indeed. Zahara *has* fallen." He brightens. "Outstanding news, is it not? Despite my misgivings, it seems that Boabdil is capable of leading an army after all. My brother said as much, though I was skeptical." The sultan laughs to inject some levity. He does not even bother to address why the elders were not informed.

Al-Qawi continues, "But sire. An unprovoked surprise attack on a major Christian fortress? The women and children sold into slavery? And a denial of ransom to the captured knights? The knights of the Order of Santiago, no less. Sire, at a time when tensions run high between Castile and Granada, the Supreme Council fears . . ." He lifts his hands helplessly. "Sire, if Queen Isabel is given good reason to feel threatened, she may well choose to attack us in retaliation . . ."

One of the guild masters adds, "Think of the devastating impact to the kingdom's prosperity, sire. The guilds simply cannot afford a war. We cannot bear the cost. We cannot." Grumbles of assent from the group.

Al-Zaghal frowns as he sees his brother's face darken.

As the sultan's eyes begin to bulge, he inhales deeply, then bellows, "YOU SNIVELING COWARDS! WHERE ARE YOUR SPINES?!"

The entire delegation recoils. Al-Qawi blanches, then mutters, "We meant no disrespect, sire."

The sultan leans forward and hisses at the man, "*I. Hope. Castile. Attacks.* I relish the chance to personally flay the infidels." His eyes bulge as he spews spittle, "FLAY THEM!"

Deathly silence as the sultan continues to stare down the chief elder, who lowers his gaze. The sultan breathes deeply, his nostrils flaring in and out, in and out. No one dares move, or say anything.

The sultan finally sits back in his throne, shakes his head with disgust. Al-Zaghal manages to make eye contact with his brother, and a silent conversation ensues. Al-Zaghal clears his throat to gather the eyes in the room. "Gentlemen, Granada's attack on Zahara was a calculated show of strength. Surprise was the key to success. That was our only reason for not informing the Supreme Council." His tone is both reasonable and firm. "Zahara served to remind Castile that Granada is not to be toyed with. That our borders must be respected or there will be a heavy price to pay. Gentlemen, let us not forget the Christian border raid on the village outside Campotéjar. Granadine women raped and beheaded. Granadine children stolen and taken back to Castile as slaves." His eyes move among the delegation to let this reminder sink in. "Zahara was a necessary and emphatic message that had to be sent to Isabel and Fernando. They have been reminded that even their most formidable castle-garrisons are vulnerable. Zahara was intended to buy us time while we prepare for the Castilian invasion that will come. And gentlemen, it surely is coming. We must prepare for the worst."

Unsettled murmurs. Even the Supreme Mullah sprouts a worried grimace.

The sultan barks, "And Zahara has achieved its intended goal!" He tries to steady his voice. "My grand vizier has news, gentlemen. News that you *lambs* will find especially interesting." The sultan looks to Venegas.

"Yes. Excellent news, I am pleased to say. We have just received word from Castile. A delegation is on its way from Córdoba as we speak. It seems that Isabel and Fernando desire a renewal of the truce between Castile and Granada."

Al-Zaghal says, "Peace. Peace through *strength*, gentlemen."

The delegation is genuinely elated at the good news.

Venegas is pleased to see that this morsel is in fact a real surprise. It seems that there are limits to Fatima's network of spies after all.

Zoraya gushes, "It is *beautiful!*" She slips the ring on, admires it from several angles. Exquisite craftsmanship. The massive stone is set in finely worked gold and surrounded by alternating rubies and emeralds. Priceless.

"For services rendered, my darling." He beams. "Your plans for Zahara worked perfectly."

She tenders her most beguiling smile. "I live to serve you, my sultan."

He pats the divan. "Come lay with me, my love."

She snuggles in close, lays her head on his chest.

His hand moves to her now visibly swelling belly. "You have made me so happy, Zoraya."

She purrs.

"We will call our son, *Abu al-Rahman*." Servant of the Merciful One. "After the first Umayyad caliph."

"Yes, I like that. Sultan Abu al-Rahman, the Magnificent. Son of Abu l-Hasan, ruler of al-Andalus, twenty-second sultan of Granada, elder of the Nasrid clan, defender of the faith."

He chuckles, pulls her tighter. "The only victor is Allah."

The Sacromonte de Granada lies just beyond the outer wall of the city to the east of the Albayzín, across the River Darro valley from the lavish gardens of the Generalife, the sultan's summer palace, a long arrow shot from the walls of the Alhambra. The hillside is dotted with caves carved into the soft stone then crafted into shanties. The Sacromonte is home to Granada's *gitanos*, her gypsies, who are denied quarters in the city proper. On still summer evenings, their raucous parties drift over the high walls and into the Albayzín and can even be heard from the towers of the Alhambra. Magical exhibitions of song and dance set to the quick-strumming of guitars, rhythmic hand-clapping and finger-snapping, anguished male vocalizations weaving in and out of the melody, and remarkable, seductive dancing by voluptuous, dark-eyed beauties, their feet blurring as they ferociously pound the beat into the floor. The crowds roar and whistle their approval.

At the very edge of the Sacromonte, just near the beginning of the royal orchards, there lives a hermit named Alfaqui. He is rarely seen but calls to mind the severe ascetics of ancient times. An unkempt bag of malnourished bones, tall and thin as a rail inside his soiled robe, hair and beard greasy and matted. In spite of this, or perhaps because of it, Alfaqui is held in high esteem by the common folk and is celebrated as an oracle of the city's future.

It has been many years now since he emerged from his cave to proclaim the coming of the plague of 1479. Since then, nothing, not a single word.

As his hooded figure limps painfully down the steep slope of the Sacromonte, he is forced to lean on his crooked staff to keep from toppling. The crowd takes notice, and soon a throng dogs his steps as he makes his way through the Faluja Gate and into the Albayzín. Word spreads like wildfire, and by the time he enters the Darro Plaza and stops, he is surrounded by hundreds. Hushed, excited whispers, and anxious anticipation. *Come quick! The hermit is going to prophesy!*

Alfaqui stops. His eyes are smoldering coals. He lifts his hands, and with remarkable power, proclaims, "Woe to Granada!"

The crowd is instantly silent. Trepidation fills the square. Breaths are held, loved ones are pulled tight.

"Granada, your hour of desolation approaches! Fools! The ruins of Zahara will rain upon your heads. Fools! The end is at hand!"

Gasps from the crowd. The news of Zahara is now known by all, but it has been widely celebrated as a great victory for the kingdom, a brilliant show of strength that has brought the Christian north to heel.

"Woe to Granada for breaking the peace! War is coming. Woe! Woe to Granada! Her fall is at hand! Desolation and strife shall smite the mighty Alhambra. Her knights shall fall beneath the gilded sword. Her children shall be led into captivity. Her maidens will be violated. Woe! Woe to Granada!"

The hermit lowers his hands, turns, and begins to limp back to his cave. No one in the crowd moves. They simply watch, numb from the shock of the old man's condemnation. As he passes through the Faluja Gate and disappears, the plaza erupts. By nightfall the whole city will have heard the prophecy.

The Gathering Storm

The sultan beams as he watches the Castilian delegation exit the Hall of the Ambassadors. He waits until they are out of earshot, then claps his hands together and laughs loudly. "These Christians are such fools!" He lifts the freshly-signed Treaty of Truce and turns his bright smile on Grand Vizier Venegas. "What say you, sir?!"

The Vizier Council is assembled in a semicircle about the throne on plush silk divans, decked out in their most formal diplomatic attire to properly receive Cardinal Mendoza and the Castilian delegation.

Venegas permits himself a rare smile. "I would say, sire, that our attack on Zahara had its intended effect. Peace. A welcomed turn of events, to be sure."

"Indeed. Peace through strength." He laughs. "My new dictum. A hundred more years of unchallenged sovereignty for Granada. My Nasrid forebearers would be proud!" He turns to al-Zaghal. "Castile fears us, Brother! Trembles in our sight. Just like in the days of old."

Al-Zaghal replies, "Indeed, sire." His exuberance is considerably more restrained.

The sultan continues unabated, "And with no annual tribute to be paid to the cursed infidels. A simple handshake that we will respect Castile's borders." He laughs again. "Fools!"

Ali al-Attar's eyes are on the floor. The military vizier soberly says, "It feels too easy to me."

The sultan looks taken aback. He glares at the old warrior.

"The Christians are not to be trusted, sire. This could be a ruse."

Venegas is intrigued. "To what end, Ali?"

The old man looks up and begins to stroke his long gray beard. "To put us at ease. To make us drop our guard. To allow us to forget that Castile is fifty times the size of Granada. To induce us to halt our preparations for the coming war. I could go on."

If this had come from someone else, the sultan might spontaneously combust. As it is, he simply frowns. "The Christians fear us, Ali. They now know that if we can take Zahara so easily, their border castles are not safe. For Allah's sake, the attack was led by my unbloodied son. An infant in arms!"

238

"Perhaps they fear us at the moment, sire. But, trust me, as soon as Isabel and Fernando are prepared, they will come calling. Granada must be ready."

Al-Zaghal finally speaks his mind. "I agree with Ali, sire. Even if this truce turns out to be genuine we must continue our preparations. Málaga's defenses are nearing completion. The border towns must make ready for war. We must be diligent."

Ali al-Attar looks up and acknowledges al-Zaghal with a tick of his head. Sharp words were exchanged between the two men when the military vizier returned to the Alhambra to find the attack on Zahara already engaged without his knowledge. Al-Zaghal's patient explanation of the true origin of the idea calmed the old man's ire, but not his disdain for the foolishness of launching a preemptive strike against Castile. Upon that, the two men were in complete agreement.

The sultan eyes his brother, obviously annoyed at having a damper slammed on his jubilation. He pouts. "Fine. We will continue with our preparations."

Venegas says, "A wise move, sire."

No answer. He is still annoyed.

Royal Treasurer al-Kamil clears his throat. "Sire, I am afraid that the treasury is getting dangerously depleted. We are in need of at least 100,000 dinars if we are to remain solvent to year's end."

The sultan waves him off. "Then raise taxes again, Tawd. The guilds can afford it."

Venegas grimaces. "The guilds are already balking about the current tax burden, sire."

The sultan eyes his grand vizier dangerously. He slowly says, "The guilds will do what the sultan needs to protect the kingdom." He sneers. "*Understood?*"

The room inhales.

Al-Zaghal glances at his brother, sees the predictable shift in his demeanor, and aims to quickly change directions before things get out of hand. "What we need is a celebration."

All eyes turn to him. The cloud hovering over the sultan dissipates as quickly as it came.

"Yes. A celebration of all that makes Granada great. Even if the peace treaty turns out in the end to be a ruse, the people should rejoice in our victory at Zahara and the truce it has facilitated. Peace through strength."

Venegas chimes in, "An excellent idea! It would be just the thing to quell the seeds of unrest sown among the common folk by that troublesome old hermit, Alfaqui."

The sultan is exuberant. "A celebration! Yes! A royal feast, with song and dance. We will fling open the gates of the Alhambra and invite the citizens to join in! And we will build a reviewing stand just outside the Justice Gate, so I can parade my victorious army in all its glory! It will be a demonstration of strength like never before seen. It will put people's minds at ease about our future." He is beaming again like a little boy.

The royal treasurer opens his mouth to interject on the cost of such a lavish undertaking but thinks better of it. Wise move.

Ali al-Attar continues to stroke his beard, but his eyes are back in his lap.

Venegas' gears are working. "Perhaps we could even invite the foreign ambassadors, sire. Word will get back to the courts of Europe that Granada is alive and well and not to be toyed with."

The sultan replies, "The ambassadors. Yes, good, I like it!"

"I will see that preparations are begun immediately, sire."

The crowd is enormous. A fevered buzz hovers in the air, the sense of expectation tangible. Peals of laughter, waving arms gathering families and friends together at a claimed spot in a prime location; back-slaps, affectionate hugs, and double-cheeked kisses. Blankets and rugs are scattered everywhere, the massive picnic baskets unpacked and carefully laid out by the huddled families, not unlike a massive Iftar gathering during Ramadan. It has been many years since Granada turned out for a citywide celebration by the common folk and nobles alike.

The plazas and streets are packed. Wide-eyed toddlers straddle their fathers' shoulders so they don't miss the spectacle. Hundreds tiptoe and jockey for position along the streets for the best view. Darting young boys flit and dance their games of tag and keep-away. Emboldened adolescents appraise the crowds in search of their heart's desire, occasionally being rewarded with a shy smile or the teasing glint of an eye. Wives gather together in throngs to titter and gossip, happy to be outside in the fresh air. The old folks are given special deference, of course, but even they have surrendered half their age to bright smiles and nods of appreciation over the coming events. Food vendors are tucked everywhere, their braziers already stoked and lit and loaded with fine fare. The delectable aromas from the drippings of the grilling meats upon crimson embers waft across the plazas and collect in the alleys like a succulent fog.

Thousands line both sides of the ashlar-paved royal road that begins at the central plaza adjacent to the River Darro on the south end of the Albayzín near the silk markets, then leads, under the steady gaze of the Bermejas Tower, on through the famous Pomegranate Gate, then up-up-up to the Alhambra. The road traverses the entire length of the palace as it slowly rises, pausing to turn into the Justice Gate, the formal entrance to the palace, then continuing on before bending southward to the al-Husayn Gate through the city's outer wall.

A three-tiered viewing stand has been hastily constructed just outside the Justice Gate. On the top tier sits Sultan Abu l-Hasan on his throne, dressed in his lavish finery, a dozen courtiers stationed nearby to attend to his every need. Also present are the Vizier Council and the most favored of the royal court. Defying protocol, Zoraya reclines at the sultan's side, her beauty radiant even through her gauzy veil, proudly displaying her now-massive pregnancy for all to admire. Fatima is nowhere to be seen. The tier below holds the city leaders and their guests—Supreme Mullah Abd Allah and the rest of the Supreme Council, the Council of Clerics, the Masters of the Guilds, and the most powerful merchants. On the lowest tier, more clerics, the most important of the qadis from the law courts, several prominent Sufi masters, a dozen teachers from the madrasa, various influence peddlers at court, three rabbis, including Zachariah al-Zuhri, and the royal physician and his two guests, Ezar and Danah. A smattering of foreign dignitaries is tucked into a corner and fussed over by a trio of courtiers. Heavily-armed, red-robed royal bodyguards are posted everywhere.

It is warm for a fall day, though not unpleasant. Perfect weather for what is planned. The celebration is to begin with a review of the elite units of Granada's army in full parade dress. Mounted knight-commanders, then cavalry, crossbowmen, and infantry. The troops will enter the city at the Elvira Gate, make their way to the central square, cross the River Darro at the Plaza Nueva, pass through the Pomegranate Gate up to the Alhambra and past the viewing stand to salute the sultan, then back out of the city. Afterward, speeches are planned, followed by a city-wide feast with music and song and dance that will stretch into the evening hours. For the privileged few, private parties will spill into the Alhambra's courtyards and gardens until the wee hours. Wine will discreetly flow, and illicit couples, emboldened by the festivities and relaxed protocols, will back into darkened crevices among the cypress hedges in the Partal Gardens, their soft groans muffled by the thousand different sounds of flowing water. It is to be a lavish affair unseen by the city since the victory of Sultan

Muhammad V over the Christians at Algeciras over a century prior.

A tickle on the back of Ali al-Attar's neck causes the old man to flinch, and suddenly uneasy, he glances over his shoulder to the west. *How odd.* He turns to assess the approaching line of clouds, then frowns. *What on earth?* The morning had been still and cloudless, crisp. Now, bulbous black clouds, swollen tight and menacing, stretch from the eastern to the western horizons on a line sharp enough to have been sliced by a dagger. The storm stretches back into the distance as far as the eye can see. No rain or lightning from within the roiling squall, which is also strange, and somehow ominous. The leading edge is just crossing the ring of mountains at the edge of the Vega. *Fifteen miles, maybe twenty.* The old man studies the stampeding storm line. His frown deepens. *Moving fast.*

He touches al-Zaghal on the shoulder, tips his head to the approaching storm. Al-Zaghal turns and studies the unsettling sight, also frowns, then leans and whispers to Venegas, who turns to look. The grand vizier grimaces, furiously whispers back. Venegas nervously looks to the flagman on the Vela Tower at the west end of the Alhambra, the highest point in the city. The man is to signal when the army passes the Pomegranate Gate. His flag is down. Venegas looks back to the line of threatening clouds and considers his options, which are practically nonexistent at this late moment, and guaranteed to trigger a sultanic explosion. He looks back to the tower. The flagman is now waving. He exchanges a communicative glance with al-Zaghal, who reluctantly nods, then turns and whispers to a courtier, who disappears. Concern is written across Ali al-Attar's face.

On top of the Justice Gate tower, a dozen fanfare trumpets are lifted in unison, then sound, resonant and loud. The brassy vibrato stills the drone of the crowd. All eyes focus on the parade ground just outside the gate. Breaths are held, and children are shushed and shuffled. *The army is coming! The army is coming!*

It takes the mounted knights several minutes to climb to the reviewing stand. The distant clop of high-stepping stallions is the first sign that the army draws near. Heads lean forward to look down the descending road to glimpse the lead elements. The cadenced *slap-slap-slap-slap* of a thousand boots striking stone joins in, growing louder and louder. As the heads of the mounted knights come into view, gushing *ooohs!* and *ahhhs!* rise from the crowd. Clapping spontaneously breaks out in a dozen places and quickly becomes deafening. Boabdil rides in the front line with the field generals. A knight victorious. Adoring whoops and hollers and whistles echo as the dashing knights approach the viewing stand. "Zahara! ZAHARA! Long Live Boabdil!" Boabdil barks a command, and in unison all the mounted knights bow to the sultan as they file past in their glory. The sultan lifts a hand in recognition. A thunderous reply from the knights, "ALLAHU ACKBAR! THERE IS NO VICTOR BUT ALLAH!" The strength of a mighty kingdom for all the world to admire.

As the review continues, a half-mile distant, on the northern side of the city, high on the ridge of the Albayzín overlooking the Alhambra, a dozen eyes, then a hundred lift to the sky with open mouths. *Dear Lord!* The brilliant azure cuts to black. The racing storm line seems low enough to reach up and touch. Loved ones are hurriedly gathered and rushed indoors.

The simultaneous flash of a thousand suns and a concussive, ear-splitting *BAMMMM!* as a jagged bolt of lightning leaps from the turbulent blackness to the belfry atop the Vela Tower of the Alhambra. In one quick recoil, ten thousand people duck and scream. In front of the viewing stand, stallions rear and whinny as the cavalrymen fight their reins for control. Several knights are bucked off, and one wild-eyed horse races off into the crowd, trampling a young girl before it is corralled. The army, which trails all the way back to the Pomegranate Gate, stops in its tracks, some units even scattering for cover, fearing they are under attack by some unseen enemy unleashing a cannon fusillade. Orders are quickly barked and units slowly reform then haphazardly resume their march.

Bamm-Bamm! A double strike to the ridgeline of the Albayzín. Booming thunder echoes off the walls of the palace. The sustained heavy rolling rumble can be felt deep in the gut.

The royal bodyguards are instantly on high alert, swords drawn, their bodies cocked into killing postures, eyes darting in search of an enemy. Archers on the walls of the palace nock their arrows and scan for targets. Within seconds a dozen bodyguards surround the sultan and Zoraya. Alarm bells in the palace begin to sound. *Clang-clang-clang!* Pause. *Clang-clang-clang!* Pause. *Clang-clang-clang!*

Bamm! Concurrent flashes and strikes begin to hit every few seconds now across the city. *Bamm! BAMM!* The city is bathed in a continuous, rolling thunder that does not let up. As day turns to night, the wind instantly changes from a gentle breeze to gale force.

Wide eyes rise to the sky in sheer terror as the monster settles its girth across the city. The crowds are transfixed by the remarkable sight, frozen in place by their shock. Incredibly, the storm line seems to slow then stop as it inhales and swells tighter still. The hickories and oaks creak and groan as they are bent over against their will and violated. Fathers have to shout to be heard above the wind and thunder as they frantically try to gather their families. *Leave the blankets! Go! Grab your sister! Hurry!* Massive, bone-crunching snaps as dozens of trees begin to give up their lives. The cypresses in the gardens of the Generalife, tall and thin as young girls, are pushed nearly horizontal then violently uprooted.

Bamm! BAMMM! Bamm!

Tables and stalls are blown down across the city, launching reams of detritus into the swirling torrent. Screams rise like smoke as people desperately seek shelter, their voices weaving together to form a horrified tapestry of trill.

The overwhelming smell on the wind shouts *RAIN!*

BAMMM! Another close strike, this time near the Hall of the Ambassadors. Panic races through the city.

The first raindrop, heavy as a marble, smacks al-Zaghal on his forehead. A smattering of heavy drops, then nothing, then a rushing *WHOOSH!* that races across the Darro Valley then up and over the Alhambra. The air instantly turns liquid, the rain so thick it cuts visibility to ten paces. The roar becomes deafening, broken only by the piercing lightning strikes and bone-rattling thunder, which continue unabated.

BAMMM! Bamm! Bamm!

Everyone is instantly soaked to the bone. The royal bodyguards have begun ushering the cowering dignitaries down off the viewing stand.

To the chagrin of the royal bodyguards, the sultan has stubbornly refused to leave until all are safely off. Zoraya is already on her way back to the Lion Palace, flanked by her mute black African bodyguards. Battle horns sound as troops begin to muster from the Alhambra's garrison in the Alcazaba.

Bamm! BAMMM!

The sultan continues to stare at the flooded parade ground before him, now empty. Pools of water a foot deep are gathering in low spots and the storm drains are quickly overrun, unleashing muddy torrents that begin to cut deep gashes down the hillside. In a dozen places the road is undercut, begins to sag, and then in one awful instant slides from the ridge, carrying troops with it. The townsfolk are still scattering like crazed ants. The sultan mutters, incredulously, "I do not understand. What is happening? I do not understand."

Al-Zaghal touches his brother's shoulder, shouting to be heard above the mayhem. "Sire! It is time to make our way to the palace. We must get you to safety." He motions to the cadre of royal bodyguards.

The sultan is lamely shaking his head. "I do not understand. What is happening?"

"Brother! We must go. Now!" Al-Zaghal turns the sultan to lock eyes with him. He sees fear. And panic. *Dear Lord.*

"I am cursed. My city is cursed. Allah despises me."

Al-Zaghal shakes the sultan's shoulders. "Brother! Brother!"

"I AM CURSED! THE CITY IS CURSED! DAMN YOU ALL! MY CITY IS CURSED!" He is raving like a lunatic.

Al-Zaghal shakes him harder. "BROTHER!"

The sultan convulses. He winces, then an ugly grimace, then he shudders. His right cheek and eye twitch violently, and then Sultan Abu l-Hasan, son of Abu Nasr Sa'd, ruler of al-Andalus, twenty-first sultan of Granada, elder of the Nasrid clan, defender of the faith, collapses into a sodden heap.

Al-Zaghal turns to the royal bodyguards. "Quickly. Carry the sultan to the Lion Palace. Quickly, men! And find the royal physician. He was on the lowest tier. Have him meet us there. MAKE HASTE!"

Bamm! BAMMM!

"Put him on the bed." David barks his orders like a veteran officer. The royal bodyguards comply. "Gently." The sultan is alarmingly flaccid, his eyes open but vacant and unseeing. His lips struggle to open and close, as if he is trying desperately to say something but can't. His body has been paralyzed by some strange malady. That, or shock from the storm. Venegas, al-Zaghal, and Ali al-Attar are there, as is the captain of the royal bodyguard and a dozen of his men. The flashes and rattles and booms of the storm continue unabated, though slightly muted inside the deep recesses of the Lion Palace.

A disheveled and veil-less Zoraya marches into the room and screams. She turns on al-Zaghal. "What has happened to my husband?"

"He collapsed. Fortunately, Hakim al-Adani was close by. We brought him here immediately."

She waddles to the side of the bed. "Dear Lord, what is wrong with his face?"

The man's eye and cheek and lips on the right side have melted into a terrible sag.

David answers, "I believe he has suffered an injury to the blood vessels in his head, my lady. The right side of his body is paralyzed."

Zoraya pivots and stares at the royal physician, unable to speak. Finally, she manages a pathetic whisper, "Paralyzed?"

"It may be temporary, my lady. I have seen this before. Time will tell."

"Who is she?" Zoraya's tone turns ugly, accusatory. "I do not want her here!" She is staring directly at Danah.

"My lady, this is Danah Amiriya. My assistant." Danah bows. "And that is Hakim al-Mufaddal." Ezar does not. "I require their services."

Zoraya is unraveling quickly. She cradles her belly and sways back and forth, unsteady on her feet. Pale and looking as if she might faint, she is frightened beyond belief, to be sure, and understandably rattled and vulnerable. A rare sight.

Danah eases to her side. "My lady, you must sit. The baby. Come, let me help you out of these wet clothes and see to you and the child."

Zoraya is wide-eyed and wary.

Danah gently takes her elbow. "Come, my lady. I must see to your baby. Hakim al-Adani and Hakim al-Mufaddal will tend to your husband. He is in excellent hands. Please. I must see to your baby. Come."

Amazingly, Zoraya allows herself to be led from the room. Her African bodyguards follow the two women to her chambers.

David turns to al-Zaghal. "I need all of you out of here. Leave us alone so we can do our work."

Al-Zaghal is hesitant.

"Now." Not a request.

"Very well. Captain. Station your men outside the door." A curt nod is returned, and with a flick of his wrist all the bodyguards except the captain evaporate.

Ali al-Attar looks up and cups his ears. "The storm appears to be weakening."

Venegas softly says, "What a fool I am. With Ali's warning to the approaching storm I should have immediately canceled the event."

The old warrior offers no consolation, but al-Zaghal says, "No one is to blame. It was a freak storm. I assumed it would simply pass over us. Who could know it would end like this?"

Ali al-Attar takes a deep breath. "I will gather the knight-commanders. We must restore order in the city. I will have the troops fan out and see to those who are injured or in need of help." He limps toward the door.

Al-Zaghal says, "Good." He turns to the captain. "I will see that the Alhambra is secured. Bring the hakim whatever he needs."

David says, "Thank you. For now, I need towels and hot water. And blankets. My medical bag and medicines are at the Bermejas Hospital. Send an escort with Hakim al-Mufaddal to retrieve those." He turns to Ezar. "Bring the henbane and hemlock pastes, and the black nightshade elixir. And my matula." He lifts a finger. "Oh, and do not forget the poppy seed and valerian root elixir."

Ezar nods.

David turns back to al-Zaghal. "Time is critical. Make haste!"

The room leaps to action.

A single hooded figure stands hunched over in the Darro Plaza, leaning on his staff against the whipping wind, soaked to the bone, defying the lightning to strike him dead. He lifts his hands to the roiling black sky and shouts, "Woe to Granada for breaking the peace! War is coming. Woe! Woe to Granada! Her fall is at hand!"

"I have done all I can for now. I need some sleep."

Al-Zaghal nods. "I will stand vigil."

"Good. I will be back at first light. He should not wake before then, but if he does, send for me immediately."

"I will." Al-Zaghal hesitates. "What are his chances for a full recovery?"

Silence. Finally, David says, "Difficult to know. His paralysis is extensive. How he fares these next few days will be key."

Al-Zaghal reaches up and touches the physician's shoulder. "Thank you for your help."

David nods, then turns and leaves.

The pre-dawn trill of the willow warblers awakens al-Zaghal. He rubs his eyes, throws off his blanket, sits up on the divan, and stretches. He cups his ears and listens. Nothing. The storm has passed. He whispers, "Praise be to Allah."

He stands to check on his brother. He lights the lamp, then turns and sees that the sultan's eyes are wide open and staring up at the dark ceiling. "Ali?" He rushes to the bedside. "Ali, can you hear me?"

The sultan's head does not move, but his eyes slowly track to the left to engage his brother's face.

Al-Zaghal beams. *There is life in those eyes.* Against his will, the grizzled warrior tears up. "All praise to Allah. I was so worried about you, Brother."

The sultan's lips begin to quiver on his half-melted face, then attempt to form a word. Unsuccessfully.

"Steady there. Rest. Your voice will come back soon enough. Rest, Brother. You need rest."

The man's lips continue their struggle. Finally, a single whispered word. "Prumm. Muss." His eyes are alive, but his body is frozen in place.

"What is it, Ali?"

"Prom-muss."

"Promise? Promise what, Ali?" Al-Zaghal leans closer.

"Prom-mess . . . mee." His words are heavily slurred. He stops to try again, and it takes everything he has to lift the words out one by one. "Prom-mess . . . mee . . . thot . . . yu . . . wull . . . surve . . . oz . . . sul-tann." A deep breath. "Til . . . bet-tor. Not . . . Bo. Ab. Dil. Nev-er . . . Bo-ab-dil." His eyes bulge, then fold closed from the exhaustion. They reopen as slits. He hisses, "Prom-mess . . . mee."

"I promise, Brother. I will stand as Sultan of Granada in your stead until you are recovered."

"Tank . . . yu." The sultan drifts back into sleep.

Al-Zaghal stares at the sultan for a full minute as he mulls the implications. He steps to the door, opens it, and says to the royal bodyguard, "Bring Venegas; I must speak with him immediately. And fetch the royal physician."

"Consider it done, my lord."

"My husband is a fool."

"Mm." The wizard fingers his cotton-white beard as he mulls this over. The sag of his cheek twitches with a life of its own. He clears his throat. "And yet it seems that your husband acted shrewdly, Sultana. After all, he managed to pass his crown to his brother and bypass his heir."

Boabdil sneers, then barks, "We will see about that!"

Fatima glares at her son, chastises him with her eyes. *Keep your mouth shut.*

The wizard observes everything and files these tidbits away for later use.

It is after midnight, deep in the twisting caverns of the Albayzín. It took Fatima two days to get a message to the High

Elder of the Abencerrajes, and another day for a reply. The instructions were more elaborate this time, and even then, mother and son were blindfolded for the final leg of the journey. This is their third clandestine meeting, the first with Boabdil present.

"Tell me, Sultana. What is it that you desire of the Abencerrajes?"

"My husband lies paralyzed in his bed, a broken man. Al-Zaghal is a warrior. He knows nothing of the nuances of court politics or how to run a kingdom. Now is the time for us to rise against him, while he is still unsure of himself and the court is in disarray."

"A coup, Sultana? A treasonous offense." His ebony eyes are sparkling.

"In point of fact, Abu al-Haytham, I intend to honor Granada's laws and traditions by ensuring that the sultan's only son and heir is placed upon the throne where he belongs. For the good of the kingdom."

"Yes, of course. Forgive me, Sultana, but I am told Zoraya is close to delivering her baby. What if the child is male? A second heir. With you and Boabdil exiled from the palace and Zoraya in control of your invalid husband, I suspect the young prince will soon be declared the new heir to the throne."

Boabdil tenses but manages to keep silent. The wizard enjoys watching the young man squirm. *So weak and undisciplined.*

"Let me worry about the Christian whore and her abomination. I assure you, there will be no legitimate heir but Boabdil. But we must act quickly, while there is still time."

"Yes. Time." He has already intuited what she has in mind. "As you know, Sultana, al-Zaghal controls the army. Any perceived coup attempt will be confronted swiftly and without mercy."

"Come, Abu al-Haytham, let us be candid. You and I both know that the Abencerrajes have infiltrated the sultan's army. You have a great many loyal officers now safely tucked within its ranks. Enough, certainly, to split al-Zaghal's chain of command and render them impotent, at least for the time it would take us to take control of the city."

"Mmmm."

"And you and I both know, Abu al-Haytham, that the Abencerrajes can muster a well-armed and formidable militia within the Albayzín at a moment's notice if you but give the word. A militia sufficient in size to storm the Alhambra if given the proper . . . opportunity." A sly smile. "I can name the commanders and their muster points if need be."

The wizard stares blankly at her, calculating. *She is bluffing; but still. Good information. Too good.* He resolves to assess how her spies have been so effective in ferreting out these tidbits.

"I ask you again, Sultana. What is it that you desire of the Abencerrajes?"

"Your loyalty. And your support."

"Ahhh, I see. Loyalty and support. Valuable things, those."

"Loyalty and support, Abu al-Haytham, to put Boabdil on the throne where he belongs. I need your help to paralyze the army. And Boabdil needs your militia behind him as a fighting force."

"I see." The wizard resumes stroking his beard. "Suppose, Sultana, just for the sake of argument, that we agree to help you. How exactly would the Abencerrajes profit?"

Good. He is coming round. "I desire what you desire, Abu al-Haytham."

"And that is?"

"To see the clan of the Abencerrajes returned to the stature they deserve. A stature they once proudly held."

He stares at her, expressionless. *Clever woman.* This is indeed his only desire.

"There will be gold, certainly. And ten percent of the tax receipts levied on the silk guilds."

The wizard lifts a finger as he shakes his head. "Forgive me, Sultana, but we already have more gold than we require."

The gears in Fatima's mind whir as she studies the old man. "The row of palaces on the south side of the Alhambra adjacent to the medina will be yours to do with as you see fit. They will be formally renamed the Palace of the Abencerrajes, and made as lavish as the Lion Palace. A permanent dwelling in the Alhambra for the elders and their families, just as your ancestors enjoyed." A wry smile. "Before being slaughtered and expelled by my husband's father."

The wizard's eyes widen ever so slightly. A presence in the Alhambra is a key piece of the puzzle of their decades-long plan to restore the clan's power and prestige. "Better. And—?"

"And two positions on Boabdil's Vizier Council."

"One of which would be Grand Vizier, of course."

Fatima echoes, "One of which would be Grand Vizier."

"Excellent." The wizard studies her. "And Boabdil's First Wife shall be chosen by the elders. An Abencerraje maiden of suitable beauty and standing. Our clans must be formally joined if there is to be lasting peace."

Fatima hesitates. She did not anticipate this move.

Boabdil's mouth opens to challenge this brazen demand, but he is silenced by his mother's intimidating glare.

The wizard continues, "She would be subject to your approval, of course."

"Done."

Abu al-Haytham, High Elder of the Abencerrajes, claps his hands together. "Very well, then. I shall take your request to the elders."

Boabdil snarls, "Be quick. Time is short."

The wizard scrutinizes the young man. *So weak. Perfect for our needs.* "Time is indeed short." He turns to Fatima. "Expect a decision by week's end, Sultana."

She nods and rises. Boabdil and Abu al-Haytham follow suit. The wizard hobbles to the door, raps out a code. The door opens, and two bodyguards enter, each bearing a blindfold.

"That is hard to believe. Why would the Moors leave Alhama so weakly garrisoned?" Rodrigo Ponce de León, Marquess of Cádiz, stares across the plain from high in the tower above the keep of Castillo de San Sebastián, castle-garrison of Marchena, forty miles east of Sevilla. He turns to his lieutenant. "Bring the man here. I want to hear it from his own lips."

"Certainly, my lord." He signals a guard, who turns and leaves.

Ponce de León links his hands behind his back and begins to pace. *Opportunity or trap?*

A moment later the man limps in and kneels. "My lord." He is gaunt and stinks, his filthy clothes in tatters, his hair knotted and matted. The man's face is bruised and scratched, as if he has been beaten.

"Rise." Ponce de León studies him. "You have seen better days, sir."

"Forgive my appearance, my lord. After I escaped I made my way through the borderlands and came as fast as I could. Nearly froze to death. I have not eaten a proper meal in a week, my lord. I knew you would want to hear the news immediately, so I came as quickly as I could."

"You did well. What is your name?"

"Pedro. Pedro de Albiz, m'lord."

"From?"

"From Paradas, m'lord. A stableman and groomer at the inn there. I joined your army to tend the horses as a hostler in your cavalry."

"I see. How long were you a prisoner in Alhama?"

"Nearly two years. I was captured on the raid outside Antequera. You may remember, m'lord. The Moors attacked our rearguard and burned the supply wagons and captured a great many of us."

Ponce de León glances at his adjutant for confirmation, and the man nods. "And how did you manage to escape, Pedro? From all that I have heard, Alhama is one of the most heavily fortified Moorish cities."

"It surely is, m'lord. High walls and many towers, perched on the edge of a deep river gorge. Praise be to God, two months ago I was released from Alhama's wicked dungeon. When the emir left with his entourage, the Moorish princes needed hostlers for their mounts. Finest stallions I have ever seen, m'lord. Purebloods."

"Go on."

"Well, m'lord, I watched, and I learned as I went about my work. The city walls along the river gorge are virtually unguarded. The Moors must feel that no man in his right mind would plan an attack from that vantage. The cliffs fall two hundred feet straight down to the river. And Alhama's garrison is remarkably unmanned. Three hundred knights, more or less. Half as many archers.

"Strange indeed for a city of that importance. You are sure, Pedro?"

"I am, m'lord. As hostler, I have been to all parts of the city, even inside the emir's palace. And, of course, the garrison stables inside the castle."

"Very well. Go on."

"Well, m'lord, I bided my time and planned my escape. I stole some rope, and late one night I climbed the wall and let myself down over the cliffs of the gorge. Alas, my rope proved too short. Nearly broke my neck when I dropped the last thirty feet. I managed to crawl to the river and then floated down a mile. I limped overland through the mountains. Had some close calls with Moorish patrols, but I managed."

"I see. And you are sure that the emir of Alhama has left the city?"

"Positive, m'lord. Just before I escaped he left for the wedding of his brother. In Vélez-Málaga, down by the coast. I saddled his horse myself. A pure white beauty, m'lord. He took half of Alhama's garrison with him. I heard one of the Moorish princes say he would be gone a month, perhaps longer."

"Interesting. And you think some climbers could scale the cliffs of the gorge and slip into the city unchecked?"

The man nods. "I am sure they could, m'lord. Security is very lax. They must figure that they have little cause for worry being so deep in Moorish territory."

"Indeed. Could you draw us a map of the walls and towers, Pedro, and the layout of the city? Where the castle-garrison is situated? And where the noble families reside?"

"I could, m'lord."

Ponce de León joins eyes with the man and stares intently, sifting the story. "Tell me, Pedro. Could you lead my army there undiscovered?"

The man considers this, then nods. "I believe I could, m'lord. We would need to pass through the wild valleys of the Sierra Alzerifa. They should prove remote enough to elude Moorish patrols, I think, provided we only move under the cover of darkness."

"Excellent. Pedro, you have done your marquess and your queen a great service. Lead my army undetected to the river gorge and into Alhama, and henceforth you will be known to all as Don Pedro de Albiz. You shall have a hundred hectares of choice pasture for your own, Don Pedro. And on it, fifty of my best horses." The man's eyes widen. Ponce de León turns to his adjutant. "Get the man a bath and a good meal, and see to his wounds. And have his family brought to Cadíz. They shall want for nothing."

"I will see to it personally, my lord."

"And gather my knight-commanders. I want them all here within the hour. We have planning to do."

"His progress has been remarkable."

David nods. "Indeed. The sultan is a lucky man."

Danah accompanies David to the Alhambra each morning to check on the sultan. Her first time inside the Nasrid palace was on the day of the storm. She is giddy still over the endless marvels of form and decoration. And the water. Dear Lord, the water! Her head adorably cranes and bends and double-takes as she walks. She points here and there, oohing and ahhing, giggling over the impossibilities spread before her. The place is a feast for the eyes. David indulges her with patient explanations of the history of the various structures and the architect's intent, the calculated dance of light and sound, the playful banter between Zamrak's poetry and the rambling arabesque foliage, the dizzying patterns of the multicolored ceramic inlays laced with hidden meanings, the understated marvels of aquatic engineering powering the magical ring of lions in the center of the marbled Lion Palace courtyard.

As they head back to the Atfal Hospital, they pass out through the Umayyad arches of the Comares Palace and into the medina. The guardsmen straighten their pikes but otherwise do not move. "It seems as if the sultan will fully recover. His limp is getting better by the day, and the sag of his right cheek is almost gone."

David replies, "Indeed. Some slurring of words still, but vastly improved. A remarkable recovery by any measure."

"He has an excellent hakim tending him."

"Soon, two excellent hakims."

They exchange warm smiles. David lowers his voice. "Even though the sultan is healing, a relapse is always possible in cases like this. The man needs rest. Something, I am afraid, he has never been especially good at."

"No."

"Did you notice that the Nasrid signet ring is back on his hand? Evidently al-Zaghal has transferred the sultanate back to him. He apparently feels he is well enough to rule again, though I have my doubts."

They walk on.

David continues, "Zoraya has taken a liking to you, Danah."

"So it would seem."

"Coming from her, that is quite a compliment. She will want you to assist with the birth."

"She mentioned it. I would be happy to assist."

He stops, turns to her. "You must be careful with Zoraya, Danah. If the gossip is to be believed, she stands willing and able to crush any living thing that gets in her way or rubs her wrongly. Or even appears to be getting cozy with her husband. A woman like that, suffering the rigors of childbirth for the first time . . ." He whistles. "Tread carefully, my dear."

Danah chuckles. "I will. Tending to her is like picking up a deathstalker scorpion barehanded."

They both laugh, then resume their walk and are soon at the Justice Gate. The guardsmen scrutinize them carefully, then raise their pikes to let them through. As they pass from shadow back into sunlight, David says, "Shall we get back to work?"

Danah smiles. "We shall, Hakim al-Adani."

"But, my lord, the queen was quite emphatic. There is to be no raiding in Moorish territory without her express permission," says Don Pedro Enriques, one of Ponce de León's field generals.

Ponce de León turns on him and shouts, "You think I have no ears, man?!"

Don Pedro blanches.

Ponce de León takes a deep breath to calm himself. "There is no time to consult with the queen on this matter, Don Pedro. We act now, or not at all. Surprise is everything. I will write to the queen, tell her of our quest and its special circumstances. Then I will beg her forgiveness."

Appreciative chuckles circle the room.

"And I will entreat King Fernando to immediately send reinforcements to relieve us. But we will need to hold the city for at least a fortnight."

"We will hold the city for a year, my lord!" cries Don Diego de Merlo, another field general. The man has always had a penchant for boasting.

"Rest assured, Don Diego, the Moors will immediately arrive in force from Granada once we kick the hornet's nest. They will have ten times our number, perhaps twenty. We will be in for the fight of our lives."

Sober nods.

"And if it proves to be a trap?" asks Don Sancho de Avila, one of Ponce de León's cavalry officers.

Ponce de León turns, hands on hips, to stare the man down. He softly says, "If it is a trap, Don Sancho, then we will all suffer an honorable death in service to the queen." A wolfish grin. "What better way to die than by fighting under Christ's banner, gentlemen. We all have our crusader indulgences from the pope. Our souls are cleansed. When we meet up again in heaven I will buy the first round of ale!"

Laughter abounds.

Ponce de León's smile runs away. "God desires this attack, gentlemen. I can feel it in my bones. Pedro's arrival was divine providence. Imagine for a moment what happens when we capture Alhama. Alhama, with its famous baths. Alhama, with its impregnable walls and castle. Alhama, guardian of the sultan's royal road linking Granada and Málaga. Alhama, lifeline of the Moorish kingdom." His eyes circle the room. "Imagine for a moment. Alhama is only thirty miles from the Alhambra, men. Thirty miles to the pride of Sultan Muley Hacén, leader of the Moors." He beams as he scans the room. His bright smile settles into an ugly sneer as he hisses. "Alhama shall suffer mightily, gentlemen. I claim vengeance for the rape of Zahara. Vengeance! Vengeance for our slain knights of the Order. Vengeance for our violated maidens. Vengeance for our children sold into slavery.

Mark my words, these Moorish heathens will pay for their crimes. Damn the Moors! God wills this attack! I will this attack! Brothers, we shall oil our swords with Moorish blood!"

Thunderous assent.

"Ready our troops; we leave at first light. And inform Ortega de Prado to gather a dozen of his best climbers. We must travel light and fast. No supply wagons will accompany us past Antequera. Each man carries his own gear and rations. I want to be at Alhama at midnight five days hence, gentlemen, ready to wreak havoc. Understood?"

Eager shouts of "Hear! Hear!"

"See to it, then. We ride for the glory of God! Long live the queen!"

"LONG LIVE THE QUEEN!"

— *THREE* —

The Sun

Look at the beautiful sun:
As it rises, it shows one golden eyebrow,
Plays miser with the other one,

But we know that soon
It will spread out a radiant veil
Over all.

A marvelous mirror
That appears in the East
Only to hide again at dusk.

The sky is saddened
When the sun leaves
And puts on mourning robes.

I believe that falling stars
Are nothing more
Than sky's gem-hard tears.

Ibn Abī l-Haytham
(d. 1232 C.E. — Sevilla)

Alhama

An hour before first light. The air is still, but damp and biting. A heavy frost will settle in by morning. Downy clouds drift lazily along without a care, their outlines kissed by the glow of the moon loitering high above. A field mouse skitters in the brush along the edge of the river, casting a wary eye over its shoulders as it flits about from shadow to shadow scrounging for food. It knows well that death stalks the night. An eagle-owl, the thing it most fears, is perched on the mottled bough of a sycamore deep within the river gorge. He stares down the hook of his beak, silent as death, his eyes like two amber moons, soft and shining under heavy lashes. He spots the mouse, but sighs, wishing for larger quarry— a jackrabbit, perhaps, or maybe some slick-skinned water creature. Suddenly forlorn, he blinks, pivots his head upstream, and calls for his lover; but he is not answered. Not a single sound rises above the soft, pleasing churn and gurgle of the river. Even the jinn have finally made their way to bed in the untroubled calm before the day's awakening. At sunrise the swallows will leap from their cliff dwellings by the thousands to unleash a deafening barrage of chatter and shriek as they playfully twist and turn and dive along the track of the gorge as it bends sharply around the eastern end of the town.

The knights trudge slowly downstream in single file, clinging to the bank for cover. The black water swirls around their numbed thighs. Pulsing jets of breath-fog punctuate the entourage as they methodically pick their way. No armor, not even chain mail or hauberks; lightly armed, only short swords and daggers. Great loops of rope circle their shoulders, and grappling hooks dangle from their belts. *Escaladors*—climbers.

Ortega de Prado lifts a hand at the sound of the eagle-owl's cry, and in unison his men halt. He cups his ears and listens as his head pivots. Nothing. His eyes slowly rise up the cliffs, surveying. High above, he can make out the silhouette of two towers, linked by a long wall topped by a battlement. Alhama's alcazaba. For nearly a minute he stares intently at the moonlit wall. No sentries to be seen. Not a single torch or lamp. His eyes scan the cliff face as he begins to methodically plot a route up to their target. Challenging, to be sure, especially near the lip of the gorge, but not unclimbable. He motions to his men, who scurry out of the water and up the bank, beginning to ready their gear.

The heady scent of wet iron rises from the neat inky circle spreading from the turbaned head of the prostrate body. The lone sentry manning the wall. From the top of the westernmost tower overlooking the gorge, Ortega de Prado lights a lamp to signal the hundred handpicked knights hiding in the grove of oaks a long arrow shot away. The edge of the tree line instantly fills, then a steady stream of men emerges at a quick trot along the lip of the gorge carrying long, skinny scaling ladders. Weapons and gear have been padded, then tied, to silence them. They make for the short stretch of wall only a tower's width from the precipice. The wall runs fifty feet due west, away from the edge of the gorge before angling sharply back to the north, safely hidden from view from all the alcazaba's towers save the one Ortega de Prado now commands.

Within minutes the first man tops the wall. Congratulations are whispered as instructions are hand-signaled and men are ushered off to allow those next on the ladders access to the parapet. The knights gather within the safe confines of the tower and assemble into squads, then begin to unstrap and ready their killing tools.

Don Pedro Enriques, knight-commander of the hundred, clasps the escalador's shoulder. "Well done, Ortega."

The man beams. "One sentry on the wall, Don Pedro. One. And only two manning the tower. Can you imagine?"

"Fools. The cliff?"

Ortega sniffs. "Child's play."

Don Pedro chuckles. "Bravo, sir. Which way to the garrison?"

"Below us, two towers down, hugging the gorge-side wall. Not a single light to be seen. Stupid Moors must be sleeping."

"Excellent. Take your men and eliminate it." He turns to his second in command. "Juan, you have the walls and towers of the alcazaba. Once they are secure, station your bowmen. Kill anyone who ventures out or tries to sound the alarm."

"Understood, Don Pedro."

"I will take my men and make for Alhama's south gate. God willing, the marquess should soon be there with the rest of the army. Hopefully unannounced. Once inside the town we will fan out and take the rest of the walls and towers, then deal with any militia the Moors manage to mobilize." He stops to lock eyes with both of his officers. "Remember. No quarter for any Moor knight who lifts a sword against us. For Zahara."

The two men nod. "For Zahara."

"Surprise is everything. Keep the killing quiet for as long as possible. Godspeed."

"Godspeed."

"Godspeed."

The sentry slumps on a stool, head down, his back to the wall, asleep at his post. Padded footfall startles him awake, but as his eyes blink open a crossbow bolt buries itself deep in his brain. The Moor's body relaxes back to sleep, his head twisting unnaturally to the side, his eyes wide and pointing in different directions. Ortega de Prado raises a hand, stilling the attackers. Swords are drawn, battle axes and maces at the ready.

He presses his ear to the door. Nothing. He turns and issues hand signals to his men. Grips tighten on their weapons. Ortega carefully lifts the latch and cracks the door. Still nothing. He opens it farther and slowly leans forward to survey the room. Without looking back, he lifts his hand and counts with his thumb and two fingers—one, two, three—then makes a fist.

Without a battle cry, the knights slip into the barracks and fan out among the sleeping mats, then begin madly swinging their weapons. The Moors don't stand a chance. As confused, sleepy heads raise from pillows they are hewn from crown to chin. The skulls of the prostrate men are crushed like eggshells; arms and legs are severed, throats slashed, lungs punctured. Truncated, terrified yelps, shocked whimpers, and helpless cries of mercy spread through the room. Trembling hands raise in pathetic self-defense, only to be sliced off at the elbows with a mighty *whoosh!* The victims stare aghast at their spurting stumps until a spiked mace finds its home, splattering brains against the wall. Others sit helplessly on their mats, hands clutching their slit throats, trying desperately to staunch the gobs of blood. As they choke on their own fluids they open and close their mouths like hooked fish tossed on a bank. The floor grows slick with gore as the knights methodically sow havoc from one end of the room to the other. Not a single Moor even raises a blade in defense. When the business is done, a dozen of Ortega's men walk slowly among the rows of mats, daggers drawn. Here and there they kneel down, whisper, "For Zahara," push their blades into beating hearts of those maimed but still alive. Gurgling sighs, then stillness.

The same scenario plays out in parallel on the first and second floors. Within minutes, the entire Moorish garrison is neutralized. Ortega exits the carnage, wipes his feet and blade on the dead sentry, and steps out onto the battlement to survey their progress in securing the alcazaba. He scans the walls and towers, sees the crossbowmen crouching at their assigned stations. The courtyard is empty except for a dozen bodies scattered about. Satisfied, he sheaths his broadsword, then lifts a hand and waves to the knights atop the tower on the opposite side of the alcazaba, and he is answered. Ortega smiles. Not a single alarm bell has sounded. Complete surprise. He turns to his second in command. "Post a dozen men on the gorge walls and towers, then gather the rest of the troops and make for the gate. Don Rodrigo and the army should be arriving any minute, and they will need our help. Now that we have the alcazaba, the town must be taken. Rest assured, all hell is going to break loose once the Moors realize what is happening."

"Understood, my lord."

In the distance, Ortega hears what he had hoped not to. *Clang-clang-clang-clang. Clang-clang-clang-clang. Clang-clang-clang-clang.* He curses. "Quickly, man!"

The distant sound of an alarm bell stirs the commanding officer of the small redoubt across the river gorge from the city. Set atop a hill a half-mile due east, the modest fortification houses a dozen troops that man an observation post charged with reporting any unusual movements on the rolling hills to the east of the city.

The officer rises, annoyed by the intrusion, lights a lamp, dresses, then steps outside into the chill. He pulls his cloak tight. Predictably, the sentry is asleep at his post. He kicks the man awake then steps to the short wall and stares into the darkness toward Alhama. He senses that something isn't right. The tepid moon is not much help; he can make out the outline of the city walls in the distance, but no more. A second, muted bell joins the first. Then a third at the far eastern end of the city walls. The officer frowns. He cups his ears and concentrates. Nothing but the bells. He looks over his shoulder. The diffuse gray of dawn can just be discerned. He curses. Sunrise is still twenty minutes away; too long to be useful.

The sentry joins him. "Trouble, sir?"

"Not sure." A fourth bell joins, and a moment later the first bell drops out, leaving three again. Then only two.

"I do not like the sound of that. Wake the men."

The sentry disappears into the building, and five minutes later all are standing by the wall, staring at the ghost of a city.

The distant sounds of battle can now be heard, faint but unmistakable—muted shouts, screams, the distinct ping of steel on steel. In the brightening gray, tendrils of smoke can be seen rising from several of the towers.

The officer calmly says, "The city is under attack."

One of his men replies, "But that makes no sense, sir. The infidels would never come this far into the kingdom. A suicide mission."

The officer grunts. "Whoever it is, Alhama appears to be in serious jeopardy."

After a few tense moments, the first golden beam breaks over the distant hills, awakening the landscape. The officer points. "See. There, by the north tower. Knights battling on the wall." He points southward. "And look. The flag flying over the garrison in the alcazaba." He curses. "Crusader cross! Damned Christians are in our city, boys!" He turns, "Jalil, saddle a horse. I want you to ride for Granada and inform the Alhambra that Alhama is under attack. Tell them that a Christian army has arrived in force and breached the walls. The city is in grave peril and must be rescued. Now ride, damn you, and ride like the wind!" He draws his broadsword. "You men, gather your weapons. We will join the fight!" The place erupts with activity.

The fight endures until dusk and is remarkably brutal given that a sizable army of veteran Christian knights face down a rag-tag Moorish militia composed mostly of poorly armed townsfolk, artisans, and field laborers. Moorish nobles and knights spring from their lavish carmens to frantically organize the militia along neighborhood lines, and the remaining troops that survived the assault on the alcazaba and the towers and walls assemble into units that are put in charge of the defense of the medina and the emir's palace. Makeshift barricades are erected, fires are lit, and crossbowmen soon line the rooftops, ready to rain havoc down upon the advancing Christians. Alhama is awash in clanging bells as the city desperately tries to discern the exact nature of the threat and organize some sort of defense. Word spreads rapidly. "Christians are in the city! Christians are in the city! The infidels are upon us! Make haste! Get your weapons! Make haste!"

Once inside the gates, taking the lightly-manned towers along the outer walls is no major feat for Ponce de León's men, but pitched battles in the medina quickly become fierce as the Moors realize that their beloved Alhama is at risk of capture. Their battle cry becomes, "Defend Alhama or die!" By any reckoning the Moors fight fearlessly, especially after they see that no quarter will be given to those who choose surrender. The fighting slowly spreads from the alcazaba eastward, creeping building by building, street by street, neighborhood by neighborhood. The Christian losses begin to mount at an alarming rate, but steady progress is made, and by late afternoon the emir's palace is the last remaining Moorish stronghold. The emir's royal guards mount a last-ditch stand, which is fierce and brutal—a fight to the death.

In the fading light, Ponce de León finally climbs the blood-drenched steps of the palace. All told, he has lost almost a quarter of his men and several of his key officers, including Don Pedro Enriques. As he reaches the tall wooden outer door, a blood-spattered Don Diego de Merlo and Don Sancho de Avila greet him with weary smiles. "The city is ours, Don Rodrigo."

A sober nod. "The Moors fought bravely, but God's Grace has prevailed. May the valiant knights who died in our service rest in peace." Both captains make the sign of the cross. "Make sure we have the gates manned and guards posted on all the walls. There is little doubt that riders are already on their way to Granada. We will soon be surrounded by a Moor army, gentlemen. No more than a day, perhaps two. We must be ready for the onslaught."

"We will be ready, Don Rodrigo."

A curt nod. "Take me to the emir's suite."

As they pick their way through the heaps of bodies, Ponce de León continues his instructions. "Release the prisoners from the dungeons and see to their care. Then round up any of the city elders still alive and put them in the dungeon for safe keeping. Make sure they have only as much food and water as they gave our men. Gather as many of their weapons as you can find; they will be needed soon enough. Oh, and confiscate all the grain and foodstuffs in the city. Store it in the alcazaba. And secure the cisterns and wells. They will be needed."

"Our dead?"

"Enlist the townsfolk to help dig the graves. Our fallen shall have proper Christian burials. We can use the gardens of the central plaza; the soil will be soft there."

"Shall we bury the Moors as well?"

Ponce de León stops to consider this. "No. Strip them and stack them outside the city gates like cordwood. There will be no burial for the Moorish knights. I want to send a welcome message to Sultan Muley Hacén that cannot be mistaken."

As they reach the top of the stairs, Don Diego says, "The emir's quarters, Don Rodrigo."

Ponce de León enters the expansive suite and stops to admire the scene. "Dear God." Incredible, ornate stuccoed walls and ceilings decorated in brilliant reds and blues and greens and whites. Elaborately decorated wooden-inlay furniture. Gold and silver fixtures everywhere. Unlike anything he has ever seen. A lavish statement of culture and wealth.

A woman's scream draws their attention. From the adjacent room they hear whimpering, then the rip of clothing, then another scream.

The three men quickly rush to the sound. Ponce de León enters and sees a young woman surrounded by three of his knights. One man has pinned her arms behind her, the other, kneeling, has her by the feet, the third is trying to kiss her. Her fine Moorish robe has been torn from her and lies in pieces in a heap on the floor. Her sheer silk bodice is ripped down the front, exposing her breasts. The knight trying to kiss her still holds her silk head scarf, which he has just yanked from her head. Even disheveled and terrified, she is a stunningly beautiful woman; lovely olive skin and long dark tresses. She heaves and gasps as the tears stream down her face. When she sees Ponce de León, she begins to softly whisper words in Arabic. None of them can understand what she is muttering, but her tone is unmistakable —the maiden is begging for mercy.

Ponce de León frowns. "What is the meaning of this?" A voice of command.

The man trying to kiss her pivots. "We found her hidden in the closet, m'lord. We were about to teach the whore a lesson." A lusty smile.

"Unhand her."

The knights are taken aback. "But she is forfeit, m'lord. Booty fairly won after a long, hard battle."

"*I said unhand her.*" Steely and dangerous. "NOW!"

The knights release her and step aside. She hugs her arms across her breasts as she backs against the wall, trembling like a leaf. Her swollen eyes are pleading.

Ponce de León removes his cloak and steps toward her. She cowers. He softly shushes her, then gently eases his cloak around her shoulders. She whispers a thank you in Arabic as she pulls it tightly to cover her nakedness. He turns to his men. "I will grant that the Moorish knights deserve no quarter, but women and children are to be spared." He darkens, then hisses. "Have you no honor? Do you knights not live by the code of chivalry? What would Queen Isabel think of your actions?!" He lifts his hand to the young woman. "This is a maiden of the emir's court. She either belongs to his harem, or perhaps is even his wife. A Moor, yes, but an innocent maiden first and foremost. She is not to be touched. None of Alhama's women are to be touched. Not one." He glares as he hisses, *"Do. You. Understand?"*

Shameful nods. "Of course, m'lord."

He turns to his two captains. "Spread the word. The men can have all the gold and silver they can carry, but Alhama's maidens are to be spared any dishonor. See to it."

"Consider it done, Don Rodrigo."

"How dare he defy my orders?!" The queen is fuming.

"How dare he?!" She thrusts the parchment at her husband, who takes it and quickly scans Ponce de León's words, then whistles. Unlike his wife, Fernando is smiling. "The man has balls made of iron, that much is sure."

Queen Isabel's only response is a quick scowl. She detests foul language.

He muses, "To strike so deep in enemy territory. And with such a small force." He whistles again. "There is no doubting the man's valor."

Isabel scoffs. "He defied my orders, Fernando. And the ink is barely dry on our peace treaty with the Moors."

"True. But he had good reason. The opportunity to strike at the heart of the Moors unexpectedly presented itself, and he seized upon it. There was no time to seek your permission or he surely would have done so. No, I do not fault the man."

She scowls again. "And what if he and his army are annihilated by the Moors? Or worse, captured and paraded in shame for all the world to see? He is the aggressor here and—"

Fernando interrupts, "No! Muley Hacén is the aggressor. Zahara, Isabel! Muley Hacén's unprovoked attack on Zahara. Let us be clear. The Moors started this. Ponce de León is merely attempting to settle the score. For his honor . . . and for yours, Isabel."

Her scowl fades, and she softly says, "I know. Still . . ."

"He will shortly be at Alhama, and soon victorious over the Moors, God willing. I will have the Great Captain gather a dozen riders to slip inside the Moorish kingdom and reconnoiter. We must have news of the outcome, and we must have it quickly."

Isabel grimaces. "Must it be Gonzalo? That sounds very dangerous." She turns and walks toward the window.

"He is fluent in Arabic, Isabel. He will need to take a few prisoners for information, so he is perfect for the mission." To soothe her he adds, "I will tell him not to directly engage the Moors. Trust me, the man is up to the task."

Without turning back, she offers a resigned, "Very well."

"In the meantime, I aim to rally our combined army at Lucena. Riders will leave within the hour to the scattered garrison camps. Assuming the news from the Great Captain is favorable, we will gather what troops we can and march on Alhama by week's end to relieve Ponce de León and his men."

She finally turns to face him. "But you said the army is not yet ready for battle."

"Not yet, no. But we have no need of heavy cannons. Speed is everything. More field training for the battalions would be useful, to be sure, but sometimes ideal circumstances just do not align with fortune's demands. Assuming Ponce de León has taken Alhama, he will not be able to hold for long against the massive army Muley Hacén will surely bring against him. We must arrive in force, and arrive very soon."

She sighs. "Yes, you must make haste."

Fernando cannot control his boyish excitement. "This is it, Isabel! This is the beginning. Conquest. Ponce de León has done us a great service. Our crusade has finally come at last. The Moors shall be beaten and banished from our land once and for all. All of Spain will be ours."

She nods, "Yes. And I will finally complete the quest my Visigoth ancestor Pelayo began 800 years ago. We will forge a Christian Spain to last an eternity."

"Go ahead, tell him what you told me." Al-Zaghal looks tense and dangerous, his ebony eyes narrowed into slits, his hand resting on the hilt of the broadsword.

The trooper hesitates. Natural for a simple warrior who is suddenly in the presence of the sultan, and bearing bad news besides.

"Come on, man, out with it!"

The sultan is not the man he once was, but physically he has mostly recovered from his injury. A little slower in thought, perhaps, with a slight limp still, and that annoying twitch of his sagging right cheek. But minor distractions, all told. The sultan tries to smile to calm the messenger, but his injury has broken the symmetry of his face, and without realizing it he projects more of a sneer than a smile. "You have nothing to fear. Speak, man." A very slight slurring of words still.

The rider's voice is quavering. "It . . . it is Alhama, sire. I . . . I . . . have ridden from Alhama. From an observation post across the gorge. I rode like the wind, sire. Ran my horse straight into the ground, sire, may Allah forgive me."

The sultan frowns. "What about Alhama?"

"Infidels, sire."

The sultan's countenance stiffens.

"The Christians, sire. Alhama is under attack. There is a desperate battle going on for control of the city. They are fighting as we speak, sire." The man looks down.

The sultan is incredulous. "WHAT?!" The rider cowers. The sultan exchanges a worried look with al-Zaghal.

Al-Zaghal replies, "It has to be the Marquess of Cádiz, sire. That fool, Ponce de León. He would be the only Christian general stupid enough to strike so deeply into our territory with no possible way to escape. My guess is a reprisal for Zahara." The brothers lock eyes dangerously. The surprise attack on Zahara remains a bone of contention between the two men. And, of course, Zoraya and her influence at court is a taboo subject. "We can assume he will not have attempted something so bold without a sizable army behind him. How an army made it all the way to Alhama undetected I have no clue. Some failure of command, no doubt. There will be hell to pay when I find out how this lapse occurred."

"Ponce de León . . ." The sultan seems confused. He shakes his head. "The Christians are in Alhama? In my Alhama? Impossible."

Al-Zaghal's voice grows steely. "This is the beginning of her war. Queen Isabel. Make no mistake, sire. This is the beginning. Granada must answer, and answer quickly."

The sultan muses, "Yes. Answer quickly." His eyes lose focus momentarily, then thankfully begin to firm up. His demeanor begins to change, his face hardening before their eyes. "Damn them. DAMN THEM! How dare they attack Alhama! DAMN THEM TO HELL!"

Al-Zaghal is relieved to see the implications congeal in his brother's mind. "Yes, damn them all. Shall I mount an army, sire? We must ride in defense of Alhama." He aims to steer his brother's thoughts.

The sultan stands, begins to smack his fist into his palm. "Ride we shall, Brother. Ride as in the days of old. Yes, we shall ride! WE SHALL RIDE!" His face darkens with rage. "Brother. Gather five hundred of your best cavalry." He begins to bark orders. "I want you at the gates of Alhama by dusk tomorrow to assess the situation. Engage the enemy only if an opportunity presents itself; otherwise, hold for my support. Understood?"

Al-Zaghal nods. *Praise Allah, he has not lost the gift of command.*

The sultan begins to pace. "It will take Ali al-Attar several days to assemble and equip an army of twenty thousand. My aim is to outnumber the Christians at least ten to one. We will follow as quickly as we can." He turns to his adjutant. "Amir, send word to Málaga. I want the Falcon brothers to ride for Alhama. Tell them to bring a thousand of their best men. And send word to Ronda. I want the emir's troops patrolling all the mountain passes between Alhama and Antequera. There is to be no escape or reinforcement for the infidels. We will crush them before any rescue can be attempted." The sultan stops. "And instruct Ronda to also send an elite cavalry force on a lightning raid of Arcos de la Frontera. In and out. With Ponce de León at Alhama, it will be lightly defended. We will teach the infidels that they are not the only ones capable of bold rides into enemy territory. Have them plunder anything they can carry with them—horses, cattle, gold, women—then burn Arcos de la Frontera to the ground. Put Moclín, Íllora, and Montefrío on high alert. Fernando may be foolish enough to attempt to provide support from Córdoba."

His adjutant is frantically scribbling notes. "Anything else, sire?"

"Inform Grand Vizier Venegas of my plans. Have him prepare documents allowing the army to commandeer whatever is needed. And tell Ali al-Attar that our rally point will be just outside the Elvira Gate. Tell him he has three days, no more. I aim to march Thursday at dawn. Tell him I want at least twenty thousand knights and infantry at my side, Amir. More if he can manage it. And plenty of scaling ladders. See that we are ready to fight."

His adjutant nods, "It shall be so, sire."

"Oh, and have my armor readied. We are now at war."

The adjutant scurries off.

The sultan turns to his royal bodyguards. "Leave us."

The Hall of the Ambassadors quickly empties.

"Come to me, Brother."

Al-Zaghal approaches to within a few feet.

"Closer." His tone softens. "Please." He stares at al-Zaghal for a long moment, then smiles his crooked smile. "Let us put our past disagreements behind us, Muhammad. Alhama needs us now. Granada needs us now. You and I, Muhammad. One flesh, one blood." His smile widens. "Together in command, we are invincible."

Al-Zaghal willingly submits once more to his brother's magnetic spell. He returns the smile. "One flesh, one blood. Invincible." *Praise Allah, he is back.*

The two men hug tightly, something they have not done in almost a year. "Together, Muhammad, we will smash the infidel devils that dare to challenge our power. They shall never tarnish our Nasrid birthright. Never!"

Al-Zaghal answers with a deadly smile. "We shall bathe in Christian blood, Ali. Depend upon it."

Mayhem

Yusef exchanges a quick glance and a nod with Umar, then raises his right hand high in the air. They have been riding since first light and their mounts need rest. "Whoa, Nasr. Whoa, boy. Whooaaa." As he pulls to a stop he affectionately slaps the slick sheen of sweat on the horse's jet-black withers. The rhythmic exhalations of the thousand stallions evoke some strange and fearsome mythical beast.

The journey from Málaga is long and grueling; first eastward through the coastal mountains before turning north through Vélez-Málaga and upward through the twisting mountain passes, skirting the edge of the forbidding Sierras de Tejeda, then finally swinging round to climb over the lip and onto the plateau of the Vega de Granada at the Zafarraya Pass. The ride from Málaga to Alhama would normally require five days. The Falcons aim to make it in under three. Al-Zaghal's communique on the remarkable turn of events stunned the brothers; they have never known the Christians to be so daring. They quickly assembled their elite strike force and left Gibralfaro Castle by late afternoon, then rode until midnight before pitching camp.

Yusef turns in his saddle to check on his men. Their cavalry ride five abreast by two hundred, the thin line stretching down the winding dusty road until it disappears around a monstrous chalky-gray stone monolith jutting from the side of the mountain. He turns to his brother. "I do not like being out of sight of our rearguard."

Umar turns and assesses. "No. But once we make the Zafarraya Pass and enter the Vega our sight lines will be miles long."

Yusef grunts his assent.

"Besides, the battle is at Alhama, not here. There is little to worry over."

"It is the reinforcements that concern me. There is no way that Ponce de León attacked Alhama without a plan for relief."

Umar answers, "One would think. The troops from Ronda should be arriving soon to seal the southern and western passes. At the very least we will know what is coming before it arrives."

"Mmm."

"How long do you think we have until Zafarraya Pass?"

Yusef looks upslope and shrugs. "Late afternoon tomorrow at this pace; early evening at the latest. The horses will need rest and the men some food and a few hours' sleep before they fight. It is no more than ten miles from the Zafarraya Pass to Alhama, and the riding will be much easier once we are on the plateau."

"Agreed."

"I want to be at Alhama by early morning the day after tomorrow, ready to engage."

Umar offers a sober nod. "And it shall be so, Brother. War is upon us now."

Al-Zaghal's cavalry has fanned out into a line two-hundred paces wide as it slowly walks over the crest of the low rise due west of the city. The knights are silent to a man as the cauldron of burnt orange slips into the horizon at their backs. In unison they behold the massive limestone walls glowing in warm relief under the dying sun. Tendrils of brownish-gray smoke rise here and there from within the walls, feathering upward until dispersed by the gentle breeze.

From this distance Alhama looks serene, but there is no mistaking the banners that have been hoisted high—the red Crusader's cross on a white field. The Granadine knights have ridden hard, leaving just before first light, pushing their Andalusian stallions to the limits of their endurance.

Al-Zaghal breaks the silence with a whispered curse. He turns to his second and says, "Alhama has fallen."

"Yes. Look, my lord." The officer points to a large pile of what appears to be cordwood stacked on either side of the city gate. Dozens of small dots flit about the stacks, jutting in here and there, then circling back and running at the piles once more. Animals of some sort.

Al-Zaghal says, "What on earth? Hold the men here." He kicks his stallion to a canter, moves down the slope and out into the plain leading to the main city gate. He studies the cordwood as he closes and at three-hundred paces he stops his mount. The sickening-sweet stench of rotting flesh is unmistakable. "Dear Allah." He squints. The stacks? Dead knights, stripped naked. The circling specters? Feral dogs feasting on the unburied. Al-Zaghal hisses, "Barbarians! You will pay for this madness. I will rip your beating hearts from your chests."

Fuutt . . . fuutt . . . fuutt. Three arrows drop forty paces in front of al-Zaghal. Just out of range, but the intent is obvious. He studies the walls to either side of the main gate. He can see now the hundreds of Castilian morions lining the battlements, the setting sun gleaming off the iron helmets. Al-Zaghal draws his broadsword and lifts it high in the air, then he kicks his stallion under close rein so it rears and whinnies. He shouts, "You infidel barbarians will pay for this madness. By Allah's Grace you will pay with your blood!" A barrage of arrows answers him. *Fuutt . . . fuuttt . . . fuuuuuuuuttttttttt . . . fuutt.* He turns and gallops back to his line.

"Have the men set camp in the lee of the hill so we cannot be seen from the towers. I want riders to circle the city and reconnoiter. I need information. Gather any able warriors they can find and bring them here. And post plenty of guards in case the Christians attempt a raid. Understood?"

"It shall be so, my lord."

"We will wait until the sultan's army arrives, and then there will be hell to pay. Pass the word. The infidels are forfeit. No quarter will be given to any Christian, whether commoner, knight, or noble. None. See to it."

His second nods and begins assigning duties.

Al-Zaghal turns back to Alhama and studies the lay of the land and the positioning of the walls and towers for possible angles of attack. He sighs. Alhama was believed by all to be unassailable. It is beyond obvious that retaking the city is going to prove very costly.

"And *then* he had the nerve to demand his gold back!" Ezar leans forward in his chair, hands on the table, eyes wide with drama. The consummate storyteller. "Can you imagine?! I told him, 'Certainly, sir, right after I put the kidney stone back where I found it!'" His head tilts back as he roars.

David, Miriam, and Danah burst out laughing. They are gathered around the table at David's home in the Jewish Quarter, a social gathering of tea and sweetmeats to celebrate the end of a long week. Miriam's idea.

Still chuckling, David playfully asks, "And did—"

Boom-boom-boom.

Someone is inflicting pain on the front door. David winks, "Ah. That must be him now. Better hide, Ezar!" He rises.

Boom-boom-boom-boom-boom.

David calls out, "Patience, please, I am coming. Have mercy on my door." He opens it to a royal courier, flanked by two heavily armed royal guardsmen. He spontaneously grimaces.

Before he can speak, the courier says, "An important message for the royal physician from Grand Vizier Venegas." A sealed scroll is thrust forward.

"I see. Very well." He reaches out and takes the scroll. Before he can thank the man, the three turn and are gone. David slowly closes the door, just staring at the thing, then turns back to the table. "Odd. What could Venegas possibly want?"

Danah helpfully offers, "Perhaps he wants you to know that Zoraya's birth pains have commenced?"

"Mmm. Not with an official document." He sits down, breaks the seal with his table knife, and begins to read. His brow furrows. "Dear Lord." He absently rerolls the scroll as he stares into space.

Concern is written on Miriam's face. "David?"

David shakes his head. "War, Miriam. Granada is at war. It seems that Alhama has been captured by the Christians. A surprise attack. The sultan is readying an army as we speak. The sultan is commandeering both the Bermejas and Atfal Hospitals. For the injured troops that will surely be coming."

Ezar says, "But they already have the Maristan."

"Evidently they are anticipating a large number of casualties. We are to ready our supplies for an onslaught of wounded troops."

Danah pipes in, "But the children, David! What is to become of the orphans?"

David looks from Ezar to Danah to Miriam. "We are to make arrangements."

Ezar replies, "How long do we have?"

"He does not say. The army marches Thursday at dawn. It is only thirty miles to Alhama. They will have to use wagons to return the wounded to Granada. Less than a week I would guess."

Miriam purses her lips, all business. "Danah, you will help me turn our home into a makeshift orphan's ward. For the young ones who need more immediate care."

Danah replies, "But Miriam—"

"Trust me, the children will not suffer. They will enjoy the vacation from their Atfal oppressor!" She winks at Ezar.

Ezar grins. "Excellent idea. And we shall do the same."

David chimes in, "But what about Rebekah and the girls?"

He spreads his arms wide. "Oh, we have plenty of room."

David seems satisfied. "Very well, then. Any we cannot house will be farmed out to the community. I will speak with Rabbi al-Zhuri. We have a plan at least for clearing the wards, but we must also focus on securing adequate medical supplies. I think it would be best if Danah and I manage the Bermejas. Ezar, you will be in charge of the Atfal. Hakim al-Fadl can handle the Maristan."

Ezar nods affirmatively. "Good man. Knows his stuff."

"We will each need to grow our staffs by three-fold, at least."

"Indeed. Five-fold would be even better."

"I will do my best. Guadix and Baza should be able to help. I will send a rider first thing tomorrow."

Miriam says, "You are forgetting something."

David looks at his wife. "Oh?"

"Yes, David. A very important detail. Danah must take her oath. If not, her presence in the wards will never be tolerated by the wounded knights. Danah must be made a proper hakim."

Danah blanches. "No!"

Miriam witnesses the panic of a sparrow who has unexpectedly flown into a hunter's snare net. It takes only an instant for her to grasp the girl's real concern. Malik. Once she is a hakim she will be free to marry.

Danah tries to recover. "I mean, I have so much to learn still, David. Too much! I am just not ready yet for my oath." She turns to her mentor, eyes pleading, then to Ezar, searching for some sort of confirmation. She is met by warm, loving smiles. "I mean, I need—"

Miriam touches her husband's arm, knowing he will be clueless about Danah's hesitancy. David says, "You are ready, Danah."

Ezar chimes in, "Readier than I ever was, Emeralds."

David continues, "Miriam is right. There is no other way, Danah. Your healing skills will be invaluable to us."

Miriam studies the girl's countenance as it deflates, so she decides to try to buoy her. "Hakim Amiriya. Think of it, Danah. You will be the first female hakim in Granada. What an amazing accomplishment! If you will permit me, I would relish stitching the Staff of Asclepius onto the sleeves of your physician's robe."

Danah's shoulders sag as she looks down, softly says, "But, I —" They watch her, waiting. Finally, she looks up, her will engaged. She takes a deep breath, exhales, then straightens her back. "Very well. I will take my oath. I will do my best to make you all proud."

"Who?" A distracted query. Enrique de Guzmán, Duke of Medina-Sidonia, reclines on a divan in his study, reading communiques from his vassal towns sprinkled across southern

Castile. A man who prides himself on attention to detail. His eyes remain glued to his papers.

"Beatriz de Pacheco, my lord."

"Who?" Impatience. He knows the name but cannot place it.

"The wife of the Marquess of Cádiz, my lord."

De Guzmán sits up, alarmed. "Dear God! Here?" Despite Queen Isabel's clearly stated wishes, the duke and the marquess remain decidedly reluctant allies. Decades of squabbling and power plays between two Castilian noble families will do that. The duke and the marquess have never once set foot in each other's castles.

"Indeed, my lord. The wife of Rodrigo Ponce de León. Beatriz de Pacheco. She is waiting in the anteroom."

"Why on earth would she be here?" The duke is incredulous.

"She would not say, my lord. She seems . . . distressed, my lord."

The duke tries to ladle calm upon his racing heart. "Very well. Give me ten minutes to dress, then bring her into the reception hall. See that she is comfortable, please. Oh, and have Alonso de Aguilar and Martin de Montemayor join us. I may need their counsel."

"Certainly, my lord."

The duke stares into space, wondering what could possibly precipitate such an unprecedented move. He finally gives up, permitting fortune's fickle hand to rest upon his shoulder. He beckons his valet to help him dress.

His quiet conversation with Alonso and Martin dies mid-sentence as the doors to the hall are opened. The door guardsmen snap to attention as the three knights rise. The duke forces a smile as he opens his hands. His welcome is formal and deliberate; calculated. "Lady de Pacheco. To what does Medina-Sidonia owe this—" He checks himself as he sees her face. "Unexpected . . . pleasure?"

Her expression is strained, stretched taut, her eyes red and swollen. She does not answer but simply steps forward, drops to her knees, and lowers her head in submission.

The duke is dumbfounded. "Lady de Pacheco?"

Don Alonso and Don Martinare stand silent, wide-eyed.

When she slowly looks up, tears are streaming, her lower lip aquiver. "You must help me. I beg you in God's name, Don Enrique. I am in dire need of your assistance." She chokes back a sob. "I know there is bad blood between our houses, but my husband, he . . . he . . . You must help me, Don Enrique!"

The duke reaches down and gently takes her hand. "Please, my lady. Rise." His voice is soothing, laden with genuine concern. Chivalry runs very deep in this man. "Of course I will help. Please sit and let us talk." He indicates the chair. "Come, Lady de Pacheco, sit. Please." He indicates the other two men. "This is Don Alonso and Don Martin, my trusted counselors."

Both men bow.

She sits.

The duke continues, "Tell me what has happened, Lady de Pacheco."

She sniffs. "Rodrigo has launched a surprise attack on the Moors, Don Enrique. On Alhama."

"WHAT?" He struggles to absorb this news. "But that is impossible, Lady de Pacheco. Alhama is only thirty miles from Granada. And well known to be impregnable—one of the strongest castles in the Moorish kingdom. Dear God, what could he be thinking?!"

Her countenance settles. She takes a deep breath and continues, "My husband received word that the Alhama was poorly defended. And the emir was away, you see; in Vélez-Málaga. An escaped prisoner reported all this to Rodrigo. My husband asked the man to lead a small force through the mountains for a surprise attack to capture the city." She tries to force a smile but cannot hold it. "As you know, Don Enrique, long odds rarely matter to Rodrigo once he sets his mind to something."

The duke actually smiles. He has no argument there; the red-maned marquess is legendary for his hot-headedness. Truth be told, he is a brilliant battlefield tactician because of it. If anyone could pull off a surprise attack deep behind enemy lines and actually capture the formidable Alhama, it would be him. "I understand, Lady de Pacheco, but Queen Isabel was quite clear to the both of us. There were to be no attacks on the Moors without her permission."

"Rodrigo sent the queen a letter informing her of his intentions, but felt he had to act immediately or lose the golden opportunity. He said he begged her forgiveness but said he trusted that she would approve of his actions when she got the news." She hesitates, then adds, "I believe he thirsts for revenge, Don Enrique. For Zahara."

The duke nods, exchanges a quick glance with the other two men. "Indeed. We all do. How long has he been gone?"

"A week and a day."

The duke frowns. "You should have come to me sooner, Lady de Pacheco. Have you had any news from Alhama?"

She begins to softly cry once more. "No. Not from Rodrigo. But yesterday . . . yesterday . . ." She begins to cry anew.

He leans forward to coax her. "What happened yesterday, Lady de Pacheco?"

She sniffs. "Yesterday, a Moorish raiding party attacked our lands. At Arcos de la Frontera. They rode in like the wind, and before you could count to ten had stormed the castle and taken it. They killed all the men who resisted. Then they plundered the town and burned it."

Don Martin exclaims, "Dear God."

She speaks in a terrified whisper. "They took the women and girls, Don Enrique. All of them."

Don Alonso flushes dark with rage, then hisses, "Damned slavers."

The duke offers a pained sigh. "Arcos is just beyond the edge of the Sultan Muley Hacén's kingdom. Easy pickings if they knew Don Rodrigo had left his lands unguarded. My guess is that the Moors retaliated for your husband's attack on Alhama. How many men did the marquess take with him to Alhama?"

"I am not sure. A thousand? Maybe less."

The duke raises his eyebrows. "To capture and hold a city the size of Alhama? Dear God. Don Rodrigo may just be the bravest man in the kingdom. That, or the most foolhardy."

Her tears begin to stream again. "Don Enrique, I beg you. You must gather an army and ride in Rodrigo's defense. He will perish without your help. Please! I beg you!"

The duke raises a hand to calm her. "You shall have your army, Lady de Pacheco. You shall have it." He turns to Don Alonso and Don Martin. "Send riders to all of my vassal towns. I will have half of their garrisons. And send word to the Master of the Order of Calatrava. Their knights shall ride with us. We will rally at Medina-Sidonia and then we will march to Don Rodrigo's aid with an army at least ten thousand strong. Time is of the essence, gentlemen. Make haste, Alhama awaits us!"

Lady de Pacheco is beaming through her tears. "Bless you, Don Enrique, bless you! God's Grace will surely shine upon you and your men. Bless you!"

The duke bows. "Let the bad blood between our noble families be ended. From this day forward, we fight as one for our queen and for Castile. Together, we shall lead the charge to vanquish the Moors. We shall rescue your brave and daring husband, Lady de Pacheco. Depend upon it!"

"There, Don Rodrigo. See?" Don Sancho de Avila points east, to just beyond the sharp bend in the river. At the gorge edge a quarter mile out, tiny scattered smudges of dancing flames. Cooking fires, hundreds, stretching back into the rolling hills as far as the eye can see.

Don Sancho pivots, sweeping his hand around to the west. "A semicircle all the way back to the oak copse that hid our initial attack. And in the center of their line, even more."

Rodrigo Ponce de León softly acknowledges their dire situation. "Surrounded. How many do you think he brought?"

The man studies the fires as he considers this. "I would say at least fifteen thousand. Perhaps twenty."

"To our eight hundred fit enough to wield a sword."

Don Diego de Merlo reaches for the positive. "We hold the city, Don Rodrigo. The Moors are master wall builders. Strong and high; not easily breached."

"Indeed. Thank God for that. When did the sultan's army arrive?"

"Not sure. It had to be well after sunset, though. The sentries saw nothing before their cooking fires were lit."

"Well, there we have it. Much as I expected. The sultan will attack at first light—depend upon it. We will be in for the fight of our lives, gentlemen."

Don Sancho says, "Your letter should have reached Córdoba a week ago. I am sure the king is already marching to relieve us."

"God willing. Assuming the queen deems us worthy of rescue, it will still take the king time to gather his forces. For now, we are on our own. If the Moors manage to scale the walls we are done for."

Don Diego replies, "At least the sultan cannot lay siege to the city. He is no fool. He knows that help must already be on its way."

Ponce de León muses. "Agreed. He will have to hope he can quickly overwhelm us with his numbers. Let us see what he thinks of our surprises. Our aim, gentlemen, is to make his losses so large that he will be forced to consider whether Alhama is really worth retaking. We must be prepared to hold for at least a week. And pray that King Fernando makes it to us in time."

Don Sancho whistles. "A week? That is likely to prove to be a tall order, Don Rodrigo."

"Nevertheless, we must make it so. Alhama must be held, even to the last man standing. The Moors will not be taking prisoners. Depend upon it."

"How *dare* he? How *dare* he desecrate the dead?!" Sultan Abu 1-Hasan's hands are balled into white-knuckled fists, his asymmetrical face flushed a deep scarlet and locked in a deadly sneer. The man's neck veins are pulsing with fury, the tendons cinched tight as a mainsail's rigging in a running wind. The officers nearest him involuntarily take a step back. "I WILL PERSONALLY FLAY THE BASTARD! I TELL YOU I WILL FLAY THE INFIDEL WHILE HE IS STILL BREATHING! DO YOU HEAR ME, BROTHER?! I. WILL. FLAY. HIM!"

Al-Zaghal allows the man's roar to clear before speaking. "Be sure that Ponce de León will get the punishment he richly deserves, sire." His voice is calm, level. "First, however, there is the task of retaking Alhama."

The sultan glares at him, fuming.

The hour is late, well past midnight. While al-Zaghal patiently waits for the sultan to recover his wits before continuing, Ali al-Attar, standing at his right, scowls his displeasure. This is no time for unbridled outbursts; there is much work to be done. He knows all too well that recapturing a city as well-fortified as Alhama will be a tall order. And very costly.

The sultan shakes his head to clear the cobwebs, flexes his fingers, then tilts his neck to crack it. "Know that I aim to attack in full force at first light."

Ali al-Attar softly replies, "That is exactly what Ponce de León will be expecting, sire."

The sultan glares the grizzled old knight into silence. "We outnumber the Christians by at least ten to one, Ali." He turns to al-Zaghal. "Tell me what you have learned of their defenses."

Pleased to see his brother's sanity returning, he says, "I have a plan, sire. Come, it is best to show you on the map."

"Riders! Pass the word! Riders approaching! Riders! Pass the word!" The news echoes down the walls. The battlements awaken with activity. Orders are barked left and right. Those that miraculously found a moment of sleep are wakened with gentle shakes and kind words. Knights stomp the cold from their feet, blow into their hands. One by one the knights don the distinctive curled crests of the gleaming morions, strap the helmets tight.

The clinks and pings of killing tools being tested for heft, the soft metallic hisses of swords being drawn from their scabbards. Archers nervously count their arrows for the tenth time, then lean them in orderly lines against the stone for easy reach when the time comes. Those few knights possessing arquebuses arrange their powder horns and lead balls. Trembling fingers struggle to cinch leather belts. The heavy *frumpf* of chain mail being draped over shoulders, the clink and clangle of armor being tugged tight and fixed. Soft, reassuring words are spoken, whispered prayers, letters to loved ones checked and rechecked in trouser pockets. These men speak with confidence about the coming battle, but you can see it their eyes: They know the odds are not good that they will still be alive come nightfall.

First light. The landscape is a murky purple-gray, nearly opaque, hushed with foreboding and otherworldly calm. Strange, effervescent mist clings to the valleys. Ponce de León stares into the void, whispers to himself, "A little luck today would be nice, O Lord. A little luck, please. Let the Moors be predictable." He turns to his left. "Don Diego, pass the word. No arrow is to be loosed until I drop my flag. I want silence on the walls. Not a peep. See to it personally."

"Consider it done, Don Rodrigo." He turns and moves down the battlement, softly repeating the order to his officers, instructing them to spread the word.

"There they are." The cavalry rides twenty across and stretches back into the distance. The blue and gold standard of Granada—Sultan Muley Hacén. The column canters forward in tight formation toward the city gate. Effortless, elegant. The Moors are famous for their horsemanship. Ponce de León counts the rows as they come into view, loses count at fifty, but the cavalry keeps coming. A second column drifts into view ten degrees to the left. Then a third column. A fourth. A fifth. A sixth. Each are ten degrees apart, each staggered to arrive just after their neighbor. For maximum impact, an assault on morale. He concedes the display of expertise with a sober nod and whispers to himself, "Impressive."

Battle trumpets sound in the distance. In a single instant the first column accelerates to a gallop, the stallions' rippled haunches pulsing with energy beneath the clenched thighs of their riders. A deep rumble reverberates off the walls, growing in strength.

Ponce de León, shouts, "Steady, boys. Just Moorish bluster. Steady! Steady boys!"

The sultan's knights raise their swords to the sky. Closer, closer. The rumble grows into rolling thunder. The column rides hard at the gate, and then a hundred paces out, abruptly breaks left, begins to shout and yell, slinging Arabic insults, daring the castle to respond. They ride along the wall, within easy arrow range, then break away in tight formation, at full gallop the whole while. Expert riding to a man. When one column is finished, the next takes up the reins, breaks into a gallop and follows suit.

In truth, cavalry is of little use against castle fortifications. The charge is mostly for show, to convey intent and intimidate by strength of numbers. And, of course, to stoke the egos of the young Moorish cavaliers, adorned in colorful Moorish silks and finely-tooled leathers, fitted with expensive inlaid battle armor and tightly woven chain mail. They wield named broadswords of ancient lineage, and gilded daggers and maces engraved with sayings of the Prophet in elegant Arabic script. Even their mounts are stylish—heavy-felt padding decorated with clan colors and crests, fancy leather saddles, silver bridles and stirrups. These purebred Andalusian stallions canter with heads held high, mirroring the egos of their masters.

The Moorish knights are young and dark and handsome; prancing peacocks. Dizzy with confidence, filled with pride. Fools. Almost to a man these brazen cavaliers have never fought in battle, have not endured the horrific agonies of close-quarter combat, where one wrong move, one tiny miscalculation, will spill your ropey guts into the dirt, sever your arm, blind you, crush your skull. Or worse. They think of swordplay as sport, having practiced for years and competed in fancy tournaments. They see this battle against the infidel as a chance to make their names, to prove their mettle, to win glory, to secure a badge of honor to help them seduce dark-eyed beauties to eagerly dole out their maidenhoods. They are certain of a quick and easy victory over the Christians. Beyond certain. Stupid fools. And so, they preen about upon their stallions, riding hard at the high wall then veering off at the last moment, swords held to the sky, whooping and hollering insults upon the Christians. Meanwhile, Alhama's walls stand silent, unimpressed, the only sign of their enemy the crests of hundreds of gleaming helmets neatly aligned and just visible above the battlements.

Sated by their pompous parade without losing a single man, the cavalry withdraws, circles back to just beyond arrow range, then gathers into formations and stops. Ali al-Attar walks his horse forward to assume command of the attack. At his word, a bannerman signals instructions, and it begins—a three-pronged infantry assault on the main city gate. Logical. To the left and right, massive phalanxes two thousand strong; first a wall of shieldmen a hundred paces wide protecting the famed Alpujarran crossbowmen bearing iron-tipped, armor piercing bolts; then pikemen, more shieldmen, then dozens of pairs of runners with their scaling ladders, more crossbowmen, and finally trailing cavalry riding in support. In the center, the same, except the ladders have been traded for a massive battering ram, a felled hickory two feet in diameter and forty feet long, spiked every foot with handholds and tipped with an iron maul. Thirty men to a side. Additional shieldmen beside each rammer, ready to provide cover for attack from above.

A hundred paces separate each of the attacking phalanxes. The flanking units are the outer pincers. They serve two purposes: first, to spread the enemy defenses thin and draw fire away from the tower gate, allowing the rammers to better accomplish their nasty work; and second, to present their own scaling threat to the battlements, crossbowmen leading the way up the skinny ladders to eliminate any defenders who dare lift a head above the wall. Once they have secured the parapet, they will fight back toward the main gate to join forces with the others. Classical Moorish tactics for seizing a castle. Tried and true. Alas, predictable.

The phalanxes move forward at a leisurely pace, slowly moving in tight formation over the crest of the hill, then down the slope, disappearing into the misty fog gathered in the shallow valley, finally reappearing, a celestial army rising from the clouds. They methodically make their way up the long, gentle slope leading to the castle gate, the marching officer chanting his rhythmic cadence. No haste, no deception; rather, a simple declaration that they have come to take their castle back.

Four hundred paces away. Three hundred. Two. The eye-watering stench emanating from the sad, decaying stacks of half-eaten dead is so heavy in the air it is almost visible, lending a sense of dread that slithers about among the ranks. The shieldmen have their tall, plated-leather contraptions raised high, but their puzzlement grows with each step. They expected a storm of arrows long before now. Nervous looks are exchanged, confused queries that race back among the units. One hundred paces out and still nothing. The walls are completely silent. Perhaps the Christians thought better of it and left the city? Commands are issued, and the three phalanxes halt.

The scene is as quiet as a graveyard. Ten seconds, twenty, then the marching officer in the center phalanx shouts, "Allahu Akbar!" and is answered with a thundering roar, "ALLAHU

AKBAR! DEATH TO THE INFIDEL! ALLAHU AKBAR!" The three phalanxes charge in double-time toward their targets. Still no response from the walls. At fifty paces out, a hail of round objects, hundreds, more, loop in high arcs over the wall in some sort of strange barrage. The objects strike the ground with sickening dull thuds and roll forward toward the attacking lines. Oddly, the shieldmen begin to break ranks and stop, horrified, as the objects roll among them. The phalanxes stutter to a halt, shredding the neat formations. The enemy barrage consists of the heads of the slain Moors, each sporting terrified death masks; mouths open and aghast, eyes plucked out, faces and hair matted with black blood. Crosses have been crudely cut into the foreheads of the dead. The troopers stand horrified. Orders are barked to try to restore ranks, but chaos reigns and a quivering panic steps close.

BOOM! BOOM! BOOM! BOOM! in tight succession. The concussive blasts are deafening, startling in their violence. Choking smoke blasts forward in bulbous gray-black clouds from the walls on both sides of the central tower. The leading elements of the center phalanx instantly evaporate into a gory crimson mist, spewing a cascade of severed limbs and body parts back through the ranks. The sleek, doeskin uniforms of the Alpujarran crossbowmen are sprayed with blood, their faces dotted with clots of flesh and lumps of brains and bits of skin and hair. Screams and moans of the horribly mutilated permeate the phalanx. Limbless shieldmen try to drag themselves backward but are trampled by those terrified few still standing in the decimated front line as they scramble to find cover, any cover. Alas, there is none to be found.

As it turns out, the emir of Alhama added four heavy cannons to his main gate fortifications just two months back. Imported from the Turks for a ridiculous sum—fine bronze beasts. They were carefully camouflaged by Ponce de León's troops, then filled with black powder, and crammed with three-inch nails, olive- and apricot-sized balls of lead, arm's length loops of heavy chain—anything to kill and maim.

From atop the walls come a dozen simultaneous commands of "READY!" The bowmen rise from behind the battlements. "LOOSE!" Three hundred arrows arc into the air. At this close range they are more than adequate to pierce chain mail. The archers duck down to nock their next arrows, rise. "LOOSE!" With the shieldmen eliminated, there is nothing to protect the phalanx from the bowmen, and the first dozen disjointed rows helplessly crumple forward in unison. Then *Pow! Pow! Pow!* as the knights with arquebuses join the fight.

BOO-BOOM! BOOM! BOOM! The front half of the center phalanx has disappeared. Panic steps closer still, and as the formation crumbles the men break ranks and begin to run. The officers scream at their charges to turn and fight, with limited success.

Ali al-Attar sees it all, curses as he watches. "Cowards." He turns to his second and screams, "Why did no one inform me that Alhama had heavy cannons?!"

The officer shrivels; no answer.

The old knight curses. "This is not going to end well." He stares into the mayhem. "Ponce de León . . . you are no fool, sir." He barks, "Any news yet from al-Zaghal?"

"Not as yet, my lord."

"Send a rider. We need to disengage here before we ruin my army. Tell him we are in retreat. Quickly, man!"

Meanwhile, the two flanking phalanxes have managed to regroup and are just arriving at the wall to begin their assaults. The shieldmen are the first to see that a ditch an arm-span wide has been dug at the base of the wall, filled with a gloppy black goo. The ditch stretches from the main gate outward, hugging the wall for almost two hundred paces. Several men step into the awful muck by mistake and sink to their shins. An oily-sticky-stinking-mess. The troopers do not seem to quite know what to make of this. Enemy longbowmen from the tower battlements are raining arrows upon them now, and large rocks are dropping from above. No time to think. The Alpujarran crossbowmen fan out to provide cover for the escaladors to plant their ladders; they begin to return fire, the air instantly rich with six-inch bolts. The crossbowmen are renowned for their skill; Christians drop into their lines from the tower. Within a minute, two dozen ladders are filling; the first are escaladors bearing rope and grappling hooks, then more crossbowmen to support them. They begin to spider up.

A torch is dropped from a tower window and lands in the ditch with a sickening *WHOOFF!* Head-high flames violently erupt, then choking black smoke blossoms and billows. Naphtha. Known to troopers on both sides as "devil's breath." The hellish cauldron races down the wall, the awful black smoke chasing close behind. The escaladors do not see the approaching danger until it is too late. The phalanx parts from the wall to permit passage of the flames, but hellfire envelops the ladders. Confronted with terrible choices, those high enough try their best to jump out across the flames to safety, breaking ankles and wrists, but surviving; those lower have no options and instead race upward as the flames lick at their heels, but with no support they are mowed down as soon as they crest the wall, an arrow through the throat, a mace to the head, a pike through the chest. Complete mayhem ensues. The Christians cut the grappling ropes and send the burning ladders crashing down into the phalanx.

BOOM! BOOM! The cannons have been rotated on their swivels and trained on the flanking phalanxes, to deadly effect. At this oblique angle, each blast cuts a swath ten feet wide by fifty feet deep, maiming or killing everything in its path, cutting down the Moors like a scythe through ripened wheat. The dead are piling up deep enough to serve as cover for the living, but this chokes off the ability of the officers to move men and deploy reinforcements. The flanking formations are crumpling.

Ali al-Attar growls, "Sound the retreat. There is no victory to be had here. Sound the retreat, damn you!"

Around to the east and just out of sight, the wall angles sharply away from the steep edge of the gorge. This land by the gorge is ragged, cut deeply by ravines eroded over the centuries; plenty of places to hide a thousand troops from sight of the towers. Two dozen scaling ladders rest against the wall between two crenellated towers a stone's throw apart, Moorish climbers scampering up as fast as they can manage. They know well that they are defenseless while trapped in midair. Crossbowmen kneel in support at the base of the ladders, firing their bolts upward at any Christian who dares show himself. A half dozen ladders have been pushed off the wall, but the Moors have now secured a foothold and the wall is rapidly filling. The troops in reserve stand ready, weapons lifted. They will pour from their hiding places and into the city when the breach is secured.

A fight to the death unfolds, a fantastical whir of maces and swords and stabbing pikes from the Christian defenders struggling frantically to staunch the flood of Moorish knights that have penetrated their defenses. Insults, screams of agony, and labored grunts contrast with the bright pings of steel upon steel, the dull thuds of maces upon shields, filling the air with the drama of desperation. The Moors are aiming to capture a tower. Secure one of those and the path downward and into the city is thrown open wide.

From the rise at the edge of the gorge al-Zaghal nods, clearly pleased. "Progress, sire. The men have secured a stretch of the wall. They will soon hold the towers, and then victory will be ours. The Christians have clearly massed their forces at the main gate for Ali al-Attar's assault. They do not have enough troops to thwart us. Victory shall be ours."

The sultan grunts his approval, his nerves are obviously stretched to the point of fraying.

This far from the main gate, the Christians are heavily outnumbered and are slowly but surely losing ground, being pushed backward along the parapet toward the towers to each side. But the alarm has been raised, the frantic clanging of iron bells clear and unmistakable. Reinforcements are already on the move.

Al-Zaghal turns to his officer. "Have the men move up into position. It should not be long now."

"Yes, my lord."

In the distance they hear the chain of deep, concussive blasts. Al-Zaghal frowns. "Cannons? But Alhama has no heavy cannons."

The sultan pales. "Dear Allah! My army will be decimated. Quickly, Brother. We must take the towers quickly!"

Don Sancho arrives at the tower just west of the breach, out of breath but with thirty knights and two dozen archers. He barks orders at his officers as they race up the narrow stairs inside the tower, taking three steps at a time. "We must hold the tower, or we are done for. Juan, take half the men out onto the wall, and with the other half form a shield around the door. No Moor gets inside the tower, understood?" He vigorously shakes a finger. "Not one! Pedro, you are in command. Godspeed!"

"Understood, my lord. Godspeed!"

Don Sancho turns. "Archers, gunmen, follow me!" They bound up the next set of stairs, pour out onto the roof of the tower. He quickly surveys the parapet and crenellations. "Fan out and choose good cover, men, their crossbowmen will be answering you soon enough. Loose from the crenels, and keep your heads low." He chops forward with his hand. "I want this half to target the Moors on the ladders." More chopping to his right. "This half target the Moors on the walls. Understood?" Sober nods. "Quickly, men—our fortune hangs in the balance. I want no Moor left standing on our walls." Determined nods. "Now make it so!"

The archers kneel down, pull their arrows from their quivers, arrange them for quick firing, then nock their longbows, lean forward into the crenels, take aim, loose, then kneel once more. Nock and loose, nock and loose, as fast as they can, the rhythm of death. The half-dozen gunmen rise up, aim their arquebuses, squeeze the triggers, fire, then duck to reload. *Pow! Pow! Po-pow! Pow-pow!* The smoke from the guns lends welcome cover. Don Sancho looks across to the other tower, sees that Don Francisco and his men have arrived, waves, then points downward and is answered. Reinforcements begin to spill out onto the wall from both towers. The tide is turning.

The air grows thick with arrows zinging back and forth, catching the Moors in a withering crossfire. Turbaned knights drop from the ladders, fall from the walls. The Alpujarran crossbowmen answer as best they can, but the steep angle works against them. Their iron-tipped bolts strike the stone crenellations, harmlessly spraying splinters of stone. Occasionally they fly true and are answered with a quick scream.

Al-Zaghal sees billowing plumes of midnight black rising in the direction of the gate. He curses. "Naphtha." He turns and studies the situation, sees that his men are quickly losing ground. Just then a rider gallops up and slides from the saddle before the horse comes to a full stop. "My lord! My lord!"

"Speak, man. What of the attack on the gate?"

"My lord, the Christians have heavy cannons!"

"I have ears, you fool! What of Ali al-Attar and the army?"

"The army is in full retreat, my lord." The man cannot bear the shame, so he looks down. "We have lost hundreds of troops, my lord. Many hundreds."

The sultan purples with rage. *"Damn the infidels! DAMN THEM!"* He kicks the dirt.

Al-Zaghal touches his brother's arm. "We must sound retreat, sire. This day is done."

The sultan dangerously hisses through clenched teeth. *"And let the infidels claim victory?!"*

Al-Zaghal presses. "We shall regroup and strike again tomorrow, sire." He locks eyes with his brother and slowly announces, "This. Battle. Is. *Over.*"

The sultan does not respond. He simply about-faces and marches back to the horses, grabs the reins of his mount from the squire, and swings up into the saddle. The sultan kicks to a gallop, headed back to his headquarters to sulk.

Al-Zaghal watches him ride away, then turns back to the waning battle. No more than two dozen of his men are still standing atop the wall, the ladders still standing nearly empty. "Sound retreat."

The trumpet blares its brassy shrill, though truth be told not a single Moor will make it off the wall alive this day.

Insurrection

Two hours before sunrise the moon finally peaks over the distant snow-capped Sierra Nevada. She kneels then stands, tall and proud, ready to stake her monthly claim to the glorious Alhambra. *Her* Alhambra. She amuses herself by flinging her silvered beams against the intricately carved buildings, cutting shadows as pointed and sharp as a needle dagger.

The damp air is cold still, and unforgiving; winter petulant as she always is, reluctant to cede any ground to the timid spring. Down near the River Darro, a dog vigorously barks at some late-night wraith slinking about, then is abruptly silenced in a blood-curdling yelp. Farther up the slope of the Albayzín, in a modest apartment above an alley, a cobbler's young wife lifts her head, instantly alert. She is not sure what exactly she has heard. Hushed voices? Footfall? Something. With small children in the house she can ill afford to sleep too soundly. She sits up, cocks an ear. Her young son has been suffering from night terrors, his muted little whimpers perfectly pitched to summon her. Nothing. Satisfied, she eases back down and snuggles up against her softly snoring husband, closing her eyes. The precious last hours of sleep before the children wake is cherished beyond all measure.

Grand Vizier Venegas has always been an early riser, but this night he has found sleep especially difficult to claim, his dreams unsettled and troubling. After tossing and turning for nearly an hour, he finally decides with a muttered curse to rise and begin his day. After all, with the recent events in Alhama there is much to be done, and little time to do it. He knows his day will stretch until midnight, and still a quarter of his tasks will remain unfinished.

After dressing he opens the door to his suite, offers a word of explanation to his two bodyguards, then, as is his habit upon rising, slowly makes his way to the Comares Palace, pensive as always, arms tucked behind his back as he begins to prioritize the decisions to be made this day. He exits the tunnel and steps out into the expansive Court of the Myrtles, admires the tranquil scene for a moment, then turns and angles around the reflecting pool, nods to the royal guardsmen at their posts outside the Hall of the Boat, and passes inside. After motioning to his bodyguards to wait for him at their usual spot, he begins his climb up the narrow tower stairs of the Hall of the Ambassadors.

Three stories up, he steps out onto the vacant crenelated platform, the highest point in the Nasrid palace complex. His cherished sunrise sanctuary. He stretches, takes a deep breath, and blasts a foggy cloud into the cold air with his exhale. He stares at the moon, just separated from the distant crags and swaggering; he smirks his disapproval of such a gaudy display. He knows that the architects of the Alhambra built the palace to serve this vain queen. Still. He pivots, and after absorbing the scene, frowns. *That is odd.* The Alhambra's walls facing the Albayzín are empty, completely devoid of sentries. His eyes jump to the observation posts atop the imposing towers of the Alcazaba. Empty. His gaze drops downward as he scans the wall from the Alcazaba on his left to the Partal Palace on his right. Not a soul. Completely unmanned. He turns back to the south wall, a long arrow shot away, and sees the familiar silhouettes of the pacing guards. His head snaps back to the north wall. His calculating engine whirs with a thousand possibilities. His heart pounds as he races for the stairs.

The baker is up early to stoke his ovens. The synchronized cacophony of boots striking cobblestone comes into focus. Curious, he unlocks the door to his shop and steps out, looks up the alley toward the ridgeline. No one is in sight, but the unmistakable cadence of marching troops grows louder. *Coming this way.* He steps back into the doorway, cracks the door to permit a quick exit. Close, no more than a stone's throw. The baker reflexively takes a half step back into the shadows.

The column turns the corner seamlessly without breaking formation, the knights tucked into neat rows of five. Chain mail and turbans; swords and daggers in their sashes; crossbows, pikes, and arquebuses on their shoulders. This is no parade— these troops are marching to battle. The baker knows about Alhama, of course, the whole city does, but this is odd indeed. The sultan's army left three days back.

As the troops approach, the officer in command catches sight of him and raises a hand, halting the column. The man turns a serious eye on the baker, who cowers.

"The Albayzín is now officially under the control of Sultan Boabdil, rightful ruler of Granada, and the Council of Elders of the Abencerrajes." His tone is official. A proclamation. "No market today. All citizens are commanded to stay inside!"

It is all the baker can do to meekly nod. *Sultan Boabdil?!* He retreats, locks his door.

The officer barks, "We march for Sultan Boabdil and the Abencerrajes!" and is answered by a thunderous roar, "TO THE ALHAMBRA!"

Boabdil steps from the long shadows cast by the moon, now a luminous bisected pearl pinned to the night sky. There is no arguing the young man looks the part. A dashing Moorish prince, with ambitions honed razor sharp, a would-be sultan by whatever means necessary. His armor is outrageously expensive—his mother's doing—his sword forged in ancient Damascus two centuries back, decorated with elaborate engravings, its silver scabbard inlaid with precious jewels.

At Boabdil's side stands the woman herself, Sultana Fatima, regal in her lavish silks, and Abu al-Haytham, High Elder of the Abencerrajes, predictably scowling, predictably in all black. The wizard has a thousand troops arrayed in ten brigades in the Darro Plaza, adjacent to the river. They stand ready to press their case and avenge a debt leveled upon them by the Nasrids so many years ago. Boabdil is in command of the Abencerraje forces, at least in name.

He motions, and the new grand vizier, a man chosen for him by the high elder, steps close. "Well, Aben Comixa?"

The beady eyes of this wry little man sparkle. "The Albayzín now belongs to the Abencerrajes, sire. Likewise, the Elvira Gate, the Fajalauza Gate, and the Hizna Roman Gate. And, of course, the city walls and towers between. As for the Alhambra, it has all been carefully arranged, sire." A sly smile. "It seems the sentries on the north wall and the Alcazaba's towers were mistakenly reassigned tonight, and I am afraid the night-officer of the Arm's Gate is Abencerraje, with loyalist clansmen under his command. The Arm's Gate should be opening as we speak, sire."

Fatima chimes in, "And the Darro crossing?"

Aben Comixa turns and points. "The Puente del Cadí and the coracha leading up to the palace are already ours." A thin smile. "Sultana, the Alhambra will soon throw open its gates in joyous welcome."

Boabdil says, "You are sure about the Alcazaba garrison?"

The little man purses his lips. He so hates to be questioned, especially by one so young and inexperienced. "Given the fortuitous events at Alhama, sire, the Alcazaba is woefully depleted of troops. And I arranged for well-placed infiltrators in their ranks to be conveniently left behind when the army marched." He sniffs. "It should fall quickly once our troops are inside the walls."

"Good."

Aben Comixa licks his lips. "With pleasure, sire."

Abu al-Haytham finally speaks. "The Alhambra shall soon be returned to its rightful owners."

A wisp of a smile from Fatima. "Indeed, it shall."

Clang-clang-clang! Pause. *Clang-clang-clang!* Pause. *Clang-clang-clang!* A royal guardsman strikes the bell on the Tower of the Gallinas, just west of the Mexuar Palace. The Alhambra's finely tuned network of iron bells atop each of its thirty-two towers lining the outer walls take up their song one after the other as the alarm quickly encircles the Alhambra. The moonlit fortress is soon awash in an unsettling metallic chorus as the palace's royal guardsmen and the Alcazaba's garrison are violently awakened. They rush to gather weapons and armor and assemble in the courtyards, awaiting orders.

The alarm bells are soon joined by the footfall of troops moving in double-time along the cobbled streets in a dozen different directions, and then the reverberating horse-clop of cavalry squadrons being repositioned to strategic locations. The base of the stairs linking the Mexuar Palace with the unmanned north wall coagulates with royal guardsmen, who race up two at a time, one breaking right, one breaking left. Within a minute these fearsome knights are in place and have their weapons drawn and ready.

The night-officer of the Arm's Gate freezes as he hears the muted song of the first set of bells. He curses. "The alarm is sounded! Quickly men, there is no time!" A slew of knights with their throats cut litter the defensive switchback that tunnels through the Arm's Tower. The ancient brickwork is a slippery mess; quick knife-work on an unsuspecting quarry. Alas, the night-officer has only seven men left to answer his commands. All depends on stealth, not numbers.

The two inner gates leading into the Alcazaba, as well as the outer gate leading down into the city, lie dangerously ajar, an affront to every imaginable defensive protocol. All that is left is to lift the massive iron *portcullis* protecting the plated oak outer gate and their work will be done. A heavy *clank-clank-clank-clank-clank-clank-clank* of the iron grate's ratchet assembly, followed by a heavy *THUNK!* One lock down—two more to go, then the grate can be levered up. "Hurry up, you fools! No time!" He hisses, "HURRY, DAMN YOU!"

The commander hears the unmistakable footfall of approaching troops. He tilts his head to assess the direction, curses again. Coming from inside the Alcazaba. *Not good.*

He barks, "How much longer?"

"Almost there, sir."

"Hurry, men!"

The footfall grows louder. Close. *Clank-clank-clank-clank-clank-clank-clank. THUNK!* One lock to go. With a sickening sense the night-officer realizes they will not make it in time. After a resigned curse he calmly says, "I am afraid that our time is up, men. Draw your swords and form a defensive line." His troops exchange terrified looks. One by one they unsheathe their weapons, then turn to stare into the jaws of death.

The Abencerraje brigade rounds the last switchback and is within a hundred paces of the Arm's Gate when the first alarm bell sounds. The officer in command issues a hand-signal and the troops halt, crouch low. He can plainly see that while the Arm's Gate door is open, the portcullis remains down. *Useless. Something has gone wrong.* He waits impatiently, knowing full well that his men are in an extremely precarious position. The traitors within the Arm's Gate come into view now as they back up against the iron grate, trapped like rats.

The heavy footfall inside the Arm's Gate is joined by the barking of orders as an attack strategy crystallizes. The royal guardsmen are in the tower tunnel now. They slow to assess the situation then ease carefully around the final right angle of the tunnel and stop, face to face with the traitors.

The night-officer shouts, "Long live the Abencerrajes!" His men echo him. "Long live the Abencerrajes!"

The royal guardsmen move forward and within a minute have cut them down.

The brigade stands as silent witnesses, helpless to prevent the slaughter. The sound of footfall is above them now, and shouts are ringing from the roofs of the Alcazaba towers as they fill with archers. The officer is not stupid. He shouts his orders, and the brigade begins an orderly retreat back down to the Albayzín.

"Make sure you only hit the Puente del Cadí. The Albayzín is not to be harmed, Prince al-Qattani. At least for now. Boabdil must have no easy means for crossing the River Darro."

The commander of the Alhambra's garrison soberly nods. "Understood, sir."

The Alhambra possesses nineteen heavy bronze cannons, eight of which can command a field of fire over the northern reaches of the city, including the Albayzín. They stare down from the Bulwark, the westernmost prow of the Alhambra.

Grand Vizier Venegas nervously paces in the castle keep of the Alcazaba. He stops and turns. "I want to send a clear message to the Abencerrajes—we can destroy the Albayzín if it comes to that. After the bridge is down, fire a few warning shots over their heads to make sure they understand their situation."

Prince al-Qattani nods.

Venegas contemplates a thousand contingencies as he resumes his pacing. He realizes full well that they have been spared a disaster by the very narrowest of margins. If he had not awakened early the Alhambra would now belong to the Abencerrajes. That Boabdil was behind this act of treason is now painfully obvious; straightforward deduction. A startlingly bold move, to be sure, and masterminded by Fatima, no doubt. That Boabdil was supported by Abencerrajes troops and its Council of Elders was not so obvious; only recently confirmed by torturing the captured infiltrators from inside the garrison. To assume that the Abencerrajes remained weak and impotent was clearly a grave error, one made by him as well as by most in the Nasrid chain of command. He realizes now that his spy networks have been exposed as woefully inadequate. He shakes his head in dismay. *We were lucky. Very lucky.* The role of Zoraya in pushing Fatima into this desperate move is not lost on him, but he knows there is little to be done about it. He has already dispatched riders to alert the sultan of the shocking developments. There will be hell to pay, that much is sure.

He again stops. "Prince al-Qattani, after you sift the palace for any more infiltrators, triple the number of troops within the Alhambra. We are at war." He frowns. "With the Christians *and* the Abencerrajes. Once you are assured of our defensive integrity, advise the city garrisons that I want the Albayzín completely sealed off."

"Understood, sir."

"There is much to be done. See to it." Venegas motions to his bodyguards and sets off for the Lion Palace.

Twenty minutes later, the Bulwark's artillery officer turns to his gun crews and shouts, "Swivel the guns, men, and set chocks to fire downward. Our target is the Puente del Cadí. Now ready your cannons!"

Just past sunrise, a deathly quiet has descended on the city. Markets are closed, businesses shuttered, even the communal ovens lie cold. The moon climbs the sky still, but she is slowly being erased by the morning light, the haughty jewel tamed to a frail, bone-white relic.

"Well?" Boabdil spits his disgust to the ground, then screams, "WELL?! EXPLAIN!" An echo of his father's antics.

It is a rare day indeed when Aben Comixa is at a loss for words. He fumbles about, "My apologies, sire. It remains . . . ahh . . . unclear how . . . umm . . . the alarm was . . . umm . . . sounded, before . . . uhh . . . the gate . . . was opened."

Boabdil hisses, "STUPID FOOL!"

Fatima looks ashen. "We are done for."

Tense silence.

Abu al-Haytham's disappointment scars his drawn face. "I will grant that fortune has not shined upon us this night. Most unfortunate. But we are not done for, not by a long shot. We own the Albayzín. And most of the merchant families are either loyal to us, or else neutral."

BOO-BOOM! BOOM! BOOM! BOO-BOOM-BOOM! BOOM!

The whole contingent instinctively ducks.

"Dear Lord!" Boabdil points, aghast. High above, thick clouds of blue-gray smoke have enveloped the Bulwark.

Abu al-Haytham sighs. "Logical. For good measure Venegas will demolish the Puente del Cadí to make sure we do not attempt another assault. And, of course, to remind us that they have heavy cannons and we do not."

Fatima's voice is strangled and shaky. "No, we do not, Abu al-Haytham. They can demolish the Albayzín, and us with it, if they so desire. Bombard us day and night until we surrender."

"I think not, Sultana." Aben Comixa has finally recovered his senses. "Destroy half of the city to save the Alhambra? No. All commerce would instantly evaporate, and businesses would grind to a halt. The merchant families would have the sultan's head within a week." He muses. "No, Venegas means only to intimidate us. We are safe. At least for now."

Abu al-Haytham says, "I agree. We have to fortify the borders of the Albayzín in case the Nasrids aim to test our defenses. And we must allow any who are loyal to the Nasrids to freely leave—without their property, of course. An olive branch. The Albayzín will become an Abencerraje fortress . . . within a Nasrid fortress."

Fatima snarls, "And what, pray, will we eat when they lay siege to this Abencerraje fortress?"

The old man snorts. "Leave that to me, sultana. We have many months of stockpiled supplies, and the River Darro is at our fingertips. There is gold aplenty. I am positive Granada has an abundance of merchants willing to barter for it. If not Granada, then Castile." A sly smile.

Boabdil straightens his back. "Very well. I will organize the defenses and continue to train my army into a lethal fighting force. For when the time comes."

Aben Comixa's eyes sparkle. "A shrewd move, sire. That time will definitely come. Let us not forget that the sultan will very quickly return with his army once he learns the news of our failed coup."

The four of them stare at one another, numb with the realization of the obvious.

BOOM! BOOM-BOOM! BOO-BOOM! BOOM!

Vermillioned Nothingness

BOOM! BOOM!

They instinctively duck for cover even though they know the cannons are not trained on them. The extreme value of cannons in this coming war, and Granada's relative lack of them, has already become painfully apparent to Ali al-Attar.

The battle rages still, but it is already obvious to the old warrior that this will be the army's second crushing defeat at the hands of the Christians. He knows full well the sultan will howl with fury when he hears the news.

For their second assault on Alhama they opted for a small auxiliary wagon gate close to the gorge rim, away from the devastating cannon fire from the main gate tower. In tandem, al-Zaghal led an assault from inside the gorge, aimed at linking up with Ali al-Attar's men once they each gained a foothold on the top of the wall. A bold move requiring both close coordination and the element of surprise.

Things began well enough, but by some miracle of engineering, Ponce de León managed to shift two of his four heavy cannons to the tower a hundred-fifty paces west of the main gate, just at the perfect angle to bring flanking fire to bear on Ali al-Attar's advancing lines. Dumb luck, but lethal nonetheless. His phalanxes are again being decimated by merciless canister loads. The Christians seem to have settled on leg-long links of chain as the most efficient manner for slaughtering Moors, and with each blast ropey tendrils of death mow down dozens of his men at a time. The old knight understands quickly that his laddermen and rammers will never reach their targets with sufficient strength to rupture the gate or scale the wall.

Within the gorge, al-Zaghal's escaladors and supporting infantry have slipped down the river undetected, and with the Christians focused on the main assault, they have managed to make it to the top of the cliff before being discovered. Alas, they were easily repulsed. Bolts of heavy felt soaked in naphtha were unrolled to thirty paces, then lit, and dropped into the gorge. The hellish streamers of flames and billowing black awfulness swept the climbers off their ropes, the air suddenly filled with sickening screams truncated by ugly, cracking thuds as their bodies broke on the rocks below. Not a single escalador made it off the cliff face.

Another disaster. Hundreds dead and wounded. Maybe more. *BOOM-BOOM!*

Excited murmurs race through the infantry held in reserve, then a few scattered shouts and finger pointing. *"Saqr! Saqr!"* Hundreds of gazes shift to the north as a thunderous cry rises: *"THE FALCONS! THE FALCONS! HUZZAH!"*

Ali al-Attar reluctantly turns his anguished face away from the frothing carnage. Remarkable how the old man's face alights when he sees them top the rolling hill in their glory. *Finally, some good news.* He softly says, "Praise Allah." The elite cavalry canters leisurely forward a quarter mile out, and then, horns sounding, begins to slowly part into five neatly formed columns. The old man recognizes this is an attack formation Yusef prefers. He frowns. "Hasan, send a rider to meet the Falcons. Tell them they are not to engage. This battle is done. Quickly now, before they come in range of the cannons. Hurry, man!" The adjutant nods, disappears.

BOO-BOOM!

The old man winces with each deep, concussive blast. "Ismail, have the trumpeter sound retreat. Send up wagons for the wounded. And make sure they are flying white flags."

"Yes, my lord. Shall I send a rider to inform the sultan?"

The old man cruelly snaps, "You think he is blind?!"

The officer lowers his eyes. "No, my lord. I just—"

"No." His tone softens. "I will give him the news myself." He curses, then mutters to himself, "Recapturing Alhama is a fool's errand. The sultan would rather see half his army slaughtered than have a few Christians fly their flag over Alhama."

The officer's eyes remain glued to the ground.

The trumpet blares.

"DAMN those infernal cannons! And DAMN the emir for buying them without informing me!" The sultan is flailing about like a madman, animated and flushed a deep scarlet, spewing venom.

Al-Zaghal watches him closely for any signs of the malady that previously felled him.

Ali al-Attar soberly says, "As long as Ponce de León can bring them to bear on our phalanxes, attacking the walls is suicide. I will not attempt it a third time without a better plan." His intense, watery eyes burn. "And if you order me to, sire, you can find yourself another military vizier."

The sultan stops and glowers but remains silent.

Al-Zaghal softly says, "Easy, old friend. How they are managing to move the cannons from tower to tower is beyond me." He shakes his head. "There cannot be more than a few hundred Christians capable of wielding a sword left in Alhama. Not nearly enough to adequately defend the walls. And yet they magically appear just in the right place at the right time . . ." His voice trails off.

Ali al-Attar finishes his sentence, "In the right place at the right time, and their cannons loaded with chain. Fifty of my men are killed or maimed with every blast, Muhammad. More. I tell you, I will not do it again."

Tense silence settles in.

The sultan has managed to calm himself and sit. "Perhaps I should send for a few of the Alhambra's heavy cannons. We could blast the gate to bits. Towers, too."

Al-Zaghal replies, "No, not possible, sire. It would take two weeks, maybe three to get them here. Let us not forget that the Christians surely have reinforcements already on the way. King Fernando's army may be on us within a week, perhaps less. No, whatever we do must be done quickly."

Yusef says, "Did you bring the limbered cannons that I designed?"

Eyes turn to the elder Falcon.

Al-Zaghal answers, "No, Yusef. We left them at the garrison in La Malahá, to make better time. But even with pelleted powder they are far too small to be of any use in breaching Alhama's walls."

"That is certainly true, sir, but I have something else in mind entirely."

His uncle says, "Tell us, Yusef."

Yusef stands. "We can use our limbered guns to pin down the Christian cannon crews. Pull them in to close range, rake their positions with canister loads. And stagger our shots one after the other, so we interrupt their reloading and aiming. Slow them down to a snail's pace."

Al-Zaghal nods appreciatively.

The sultan replies, "Go on."

Yusef continues, "Our cannons are horse-drawn, sire, so we can quickly deploy them at any point on the battlefield. Move in close, fire, then move again, before the Christians have time to aim their cannons at us. We stay one step ahead of them."

Umar chimes in, "They may get off a few shots at our phalanxes, but not enough to stop the assault. Fire and move, fire and move. I like it!"

The old man grunts his approval. "Finally, an idea."

Yusef says, "How many cannon and limbers were completed, Uncle?"

"Eight." He raises a cautionary finger. "But they have not been test-fired or seasoned, Yusef."

"Mmm." He turns to the sultan. "Sire, I would suggest sending your fastest rider to La Malahá, and bring the limbered cannons and the gun crews. They should be able to be back here in two days if they ride hard. One day for preparations, then we attack again on Thursday morning. I will lead the cannon crews during the battle, and Umar will command our cavalry. Uncle will assault the same gate as this morning. Perhaps they will still have only two cannons capable of flanking fire. And this time, Prince al-Zaghal will assault the wall where he first attacked. On the opposite side of the city. The Christians do not have enough numbers to defend both. We shall have victory, sire."

The sultan beams. "And by Allah, it shall be so! Well done, Yusef. Well done!" He turns to al-Zaghal. "Brother, I want a rider in La Malahá by tomorrow morning." He claps his hands together. "There is no victor but Allah!"

"There is no victor but Allah!"

IN THE BORDERLANDS OF THE KINGDOM OF GRANADA SOUTH OF LUCENA, NEAR BENAMEJÍ.

Three riders walk their mounts from the edge of the dark woods and stop in plain sight, a loaded pack-horse trailing behind. Full beards trimmed in the Andalusian style. White turbans and colorful Moorish clothing; not lavish, but not poor either. No armor. Daggers and unimposing short swords are their only obvious weaponry. Moorish traders, trafficking illegal wares of some sort across the border. Common enough.

The Castilian army stretches back into the distance. Swords drawn, the cavalry vanguard races up and surrounds the men. Word is quickly passed back to King Fernando, who gallops up to investigate. He stops and surveys the Moorish riders in silence, his expression stern, his palm resting on his sword hilt.

One of the Moors walks his horse forward three steps. He nods to the king. "*As-salam alaykum.*" Hello. Peace.

The king frowns.

"*Kayfa ḥalak.*" How are you?

No response.

The Moor looks perplexed. "*Hal tatakallam al-lughah al-arabiyah?*" Do you speak Arabic?

Fernando begins to chuckle, then laughs loudly. He rises in his stirrups. "And how fares the Great Captain?"

Gonzalo de Córdoba beams that handsome smile, makes a sweeping bow in his saddle. "No worse for wear, majesty."

"You make a fine, Moor, Gonzalo! What say you, sir?!" The king's affection for his trusted general is unmistakable.

The Great Captain smiles. "I say that Castile's army is a welcomed sight indeed, majesty."

"Tell me you have good news from Alhama, Gonzalo."

"Indeed I do, majesty. Ponce de León holds the city still, but by the narrowest of margins." His smile relaxes. "Sultan Muley Hacén has him surrounded. An army of fifteen thousand, perhaps twenty. I fear our friend will not last long."

"Then we must make haste to relieve him. The queen insists that Alhama be held, Gonzalo, that Ponce de León's valor be matched by our own. I rallied as much of the army as I could at Lucena before marching, but many of our units are still scattered across Castile and Aragon. We are barely at a quarter-strength."

"I was afraid of that. It would be perilous to enter the Moorish kingdom ill-prepared, majesty. We must not underestimate the sultan's capabilities to defend his realm. I would suggest we return to Lucena and hold our assault until we are at full strength."

The king considers this. "Ponce de León is depending on us, Gonzalo. We have no choice but to strike for Alhama, prepared or not."

A sly smile. "There is more good news to tell, majesty."

The king queries with his eyebrows.

"As we speak, the Duke of Medina-Sidonia also marches to relieve Alhama, majesty. From the west. I am told he has his entire army at his call, and the knights of the Order of Santiago at his side. They thirst to avenge Zahara."

The king shakes his head incredulously. "Praise God. How did this miracle come to pass?"

"It seems Ponce de León's wife made a personal appeal to the duke's honor. One, it seems, he could not refuse." The Great Captain smiles. "She threw herself at his feet and begged in God's name for his help in saving her husband from the blood-thirsty Moors."

The king chuckles. "Lady de Pacheco is quite the woman."

"Indeed she is. The duke's army should be in Antequera by now, I would think. They should reach Alhama by Thursday if all goes well. God willing, the duke's arrival should give the sultan pause. Forces joined, the duke and Ponce de León should be able to defend Alhama. Let us turn back for Lucena and regroup, majesty. Once the army is at full strength we should march first on Loja. My sources tell me that it is lightly garrisoned. Once we capture it, we can use Loja as a staging ground for a final push on Alhama. A two-step assault. Then, with a march to Málaga we can cut the sultan's kingdom in half, and the war will be over almost before it has begun. There is much to discuss, majesty, and plans to be drawn up."

"Yes. It is good to have you back in my company, Gonzalo. I depend upon your good counsel."

Gonzalo tips his head. "You honor me, majesty."

King Fernando turns in his saddle. "We will make camp here tonight. Spread the word."

The knights whose wounds are judged to be sufficiently minor are hastily bandaged and sent back to their battalions. The badly injured are loaded into wagons and sent to Granada for care. Two days of agony in route, the air cold and biting, the bumpy roads punishing. Over half will die in transit, their broken bodies delivered to their wailing families outside the city gates. Mothers screaming at the sky as they cradle the sweet faces of their dead twenty-year-old sons whose bodies have been so cruelly abused. Fathers and sisters and young wives and those betrothed will gather in a tight circle round their dead loved ones, wailing. A spirit-crushing sight to behold.

The survivors are divvied between the Atfal and the Bermejas hospitals, each now nearing capacity—it is a mad scramble to find sufficient beds for everyone. Under a flag of truce an appeal is made to Boabdil by Venegas to permit Hakim al-Fadl and his staff at the Maristan to carry on with the business of tending the wounded. Boabdil and the Council of Elders reluctantly agree, though only for the wounded whose families still reside in the Albayzín. The wagons are stopped at the barricaded border and thoroughly searched, then are waved through. Though one might naively assume that compassion can sometimes outweigh politics, truth be told, almost all of the families that still remain in the Albayzín are loyal to the Abencerraje cause.

None of them, even Ezar and David, are prepared for the cruelty of the wounds, the awfulness that battle can inflict upon a human body. After all, Granada has not been at war since the Battle of Jaén, one hundred and twenty years ago. It is history's terrible irony that the hell of any war, of all wars, is so quickly forgotten, so neatly packed up and tucked away, empowering innocent youth to once again take up their swords so willingly and stake their lives on the false promise of glamor, of glory, of honor. For many, for most, this cruel deception will end tragically in the harsh reality of suffering and anguish, of lost friends, of heartache and tears. In hurt beyond all hurt. Even those who manage to walk away seemingly unscathed will bear deep, invisible scars for the rest of their lives. And yet, amazingly enough, their children's children will likely never learn of the horror they endured, of the truth about war, because their grandfathers will refuse to speak of the unmentionable ordeal they lived through. And when we forget, we are doomed to retrace those cruel steps once again. History's terrible irony come full circle.

The surgical ward is clean and well lit, the braziers pumping out heat, but the smell is unmistakable—death. Soft, tortured moans; strained grunts of agony, so arresting in their odd rhythms; pathetic whimpers; quiet calls for loved ones; delirious, piercing screams—a cacophony of anguish fills the Bermejas. Some hellish nightmare unleashed.

Danah glances at the young knight's face. Handsome; not much older than her. Unconscious, thankfully, but his face is flushed, his brow beaded with sweat—never a good sign with a wound. She begins to unravel his sopping bandages, the blood so bright and alive it might have been dyed in a vat of expensive cinnabar that morning. She gasps. The young man's shoulder is completely torn away, the ball joint exposed and crudely disconnected from the socket where it belongs, as if some macabre dissection lesson has gone horribly wrong in the hands of an amateur butcher. She scans the wound. Thankfully, no active bleeders; just raw meat. *Miraculous that no major vessels were cut.* She takes a deep breath, exhales, then begins to carefully remove the blood-soaked bandages on his arm and hand. The young man begins to moan. Her hands freeze. She watches him carefully. Fortunately, he does not break the plane of consciousness, and finally the moans cease. She continues, wincing. The bone of his upper arm is shattered, the finger-length jagged end protruding through the skin. *Ugly; a compound fracture.* Two crisscrossed lacerations on this forearm link his wrist to his elbow, deep enough to see tendons and white bone beneath. Still oozing blood. Thumb and forefinger missing. *He will never hold a sword again, that much is sure.* She wrinkles her nose, leans closer. The sweet stink of infection has already set in.

Her lip begins to quiver. *Dear Lord. What am I supposed to do with this?* Her world slows, the colors fading to gray. She simply stares, paralyzed, her mouth agape.

From across the room, David sees her and comes to her side. "Danah."

She simply stares at the massive wound, catatonic.

He touches her shoulder. "Danah!"

Nothing.

He shakes her.

She slowly turns. Her face is ashen, her eyes terror-filled. She helplessly whispers, "David. Dear Lord. Dear Lord."

He glances down at the awful mess. "Wake him. Give him some poppy seed and valerian root elixir. Try to stitch what you can, then set the arm and treat him for infection. Quickly now, Danah, time matters. There are a dozen more who need you."

She is not there.

"Danah. You can do this."

No response.

"Danah, look at me. Danah!"

Her eyes wander to his, but she does not seem to recognize him.

He snaps, "Hakim Amiriya!"

Thankfully, this thaws her. Her focus returns, her eyes brighten. A weak nod, then her expression tightens. She purses her lips and whispers, "I can do this. I *will* do this."

David nods.

She clears her throat. Her color is coming back; she is herself again. "Forgive me, David. I am fine." She reaches for her medicine vial, scans the label, pours it into a measuring spoon.

Satisfied, he turns and moves to the bed next to her. An officer. The man's leg has been severed mid-thigh, ropey tendons and long strands of skin and meat still attached and hanging limp on the blood-drenched sheet. A crudely applied tourniquet made from a leather belt is the only thing keeping the man from bleeding to death. Amazing that he made it to Granada still alive. David shakes his head and mutters, "Dear Lord, help us."

Yusef's gun crews are tucked safely behind the crest of the hill, out of sight. These cannons are little things compared to the monsters they are up against. Five feet stem to stern, three-inch bores. He has eight functional guns, each carriage pulled by a single draft horse. Six-man gun crews, each with a mount for rapid deployment—one on the draft horse pulling the gun, one gunnery officer, one swabber, one powderman, one shotman, and one primer. Cannon number nine broke the wheel of its carriage on the road to Alhama; number ten was not yet mounted. They will fire canister loads, each three-inch cylindrical bag bearing forty olive-sized hunks of lead. He figures that with carefully overlapping fields of fire, his eight guns should be enough to pin down two fixed cannons trained on them.

He has ridden forward with his gunnery officers far enough to see the action unfold. It is vital that he knows what they are up against before revealing his strategy to the Christians. Umar has command of their cavalry and is riding in support of al-Zaghal's force on the opposite side of Alhama.

Ali al-Attar's phalanxes are once again on the march toward the wagon gate. The only difference this time is their marching speed—much more spirited than before—an attempt to quickly cover the distance before the cannons can have their say. Still no response from the tower, but the walls are ominously filling with dancing iron helmets as reinforcements are brought up. Three hundred paces. Two hundred. One hundred.

BOO-BOOM!

The pair of fiery flashes and a thick billowing cloud of smoke consumes the tower. Parallel swaths of death slice through the center phalanx, each scything four-dozen troops. The phalanx stops momentarily to close ranks, then resumes its march. The waves of archers on the walls begin to loose, and are soon joined by the arquebuses. *Po-pow! Pow! Pow-pow!*

Good, still there. One, two, three, four, five . . . Yusef stares hard at the tower as he counts to himself. Finally, the smoke begins to thin and clear. He sees what he is after; on the secondary platform on the south side of the tower the scurrying of iron-helmeted troops wrestling the beasts. At the count of fifty-two, the shiny barrels of the cannons peek through the wall as they are pulled forward with ropes and pulleys to be aimed. He sees that, due to their oblique firing angle, two gaps in the crenellations have been widened by several feet to give them better fields of fire. Not exactly exposed, but definitely vulnerable.

At sixty-seven, a concussive *BOOM!* Five seconds later, the other *BOOM!* He nods. A full minute for his men to load, fire, and move. He again waits for the smoke to clear, then points, "See them nosing out! Second platform down from the top, the two gaps in the crenellations. Got it?!" His officers acknowledge. "Our time has come, men! We must fire and move as quickly as we can. Sixty seconds, no more. Keep careful track of the time. Remember, only half-charges of powder. These guns have not been properly seasoned. Careful aiming. Make each shot count. And stay in pairs and maintain firing order so that we can keep a steady barrage on them. The goal is to fire in pairs, repeated every half-minute. Pace yourselves and adjust as needed. I will be riding with gun crew number one. Do me proud, men! To victory!"

"To victory!"

"No! Stay away from me! Someone! Keep her away from me!"

At first Danah is surprised by the man's words, then she is taken aback, but then her nostrils flare as her face settles into stone. Her emeralds blaze as she begins to fume. Her words emerge slowly, dangerously. "If you wish to live, sir, I suggest you allow me to tend to your wounds. I can assure you—"

"Stay away from me, green-eyed devil! Someone, help me! Help!"

David is instantly at her side. "What is the problem here?"

The man's eyes are wide with terror. "Blasphemy! Why is this she-devil tending my wounds? I will not have a woman hold a knife over me. Never! I will not!"

David's jaw muscles tighten. He hisses, "Fool. Do you not see the robe she wears? This is Hakim Amiriya, a skilled physician. She is one of the finest healers in the kingdom. If you value your life, I suggest you keep your mouth closed and let her do her work. Understood?"

"But she is a woman—"

"I will say this once more, and only once more. If you value your life, you will keep your mouth closed and let Hakim Amiriya do her work."

The man falls silent and turns his head away from them.

Danah and David exchange a quick glance. She nods, and he turns and walks back to his patient. Her voice softens. "Here, you must drink this. It will help you sleep while I work. Please."

He refuses to meet her eyes, but he does allow her to lift his head. He drinks the elixir, then looks away again.

He tenses as she lifts the blanket to examine his wounds but otherwise does not resist. She carefully unwraps the bandages. The man's upper arm has been sliced to the bone from his elbow to his shoulder, and he has taken an arrow just below his collarbone; the shaft crudely snapped off, the arrowpoint foolishly left in place. A wide ring of swollen, angry-red flesh encircles the shaft. Infection has set in. She leans to see his face. Asleep. She turns to her tray of tools, lifts her surgical knife, and gets to work.

David slowly walks through the main ward, surveying the day's work. It is deep into the night now, and the place has thankfully quieted, except for the occasional whimper or soft groan. He is weary beyond belief. Seventeen hours on his feet. Of the twenty-three wounded who arrived that morning, sixteen are still alive, though three are not likely to survive the night. He shakes his head as he recollects the frightful wounds they faced. The knights arrived chilled to the bone and to a man in some stage of shock, most having lost large amounts of blood. Some had clear signs of infection festering in their abused flesh. And the wounds, dear Lord. He is well acquainted with the deep sword slices and dagger cuts and the ugly puncture holes of pikes and lances, but these injuries from cannon fire are different. Devastating, many simply beyond his skills—beyond any hakim's skills. A death sentence.

Danah shined, as he knew she would once she got over her initial shock. Thankfully, there were no more incidents related to having a female working in the ward. His staff of eight medical assistants was exemplary. They have spent the past hour mopping up the blood splashed over the floors, then boiling the sheets and bandages and surgical cutting tools, as well as preparing bread and soup for the next day's arrival of wounded. Order has mostly been restored. He has instructed them to sleep in shifts, four on, four off, so that there is always at least one set of eyes in each ward to summon him or Danah in an emergency.

He turns the corner, opens the door, and enters the smaller room where they opted to put the most grievously wounded, the ones unlikely to last the night. He stops as he sees her. She is kneeling on the floor beside a knight, cradling his hand between her two. He remembers the injury. Danah worked for hours on the young man. Left leg hacked away below the knee, chest ripped open, his liver badly damaged, stomach chewed up. He will not live long.

The young man's eyes are closed, his face pale, so pale. She is leaning over him, whispering into his ear. David cannot hear her words, but it is clear that she is praying for the dying knight. On and on she goes.

He steps to her, touches her on the shoulder, softly says, "Danah." She does not acknowledge her mentor. Her whispers grow more urgent. "Danah. You have done all that you can. Some wounds are just not possible to repair. I will see that Baruch checks on him."

The prayers cease, and she slowly rises. "So young. So young to die, David. What is this world coming to? Tell me." She looks up at him, suddenly angry. "War is so insane, so horrible!"

"I know. How soon we all forget." She looks so tired. He lays a fatherly arm across her shoulders. "You have made me very proud today, Danah."

She calms herself. "Thank you."

He manages a smile. "Your training is complete. Come, Hakim Amiriya, we both desperately need rest. More wounded will surely be arriving in the morning."

The rider gallops up and is directed by the sentries to the sultan's large tent. He dismounts. "I must see the sultan. An important message from the Alhambra."

The commander of the royal bodyguard eyes the man cautiously. Disheveled, clearly having ridden through the night. Horse ridden to the ground. He looks back at the man. "The sultan is unwell this morning. You may leave it with me. I will see that he gets it when he wakes."

The rider grows frantic. "But the letter is from Grand Vizier Venegas, my lord. An urgent matter! For the sultan's eyes only, my lord. Grand Vizier Venegas was quite emphatic. Please, my lord."

The commander considers this. "A moment." He motions, and three of his men step forward to wait with the rider; then the commander turns and enters the sultan's tent.

As the messenger waits he hears heavy cannons fire in the distance. *BOOM! BOOM!* He turns in their direction. A pair of smaller blasts answer. *Blam! Blam!* While he cannot see the city walls from here, there is clearly a vicious battle raging. *Bla-blam!*

The sultan's private secretary is frowning as he steps from the tent. "What seems to be the trouble?"

"I have been sent by Grand Vizier Venegas, my lord. An urgent letter for the sultan's eyes only. All hell has broken loose in Granada, my lord."

The secretary lifts his brows in surprise. "Very well. I will wake the sultan. Wait here."

Ten minutes later, the sultan lifts the tent flap and steps into the sunshine. The man looks decidedly unwell. Pale, and with a prominent limp. He curses the light, then squints at the rider; clearly in pain, the sultan rubs his right temple. "Speak." His pronunciation is odd, a bit slurred.

The messenger bows. "Sire. A message from Grand Vizier Venegas." He thrusts the scroll forward, bows once more.

The sultan breaks the seal, begins to read. He winces, reads some more, then stops and curses, continues to the end, curses again, then crushes the letter in his hand. As his face flushes dark with fury, he shakes his fist at the sky. "What have I done to deserve such treachery, O Lord? TELL ME, PLEASE! WHAT?!" He takes a deep breath, holds it, then exhales. "It seems I have spawned a traitor, gentlemen. A TRAITOR! MY SON BOABDIL IS A DAMNED TRAITOR!" His right cheek begins to twitch uncontrollably. He motions to the commander of the royal bodyguards, who comes to his side.

"Sire?"

"Granada is in revolt, Ahmad. It seems that Boabdil has somehow won the support of the Abencerraje dogs. He now has troops under his command, though no one seems to know how many. They attempted a surprise attack on the Arm's Gate. Thankfully, Venegas managed to thwart the attack, but it seems that Boabdil and the Abencerrajes are now in control of the Albayzín. Sealed off and fortified."

"Dear Lord."

"Venegas had to use our cannons to destroy the Puente del Cadí."

The commander sees that the sultan's lips are quivering. The man looks unsteady on his feet. "Sire. You need rest."

He slurs, "No time." The sultan places a hand on Ahmad's shoulder to steady himself. "I must send troops to Granada to reinforce Venegas and the Alhambra in case Boabdil decides to attack again. How goes the battle?"

"So far Yusef's cannons are doing their job, sire. The firing from the tower cannons has slowed to a crawl, enabling Ali al-Attar to engage the wagon gate. Al-Zaghal is about to begin his assault."

"Good. Umar's cavalry?"

"In reserve, sire."

"Good. Send word. I want him to ride for Granada as fast as the wind. Tell him the Alhambra is under attack, and he is to place his cavalry under Venegas' command. And make sure Ali al-Attar and my brother are informed." The sultan's slurring is getting worse.

"I will see to it immediately, sire." Ahmad ticks his head, and one of his men is instantly at his side. He whispers his orders, and the man turns and calls for a mount; he gallops off. Ahmad then motions to two of his men to help the sultan. "Sire. You require rest."

The sultan grimaces, waves them off. He turns to his secretary. "Hatim, draw up orders. After this battle is finished, part of my army must be returned to the city to lay siege to the Albayzín. Choose brigades that are at full strength."

The sultan's secretary replies, "Of course, sire." He exchanges a worried glance with the commander. "Sire. You must rest until this headache passes. I *must* insist."

The sultan looks confused, weary beyond belief. "Perhaps you are right. Just a few minutes' rest." He allows Hatim and the two bodyguards to lead him back into the tent.

David scans the letter, frowns.

She is carefully measuring out antiseptics into a graduated flask on a bench across the room but senses trouble in his silence. Without taking her eyes from her work she says, "Tell me."

"Your parents."

She turns now, sees his expression, resumes her work. "They want me to come home to the Albayzín."

"They do. At noon today." He manages a chuckle. "I would say more of a command than a desire. They even included a safe conduct pass to get you through the sentries at the gate. Would you like to read it?"

"No."

"They *are* your parents, Danah."

No hesitation. "I am not going, David. As we both know, I am sorely needed here."

"That is true. Still, they have a rightful say."

She turns again to face him. "They will confine me to the carmen until this insurrection is settled. Meanwhile, the wounded from Alhama will continue to arrive."

"I know." He considers her situation. "There is the Maristan Hospital. Boabdil is letting at least some of the wounded into the Albayzín for treatment. I could write a letter to your parents saying that I am reassigning you there. A compromise."

"As you and I both know, only the Abencerraje wounded are being allowed in, David. As a hakim of Granada, I cannot show any preference for whom I treat. *I will not.*"

Softly now, "Yes." He studies her. "Are you sure?"

"My mind is made up."

"Then will you at least write them a letter explaining that you are safe and are needed here. And that you are under the direct care and protection of Royal Physician al-Adani and his wife. I will add my own letter to try to ease their minds. Please?"

"Very well." She returns to her work.

The Christians greeted them with arrows and scattered arquebuses when Yusef's cannon crews strutted onto the battlefield like little chariots, but they are safely beyond reach. Yusef stands in his stirrups on his stallion Nasr, adjacent to his gun, and is intently studying their target. *There!* He sees the bronze barrel inch forward into view. He shouts, "Fire, Jalil!" The gunnery officer barks, "Stand clear!" As the primer steps forward, they plug their ears with their fingers. The primer presses the smoldering rope to the touch hole.

BLAM!

The gun carriage jerks upward and rolls back. The dense cloud of smoke obscures their view for a moment, then begins to dissipate in the breeze. With half-charges of pelleted powder, the velocity is slow enough that he can actually see the swarm of canister balls fly at the tower like angry bees. They strike the crenellated wall of the platform full on, felling several soldiers and showering the battery with shards of masonry. The heavy cannon remains stationary; exactly the intent.

His gun crew shouts, "Huzzah!"

BLAM! goes the second gun, as their mate, deployed thirty paces to their left, fires. The timing is a little late, and he sees that their load sails high.

Yusef barks, "Hook the carriage and move! Quickly, men!"

Within twenty seconds the carriage is attached to its mount and they are rolling away, Yusef leading. "Hyah, Nasr, Hyah!" The second gun is soon giving chase. He takes them in an arc closer to the phalanxes, but the same distance from the tower. He raises his hand to signal them. "Whoa, Nasr!" The gun carriage grinds to a halt. "Ready the gun, Jalil!" The men methodically begin their work.

BLA-BLAM! The next pair of cannons fires, three and four. Perfect timing, and on target. Then five and six. By the time all eight guns have fired the tower has still not answered. Ali al-Attar's men are at the gate now with their ram, and the outer phalanxes are readying their ladders. So far, so good.

The shotman cries, "Charge ready!"

The gunnery officer sights down the barrel at the tower, sees that they are on target side to side. "True! Elevation, twenty degrees!" The powderman pounds a wooden chock to elevate the barrel, *slap-slap-slap-slap*, then stops. "Ten degrees more!" He gives two more hits to his chock. "Sighted! Primer up!"

The primer steps forward and rams his iron pick into the touch hole, jerks it back and forth, pulls it out, then fills the hole with powder. "Primed!"

The officer turns to Yusef. "Ready, sir!"

Yusef lifts a hand, looks to his adjacent cannon crew. *Almost there.* He holds until he sees the other officer raise an arm, then he drops his own hand. "Fire, Jalil!"

"Stand clear!"

BLAM! Only a single heartbeat, then *BLAM!* Yusef nods. Much better timing.

BOOM! BOOM! From far to their left. Yusef's eyes whip around just in time to see the carnage unleashed on the third and fourth cannons. The horses, the gun and its carriage, and the crew of the third gun disintegrate in a spray of splintered wood, body parts, and chunks of crimson gore. The incredulous gunnery officer staggers toward the awful mess, armless and faceless, then keels over in a heap. He sees that its twin, the fourth gun, is leaning unsteadily on one wheel but still standing. The massive draft horse, however, has been eviscerated, the poor thing's ropey guts spilled out across the ground. It screams as it tries to move, gets tangled in its own guts, begins to wobble. It settles to its knees, then flops over. Yusef counts. Three men and four horses down. The officer and shotman shuffle about in a daze, unsure what just happened.

Yusef curses. Two of his cannons are now out of commission.

He quickly searches Alhama's walls, spots the cloud of heavy smoke in the distance to his far left, and instantly realizes his error. The blast came from the tower on the main gate. The two other cannons are still there. An extreme oblique angle for a flanking shot, but he miscalculated—his gun crews are still perilously in their field of fire, and at this angle both of the gun crews in each pair can be hit with a single volley. He curses himself as he searches for their best course of action. Too far to reach with a canister load. He knows he cannot move closer to the wall to cut the angle without coming within range of the archers and arquebuses. His own gun crew is still staring open-mounted at the havoc leveled upon their comrades. Yusef realizes they have been in place much longer than sixty seconds, and shouts, "MOVE! MOVE! MOVE!" The gun crew frantically snaps into action, and they are again racing away.

They grind to a halt and quickly unhook the draft horse and pivot the cannon. On Yusef's orders, cannon number two is now fifty paces to the left-rear so that one shot from the tower cannot take out two crews. He glances at the distant tower, curses again. *Still in their field of fire.*

"Jalil! Ready the gun to fire on the tower of the main gate. Jalil!"

"Sir?" The officer is numb.

"Ready the gun to fire on the tower of the main gate. Solid shot this time. And full charge."

It takes the man a moment to collect himself. "But, sir, you said—"

"I said solid shot and full charge."

"Solid shot and full charge, sir."

The officer turns to his crew. "Turn the cannon, men. Main gate. Solid shot, full charge." They frantically scramble to complete their tasks, knowing that they are now the quarry being sighted, and that time is against them.

"Ready, sir!"

"Fire, Jalil!"

"Stand clear!"

BANG! The difference between the half charge and full charge of pelleted powder is striking. The gun carriage kicks up high into the air like a bucking bull, then glides back six feet, almost rolling over the shotman, who has to jump aside.

Yusef squints at his target. The three-inch iron ball strikes the base of the tower four feet above the ground with a cascade of broken masonry. He mentally calculates the required angle and shouts, "Your aim is true, Jalil, but twelve degrees more elevation!"

Gun number two fires its canister at their original target. *BLAMM!*

"Shall we move, sir?"

Yusef weighs this. "No, we need to strike home to protect the others. Fire once more, then we move. Solid shot, full charge! Twelve degrees up!"

BOOM! BOOM! The cannons from their original target finally manage to fire, to devastating effect. Huge swaths are cut through Ali al-Attar's center phalanx. Yusef sees that the battering ram has been dropped. His gun crew is frantically racing to reload.

BLA-BLAMM! Yusef glances up. Cannons five and six.

BOO-BOOM! He can tell without looking by the change in pitch that those are the cannons on the distant main gate tower. The gun crew instinctively crouches. The powderman moans as he wets himself. The raspy whistle of the lead balls and nails and links of chain grows louder and louder. They have seen firsthand what it can do. Breaths are held as the eerie whistle strengthens. The ground twenty paces to their left erupts in a ripping spray of black earth and tufts of grass, two twenty-foot wide cuts, each slicing sixty paces long. Near misses.

That was close. We must move! He slaps Nasr with his reins and is instantly beside the gun. "Jalil! Quickly, man. We must be gone before they reload! They have our range now."

"Almost there, sir!"

Seconds turn into hours, days.

Slap-slap-slap-slap-slap. "Sighted! Primer up!"

"Ready, sir!"

"Fire, Jalil!"

"Stand clear!"

The touch hole fizzles, but the cannon does not fire. The primer frowns, steps forward again, and presses the smoldering rope to the touch hole once more. Nothing. The primer shrugs, uncertain what to do. The gunnery officer steps closer, turns to the swabber. "Bring the water bucket." They are all looking at the gun expectantly when they see another weak puff of smoke and then a sudden, deafening *CAH-POWWWW!*

Time stops. The sounds of battle evaporate. Only burning, acrid smoke and stark, unnatural silence.

The primer and the gunnery officer are torn to pieces by the breech blast. The only thing left of them are the four feet still on the ground, bloody stumps sticking out of the tops of their boots. The powderman is decapitated and pitches forward into the dirt like a felled oak. The shotman is viciously torn asunder by a jagged, fist-sized slab of sizzling bronze, ripping his lungs and liver from his chest. The swabber loses both arms and half a leg. Thankfully, a coin-sized sliver of metal hits him square between the eyes, sparing him the protracted agony of bleeding to death.

All Yusef will ever remember is the brilliance of the flash, a thousand suns searing into his eyes, boring directly into his brain. It is a miracle that he survives the explosion at all. A tiny twist of shrapnel grazes his forehead. An inch to the left, and it would have explored his brain. A second, button-sized piece of bronze bores through the meat of his right forearm, his sword arm; but the strike is clean, missing any major vessels.

Nasr rears up violently when the thick slab of bronze slices through his neck like a hot knife through butter. Yusef manages to hang on to the animal's mane, but the stallion loses his balance and pitches backward awkwardly, landing on his master's leg with a gut-wrenching *crack!* Yusef screams.

He blacks out from the searing pain in his thigh, then comes to, dazed, ears ringing ferociously, still not sure exactly what has happened. He tries to lift his head but cannot. He opens his eyes and stares up at the sky. Vermillion. *How odd.* The reddest red he has ever seen. He blinks to clear his vision. Vermillioned nothingness. He touches his forehead, feels the wet wound; closes his eyes and feels them too. Intact. He opens his eyes once more. Only vermillion. A biting pain in his lower arm, but he is able to flex his fingers. He tries once more to lift his head. An inch, two, then he lies back. The ringing in his ears is easing, the sounds of battle slowly returning.

A muted, *Boo-boom!* Terrifying, raspy whistling; then awful screams.

He remembers now. *Breech blast. I was a fool for using full charges in an unseasoned cannon. My fault. My fault.* The heady smell of blood mixed with gunpowder and charred wood hangs heavy in the air. He suddenly becomes aware of a puddle of hot liquid in his lap. He frantically checks himself for more wounds. Nothing obvious. It finally dawns on him. "Nasr!" A soft, pathetic nicker. He tries to pull himself out from under the horse, but he cries out as he disturbs his shattered leg. Trapped. With his good arm he reaches up and feels for the horse's head. Wet and sticky. The beast's hot blood spurts across his arm. "Easy, boy, easy." The answering nicker is weaker now. "Easy, Nasr. Easy, boy."

Yusef blinks at the sky. The vermillion is slowly changing, darkening—vermillion flows into crimson, then carmine, finally maroon; then grays begin to mix into the palette. Yusef is wide-eyed, fascinated by the evolving colors. After a brief struggle, maroon surrenders to charcoal gray. As darkness approaches, his heart begins to pound with a sickening realization. *I cannot see.* All that is left now is jet black. The abyss. Yusef feels panic rise in his chest. *Dear Lord, I am blind!* In his desperation, he cries out for her, "Danah! DANAH!"

BLA-BLAMM!
BOOM! BOOM!

Her eyes dance beneath closed lids, back and forth, back and forth. She winces, her mouth opens as if to silently scream, then closes. A soft groan as she rolls from her back to her side and tucks her knees to her chest like a little girl and rocks herself, trying desperately to escape the clutches of her nightmare.

When David finally ordered her to lie down and rest her eyes on a makeshift mattress in the stockroom, she made him promise to wake her in a half-hour. It has been almost an hour now, and the demons are having their way with her.

She yelps, flips onto her back again, groans once more, and then her eyes fly open wide as she cries out, "No. No-no! NO!" Her heart is pounding so hard it feels like it may jump from her chest. Disoriented, she lifts her head and struggles to remember where she is. *Bermejas Hospital. Nightmare. So real.* She takes a deep breath, guards it jealously, then finally relents and exhales. She whispers, "So real." She sits up, takes another deep breath. "Dear Lord."

It has been five months now since she has dreamed of him. Since the day of her betrothal to Malik. The specifics of the dream are already fading, though the terror lingers on, as is the way of nightmares. She closes her eyes, tries to grasp what is left. She sees him lying on the battlefield, trapped beneath his horse. She sees him look up at the sky, eyes wide with terror. She hears him scream her name.

Her eyes fill, streak her cheeks. She softly answers him, "Yusef, I am here. Yusef." She clasps her hands in prayer. "Dear Allah. Let it not be so, let it be only a dream. Let Yusef be safe, O Lord. Please, O Lord, protect him. Please, O Lord. Let Yusef be safe."

BOO-BOOM!

Ali al-Attar is beside himself. With the cannons of the main gate successfully pinning down Yusef's horse-drawn cannons, the two guns trained on his phalanxes are now having their way. The attack on the wagon gate has all but collapsed under the withering fire, and the left phalanx has suffered heavy casualties, their ranks in disarray. The right phalanx managed to top the wall and make some headway but then were driven back by the archers and the arquebuses. No more than a dozen ladders are still standing.

The old man curses. "Another defeat." He turns to his adjutant. "Hasan, send for Yusef."

The officer looks pained.

"What? Speak, man!"

"We just received word, my lord." He hesitates. "Prince Yusef has been . . . badly injured."

The old man blanches. "Oh, dear Lord, no. Where is he? Where?!"

"He was pulled from beneath his stallion, my lord, and taken back to camp. It seems his cannon exploded. He was the only man in his crew to survive."

Ali al-Attar's eyes fold closed. "I see."

A shout from behind them. "Rider! Rider approaching!"

The old warrior opens his eyes and turns to their rear to see a scout riding hard across the plain. The man stops in a swirl of dust and jumps from his mount. "My lord! My lord! A Christian army approaches!"

Ali al-Attar shakes his head in dismay. *What else can possibly go wrong this day?* "How many, and how far?"

"A large Christian army, my lord. At least six thousand strong, maybe eight. No more than six miles to the west. They are marching with a purpose, my lord."

"To the west? But King Fernando should be north of us. Are you sure?"

"Positive, my lord. Due west."

He mulls this over. "I see. Very well. Bring my horse; I must inform the sultan and al-Zaghal. Hasan, have the trumpeter sound retreat. Gather as many of the wounded as you can into wagons, and have the men quickly form ranks for marching. If I have my say, we will leave Alhama within two hours. I want a reserve brigade protecting our rearguard in case they send cavalry ahead of the main army."

"Understood, my lord."

"And gather all of the cannons, even the damaged ones. We will take them with us."

"Understood, my lord."

Once the second rider arrived, informing them that King Fernando's Córdoban army had crossed into the kingdom near Zagra, no more than a three-day hard march, it was a simple matter to convince al-Zaghal. They are simply not prepared to engage two Christian armies simultaneously on the field of battle. Even so, it took an ugly, heated argument for the two of them to convince the sultan that retreat was their only viable option. In the end, the old man's crude logic prevailed—live to fight again another day.

They agreed that al-Zaghal and Ali al-Attar should take part of the army to reinforce Loja and hopefully deter King Fernando from a deeper incursion into their territory from the north. Then, once the sultan was back in firm control of Granada, he would bring the rest of the army to rejoin forces, and they would go on the offensive, strike into Castile, perhaps even attack Córdoba. For the time being at least, the decision is made to cede Alhama to the Christians.

The Moorish army that marched on Alhama so confident and invincible, is leaving bloodied and beaten, the heads of the brazen knights bowed low in shame.

As the vanguard cavalry finally spills onto the plain of Alhama from the west, a mighty cheer rises from the walls. Fewer than three-hundred haggard knights remain standing, half of those bearing some sort of injury. Only a quarter of his original force.

Ponce de León looks up when he hears the cheering, searches the horizon for the flagmen, sees the red-cross-on-white of the Order of Santiago and the gold-castle-on-red of Medina-Sidonia. His eyes fill. All he can mutter is, "Thank God you came, Enrique. Thank God." He knows full well that they could not have withstood another Moorish assault.

The duke's army grows silent to a man as they ride through the awful carnage left behind by the retreating army. Hundreds of dead and dozens of mutilated horses scattered upon the field of battle, wisps of smoke still rising from the embattled city.

Reunion

"Now that things have calmed a bit I need to go check on Ezar and make sure that all is well at the Atfal. I am leaving the Bermejas in your capable hands, Hakim Amiriya."

She smiles. "Tell him I asked about his woolly worms."

David chuckles. "I will."

"And tell him I miss him."

He smiles. "Of course. I should be back by noon." He turns to leave, then stops and pivots as he recalls something. "Oh, and Danah. A letter from Málaga came while you were in the ward. I left it on my desk."

She nods. *Malik.* He writes to her every third day, as certain as the rising of the sun. If anything, Malik is meticulous. What should be endearing she instead finds tedious. *Malik.* Without thinking, the word *"boring"* jumps into her mind. As she sighs with the truth of this recognition, she also feels a twinge of guilt. Still, the content of his letters never varies. First, he will declare that he misses her. Then he will give news of Málaga and his family. Next, a litany of the things he is studying, new techniques he has learned. He will end with some timid, sweet profession of his love, and beg her to write more often. Occasionally, he will make some reference to setting a wedding date. Never direct, always oblique. Predictable.

She finishes her paperwork then ambles through the main ward offering kind words here and there, whispering instructions into the ears of the attendants about the most serious cases. Those who were destined to die have mostly done so already. The young man with the horrible shoulder wound, Danah's first patient, passed two days back. A massive infection they simply could not control.

The remaining injured have been sorted by the severity of their wounds and their likelihood of recovery. The main ward houses the least serious, those who can eventually be transferred out to family homes once they are sufficiently stabilized. And, of course, the sad dying ward. There are five rooms off the main corridor; the larger one is the surgical ward, with four smaller wards for recovery.

There are a total of thirty-seven wounded in the Bermejas as of this morning. With a little luck, these young men have some hope of recovery, at least most of them, though many will never fight again. The worst of the lot remain sedated with an elixir made from poppy seed resin and valerian root. Infection is their greatest worry now; it is a steadfast killer. The staff is diligent in maintaining cleanliness throughout the wards, liberally applying what antiseptics they have at their disposal: myrrh and balsam-infused oils, vinegar, diluted naphtha, pastes of ground cloves and rosemary—recipes traceable back to the ancient Greeks but refined over the centuries by the great medical minds of al-Andalus. Bandages are changed daily, and wounds are bathed and aired out. Careful attention is paid to any foul drainage or dark discolorations of the skin near incisions, and especially the sickly-sweet smell marking the beginnings of lethal putrefaction. They have already had to reopen several especially angry wounds, excise festering dead flesh, and treat again for infection.

They are not expecting the next load of wagons from Alhama until late afternoon, and the minor reprieve is welcomed by all. A chance to catch up and take a deep breath.

She exits the main ward, walks down the hall, and opens the door to David's office. She has not been able to shake her dream, and she finds her thoughts drifting to Yusef, almost against her will. She feels guilty each time, reminds herself that she is betrothed and that there is nothing—less than nothing—between them.

She sees the letter on David's desk but does not move to pick it up. She knows she should write Malik more, and with the coming of the war, and especially her new role at the Bermejas, she has a thousand things she could say; but it has been over two weeks now since she has put quill to paper. She feels guilty about this too, but truth be told, she is just not ready to tell him that she has taken her physician's oath. She knows well enough the chain of events that detail will precipitate. And so, she stakes a claim to busyness and puts off writing.

She casually picks up the letter and fingers it but then raises her eyebrows. The handwriting on the outside does not belong to Malik. She scans the imprint in the sealing wax. *Madrasa of Málaga.* Abd al-Salam, her Sufi mentor! This unexpected news prompts instant glee. She sits, eagerly breaks the seal and smooths the stiff paper with her hands. His handwriting is amusingly atrocious, and she has to slowly tease apart the puzzle word by word.

My Dearest Danah. Please indulge a forgetful old man. I have heard tales of a beautiful young maiden in my beloved

*Granada. One with a Sufi heart and amazing gifts for
healing. Supposedly she aspires to be Granada's first
female hakim. Can you imagine?! Alas, I cannot seem to
recall her name. Perhaps you have met her?*

Danah cannot help but laugh. She so misses this man. Wait
until he learns she is already Hakim Amiriya!

*Forgive your favorite matchmaker for not writing sooner, my
dear. Reorganizing the madrasa takes my every waking
moment, and then some. These young stags will be the
death of me! Thankfully my work here is nearly complete,
and I shall soon return to fair Granada. The students of
Málaga will be cursing my name for years!*

Danah smiles.

Your betrothed is well.

Her smile relaxes.

*I see Malik quite often since the Royal Hospital is not far
from the madrasa. He says he will take his oath this spring,
and then your lives can finally proceed as planned. I am
happy for you both. He speaks of nothing but you, of course.
It seems you bewitched the poor lad, my dear! Do us both a
favor and ease his misery and write to him. He is a fine
young man. Blessings be upon you both.*

*Events of late are so troubling, Danah. First Alhama, and
now this awful civil strife in Granada. How soon we forget
the evils righteous men can inflict upon one another. With
your father an Abencerraje elder, I can only imagine the
anxiety you have felt, my dear. David sent word of your
decision to stay at the Bermejas against your parents'
wishes. I have sent a letter to them on your behalf.*

*No doubt you and David have your hands full with the
Alhama's wounded by now. My prayer is that the numbers
are small. Open your heart, dear Danah, and focus on using
the great gifts Allah has bestowed upon you. Remember, the
Sufi Way is to serve. You will shine, my dear.*

*I am afraid Málaga is on edge as well. To be expected, I
suppose. The city knight-commander, Hamete Zeli, says the
Christians will soon be knocking at our gates. Who can*

know for sure, but the city is frantic in its preparations. At the sultan's command the Falcon brothers—

She tenses, holds her breath.

At the sultan's command the Falcon brothers took a thousand of Málaga's finest cavalry and rode like the wind for Alhama.

A haunting image from her dream jumps into her mind's eye: Yusef trapped beneath his horse, frantically calling for her. She forces herself back to the letter.

How funny that you and the Falcon brothers know each other. It seems you made quite an impression on them, my dear, Yusef especially. I had mentioned that you and Malik were to be betrothed back when he and Umar first arrived in the city five months ago. Well, all the blood drained from poor Yusef's face. The lad seemed absolutely shattered that you were already spoken for. As your matchmaker, I had to set him straight, of course, and tell him that you were taken, and he needed to find another fair maiden. He was not amused. If I did not know better I would say the young man has feelings for you, Danah. Or, I should say, did. You must contain your charms, my dear!

Her mouth falls open as her heart begins to race. Danah stops, re-reads the old Sufi's words.

I had mentioned that you and Malik were to be betrothed back when he and Umar first arrived in the city five months ago.

The room tightens, making it hard for her to breathe. Her hands begin to tremble like leaves in the wind. Her heart slowly implodes as the bone-crushing realization settles upon her. She numbly recites Yusef's words, the words she knows by heart, the words that so devastated her . . . five months ago: "I am honor-bound to inform you that the feelings I expressed to you were misguided and false. The chasm separating our stations in life is much too wide to ever bridge." Her eyes flood then spill. "Miriam was right. Something *did* happen." She chokes back a sob. "I am honor-bound . . ." she whispers. "Abd al-Salam told him I was to be betrothed to Malik. Dear Lord, no. No . . ." Her lower lip begins to quiver. "Yusef. Oh, Yusef. Forgive me." Her shoulders softly shake as she begins to cry. Consumed by grief, she lowers her face into her hands and sobs.

The door opens. "There you are."

She looks up, still in a daze. She has not moved. For the past hour, she has simply stared into space, numb.

David removes his cloak and hangs it. "Ezar sends his best. He misses you."

A perfunctory nod, then she looks away.

"He chastised me for not bringing you, of course." He shifts to his best Ezar voice. "Tell Emeralds to leave my woolly worms out of it. All I need is a good joke and a little teasing to set me right. Is that too much to ask of Granada's newest hakim who has decided to neglect me?"

No response. David frowns his disappointment. His impersonation of their friend is actually quite good.

He sees the letter. "Malik is well?"

Confusion. "Malik?"

"The letter."

"Oh. No. I mean . . . the letter is from Master Abd al-Salam."

"Ah. He must have received my letter. I asked him to write your parents. And how is our old Sufi friend?"

"Well." Her tone is limp, deflated.

"With all that has happened Granada could certainly use his voice of reason. Did he say when he expects to return to us?"

"What? Oh. Soon." Her eyes retreat to the safety of her lap.

He studies her, concerned now about a possible relapse. "Danah?"

She reluctantly looks up.

"You look like you have been crying. Are you all right?"

"Yes. Of course." She tries to force a smile but does not make it. "Just tired."

He continues to study her. "Yes. Tired, I understand. You must pace yourself, Danah. And rest at every opportunity. Please." Fatherly concern. "The next group of wounded should be here this afternoon. It will be a long night."

"Is Miriam at home?"

"She should be." He chuckles. "She told me she and Samra aim to see that every one of those rascals is bathed today. They were headed to the hammam this morning. I am sure they are back by now." A satisfied smile as he thinks of her. "Having the orphans come live with us has been such a gift. She loves them like they are our own. Yehovah works in such interesting ways."

Danah stands and rushes to the door. "I need to speak with her."

"Danah?"

She does not look back, just turns the corner and says, "I will be back," and is gone.

David frowns once more, then shrugs. He makes a mental note to query Miriam on Danah's odd behavior.

Mayhem. The din of a hospital assailed by dozens of freshly delivered wounded is bone-chilling. The now-familiar sad chorus of groans and curses and whimpers and screams. Attendants rush about shuffling supplies to where they are most needed, press down to staunch new bleeders as wounds are unpacked, apply temporary bandages to cover gaping slices through flesh. They know survival for many of these men is a race against time, and thus they dart from one bed to the next to the next. As they move they offer soothing words, pass on requests to their co-workers—"Third bed on the right. Left arm." Orders are impatiently barked at confused stretcher bearers who have veered off course—"Surgical ward, not main ward! That way!" This is the fourth wave of wounded they have dealt with, and the Bermejas staff has grown efficient in dealing with the ensuing challenges. Everyone knows his role. Chaos, yes, but organized chaos. A tribute to David's leadership and his insistence on relentless training.

Recovering wounded in the main ward who are able, sit up to watch the dizzying sight, silent and wide-eyed with awe. They search for comrades, offering soft, kind words of compassion to their brothers-in-arms as they pass. There is not a speck of bravado remaining in this hall of suffering.

The wagons arrived later than expected, and it is already dark outside. As the stretcher bearers bring a fresh batch of wounded knights in from the cold, David stops them in the vestibule. With his assistant holding an oil lamp close, he lifts their blankets to quickly inspect the severity of the wounds, then indicates which ward they belong in. "Surgical ward. Next."

The stretcher bearers make their way down the hall and are met by an attendant. "Room one, empty bed on the far left." Danah is there, already hard at work on a terrible neck and face wound. The young man's left jaw and cheek are mangled, an empty gap where his teeth should be. She is quickly suturing a series of deep lacerations in his neck that are perilously close to the main artery.

"Main ward. Next." Another is delivered. David lifts the blanket and winces. He places his fingers on the man's neck to feel for a pulse. He looks up at the stretcher bearer and shakes his head. "Next."

David sighs. "Quiet ward." Their euphemistic name for the dying ward. "Next."

The stretcher-bearer announces, "Hakim al-Adani, this is Prince Yusef al-Makki."

David frowns and whispers, "Dear Lord." He immediately thinks of Danah and is thankful she is not present. The patient's head is shrouded in bandages like an Egyptian mummy. "Tell me."

The man says, "Badly broken thigh, Hakim. His horse fell on him. A piece of shrapnel through his forearm." The man stops.

David asks, "And the head wound?"

"Laceration to his forehead. Not serious. But, his eyes . . ."

David raises his eyebrows expectantly. He kneels beside the stretcher. "Yusef? Can you hear me?"

The moment stretches out.

"I can hear you." His words are tense with pain, laced with fear. Anger?

"This is Hakim al-Adani. Tell me about your eyes."

Another long pause. "I am . . . blind." It requires serious effort to claim the word.

"How?"

The seconds tick by. "Breech-blast of a cannon." The wounded prince is listless.

David thinks for a moment, then turns to his assistant. "Take him to the recovery rooms. Room four should be empty. As soon as I am finished here I will come. See that he stays warm. And do not disturb his head bandages."

The assistant motions the stretcher forward.

"Next. Quickly, please."

Yusef bitterly complained about having to drink the poppy seed and valerian root elixir, but David was insistent. "Yusef, you must. It is not just the pain—it will make my job far easier. And the sooner I am done with you the quicker I can get to the other wounded." A compelling argument to a man like Yusef. He finally acquiesced and drank the bitter potion.

Up first is Yusef's arm. David removes the bandage and lifts it to examine the wound. The flow of blood has nearly ceased. *Good, no major vessels severed. And no sign of infection.* He rotates the arm. A neat puncture right through the muscle of his forearm. In one side, out the other. He bends each finger to test the tendons. *Lucky.* David takes a hooked probe and explores deep inside to make sure that no foreign matter remains, which would invite festering. Satisfied, he cleans the wound, uses a needle and catgut to suture both sides closed, then bandages it. *As long as infection is held at bay, nothing serious.*

He folds back the blanket and removes the field splint from Yusef's bare leg. Significant swelling and already black-and-blue from groin to knee, but it looks like a clean break. *Fortunate, given a horse fell on him.* He lightly traces his fingers over the break, then gently presses on either side to feel the position of the bone. Yusef moans from his drugged sleep. *Thankfully, reasonably well set. No need to disturb it again. A long time to fully heal, but with some luck, there should be no permanent limp.* He cleans the leg, applies a more stable splint, and ties it off. With the help of his assistant, he lifts Yusef's thigh and wraps it in linen soaked in cerate to form a hard cast to immobilize the break.

Finally, the head. David carefully removes the bandage. An odd, arcing slice across his forehead, an inch above his left eye. He can see bone, but the tear is clean, as if sliced with a knife, and the bleeding has stopped. *Just grazed him. An inch to the left and he would be in the ground now.* He dabs the oozing clear fluid with a cotton cloth and continues his inspection. *He will bear an unusual scar, but nothing worrisome.* He disinfects the wound and sutures it closed with carefully-placed stitches to minimize the scar, then applies a small cotton pad to keep it clean.

David stares at Yusef's eyes from various angles. Significant bruising around the eyes, but no obvious wound. He turns to his assistant. "Joshua, hold the lamp close. I need more light." With thumb and forefinger, he gently parts the lids of the left eye. The pupil instantly constricts. *Good.* The white of his eye is heavily laced with bloodshot, but no obvious tears or punctures on the eyeball itself. "A little less light, please. Hold it steady right here." He lifts a magnifying glass and a lit taper and leans in, peers into the pupil as he moves the flame from right to left. Healthy, no obvious blood or debris inside the eyeball. *Good.* He repeats these steps on the right eye. He removes some crusty dirt trapped under the lid, but again, there is no obvious injury to the eyeball. David frowns. *So why the blindness?* He knows that the concussive shock from an explosion can produce odd traumas to the body. *At least without any major injury to the eyeballs, there is some hope for recovery.* He flushes each eye with water, dries them, applies cotton patches, then gently lifts Yusef's head and wraps him like a mummy down to his nostrils. *Impossible to recognize now.*

He turns to his assistant. "He should sleep until morning, but check on him from time to time." The man nods. "And, Joshua. I would prefer that you not mention his identity to Hakim Amiriya."

"Of course, Hakim al-Adani."

David stands and stretches. It will be a long night. He mutters to himself, "So how do I tell Danah?"

Three hours later they finish the last major surgery. A terrible sucking chest wound. Chain mail is little help against a violent pike thrust. Since this was the last of the serious cases, they work together. As she knots the last suture, David motions to his attendant to disinfect and bandage the wound. He and Danah exchange a somber glance. They both know that this young man is destined for the dying ward.

They remove their bloody surgical gowns then wash their hands in the basin. A resigned exhale from David. He knows what he has to do. He touches her on the arm, tells her they need to talk in private. She nods, instantly cautious, and the two of them step out into the hallway. Too many people, so he ushers her into his office.

David closes the door and turns to her, softly speaks her name. Her wariness grows. Then he tells her. She gasps; he stops. She remains silent as he continues, but the color drains from her face. Before he can finish she unexpectedly snaps at him angrily for hiding this information from her. He recoils, then tries again to explain, but she cuts him off and fires a barrage of harsh clinical questions, her only hope at mounting some sort of defense. David answers, methodically retracing his steps. First the details of the arm, then the leg, then the forehead. Face pinched with worry, she nods as he goes, and you can see her relief when he finishes. At least nothing that is life-threatening. But then he stops and simply stares at her. He can't bring himself to say it. She sees trouble brewing in his strained features. Her eyes fill as she whispers through trembling lips, "Tell me." And so he does. She gasps once more, tries to muster another question, but does not get it out, then tries again, her query tentative, fearful. His hands lift and indicate his own eyes as he explains the medical nuances, the possibilities. Her features lock into crystallized stoicism. A pathetic nod is all she can manage. Tears course down her cheeks. He tries to interject some hope, but she is first dubious, then despairing. He tries once more, a different angle this time.

She whispers one last awful question to clarify his words. David considers this, then answers her truthfully. She begins to heave. He steps forward and hugs her to his tired body. She begins to wail. He pulls her tighter, then tighter still as he tries to comfort her.

She is at his side when he awakens. She sits on a stool to his left, her head resting on the edge of his bed. She has dozed, though fitfully. David came by earlier and draped a blanket across her shoulders.

He jerks and grunts in his drugged sleep as he slowly edges closer to consciousness.

She lifts her head.

His body twitches as he softly groans. The fingers on his good arm slowly curl one by one, then ball into a fist and relax. He struggles to lift his bad arm, moans, leaves it where it lies. His head rolls to his right, then his left, as if he is surveying the room. He lifts his good hand to his face, feels the bandages, then drops his arm back flat again. He takes a deep breath and exhales, croaking, "Water. Water, please."

Without saying a word, she stands, moves to the table, and pours some water into a glass. His head tilts toward the sound, searching. She comes to him, lifts his hand, and places the glass in it, then slides her palm beneath his head, lifting him so he can drink. She helps him guide the glass to his lips. He spills a little but manages to slurp most of it down. He licks his lips. She lowers his head to the pillow and takes the cup from him.

Tense silence fills the small room.

"Thank you." The right words, but sheathed in despair.

Her mouth opens to respond, but then she closes it. She cannot find the words. She sets the glass back down on the table, then sits.

Yusef's head tilts in her direction, his shrouded face staring straight at her.

Her eyes fill.

"Danah." Not a question.

Tears slide down her cheeks. "I dreamed that you were hurt. That you called my name." A breathless whisper.

He says nothing.

"Yusef." So tender. She lays her hand upon his, squeezes.

"My life is over now." His words are stilted, awkward things, half-angry, half-resentful, totally devoid of life. The finality is startling. He retracts his hand.

"Yusef, no . . ."

He does not respond, simply turns his head away from her. She begins to cry.

They have received word that the army is returning from Alhama, beaten, heads bent low in shame. News of the defeat casts a pall across the city, but the hospital staff are elated for the respite, even if temporary. They have already released a dozen patients back to their families. Predictably, the Abencerrajes and their loyalists leverage the news, ideal propaganda for trumpeting their mandate for regime change. The city is locked in a tense stalemate, the Albayzín now a walled fortress, the cannons of the Alhambra trained on it menacingly.

David is making his morning rounds and stops by to check on her. He opens the door, sees that she is on a floor pillow by Yusef's side, reading.

Danah looks up.

He softly says, "How are you, my dear?"

A lifeless shrug.

She is answered by a sober nod. "And our patient?"

"The poppy elixir keeps him asleep, but he still cries out. Nightmares are understandable, I suppose." Her eyes fill. "He said his life was over, David."

"I am sure he just cannot imagine a life, any life, without his sight."

"But . . ."

David lifts a hand.

"As I told you, there is still some hope his vision may return, though you must understand, Danah, that with each passing day the odds diminish. In the meantime, you must use your gifts to help him imagine another life for himself, a different life than what he has known. We must prepare for the worst."

She dabs her eyes and slowly nods.

"I want to keep him on the poppy elixir for another two days. Sleep is the best medicine for now."

"Yes."

"With no more wounded coming for a while, I see no reason why he cannot stay in here by himself. We have room, and I am guessing a prince of the Alhambra might enjoy some private care." Miriam's suggestion.

She brightens. "Thank you, David."

"I came as quickly as I could. The tensions in the city are high, and with the Abencerrajes in control of the Albayzín . . . well, you can imagine how busy things have been."

David answers, "Of course."

Umar lifts his hand. "My wife, Faynan. Faynan, this is Hakim al-Adani, the sultan's royal physician."

David bows. "I am pleased to meet you. Please call me David."

"The pleasure is mine, David."

Umar continues, "May we see him?"

"Certainly. This way." The three of them walk down the hall. "I have him in a private room."

"Good."

"He is under the care of Hakim Amiriya. You remember Danah, Umar."

Umar and Faynan exchange a knowing glance.

Umar says, "So Danah has taken her oath. Excellent to hear." He muses. "A spirited young woman."

David chuckles. "That she is. And as fine a healer as you will ever meet. Yusef is in good hands."

A smile tickles the corners of Faynan's mouth.

Umar touches David's shoulder and they stop. "Tell me, David, how is he, really? The truth, please."

"Well. A piece of shrapnel passed through his lower arm, and a small laceration on his forehead. There is no apparent structural damage to the arm, and no infection. Both should heal nicely. He has a nasty fracture of his thigh-bone where his horse fell on him, but a clean break. He will limp for some time, though I do expect a full recovery." David stops. "His eyes, however—"

"What about his eyes?" Umar's concern grows.

"I am afraid he is blind, Umar."

Faynan gasps.

"Dear Lord, no. How?"

"Evidently, he was staring straight at a cannon when a breach-blast occurred. I was told the explosion killed everyone in his gun crew but him. He was lucky. But the force of the blast has blinded him."

Umar sadly shakes his head as he considers this. "Is it permanent?"

David does not immediately answer. "Difficult to know. There was no obvious trauma to his eyes, which is good, but he is unable to see. There is always some hope that his sight will return—I have seen it before. But I am afraid that likelihood will diminish with each passing day. Come." They resume walking. "As you can imagine, his spirits are very low. I know he will be so glad you came." This is a lie. Yusef has not asked for his brother once.

"Here is his room." David opens the door. Danah looks up from her book then rises from her floor pillow. "Danah. I believe you know Prince Umar."

Yusef's head rotates to the voices but then turns away.

Umar bows dramatically. "It is good to see you again, my lady." There is that twinkle in Umar's eyes. "Congratulations on taking your oath. I know that my brother is lucky to be under the care of such an able hakim." He unleashes that disarming smile.

Danah blushes. "Thank you."

Umar lifts a hand. "This is my wife, Faynan. Faynan, this is Hakim Amiriya. Danah."

"I am pleased to meet you, Faynan." Danah sees that Umar's wife is simply stunning; one of the great Arabian beauties who helped earn the kingdom's fame in such matters. She instantly feels self-conscious.

Faynan smiles. "How wonderful to finally meet. I have heard so much about you, Danah."

Danah listens as David and Umar's conversation drifts to the army's return, his other patients, and the city's civil unrest.

Faynan, instantly intrigued, begins to discreetly study the young hakim her brother-in-law is so taken with. *Plainer than I would have guessed, though Umar said her smile is absolutely captivating. Mmm . . . her face is alluring in a way that is hard to place. Always the best kind. Those eyes! Dear Lord. Cut jewels. They lend her an exotic air . . . though she would benefit from some good makeup to embolden them. Unmistakably intelligent, but with something more. An inner strength, and determination, certainly, though shrouded in . . . in what exactly? Ahh. Vulnerability. Endearingly self-conscious about her looks. A plus.* Faynan smiles. *And she has a temper. All this, also a gifted healer, and with Sufi ambitions?* Faynan nods her approval then smiles. *Exactly the kind of woman Yusef would fall for.*

As the conversation wanes, they return to the purpose of their visit. David turns. "Yusef?"

No movement.

He turns to Danah and mouths, "Asleep?"

She shakes her head.

"Yusef, your brother and his wife are here to see you."

Still nothing.

"I am sure you want to greet them."

It is more than obvious that he does not.

Umar steps close, begins to lovingly stroke his brother's bandaged head, which is still turned toward the wall. He leans down and begins to whisper into his ear. On and on he goes. He stops finally and kisses his brother's head. "Uncle is with al-Zaghal in Loja now. He sends his best wishes for a quick recovery. I will come again as soon as I am able, Yusef. *As-salamu alaykum.*" May Allah's peace, mercy and blessing be upon you.

As they turn to leave, Faynan leans into Danah, joins their hands, and whispers something into her ear.

Danah's eyes widen as she looks at Faynan incredulously. Faynan smiles, nods. As David leads them out, Danah turns back and studies Yusef, her heart now racing.

Outside, David apologizes. "We must give him some time. He is still coming to grips with his condition."

Umar sighs. "I know. I am sure he feels that his life as a knight is over now. I would."

A sober nod from David.

Faynan says, "It is important that Danah continues her care for Yusef."

David nods again in agreement. "Yes, of course."

As she opens the door, his mummy face turns to track her movements. He has somehow managed to prop himself up with his pillows into a sitting position.

"Good morning." She waits for a response, and when it doesn't come, she continues, "I need to change your bandages. It is important that we let your wounds air out and dry." She is beside his bed now. "Afterward, David wants to examine your eyes again."

Nothing.

As she begins to remove the bandage on his arm, her tone shifts to clinical. "Healing nicely. No sign at all of infection. Flex your fingers one by one, starting with your thumb."

He does, with sharp intakes of breath as he goes.

"Excellent. Some pain is to be expected. There does not appear to be any permanent damage. Now for the head."

He grunts.

She begins to remove the linen wrappings. When she is finished, she pulls the cotton patches from his eyes. "Open your eyes." He does. "Anything?"

He impatiently shakes his head, folds his lids closed.

She purses her lips in irritation, almost decides to challenge him, but then thinks better of it. *Too soon.* She peels the pad from his forehead and immediately gasps.

His blind eyes open and turn to her. "What?"

The laceration, all puckered and everted by the fine stitching, is shaped like a perfect crescent moon. The words of Tetta Layla jump into her mind.

> *"Tetta, how will I recognize my Great Love?"*
> *"Look for the crescent moon, dear one. The crescent moon."*

He repeats, "What?"

Her heart is racing. "I am sorry, Yusef. The wound is healing nicely. It is just that . . ."

"Just what?"

She swallows hard. "The laceration is shaped like a perfect crescent moon."

Another grunt.

She mulls her options—to speak the truth or remain silent—and opts for the safer path. "It is just that you will bear a distinctive scar."

All she gets is an exasperated sigh. "A distinctive scar is the least of my worries." Resignation slithers between his words.

"Faynan is right, you know. You two do belong together." Miriam smiles. "And now the crescent moon? How much clearer could it be, Danah? You must tell Yusef the truth. All of the truth."

"Miriam, how? How can I possibly? I barely know him. We were together one day. One, Miriam! I was a fool to think there was something between us."

She studies her, sees the confusion, the fear. "And yet you dream of him constantly, you think of him day and night, and cannot keep him out of your mind. Or your heart." Her words are warm, compassionate. "Danah, you love Yusef. Deep within, you know this to be so." A motherly smile. "One year, one day, one hour, one minute. Who can know the manner in which love will visit us? New feelings are frightening, Danah, I understand that. It was no different with me and David."

Danah looks up, her eyes full, helpless against the torture her feelings are inflicting.

"Dear, dear, Danah. You must find the courage that we both know lies within you. Then, tell him what you felt when he took your hand and looked into your eyes that day at the Atfal, what you felt when you read his first letter. *And* the second. And tell him of your dreams, your tetta's words, Abd al-Salam's letter, the misunderstanding. Your regret. What you felt inside when you saw him lying on the bed, broken. You must tell him what you feel in your heart for him. All of it. You must tell him the truth."

Danah is wide-eyed, shaking her head. "But Miriam . . ."

"You must embrace the life you were intended to live, Danah, the love intended for you both, no matter how much that scares you. You must be honest; with yourself and with Yusef. It seems more than obvious to me that you and Yusef are destined for each other. Great Love is Yehovah's Grace. Embrace your destiny . . . no matter where it leads you." A warm, loving look. "Remember what your tetta told you. 'You must build a bridge within your heart . . . then close your eyes and cross it.' Even though it scares you. Especially because it scares you."

She looks up. "And what if he rejects me? He is blind, Miriam. He thinks his life is over."

"Yusef needs you more than he can know. Love can save him, Danah. Perhaps *only* love can save him."

Danah chews her lower lip as she considers this.

"You must gather your strength and take a risk, Danah. Build a bridge within your heart. Yusef needs you now. Your love can show him that there is a way forward to a new life. You must embrace your destiny."

"And what about Malik?"

"What *about* Malik?"

"The betrothal, Miriam," Danah replies, exasperated.

"That was my doing, Danah. I involved Abd al-Salam. I am to blame."

"No, Miriam."

"In the end, though he will be heartbroken, Malik will want what is best for you. And marrying him when you are in love with Yusef? No, he will not wish for that, not if he cares about you. And clearly he does."

"I feel terrible. My parents will hate me."

She shakes her head. "Despite what you may think, your parents love you. They want you to be happy, Danah. You must tell Yusef the truth. All of the truth. And beg Allah to stand beside you when you need strength."

After a silent prayer, Danah swallows hard, then reaches out and lightly touches his forehead. He flinches, his body tensing, but then he relaxes as she begins to slowly trace her finger along the outside arc of the crescent moon, back and forth, back and forth. Her touch is tender. She leans close, stomach churning with the wings of a thousand butterflies, and in a low voice she says, "In a dream, many months ago, my tetta came to me, as real as if she were standing next to us both right now." She stops to gather her strength. "You may have heard of her. Layla al-Khatib, daughter of Lisan al-Din ibn al-Khatib, the grand vizier of Sultan Muhammad V." She stops again, giving him space. Her hand lowers to his shoulder, hovers there indecisively, then settles. He does not flinch this time.

After an interminable wait, he finally replies, "That is impossible. Ibn al-Khatib was banished from Granada over a hundred years ago."

"Yes, he was. But I have come to know that his daughter, Layla al-Khatib, is my great-great-great-great tetta. Was."

A skeptical grunt.

"She married Shahab Chandon, the Christian convert who died at the battle of Jaén saving Granada from the Castilians. During the Nasrid Golden Age. And she founded the Atfal Hospital. For the orphans of the city."

"Every knight of Granada knows the legend of Shahab Chandon." Matter of fact.

"Layla and Shahab were married on the twenty-sixth day of September, in 1368, to be exact. Less than a year before he died."

"You are telling me that you are an heir of Shahab Chandon?" Despite his natural inclination toward skepticism, he is impressed. Incredulous, but impressed. Chandon's valor and exploits are legendary.

"My eyes, Yusef. Layla was known as the 'Emeralds of the Alhambra'."

Yusef absorbs this, his curiosity piqued. "She came to you in a dream?"

"Yes, more than once."

"Why?"

"She said she came to tell me the truth about her father, who was wrongly accused of treason and banished to the Maghreb. And to tell me my true heritage, which has been hidden from me, for reasons I do not yet understand."

"She told you this in a dream?" More skepticism.

"Yes, Yusef, in a vivid dream as lifelike as any waking moment I have ever experienced. I am Abencerrajes, Yusef, but Tetta Layla was Nasrid." She treads delicately upon eggshells. "She also wanted me to know the real story of the man she fell in love with —William Chandon. Shahab. She called their love 'Great Love.' A divine love. A gift directly from Allah." She stops, says another silent prayer. "Tetta Layla said that I, too, would find Great Love,

Yusef." She inhales, jealously guards her breath, reluctantly releases it. "When I asked her about the man I was destined to fall in love with, the man I would spend my life with, she would not answer me. She would only say . . ." Danah steels herself for the plunge. "She would only say, 'Look for the crescent moon. The crescent moon.'" She lets this sink in. "I could never figure out what she meant by it."

His blind eyes open and turn to her.

Heart pounding, she reaches up and delicately fingers the wound once more. Her voice fills with emotion. "And now I know."

The silence stretches out. He chooses his next words carefully. "And now you know." He starts to say something more but then closes his mouth, undecided. As the seconds tick by she stands beside him, waiting, hoping. His blind eyes return to his lap. He purses his lips, shakes his head in frustration, as if he is wrestling with some weighty decision. He opens his mouth to speak again, then closes it, then tries once more. "I have thought about you day and night since we met that day in the Atfal, Danah. Always you. Only you." He takes a deep breath, holds it, then releases. "Something remarkable happened to me that day, something I still do not understand. For the first time, I felt . . . I felt . . ." His words desert him.

Her hand tentatively seeks his, and their fingers twine together. "Yes, for me as well." Without thinking, she leans into him, lays her arm across his shoulder, and holds him. An innocent gesture, but profoundly intimate. Their hearts are both pounding. Spontaneity is not something she believed herself capable of, and yet here it is, staring her down, willing her forward. Before logic can take hold and change her mind, she softly whispers, "*Ana behibak.*" I love you.

Yusef looks up and turns to her. His eyes are full. "*Ana behibek.*"

"Your letter melted my heart, Yusef. Suddenly, everything that I experienced, all those confused feelings . . . they finally made sense."

"Yes."

"I dreamed of you each night." Her voice grows husky. "You came to me, Yusef."

He squeezes her hand. "It was the same for me."

A long pause as they both recollect these sweet memories. "Until . . ." Her words trail off. "Until the second letter."

His body tenses as his eyes sink back to his lap. He croaks, "I was a fool. I am a fool. Worse than a fool. When Abd-al-Salam told me that you were to be betrothed, my pride . . . my pride . . ." His voice begins to quaver. "Umar told me to profess my love once more, to fight for you, Danah." His voice wilts. "And I did not. I let my pride, my honor, lead me to a terrible choice. I forsook what my heart was screaming at me. So, I took the coward's way and sent the letter. It killed me to write those words, to lie to you. Forgive me. Please, Danah, forgive me."

Her eyes fill. "I was crushed. Then angry. Beyond angry."

"And I deserved every bit of it."

Silence.

"And so, I agreed to the betrothal with Malik." She pleads, "You must understand, Yusef. I had no choice. My parents. I promised to honor Abd al-Salam's choice."

"I do understand. The fault was mine, not yours. I should have fought for you."

"After the betrothal I did not dream of you again . . . until I saw you on the battlefield, calling for me. And then I received a letter from Abd al-Salam. Just before you arrived. He mentioned that you seemed distraught when you learned that I was to be betrothed. It all became clear in an instant. A terrible instant."

"I made a horrible mistake by sending the second letter, Danah. The stupidest, most cowardly thing I have ever done."

"And I made a horrible mistake by accepting betrothal to Malik. He is a good man, Yusef, a kind man." She pauses. "But I do not love him."

Their fingers tighten as the stillness closes in around them.

"And now this." Pain enfolds Yusef's whisper. He helplessly points to his eyes. "Danah, I am blind. My career, everything I trained for, everything I know, everything I believe in, is over, gone. Taken from me. I am a prince of court, a knight-commander. I will never lead men into battle again. I have nothing to offer you, Danah, not a single thing. I am worthless without my sight. I am nothing. Less than nothing."

"No, Yusef, you are mistaken. Tetta Layla told me, 'You must build a bridge within your heart . . . then close your eyes and cross it.' Perhaps she meant this for you, Yusef. We were destined to be together. I know this now. Allah has a plan for us, Yusef. Together, we can find it. We *will* find it. You must put your trust in that. Can you do that for me?"

A pained moment passes. "I can try."

The door opens, and they instantly separate, though not before David notices the untwining of their fingers and does a quick double take. Danah looks away. David clears his throat. "Good morning, Yusef. I trust that you are receiving adequate care?"

"More than adequate, Hakim al-Adani."

"Dear Lord, the man speaks! You have worked a miracle, Danah."

Yusef actually smiles.

When Danah turns back, she is still blushing. But beaming.

David can't help but smile. "Let me take a look at those eyes again."

Danah lies sleeping on her floor mattress in the small room off the main hallway they have converted for her. Not large, but more than enough to fit her bed, a sitting pillow, and small writing desk. A welcomed refuge—her new home. As the jinn's hour approaches, Danah's pupils begin to pace beneath her lids, then they run. The lamp's dead nub of wick suddenly bursts into flame, the darkness instantly lifted, like a lightning strike on a moonless night. The flame bends and flickers as if caught in a stiff breeze, lengthens, then contracts and settles, lending a soft glow to the space. The air stills, and a tomb-like silence fills the room. One by one, pinpricks of gold shimmer forth and begin to coalesce in the air.

Danah's eyes slowly open. Her tetta sits cross-legged on the pillow, close enough to reach out and touch. The old woman's brilliant emeralds are radiant above a smile stretched ear to ear.

"Tetta Layla."

"Dear girl. I have missed you."

"Why did you leave me when I needed you most, Tetta? I called for you, but you never came. Why, Tetta?"

Layla's smile relaxes. "I was never far from you. But sometimes, my dear, we must walk alone on the path that destiny requires of us. 'You must build a bridge within your heart . . . then close your eyes and cross it.'"

Danah absorbs this. "The crescent moon. I know now what you meant, Tetta Layla."

"Yes, you do."

"After all those months of not dreaming of him, he came to me when he was wounded. He called for me, Tetta."

"Yes, he did. And you answered, my dear, at a time when he needed you most. He, too, must fulfill his destiny. And now your paths have once again crossed. As was intended by Allah from the beginning."

Danah considers this. "You sent the dream of him to me."

She is answered only with a smile.

"I told him I loved him, Tetta. I do not know how I found the courage, but I told him. I told him the truth, that I love him." Her eyes fill. "He returned my words."

"Great Love is the destiny you two share, my dear. Just as it was for me and my William."

"But his eyes, Tetta. Will he recover his sight?"

She does not answer. "There are many things Yusef must still learn, Danah."

"But—"

"And there are many things you must still learn, dear girl. About Yusef. About yourself. About Great Love."

Danah considers this. "But how, Tetta? What must I do?"

"Follow the Sufi Way, Danah."

She shakes her head. "I do not understand."

"Each of you must build a bridge within your hearts . . . then close your eyes and cross. Together." The old woman smiles. "Follow the Sufi Way, child."

"But Tetta—"

"I must go now."

"No . . . please do not leave me again. I need you. Tetta, no." She reaches out.

Layla takes her hand, her brilliant emeralds brimming with warmth and love. "Follow the Sufi Way, Danah. I will be close by, my dear. Always close by." Sparks of gold begin to sizzle above the pillow as Layla's image fades.

"Tetta, no, do not leave me. No. Please."

The old woman smiles once more, then winks out, gone.

"Danah. Danah." Someone is shaking her shoulder.

She jumps like a startled cat. "Tetta! No!"

"It is David, Danah. You were dreaming, Danah. Danah."

She lies back. "David. A dream, yes. So real. I dreamed of my Tetta Layla. It has been many months."

"I am sorry to wake you, but I need your help. That nasty leg wound we worked on three days back. I am afraid putrefaction has set in. We need to reopen the wound immediately if he is to have a chance. I need your help."

"Yes. Yes, of course. Let me change. I will be there in a moment."

The Sufi Way

A heavyset man with a flowing dark beard and a gold front tooth heavily pants as he tops the last step of the spiral staircase. He stops for a moment to gather himself, and when his breath is again steady he slips silently from the shadows and turns to his side to squeeze through the narrow red-and-white-striped Umayyad arch and onto the small platform on the thin ledge. A stunning view of the city and the Granadine Vega beyond unfolds below him, a sight of which he never tires. The pre-dawn light is still pale and diffuse, but soothing. Soon the swallows will jump from their nests into thin air like rowdy children dashing about in playful glee, squealing their delight. But for now, at least, the quiet holds, instilling a reverent tone, a holy silence.

Due east, the jagged peaks of the Sierra Nevada strain heavenward in their majesty, lording over the glorious Alhambra. The air is crystalline and pure as a mountain stream, cool and crisp, full of promise. A beautiful early spring day will soon nuzzle the city, oblivious to the discord that has pitted father against son, brother against brother, Nasrid against Abencerraje.

The Royal *Muezzin* studies the light with the careful eye of a landscape painter. Timing is everything, and his is impeccable. Satisfied, he takes a half-step forward to the edge of the precipice, silently recites a prayer, bows toward Mecca, then cups his right hand beside his mouth, closes his eyes, and begins his call: the *Fajr salah*, the sunrise call to prayer. His warbled melody is piercingly pure and beautiful. He stretches and bends and folds and twists the notes with great power and dexterity. He is a master of his holy craft, a craft he has trained for all his life. Here is an artist who paints with his voice. As the call pauses, the echo off the buildings below lingers on for seconds. He starts once more.

In the distance, another muezzin awakens, then another, and within a minute the call to prayer spreads from mosque to mosque across Granada like some mighty reverberating chant. Even for a city at war with itself, all muezzins defer to the timing of the Royal Muezzin.

First a truncated, birdlike squawk, then a pathetic crying jag bordering on adorable; but finally, a full-throated, caterwauling wail that commands attention. She's a crier, this one. A beautiful little thing, but a crier. Even at this tender age she looks like her mother, the sultan nowhere to be found. Wispy blond hair, the coloring identical to her mama's, same enchanting almond eyes. Even as an infant you can tell she will grow into a lovely creature.

Zoraya has insisted on keeping the babe by her side at all times and has had an ornate cradle brought to their quarters. Perhaps she fears assassins still, though truth be told, she has gone to great pains to rid the palace of all would-be threats, both male and female alike. The royal court treads lightly these days.

She has shunned the royal harem, her mandated domicile. First, she emptied it of nubile young playthings, then slowly but surely transformed it into a dull abode inhabited only by bored and dour eunuchs. Instead, the two of them share his suite in the Hall of the Abencerrajes just below. An unprecedented choice to be sure, but then again, she is a most unusual sultana. He was reluctant about the arrangement at first, but she has made it worth his while.

She nurses the babe herself, another odd choice for a sultana, and one might add, a decision not especially pleasing to her husband. He is a jealous master of her breasts, after all, which have somehow managed to become even more luscious with the sweet swell of motherhood and a darkening of her areolas.

She rises and looks skyward to the honeycombed heaven high above. Still dark. She retrieves her baby girl, brings the little one back to their bed, unties her nightgown and slips it from her shoulder, begins to feed the babe. The room grows still once more, silent except for the little thing's endearing soft suckle-sighs.

"Are you awake, my sultan?" Only a whisper.

"I am now." Annoyance buried in a shallow grave beneath his words.

Zoraya turns toward him and shifts the babe to her other breast. "She will soon be sleeping through the night, my sultan."

"Let us hope so. Sleep is not a luxury for me, Zoraya. I am weary to my bones."

"I know, my sultan. Do you feel any better?"

There was an episode after supper while he was railing against Boabdil and Fatima. Grand Vizier Venegas took the brunt of the sultan's wrath. It seems the Abencerraje Council of Elders has tendered a set of demands. Not unexpected, at least by Venegas, given that the city remains locked in a tense standoff. The sultan's response was instantaneous and incendiary. He paced and screamed until he grew faint and nearly collapsed. The royal physician was summoned, who put him to bed with some sleeping concoction. Before he left, he scolded Venegas. "These outbursts will eventually kill him, you know. He *must* rest. He *must not* grow so excited." Venegas could do little but nod his acquiescence.

The sultan sighs. "Some. That wicked headache is gone, praise Allah. I am still weak, though, no energy at all."

"Should I send for Hakim al-Adani again?"

"No." Clearly not open to debate.

His disappointment in learning that his new son and heir is actually a girl lingers like an unacknowledged bad smell between them—always there, never named. In fairness, she, too, was shocked. She was so confident the child would be male; she could feel it in her bones.

Danah and David were present to help bring the royal baby into the world, thankfully with no serious complications, other than having to deftly manage a young mother's shocked disbelief at the sex of her child. Danah was instrumental. But truth be told, Zoraya has warmed to the little thing, whom she has named Kinda. Still, she knows full well that without bearing him a son and heir to replace Boabdil, her future, their future, is precarious. Especially now that his health is in doubt. Desperate is not yet the right word. Determined would be more apt.

They lie in silence until she is finished. She rises, paces as she burps the baby, then lays the little one back into the cradle, pats her to sleep, and tiptoes back to bed. She unties her silk gown and lets it slip to the floor, then snuggles up to him, presses her breasts against him.

He does not respond.

She nibbles on his ear lobe and whispers, "I ache for you."

"Please, woman. Not now. I need sleep." He turns away from her.

She lies still for several moments as she plans her attack. Decisions made, her hand shyly glides across his belly, lingers to twirl a finger into his navel hair, then submerges beneath his pants. She carefully watches his expression as she flirts and teases until he stiffens. With a devious smile she sits up, leans over and bares him, commences doing things that would make many a wife blush. All he can do is helplessly submit. She is a master, after all; an artist practicing her art. His groans and writhing intensify as she has her way with him. When she knows he is close, she abruptly swings her leg over and straddles him, guides him inside her, and with only three quick thrusts he cries

341

out in sweet agony and the deed is done. She gently kisses him, eases herself off and lies on her back.

He lies panting, drained of every single ounce of energy he possesses.

Truth be told, she is not yet ready for this, the sting of it still raw and pulsing in her tender parts. But she is determined. When she hears him begin to softly snore, she pulls her feet in and raises her knees, slides a hand under each buttock, and lifts her generous hips into the air to cradle his seed.

Mayya dismisses the letter, dropping it to the table as if it carries the plague. "They are all against us. First the royal physician, and now Abd al-Salam. They have poisoned her mind against us, Battal."

His eyes slowly rise from the document outlining a second round of demands the Abencerraje Council of Elders will vote on this evening. He chides her. "Mayya. No. That is not true, and you know it."

Danah's mother backs down but then thinks otherwise and purses her lips. "She has forsaken us, and our home, for a *hospital*. She tends the wounded, Battal. *Men* who are wounded, Battal. *Men!* Our unmarried, only daughter, Battal, tending to half-clad men. Think of the scandal!"

He frowns. "She is under the care of the royal physician, Mayya. And she has taken her oath. Our Danah is now Hakim Amiriya. She serves the wounded from Alhama. She does her duty. You and I both know Danah has dreamed about doing this her whole life. Her decision to stay at the Bermejas, much as we might prefer it to be otherwise during this trying time, is quite easy to understand."

His wife is defiant. "And what about Malik? What about him?"

Battal sighs. "I am certain Malik would be proud of her, darling."

"Well—"

"Listen. Those two are betrothed. It is a wonderful match for both of them. Danah has taken her oath now. Malik will soon take his. And then they will be married. Two hakims. All will be well, you will see."

"There *is* a war going on, you know," she retorts with unkind sarcasm. "Not to mention what is happening in the city. Or did you forget that we are living in the middle of an armed camp?"

"The Christians have not threatened Málaga, or Granada, and are unlikely to anytime soon. From all that I have been told,

Alhama was a fluke; pure luck. The Christians simply do not have the means for a full-scale invasion of the kingdom. They would be fools to try. As for the city, my sense is that things will be resolved soon enough. The sultan has little choice. The Abencerraje command nearly half of Granada now, and we have demonstrated that we are capable of defending it. We have most of the merchants on our side and therefore the ability to control the taxes that the sultan can collect. Things will have to change, Mayya. The people are turning against the Nasrids. You will see."

"Mmm."

"Darling, you must be patient."

She mulls this over. "I want a wedding by the end of the summer."

Battal smiles. "And so do I. Patience, my love. These two will be married soon enough."

"Go ahead and tell Umar, Venegas."

Sultan Abu l-Hasan, Grand Vizier Venegas, Royal Treasurer Tawd Ibn al-Kamil, and Umar are gathered in the Hall of the Kings. The sultan is grim-lipped and pacing. The man has a worryingly unhealthy pallor and sagging bags beneath hollowed eyes.

The grand vizier nods. "Al-Zaghal and your uncle made it to Loja while Fernando's main army was still assembling at Lucena. Praise Allah. Loja's defenses are whole now. Your uncle has spies combing the borderlands for news of when and where Fernando plans to attack us."

"Wise."

Venegas continues, "We just received word by rider. Fernando is finally on the march. His army is presently just north of Zagra."

Umar smirks. "Through the mountains? Surprising. I would have expected him to approach Alhama along the road through Archidona. Much easier and quicker."

"Indeed. Your uncle is convinced that he plans to attack Loja first, then move on Alhama via the road passing through Salar. Loja would give him a major foothold in the kingdom, and an ideal staging ground for ravaging the Vega at will."

Umar weighs this. "Yes. Sound strategy."

"Your uncle is requesting six thousand troops; three thousand cavalry and three thousand crossbowmen."

"To bolster Loja's garrison?"

"No. He aims to go on the offensive."

Umar's eyes widen.

"He plans to leave the safety of the castle and attack Fernando on open ground. Something he believes the Christians will not be anticipating. He wants our army to launch a surprise attack on Fernando's rearguard when the two sides have their horns locked."

"I see."

"It would require careful coordination, of course. But if successful, a retreat back to Lucena would be Fernando's only option."

The sultan glares at his grand vizier. "Unless we destroy him first."

Venegas ticks his head, "A desirable, outcome, of course, though in my opinion, unlikely."

Umar muses. "And suppose he does not turn to attack Loja, but instead races straight for Alhama?"

No immediate answer. Finally, Venegas offers, "There are no certainties in war, Umar. That said, your uncle knows the strategy of battle like few others in this land."

Umar replies, "Indeed. And who will lead this surprise attack?"

The sultan answers, "You will, Umar."

Umar bows. "You honor me with your trust, sire. I only wish Yusef could command with me."

"We all do, Umar. Sadly, that is not to be."

"I live to serve Granada, sire. When will we fight?"

Venegas replies, "Too soon to tell. Your uncle thinks Fernando will be at Loja within four days, more likely five. Plan on four. Two days to prepare, two nights for travel. I will instruct al-Zaghal to send a small detachment to meet you and guide you to the proper location to await the attack. We dare not move an army that size during the day."

"Understood."

The sultan nods. "Very well, then. Venegas, send word to my brother. Coded, obviously. In the meantime, Umar, begin your preparations. Tawd, give him any resources he needs." He resumes pacing.

The royal treasurer looks worried. "With all due respect, sire, our coffers are dangerously depleted." He lifts his hands helplessly. "Alhama, sire."

The sultan stops and turns. "Empty the treasury if you must, Tawd. We must have a victory, and soon. Understood?"

"Of course, sire. But what of the Abencerrajes?"

Venegas studies the royal treasurer. Brave to enter such dangerous waters. That, or foolhardy. He decides on the latter, begins to calculate how to best diffuse the growing tension.

The sultan turns on the man as he darkens. He hisses, "What *about* them, Tawd?"

The man presses onward but then begins to sense his peril. "Just that if the army leaves, the Abencerrajes may feel . . . emboldened, sire."

The sultan stares the man down until his eyes retreat to the floor. He's fuming, jaw muscles clenched tight.

Venegas steps in. "We have already discussed that contingency, Tawd. Even with Umar's army leaving Granada, more than eight thousand troops will still remain in the city. Almost the same number as when the army was engaged at Alhama. And the garrison in the Alhambra has been quadrupled. That should be more than adequate to keep the Abencerrajes in check. What we most need now, gentlemen, is a decisive victory over the Christians. At all costs, we must reassure the citizens of Granada that we are capable of successfully defending the kingdom against King Fernando and his forces." He muses. "In any case, the Abencerrajes will not dare to attack us while our heavy cannons are trained on them. We could level the Albayzín if we are forced to, and Boabdil and the elders know this. By destroying the Puente del Cadí we delivered an unequivocal message regarding our capabilities." His own decision, of course.

The royal treasurer looks unconvinced but nods nevertheless and backs down.

The sultan remains silent, but his eyes have not left the man's face.

Umar says, "I agree. I can remove the troops I need in a manner that will not raise undue attention or compromise our defenses." He turns to the sultan. "Sire, I would suggest tripling the guard around our heavy cannons. They are an asset we can ill afford to lose."

Venegas answers for the sultan. "Agreed. I will see to it today." He turns to the sultan and frowns. "Sire?"

The sultan looks confused. "What? Oh. Yes, make it so."

"Good morning!" She opens the door all bright and sunny, effervescent with the glow of young love. Knowing smiles and amused nods dog her steps these days. The hospital staff have enjoyed watching the new hakim as she makes her rounds with her patients each morning, inevitably ending at Yusef's room. What might have proved a distraction in normal times is instead welcomed with open arms, a splash of light painted across the ward's dreary shadows. A fine tonic for the hospital's sagging morale.

He offers only a grunt in reply.

This stops her in her tracks, wilts her smile. "Is something wrong?"

No response.

She comes closer, forehead furled. "Yusef. What happened?"

"My brother was just here." His words drip resentment.

"Oh. I am sorry, I did not see him. But it is good that Umar comes to visit you, Yusef."

"You do not understand."

She frowns. "What do I not understand?"

"It is just that . . ."

"Go on."

"The sultan has put Umar in command of the army, Danah. He will march under cover of night to join ranks with al-Zaghal and our uncle at Loja."

"I see. When?"

"Tonight. There is to be a surprise attack against King Fernando and the Christians."

"You are worried about him."

He turns to face her. "No. Yes. Of course I am worried about him. But . . . I should be at his side. The Falcon brothers fight together, Danah. We command together . . . we always have."

"I see."

"And I am here, stuck in this hospital bed. An invalid." Frustration digs in its talons. "A useless invalid, Danah. Just when Granada needs me most."

Her voice softens. "I understand."

He turns on her, his tone searing. "I am not sure you do. I am blind, Danah." He jabs at his sightless eyes. "Blind! It is stupid to pretend otherwise. What am I to do with my life now? Sit in a bed all day and be nursed?! How can we possibly build a life together? How? HOW?!"

She takes his hand. "Yusef, Allah has a plan for us. I am certain of this. Together, we will find a way. You must put your trust in Allah's Merciful Grace. You must trust Allah."

He scoffs. "Trust Allah? If only it were that simple. Will Allah bring my sight back? Will He?! Well?!" His words are searing.

She is pained. "Oh, Yusef. With Allah all things are possible."

His voice is strangled by resignation. "Perhaps for you, Danah, but not for me. I was raised by Uncle Ali to respect matters of faith. There was a time when I believed, when I prayed. But no more. Allah gave up on me long ago."

This clearly troubles her. "Yusef, Allah never gives up on us. He is always present. Always. Like the sunshine. It is only us who give up on Him. We choose to walk alone into darkness."

"You do not understand. The things I have seen done by men . . . the things I myself have done. There can be no forgiveness." He shakes his head vigorously. "None."

She studies him, wondering what could have happened to shatter his faith. She debates whether to pry but then decides to change the subject. "Since I was a little girl I dreamed of becoming a physician. I used to practice medicine on the neighborhood pets." She forces a chuckle to lighten the mood. "I once even treated a boy who fell and hurt his leg. I turned him into an Egyptian mummy!" She laughs and waits for him to join her.

Finally, he relents and softly says, "I would have liked to have seen that."

Encouraged, she continues, "I was permitted to go to Saturday market by myself when I came of age. The one near the Royal Madrasa. Baba would give me a *dirham* to spend. I refused to use it on perfumes or clothes or makeup like the other girls my age. Instead, I would visit the spice and herb market, and I always spent my silver on medicinals and herbal remedies. I even started my own collection. Mama was furious, of course. But Baba . . ." She smiles with the recollection. "Well, Baba indulged me. Without Mama knowing he doubled my allowance. He is the one who introduced me to Abd al-Salam. My parents would have the Sufi master over for dinner. Sometimes he would bring his apprentices who were studying at the madrasa. What fascinating conversations we had. He and I became good friends. And then one day he surprised me with a book. Hippocrates' *On Ancient Medicine*." She turns to him. "Do you know it?"

"No."

"Well, I devoured the codex in three days. It was the most fascinating book I have ever read. From then on, Abd al-Salam encouraged my ambitions in the medical arts. He even managed to talk Baba and Mama into letting me become an apprentice to Hakim al-Adani. David." She studies him. "Medicine is my calling, Yusef. Like the Sufis, I live to serve."

"And you are a gifted healer, Danah."

"You are kind. I still have much to learn, of course. I almost fainted when I had to perform my first surgery on the wounded from Alhama."

"But you did not." A statement of fact.

"No, I did not." Silence slips in as her eyes well up. "He was younger than you. A grievous shoulder wound. I had seen nothing like it before . . ." Her words trail off. "Despite my best efforts, he died three days later."

"I am so sorry, Danah."

She sniffs, dabs her eyes. "War is a terrible, terrible thing, Yusef."

His words suddenly become laden with emotion. "Yes. Yes, it is."

"And now it has laid its cruel touch upon you. Upon us."

"Yes." He barely gets this out.

She permits the silence to settle in, hoping he will step into the space between them. She sits on the edge of his bed and cradles his hand between hers. The moments pass.

A resigned exhale. "It was three years ago, mid-July. Blistering heat. I was on a cavalry patrol in the borderlands east of Jaén. North of the castle at Huelma, in the Sierra Mágina Mountains. Uncle had gotten word that several bands of Christian mercenaries were raiding the mountain villages, stealing cattle, terrorizing the local population. Typical border incursions, hit and run, certainly nothing overly concerning. He decided to send me with a hundred riders to investigate, and if necessary, to chase the marauders back into Castile. It was my first command."

"Umar was not with you?"

"No. Uncle had sent him to Ronda to retrieve a herd of stallions purchased from the Maghreb."

"Go on."

"I was so puffed up and proud. And so intent to do my duty, to serve honorably. I wanted Uncle to be proud of me." He stops, stares into space as the memories awaken.

She squeezes his hand. "Do not stop. Please."

"The name of the village was . . . Mata Bejid. A tiny place in a narrow canyon just at the edge of the mountains, maybe three dozen villagers all told. When we stopped to water our horses, the elders were emphatic that they would soon be attacked. They begged us to stay and protect them. I was certain that they were not in any danger—too close to Huelma and its garrison—so I decided to leave them unguarded as we rode to the castle for better information on where the marauders might strike next." He sadly shakes his head. "My pride undid me. As it turned out, the elders were right." He hesitates. "When we returned the next day . . ." He stops.

"What?"

"The mercenaries were there. Eight of them; heavily armed. First they rounded up the villagers and put them in the corral, then they proceeded to steal the cattle. We surprised them. I am not sure why they did not hear us coming, but when they finally saw us they panicked, and instead of dropping their booty and riding for the hills, they grabbed hostages and held knives to their throats. They went for the children, Danah. The little ones."

"Dear Lord."

"By the time we rode up, the mothers and fathers were berserk, screaming and shouting at the Christians to release their children." He shakes his head. "I should have turned the squadron and retreated. Perhaps that would have changed things. But I stood my ground and ordered my men to draw their bows. I dismounted and approached the group on foot, my hands clear, broadsword still in its scabbard. It was obvious we had them surrounded, that there could be no escape. I told them in Arabic to release the children and they would be treated fairly. No response. I tried again in Castilian. Nothing. One of them stepped forward with a little girl in his grasp, his blade at her throat. She could not have been more than five years old. And so frightened. I will never forget the look on her face. The man sneered at me, then unleashed a barrage of words I did not understand. Some northern tongue. I motioned to him to give me the girl. He pulled her tighter, screamed at us again. And then . . . and then I could see it in his eyes, Danah. The angel of death. And in that instant, I knew he would kill the girl. I pulled my dagger and leaped for him, but I was not quick enough. He slit her throat and dropped her. It happened so slowly, as if time was frozen. He tried to fend me off, but I had no trouble putting my dagger in his guts. But then it started in earnest. A shout rang out from the mercenaries, and the rest of them began to . . ." His words trail away. "I screamed 'LOOSE!' and in an instant all of them were slain. But not before . . ."

She finishes for him in a quavering voice. "Not before they had murdered the children."

His eyes fall to his lap. "All eight of them."

Danah gasps.

"The fathers and mothers rushed to cradle their dying children, their little bodies limp and growing cold, their eyes already vacant. Dear Lord, it broke my heart. The blood, Danah. Rivers of innocent blood. Children, Danah. Children." His unseeing eyes are wide with horror.

Danah is crying.

"That was the last day I prayed, Danah. The very last. What kind of god allows such a thing to happen? To little ones. To innocent little children. What kind of god? Tell me, please? What kind of god?!" His voice catches again. He gathers himself and continues to the bitter end. "We were shaken. To a man we were shaken. I grew bloodthirsty. We all did. We swore revenge upon the Christians. We spent the next week hunting down the other mercenaries operating in those mountains. Three different bands of them. We hunted them like quarry, Danah. When we caught them we showed no mercy, even when they dropped to their knees and begged us. No mercy. None." He begins to shake. "We killed all of them, Danah, shouting, 'For the children!' We killed them, and we *enjoyed* it." He hisses through clenched teeth, "Then we mutilated their bodies. In terrible ways. I gave the command that none were to be buried, they were to be left as food for the wolves. It was pure bloodlust, Danah. Evil bloodlust. I died inside that day. My heart turned to stone . . . to stone." His eyes sink. "For three long years—nothing but stone." He shakes his head. "But that day I met you . . . I felt . . . I felt . . ."

"What did you feel, Yusef?"

"I felt . . . my heart begin to melt. You saved me, Danah."

She whispers through her swimming eyes. "Allah melted your heart, Yusef. He melted it. Allah's Merciful Grace, Yusef." She holds him as his tears finally arrive. He cries silently at first, then gives up and lays his head on her and sobs. She holds him tighter still, will not release him. "Allah forgives you, Yusef. He does. Allah forgives you. You are forgiven, Yusef, you are."

THREE DAYS LATER.

She sits cross-legged on her floor pillow in her tiny room, back straight as an arrow, eyes closed, face relaxed and at peace. Her palms are cupped and turned upward in her lap in patient waiting as Abd al-Salam has taught her. "A Sufi must invite Allah's Grace, Danah, moment by moment." She imbibes her breath, slowly, evenly, holds it, one-two-three-four-five-six, then exhales in mirror image; in and out, in and out, in and out. The world stills; the silence bends close and envelops her.

The heavenly palette timidly steps one by one from the abyss of darkness to shyly stand before her, each in its own perfection—the Sufi Muraqaba of Light. Her mind's eye fills first with a violet so pure and intense it makes a mockery of the color. The light surrounds her, bathes her, then gradually returns to midnight black. Nothingness. Next comes indigo, her favorite. Then blue, then green, then yellow, then orange, and finally red. Vermillion. Her heart stirs. Piercing vermillion. Yusef's vermillion. Her eyes fly open, brilliant green set upon white. "The Sufi Way! Dear Lord, of course! Tetta Layla, I understand. Tetta, I understand!" Still in her bedclothes she leaps up, throws open the door, and makes for his room, slipping and sliding in her silk stockings.

She breathlessly races through her explanation of what just happened: the meditation form, the insight, the answer, Allah's Grace, all of it.

He does not seem himself.

"The Sufi Way, Yusef. To serve. Yusef! You must serve!" Her hands dance as she gushes. She is so excited she can barely contain herself.

He just shakes his head, baffled.

She slows, she tries again.

He grows increasingly frustrated. "Serve? Who do you want me to serve?! Danah, how can you even pretend I am capable of serving—I am blind. Blind! Have you forgotten that simple fact? Have you? Well? I cannot even feed myself." His words grow unkind, "How am I to serve? HOW?!"

She takes his hand, presses it to her cheek. "You must see, Yusef. You must. Please. The Sufi Way, Yusef. Tetta Layla's words. We will serve together. It is what Allah intends for us. It is our fate. We are being called to use this Great Love we have been graciously given. Yusef!"

He retracts his hand. He sneers as his words bend ugly. "You would have me grovel, Danah? To bumble through the streets like some blind gypsy, begging? Would you? And have all the people of Granada pity me? 'There goes the poor blind Falcon. Poor Yusef. Here, toss him a crumb so he does not starve.' Is that what you wish me to do, Danah? Is that it?"

Who is this person that I love? "Yusef, no. Please. We will start with the wounded. Right here in the Bermejas. These wounded men need you. Let them know you are here, that you too are injured, that you feel their pain. You must serve Allah, Yusef, it is the Sufi Way. I know that you are afraid—"

He recoils as if struck, then flushes dark. "Afraid? AFRAID?!" He puffs up. "I am a Nasrid prince of the realm. I am a knight of Granada, sworn to bravery and honor and chivalry in my thoughts and deeds. Do NOT forget that." He flicks his wrist dismissively. "Why would you insult me so?"

His words reach out and slap her, the sting filling her eyes. *Why does he not see? Why, Lord?* She is devastated. Beyond devastated. "Yusef, no. You do not understand. Please. I am only trying to help you. Please, Yusef."

"Trying to help me? You wish me to grovel. I WILL NOT! I WILL NOT! Now take your Sufi imaginings and leave me." He turns away from her.

Danah steps back in horror. She is a mess. She makes her way down the hall in a teetering daze, opens the door, and throws herself onto her mattress.

She is still sobbing a half-hour later.

The entire staff notices the change. She is as attentive to her patients as ever, but the light behind her eyes has departed. One-word answers, listless queries, forced smiles at jokes that would normally cause her to cackle with delight. David repeatedly asks her what is wrong, if she is feeling ill. She assures him that she is fine, just tired. Feeling out of his depth, he gives up and decides to consult with his wife.

"It is time to change the bandage on your arm. Afterward, Joshua will come to bathe you." As stiff and lifeless as starched cotton cloth pressed flat under a heated iron.

"Good morning." He is tentative, polite.

No response.

The tension between the two of them has stretched taut, then tauter still. As the days have dragged on, she has grown colder, more distant. He is still unsure what exactly came over him. He has increasingly suffered over his words, is filled with regret for slamming the door on her excitement. *My pride, damn my stupid pride!*

She begins to work on his arm. His sightless eyes follow her movements. She gives a quick glance then ignores him.

Unexpectedly, he smiles. "I would prefer you."

She frowns without looking up. "What?"

"I would prefer that you bathed me." Impolitic words, to be certain. His feeble attempt to lighten her mood.

She smirks, ignores his playful overture. She continues her work, lifting an instrument to probe the exposed wound.

"Can you feel this?" She touches the probe to his skin next to the suture line.

"Yes."

"Here?"

"Yes."

"Here?"

"Yes."

"Good." All business. She begins to rewrap the wound. "David says it is time to get you out of bed and up on crutches. To keep your muscles from withering. It will be a little while still before you can put weight on your broken leg, but at least you can get out for some fresh air."

"That would be nice." He chews his cheek. "Danah?"

She does not answer.

"Danah?" More insistent.

She relents. "Yes."

"I am sorry. I let my stupid pride . . ." He stops, searching for the right words.

"There is nothing to be sorry for, Yusef. It was wrong of me to imagine that I had any answers."

He paws the air until he finds her arm, slides his hand down upon hers. "Danah. I am sorry. Forgive me."

She pulls from his grasp. "There is nothing to forgive." He cannot see that her eyes have welled up. "I have patients I must see."

As he hears the door close he curses himself for the tenth time.

On her regular rounds two days later, she opens the door to his room and stops with a puzzled frown. No Yusef. Her eyes track to the corner. No crutches. She left strict orders that he was not to leave his room without assistance. Annoyed, she exits, turns left, and marches to the attendant's station. "Aaron?" There is a sharp, accusatory edge to her tone.

The man looks up. "Yes, Hakim?"

"Yusef is not in his room."

"No, Hakim."

Her hands find her hips as she frowns her disapproval; rarely a good omen. "My instructions were quite clear. Prince al-Makki is not to leave his room without someone at his side. He is not used to crutches. If he falls and re-breaks that leg . . ."

"I understand, Hakim."

She is perturbed. "Is he in the courtyard?"

Joshua walks up to join them. "He is in the ward, Hakim Amiriya. I saw that he got there safely."

"In the ward?" Her brows knit their puzzlement.

"Yes, Hakim. He was insistent. I saw that he got there safely."

"I see." A frustrated wag of her head as she sets off down the hallway, leather heels clicking behind her.

Aaron and Joshua exchange amused smiles.

353

She pushes the door to the ward open, ready to chastise him for taking advantage of the attendants, but stops in her tracks, breathless. Six rows down and to the left, Yusef sits on the edge of a wounded knight's bed, his back to her, crutches leaning against the wall. Danah remembers the injury. Terrible head wound that David worked on. Left eye, nose, and ear ripped from the young man's face.

Yusef is leaning close, whispering into his good ear. She sees the young knight nod, nod again. Yusef lays his hand upon the young man's shoulder as he continues to speak. His words grow more emphatic, as if he is issuing the young knight a command. She hears the young man answer, "You have my word, my lord. Thank you."

"Prince al-Makki?" A shy query from the adjacent bed. The ward is becoming aware of the presence of a Falcon.

Her emeralds melt then spill. She murmurs, "The Sufi Way. *Alhamdulillah.*" Praise be to Allah. "Alhamdulillah." Lower lip trembling, she slips from the ward. As she dabs at her eyes, a brilliant smile dances onto her face.

Loja

By the time the patrol sent to reconnoiter the enemy positions approaches, the sun is already high, the morning mist long departed from the network of irrigation canals crisscrossing the valley floor.

The fertile Granadine Vega stretches into the distance from the banks of the River Genil. Oddly, not a single laborer can be seen fussing over the dense patchwork of wheat fields and citrus orchards, as if nature's plush bounty magically burst forth of its own volition. Verdant serenity as far as the eye can see, but an eerie, unmistakable tension hangs heavy in the air. Beneath the blistering sun the incessant drone of insects has kicked in with a vengeance. Not even a hint of breeze. Heat wrinkles obscure sightlines, a portent of the coming summer swelter for which the Kingdom of Granada is infamous. A solitary kestrel skates upon the currents, bow-bending southward, scanning, hoping.

The two men rise from their seats as the riders gallop up. The lead scout slides from his mount, steps forward out of the cloud of dust, and bows. "My lord."

Ali al-Attar mops his brow with a cotton cloth. His white turban is darkened with sweat where it wraps across his forehead. "I had about given you up for dead, Ahmad. Well, what news?"

"You were right, my lord. The Christians have taken the bait. A third of his army is making for the Hill of Albohacen as we speak."

"Excellent."

Ali al-Attar strokes his beard. "Fool. I knew Fernando would lust over the high ground for his infernal cannons. As tempting as a honeyed almond. The man's arrogance does not allow him to stop and consider why we would leave such a strategic position undefended. Their pace?"

"Slow and steady, my lord, to stay with their cannons. Cavalry flanking the infantry column. They went upstream a mile for an easier crossing of the Genil, then back down and into the forest." He turns and points. "There. Behind the cover of the ridge. My guess is that they will reach the peak of Albohacen by mid-afternoon."

"Good. As expected."

Al-Zaghal nods, impressed. "I will concede that you were right, and I was wrong."

The grizzled warrior offers a wolfish smile. "These old eyes have seen a few more battles than yours, Muhammad. This is what we have been waiting for—a battle on open ground. The Christians trust too much in their plate armor and monstrous stallions. Prancing dandies in metal costumes. Painfully slow at maneuvering in space. We will make them pay a price for their vanity." He turns back to the rider. "How many cannons?"

"We counted only three, my lord. Massive beasts. Very slow moving."

Ali al-Attar grunts. "I would have guessed more. There is nothing to worry about, Muhammed—they will never get the chance to fire on Loja."

Al-Zaghal replies, "Let us hope not. We will have ceded them the high ground."

Ali al-Attar grunts. "We will see about that. Is the king in command?"

"No, my lord, the king is still encamped in the valley. From our vantage we could clearly see his tent and the queen's royal standard. The force making for Albohacen rides under three banners: the Marquess of Cádiz, the Marquess of Villena, and the Master of the Order of Calatrava."

Ali al-Attar snorts. "So, Ponce de Léon has arrived from Alhama to join the fight after all. Excellent news. That one is due some payback. He will be in command, and with no stone wall to hide behind this time. Villena I do not know. But the Master of the Order of Calatrava I do. Rodrigo Girón. I have fought several border skirmishes against that one."

"And?"

"An able commander." He turns to the lead scout. "You have done well, Ahmad. I want you to keep track of Ponce de Léon's movements. Discreetly, please. Send word when they are nearing Albohacen's summit. I do not want them to have time to dig in. You know where to find me."

"Understood, my lord."

The old man watches the patrol ride off, then draws his sword with a cool, metallic hiss and begins to etch their battle plan in the dirt. First, the wavy line of the River Genil as it makes its way out of the forest and wends along the edge of the fertile valley past Loja. Next, the Christian encampment, then the city; finally, the Hill of Albohacen. "Fernando does not appreciate the precarious position in which he has placed himself. The run of the irrigation canals into the Vega will prevent his heavy cavalry from massing for an organized charge. You will need to swing around wide and slip your men in from the southeast, then weave your way through the canals onto his rear before he has time to reposition or retreat. Use the orchards to cover your approach. You will attack here. Once you have fully engaged the Christians, have your bannnerman signal Umar to commence his attack. Here. In the meantime, I will remind Ponce de Léon that Granada still remembers how to fight. When Albohacen is ours we will move to attack his flank and finish him off. Here."

"And if your plan fails?"

The old man's eyes sparkle. "The day is ours for the taking, Muhammad. Allah has willed it."

Al-Zaghal nods. "Then let it be so, old friend. *Fi Amanullah.*" May Allah protect you.

Ali al-Attar nods, turns, and signals his adjutant. "Alert the troops. We ride!" With his boot he erases the battle plan.

Yusef sits on the stone bench blankly staring in the direction of the courtyard fountain, head slightly cocked to one side. Without any perceptible movement, the cool elixir effortlessly folds over the polished marble edge, a perfectly pressed, translucent curtain draped from the reservoir to a thin, turbulent white line in the catch basin. Seductive curves and marvelous symmetry, the sound crystalline, majestic.

She stops when she sees him through the window, then backtracks and opens the door and enters the courtyard. The slow, plush crunch of soft leather upon pea pebbles marks her steps.

His blind eyes do not move from the tranquility of the falling water. "I never realized just how beautiful the sound of water can be. Ever changing, but always the same. Like life."

The moment stretches out.

"You were thinking of your brother."

A long pause. "Yes."

"I pray every day for his safe return."

He does not respond.

She leans forward and whispers into his ear.

He listens, nods, then nods again. "I know. Thank you, Danah."

As the soft cadence of stone-crush retreats, his hands fold together in prayer, something they have not done in years.

"Damn this heat." Ponce de León turns in his saddle to assess their progress. Down the slope, his rearguard is finally in sight. One less worry. Orders have been issued, and the infantry that have already crested the mountain are beginning to reassemble into their brigades. The cannon crews have chocked the iron wheels on the massive limbers to hold them steady. Heavy cavalry rumbles menacingly along the flanks at the edge of the forest. He cocks his head toward the sun to assess the hour and nods— ample margin to fortify their position before dark. Satisfied, he removes his visored helmet to cool off, resting it on his saddle in front of him. His officers follow suit. His elaborately engraved plate armor, polished to a brilliant sheen, weighs forty-eight pounds, not including his heavy-felt undergarments and weaponry. His stallion's burden is triple that.

He surveys the crest of the Hill of Albohacen, now in their possession. The climb was grueling, the army's progress slowed to a crawl by the heavy cannons. In the end he had to use a dozen of his cavalry mounts to help pull the ungainly bronze beasts up the final sharp rise to the summit. Thankfully, the mountaintop is almost bald and reasonably flat before it slopes back off to the south in the direction of Loja. Like many of the peaks ringing in the Granadine Vega, Albohacen is covered mostly by wild grasses and clumps of low scrub, separated by isolated tracks of dense forest running downslope to the valley. His eyes settle on the castle nestled on the banks of the Genil far below. He can see the troops on the ramparts, the bustle of activity on the parade ground of the garrison. As expected, Albohacen has a beautiful sightline down onto Loja's castle. "Spectacular spot for an artillery battery."

Don Rodrigo Tellez Girón, master of the Order of Calatrava, answers, "Indeed. We will have their wall down in two days. Maybe less."

Don Alonso de Aquilar, the Marquess of Villena, adds, "The Moors were fools not to garrison this peak."

Ponce de León frowns as a tingle races along his spine. He has learned to rely upon his battlefield intuition, and the man's remark unsettles him. *It is indeed strange that this peak remains unguarded.* He turns to his second. "Juan, deploy the cannons so they have a clear firing line on the castle, then have the men dig in. Have trees cut and brought up so breastworks can be laid. I want this mountain turned into a fortress by dusk, understood? The Moors will surely soon be—"

"ALLAHU ACKBAR!" Below them, toward the castle, from within the run of dense forest downslope. Alarmingly close.

Girón's stallion rears and whinnies, nearly bucking him off, his helmet striking the ground with a dull thud. Conversations within the ranks instantly halt. The birdsong trails away, and the drone of insects ominously stills. Sphincters clench as eyes snap to the unmistakable battle cry of the Moors. The hands of the veteran men-at-arms instinctively reach for their sword hilts. Tense silence binds the landscape. The sting of sweat runs into unblinking wide eyes and uneasy glances are exchanged. Girón's squire trots up to retrieve his helmet as all the knights hastily begin to lock their armor back in place.

Ponce de León cups his hands to his ears to try to pinpoint the direction. Nothing. He rises up in his stirrups. Not a sight or sound of their enemy.

"ALLAHU ACKBAR!" Closer now, just inside the edge of the tree line.

He turns in his saddle to the dozen officers gathered behind him. "Form ranks! FORM RANKS! PREPARE FOR BATTLE!" Girón, Aquilar, and the other officers race to rejoin their men. The summit erupts in frantic motion and shouted orders. Footmen donning arquebuses assigned to guard the cannons race to the limbers, take up station and kneel, then begin to charge their weapons. The infantry brigades form staggered phalanxes; pikemen to the front to thwart a cavalry charge, archers to the rear. Plate-armored knights on foot provide protection for the flanks of the infantry cohorts. To the front of the infantry and cannons stands a battle line of lethal war machines, knights atop monstrous stallions, the afternoon sun reflecting off the mass of polished plate. It is an imposing sight to be sure, intimidating to any rational foe. Precisely the aim. The cavalry stands two hundred paces wide and five horses deep, their commander front and center.

Ponce de León's hand rises. In response, the mounted knight's visors are lowered, and swords and maces are drawn. Battle ready. He turns to his adjutant. "Send word to the rearguard to make haste. I want them in reserve but ready to defend our flanks if called upon." The man nods, kicks his mount, and gallops back down the slope. The landscape stills, but the tension in the air is as oppressive as the scorching heat. Ponce de León walks his mount forward a short distance and stops.

"ALLAHU ACKBAR!" All eyes are glued to the woods, four hundred paces downslope.

"Knights of Castile, stand tall! Long live the queen!"

"LONG LIVE THE QUEEN!" The refrain is thunderous.

A line of cavalry slowly emerges from the forest shadows. Moorish knights riding small Andalusian ponies, four hands shorter and smaller-boned than the Christian monsters. The horses sport no armor beyond oversized heavy-felt saddle blankets and boiled leather leg casings. Granadine cavalry is celebrated far and wide for their superb riding skills and the speed and endurance of their diminutive stallions. A mobile, lethal fighting force. Ponce de León knows this better than anyone. No match in a head-to-head fight against a plate-armored knight, but far more agile, and dangerous for exactly this reason.

The Moors are dressed in colorful, flowing, silk-embroidered robes, mostly browns and blues and greens; expensive stuff; courtly attire. Despite its prevalence in European warfare, the Moors share a disdain for plate armor—too heavy and burdensome—though most do wear chain mail hauberks to blunt a sword or pike thrust. A stark contrast to the heavy and motion-constraining polished plate of their adversaries. The tails of the Moors' cotton-white turbans stretch down their backs, each rider a sleek bannerman at full gallop. Unlike the Christian knights, who enlist broadswords or maces to crush their enemies, the Moors prefer crossbows and javelins and are trained to throw or loose at full gallop. They carry crescent-hilted Granadine broadswords, sash daggers, and small but distinctive, heart-shaped leather-over-wood shields for close-in fighting.

One hundred Moor knights slowly walk their horses forward in an impeccable line. Then another hundred. Then a third. They stop. The Moor cavalry stretches back into the woods, deliberately obscuring their actual numbers.

Ponce de León frowns his distaste for uncertainty of odds.

In the center of the first Moor line Ponce de León trains his eyes on a grizzled old knight dressed in all red, recognizing him from Alhama. He knows this is their commander, a veteran Moorish prince whose name he would very much like to know. After all that he witnessed at Alhama, he greatly respects the man's valor.

Ali al-Attar raises his ancient broadsword and shouts, "There is no victor but Allah!"

He is immediately answered by an Arabic roar, "THERE IS NO VICTOR BUT ALLAH!"

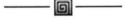

"Majesty, our position is precarious, and we are severely undermanned!"

Fernando and his commanders are gathered in the king's tent for a war council.

Don Alonso of Aragon, the Duke of Villahermosa, is seething. "The River Genil is too high-banked to be easily crossed if, God forbid, we are forced to retreat. And the damned irrigation canals cut up the whole countryside! If the Moors decide to challenge us on open ground, our heavy cavalry will be unable to mount any kind of effective fighting force. It will be nearly impossible for our stallions to jump these canals. I repeat, our position here is precarious." The duke is a seasoned veteran of a dozen campaigns under the Aragonese flag. A man respected for his tactical skills, not easily discounted.

The king nods his acknowledgment. "I understand your concern, Don Alonso. I have ordered three bridges to be built across the Genil."

Don Alonso grunts his disapproval. "That will take days, majesty."

"Mmm. Don Diego?"

Don Diego de Merlo vigorously shakes his head, clearly disagreeing with the Aragonese commander's opinion. That their present encampment on the Vega is so close to the enemy castle was his brainstorm. Meant to intimidate the Moors and distract them from Ponce de León's push up Albohacen with the cannons. "The Moors do not want to fight us on open ground, majesty. Why would they? No, they will assume they are safe behind their castle walls, and after Alhama, how could they possibly not believe that? They will not dare to challenge us in open battle."

Don Alonso blurts out, "Why tempt fate? The Moors are not stupid, you know." The two men lock eyes. Their expressions convey their differing positions quite clearly.

Don Diego softens his tone. "Majesty, in any case, Ponce de León will command Albohacen by nightfall, and in the morning our cannons will fire on Loja's walls. By then it will be too late for the Moors to act. Within a few days Loja will be ours for the taking. The Moors cannot possibly know that we are about to train our heavy cannons on them."

The king mulls this over. "So be it. We stay. But I want bridges built across the Genil and our fortifications bolstered. As quickly as possible." He turns to his adjutant. "Any news on the Great Captain?"

"He is not due back from Alhama for two more days, majesty."

Fernando frowns. "Inform me as soon as he arrives, I must speak with him."

"Of course, majesty."

As Ali al-Attar lowers his sword his cavalry leaps to a charge in perfect formation, each man screaming, "ALLAHU ACKBAR! ALLAHU ACKBAR! ALLAHU ACKBAR!"

Ponce de León shouts, "Archers, nock arrows! Hold for my command! Pikemen, up!" Orders pass down the ranks.

Rolling thunder rises from down the slope.

The Moors have halved the distance to the Christian line by the time the pikemen reach position and kneel in a double row in front of the cavalry line, pikes braced at forty-five-degree angles. A wall of death to the Moorish stallions who do not sport chest armor.

The thunder grows louder.

Officers ride back and forth behind the ranks barking, "Steady, boys! Hold the line! Steady, boys!"

Still the Moors come.

"Stand firm! Hold the line! Stand firm!"

The thunder grows deafening as the Moors crest the mountaintop and bear down on the Christian line.

Fifty paces out, the Moor cavalry abruptly yank their reins in unison, pulling their mounts to a sudden stop. Locked legs slide to a grinding halt in a choking cloud of dust. As the air begins to settle, it becomes clear that the Moors have reconsidered trying to run the gauntlet of pikes. They begin to turn and race back toward their forest hideout.

As Ponce de León expected. He turns and shouts, "ARCHERS, LOOSE!" A cloud of arrows whoosh past, dropping several dozen Moors from their saddles.

Ponce de León raises his sword. "KNIGHTS OF CASTILE! ATTACK!"

"LONG LIVE THE QUEEN!" The pikemen rise and part, allowing the Christian heavy cavalry to burst forth, their monstrous stallions giving chase, hooves tearing the earth as they roar forward.

Ponce de León leads the charge. His eyes dance between the retreating Moor cavalry and the forest, calculating. He quickly realizes the Moorish ponies are too fleet to catch before they enter the safety of the forest cover. He knows well that it would be foolish to give chase into such close quarters.

Unexpectedly, the Moors bend right and tighten their formation, making for a narrow clearing separating the dense forest from which they emerged and an adjacent line of trees. As the Moors begin to disappear between the two banks of forest, Ponce de León makes a split-second decision and decides to give chase. As his cavalry follows, both of his flanks are hemmed in by the thick woods. The clearing tightens down and bends hard left as it funnels down, and the racing Moors disappear from sight. Instantly sensing danger, Ponce de León raises his hand and reins his mount, his knights following his lead. The cavalry slows then stops in the thick dust cloud. He shouts to his second. "I do not like the feel of this. Turn the cavalry and make for our lines. Quickly. Pass the word! Retreat! Pass the word!" Shouts ring out down the line. Alas, the space between the trees is too narrow for any organized maneuver, forcing each knight to awkwardly try to pivot his stallion. Ponce de León curses. *Too slow. Too slow!*

The hairs on the back of his neck are standing at full salute now. Ponce de León anxiously glances over his shoulder at the point where the Moors disappeared. He curses again as he sees his enemy slowly walk from their hiding place around the bend, the old prince in the vanguard holding his sword high and proud. With a sinking feeling in his gut, the old Moor's battle plan comes into focus. *Trap.* Ponce de León shouts, "Ambush! Make haste, men, ride for our lines! Ambush! Ride now! AMBUSH! MAKE HASTE!"

At that moment, the first crossbow bolt strikes the master of the Order of Calatrava, whose knights anchor the left flank. He is close to the tree line, dangerously close. The bolt strikes between the lip of his helmet and his plated shoulder guards, severing his spine. Expert marksmanship. A surprised grunt is all the marquess manages as he slips from the saddle like a ragdoll and hits the ground in a sickening metallic crush.

Several, then dozens, then hundreds of bolts sail through the air from both tree lines. Caught in a deadly crossfire. Because decent plate armor is thick enough to thwart a small crossbow bolt, those are aimed at the haunches and thighs of the stallions; any vulnerable piece of horseflesh. But the Moors are also firing heavy crossbows standing half the height of a man and requiring a special bracing tool to cock. These beasts fire an iron-tipped, foot-long bolt an inch in diameter. Designed specifically to puncture plate armor—a recent and lethal Moorish innovation. The Christian cavalry dissolves into mayhem. The lead elements attempt to retreat, but wide-eyed mounts rear and buck as the bolts drive home into soft meat, clogging the escape route. The trapped knights frantically twist and turn, attempting to wriggle free as the bolts continue to sail from the dark woods. In alarming numbers, the Christian knights begin to hit the dirt, massive bolts sprouting from their armor, the thick shafts buried half their length in shiny plate, plenty deep enough to find vital organs. To a one these brave men, nobles of court and landed gentry, are shocked at this turn of events, having naively assumed their armor guaranteed safety from bolts and arrows of any kind. They do not even bother to carry shields. Fatal mistake.

Ponce de León curses the ugly carnage unfolding around him and fights to rally his men to an orderly retreat. He glances back and sees that the Moor cavalry is now charging on his position. "Damn these Moors!"

"ALLAHU ACKBAR!" Closing quickly. "ALLAHU ACKBAR!"

"Ride, damn you! RIDE! RIDE OR DIE!"

As the mounts of the dead and dying Christians sprint wildly in all directions, the killing field thins enough that the remaining cavalry can begin to free themselves, and in small clots the knights attempt a disorganized retreat, many having no choice but to trample their fallen comrades. A stuttered cadence of gut-wrenching, hammered-metal clunks and crunches is followed by dust and rising thunder as the retreat gains momentum.

As his decimated cavalry approaches the entrance to the funnel between the trees that ensnared them, an odd glint of reflected light draws Ponce de León's eyes to the right tree line a hundred paces to their front. The new danger is unmistakable to his seasoned eye—bronze barrels protruding from blinds. His recognition is instantaneous and sickening. *Cannons! Dear God, how?!* He quickly scans. *One. Two. Three. Four. Five.* All neatly aligned to ensure overlapping fields of fire. He turns in his saddle and sees that the Moor cavalry is closing rapidly. *No time.* He screams, "RIDE LIKE THE WIND! RIDE FOR YOUR LIVES!" He kicks his mount with bloodied spurs and screams, "HYAH! HYAH!"

The world slows to a crawl and for an infernal moment he thinks they may even manage to slip pass the cannons unscathed. *Maybe they are not yet primed.*

BLAMM! BLA-BLA-BLAMM! BLAMM!

Thick ribbons of dense gray smoke billow from the woods just as Ponce de León and the lead element pass. Even at half charge the canister loads are lethal at this point-blank range, capable of puncturing neat, finger-sized holes in the most expensive French tempered plate. A swath of destruction forty paces wide is instantly hewn through the core of the disheveled cavalry, the stallions and knights alike issuing horrified screams that are abruptly truncated as they are riddled with lead balls. They buckle earthward in one massive rolling wave of death. Those behind have no choice but to try to jump the tangled bloody mess. Most just ride right over.

And still the Moor cavalry comes. "ALLAHU ACKBAR!"

Al-Zaghal's knights have slipped undetected to within a long arrow shot of the Christian encampment on the south side of the River Genil. It is a small strike force, but well-trained and agile. Al-Zaghal has exploited the cover of the lush citrus grove masterfully and has halted his men just inside the dense cover. He and his two commanders crouch at the base of a tree to survey their best angle of attack.

The Christian sentries are clustered between the castle and the encampment, conveniently on the side opposite al-Zaghal's position. Fools. The perimeter in front of the Moors is weakly garrisoned, and the low-walled wooden defensive barriers appear to have been hastily assembled. Weak.

He whispers to his two commanders, "Follow the line of the canal." He points to his right, traces its path toward the encampment. "See how it switches back just outside their perimeter? Maybe six feet wide. And deep."

"I see it."

"Yes. Perfect."

"Too wide for their big-boned stallions to jump without room for a decent galloping approach. When I give the word, we strike there. Tight formation. My aim is to puncture their lines before they can shift their forces for a proper defense. That jump should give your cavalry no pause, Ashab."

A leering grin. "Child's play."

"Garib, the cavalry will hold pace and flank your footmen as they approach the Christian line, then jump the barricades and set a perimeter for you. Let the crossbowmen lead and do what they do best. Once we secure the breech, we will fight northward toward the king's tent."

"Understood."

"Remember, gentlemen, no quarter for any Christian knight. For Alhama."

"For Alhama!"

"For Alhama!"

"ALLAHU ACKBAR! ALLAHU ACKBAR!"

The loitering Christian troops turn to the sound, confused. Word quickly begins to spread.

Hearing the commotion, Fernando steps from his tent and looks southeast, away from the castle. Moor cavalry are jumping their barricades and spilling into the encampment. "Holy God. Sound the alarm!"

A bronze bell clangs. Another. A third. The camp bursts into action as half-armored infantry gather their weapons and race to the fight. Squires frantically saddle stallions as the knights begin to lock their armor in place and rush to their mounts.

"ALLAHU ACKBAR! ALLAHU ACKBAR!"

Don Diego Lopez de Ayala, Ponce de León's commander of infantry, is up in his stirrups trying desperately to assess what is happening downslope. All he sees are panicked, riderless stallions veering right and left from the opening between the trees. Heart pounding, he turns to his officers. "I do not like this. Prepare for attack! Pass the word. Prepare for attack!"

"ALLAHU ACKBAR!" From the tree line on his left flank.

"ALLAHU ACKBAR!" An echoed answer from his right flank.

Don Diego's head snaps in one direction and then the other just in time to see Moorish cavalry roar from the forest, weapons raised and ready. "Dear God, help us." He croaks at his adjutant. "Is the rearguard up and in reserve yet?" Fear drips from the man's words.

"No, my lord, not yet."

"Swing the brigades to the flanks and mount a defense! Quickly, man, before all is lost! And send a rider for the rearguard and tell Don Luis—" With an awful *THRUMP!* a bolt shatters Don Diego's cheekbone and burrows itself deep in his brain. Stupidly, his visor is still open. The handsome young man's mouth opens and closes like a fish tossed upon the bank, then he folds backward off his stallion, one foot awkwardly caught in his stirrup. His mount screams and rears as a bolt finds his withers. The horse races white-eyed down the slope, his dead master's bloody head bouncing along in the dirt.

Specks of blood dot the adjutant's shocked face. White as a ghost, he stands motionless, limbs paralyzed by fear.

"ALLAHU ACKBAR!"

The Christian infantry are dropping like flies in the barrage of bolts as the Moor juggernaut bursts through their lines, the mounted knights viciously swinging their broadswords in wide, looping arcs, severing arms, crushing skulls, cleaving necks.

Most of the Christian men-at-arms on foot are simply toppled by the on-rushing stallions or else kicked over by Moor riders. As the prostrate knights awkwardly attempt to rise and give fight, special Moor footmen race to their sides and kneel, needle daggers drawn. Some flip back helmet visors and ram their blades into widened, horrified eyes and deep into their quarries' brains, while others wiggle their daggers into the open gaps beneath the shoulder armor, through the ribs and into pounding hearts. Quick, terrified screams and it is over.

The battleground is bathed in awful cries of agony and the clenching terror of impending death. The gamey smell of fresh blood mingled with fecal reek hangs heavy in the sweltering air, the ground a tangled mess of crimson guts and gore.

The Christian ranks dissolve in panic. One man runs, then a few, then dozens, then hundreds. They fling their weapons to the ground and scatter, racing for some semblance of safety back down the slope from whence they came, preventing any organized movement by the rearguard to join the fight. The gunmen protecting the cannons fire their arquebuses only once, most missing their targets, then are ravaged with broadswords, javelins, and crossbows. After the artillery officers are cut down, the cannon crews desert their bronze beasts and sprint for cover. Most are dropped before they can leave the mountaintop.

By the time Ponce de León arrives with his remaining cavalry the battle is clearly lost. Aghast, he slows to survey the devastation, but with Ali al-Attar on his heels, he has no choice but to kick his stallion and vector his decimated cavalry back down the mountain to rejoin the king's army. Full retreat.

The desperate fight inside the king's encampment has devolved into a vicious hand-to-hand melee across blurred battle lines as the element of surprise slowly gives way to an organized Christian counterattack led by Don Alonso of Aragon and the king. Dead and dying knights are stacked two and three deep in places, making organized movement by either side difficult. Don Diego de Merlo, champion of Alhama, lies dead in the mud, the back of his helmet crushed by the shoed hoof of one of his own men's stallions, which trampled him after he fell. With limited room to maneuver, the Moor cavalry is no match head-to-head against the mounted Christian men-at-arms, and the tide of battle begins to turn.

Broadsword still in hand, al-Zaghal raises both arms high, crossing them at the wrists. The waiting bannerman across the canal raises a bright red flag on a long pole and begins to wave it furiously back and forth.

Rolling thunder rises as Umar's cavalry races from the orchard shouting, "ALLAHU ACKBAR! THERE IS NO VICTOR BUT ALLAH! ALLAHU ACKBAR!"

Don Alonso is the first to see the new threat. He shouts at the king, "Another Moor attack, majesty!" He points.

Fernando curses.

"We will soon be outnumbered. Our position is untenable, majesty."

Grim-faced, Fernando assesses the situation and reluctantly nods. He quickly surveys the battlefield then makes his decision. "Sound retreat. Sound retreat, I say! Pass the word, ride for the banks of the Genil, then west. I want the cavalry protecting our rearguard. MOVE! MOVE! MOVE!"

From the fray, heads turn as bugles sound. The Christians begin to disengage, and the officers struggle to organize their men to move. By the time Umar's cavalry jumps the canal and crashes through the barricade, the king's army is already streaming out of the encampment in full retreat.

Umar reins his mount then turns and locks eyes with al-Zaghal, who smiles, then thrusts his sword in the direction of the retreating Christians. "ATTACK!"

Umar shouts at his men. "LONG LIVE GRANADA! CHARGE! CHARGE!" He kicks his stallion in hot pursuit. "HYAH! HYAH!"

By the time the bloodied Christian army manages to extricate itself from the Loja valley, what little is left of Ponce de León's cavalry rejoins the severely depleted main force. Hundreds of the king's men fall during the disorganized retreat as Umar's cavalry continues to harass their rearguard inch by painful inch. To add insult to injury, Ali al-Attar's cavalry arrives fresh from victory at Albohacen and joins the rout. The Moors do not break off their attack until the king reaches River Frio and finally has the opportunity to set a hasty defensive line. With one final massive shout of "THERE IS NO VICTOR BUT ALLAH!" the Moors turn and ride back to Loja, exultant over their stunning victory.

Proud and arrogant after Alhama, Christian heads are now slack, bent low in shame, eyes glued to the ground in bewilderment. The king's army is quiet to a man. As the army begins to limp back to Lucena to regroup, the obvious starts to sink in to knights and commanders alike—the Moors are a more than capable adversary after all. Something that should have surprised no one. This will be a hard-fought and bloody war.

High above, on the summit of Albohacen, the blistering sun beats down upon the bloated bodies of the Christian dead, stripped bare of their valuable armor and left to rot. The corpses stink unbelievably, and they sing with flies; the bodies are

ribboned with slopes of white fat and black ropes of blood—
hellchunks in the growing heat.

Heartstrings

"Danah?"

She looks up from rewrapping her patient's bandages and raises an eyebrow expectantly. They have all been on pins and needles awaiting word from Loja—something, anything.

David's face does not betray the answer. He simply ticks his head, indicating he wishes to speak with her privately.

She nods, finishes with the bandage, and offers her patient a kind word, then she rises, heart suddenly pounding, and joins him in the hallway.

"I just received word from the Alhambra."

She searches his face with held breath, sees the answer just before it arrives.

"Good news."

She slowly exhales. "*Subhanallah.*" Glory to Allah. "Tell me."

"A decisive victory over the Christians. King Fernando is in full retreat back to Lucena."

She absorbs this. "The wounded?"

"They should begin arriving within two days, I would think. But nothing like Alhama. The word is that the Christian losses were staggering compared to ours."

"I see." In her mind's eye she sees dead and maimed young men splayed across the killing fields. "I hate war."

A somber nod of agreement. "Yes."

"Umar?"

"He and his uncle are both fine. Evidently Umar and his men were instrumental in carrying the day."

She nods. "I will give him the news."

"Yes. We have preparations to make."

"Of course. I will alert the staff and check on our supplies." She turns to leave.

"And Danah?"

She stops, looks back. "Yes?"

David hesitates, as if trying to decide whether to mention something, then shakes his head and waves her on. "It can wait."

She stops when she sees him, content to watch the miracle transpiring across the courtyard. A smile settles onto her face as her emeralds gloriously sparkle.

He sits on a stone bench and stares into space as he regales two knights with some story, his hands stretching wide for emphasis then contracting as his tale ebbs and flows. At the end he laughs loudly, eliciting chuckles from the two knights. One man is missing his forearm, neatly cleaved just below the elbow. The other took a lead arquebus ball to his shoulder, permanently ruining the joint and use of his arm. The wards have slowly emptied over the ensuing weeks, but these two are remaining stragglers who have not been sent home yet due to the severity of their wounds. It is clear now that both will live, but it is also painfully obvious that neither man will live the life he imagined.

There has been a remarkable change in Yusef's demeanor since the day he decided to step beyond his own cruel fate and enter the pain of his fellow wounded. He serves in the only manner he is able: with empathetic ears and compassionate, caring words. She continues to marvel that his mere presence among the wounded men manages to sow such powerful rays of hope where previously there were none. No small feat. He listens, he offers words of encouragement, and at times he challenges them when he realizes this is required. And of course he tries to lighten their burden by getting them to laugh, or at least to smile. He leads by example, as he always has. The fallen Falcon prince, whose wings have been so rudely clipped, has learned how to become a powerful salve for those in dire need. He follows the Sufi Way, a miracle indeed. She has watched this daily unfolding with great amazement, with prayerful thanksgiving, and with a deep appreciation that Allah is sculpting the man she loves moment by moment into something new, something wonderful.

Truth be told, the changes in the ward of the Bermejas have not all been Yusef's. There is a playful, coltish jounce in Danah's step these days, and David has caught her more than once just staring into space over her work, beaming like a little girl as she daydreams about who knows what. Time and again that radiant smile of hers just seems to unexpectedly blossom for no apparent reason. The girl has probably smiled more in this past week alone than she has in her whole life. She unleashes that cute laugh in response to his teasing and has even begun to indulge in the fine art of flirting. Who would have thought such things possible?

Still, they are both delightfully inexperienced in the ways of love. It is almost comical to see her facial reaction when he

371

musters the courage to lean close and murmur some sweet words meant only for her, his breathy whisper gently caressing the fine down gracing the lovely arch of her ear. The shyness of it all is quite endearing. The poor girl seems deliciously unaware that love frames her face in a lovely, ethereal glow when she steps into the young prince's presence. Her feelings transform her beauty into something quite stunning. Love is wonderfully sneaky that way.

All this comes to the great amusement and delight of the Bermejas staff, of course; how could it not? David passes on tidbits to both Miriam and Ezar, eliciting squeals of glee from one, and from the other, an overly dramatic, wide-eyed surprise chased by a pleased, hearty chuckle. What is not to like about young love?

She continues to watch him until the two wounded knights rise and walk back to the ward. Yusef gathers his crutches and makes his way along the stone path to the fountain, his new refuge. She opens the door and silently follows.

"Sire?"

No response.

The melodic tapestry woven by the guitar virtuoso and his accompanying reed flute hangs in undulating ripples from the balcony in the anteroom, tranquilizing the warm, humid air. High overhead, the star-shaped portals of red glass lend the space an eerie sunset glow. The Royal Hammam is tucked neatly between the Courtyard of the Myrtles and the Lion Palace, and is the exclusive domain of the royal family. The head eunuch of the hammam turns to the balcony and lifts his palm, then flattens it. The music instantly ceases. The eunuch seems especially tentative, reluctant to disturb the sultan. No doubt from prior experience.

"Sire?" Slightly louder.

Zoraya's frowning face parts the hanging beads covering the door between the hammam's warm room and the outer anteroom. The eunuch recoils ever so slightly. She hisses, "You were told we were not to be disturbed, Fatik." That Zoraya is together with the sultan in the hammam breaks several levels of centuries-old court protocol; but then again, what protocols have not been broken of late by these two?

The eunuch lowers his eyes in submission. "Forgive me, Sultana. Grand Vizier Venegas says he must speak with the sultan immediately. An urgent matter."

She mulls this over. "Loja?"

"He would not say, Sultana."

Zoraya's face retreats from the beads, leaving the eunuch standing where he was, frozen in place.

She had the sultan bathed and scrubbed in the hot room, followed by a deep massage in the warm room. Before he had a chance to fall asleep, she dismissed the bath attendants, rolled him on his back, dropped her robe, and after coaxing him to life, mounted him. He is now softly snoring on the divan with a towel draped across his sad, flaccid manhood.

She leans down and touches the sultan's shoulder. "My love?"

Nothing.

"My love?"

He snorts, then grumbles something unintelligible.

"Ali?"

His eyes flutter open. Even after a bath, massage, and love making, an unhealthy pallor clings to the man's face. He looks confused. "What? What?"

"My love, Venegas says he must speak with you. He says it is urgent."

"Who?" Furrows slice into his forehead.

"Grand Vizier Venegas, my love. He says he must speak with you. I would assume concerning Loja."

The confusion slowly evaporates. "I see. Where am I?"

Zoraya studies him. *This is getting worse.* "In the Royal Hammam, my love. You begged to be inside me, remember? You are still as virile as a teenager, my love." She even manages a demure, girlish blush to drive the point home.

This rouses him, producing a wicked grin—her intent. He sits up. "Yes, well, you are the most desirable woman in my kingdom."

She answers him with her most alluring smile. "You are too kind, my love."

"Give me a moment. Have hot mint tea brought and then send Venegas in."

"Of course, my love."

"Sire." A frown tickles the corners of the grand vizier's mouth when he sees Zoraya planted on the divan next to the sultan. At a height equal to the sultan. For a culture that lives and dies on precept and protocol, this is something simply unheard of, even in the hammam. Especially in the hammam. Though her expression remains unreadable, Zoraya eyes the grand vizier menacingly, almost daring him to challenge her presence. He recovers instantly and bows. He, above anyone, appreciates the danger of involving such a formidable schemer in delicate state matters. Any state matter. But an explosive confrontation with the sultan and the possible threat to his health is not something he dare risk. He decides to ignore her, though he does make a mental note to speak with the head eunuch.

"Sit, Venegas, have some tea." Aside from his awful pallor, the sultan's eyes are alert.

Venegas settles onto the floor pillow. "No thank you, sire."

"News from Loja?"

"Indeed, sire." He relaxes. "Good news, I am pleased to say."

The sultan brightens. "Finally. Tell me."

"We have soundly defeated King Fernando's army, sire. A complete rout, in fact. Evidently, Ali sprung a trap that Ponce de León fell for. And then your brother launched his surprise attack on the king's camp. He had a tough go after the Christians managed to organize a defense, but then Umar joined the fray and together they crushed our enemy. Fernando was forced to make a hasty retreat, with heavy losses."

The sultan stands, begins to pace. "Excellent. Excellent! I hope my son and his Abencerraje conspirators choke on the good news."

"Indeed, sire, they should have heard by now, I would guess. We even managed to capture Fernando's heavy cannons. Three bronze monsters. I have directed Ali al-Attar to keep them in Loja for defensive purposes, at least for now."

"Good."

"Sire, I suggest we send a formal announcement of the victory, in my finest calligraphy, to Supreme Mullah Abd Allah, the Supreme Council, the Council of Clerics, and of course the Masters of the Guilds. I will craft the language to be a not-so-subtle reminder of who it is that protects the kingdom and the people of Granada, followed by a carefully worded statement that their loyalty to the legitimate ruler of the kingdom is required. As well as their taxes."

"Yes. Yes, I like it. Make it so."

"There should be a triumphal parade." Zoraya finally speaks.

Venegas turns to eye her suspiciously.

She continues, "To celebrate the great victory. Let the army march through the streets of the city to be cheered by the crowds. Your brother, Ali al-Attar, and Umar can lay captured Christian banners at your feet. Easing the people's anxiety over the Christian aggression is just as important as reining in the Grand Mullah and his lackeys. Perhaps more so. Where the people of Granada go, so goes the Alhambra."

The sultan grumbles. "Mmm. The last parade by the army did not end well, as you will no doubt recall."

"My love, that storm was a freak, something that will never be repeated in our lifetime."

Venegas weighs her words and is forced to concede the logic. "I agree with Zoraya, sire, that—"

"Sultana." She cuts him off.

Venegas turns and studies her, his expression blank.

"You will refer to me as Sultana."

A thin, strained smile is his only answer. He turns back to the sultan. "I agree with the sultana, sire. A triumphal parade would also send a clear message to the Abencerrajes, especially if we route the parade past the walls of the Albayzín."

The sultan considers this. "Very well, make it so."

Her dreams have returned to torture her nights. They have taken on a life of their own once again, as if she has become the plaything of some impish jinn. When she sets her book aside and closes her eyes, he comes to her; sometimes seeing, sometimes blind. Never as a knight dressed for battle. She dreams of their future together: of working side-by-side in the hospital; of their home, spare, not lavish; of their children, sometimes as infants, sometimes nearly grown, but always three, a boy first, then two girls; of shared prayer and worship; of their beautiful life of love and commitment.

Oftentimes, though, her nights are sweaty, heart-pounding affairs that mercilessly tease her nerves into a throbbing mess. From the former she wakes with a languid stretch and a satisfied smile. From the latter she wakes twisted into her covers, aching, wanting. She can only manage a weary sigh, a pleading whisper of his name, an embarrassed, guilty smile.

"I simply cannot understand why she refuses to at least write to us. We are her parents, after all. One letter since she has been gone, Battal. One! And then just to inform us that she will not be coming home. Informing us, not asking our permission! I tell you, the girl has forsaken us." Mayya's tone is biting.

Battal looks up from his papers and studies his wife. "She has been busy, Mayya, that is all. First Alhama, now Loja."

"I tell you, she has forgotten us, completely forgotten us."

"Mayya, all the hospitals are full, and there are many wounded to treat. From what both Abd al-Salam and Hakim al-Adani have told us, Danah has become indispensable. You should be proud of her, not angry. When things calm down I am sure she will reach out to us." He looks back to his work.

She shakes a finger. "But what about Malik? You saw what his father said. Her letters to her intended are very infrequent. They are betrothed, Battal, betrothed!"

He sighs, looks back up. "Yes, I know. These are difficult times, Mayya. With the stalemate in the city, and the threat of Christian invasion, well . . . we must be patient. Things will happen in due time."

"I can only hope." A rattling exhale as emotion overtakes her.

He sees the battle raging within his wife. Anger and exasperation come so easily for her when she speaks of Danah, but she is her mother, after all, and she loves and misses her only child. In truth, they have much in common when it comes to willfulness and defiance.

"I so hoped those two would be married by now, and . . . and . . . perhaps even a baby on the way." Softly now, dejected.

"I know you did." He tries to soothe her. "The time will come."

Mayya's face wilts as her eyes fill. Her voice quavers, "I miss my girl, Battal." She begins to cry.

He rises and comes to hold her. "I know. I know. All will be well, you will see."

Mayya sniffs. "Can we not visit her at least? Just to say hello."

Battal frowns. "You know that is impossible. I am an elder of the Abencerrajes, Mayya, what would people think? In all likelihood I would be arrested by the Nasrids as soon as I left the safety of the Albayzín."

"I understand." She is completely deflated.

The moments pass as he ponders his wife and daughter. "I cannot visit her, but there might be another way."

She looks at her husband. "What do you mean?"

"My face is known to the Nasrids, but yours is not, darling. I could have papers prepared to get you through the blockade. What if your son was wounded at Loja and was mistakenly sent to the Bermejas instead of the Maristan? Even the Nasrids would not dare deprive a mother of seeing her wounded son, no matter her clan."

Her face brightens. "Yes . . . Yes!"

"But Mayya, this would not be without risk, you must know that."

"I understand." She pleads, "Battal, this would make me so happy!"

He smiles. "Your happiness, darling, is my happiness. I will check on what would be entailed in preparing the appropriate papers and making the arrangements. This may take some time." He lifts his eyebrows for emphasis. "And not a word to anyone."

She is beaming. "Of course not. Thank you, Battal. Thank you!"

The two of them sit side by side in the medicine preparation room. Alone. A bending of decorum, true, but given the relaxed nature of the Bermejas and its staff, no special cause for concern. Danah is at the workbench patiently grinding herbs into a paste using a mortar and pestle. These two have grown as comfortable in silence as they are in conversation. She throws another handful of herbs in, measures out a small dram of green liquid, continues to grind. Arduous work, but after sharing what they have with Ezar and the Atfal, their stock of anti-infection ointments is marginal, and Loja's wounded are en route.

By the way he has been attentively staring, apparently watching her work, you would never guess that he is blind. In truth, he is rapidly becoming adept at using sound for locating things. All of his other senses have miraculously come alive, presumably compensating for what has been taken away. Sounds, even subtle ones that are easy to miss, have developed a life of their own, each telling a new story. The flavor and texture of food fascinate him. He has acquired the ability to pick apart a mélange of aromas, sifting out a particular subtle element. The bitter herbs Danah is patiently grinding scream at him; pungent, yes, though the sensation is not unpleasant. When he lightly touches things with the tips of his fingers the feeling is electric, sizzling with energy. With each day that passes he notices something new and surprising, something wonderful.

"David came to talk to me." Yusef's tone is nonchalant, but his eyes sink to his lap as if what he must say has been weighing on him.

"Oh? About what?" She does not bother to look up from her work.

"Well . . ." He gathers up his courage. "Actually, he told me that as soon as I am off my crutches I am free to return to my quarters in the Alhambra."

The pestle freezes mid-twist. Her eyes remain locked on the mortar. Softly, "I see." A wistful sigh. "Soon, then."

He struggles for a casual, even tone. "I would obviously need an attendant to see to my needs."

"Yes." The word hangs limp in the air.

"And he said he wants me to visit regularly so he can check my eyes."

"Of course." Listless, tinged at the edges with despair. She struggles with what to say next. "I suppose you cannot stay in the ward forever, it is just that . . ." Her words trail off. She grabs a handful of herbs and tosses it into the mortar, wills herself to resume grinding.

The silence stretches out.

He looks up. "I told him I wanted to stay here. So that I can assist with the incoming wounded from Loja."

Her eyes rise to study him, her face radiant with relief. "*Really?*"

He smiles as if he can read her expression. "Really. I have found something here to call my own, Danah. You have shown me a way to do some small amount of good for others in their time of need. I cannot leave that now." He swallows hard. "Or you."

She sets the pestle down, wipes her hands, turns to him.

He continues, "David agreed. He said he would be happy to have my help. He did say I will need to move out of the ward and into my own room. He suggested clearing out the small storage closet at the end of the hallway. There should be room for a mattress. Barely. It even has a tiny window that can be opened for a breeze."

She is still staring at him, eyes now full. "I am not sure what I would do if you were not here with me, Yusef. My feelings have . . ." She stops, looks down, suddenly self-conscious. "Thank you."

He slides closer to her, paws the air and finds her. He whispers, "My feelings have grown for you too, Danah." They sit together, holding hands. Finally, he says, "I am afraid there is one thing I must confess to you."

She looks back up, now with trepidation. "What?"

"I can think of nothing but running my fingers through your glorious tresses."

Her eyebrows arch their puzzlement, and then she unleashes a hearty laugh.

"Day and night. It is murdering me." He sheepishly smiles. "I have always imagined a waterfall of dark curls trailing down to the small of your back." He chuckles. "When I was in Málaga, you see, it became a serious obsession."

She is beaming. "You cannot be serious, sir. My hair? That is all you yearn to touch?" Who can know where her newfound penchant for flirtation comes from? A marvel.

He actually blushes. "Well, as I said, it was something of an obsession."

She aims to tease him for his foolishness. "A very bold request, sir, even for a prince of the Alhambra. I wonder what my father would think. I assume you asked his permission?"

He is beaming now. "Indeed, my lady, a very bold request. Alas, I am afraid I have not yet had the occasion to ask your father. Still . . ."

Her emeralds are blazing. She cuts her eyes to the door and sees that it is cracked open. She chews her cheek for a moment, wondering, calculating, amazed that she is even considering this madness. She finds herself whispering, "Wait here." She steps across the room and fingers the latch as she silently eases the door closed, her heart pounding merrily away. She frowns as she sees that, alas, it has no lock. She shrugs, comes back to him wearing a cute, impish smile. She reaches up and one-by-one removes the long pins holding her head scarf. She lays the first upon the table with no discernible sound.

His eyes widen as they track to the exact spot where she laid them.

She smiles, pleased with herself.

He silently counts as she discards each pin. *One. Two. Three. Four. Five. Six.*

A long run of white silk slides to the floor with a soft swoosh.

His eyes follow the sound. He swallows hard.

She removes the olive-wood combs holding her hair up in a bun. Tresses liberated, she tilts her head back and shakes it vigorously, the dense jumble of dark curls spilling down to the small of her back.

He is grinning like an idiot.

She steps close to him, then closer still, and with her fingertip she gently traces the crescent moon on his forehead. His grin relaxes. She takes both of his hands, brings them to her face. She whispers, "Your wish has been granted, sir."

His fingertips begin to explore her face, moving delicately over the sculpted contours. Her eyelids begin to droop, then fold closed. First, her cheekbones, then her nose, then her eyes. He traces the soft arch of her eyebrows. Her breathing grows quick and shallow. Next, his fingertips float across her forehead, then on down to her ears, pausing to gently finger her earlobes, then back along the line of her jaw to her chin. Her heart is thumping so hard she can hear her pulse in her ears. He comes last to her lips, which part ever so slightly as his fingertips feather between them.

Her knees bend under the weight of it all, threatening to buckle. Better than her dreams.

He whispers, "You are so beautiful." Fingers slightly trembling, he weaves his fingers into her thick hair, tenderly caressing the back of her head. He slowly runs his hands down to the glorious inward curve at the small of her back, gauging the length of her hair. She shivers. He offers a heavy, satisfied exhale. "I knew it. Magnificent curls, and so long. Chestnut-brown, if I had to guess?"

She opens her eyes, incredulous. "How on earth did you know that?"

He laughs. "The day we first met in the Atfal. I saw a single curl peeking from behind your ear. Impossible to forget."

He begins to caress her tresses once more, then suddenly stops, gathers her hair and pulls it to her chest. As he leans down he pulls the jumble to his nose and inhales deeply. "Dear Lord, you smell like heaven."

She giggles.

"You washed your hair this morning." He slides his arms around her and pulls her against him.

"Yes." Her voice has grown husky, laden with emotion. Desire. "Yusef, we should not . . . the door has no lock . . . and . . ."

He releases her, then with his finger lifts her chin, stares directly into her eyes. "I love you, Danah."

Her lower lip is quivering. "And I love you, Yusef."

"You saved me."

Her lids slowly fold closed once more. He leans forward and brushes her lips with his own, then pulls back. "I have dreamed of this moment for so long."

"Yes . . ." Breathless.

He kisses her again, softly, tenderly.

Their lips part. He pulls her harder against him, and they kiss once more, this time more urgently, deeper. Sublime torture. As her organs melt, she is helpless to prevent a soft moan from slipping from her.

A shimmer of electric blue begins to sizzle the air just above their heads. They part again, hearts pounding. His hands circle her hips then pull her hard against his ache. Desire begins to devour them limb by limb, taking on a life of its own.

He whispers, "I love you."

"And I love you." She is delirious with desire.

Knock-knock-knock. "Hakim Amiriya?"

Danah's eyes fly wide in horror. She pulls back from him and turns away from the door.

Knock-knock-knock.

She grips the edge of the table, fights to compose herself, commands her voice to behave itself. "Yes?" Close, but not quite.

"Hakim al-Adani sent word that the wounded have just entered the city gates. They should be arriving shortly. He asked if you would join him."

A long pause. "Thank you, Aaron." Better now. "I will gather my things and be there momentarily." She takes a deep breath, shakes her hands, and exhales through pursed lips. After she has collected herself, she begins redoing her hair and head scarf.

He listens to her quietly work, and when she is done he reaches out and takes her hand. He whispers, "That was close." A boyish, wincing smile.

"Yes, *too* close." Her tone is scolding, but in the end, she finally manages an embarrassed giggle. "I am a fool."

"You are beautiful. And I love you."

She smirks, but her tone turns playful, "You are a bad influence, sir. Shame on you for attempting to corrupt one of Granada's innocent maidens."

He laughs loudly. "Forgive me, my lady, but I fear that the innocent maiden in question has cast a spell upon this gentle knight. She tortures me with her charms."

She chuckles on her way out the door.

Without crutches he moves as if he is balancing a sword within his body. Inch by awful inch, Yusef creeps along with one of the attendants always discreetly in sight—Danah's doing. In his stubbornness he has predictably been emphatic that no one move to help him unless he calls for it himself. She honors his request but constantly worries that he will fall and do more harm.

When he enters the ward, she will come to him and fill him in on the various new patients. He listens intently as she whispers about each man's wounds and the prognosis, seeking clarification here and there, and then asks her to point him in the man's direction and sets out. *Down three rows and two beds to the right.* He makes his way as far as he is able, then stops and asks for more directions, continues on. It can take him ten minutes to cross the room. The leg is very tender still, and he winces each time he eases weight onto it, sometimes having to stop to hiss the pain through clenched teeth. He has traded his crutches for a simple reed cane, not for support but as an aid to help him feel his way. David's idea. He slides it back and forth, back and forth, to encounter obstacles before they trip him up; the edge of a bed frame, a slippery rug, a step up or down.

When he reaches his destination, inevitably the most grievously wounded man first, he feels the mattress to make sure he will not to sit on his patient, then gingerly eases himself down, careful to keep his leg outstretched. The conversation always begins with, "I am Yusef al-Makki. I thought we might talk." An unnecessary formality; every knight knows who the Falcon Prince of the Alhambra is. He does not mention his own wounds unless asked, but it is more than obvious that he is blind.

There is an endearing, tactile sense that has come to Yusef in his injury. He will reach out and tenderly touch the man's face, hold his hand while he speaks. When he finds out who he is and his rank and unit, he will often tell a story based on some tidbit of truth or fanciful legend about the men he served with, its commander, some adventure that was had in days of old. Anything to distract from the present situation.

As only a naturally gifted healer can, he feels his way into the conversation, and when he intuits that the time is right, he will say something like, "Thank you for your brave service in defending our beloved Granada." Then softly, confidingly, "Tell me what happened." Together they will relive the horror of the battle and how the man was injured, in itself deeply therapeutic and often tearful. Then on to what the man is dealing with, especially the conflicted emotions. Here Yusef will often share his own story; the things he felt and had to deal with after he himself was wounded; how he came through it into the light; Danah. The wounded knights listen, mesmerized. Then on to the man's family, the maiden he loves or dreams of loving one day. Perhaps some gentle teasing to lighten the mood. Only at the end will Yusef speak about what the future holds and the courage that will be required to reclaim some semblance of a normal life.

All told, the Bermejas receives twenty-nine wounded from Loja, less than a quarter of what they received after Alhama. A collection of ugly sword cuts, pike thrusts, and buried arrow points, two with lead balls that had to be extracted; but nothing like the horror inflicted by the cannons. All but three have survived thus far, though fully a third are unlikely to fight again in the foreseeable future.

Danah and David work from before dawn until evening prayers with barely a chance to breathe. Yusef's days are full as well, and draining. He tries his best to visit each man once per day. This is difficult at the beginning when the wards are beset with wounded, but it becomes easier as the less-grievously injured are sent home for their extended care. The knights have begun to shyly call his name when they see him enter the ward, beckoning him over. He smiles, then awkwardly shuffles toward the voice. He has a firm mental image of the layout of the room now, and his navigation skills are becoming remarkably adept for a blind man with a broken leg.

To a man, the wounded find comfort in his visits and the courage to begin the journey of healing from the deep scars of battle; the physical wounds, yes, but more importantly, the emotional trauma inflicted.

And what of the kiss? Well, with the sudden influx of wounded and the rigors of tending those in their care, these two have not had a quiet moment alone for days now and are so fatigued by the relentless hours of work that they fall into a deep sleep as soon as their heads rest upon their pillows.

Still, a careful observer could note several interesting things, if so inclined. When these two pass each other in the hallway several times each day, she on her way back to the surgical ward or to retrieve medicinals, he inching toward the ward with his cane, they will stop for a precious moment and huddle together, a step closer than mere colleagues would stand. They whisper kind words of encouragement to each other, and on occasion, delicate murmurs of their feelings.

They face each other, her liquid emeralds searching for him in the depths of his sightless pupils. They switch to cute, self-conscious smiles, then back to serious again. Needless to say, the sweet gnaw of desire growing between these two has grown into a living presence, the pent-up tension always threatening to boil over unexpectedly.

If an attendant happens to approach them during these brief moments together, she will look down at her medical charts and share some new bit of information about a patient until the coast is clear. He will nod somberly, as if intently listening, which he is not. They break into smiles when alone once more.

Before they part they will step closer still, and their fingers will manage to find each other, an electric brush of fingertip to fingertip, skin upon skin. From the tender looks on their faces all can tell that whole conversations are being had.

Things have calmed down, thankfully, and their busyness has eased to a reasonable level. On his way back to his office, David catches sight of them and stops to gawk.

They sit hip-against-hip on the stone bench, staring at the fountain, talking, she kicking her feet back and forth like a young girl on a swing. This is their new favorite place to be together when a lull in the storm permits. In plain view, so safely proper, but with enough privacy to permit eavesdropping-free conversation. David shakes his head and smiles. *Young love.* He has never seen Danah so happy. And Yusef's ability to help the injured deal with their wounds and begin the long healing process . . . well, it has been nothing short of remarkable. A fine addition to his staff. Needless to say, Ezar is jealous and constantly pesters him for a loan, which, in deference to Danah, is a request that he has thus far ignored.

His smile evaporates. If only he could find a cure for the man's blindness. His original optimism for a recovery is fading.

She is chattering away about something, so cute and animated, her hands up and flitting about, dancing around her words.

David's smile returns.

Yusef nods, a huge smile plastered on his face, nods again, then offers a retort of some sort.

She abruptly stops, mouth open, aghast, her face a portrait of mock-offense. Then she smiles and playfully elbows him, says something.

He bursts out laughing.

Her answering raspy laugh works its way through the window, and David himself is forced to chuckle. He makes a mental note to fill Miriam in. She so enjoys the new Danah.

Torquemada

"But, my queen, Tomás de Torquemada? Surely you must know his reputation." Almost a plea. Hernán de Talavera has his hands behind his back, staring out the window. A location chosen so that he does not have to reveal the frustration written across his face. He marched to her chambers as soon as he received word that the Dominican friar had arrived at the palace for an audience with the queen. At her invitation. Ferreting out the identity of the visitor was trivial for a man of Talavera's skills. The monk is more than a little hurt that he was not consulted before the decision was made.

Queen Isabel is sitting at her desk reading the letter from her husband, which has just arrived from Lucena. Her hand cradles her ripening belly. She looks lovely, her cheeks brushed with a pleasing touch of peach. Even though this is Isabel's fifth child, she is as radiant as a first-time mother. She reads on, determined not to respond to her piqued confidante. When she finishes, she lays the letter down and smiles, pleased with Fernando's positive response to her suggestion for an attack on Málaga using Antequera as a staging ground. The only salve for the unfortunate disaster at Loja is a quick victory. It seems that all of them underestimated the Moors' fighting capabilities. She looks up. "Of course I do. He was my confessor, Hernán."

The monk turns. This is news to him, and he makes it his business to know everything there is to know about Isabel. "Really?"

"Yes. For a time. Back when I was sequestered in Arévalo."

He considers this revelation. "He must have just been named *prior* of the monastery of Santa Cruz in Segovia."

"Yes. His name was suggested by Cardinal Mendoza."

"I see. Then you are well aware that he is regarded in clerical circles as an uncompromising zealot in all matters of church orthodoxy, my queen."

"Indeed I am, Hernán. It is what I recall most about him." She muses. "They say people are calling him 'Hammer of Heretics'."

"Trust me, it is not meant as a compliment. People fear him and his tactics, my queen. He is known for the severe austerity he imposed on his *novices* when he was prior. Bordering on cruelty. Some say, torture. Evidently, he believes punishment is the best way to cultivate the extreme piety and orthodoxy the Dominicans prize." It is clear that the friar does not approve of the man or his methods. Or the Dominicans, for that matter. "Whether that actually cultivates a genuine faith is another matter entirely."

"Mm." The queen appears uninterested. She glances back at the letter before her.

"A person who embraces cruelty as a means to an end is a person that cannot be trusted, my queen."

No response.

"Torquemada has lived in a monastery since he was a young child, you know. He has had little interaction with the complexities and nuances of the real world."

"Mm." She does not seem to want to engage him.

"I am told he is deeply suspicious of *any* convert to the faith, whether Jewish or Muslim." The monk holds for some type of acknowledgment, but this does not come. Her eyes remain fixed on the letter. He continues, "Ironic, given that he himself has conversa blood in his veins. His uncle's grandmother was a Jewish convert."

She must know that. But, still nothing.

"You *do* realize that he holds extreme views."

She finally looks up and frowns, suddenly perturbed with her confidante. "Yes, Hernán. And these are extreme times. The church has been infiltrated by false converts, no one disputes that. Heretics, Hernán, *heretics*. To cleanse my kingdom, Pope Sixtus IV has granted me the unprecedented right to name my own inquisitors. I do not intend to squander the opportunity. As Grand Inquisitor, Torquemada will be put in charge of all Inquisition tribunals, in both Castile and Aragon."

Grand Inquisitor? The monk frowns. "Do you really think that is a wise decision, my queen?"

"If he is subservient to me . . . then, yes, I *do* think it is a wise decision, Hernán. And Fernando agrees that Torquemada is well-suited for . . . our needs."

"So much power in one man's hands is cause for concern, my queen. I fear that once Torquemada tastes absolute power he may be difficult to control, even for the queen of Castile."

She purses her lips. "Leave that to me." There is a sharpened edge of finality in her tone.

He knows her well enough to realize the conversation is ended. "Of course, my queen."

"Have the guards summon him."

He hesitates, then gives up. "Very well." He moves to the door, opens it, whispers to the guard, then recloses it and moves back to his perch by the window.

Talavera turns to scrutinize the Hammer of Heretics as he enters the queen's chambers. Short and squat, with the tonsured hair typical of a Dominican friar. Standard black woolen robe stretching to the floor, thick and scratchy and punishing. A small leather document pouch is slung over his shoulder. A large, gold pectoral cross is his only adornment. The man's crooked, bulbous nose is his most prominent feature. He bears a hostile scowl that appears to be fixed permanently to his face—as if he had never thought to smile once in his life. Quite a repugnant little man.

Torquemada stops and formally bows. "Queen Isabel. I am honored."

The queen remains sitting. "It is good to see you again, Tomás. This is my counselor and confessor, Hernán de Talavera." She lifts her palm.

Talavera returns the bow, ever the consummate diplomat. "Pleasure." No hint of disdain.

Torquemada sizes up his competition and sniffs. "Talavera. Order of St. Jerome, I believe." Overtly dismissive. The Dominican Black Friars are well known for their air of superiority, especially in Castile, their principal power base.

"Quite so. Torquemada. Order of St. Dominic, I believe." He cannot help himself. A giant smile to add an exclamation point.

Torquemada does not acknowledge the jab. "I came as soon as heavenly possible, majesty. If I might say, majesty, you look exceedingly well. Congratulations on your . . . ah . . . coming child. The kingdom rejoices. I am sure God will grant you another boy."

"My husband and I are richly blessed." She smiles. "Thank you for coming so quickly. You already know my intent. I wish to name you Grand Inquisitor in charge of the Holy Office for the Propagation of the Faith. You will have personal control over all Inquisition tribunals in both Castile and Aragon."

The scowl remains set in stone. He bows. "You honor me, majesty. I am pleased to . . . ah . . . accept your offer."

"Excellent."

"If I may, majesty."

The queen nods for him to continue.

"I have taken the liberty of composing . . . ah . . . a handbook for use by my tribunals." His use of the possessive pronoun does not escape Talavera. "I felt it necessary to . . . ah . . . further hone the means by which my inquisitors encourage identification of heretics by their own communities. Inducements, shall we say. I also detail the telltale signs to look for when questioning those identified as possible heretics, as well as the best . . . ah . . . methods for obtaining a confession, as appropriate." He opens his satchel and pulls out a small book, places it in front of the queen, and bows.

"Thank you, Tomás." She does not move to retrieve it.

"Majesty, I have in hand disturbing reports of heretical activities rampant in your cities. Sad to say, both Jewish and Moorish false conversos abound in your kingdom, many hidden in plain view. Men and women who have been baptized in the faith but secretly continue to worship their renounced religions. They make a mockery of the Church, majesty, and they insult Christ the Savior. They are heretics, pure and simple. I intend to . . . ah . . . establish new Inquisition tribunals in Jaén, Ciudad Real, and Córdoba herself. As a beginning."

Talavera notes that Torquemada does not seek permission and says, "You may have heard that Inquisitor de Portillo has just condemned six conversos in Sevilla to death. To a one, prominent men from good families. And exceedingly wealthy." Talavera decides to bait his adversary as an attempt to reveal his true colors to the queen.

Torquemada lifts his eyes to Talavera, sniffs. "False conversos, *friar*." The honorific is twisted derisively. He is already talking down to a lesser human being. "Marranos. The six were found to be secretly practicing as Jews, subverting the . . . ah . . . true and pious Christians of that great city. Neither status nor wealth shall be a shield for heresy, *friar*."

"Given that no proof is required of the tribunal, how exactly can one be sure that they are indeed secretly practicing Jews . . . *friar*?" Talavera's practiced diplomatic veneer is beginning to crack at the edges.

He stares Talavera down, then dismissively sniffs. He turns back to the queen. "I can assure you, majesty, that the methods of Inquisitor de Portillo and his tribunal are sound. In fact, my sense is that he has perhaps become . . . ah . . . too lenient in punishing repeat transgressors. A weakness we can ill afford, I am afraid. I aim to pay him a visit to . . . ah . . . rectify the situation." Torquemada's intent is clear.

"And how many false converts would you guess reside in the queen's kingdom?"

Torquemada's eyes turn on Talavera and dangerously narrow. "Certainly more than six. Sixty. Six hundred. Six thousand. It matters not, *friar*. What matters is that the Church is purified of heretics. *All* heretics. I will not stop until every marrano and every morisco is rooted out and . . . ah . . . properly dealt with." The two men's eyes remain locked on each other.

"Enough banter, gentlemen. Tomás, you will keep me informed of your actions. I want weekly reports. And a careful accounting of all that is confiscated, both gold and property. I am authorizing twenty percent for the Inquisition and the pope. The rest goes to my treasury. As you know, I have a war to fight, and it just got more difficult. Conquest of the Moorish lands will be my gift to the pope and his Church."

"And a fine gift it will be, majesty."

"Thank you again for coming, Tomás. I am afraid I must now pen a letter to the king."

"Of course, majesty. Farewell." Torquemada does not bother with acknowledging Talavera. He bows deeply, turns, and is gone.

The two remain silent for some time.

"You have made an enemy, Hernán. How uncharacteristic of you to show your hand so plainly."

Talavera sighs. "I fear where this will all end, my queen."

"Mm. Leave me. I must share my plan for the Málaga campaign with my husband."

The monk frowns, then bows and withdraws.

Ya Amar—My Moon

With a soft knock he shows himself in.

Their heads turn together.

"Hakim al-Adani said you would be here. It is good to see you again, Danah."

"Umar." Her greeting is warm and affectionate. She is clearly pleased he has come.

Yusef's sightless eyes retreat to the floor.

Umar offers her an elaborate, playful bow, which elicits a smile. He is dashing as always, and dressed in his finest princely attire, sans broadsword. Take-your-breath-away handsome. Little wonder the young maidens swoon when they catch sight of him. Somehow, though, the new Danah remains perfectly at ease, unfazed by it all.

"Thank you for coming. We were both so worried about you." She cuts her eyes to Yusef.

"I just got back to the city. I wanted to—" He stops, suddenly unsure of himself as his eyes drift to Yusef. "I wanted to check on my brother."

Danah nods. "Yes. Of course. If you will excuse me, I need to make my rounds. I will be in the ward if you need me."

Yusef visibly stiffens, opens his mouth to say something to detain her, then closes it.

Umar replies, "Thank you, Danah."

She turns and leaves, closing the door behind her.

Umar studies his brother for a moment, then moves to the table where he is seated. Yusef's eyes rise to track his brother's movements, then settle back to his lap.

"May I sit?"

A slight hesitation, then a guarded, "Certainly." Too formal.

They sit in silence for what seems like a lifetime, then finally Umar gives up and says, "The sultan and Venegas have decided that there is to be a triumphal parade."

No response.

"A waste of time, if you ask me, but they seem to think that a strong message needs to be sent to Boabdil and the Abencerrajes."

Still nothing.

Yusef clears his throat, then says, "Victories should be celebrated. From what I have heard, you and your men carried the day at Loja." His words are twisted tight.

"Our men, Yusef. *Our* men. We trained them together; they are as much yours as mine."

No reply.

"Hakim al-Adani tells me you are walking again."

A lengthy pause. "Yes. My leg still hurts like hell when I put pressure on it, but at least I am up and out of bed."

"Yes. Good." Umar smiles. "He also says you have an amazing gift, Yusef." The love, and the need for reconciliation, is so plain to see on the younger man. "And that you have helped so many of our wounded to begin their healing. Not the wounds we see, but the deeper ones that can fester for a lifetime."

Yusef grunts. "I am trying to do my part, however small."

Umar decides on a different tack. "Danah looks beautiful. If I did not know better, I would say it was the glow of love." There is a playful edge to his words; the bantering Umar of old.

Yusef looks up and stares intently in the direction of his brother's voice. "I *do* love her, Umar. With my entire being."

Umar beams. "Now that is the best news I have heard in a long while. You have changed, Brother, and for the better." He whistles. "So, Faynan was right all along. How do women always know these things?"

Yusef's voice thickens. "Danah saved me, Umar. I was drowning in my self-pity. She helped me find a path forward and learn to serve in ways that I am able. I am finding that it suits me."

"Yes, I can see that." He smiles. "Danah is the kind of woman a man could make a very happy life with."

Yusef frowns. "She is still betrothed, Umar."

"For the moment, perhaps. It is plain that the girl loves you."

"Mm. She is Abencerraje. Think about that for a second."

"Love is complicated, Brother. Always complicated." As he reaches for his brother's hand, his expression grows serious. "Listen, Yusef. Injury or no injury, sight or no sight, there must be peace between us. Even if you cannot ride beside me in battle, you are still my big brother." His voice catches. "You are my hero, Yusef. I am nothing without that."

Softly, Yusef responds, "I have missed you, Umar." He opens his arms, and Umar rises and comes to hug him. They cling to each other with tears in their eyes.

Yusef sniffs. "And Uncle? How is the old buzzard?"

Umar laughs. "You should have seen him, Yusef! The old goat was brilliant. Tricked poor Ponce de León into a baited trap, with devastating consequences. Nearly wiped the Christians out. He is the true victor of Loja, not me."

"Uncle is the best battlefield tactician Granada has."

"Indeed. He said he will stop by tomorrow morning to check on you. By the way, al-Zaghal told me to ask if you would join the sultan's war council when we meet. Assuming you are up to it. He and the sultan greatly value your opinion, you know."

Yusef mulls this over. He has not been to the Alhambra since Alhama, so this is a big step. He finally relents to the call of duty. "Very well. Send a cart."

"Good, al-Zaghal will be pleased." Umar stands smiling at his brother. A load of bricks has been removed from each man's shoulders. "How long will you stay at the Bermejas? I am happy to have you join me and Faynan in the Alhambra. Our suite has plenty of space."

"Thank you, but I have decided to stay here. For a while." A sheepish smile. "There is much to be done still." Yusef actually blushes.

Umar punches his shoulder. "And a young hakim to be wooed. You dog!"

Both men laugh.

Each Tuesday Danah joins David and Miriam for dinner. She comes early to check on the orphans housed there and tend to any of their medical needs. And to chat with Miriam, of course, and visit Samra, the oldest of the dozen orphans staying with the al-Adanis. She has become a great help to Miriam in tending to the little ones.

Caring for the displaced orphans is a task Miriam relishes, but which can still prove overwhelming at times. Samra has taken to her added responsibilities, and while Miriam will occasionally catch the girl staring into space with a startled, fearful expression, or jumping at a sharp sound, the devastation of her trauma has miraculously eased. Not exactly talkative, except to Danah, but better. Much better.

Danah finishes wrapping the foot of four-year-old Kanza, who managed to twist an ankle yesterday playing chase. "There. Good as new, my dear." Danah mock frowns and waggles a scolding finger. "No running, please. Do I make myself clear?" Adorable little Kanza nods. She is all giant almond-eyes and a dense jumble of dark curls. "Yes, Hakim."

Miriam turns to Samra and says, "Would you take the children out to play until dinner?"

The girl nods and sets about the task. A moment later, she herds the squealing horde out the back door. Warm sounds of children at play fill the spacious courtyard.

Miriam shakes her head and laughs. "Finally, a moment of peace."

"You are so good with the children, Miriam."

A warm smile. "Yes, well . . . it has been almost like having my own. Though bearing a dozen would not have been my plan." She playfully rolls her eyes. "Poor David is not sure what to make of it all."

Danah laughs.

"I make him read to them at night. They gather round and hang on his every word. He will not admit it, but I know he has come to enjoy the ritual. How are things at the Bermejas?"

Danah avoids Miriam's gaze by starting to repack her medical bag. She strives for nonchalant, and almost gets there. "Oh, the usual. No more wounded have arrived, praise Allah, and we are down to eleven patients from Loja."

"Good. So not as busy." Miriam studies her. "Are you sleeping any better?"

She continues to fiddle with her medical kit, refuses to look up. Finally, her hands still and she sighs. "My dreams are torturing me, Miriam." An embarrassed whisper.

Miriam eyes her with an amused smile. *Poor girl.* "With the two of you under the same roof, I expect so. Anything more than dreams?"

When Danah finally looks up, she has flushed a deep scarlet. Even her earlobes are blushing.

Miriam's smile widens. "I see."

Danah stammers, "I mean, nothing bad. It was not anything, really. Just a kiss." Her eyes settle on the floor, weighed down by embarrassment.

"Just a kiss . . ."

She jounces on, "It was not something we planned. I mean . . . it just happened."

"Mm."

Danah's expression turns pained. "Then we almost got caught."

"You two must be discreet, Danah."

"Trust me, we are. No one in the Bermejas suspects there is anything between us."

"I am sure you are right." Miriam's amusement grows. David brings home stories of the two of them almost daily. All of the Bermejas knows, even the patients. How could they not? "Look at me, Danah."

The younger woman's eyes rise, then she sheepishly smiles.

Miriam lifts her eyebrows. "You are glowing, Danah. Love suits you."

She whispers, "The intensity of my feelings for him sometimes scares me, Miriam."

The warm, motherly smile returns. "Love is like that, Danah. You must embrace the feelings, unsettling though they may be. Still, I would suggest you two spend your time together in public view. Gossip is not something you want to attract. And besides, kisses can easily lead . . . to other things." She chortles. "Take it from one who knows."

Danah blushes once more. "I know."

Miriam decides to change the subject. "From what David says, Yusef seems to have really taken to his new role."

Danah brightens. "He has, yes. He has the gift of healing, Miriam—you should see him! He follows the Sufi Way. He is even praying again. We do salah together. Some days it is almost as if he has forgotten that he is blind. Almost."

"Mm. And what of the future?"

Danah falls silent.

"You *have* written to Malik, yes?"

She wilts. "Not yet. I have tried, but I just cannot find the right words ... I feel so much guilt, Miriam. He does not deserve this."

"This must be done. *And* your parents. You know Yusef, Danah. He will never ask for your hand while you are officially betrothed. Waiting is not fair to either man."

A dejected, "I know."

Miriam says, "I have written to Abd al-Salam. He knows the whole story now. Or soon will."

"Did you ask him to speak to Malik?"

Miriam frowns. "Danah. Of course not. That is for you to do."

"I know." Resigned.

The front door opens and swings wide. David says, "Miriam! Danah! Look who I found wandering the streets. I figured one more stray at the table could not hurt."

Ezar enters with an exaggerated scowl and shrugs.

Danah beams when she catches sight of him. "Frizzles!" It has been almost a month since she has seen him.

"Emeralds." Nearly a smile. "I know a young hakim who has not visited me in weeks, so I decided to come find where she was hiding." He studies her. "Dear Lord, you look different, girl. Are you behaving yourself at the Bermejas?"

She blushes dark once again and desperately looks to Miriam for help.

Ezar arches a wooly worm. Usually his playful jabs bounce right off the girl.

Miriam comes to her aid and scolds him. "Leave the poor girl alone, you fool!"

Ezar wilts. "I meant no harm, Miriam. It is only that I have missed her so." He is uncharacteristically serious.

Danah recovers. "And I, you, Ezar. It is so good to see you."

"Indeed it is. Come here and give an old man a hug." He opens his arms wide. "Let us catch up, my dear."

Later, after the maelstrom called dinner has passed and Ezar has since departed for the Atfal, David is upstairs reading to the orphans. They can hear his muffled voice rising and falling with a sense of drama that only a natural storyteller possesses. A somewhat unexpected skill, but endearing nevertheless. The two women are together chatting over the dishes—Miriam washes; Danah dries.

Miriam says, "I was thinking."

"Yes?"

"Perhaps it would be good to bring Yusef here. He could visit the children."

"The children?"

"Yes. From what you told me about the tragedy years back, it might be good for him. To meet some children the age of the young girl who died."

Danah stops drying and considers this. "Mm. An interesting thought . . ." Danah muses, "He has not yet left the safety of the Bermejas grounds, so that would be good, too." She nods approvingly. "A next logical step. I like it. Perhaps I could convince him . . ."

Miriam stops her washing. "My dear, I am certain that with the promise of another kiss you could convince poor Yusef to do just about anything."

They exchange a quick glance and then simultaneously burst out laughing.

The old man has tears in his eyes, by any reckoning a remarkable thing. The old man who, in the fevered pitch of battle, has killed seventeen Christian knights, their limbs cleaved or bodies punctured with the tempered Damascus steel of his ancient broadsword. He has maimed countless more, and even strangled one with his bare hands after he was knocked from his mount by a lucky swing of a mace, then nearly trampled. Pulled the poor soul out of his saddle and throttled him as the battle raged around them. The old man who led armies in thirteen major battles and twenty-six skirmishes; who first led a cavalry charge at the tender age of eighteen—to victory, of course; who rode his prized midnight-black Andalusian into the ground to win a fight, then knelt beside the broken, foaming beast and wailed like an infant; who has seen every tactic of every able commander devised to vanquish a foe, and pioneered many himself. Witness Loja. All to defend his kingdom, his homeland. He has fought for seven different sultans, many—most—of questionable character. This old man feels less allegiance to the Nasrid who presently occupies the Alhambra throne than to the land herself. His beloved Granada.

This old man has tears in his eyes as he hugs Yusef to his chest and whispers soft words of consolation. He feels guilt, of course. How could he not? After all, it was his idea to leverage the pelleted black powder for better cannons. And he quickly acquiesced to Yusef's plan at Alhama.

This grizzled old warrior long ago lost his smile to the horrors of war, and these days feels his age with every step he takes. His wrinkled body is riddled with scars, his joints worn out. When he is alone at night, even in his tent on the eve of battle, he reads ancient ghazals from the Golden Age of Umayyad Córdoba, poems of love and desire, and recalls his days as a young man with his lovely bride Muzna, who passed less than two short years after their marriage—during childbirth. Neither mother nor baby boy survived. This was a lifetime ago, but devastating still to the old man. Time does not heal such wounds. His nephews are gold to him, all he has left of his dead brother.

After the haze of emotion clears, they sit and talk at length. Ali al-Attar retraces his steps at Loja for his nephew, something he relishes because he knows Yusef has a more discerning ear for battlefield tactics than his younger brother. When queried he shares his thoughts on what may come next from Fernando. Yusef nods appreciatively as he intently listens, offers a probing thought here and there.

The old man asks about his nephew's new role at the Bermejas. Umar has filled him in, of course, but he wants to hear it from Yusef himself. He is pleased with what he learns, tells the injured young man that he has chosen an honorable path for his new life. This is welcome news to Yusef. His uncle's opinion matters greatly to the young Falcon.

In the end, when asked, Yusef shyly speaks of Danah, the new hakim who has helped him find the Sufi Way, though he avoids any mention of her clan. As he dances around the edges of his true feelings for her, the old man patiently listens, nods, and even manages to crack a smile; not once, but twice. All his uncle says is, "About time some young maiden captured your heart, you scoundrel."

Yusef abruptly stops, chagrined that he has become so transparent. In desperation, he simply shrugs and offers a goofy smile.

When they are done, Yusef feels for his uncle's hand, kisses the back of it and presses it to his forehead. "May Allah's blessings be upon you, Uncle."

"And upon you, dear boy. Next time I come I want to meet this girl. She sounds rare."

"Of course, Uncle." Yusef smiles. "She is. Very rare."

The old man studies his nephew for a long moment, then grunts as he offers an approving smile, more of a grimace, really, and is off.

She twists into her covers, her hands first clenching then unclenching, her legs twitching and bending and stretching. Her head flips side to side, her brow knitted tight, her face terror-stricken. She opens her mouth and tries to speak, but nothing comes out. Instead she just groans, then finally blurts out, "No. Please no!"

The pyre is large, a great stack of wood. She groans once more, hisses, "Say it, just say it!" She smells the smoke before she sees the flames. Then tiny bursts of orange lick at the center of the pyre. "No. NO!" Her hands frantically grab at the air. "Just say it!" She whimpers. "Dear Allah! No! NO! PLEASE! I BEG YOU!" She flinches when she hears the first scream. She moans her desperation as she tosses and turns. There is a frantic cry for help. She is sure she knows the voice. She knows. She knows! The flames are lapping higher now, have broken through the pyre to claim it. They rise out of the neat stack of logs, leaping, cracking, popping. "NO! NO! PLEASE STOP! PLEASE! I BEG YOU! NO!" Her eyes fly wide and she yelps like a struck puppy, then begins to sob. "Who? Who are you? Please tell me. Please."

She fights to console herself, to calm her panic. "It was a dream . . . only a dream . . . oh, Lord, help me . . ." She groans her misery, exhausted, eyes still wide with terror. "Help me, Lord, please help me."

And then it comes to her: an irresistible force, an uncontrollable need. Without thinking, she rises in the blackness, reaches for her physician's robe, opens the door, looks both ways, then slips into the hallway.

His blind eyes reflexively open when he hears the door latch lift. He listens. Nothing. He grows keenly aware that he is only wearing thin cotton bed trousers. "Danah?"

She eases down beside him without a word. As she turns onto her side away from him, her shoulders gently shake as she begins to cry. She mutters, "I had a terrible, terrible dream. So real . . . so real . . ." She whimpers like a child. "Hold me. Hold me, Yusef."

He pulls her tight to him and wraps his arms around her as he tries to soothe her. He gently strokes her hair. "Shhh . . . shhh, Danah. It will be all right. Shhh . . . I am here, Danah. Shhh . . ."

It breaks his heart to see her so upset. Love wells up within him, fills him, and spills over. He pulls her tighter still. "Shhh . . . Danah. I love you. I love you, Danah. I am here. Shhh . . ."

After a few moments her crying eases, first to a shivering heave, then another, then she mercifully quiets. They lie together silently for what seems like an eternity.

Both lie wide-eyed in the dark. Both are afraid to move a muscle, lest the trance be broken. Finally, she softly says, "I have never had such a frightening dream."

"Tell me."

"There was a funeral pyre. Someone was on it, but I could not tell who it was. I begged them not to light the fire, but they did. The person on the pyre began to scream as the flames rose . . . they were still alive. It makes no sense . . . why would someone alive be on a funeral pyre?" Her voice catches. "The flames, Yusef. The person was screaming for me to help them. I tried, but I could not. My arms and legs were bound. It was so real, so awful."

"Shhh . . . shhh . . . it was only a dream, Danah. Shhh . . . I am here. Shhh . . ."

She stills once more as he holds her close and delicately strokes her cheek.

"I should not be here. What would people think? Forgive me . . . I should not have come. But I just needed . . ."

"Please stay, Danah. Please."

"Yusef . . ."

His voice thickens as he says, "*Ya Amar.*" My moon.

She lifts herself up on her elbow. "I am not sure what I would have done if you were not here." She turns and softly kisses his forehead, then rises from the floor mattress. He hears the door open, then close.

He relaxes onto his back, his blind eyes wide and searching the abyss. "Danah . . . my Danah."

An hour later, she is still staring at the ceiling in the pitch black of her room, wide awake. How could she not be? Her thoughts are of him, of course; of them. She replays every movement, every word, over and over. The more she permits her imagination free reign the harder her heart pounds. In the end, she steels herself and wills the decision, for once permitting her feelings to carry the day. No small feat. Her daring at first surprises her, then promptly fills her gut with an unsettling, tingly flutter that is both terrifying and exhilarating at the same instant. She rises once more and finds her robe, quietly opens the door, and is again in the hallway.

He is still on his back, his unseeing eyes wide open, thinking of her, wanting her. He freezes when he hears the latch lift. He hears the door open, then close. He hears the raspy slide of the lock as it is set. He hears her robe drop to the floor in a heap. Paralyzed, his heart begins to race.

She silently eases down beside him, clothed only in her nightgown. She rolls onto her side, head on the pillow beside his, but this time she faces him. He turns toward her.

She whispers, "I love you."

"I love you more than life itself."

"I could not stop thinking of you."

"Nor I, you."

"You called me, 'Ya Amar.'"

"The full moon, in all her glory, would be jealous of your beauty, my love." Since when has Yusef ever been given to poetry?

It starts predictably enough, though to these two the newness of it all is beyond intoxicating—first they scoot closer together so that their faces are only inches apart, toes mingling, knees touching, her breasts pressing against his bare chest. Sweet words of love are exchanged, and then their lips meet in a gentle kiss.

Their kisses quickly grow urgent and impassioned, and without even considering it their limbs begin to twist together, their bodies pressing themselves into a seamless whole. His hands inevitably begin to explore her lovely curves. A shimmer of tiny, electric-blue sparks ignites in the air above them and hovers there, waiting, hoping.

As they continue to kiss and touch, soft love murmurs fill the tiny room. Their movements intensify, their frayed nerves roasting upon the bed of crimson coals raked beneath them. In her desperation she awkwardly slides her free hand between them to search out the tie of his bed trousers. She accidently brushes against him in the process, which gets his attention. She inexpertly tugs on the string.

His lips pull back from hers, both of them a tangled mess of breathless panting. "Danah. Danah, no." The electric-blue sparks dim momentarily, then begin to vanish one by one.

"Yusef . . ." The pleading in her voice is not buried deeply.

"We cannot. I am sorry, Danah."

"Yusef, I love you. Do you not want me?"

"I want you more than you can possibly imagine. Dear Lord, you *must* know that. It is practically all I think about."

"Then what . . ."

"We are not betrothed, Danah, and I will not compromise your honor. What if we beget a child? Your parents, Danah, think of them." He rolls back from her.

She is shocked, then hurt, then embarrassed by her forwardness. She stammers, "Yes, of course. You are right. We are not betrothed . . ." Her embarrassment grows. "I am not sure what I was thinking when I came back. Forgive me."

He reaches for her, pulls her tight. Without thinking he says, "Trust me, when I ask for your hand and you say 'yes,' and we are finally betrothed, you will find it impossible to keep my hands off you. That you can depend upon. You drive me crazy with desire!" This is the first time he has been so explicit about his intentions, though they have obliquely tiptoed around the topic several times. Alas, the shadow of Malik looms over them. Yusef will not act until that knot is untied, and she knows this all too well.

His words thrill her, of course. She tries to force a smile, and almost gets there. "I understand." A tad too stiff. She is sitting up now, fumbling with her discarded robe. "You are right. Of course you are. I should go."

"Danah . . . please. Stay for a while. We can just lie together. Please. Danah."

"You are right, Yusef. This is not something we should do. Not now. I need to go. We can talk tomorrow." Her tone is strained.

"Danah . . ." He silently curses himself, fearing he has hurt her. Again. He follows her to the door and they kiss once more, though this one is perfunctory. She slides the lock, lifts the latch, eases her head into the hallway. After seeing that the coast is clear, she slowly plods back to her room, weak-kneed and perceptibly teetering.

Back safely in her room, her thoughts drift to Malik. She curses her stupid procrastination, and then the guilt sets in. Again. Malik is a good man. But then she recollects Yusef's words. His declaration. A satisfied smile settles onto her face. She begins composing in her head the letter that must be sent. She vows to send it tomorrow. She will worry about her parents soon enough, but first things first.

Her thoughts of being free of the entanglement and then betrothed to Yusef are . . . well . . . titillating. Her thoughts find their way back to him—How could they not? She whispers his name over and over as she begins to squirm against her ache.

Healings

Within no time, things between them are back to normal. Oh, it was a tad awkward at first, of course. She nursed her lingering embarrassment and bruised ego for an entire morning, but she knows he was right, after all.

In truth, the memory of that night still tortures them both. Mercilessly. But in the end, she set that iron will of hers upon the matter and decided to make a cute inside joke about the whole thing. This relieved him of his guilt over hurting her, which was her intent. He quickly joined in and together they laughed about it. Since then, it has become something of a running joke between them, a playful banter back and forth no one else is privy to. She —"Who only wears trousers to bed?" He—"I was sure I had locked the door to keep lusty maidens out." On and on it goes.

There has been no attempt of another late-night rendezvous, though these days they struggle to resist the temptation to kiss and touch when they find themselves alone. So far, they have succeeded. Mostly. The dwindling population of Loja's wounded helps afford them more free time, and the staff has grown used to seeing the two side by side at the fountain talking in hushed voices, sometimes for hours at a stretch. They talk about all manner of things: the medical arts and their remaining patients, of course, but also seminal events from their pasts, the things they care most about in life, their favorite foods, their families, city gossip, the Abencerraje insurrection, the unfolding war. Serious matters. But they also laugh and play and tease. They are becoming best friends, these two; a rare and healthy turn of events for would-be lovers. Very occasionally they will edge close to plans for a future life together, though both are careful to not step too near the specifics.

The letter has been dispatched. She lets it slip, of course. Who wouldn't? They are at their favorite haunt when she tells him. A casual mention is all she makes, though she has rehearsed her precise words a dozen times.

He nods, pleased with her revelation. "What did you tell him?"

"I told him the truth. I owe him that."

"And what truth is that?" His tone bends playful.

A coy smile answers him. "That a roguish prince of court somehow seduced me."

He laughs loudly.

Her face grows serious. "I told him that my heart and soul belong to another. He will be hurt. And for that I have begged his forgiveness. But he will realize there is no future between us. I told him I will not marry without love."

"Will he realize who it is?"

She considers this. "Yes. Malik is smart. He will know."

"And will he honor your wishes and break the betrothal?"

"Miriam is certain that he will."

"Miriam is certain?" There is a wary edge in his voice.

She looks at him and sees the concern. "Yusef, Miriam is as close to me as my own mother. In some ways, much closer. She knows all of this. She is my confidante; there are no secrets between us."

He relaxes. "I know."

They fall into a comfortable silence. Finally, Yusef says, "When do you expect to hear back? From Malik, I mean?"

Her thoughts race to her favorite visual image of Yusef asking for her hand. She has imagined the scene a hundred different times, in a hundred different ways. She strikes for nonchalant. "I would hope within a couple of weeks. Perhaps sooner. David kindly arranged for the letter to be placed in the Alhambra's weekly dispatch to Málaga. It will travel by royal courier."

"Excellent." He sounds relieved. "I look forward to the moment when you are once again an unattached maiden of Granada." A boyish smile.

"I am counting the days." She is beaming inside. The silence stretches out. "By the way, Miriam has a request that I have been meaning to mention to you."

"Oh?"

"She needs your help."

"My help?" He is incredulous.

"Yes. With the orphans. She has a dozen boys and girls staying with her, you know. One of the boys, Rashid, is giving her some trouble. Nothing serious, but she thought a word from you would be very helpful." It is the plan the two women eventually concocted.

He grows silent. "Danah . . . helping the wounded is one thing, but I have no experience with children. None whatsoever."

"I understand, and I told her as much. But she is convinced that you can be of great service."

"My blindness may scare them. It would scare me if I were a child."

"That is silly, Yusef. Please? It would mean a great deal to her. And to me."

"Danah . . . no . . ."

She leans into him. "Are you sure there is nothing I can do to convince you?" She glances over her shoulder, then with a wicked grin proceeds to press her palm down upon the middle of his thigh. The girl is beginning to enjoy this latent boldness she has discovered within herself.

The shock on his face is almost comical as electric fire races from her hand to his groin as she blackmails him with her touch. He can feel the heat of her palm through his trousers. After a moment he recovers his wits and manages a playful tone as he says, "Tell me, my lady, do beautiful, emerald-eyed maidens always conspire to get their way?"

She feigns complete innocence. "Whatever can you mean, sir?" She slowly slides her hand down between his thighs.

He winces under the exquisite torture. "Fine, I will go. But only if you stay at my side the entire time."

"Deal." Her hand slowly withdraws back to the top of his thigh. "How will we get there?"

"We can walk together. It is not far from the Bermejas."

"Yes, but . . ."

Her hand begins to creep down once more. "Yusef. I will be with you the whole way."

"Mm. If you say so."

She squeezes his thigh as she leans close, directs her warm, moist breath into his ear, and whispers, "I do say so."

He shivers, then involuntarily chuckles at the madness of it all and is instantly joined by her cute laugh.

"It was only a parade, sire. A meaningless spectacle."

Boabdil halts his pacing and turns on his grand vizier. He snaps, "No, Aben Comixa. It was a triumphal march by a victorious army. There is a difference." He resumes his pacing.

The mood in the room is sullen and tense. The tide has turned against them.

For once, Fatima agrees with her son. "A *very large* difference, Aben Comixa." Not for the first time, she questions the judgment of her son's new Abencerraje-appointed grand vizier. "From what my sources tell me, thousands lined the streets, and they were cheering wildly while we sit, idle and impotent, behind the walls of the Albayzín. The victory at Loja has re-instilled confidence in my husband's ability to defend the kingdom against the Christian hordes. The irony, of course, is that he had nothing to do with the battle. No doubt he was humping that whore of his during the whole thing." The bitterness is very raw still. A wicked smile curls her lips. "At least the bastard child was a girl. Of little use in the whore's grand plan." A biting laugh. "Stupid fool. Serves her right." She continues, "Loja is a problem for us, gentlemen. Another victory by my husband will likely seal our fate. That cagey old lizard Ali al-Attar, and my husband's brother—those two are the ones to be reckoned with. Unlike us, it seems that they know how to fight." She scowls at her son.

Boabdil stops again, but chooses to ignore her chiding. "Do not forget that cursed Falcon. I am told he carried the day." Umar is only two years older than Boabdil. Despite his bluster, Boabdil secretly envies his contemporary and even fears him a little. A fact that does not escape his mother's attention or her derision.

She relents and concedes his point with a tick of her head. "Indeed. The al-Makki brothers will have to be dealt with."

Aben Comixa adds, "I have good word that the elder Falcon has been removed from the chess board. Blinded at Alhama."

Fatima has heard the same rumor. She was probing the competence of the Abencerraje spy network. She replies, "Good riddance. Abu al-Haytham, you have been quiet. What do you hear from the guilds?"

The High Elder of the Abencerrajes answers with a wet cough into his hand. "The guilds are unhappy, Sultana. This stalemate is hurting business. Profits in the silk markets are down by thirty percent."

Fatima says, "I was afraid of that. Degrading their margins is not sustainable."

"No, it is not." Matter of fact.

"And our food stores?"

"Water is no issue, obviously, but meat and grain are quickly becoming a problem. We have perhaps two months remaining before we will be forced to begin rationing." He frowns. "Not a single member of the Council of Elders will relish spending our hard-won gold to import food from the Maghreb when we are but a stone's throw from the most fertile land on earth."

"No."

"Sultana, I am afraid our window of time to act is quickly closing."

She has reached the same conclusion. "And winter will soon be upon us."

"Indeed."

The room falls silent.

Boabdil says, "I should make another assault on the Alhambra, but this time in force."

The high elder replies, "Too risky, at least for now. Remember the cannons. Besides, the bulk of the army is back in the city now. How they managed to slip in under our noses is beyond me. Heads have rolled. No, the odds are not favorable for attacking the Alhambra."

The young man falls silent in the face of the obvious facts.

Aben Comixa says, "Just this morning I heard some interesting news." Eyes turn to him. "It seems the Christian forces are rallying in Antequera."

Boabdil scoffs, "Antequera? Why, when they have Alhama? Besides, Fernando is still at Lucena with his troops."

"My sources tell me that Fernando has directed Ponce de León and the Duke of Medina-Sidonia to launch an attack on Málaga."

This is news to Fatima. She frowns.

Boabdil is skeptical, "Málaga? But that is on the other side of the kingdom. That makes no sense, Aben Comixa, none at all."

Fatima immediately grasps the implications, and as usual is dismayed by her son's stupidity. "It makes perfect sense. The Christians intend to destroy our economy. The lion's share of Granada's import and export trade flows through the harbor at Málaga. Close our trade routes, and we will wither on the vine." She turns to the grand vizier, clearly impressed. "It would be a smart move on their part. Go on."

A hint of a smile as the man's beady eyes narrow. He is pleased with himself. "If this rumor is true, then al-Zaghal will have to lead the sultan's army to challenge the Christians and—"

Boabdil jumps in, "And then we attack the Alhambra!"

Fatima sighs.

Aben Comixa possesses the stoic patience of a teacher in the madrasa. He says, "No, sire. Then you take our army, slip out of the city at night, and secretly march to Lucena for a surprise attack. It will be the last thing Fernando suspects. At best case, we lay siege and capture King Fernando and end this war. At worst case, we defeat his army and return to Granada with our own victory to brandish about to the citizens of the city."

Fatima nods, "Interesting." Perhaps she misjudged this scheming little man's capabilities.

Alas, Aben Comixa's plan is the brainchild of the high elder. The old wizard studies his quarry, sees that she does not make the connection. *Excellent. Her obsession with Zoraya will be her undoing . . . when the time comes.*

Aben Comixa continues, "There would be nothing like a victory to silence the grumbling from the guilds. At least for a while. And with Fernando as barter, we would have food aplenty from Castile. Perhaps even our own cannons. There is some chance that al-Zaghal will be defeated in the battle, but even if not, he will be too far away to aid Granada. With a victory in hand and the citizenry back on our side, the odds will again be in our favor. *Then* we will attack the Alhambra, first destroying their cannons, of course."

Boabdil's dour mood has brightened considerably. "Finally! A real fight. I will crush the Christians and parade their king along the streets of the Albayzín for all to admire." He begins to spew bluster and bravado about his coming exploits against the Christians.

Aben Comixa and Abu al-Haytham exchange a knowing glance.

As Fatima watches her son, her concerns surface once again, though she would not dare to share them in this company. Concerns not on this new strategy, which seems to her to be sound, but rather on her son's ability to perform as required when the time comes. She chews her cheek as the gears whir, and she begins scheming their next moves upon the chessboard. *If only I had better raw material to work with. The younger Falcon would do nicely. If only . . .*

The normal market day frenzy unfolding on the packed plaza beside the Bermejas Hospital stills along the crest of a slowly parting wave. Conversations cease, heads turn, people stare. Of course they do. After all, how often does one see a blind Nasrid prince, a Falcon no less, arm in arm with a lovely young female hakim, feeling his way along the street with a cane like an old man. The brazen among them whisper to their neighbors, and one or two even dare to snigger. One by one they lower their eyes as Danah locks her smoldering emeralds upon them, glaring them into submission.

Even so, he is acutely aware of the attention leveled upon them—upon him. His hearing is so acute now that little is lost. He does his best to ignore the whispers of gossip and rumor and trudge on. This takes guts. He wills his head high, his eyes open and apparently searching their path. Hard-won pride is a difficult thing to shake, even for a blind man.

Every few moments she offers him encouraging words, trying to lighten his load, then returns to scanning the crowd with her intimidating glare, jaw clenched, lips pursed, a green-eyed tigress with her claws exposed, ready to pounce in defense of her wounded mate. Thankfully, the crowd soon tires of the spectacle and moves on about its business.

Despite the short distance to David and Miriam's house, it takes them nearly a quarter of an hour to complete the journey. Miriam opens the door and greets them both with a ready smile and open arms. She has been patiently watching for their arrival. She realizes what she has asked of the man. She hugs Danah, then turns to her guest. "How wonderful to see you again, Yusef. You look well." She kisses the young man affectionately on both cheeks.

He releases his guide's arm and bows. "Always a pleasure, Lady Miriam. I trust that you are well?"

"Yes, thank you, very well."

"I have missed your company. Danah tells me that your new children have been keeping you busy."

Miriam laughs. "Busy would be an understatement. The little scoundrels are running me ragged!" She rolls her eyes then smiles. "But I would not change it for the world." She motions to them. "You two come in. The children are so excited to have visitors. They have been talking about you all morning."

Yusef's expression tightens. Danah sees his anxiousness, squeezes his hand to reassure him, then takes his cane and leans it against the wall. She is suddenly nervous for the man she loves.

Samra walks into the room and abruptly stops. And stares. Her wretched past safely behind her, Samra has healed, though she's now reached the dreamy-eyed age in a young woman's life when she grows acutely aware of the opposite sex and thinks of little else, yet she is still painfully shy and awkwardly self-conscious about herself and her looks and what to say and do around a man. One this handsome is guaranteed to stupefy.

Danah says, "Good morning, Samra. You remember Prince al-Makki."

To Danah's amusement, the girl blushes. Samra manages an off-kilter curtsy. She mumbles, "Pleased to meet you." The girl winces, as if she has said something entirely inappropriate. "My lord."

Yusef formally bows. "Please call me Yusef. Danah tells me you are a great help with the orphans, Samra."

The girl's blush darkens as her eyes retreat to the floor in hiding. After a painful stretch of silence, she manages to look up and offer a shy, "Thank you, my lord."

He smiles warmly, repeats himself. "Yusef."

Miriam frowns at the silliness of the girl's tortured plight and decides to save her from her misery. "Samra, you may bring the children."

"Yes." Samra stands frozen, just staring at him.

Miriam quizzically raises her brows and motions the girl away with her wrist. Samra catches herself and turns to leave.

Miriam and Danah exchange smiles.

From upstairs come gleeful squeals and peals of bright laughter, followed by a herd of foot-patter above them.

Miriam chuckles. "Prepare yourself for the onslaught, Yusef. I can assure you that, despite that racket, they are actually quite harmless."

The elder Falcon unconsciously stiffens.

Down the stairs tramples the stampede. Samra does her best to corral the children and hold them back, but this proves futile, of course, and they spill into the room in a giggling throng, the littlest in front, fearless, the young boys to the back, all serious and preening like young cocks on the strut. The boys have never met a Nasrid prince, much less a famous Falcon. Amazingly, the gaggle comes to a screeching halt and instantly falls mute. All ten of them stare wide-eyed at their visitor.

Miriam is dumbfounded. She manages, "Come, children. I would like to introduce Prince al-Makki of the Alhambra."

Nothing.

Yusef stammers, "I—I am pleased to meet you." Very stiff.

Still nothing. Statues locked in stone.

Danah begins to think this was a terrible idea. Just as she decides to put an end to it, a little girl, barely five years old, bravely steps forward from the paralyzed cohort. Precious little Ummah, a tad odd and always unpredictable; a precocious young thing. She stops, then tentatively shuffles forward, then halts in front of Yusef and studies him. "You cannot see." A proclamation.

Both women are shocked by the child's impertinence. Miriam exclaims, "Ummah! Mind your manners!"

Interestingly, however, Yusef laughs. "That is right, Ummah. I cannot see."

The little girl reaches up and takes his hand. "How did it happen?"

"I was wounded in battle."

The murdered village girl in Yusef's awful story jumps into Danah's mind. *About the same age.* She grows fearful of what may unfold, then protective of him. She decides to move to Yusef's side, but Miriam reaches out and touches her shoulder, shakes her head. Danah remains where she is, wary, ready to step in if required.

Ummah thinks his answer over, then nods, satisfied. "I will make you better." She tugs on his hand to force him down to her level. Yusef looks confused as he kneels in front of the little girl. In a quick motion Ummah flings both arms around his neck and hugs him tight.

Yusef is clearly shocked by her action, but remarkably, he does not recoil; he simply lets the little girl hug him. A spell has been cast. Magically, time slows, and the room stills. Not a person moves or says a word. Slowly, one of his hands finds its way to the little girl's back, then the other, and he returns her hug.

Danah and Miriam look on with amazement.

Ummah whispers, "Mercy."

Yusef squeezes his eyes tightly shut.

Ummah kisses first one eye, then the other, then leans back and studies his face. She says, "You are forgiven." Such an unexpected choice of words from the little girl.

Yusef chokes back a sob.

Ummah traces the scar of the crescent moon on his forehead. Yusef opens his eyes, spilling a tear down each cheek. Ummah wipes each tear away, then says, "There. All better. Now, will you play with us?"

Yusef laughs. "Will you show me how?"

Miriam and Danah are both wiping their eyes.

Ummah releases him from her hug and takes his hand. "Come. I will teach you." She leads him across the room toward the courtyard. The trance is broken, and the other children begin to merrily chatter and follow the two of them out the door.

Danah and Miriam simply stare at each other in bewilderment, wondering what exactly they have just witnessed.

Miriam says it first. "Grace."

Danah agrees. "Yes. The miracle of Allah's Grace. Praise to you, O Merciful One."

The two women listen to endearing sounds of children at play, punctuated every few moments by a blind Falcon's laugh.

The women have been sitting and talking over their hot tea for nearly an hour. Danah fidgets; she cannot help going to the window every few minutes and checking on him. She shakes her head and chuckles. "You would not believe what I am seeing, Miriam."

Miriam gently chastises her. "Sit, Danah. Yusef is fine. He is in good hands now."

"I know." She returns and sits. "How did you know this would happen?"

"I did not. But after you told me his horrible story I had a hunch that being around young children might help him."

"And Ummah?"

"That was as much a surprise to me as it was to you."

Danah says, "It was amazing."

"Yes. Grace is a mysterious thing. Who could have possibly guessed it would be little Ummah?"

"Remarkable."

Miriam studies her friend. "He will be a good father, you know."

Danah looks up, offers a radiant smile. "Yes, he will."

"I assume no word has arrived from Malik?"

Danah wilts. "No. I thought I would have heard by now, Miriam." A thinly veiled wisp of desperation clings to her words.

"Patience, my dear. Malik will do the right thing. Trust me."

"I know, but . . ."

"Patience, Danah. Soon."

The courtyard door swings open, and a sweaty Yusef emerges, escorted by the two elder boys—Rashid, ten, and Jattab, nine. Each boy holds a hand to lead him.

Danah brightens and rises. "You survived!"

Yusef laughs. "Barely. First, Ummah and the girls insisted I help them dress their wooden dolls! Then the boys had to demonstrate their spinning tops. In the end it was blind man's bluff with all of them. I was the blind man!" He laughs loudly. "These two young pups took forever to find."

The ladies laugh. The two boys shyly smile, clearly pleased with themselves.

"By the way, young Rashid and I have chatted. He assures me that you can expect his best behavior from now on, Miriam. Is that not right, Rashid?"

The boy looks down and mutters, "I am sorry for the trouble I caused you, m'lady. It will not happen again."

Miriam smiles. "M'lady? My, my . . . I could get used to this!"

Rashid looks up at Yusef and says, "Will you come again and play, m'lord?"

Yusef beams. "You may depend upon that, sir. After all, I know two young knights who need some training."

Both boys beam.

"Now go. Go!" He playfully shoos them out.

Danah guides him to a seat. Both women are still smiling. Miriam says, "You have quite the gift with children, Yusef."

He shakes his head as he chuckles. "Lord only knows how. I have never been around little boys and girls." His expression grows serious. "Tell me about Ummah."

Miriam sighs. "Well . . . actually, we know very little about our Ummah. Ezar found her sitting outside the Atfal, nearly five months back. She would not say who left her there. When we asked about her family, she simply shook her head and said, "I have no family." We put word out across the city, to no avail. My guess is she is from somewhere in the Vega. Girls are not especially valued by farming families, sad to say."

"No, I suppose not."

"But she is a precocious little thing. Uses words far bigger than her age would warrant. And she has an odd, knowing look about her. She stared at you that way, Yusef. She was clearly intent upon something."

"Mm."

"She is liked well enough by the other children, but she tends to be a loner. At least most days. And despite her forwardness today, definitely not a leader."

"But how did she do what she did? I mean . . ."

The healer in Danah is intrigued. "What exactly did you feel happen?"

"It felt . . . well . . . like . . ." He sighs. "I am not sure what I felt, exactly." He shrugs, unable to precisely define the sensation. "Warmth, I guess. Especially in my eyes when she kissed them. But also in here." He taps his chest. He stares into space as he tries to recreate the complicated feelings he experienced. "And why would she trace my crescent scar? When she did that it was almost as if an ancient yoke that had been laid upon me . . . was lifted from my shoulders."

Danah gently offers, "She is about the age of the little girl who was murdered in front of you so long ago."

He weighs this. "Yes, I suppose she is. Interesting . . . the deep sense of peace was so striking, Danah. Peace, yes; that was it. And the tears . . . dear Lord. Where did those come from? How do such things happen?" He shakes his head, puzzled.

Danah offers, "Allah's Grace."

Miriam muses, "Perhaps Ummah was simply a vessel of Grace the Lord sent to heal your old wounds. The Lord's ways are mysterious."

"Mm." He nods. "Grace. Perhaps so. *Alhamdulillah.*" Praise be to Allah.

"Thank you both for coming at so late an hour." Barely a whisper. The room is lit by a single taper, the soft sway of the flame bending and stretching shadows across the sculpted stucco walls. Rabbi al-Zuhri is grim-faced. He seems to have aged a decade in a day.

David's concern shows when he sees his friend. "Dear Lord, Zachariah, what happened?"

The old man's eyes settle on the scroll on the desk before him. He struggles to lift it in his trembling hands, as if the sheet of paper was instead made of lead. The rabbi is quivering like a leaf. He opens his mouth to speak but cannot. His eyes helplessly fill. He cannot bear its weight and lowers the thing back to its resting place.

Ezar implores him, "*What* is in the letter?"

The rabbi croaks, "Word from Sevilla. From Rabbi Hananel. It seems . . ." He closes his eyes.

David touches the old man's arm to gently encourage him. "Speak, Zachariah. What did Rabbi Hananel say?"

It takes everything he has to utter the word. "*Shoah.*"

Ezar raises his wooly worms, incredulous.

David is perplexed. "What do you mean?"

As the rabbi opens his eyes, tears spill down his cheeks. "They burned them, David."

David shakes his head. "Who? Who burned them, Zachariah?"

"The Christians. The Inquisition." The old man struggles to get the words out. "Another auto-da-fé. But this tribunal ended differently." The rabbi falls silent.

Ezar says, "Go on."

"Six Sevillian conversos were sentenced to death by the Inquisitor. A Dominican friar by the name of Alfonso de Portillo. His claim was that they were still secretly practicing as Jews, though no evidence was presented. The tribunal condemned them. All six vehemently denied the charge, to no avail. They were tortured to extract false confessions, then burned at the stake in the public square."

David grows limp. "Dear Lord, no."

Ezar asks, "Do we know who they were?"

"Rabbi Hananel said that four were well-known merchants. Wealthy. The other two were bankers, who also served on the town council. Isaac al-Tuati and Jacob ibn Awkal. I have never met them, but I know the names. Well respected."

David says, "But if the queen is only after their gold, why kill them?"

Ezar responds, "No, David. These things never end where they begin. Once the tiger is loosed from its cage and develops a taste for blood, it will not be caged again." Ezar follows the facts to their logical conclusion, a fear that he has held but never shared with his friend. "The queen is trying to strike fear in all converts to Christianity, both Jewish and Muslim. The Jews forced to convert in the 1391 pogrom are especially easy targets. The inquisitors can simply claim that those conversos of sufficient rank and wealth to be of political use are secretly practicing as Jews in defiance of the queen's decrees. And if they refuse to play along, the Inquisitor and his tribunal will condemn them. I feared all along that the queen would wield the power bestowed by the pope as a weapon of political expediency. What better way to suppress would-be challengers to her power? To make a population cower?" He stops to let this sink in. "I strongly suspect that by extension she aims to send a message to *all* Jewish conversos in Castile—that they are lesser Christians, less pure because of their Jewish roots, and are no longer welcome in her kingdom." He waggles his finger. "Mark my words, Zachariah. In the end, the Inquisition will turn its eyes on the practicing Jews, even those of high rank at court. And heaven help us if the Christians manage to conquer Granada."

David's head bows under the weight of it all. "But dear Lord, man, why burn them?"

"The Inquisition, and by extension the king and queen themselves, aim to send a message that cannot possibly be misinterpreted. Stand in our way and you will suffer the consequences. They have carefully crafted the ideal means of intimidation."

The three fall silent as they absorb the shock.

Rabbi al-Zuhri manages to collect himself, then finally says, "I fear Ezar is right. I will write to Rabbi Hananel and tell him that his congregation is welcome in Granada."

"No." Ezar is shaking his head. "Not enough, Zachariah. You must implore him to gather the whole Jewish community and leave Sevilla immediately, before it is too late. Trust me, this burning will not be the last. It is only a matter of time before the Inquisitor turns his attention from the conversos to the Jews. After all, they hold the lion's share of Castile's gold."

The three men numbly stare at each other, the sense of foreboding weighing heavily upon them. Deep within, each man senses the dawn of a terrifying new era for the Jews of Spain. Bitter irony, given that the land upon which they now stand, their land, shepherded in the Golden Age of Judaism some five hundred years ago. The shimmering paradise that was Umayyad Córdoba at its zenith is now nothing but dust.

Joshua, a young attendant on the staff of the Bermejas, leads the woman into the ward. A matron, dressed head to toe in the all-black preferred by the mountain clans. Her black veil is pulled tightly across her face, leaving only her almond eyes exposed.

"There she is." The young man points to the end of the cavernous room. "When Hakim Amiriya is finished tending her patient you can approach her with your question. She knows all of the orphans."

"Thank you for your kindness."

The young man is clearly anxious to be about his business. "I am afraid I have work to do."

"Please, I will stand here quietly until the hakim is finished." Her eyes implore him. "Please."

Joshua looks torn. He knows protocol. "Where did you say you were from?"

"Nigüelas. South of the city, at the edge of the mountains."

"Yes, I know the village. I suppose I should wait with you . . ." Still undecided.

"Please, no. My question will only take a moment of her time. I have been searching for my grandson for so long. He needs me. Please. I can see myself out. I swear I will not be a bother to anyone." The irresistible plea of a determined tetta.

Joshua considers her request, then finally relents. "Very well. Please do not disturb the hakim until she is finished with her patients."

"Of course."

"It may be a little while."

"I understand. Thank you."

Joshua turns and is gone.

Mayya Amiriya sighs her relief, then melts into the wall, dark upon dark, and takes in the scene. Only a few of the sea of beds are occupied, all at the far end of the room. Danah sits on the edge of a bed, her back turned to her mother, removing the bandages from the arm of her patient. Mayya's lips purse with disapproval beneath her veil as she realizes that her daughter tends a wounded . . . man. The two of them are talking, but too softly for her to make out the words. She cannot see Danah's face, but she can see the man's. He is clearly relishing Danah's attention. Mayya frowns. When Danah is done removing the bandages she lifts his exposed forearm, carefully scrutinizes it, then leans close for a sniff. She lifts a probe from her bag and teases the stitches. Satisfied, she begins to test the mobility of his elbow, bending it back and forth, back and forth, then rotating it ten degrees in either direction and repeating the motion.

Mayya has never seen her daughter at work. Danah moves about her tasks confidently, without the slightest hesitation. What Mayya knows as fact begins to sink in to the mother within—

415

Hakim Amiriya. My little girl is the first female hakim in the city. The seeds of pride swell within her.

Next Danah supports the elbow and bends the man's fingers one by one, ending with the thumb. On this last one, the man winces. She says something unintelligible. The man laughs. She tests the thumb again, this time pressing down on a spot on his palm using her other hand. The man does not wince this time. Evidently, she has eliminated the pain. He returns a comment that elicits a soft chuckle from her daughter. Mayya frowns once more. Her betrothed daughter touching a man's exposed body. *What would Battal think? What would Malik think?!*

Mayya continues to watch as Danah rewraps the man's forearm with fresh bandages. When she is almost finished, the man propped up on a pillow on the bed two down from her current patient calls for her. Danah's head raises. She says something to the new patient, who nods. Mayya inches to the right to see the other man's face. The left half of the young man's head is covered in white bandages. No doubt some disfiguring wound.

When Danah is finished with the arm, she offers her patient a kind word, then she rises, steps to the side of the other man, and sits down. She takes his hand and holds it between both of her own, speaking in soothing tones. She presses a hand on the unbandaged part of his forehead to check for fever. Satisfied, she begins to gently stroke his hair while she hums a song. Mayya's eyes widen. She recognizes the tune. It is a song that her own tetta taught her, and which she herself sang to Danah when she was a young child and needed consoling. The man relaxes, and within a few moments his lone eye begins to flutter, then finally closes.

Mayya's pride in her daughter returns. *Hakim Amiriya. My daughter the healer.*

Danah continues to hum her tune and stroke the man's head to be sure he is asleep. At the far end of the room the door opens. Mayya freezes.

A man with a cane enters the ward at the far end of the room. Mayya squints. *Princely attire. Very handsome.*

Danah immediately looks up and says something, but Mayya cannot see her expression. The man's face instantly brightens upon hearing Danah's voice. And something more, though she is not sure what. Something. Mayya chews her cheek as she considers his reaction to her daughter. Wary, as only a protective mother can be. *Not a casual acquaintance, that much is certain.*

The man's cane slides back and forth as he slowly crosses from the door toward Danah. *Blind. What a shame.* Mayya studies him. The man looks familiar, but she cannot place who he is. Clearly someone of importance; from some noble family, no doubt.

Danah checks to make sure her patient is asleep, then rises from the bed and moves to greet the blind man. They do not embrace when they meet, but Danah stands much too close for decorum. She tiptoes to whisper in his ear. The blind man beams as he nods. Clearly an intimate exchange of some sort. Mayya's wariness returns. *Too familiar.* Mayya studies their body language. She frowns yet again. She almost misses it, but then she sees her daughter's fingers brush against his, linger, then part. Then once again. The man's bright smile returns. With an unnerving flutter in her gut the realization hits Mayya full force. *There is something between these two.*

They continue to whisper as Mayya narrows her eyes and hawks over them, her alarm growing by the moment. The man says something, then they brush fingers once more, and he turns to leave. He makes a straight line for the door, as if he knows the way. Danah does not take her eyes from him. Back and forth, back and forth goes the cane, then he is gone. Danah stands for a moment longer, then pivots, and for the first time Mayya sees her daughter's face. *Oh dear. No.* She knows that look. Her heart begins to race. The glow of love.

Mayya's alarm at what she sees bends in a predictable direction. Fury. She steps from her hiding place on the wall and loudly clears her throat.

Danah immediately turns to the sound, instantly all business. "Excuse me?"

Mayya is afraid to speak, but she is livid. How *dare* she?!

Danah begins to walk toward the woman. "You are not supposed to be in here. Who brought you here?" A more challenging tone. The distance between them is vanishing.

Still no response.

Danah stops in front of the black-robed woman and sizes her up. Satisfied that the woman is no threat, she softens her tone. "May I help you?"

Mayya reaches up, unclasps her veil, and slowly peels it back.

Danah's face collapses. "*Mama?*"

Mayya scowls. "Who was that man?" Biting.

Danah blanches but does not reply.

"The man with the cane. Who was he?"

Danah searches for solid ground. "Mama. How did you get here? I did not expect you."

"Obviously."

"Mama . . . I have missed you."

417

"Who." Not a query.

Danah swallows. "Yusef al-Makki."

Mayya nods as she finally places the face. "The elder Falcon prince."

"Yes, Mama."

Mayya is amazed that Danah would attract the attention of such a famous knight. Status beyond her wildest imaginings. But then the obvious hits her. "A Nasrid." Her tone is not kind.

"Yes, Mama, a *Nasrid*." Danah's bile rises to coax her resolve.

Mayya backs down with a weary exhale. "How was he blinded?"

"At Alhama. I was assigned by Hakim al-Adani to assist with his recovery." A half-truth is all she can manage.

The judgmental scowl returns. "From what I saw, I would say you have done more than that, young lady."

Danah is helpless to prevent her cheeks from coloring. She lowers her eyes. "Mama . . . please."

"Danah. Dear Lord. You are betrothed. What would Malik think? The scandal, Danah, think of the scandal."

"Mama—"

Mayya hisses, "You are betrothed! What of your intended? And what about your father? His heart will be broken, Danah, broken. Dear Lord, help us all."

Danah takes all this with her head bowed in submission, but finally she looks up. "Mama. I love Yusef. With all my heart I love him." Her eyes fill. "He is the first thing I think of when I wake each morning, and the last thing I pray for when I go to sleep. Yusef is my best friend, Mama. We understand each other. We belong together. Allah has blessed the two of us with Great Love, Mama. Just as Tetta Layla told me in my dream. She was right, Mama. Tetta Layla was right. I love Yusef, Mama, body and soul, I love him." Her tears spill. "I love him. *I love him.*"

What is a mother to say to such words from her daughter? Mayya opens her mouth to speak, then closes it, dumbfounded. Instead, she does the only thing she can—she opens her arms. "Come, child. I have missed you. Come."

Danah flings herself into her mother's arms and begins to sob.

Mayya holds her tightly as she cries. Her little girl is a woman. "Shhh . . . shhh. It will be all right, Danah. Shhh . . . shhh . . ."

418

Gyrations

Antequera is an ancient city, tracing its lineage back to
Imperial Rome. A mere thirty-one miles north of Málaga, as the
crow flies. Conquered by an ambitious, some say lucky, Aragonese
prince in 1410, Antequera is the largest of the Christian-held
cities in the borderlands separating Castile and the Kingdom of
Granada. Its imposing fortifications were constructed by the
Nasrids nearly two centuries back, and as a result, Antequera has
emerged as a strategic stronghold for Castile; an ideal staging
ground for an attack on Málaga.

Between the two cities reside the Moorish-occupied Ajarquía
Mountains, an impossibly rugged land of jagged, soaring peaks,
dusty ridges choked with thickets of scrub, and deep, water-
carved valleys lined with precipices that drop from dizzying
heights into roiling white-water sluicing around sculpted
boulders. The mountains are infamous for being treacherous to
navigate, and as a result the locals almost exclusively use sure-
footed mules to traverse the steep switchbacks of their crude
trails. These uninviting lands, though sparsely populated, are
inhabited by simple mountain-folk, sheep herders and farmers
mostly, who manage to scratch a living from the arid wasteland.
They are a fearsome people bound in tightknit clans, tough and
seasoned by the adversity of their surroundings. Ajarquíans speak
an odd Arabic dialect, quite distinct from Andalusi, and are
anything but strictly observant Muslims. They are, however,
fiercely protective of the mountains that they have for centuries
called home, and they are steadfastly loyal to the Nasrid sultan.

In the castle keep of the old Nasrid alcazaba in Antequera sits
the largest Christian war council ever assembled this close to the
Moorish lands. Fernando and his generals are here to plan the
coming assault on Málaga. In attendance are the Great Captain;
Ponce de León; the Duke of Medina-Sidonia; Don Alfonso de
Cárdenas; Don Juan de Silva, Count of Cifuentes and royal
standard bearer; Don Alonso de Aguilar of Toledo and childhood
friend of Ponce de León; and Don Pedro Henriquez of Galicia,
garrison commander of Antequera.

Their combined army is camped just beyond the city walls. It
is a force of modest size, only twenty-seven hundred strong, but

almost exclusively men-at-arms mounted on massive war horses. Oddly, no infantry, no archers, no artillery, no miles-long baggage train. This is an army intended to be easily concealed on the march, an army honed for maneuverability. Among their ranks are the best and the brightest knights that Castile and Aragon can field. And to a one they are out for revenge upon the Moors, pure and simple. They aim to atone for their heavy losses at Loja.

It was Queen Isabel's stroke of brilliance that focused their attention on Málaga and drew them to Antequera, though truth be told, her plan is a reasonably obvious move by any thoughtful strategist. The intent is to avoid a direct assault on Granada proper and to instead divide the Moorish kingdom in half, strangling the city by cutting off its trade. It is, of course, unknown to the queen or Fernando or his generals, that this was precisely Sultan al-Hasan and al-Zaghal's *first* concern, and why they sent Yusef and Umar to shore up the sagging defenses of Málaga—and at great expense hire a Berber army to help defend it. The Christians are ignorant of the fact that at this moment Málaga is more formidably defended than even Granada herself.

Fernando clears his throat and raises a hand to quiet the room. "Rodrigo, please fill the others in on our plans."

Eyes turn to Ponce de León. After Alhama, he is the most experienced knight-commander among them, and even after the debacle of Loja, is universally respected. "Certainly, majesty. Gentlemen, we aim to strike for Málaga, but not along the principal Moorish trade route linking the Granadine Vega to Vélez-Málaga and the coast through the Zafarraya Pass, but directly through the wilds of the Ajarquía Mountains, attacking the city from the rugged mountains where they will least expect it. We will follow the contours of the valleys to remain undetected until we arrive at the city gates."

Don Pedro Henriquez interrupts, "And what about the Gibralfaro Castle that lords over the city? It is known to be impregnable."

"We do not intend to lay siege to the city, Don Pedro. We will attack from the west, opposite the castle. Our goal is the harbor, not the city proper. We aim to burn the docks, gentlemen, and wreck their ship moorings. We will destroy Málaga's harbor. Our aim is to sever Granada's trade with the world."

"How, is what I want to know?" Don Alfonso de Cárdenas. Eyes turn to the master of the Order of Santiago. "*How* will we get to the harbor? The city walls will be between us and our target."

"Indeed. We will feign a charge on the city's Antequera Gate, then vector south along the Guidalmedina River, travel past the

Atarazanas Gate and its fortifications, then ride back along the beach to the harbor. Málaga's defenses were constructed to defeat an attack by sea, not this. It should be a simple matter to breach the harbor from our vantage and put it to the torch. We will be bringing casks of both gunpowder and heavy pitch for that purpose.

Don Alfonso looks skeptical. "What makes you sure there will be room for our cavalry between the seawall and the water?"

Ponce de León smiles. "I have been assured by my sources that there is ample room . . . at low tide. There is a point in front of the fort where it narrows down, but even there, four horses abreast can squeeze through. And the fort's cannons are placed to fire on sailing vessels; they will be too high to train on us."

The Duke of Medina-Sidonia clears his throat. "Very risky, if you ask me. Success will hinge on achieving complete surprise. Who can guarantee that? In addition, the Ajarquía Mountains that you are talking about, sir. Have you ever traveled them?"

Ponce de León concedes, "I have not."

"*I have.* Treacherous. Trust me, our movements will be painfully slow through those mountains. The odds of us being seen, and of that information being relayed to Málaga in advance of us . . . well, they do not seem small to me, sir. The thought of being ambushed in those mountains unsettles me. Our lines will be stretched thin, with little room to maneuver. If we are attacked by the Moors on the march, we will pay dearly in blood."

Ponce de León is an able commander, certainly not one to be blinded by his own bravado, especially after Loja. "I understand your concern, Enrique. To that end, I sent a scouting party of local militia to find the safest route through the mountains. They returned undetected two days back. They have a route mapped out for us. Nothing is guaranteed in war, obviously, but I believe the risk is manageable, and one that we must take to secure a strategic advantage."

"Mm." The duke seems unconvinced.

The king chimes in. "Enrique, think of the message we will send if our army successfully launches a surprise attack upon an unsuspecting Málaga and succeeds in destroying its harbor. I aim to personally lead the charge."

Rumbles of agreement.

The Great Captain finally speaks. "Majesty. With all due respect, you and I must return to Lucena and withdraw the army back to Córdoba."

Fernando frowns.

Eyes turn to the Great Captain. "Majesty, hear me out. Our army at Lucena is the only thing standing between Queen Isabel and Sultan Muley Hacén. After our losses at Loja, we can all agree that the army is in need of serious refitting and fresh troops. Alhama is secure now and well-garrisoned, so there is no special need for the army to stand ready to reinforce them. Besides, the time will soon be upon us when we require heavy cannons to lay siege to the Moorish castles. Sad to say, we lost the only three we had at Loja. As you know, majesty, their replacements, and a dozen more, will soon reside in Córdoba. Preparations for their transport with our army when it marches must be properly secured. Majesty, I repeat. We must withdraw from Lucena back to Córdoba and make ready for the coming campaign."

The king does not respond.

Ponce de León concurs. "I agree, majesty. You and Gonzalo must return to Lucena and withdraw the army for refitting. I would suggest that we leave a garrison at Lucena to dispel any temptation by the Moors to invade, remote as that may be. And I would suggest departing under the cover of dark so that the sultan's spies do not learn of your withdrawal. No need to tempt fate."

The Great Captain nods. "Sound advice."

The others voice their agreement.

"Majesty, it must be so." The duke weighs in. "Gonzalo, I would alert Diego Fernandez de Córdoba, Count of Cabra. He is not far from Lucena, and he can provide support to the garrison in the unlikely event that it is required."

The Great Captain replies, "Agreed. I know the man. He is a worthy knight with capable men under his command."

Though he yearns to lead the raid on Málaga, Fernando sees the wisdom of the advice. "Very well. I will return to Lucena and lead our withdrawal to Córdoba for refitting." His eyes circle the room. "But when the time finally comes to lay siege to Málaga, and level its walls with my new cannons, I will be leading the charge. Understood?"

The Great Captain is pleased that the king has seen the logic. "Of course, majesty. That day will come soon enough."

In point of fact, on Yusef's advice, Hamete Zeli, knight-commander of Málaga, has been paying the Ajarquíans to watch the mountain passes for many months now. Ponce de León's scouting party was sighted by Ajarquían shepherds, then followed back to Antequera to assess their intent. An army of three thousand mounted knights is not easily hidden.

Miriam was insistent that Danah's mother stay with them.

To be sure, Danah was delighted to have her mother's watchful eye out of the Bermejas, but still, she was concerned about adding more work to Miriam's already heavy load. But Miriam was predictably persistent, and in the end Danah relented to her friend's request, though she insisted on no more than a week or two.

Mayya balked at the arrangement, of course, but eventually she gave in. After all, she is not given to sleeping in a hospital ward with no privacy. It was either acquiesce or return to the Albayzín, and with the revelation from her daughter, how could she leave with things so unsettled still?

Mayya has no close Jewish friends, but the al-Adanis have been very welcoming indeed. The home is noisy, chaotic even, with the children's constant antics, but while she would not admit it, she has come to actually enjoy the banter, especially around the dinner table. She pitches in where she can, tries to make herself useful. Danah comes each day to visit her after her work duties are completed.

Interestingly enough, Miriam and Mayya have actually begun to develop a friendship of sorts, despite the fact that it became readily apparent to Mayya that Miriam knew much more of her daughter's new life, and her heart, than she herself did. Not to mention the inescapable fact, all too easily deduced, that the original idea for soliciting Abd al-Salam to choose a match for Danah clearly originated with Miriam. This realization initially rankled Mayya, especially given the knot of current circumstances, but she has moved past it now. There are more important matters to deal with at this late stage of the game—namely, a blind Falcon prince. Mayya has tried on several occasions to broach the subject of Danah's future with her new friend, but her attempts thus far have been unsuccessful. And this weighs on her, as it would any mother.

"Tell me, Miriam. Do you think it would it be possible to get word to my husband that I am well and staying here with you for a few more days? I know he must be worried sick since I did not immediately return as we had planned."

Miriam considers the options. "Yes, I think so. David sends a regular shipment of medical supplies to Hakim al-Fadl at the Maristan Hospital. I am sure he could include a letter for your husband. We can ask him when he gets home."

"Thank you."

"Of course, think nothing of it."

"Miriam?" Mayya chews her cheek, debating what exactly to say.

She looks up. "Yes?"

"I wanted to . . . thank you. For being such a good friend to Danah. I know you had her best interests at heart in all that you have done."

"I care deeply for Danah. She is a rare young woman, Mayya. So gifted, and such a beautiful heart. She is a fine reflection of both you and your husband. You should both be very proud."

"You are too kind. But yes, we are very proud. I will admit it took some time for me to see Danah's gifts, and her calling. Although she cannot see it, all I really wanted was for her to be happy, Miriam. Sometimes . . . well, sometimes that may have come out the wrong way."

"I understand. All mothers want the best for their daughters." There is such warmth and tenderness in Miriam's words.

They fall silent.

"May I be truthful, Mayya?"

The two lock eyes. "Of course."

"Danah is discovering the depths of her heart for the very first time. Such things are always delicate matters. It was for me. And I am sure it was for you."

"Yes."

"Mayya, Danah had feelings for Yusef before she and Malik were betrothed."

Mayya's jaw goes slack. This is news. "But . . ."

"They met at the Atfal Hospital. Afterward, he wrote to her, professing his feelings. Just before he was sent away to Málaga. She received Yusef's letter the same day Abd al-Salam wrote you with news of Malik. Danah felt she had no choice but to honor her promise to you and your husband. She felt trapped."

"I see." This saddens her.

Miriam looks troubled. "I am afraid getting Abd al-Salam involved was all my doing. It seemed like the best way to satisfy you and Battal, while giving Danah the time she needed to complete her training. Forgive me for stepping in where I did not belong."

"All is forgiven, Miriam. I inferred as much. I know you were only thinking of what was best for Danah. You have been a great friend to her, at a time when a wall stood between the two of us. Thank you."

"Mayya, I have never seen two young people so deeply in love. As you have now witnessed yourself, their feelings for each other are plain to see. While I realize that the complexities presented by such a relationship are very real, I have always believed that true love will find a way."

"Mm."

"They deserve our help. Especially yours."

Mayya's eyes fill. She whispers, "I know. It is just that . . ."

"Danah longs for your approval, Mayya. Her great joy at finding love will not be complete if you hold back your approval."

"But this places Battal in such a precarious position, Miriam. My husband is an *elder* of the Abencerrajes."

"Sworn enemies of the Nasrids. I know."

"That might be an understatement. Tell me about Yusef."

"He is such a fine young man, Mayya. Well educated and cultured, as you would expect of a prince of the Alhambra. David says he is a great leader and is known to be one of the finest tacticians of all of the sultan's knight-commanders. He inspires confidence and great loyalty in those who serve under him." She smiles as she recollects the young man. "But so shy and tentative around her, Mayya, like he is walking on eggshells. It is obvious he has little experience with women, and clearly has never loved before. They are discovering their feelings together." She laughs. "Trust me, it has been fun to watch. The young Falcon prince has a heart of gold, Mayya, and nothing but respect for your daughter. And they have become such good friends. As we both know, friendship is such an important ingredient to lasting happiness. Danah has finally stepped out of her shell and is so filled with joy. Dear Lord, the girl is either smiling or laughing nearly every moment the two are together."

Mayya smiles. "I would never have believed such things possible."

"These two were meant for each other, Mayya."

"But what kind of life together can they possibly have, Miriam . . . with him being blind, I mean?"

"Well. They seem to have already moved beyond that fact. As they say, love knows no bounds."

"But still . . ."

"They intend to serve together in the hospital. From what David has said, Yusef has a real gift for helping the wounded deal with their pain. Not the wounds; she does that. The hidden pain, the lingering hurt." She grows animated. "And you should see Yusef with the children, Mayya! He will be a wonderful father."

"But what of Malik? The scandal, Miriam. Think of the scandal." She sadly shakes her head.

"Danah has written to him. And I have written to Abd al-Salam. Malik cares too much for Danah to cause her trouble. She told me she was truthful with him. He will be hurt, no doubt, but in the end, he will understand. I am sure there will be no scandal. A quiet breaking of the betrothal, and then Yusef will be free to ask for her hand. Abd al-Salam will help. I know he will."

"I hope you are right."

"Trust me, Mayya, Yusef will not ask for Danah's hand without your husband's and your permission. He is a chivalrous young man, perhaps to a fault."

"Well . . . it is good that he would feel that need. Convincing Battal may be a different matter altogether."

"With your help, Mayya, your husband will see that Danah must follow her heart, no matter where it leads. Abd al-Salam will help us through this, I am sure of it. David received word yesterday that he is finally on his way back from Málaga, thank goodness. All things are possible with love, Mayya. All things."

"I know."

They hear a latch slide, then the door cracks open. A young woman. "May I help you?"

Both men bow, chased by friendly smiles. "Ah. You must be Beatriz."

She seems wary as she opens the door. There is no mistaking that she is heavy with child. Finally, she manages, "Yes. I am Beatriz Enríquez de Arana."

"If I might say, my dear, mazel tov."

The young woman clearly does not understand the word.

"Congratulations . . . on your coming child. I am Abraham Seneor, chief tax collector of Castile and court rabbi. And this is Don Isaac Abrabanel, court financier and legal counsellor to Queen Isabel. We have come to see your husband."

Before she can check herself, the young woman's face visibly wilts. "Please come in. I will inform the captain." She indicates two chairs in the anteroom and then leaves the room.

The friends' eyes meet. These two do not need words for conversation. Unmarried, and soon with a bastard. Abrabanel says, "Pretty."

Seneor answers, "Indeed. I wonder if he will claim the child."

"Let us hope."

Their eyes circle the room. Modest would be overly generous. But then again, his royal stipend is intentionally meager. They hear him coming down the stairs and rise.

"Gentlemen." Not unkind, but not especially welcoming either.

Both men bow. Seneor says, "A pleasure to see you once again, Captain Colón. Congratulations on the coming birth."

Colón grunts an acknowledgment, then turns to the young woman who had escorted him back to the room. "Leave us."

"Let us hope it is another son. You remember Don Isaac Abrabanel."

Colón smirks. "I can assure you that my memory is sharp. I trust you have brought good news. It has been over two months since my audience with the king and queen. And a very brief one at that. I am sick of these interminable waits." The man's disdain has not even been partially buried.

The two old Jews exchange a quick glance. Still the same rude man. What was once amusing is quickly growing tiresome. His lack of proper etiquette in the presence of the queen was the final straw.

Seneor says, "Let us sit and talk, Captain Colón."

"You sit. I will stand."

Another quick glance is exchanged. "Very well." The two men sit. No offer of tea or treats. Colón was clearly never schooled in the art of hospitality.

The captain's hands find his hips. "What news have you?"

Seneor begins, "After your audience, Queen Isabel and King Fernando acquiesced with your recommendation and once again submitted your proposal to their Council of Geographers and Astronomers for careful consideration. But this time with the attachment of some of your own calculations, of course, and your notes on the westerlies."

"Good, good. Hopefully they know enough geometry to follow my numbers. So, they agree with me, then."

Abrabanel hesitates, then clears his throat. "I am afraid, Captain Colón, that they again came to their prior conclusion."

The mariner manages to frown through his incredulous expression.

Seneor helpfully adds, "In their view, your estimation of the distance to the Indies is much too short."

Abrabanel continues, "Unreachable by caravel, even *with* the westerlies."

"I am sorry to be the bearer of bad news, Captain Colón." Seneor reaches into his cloak and withdraws a bundle of folded parchments. "I have taken the liberty of bringing some of their calculations with me. So that you might peruse them for errors." The old rabbi knows that searching for mistakes in their work is a waste of time. He is intimately acquainted with their formidable mathematical skills.

The man remains staring at the floor as his face darkens. His hands ball into tight fists. He hisses, "Then I have wasted many months in this *God-forsaken* land. From what my brother tells me, I may find a welcome ear in England." This has the air of a threat.

Seneor attempts to calm him. "Captain Colón, despite the advice of the council, I can assure you that the king and queen are not unfriendly to your proposal. It is just that they are presently preoccupied with matters of state. The conquest of the Moorish lands, you see. You must understand, these things take time to work themselves out."

He simply glares at the old rabbi.

Abrabanel says, "There *is* some good news, Captain Colón."

He shifts his glare but does not speak.

"The king and queen have assured us that they will support your proposal after they have dealt with the Moors." A calculated lie. "They would like you . . . and your family . . . to remain in Castile. As personal guests. Your royal stipend will be tripled to twelve-thousand *maravedis*." Quite generous—enough for a reasonably plush dwelling, perhaps a servant or two. Needless to say, provided for by the two Jews. "In addition, you will receive a royal decree from the queen granting you free lodging and meals anywhere you travel within Castile." Again, paid for by the two men.

He grumbles. "The least they can do for delaying my voyage."

The two men do not bother to respond.

On their way back to court, Seneor begins, "That went well."

Abrabanel replies, "About as I expected."

Seneor chuckles. "That was some lie you told, sir."

"It seemed necessary. We cannot have him peddling his wares to England."

"Mm. Any news from your contacts in Genoa?"

"No trace of the captain's roots is to be found. But despite the lack of evidence, I still suspect he has a converso ancestry. I will continue to turn over rocks until I find what I am after."

"But what does it matter now?"

Abrabanel replies, "One never knows, my friend, how a tidbit of incriminating evidence might serve its master."

Seneor laughs. "No argument from me."

Abrabanel stops. "Abraham, we must not let this man disappear into oblivion. Coarse though he may be. Even a one percent chance that he is right about a western route to the Indies makes it worth the queen's consideration. Even if she is deeply skeptical of the merits of sponsoring his voyage."

"It sounds to me as if our intercession may well be required if this is ever to happen."

"Agreed." The old lawyer smiles. "Trust me, my friend, the queen will listen to our logic once she manages to defeat the Moors and is left holding an empty treasury and all of Spain waiting for her to govern. We must be patient."

Seneor nods his agreement.

The two men continue walking.

Battal does not sit, he just rips open the letter, desperate for news of his wife and daughter. It has been days now with no word, none at all. He begins to race down the page, scanning the contents, the expression on his face unfolding line by line. First, relief, then the hint of a smile, which promptly relaxes, then a quick frown, which deepens, then a furrowing of his brow. He stops halfway through, begins to reread. Surely, he has misunderstood her words. He has not. He reads on, more slowly now. The sag of his shoulders deepens with each passing line. When he reaches the end, he lets out a long sigh of despair. He turns the letter over to make sure there is no addendum. There is not. The hand that is clutching the letter trembles ever so slightly. His heart is racing. He stares into space as he wrestles to absorb this news. He helplessly whispers, "Dear Lord, Danah . . . dear Lord . . ."

"Yes, Grand Inquisitor, six conversos. They were found to be secretly practicing as Jews."

"And they confessed to their heresy?"

"They did." He adds, "Under torture."

Torquemada sniffs. "Good. And they repented their sins before they were burned?"

Inquisitor de Portillo hesitates. "They did not, Grand Inquisitor. Not one."

"I see. Eternity is a long time to burn in hell, would you not agree, Inquisitor de Portillo?"

"Indeed, Grand Inquisitor."

As Torquemada continues to stare down the friar, his beady eyes narrow. "Six. Only six . . ." His scowl deepens. "And that was all you could manage to . . . ah . . . root out, Inquisitor de Portillo?" He sniffs. "It makes me wonder about your methods. I

have it on good authority that Sevilla is rife with heretics. *Rife.*"
There is no mistaking the man's disdain for his fellow Dominican.

Inquisitor de Portillo blanches. "The tribunal sought to set an
example, Grand Inquisitor. So that others would confess more
readily. We felt—"

Torquemada cuts him off. "After the next auto-da-fé, it will be
twelve. Understood?"

The friar frowns. "Of course, Grand Inquisitor. Twelve will be
burned."

"And for the one that follows that, twenty-four."

Inquisitor de Portillo remains silent. *Dear God.*

"Do I . . . ah . . . make myself clear, *Inquisitor* de Portillo?"

"Yes, Grand Inquisitor."

"We must send an unequivocal message to . . . ah . . . all Jews
in Castile. What better place than Sevilla to begin, yes?" He
attempts a sinister smile, which comes out as little more than a
mangled scowl.

"Understood, Grand Inquisitor." The friar's tone has wilted.

Torquemada steps forward and drops his handbook on the
friar's desk with a loud *slap!* "A new manual detailing the
authority and actions of my tribunals. See that your entire staff
reads this and follows it to . . . ah . . . the letter."

"Of course, Grand Inquisitor."

"I will need to see your ledgers detailing all confiscated
property, and . . . ah . . . gold. Have them brought to my room
immediately." Torquemada turns and leaves without waiting for
an answer.

"Of course, Grand Inquisitor." The friar's face is ashen.

There is a quick, announcing knock, and then the door slowly
creaks open. "Miriam. Mama. We are here." Danah. Her voice is
husky, oddly strained.

The two women are seated at the table, talking while they
enjoy tea, still recovering from their trip to the hammam. Always
an ordeal with so many children to be bathed. The two women
exchange heartfelt looks. Miriam smiles encouragement at her
new friend. Mayya nods, takes a deep breath to steady herself.
They rise to greet their guests.

As Danah enters she can't help but catch her mother's eye,
just for an instant. Mayya instantly recognizes her daughter's
nervousness. No surprise there; they both are apprehensive. But
there is no use denying it: The girl is absolutely radiant with the
glow of love.

Yusef steps into the room. Danah takes his cane and leans it in the corner, then takes his hand to guide him forward.

Miriam is the first to speak. "Good afternoon, you two! I am so glad you are here. The children have been asking for you constantly, Yusef. Come in. Come in."

The young man smiles. "It is good to be back, Miriam. I have missed the children. I trust that Rashid is behaving himself these days?"

Mayya is glued to his face. *So handsome.* Of course she has heard the idle gossip about young maidens swooning in the presence of the Falcon brothers. She now sees why. *Dashing. And that smile is positively magnetic.* Still, she is certain Danah is not so shallow as to be swayed by looks alone. She knows in her heart there must be great depth of character to be found in this young man. Yusef's eyes are open and appear completely normal. Seeing him up close without his cane, one would never guess that he is blind.

Miriam responds, "I am pleased to say that Rashid has been a perfect gentlemen, Yusef. Thanks to you."

"It was nothing. I merely reminded him of a few things that all young knights must learn. And Ummah? How is she?"

"Oh, strange and precocious as ever. I am afraid the girl has taken to referring to you as 'The Man with No Eyes.'" They both laugh.

Danah says, "Mama, I would like to introduce Yusef al-Makki."

As Mayya steps forward Yusef's eyes track her movements via sound. Danah eases back to give them space. Both she and Miriam are holding their breath. "*Sayyeda Amiriya.*" Mrs. Amiriya. He formally bows. "It is a great pleasure to finally meet you. Danah has told me so much about you and your husband."

"It is good to finally meet you, Yusef." Her words have climbed up on stilts and are now precariously balanced.

Yusef unexpectedly says, "Your daughter loves you so."

Danah's emeralds are swimming. *This* she did not expect.

Miriam is beaming.

"And I love her. She is my only child, Yusef. Flesh of my flesh. I am incredibly proud of the person Danah has become. Hakim Amiriya. Who could have known?" Mayya's voice has thankfully recovered. She hesitates, debating with herself. Decision finally made, she just says it. "I am delighted that you and Danah have become such good friends. Battal and I have always felt that friendship is a solid foundation for building a life together."

Who can know where such miracles are born? No doubt in the deep reaches of the heart, where the divine spark resides.

Yusef blushes.

Danah's jaw has dropped. She never dared hope for so much from her mother.

Even Miriam is stunned.

No one says a word.

Thankfully, Miriam comes to the rescue. "Perhaps the four of us can sit for a few minutes and talk before the children drag Yusef to the courtyard to play. I will put some tea on and bring out some sweetmeats."

Everyone relaxes.

Danah makes eye contact with Mayya. Both mother's and daughter's eyes are brimming. Danah silently mouths, "I love you, Mama. Thank you."

Before she can catch herself, Mayya spills a tear.

And so it begins.

Umar and Yusef are the last to arrive. The pair of bodyguards straighten their crossed pikes to permit the entry of the Falcons.

Ali al-Attar rushes to the door to fuss over his elder nephew and help shepherd him to a waiting pillow. Venegas and al-Zaghal exchange amused smiles. The old warrior is not given to doting on anyone.

Umar says, "I am sorry that we are late, sire. The cart ride from the Bermejas was much slower than I anticipated."

Al-Zaghal replies, "No matter, Umar. We have not yet begun. Yusef, it is so good to see you again. You look well."

"Thank you, my lord. I *am* well." He wonders if they know about Danah. Umar insists they do not, but Yusef is not so sure.

"And the leg?"

"Completely healed. Not even a limp."

The sultan chimes in, "The royal physician tells me you have helped many of the wounded knights recover their lives. Know that I am grateful for your service."

"Thank you, sire. It seems that Allah has plans for me after all, even without my sight. For that I am thankful."

"Yes. Good."

"Shall we begin, then?" Venegas seems uncharacteristically impatient. The sultan's war council is seated in a circle in the Hall of the Kings within the Lion Palace. He continues, "Gentlemen, the sultan has just received a dispatch from Hamete Zeli. It seems the Christians have assembled an army in Antequera and are readying to march on Málaga."

Al-Zaghal nods. "Just as my contact suggested. They aim to deprive us of our trade. Cut the kingdom in half and starve us."

Venegas replies, "Indeed. Zeli is confident the report is trustworthy. Remarkably, the Christians apparently intend to attack us through the wilds of the Ajarquía Mountains. They sent scouts to locate the best route."

Umar says, "Is he sure? Yusef and I have ridden in those mountains. A difficult journey, even for us, much less with an army in tow."

"Zeli's men claim they have nearly three thousand cavalry, but apparently little, if any, infantry or archers. And no baggage train in sight. They are camped just outside Antequera's walls."

Ali al-Attar mutters something unintelligible, then, "Why no cannons?"

"I am not sure. But they saw none. He was quite clear about that."

The old man scoffs. "That makes no sense. How will they lay siege? Surely they know that Málaga's defenses have been shored up."

Venegas shrugs.

Al-Zaghal says, "Mm. A risky move to be sure. But then again, Ponce de León did a similar thing at Alhama. They had no cannons or baggage train then either, and that did not prevent their victory, as we know all too well."

Grumbles circle the council. The sultan scowls at the unpleasant memory of their defeat.

Umar says, "I suspect their sole aim is speed, sire. They are not fools; they see the danger if they linger too long in the mountains."

Yusef muses, "Actually, I have always suspected this would be their strategy. Which is why I had the passes watched. Tactically, it is a wise move, sire. Such an approach allows them to move undetected to just outside the city walls, at its weakest point, and safely out of range of the guns of the Gibralfaro. My guess is they do not aim to lay siege to the city, Uncle, but rather to destroy the harbor, then make a hasty retreat from whence they came. A lightning raid. Needless to say, such a plan requires complete surprise. Quite daring, actually. I am impressed." He nods to himself as he imagines the plan unfolding. "This development provides us with an excellent opportunity, sire. One that we must seize."

"I agree, sire. The journey through the mountains will be riddled with endless places for ambush. We should be able to easily prevent them from reaching Málaga in force," Al-Zaghal follows up.

Venegas studies Yusef's expression. "What, then, should our strategy be, Yusef?"

He considers the options. "The Ajarquíans are loyal to you, sire, and from what I have been able to learn, they are fierce warriors, at least when provoked. But they must not harass the Christians on their journey to Málaga. And no ambushes by our forces either."

Al-Zaghal frowns but remains silent.

"When the Christians arrive at our gates they will believe they have achieved surprise. Alas, our army will be waiting for them. Outside the walls so our overwhelming numbers can be readily appreciated by their generals. Triple their strength would be good. Or more. And we can move several of the cannons from the harbor and bring them to bare. The Christians will immediately realize their plan has been foiled, and they are now at risk of annihilation. We will attack and force them to make for Antequera as fast as they can ride. Half of our army will be waiting in the mountains for their return journey. *Now* we ambush them. Hit them hard in the passes. And mobilize the Ajarquíans to harass them every step of the way as they scatter for cover."

Al-Zaghal is smiling now. "Yes. Excellent. Excellent."

Yusef muses. "Sire, I would suggest we have the mountainfolk construct signal fires on all the passes through the Ajarquía, and place lookouts at key valley junctions. That way our ambushing army can instantly know the exact route the Christians choose for their escape."

Ali al-Attar is beaming. "Masterful."

Yusef says, "With a little luck, we can achieve a complete rout. Worse than Loja."

The sultan has been patiently listening with no visible emotion. His brother turns to him. "What say you, sire?"

The sultan begins to nod . . . then a wolfish smile. He roars, "I say brilliant! BRILLIANT! I shall have the standards of the Order of Santiago and parade their officers naked through the streets of Granada. I aim to lead this fight."

Venegas frowns. "Sire, I do not believe that is wise given your health."

The sultan turns on his grand vizier and darkens. "I will lead this fight. *Understood?*"

Al-Zaghal tenders a compromise. "I will ride beside the sultan, Venegas. We will bring fifteen thousand cavalry to the defense of Málaga. Ten for the city, five for the mountains."

Venegas recoils. "Surely not. Have you forgotten the Abencerraje menace? We cannot leave the city so poorly defended. Boabdil will exploit any perceived weakness, perhaps even attempt to storm the Alhambra again."

Yusef says. "I agree, sire. It would be unwise to remove too much of our army. And there is another consideration. King Fernando still has his army at Lucena. Beaten, yes, but not broken. My guess is that it will be held out of the fight since it alone stands in defense of Córdoba. Sire, I would suggest that you only take, say, six thousand cavalry to Málaga. Hamete Zeli can supply at least three thousand more. *And* the Berber army. You will be more than a match for the Christians. That will leave five thousand to guard the city, and my uncle and brother will take the other three thousand and return to Loja. They will make sure to be seen by the Christian scouts. Their presence in Loja will guarantee that Fernando's army stays in Lucena. If he rashly decides to move on the Vega, Uncle and Umar will leave Loja and take to the field to challenge him. After what happened at Loja, he will not dare face us on open ground. In the unlikely event that Boabdil decides to attack the Alhambra, they will still be in striking distance to reinforce as needed."

Venegas looks relieved. "Good, yes. I like this plan."

Al-Zaghal nods. "Very well. Ali? Umar?"

"Agreed."

"Agreed."

The sultan weighs the strategy. "Make it so. Summon the troops. We ride for Málaga."

The reed cane slides along the stone floor of the narrow hallway, back and forth, back and forth, each wide arc searching out the wall to either side. When he detects a doorway he pauses, then continues on. He is counting doors. Yusef has grown quite adept at traversing the Bermejas unaccompanied.

At the fourth door on the left he stops; he listens. Nothing. He feels for the latch, lifts it, steps into the medical supply room, turns, and quietly closes and locks the door behind him.

She is standing just inside the door to the right, leaning against the wall, waiting for him. Her glorious curls spill down her back. A prearranged meeting time just after noon prayers, when most of the staff have gone home for their midday meals.

He pivots toward her and remains still. She slides up to him and hugs him. Her eyes close as his hands weave into her hair. When he is sated he gently cups her face, begins to finger her eyes, her cheeks, her lips. Her arms encircle his waist then lock themselves behind him while he performs this remarkably sensual ritual. They do not speak.

He lifts her chin and leans down to kiss her. Their lips touch, part, press together, then part once more. There is a telling ease to their motions—it would appear that they have walked this path more than one time. Her mouth opens slightly to permit a warm, moist exhale of desire. He kisses her again, harder, deeper, their tongues flirting as their passions begin to devour them. Her arms pull him tighter to her. He backs her against the wall, presses himself against her. Weak-kneed, their helpless love-murmurs caress the air as their kissing intensifies. A flurry of electric-blue fireflies flits about in the air above their heads.

Clearly, things have progressed. Surely no surprise.

This goes on until neither can stand it any longer, and they release their kiss, panting. Still no words, just weary love-sighs as she rests her head upon his shoulder.

He whispers, "I ache for you, my love."

"I love you, Yusef. Dear Lord, this is getting unbearable."

"Yes."

"We should sit and talk."

"Yes, we should." Still, neither makes a move to part.

As Yusef reluctantly backs away from her, she locks her fingers in his and leads him to the chair at the workbench. The electric-blue crowd hovering above them winks out, one by one.

As their bodies calm, they begin to quietly talk. Soon they are up to their usual banter about all manner of things, all but the obvious: their future. She—chattering away, her hands up and dancing. He—listening, smiling, adding his thoughts here and there. Their patients, the children, Miriam and David, Ezar, her mother, her father, Abd al-Salam's impending return. By mutual agreement they permit themselves only thirty minutes alone together, and only twice a week. No more, lest they arouse suspicion. Or succumb to their desires.

"By the way, where were you this morning? You did not make your usual rounds in the ward."

He hesitates. "No."

She lets the word hang, waiting for him to explain, but he does not. "Ali was asking for you." She turns to study his face.

He senses this and averts his eyes. "Umar came for me. The sultan requested my presence in the Alhambra. I went by cart."

She frowns. "I see. For what?" Odd that he did not tell her.

Again, he does not answer.

"Yusef? For what?"

"A war council."

"*A what?*"

"Danah, the sultan has learned that the Christians are massing an army in Antequera. For an attack on Málaga."

She sadly shakes her head. "Dear Lord, more fighting? And so soon?" She groans. "More maiming, more dying. More fatherless children. Did the sultan learn nothing from Alhama and Loja?" There is a chiseled edge to her tone which is quickly approaching anger.

He does not respond.

"When?"

"Soon."

"What could the sultan possibly need from you?" A little too biting.

This prods him to look at her. "Danah, please. I cannot fight, but I *can* strategize. My opinions were sought."

"And you offered them." She is fuming now.

"And I offered them."

She absorbs this. She softly says, "I see. It is just that . . ." Her tone has reversed course, become flattened, vulnerable.

"Just what?"

"Well, your place is here with me now, Yusef. In the hospital. Saving lives, not helping end them. I thought . . ." She stops. Her eyes are filling.

"Danah. If the Christians cut off trade with Málaga, Granada will starve. Our patients will starve. *We* will starve. Queen Isabel aims to destroy Granada. Surely you can appreciate that. The Christians want to erase our civilization from history. I must help in any way I am able. A tactical advantage is the only thing I can give the sultan now. And I must do that, for the good of the kingdom. For us. You *must* see that."

Silence.

"Danah?"

The vulnerability wins out. Her voice quavers. "What is to become of us, Yusef?"

He reaches for her hand, enfolds it between both of his. "Look at me." She does. "I have told you a dozen times. When the letter arrives, I will ask for your hand. Then we will marry and finally be able to live as husband and wife. We will serve together, at the Bermejas, or wherever they need us." He smiles to lighten her mood. "We will make love every day, twice a day, and we will bring our children into this world, inshallah." He pulls her closer to him. "Little emerald-eyed girls as beautiful as their mama. You will be a wonderful mother, Danah."

"I live for that day, Yusef." Tears spill. "But there is still no word, no—" She cannot bring herself to finish the sentence.

"Patience, my love. His letter will come." He lifts her chin, kisses her tenderly. "I love you. We *will* be married. You may depend upon it, Danah."

"Yusef?"

"Yes?"

"Will you join me for prayer? So we can pray for our future. Please?"

He does not need time to think. "Of course, my love."

Ajarquía

The shepherd touches his companion on the shoulder to wake him. He points downward from the crag where the two are perched. In the depths of the dark valley below them the faint outline of a silvery snake slithers along. The reflection of the waning moon upon polished plate. The ethereal serpent shimmers as it moves, its tail stretching back far to the north until it bends out of sight. A lone torch at the head of the beast tongues the trail meandering beside the fitful tumble of rushing water, a series of broken cascades clinging to the crinkled gash at the vertex of the steep valley cutting through the ancient mountains.

The two men exchange a few words, then one of them rises and picks his way down the opposite side of the peak to where their mules are tethered.

The cavalry thunders through the Zafarraya Pass leading down from the Granadine plateau through the mountains to Vélez-Málaga and the coast. Sultan Abu l-Hasan and al-Zaghal ride side-by-side at the front of a cantering column eight riders wide. They are flanked by bannermen flying the blue and gold Nasrid battle standards. The Moor army is six-thousand strong, not a single footman. They do not bother to stop at the Zafarraya way station but instead urgently press onward down through the mountains and to the sea. The dust cloud they kick up chases their movements and can be seen for miles.

The armored knights walk their monsters in single file, weapons lashed to their saddles to quiet them. What could be ridden in a day and half over open ground will take them four through the Ajarquía Mountains. Their guides have assured them that the locals do not venture far from their villages at night, and thus they travel only by moonlight. With no easy place to camp by day they are forced to hobble their horses on the trail, tie a tarp to their saddles for some shade, and try their best to nap. No cooking fires, just jerky and wheat biscuits hard enough to break a tooth. They are dangerously exposed. They know this, of course; to a man they are seasoned warriors. It is a risky gamble upon which the Christians have embarked. At twilight they mount up once more and proceed onward down the treacherous valley.

Heads nervously scan the darkened slopes rising high above them, eyes tracking left to right, right to left, forward, backward, searching for any hint of danger; a campfire, perhaps; voices; anything. An owl cries from across the stream, and a hundred heads turn in unison as hands involuntarily grip the hilts of broadswords. From time to time the reverberating echoes of small rockslides from the unstable cliffs prompt the raising of an officer's hand while, one by one, down the line, the knights stop and cup their ears to listen for endless minutes as their hearts pound away. Bird trill passes down the line, and again they are moving.

Anxiety feasts upon the unknown. Nerves fray; mounts grow jumpy and have to be reined in. The pious pray to the Virgin Mary for courage and protection. The sinful curse the foolishness of their endeavor . . . and their commanders. The sense of foreboding is oppressive and deeply unsettling. They grow silent and sullen, wanting nothing but to be back on open ground.

Three days after the sultan and al-Zaghal lead their army out of Granada, ample time to guarantee they reach Málaga and thus ensure that they are too far away to threaten him, Boabdil's army leaves the city under cover of night via the Elvira Gate. His aim is the siege of Lucena and hopefully the capture of King Fernando, and thus his army is ten-to-one infantry to cavalry. Slow on the march.

On the fourth day, the Christians emerge from the foothills of the mountains less than two miles from the western wall of Málaga, two hours before sunset. Impeccable timing. The aim is to burn the harbor and retreat back into the cover of the mountains by nightfall before the Moors are fully aware of what is happening.

Ponce de León, the duke, and the other knight-commanders congratulate themselves on having emerged from the Ajarquía unscathed, the element of surprise intact. They stop to rest, water the horses. After readying their weapons, the squadrons form rank, and final commands are issued.

The cavalry arranges itself into a staggered phalanx of individual squadrons and begins to canter for the city, broadswords, studded maces, and battle axes at the ready. They rumble past the small outlying villages. When the locals catch sight of the red-on-white crusader crosses they first do an incredulous double-take, then stare long and hard as alarm sets in. It takes no time at all to gauge the intent of these armored horsemen. Shrill screams erupt as panic ensues. People begin to race about, hurriedly gathering children and loved ones and locking themselves in their homes. But their fears are unfounded, at least for now. The cavalry bypasses the villages; they have no time to pillage. That pleasure will be saved for the return journey, after their victory.

As the cavalry exits from between the last two foothills bending into the city, a panoramic view of Málaga opens all at once, drawing their eyes. The impressive semicircular city wall directly to their front arcs around to the right, stretching back to the deep blue of the sea. To the left, north, it bends around to the double-walled Alcazaba, the palace of the emir, which straddles a protected knoll overlooking the city. High above the Alcazaba on the top of the mountain is the Gibralfaro Castle, which lords over everything. It is an inspiring sight to behold; a large, lovely city never seen by these men, not one.

Ponce de León's eyes track back to the Antequera Gate, the target of their feigned attack before breaking for the sea. He instantly frowns and raises a hand. The knight-commanders follow suit, and the cavalry squadrons slow in formation then stop. They are a little less than a quarter-mile out from the gate.

Arrayed in close quarter and perfectly stationary to either side of the gate are massive rectangles of Moor cavalry. Ponce de León's quick estimate is four, maybe five thousand mounted knights, nearly twice his strength. He studies the scene for clues. As he sees Sultan Muley Hacén, flanked by Granada's battle standards, his frown is replaced by concern. The Moors do not move. They seem to be simply standing watch, but their presence alone is a sure indication that the Christian plans have been anticipated. He wonders to himself how Granada's army managed to arrive so quickly. A sense of despair wells up within him until he recalls his duty and chokes it back.

The duke kicks his horse up, and a heated exchange commences. The other knight-commanders ride up to join the debate. Don Alonso de Aguilar sides with the duke in demanding a hasty retreat, while the Count of Cifuentes and Don Pedro Henriquez want to stand and fight to prove their mettle against the Moors and defend the honor of the queen.

But Ponce de León is no fool, and in the end, logic prevails. Decision made, he curses his own folly in thinking he could achieve surprise. He turns to his second and gives the command, who relays it to the bugler. The man raises his horn and blows a quick burst of shrill notes. Retreat. He repeats the phrase. Again. Word passes through the ranks to turn about, hold formation, and make for the mountains with all haste. Ponce de León's men are assigned to the rearguard to ensure an orderly retreat. As they learn of the decision the knights are torn between disappointment and terror. Even as the orders are given all eyes remain glued on their menacing enemy. Officers bark for attention, and the cavalry reluctantly begins to come about so it can commence withdrawing. Ponce de León continues to glance back at the sultan's cavalry arrayed at the wall. They have not moved, something both surprising and ominous.

Just as the lead squadrons finish turning, the top of the wall to either side of the gate erupts with six, bright-orange flashes, instantly followed by thick billows of ivory smoke, a years-long moment of delay, and then a throaty, concussive BOOM! The harbor guns have been moved. The Moors learned a valuable lesson at Alhama. Their cannons are packed not with solid shot but with arm's-length ropes of chain anchored on either end by fist-sized iron balls, a design intended to devastate rigging on a sailing vessel. Mixed with the links of chain are many dozens of lead balls the size of walnuts.

The Christian knights spontaneously duck in their saddles when they hear the deep blast, then swivel, confused, trying to see exactly what happened. An awful whistling hiss grows louder and louder, seeding a terrible, gut-wrenching expectation, then it is upon them. Heads, arms, hands, large chunks of horse flesh, broadswords, and assorted pieces of crinkled armor scatter through the air in a gory, crimson rush of windy clatter. Horses scream as their legs are cut from beneath them by the looping chains. Some of the massive beasts bite the dust at full gallop, others are toppled like mighty oaks, dumping their riders and mercilessly crushing them.

The cannons are on target; they have clearly been ranged in advance. Ponce de León's rearguard squadron is decimated by the first volley. He slows to survey the damage. The long, tattered swaths of churned earth are now a wriggling mess of bloody gore and hewn flesh choked by groans of the dead and dying. A hundred down, maybe more. Just then he hears the faint cry rise from the city, "Allahu Akbar! Allahu Akbar!" He pivots in his saddle to scan the Moor cavalry just as they begin to leap forward in pursuit. He jabs at the gap between the two foothills and screams commands until he is hoarse. He kicks his mount to a gallop once he sees that the army is again moving.

Another withering volley is loosed. Another hundred drop. Just before the fleeing Christians slide out of range, the guns fire on each spreading flank to hem them in and tighten their retreating column. To devastating effect. The cavalry begins to break ranks, its squadrons dissolving into a frenzied mass as they race for safety. Disorder among cavalry is a dangerous thing indeed.

The duke is in the lead squadron and is the first to see the peril emerge to their right and left. Moor cavalry brigades are spilling across opposite sides of the flanking foothills to block access to the mountain valley. Their javelins are up and ready, arrows nocked, bows at full draw. A pincer movement designed to thwart their escape. The skill of Moor cavalry in unleashing a reign of terror at full gallop is legendary, and rightly feared. The Christians are facing the finest riders in the land. It is instantly obvious to the duke that the Moors have the angle and cannot be outrun except perhaps by the lead squadrons. Half the army will be cut off and trapped. The stragglers will have to fight their way through. He knows firsthand that the heavily armored Christian knights on their massive beasts are no match on open ground for the much lighter and nimbler Moors. He screams at his men to ride like the wind. As the retreating army realizes what is unfolding, panic begins to set in. Always a lethal turn of events in battle.

Only twelve hundred and seventeen knights, less than half their strength, make it off the plains of Málaga and back into the Ajarquía Mountains, and by the time nightfall provides some modicum of cover, the Christian army has dissolved into small clots of riders, ten, twenty, fifty, a hundred, and splintered in a dozen different directions. What else could they do? The sky is overcast, and what moon there was, is no more. Good for hiding, dangerous for navigating unfamiliar mountains.

A large, leaderless group that unwisely opts for the same route through the valley by which they arrived rounds a bend and comes face-to-face with five hundred Moors led by al-Zaghal. Their fighting days are over with the snap of a finger. The first captives of the day, but certainly not the last. The Moor cavalry triumphantly shouts, "AL-ZAGHAL! AL-ZAGHAL! AL-ZAGHAL!"

The group that encounters the mercenary Berber knights in the adjacent valley are not so lucky. The fearsome warriors of the

Maghreb loathe the concept of surrender and ransom, long considered by the desert Bedouin to be a level of cowardice deserving of summary execution. Many of the bodies are mutilated to atone for the insult. The Christians quickly learn Berber predilections and instead begin to fight to the death, which for most comes swiftly, and often cruelly.

Those bands led by veteran commanders—Ponce de León, the duke, the count, a half-dozen others—know to stay away from the valleys, which are patrolled by the Moor and Berber cavalries. Instead, they do their best to scale the heights to the tops of the ridges, no minor feat. In most cases the slopes are much too steep to ride up, so instead horses are dragged by the reins, up-up-up. Armor becomes nothing but a burden under such circumstances and is quickly shed. Even the knight-commanders strip down to their chain mail and tunics.

The lucky rejoice when they manage to cross the paths used by the Ajarquians. They mount up again and start to follow these, hoping for a quick way back to Antequera, a village to mount a defense, a house, anything that provides an ounce of safety. Sad to say, most of these winding paths are unsafe for travel by horse, especially at night. An unlucky slip of a hoof upon loose gravel, a misplaced step, a quick, horrified scream, then nothing. No one can see the cascade of man and beast as they tumble down the slope, only the awful sound left in its wake, which goes on and on, slowly growing fainter and fainter until the victims crumple to a stop hundreds of feet below. Beyond exhausted, the riders reluctantly dismount once more. Most opt to just release their stallions and trudge onward by foot.

The peaks looking down upon the spiderweb of escape routes begin to catch fire one by one, as if by some sorcerer's magic. The bright orange of the pyres of hewn scrub leap and dance skyward in tongues of flame, casting strange shadows over the alien landscape. Soon, dozens of bonfires sprout in the mountains, marking the clots of the retreating knights. The stricken knights stop and stare, numb from shock. Even those not given to piety mutter prayers for deliverance, for mercy. The youngest among them have been brought to tears by the hopelessness of it all. Some of the stragglers simply collapse into a heap, paralyzed, and refuse to move a step farther. They are left behind. In the distance, the silence is interrupted from time to time by the faint pings of metal upon metal, then curses and quick screams. Skirmishes. Some of the Christians manage to escape capture by slipping into the shadows. Most do not. And so it goes.

The Ajarquían shepherds lie in wait and sow havoc through the night, rolling boulders down upon the hapless Christians, raining arrows, sneaking up behind stragglers and slitting their throats, shoving the victims into the abyss, then disappearing. The low point comes just before dawn when a band of seven frazzled knights, veterans to a man, stumble out onto the saddle of a ridge into an enclave of mud huts circled around a communal cooking fire. They begin to search for water. The thirst, dear God, the thirst. It is a tiny mountain village; home of a single clan. The bewildered knights stop and stare, mesmerized, as a group of women step from the shadows bearing sickles and pitchforks and spades. The women do not speak; they simply move to encircle the knights. The men's spirits are broken; they do not resist. They simply drop their swords, lower their heads in shame, and kneel in submission. Their fight is done.

Minor miracles occur. Ponce de León, the duke, and Don Alonso de Aguilar make it out via different escape routes and make their way to Antequera. Haggard, but alive, by the skin of their teeth. Ponce de León manages to extract a hundred-twenty men with him; the others, only half that. Don Pedro Henriquez and the Count of Cifuentes are not so lucky. Don Pedro is struck down by the Berbers, his belly opened with a bejeweled Bedouin dagger and ropey guts spilled beside a stream for the wild dogs to gorge upon. Cifuentes is knocked unconscious and captured by al-Zaghal's men, along with Castile's battle standards. Losing one's standards, whether now or in Roman times, is nothing less than shame heaped upon shame.

Ghost-eyed stragglers in threes and fours and fives continue to drag into Antequera for days. Amazingly enough, three weeks hence, a wild-eyed pair of emaciated knights with only the rags on their back will limp into Alhama. The last of the survivors, lost in the wilderness, subsisting on berries and roots. Many hundreds of men-at-arms who entered the Ajarquía will never be heard from by their families again. Such is war.

The raucous celebration, marshaled by Sultan Abu l-Hasan, the emir of Málaga, and al-Zaghal, stretches on for three days. The citizens are positively delirious with joy at their deliverance from the infidels. The vanquished Christian knights are paraded behind the victorious army, and are bathed in curses and jeers. On foot, Castile's best and brightest, stripped of their armor and weaponry and locked in leg irons, look quite tame. Rotten vegetables sail from the crowds, pummeling the dejected men. Over al-Zaghal's strong protests, the highest-ranking officers are ransomed after all, though they are thrown into the Alcazaba's dank dungeon until the requisite gold for prisoner exchange arrives by emissary some months later. It seems that the sultan required gold to pay his Berber mercenaries for another year. The rest of the knights, however, are either sent as gifts to the emirs of the other cities in the Moorish kingdom, sold to slavers, or locked away in dungeons to rot.

Ya Hayati—My Life

The door opens.

She is concentrating on the transfer of an amber liquid from a mixing beaker into a graduated flask and does not bother to look up.

"Danah?"

Her eyes remain glued to the etched line on the flask as the level slowly rises. Precision is required for this elixir. "Yes, David?"

"Something came for you."

She freezes, though only for an instant, then continues her careful pouring.

"A letter." He opens his mouth to say something more, then thinks better of it. "I will leave it on the table."

Silence, then, "Thank you." Her heart is pounding.

He turns to leave, quietly closes the door behind him.

To her chagrin, her hands have grown unsteady. She frowns her frustration and realizes she will not be able to continue. She sets the flask and beaker down, takes a deep breath, holds it, exhales. She stands, moves to the table, and stares at the thing. A small scroll. She lifts it, examines the red wax. The al-Karim family seal. Malik.

She does not hesitate; she simply rips it open, unrolls the coarse paper, and begins to devour Malik's words. Six lines in, she stops, looks heavenward, and softly mutters, "Thank you, Lord. Thank you."

She returns to the page and reads on, slowing as the weight of his words grows heavy. The young man spills his guts, pours out his wounded soul upon the paper—his disappointment with her, his devastation, his anger. Danah's lower lip begins to quiver. So much honesty, so much hurt. Her emeralds begin to swim, threaten to spill. She rapidly blinks back the tide. She forces herself to read on to the very end. She knows she deserves it, every word of it. She sniffs, thumbs the tears in her eyes. "I am so sorry, Malik. Forgive me. Please forgive me." Her shuddering gasp catches her off guard, then another, then she is weeping, then heaving and sobbing. Breaking the heart of another is a terrible, terrible thing.

Yusef is dressed in his finest courtly attire, sans broadsword and dagger. A dashing prince of the Alhambra. He stands by himself, fidgeting, clearly nervous. But he breaks into a wide smile as he hears them stepping down the stairs.

Mayya comes across the room and stops, facing him. Danah is just behind her, veiled in white silk and wearing her physician's robe. David, Miriam, and Ezar stand to the side, beaming. They will serve as witnesses. The children are seated in a semicircle on the floor, staring wide-eyed, quiet for a change. Samra and the older girls are mesmerized by the romance of it all, of course, but even the boys are awestruck, slack-jawed and rapt.

Yusef takes one step forward, formally bows. "Sayyeda Amiriya."

Mayya returns the bow.

Yusef's face grows serious. "I, Yusef al-Makki, with my whole heart and soul, publicly profess my love for your daughter, Danah. I seek your permission that we might be betrothed and soon marry." He bows once more.

Mayya is fighting back tears. "I, Mayya Amiriya, as Danah's mother and *wali*, and Battal Amiriya, her father, though here in spirit only, grant you, Yusef al-Makki, our permission to ask our beloved Danah for her hand in marriage."

All lower their heads in prayer.

She continues, "May the betrothal vows you both exchange this day, and this coming marriage, be blessed. May this marriage be sweetened with milk and honey. May this marriage offer fruit and shade like a date palm in the desert sands. May this marriage be full of laughter and joy, your every day a day in paradise. May this marriage be a sign of your love and compassion, a seal of happiness both here and in the hereafter. May this marriage have a fair face and a good name, an omen as welcome as the full moon in a clear evening sky. May Allah enter and mingle in this marriage. May your love for each other grow without bound. Amen."

All join in. "Amen."

Mayya turns and lifts the veil from her daughter's face, then steps aside, sniffling. Both she and Miriam are already crying.

Yusef slowly steps forward and lifts his hands so that she can take them. Facing him, Danah stares deeply into his unseeing eyes as they begin their declaration of love.

"Danah Amiriya. With the blessing and guidance of Allah, and with our friends as witnesses, I betroth myself to you, and desire with my entire being that we be joined as husband and wife forevermore." His voice begins to quaver. "My heart and soul will always belong to you, Danah, *ya hayati.*" My life.

Tears begin to leak from her dazzling emeralds. "Yusef al-Makki. With the blessing and guidance of Allah, and with our friends as witnesses, I betroth myself to you, and desire with my entire being that we be joined as husband and wife forevermore. My heart and soul will always belong to you, Yusef, my love and my light."

Tears of joy roll down their cheeks. Together they recite, "We ask Allah, the Loving, the Generous, the Shaper of All Things Beautiful and Holy, to bless our coming marriage. May we always respect each other, always honor and preserve each other, always defend and stand by each other, always seek guidance and advice from each other. May we each find strength in each other's strength, and joy in each other's joy. May your successes be my successes, and may our love for each other grow without bound for all time. We ask Allah, the Glorious, the Light, the Creator of All Goodness, to bless our coming marriage. Amen."

A rousing, "Amen!"

Instantly the room is upon the two of them, shrill squeals and bright laughter from the children, and tears and hugs and back-slaps and congratulations from the others. Such joy is so contagious. Even Ezar, who is not given to such things, is wiping his eyes. David is beyond proud of his new hakim. Little Ummah has wrapped herself around Yusef's leg, holding on for dear life, and even Rashid timidly sidles up to Yusef to bask in his glow.

There is a knock at the door, and eyes turn. In walks a confused Abd al-Salam. "Dear Lord, what is going on in here? From the alley it sounds like a gathering of drunkards that would make even Rumi proud!"

The room bursts into laughter and they rush to encircle the old Sufi master. Danah enfolds him in a bear hug, exciting even more laughter. The old man is adorably taken off guard, but soon he is cackling with the rest of them. Who wouldn't relish the affections of such a beautiful young woman just betrothed.

Miriam raises her voice above the crowd, "Children! Out in the courtyard, time to play. Hurry along now. Samra, please see that they behave. We need some peace and quiet in here."

Ummah chirps, "Can the Man with No Eyes play with us?"

"No. Now go! Shoo! Shoo!" Miriam follows them, waving them out the door. Mayhem departed, she turns and smiles. "You would think they had never seen what love looks like."

They all laugh.

Danah releases her Sufi mentor and returns to the side of her betrothed. The two of them lock hands. David steps forward to greet his friend with a warm smile and an embrace. Abd al-Salam kisses the royal physician on both cheeks, something he has done for many years.

David says, "I thought you would never return to the roost, old friend. It is so good to see you again. Granada has been diminished by your absence. There are many things that you need to catch up on."

"So I hear, David, so I hear. The rumors . . . well, some of them seem hard to believe. But in any case, it is good to be back home. I am afraid it took longer to straighten out Málaga's madrasa than I originally thought. What a mess they made of their curriculum!" He shakes his head. "Now the students will be cursing my name for years, praise Allah." He chuckles.

David says, "You will stay with us tonight." Not an invitation but a friendly command.

The old man beams. "Of course. I would not miss one of your lovely wife's fine feasts."

Miriam playfully says, "The children will insist upon a Sufi tale before bedtime, and their chatter will probably keep you awake half the night."

"Yes, well, I long ago gave up sleeping. Bad habit."

They all laugh.

"Ezar. All is well, sir?"

Ezar mumbles something under his breath, but then his wooly worms arch their backs and he reluctantly smiles. "Best as can be expected I guess. It is good to see you, old friend."

The Sufi's eyes sparkle as he turns to Miriam. "My dear, my heart swells in your presence." He sighs. "If only I were twenty years younger. You are a lucky man, David, a very lucky man." He mock-frowns. "Despite reading your letter a dozen times, Miriam, I cannot for the life of me figure out what so urgently required my presence." He jests. Her letter spelled it out in gory detail. Her principal aim, of course, was to solicit his help with Malik's father in smoothly breaking the betrothal. But she also filled him in on all-things Danah: her becoming hakim, treating the wounded of Alhama, the arrival of Yusef, her dreams of Tetta Layla, the discovery of Yusef's calling, their unfolding love story. She ended by begging him to return to Granada where he rightfully belongs. "How can I be of assistance, my dear?"

Miriam answers with a bright smile, opens her palm to indicate the two of them, then helplessly shrugs.

"Ah." He faces the young couple. "Dear Lord, Danah, you are glowing with the light of a thousand full moons. Could it be love?"

Yusef laughs as Danah blushes.

He correctly infers that Malik's letter breaking their betrothal must have just arrived. Quicker than he would have guessed, but still a welcomed event. After he received Miriam's letter he spoke with Malik's father to smooth things over as best he could—the young man was understandably devastated. Abd al-Salam steps forward and hugs the Falcon prince. "Yusef. It is so good to see you."

"The feeling is mutual, sir."

"That wily old uncle of yours is in good health?"

"Indeed he is. He and Umar are back in Loja."

"Mm. This infernal war with Castile, no doubt. It weighs heavy on my heart."

"Yes, for me as well."

The old Sufi's face grows serious. "I was so pained to hear of your injury, Yusef." The old man sizes him up. "But I must say, you look well. No doubt you have been receiving ample attention from a certain new hakim." He winks.

Yusef smiles—Danah laughs. "I have, sir. And thanks to Danah I have found my calling. A Sufi calling, you will be pleased to hear. Not to be lived with a broadsword in my hand, but by helping those in their time of great need."

Danah cannot stifle her glee.

"Indeed. The Sufi Way. Now that is good news, my boy; fine news. Discovering one's true purpose in life is a Grace we should all desire. Allah is smiling upon you two, I can see that plain as day."

His eyes twinkle as he turns to her. "Danah, you should have seen the look on this young Falcon's face when I informed him that your hand was already spoken for. He blanched white as cotton. I was worried the poor boy was going to faint right there in front of me. I can tell you, it was a sight to behold. I knew in an instant he was smitten with you."

His turn to blush.

She laughs.

Abd al-Salam studies the two of them and reaches the obvious conclusion. "You were betrothed just now."

They beam their answer as they both nod.

"Well, that is enough to make an old man smile." And he does. "Yusef, your uncle and Umar knew of this happy turn of events?"

Yusef replies, "About Danah, yes. About the betrothal . . . alas, no. Danah just received word from Málaga yesterday. We were not sure when they would return from Loja, and well . . . we did not want to wait."

"Mm. Such is young love. They will not be pleased to have missed witnessing this event. Your uncle, bless his soul, never thought he would live to see the day when a beautiful young maiden captured his elder nephew's heart."

"Nor I, sir. I have written to them already. And we will make sure our marriage ceremony includes them."

"Good." The old Sufi turns to Danah's mother. "Mayya. I certainly did not expect to see you here." Their relationship over the years has been tense at times, even acrimonious, particularly in relation to Danah and her future. He knows from experience to tread carefully with her.

"I came to check on Danah."

"I see. No small feat to cross the battle lines, I am guessing."

"No, it was not. Battal arranged it."

"Mm. And when you arrived you found a girl deeply in love." She hesitates. "I did."

"With a young man you did not know."

"Yes."

"And yet you gave your permission."

"I did. When all is said and done, Danah's happiness is my only concern."

He considers her answer. "You did the right thing, Mayya. True love is from Allah and must always be acknowledged as such, despite what protocol tells us, or even what good sense dictates." He ponders this remarkable turn of events. "You have grown as a mother, Mayya. And as a woman. That pleases me deeply."

"I had the help of . . . a friend." She cuts her eyes to Miriam.

He nods his understanding. "The world would be a better place if we all had such friends. I trust Battal is well?"

"He is, thank you."

"And he approves?" He tips his head to the young couple.

"He does. I explained in my letter what I had witnessed firsthand, what I had learned about our daughter. I told him I thought this union was meant to be. Once he got over his shock, he agreed." Her eyes well up. "I just wish he could have been here, Abd al-Salam. This fighting between the Nasrids and the Abencerrajes must end before it—" She stops herself; she does not want to spoil this happy occasion.

"Indeed. I weep for our divided Granada. We must find a path forward and put an end to this reckless strife before lasting harm is done. Alas, tomorrow morning I must brave the wilds of the

Albayzín and attend to the needs of the Sufi madrasa. They have been too long without my guidance. It will afford me the chance to see firsthand how the division of the city is affecting the people. I will also plan to visit Battal and fill him in. Mayya, rest assured, he and I will work together to find some means to get him to the marriage ceremony when the time comes. Leave it to me."

Mayya is crying again. "Thank you."

"David, I would love to have some time catching up on the life of this new hakim in your charge whom I have heard so much about. The one with the Sufi heart who has discovered what it means to love another." He turns expectantly to Danah. "What say you, my dear, are you game for some late-night shared prayer and conversation with a Sufi as old as dirt?"

She is beaming. "I would love nothing more."

"Miriam, would it be a problem for Danah to spend the night here? I am afraid I must leave at first light."

"Certainly not, she can stay with Samra and the girls."

"Excellent, then it is settled."

Danah and Yusef exchange a furtive glance, then look down to evade notice.

Not something to be missed by a Sufi master. Abd al-Salam raises his eyebrows into an exaggerated query. "Unless, that is, you two have some objection to sleeping apart?"

Both of them flush a deep scarlet as they simultaneously blurt out, "Of course not!"

Mayya casts a suspicious eye upon her daughter, as only a mother can.

"Mm. Good. Never fear, you two. It will only be for one night."

David playfully adds, "I would be happy to escort Yusef back to the Bermejas after our feast . . . and see that he gets properly tucked in."

Abd al-Salam continues to scrutinize the two of them with an amused smile. "Miriam, I do believe we better get these two married sooner, rather than later." He tilts his head back and roars.

The rest join the fun at their expense.

The old Sufi opens his arms wide. "Come, let us rejoice and celebrate this marvelous day!"

Following *Isha salah*, evening prayers, the two of them settle side by side upon pillows and together enter the sacred space of Danah's beloved *Muraqaba of Light* that Abd al-Salam taught her so long ago. Later, they retire to the courtyard with steaming mint tea, to be alone and talk beneath the pulsating stars. Their conversation indeed stretches deep into the night.

With a loving smile he gently probes her feelings with his questions, some subtle, some less so. Her hands flit about as she chatters away with pure glee about Yusef, an endearing habit Abd al-Salam has always loved about the girl. The old Sufi says little, simply nods as he listens, from time to time asking another question to lead her onward, deeper. But then she abruptly stops and gets choked up with the sheer intensity of feelings she holds for this young man. A good sign, clearly, and deeply pleasing to him. He reminds her that love is a beautiful gift to receive from Allah. The most surprising thing to him is her ease in sharing about her growing love for Yusef, the absolute certainty of it. She has clearly learned much about herself in the process of falling in love, and has grown in remarkable ways as a young woman since they last were together. Yusef has grown profoundly as well. Abd al-Salam rejoices at the power of love to transform the human heart. He, better than most, knows that if only all people could discover the miracle of love the world would be a much better place.

He was surprised upon reading Miriam's letter to hear about her dreams of Layla al-Khatib, and he asks her about this. Danah relays the whole remarkable encounter in a casual manner, as if a long-dead relative coming to her with advice during her dreams is a normal occurrence. She tells the old Sufi about the lie perpetuated concerning Layla's father, the crescent moon, the Sufi Way, Great Love. She wonders aloud how she came to be Abencerraje given that her ancestry is Nasrid. He notes that she states this as fact, not speculation. He listens intently, brows furrowed. He knows the legend of Lisan al-Din ibn al-Khatib's fall from grace, of course, but makes a mental note to search the records of the Sufi madrasa for any mention of the daughter, Layla. He interrupts her to do some mental calculations. He realizes that Layla must have been under Mansur al-Mussib's tutelage, a legendary Sufi master during the reign of Sultan Muhammad V. If she was indeed a Sufi, there should be some record of her in the madrasa library.

Afterward, he speaks to Danah of tawhid, that mystical union with Allah sought by all Sufis. An extinction of the self to mystically join in unity with the Divine Presence. "Over the centuries many have said that the easiest path to tawhid lies through the sacred love of another, Danah. I pray that you and Yusef have that experience."

"How will I know?"

He pats her hand. "You will know."

Eventually they fall into a comfortable silence, enjoying each other's company under the moonless sky.

"I am counting on you to preside at our marriage."

A warm smile. "I would be honored, my dear. And do not worry, I will find some way for your baba to be present. Otherwise, I am afraid I would suffer the scorn of your mama until my dying breath." They both laugh.

He slaps his thighs. "I have kept you up far too late, my dear. How selfish of me. Off to bed with you now! When I get back from the Albayzín we will talk again. I have so missed our conversations."

"I love you, Abd al-Salam."

"And I love you, my dear."

"Thank you for all you have done for me."

"Danah. Helping you discover your calling, both as hakim, and soon as wife and mother, has been one of the great joys in my long journey back into the loving arms of Allah."

The two of them embrace, and she heads upstairs to bed. He remains where he is and casts his gaze upward into the magical canopy of sparkling diamonds. He chuckles to himself. "Dear, dear Danah. Who would have thought?" In seeming answer, a brilliant streak of emerald slices across the sky toward the horizon, then is gone. He smiles, offers a prayer of gratitude.

She lies awake on her floor mattress listening to Samra's soft snoring. She is beyond exhausted, but her mind is racing still, and sleep is slow to come. Inevitably, her thoughts move to the Bermejas, to his room, to him. She smiles. She sees him curled on his side, sleeping. Or, she thinks, perhaps he is still lying awake too, thinking of me, remembering the words about his desire he spoke that night in his room—*'Trust me, when I ask for your hand and you say 'yes,' and we are finally betrothed, you will find it impossible to keep my hands off you.'* Needless to say, such things to a young woman in love are, well . . . arousing. But she wisely refuses to indulge the fantasy and wills herself back to prayer. She offers silent words of thanksgiving to Allah for the gift of Great Love, for the life of service they will soon share together, for the children to come, inshallah. As she whispers his name over and over—"Yusef, I love you. Yusef, I love you. Yusef, I love you." Her eyes begin their inevitable droop, then close, then open once more, then close for good.

Shimmering gold sparkles hovering next to her in the air awaken her. She rubs her eyes, sits up, and looks to her right. Samra and the girls are sound asleep. She turns and sees that Tetta Layla is coalescing on a floor pillow beside her mattress. She is looking past Danah into the distance, deep in thought. Danah reaches out and touches her tetta's knee. The old woman turns to her and smiles. "My cherished one."

"Tetta Layla. I have missed you so."

"And I, you, my dear." The abiding love the old woman feels for the girl is so plain to see. "You have been busy learning about love."

"Tetta, I was betrothed to Yusef today!" She is effervescent.

"Yes."

"I wish you could have been there."

"I was, my dear, of course I was. I am so happy for you, dear girl. Great Love has found you at last. Allah smiles upon you and your Yusef, Danah. Each of you has found a way to build a bridge within your hearts. Each of you has closed your eyes and crossed the chasm to be together."

"Yes, we have, just as you said we must."

"All praise to Allah."

"All praise to Allah. Tetta, Yusef is Nasrid, and so am I." A statement of fact.

"Yes, Danah, you *are* Nasrid." A drawn-out pause. "And also Abencerraje."

Danah frowns her puzzlement. "How, Tetta? How can that be? I am ready to hear the truth. *Please.*"

The old woman studies her carefully. "Yes, I believe you *are* ready to hear the truth."

"Tell me, Tetta, please. How I can be both Nasrid and Abencerraje?"

The old woman stares into the distance again, recollecting an ancient memory. "After William passed, it was not more than a week before he came around again."

"Who?"

"Zamrak."

"The poet of the Alhambra."

"The one. He said he wanted to console me in my loss, but I knew better. He loved me, you see, or so he said. The night William and I were betrothed he found me alone in the Generalife and professed his love for me. He told me I was a fool to marry a Christian. Alas, Zamrak had no clue about Great Love."

"How did he come to know you?"

"Well, Zamrak was discovered by my father as a young man. Baba took him under his wing and educated him, then saw that he received an appointment at court. Zamrak owed everything that he had to Baba, even his role as court poet. He had known me for years, of course, though to my mind I never did anything to encourage him to fall in love with me. But, such is fate."

"What did you say when he came to visit you?"

An amused smile. "I was livid that he could not find it in himself to respect the memory of my beloved William. I scorned his pathetic overtures." Her smile widens. "No, that is much too weak a word. I eviscerated the poor boy." Her smile fades. "So he had his revenge upon me."

"What did he do?"

"Well, first he went and pleaded his case to my father. I suppose he thought Baba held some sway over me. But that got him nowhere. Baba kicked him out of the apartment and told him not to return. So Zamrak began to scheme, and it turned out he was quite adept at skillful manipulation of others to advance his sadistic plans. He aimed to destroy Baba's good name and reputation, and of course, have his revenge upon me for spurning him. You see, dear girl, by this point Baba had arranged for Zamrak to be appointed private secretary to the sultan. A fatal mistake, sad to say. It gave him ready access to the sultan's ear . . . which he quickly used to his advantage. I warned Baba about this, but he shrugged it off and paid no heed. Baba had too kind a heart for his own good."

"So, what happened?"

"Zamrak began to plant seeds of discord by insinuating that Baba was sympathetic toward the Marinid Empire in the Maghreb and thought that Sultan Muhammad was making a serious mistake by not honoring their entreaties for an alliance with Granada. There was a thread of truth in this. The sultan resented this insinuation, of course. Next, he let slip that Baba was secretly corresponding with the Marinid court without permission. A complete lie. What Zamrak suggested Baba was engaged in would constitute treason, punishable by death. The sultan was skeptical that Baba would be so brazen. After all, Baba had been his trusted grand vizier for many years, and always loyal. Shrewdly, Zamrak also planted this seed in the ear of Granada's ambassador to the Marinid Empire. The ambassador brought his concerns directly to the sultan. Independent confirmation of Zamrak's suspicions. Quite clever. This sordid sowing of seeds went on for some time.

"The suspicions were carefully crafted and honed until Zamrak was ready to make his move for checkmate. Then he arranged to have a forged document drafted and hidden in Baba's apartment. A letter supposedly written by the Marinid sultan and sent to Baba. A letter that revealed state secrets only the sultan and his grand vizier knew. Unbeknownst to the sultan, these state secrets were also discovered by his private secretary while he was supposedly transcribing official court documents. The sultan was a fool to be so easily duped.

"Now convinced of Baba's guilt, the sultan had his apartment searched. They found the letter, of course, and had Baba arrested and brought to trial. It became gossip fodder for the city, for the kingdom. It was a quick conviction by the jury, even with the counter testimony on Baba's behalf by the royal physician, Salamun, and my Sufi Master, Mansur al-Mussib. There was hard 'evidence,' after all, even though Baba swore that it was clearly a forgery and presented arguments to this effect. The qadi did not believe him, and neither did the jury." The old woman sadly shakes her head. "Even Zamrak, the devil, testified on Baba's behalf! Can you imagine?! He wept in front of the jury, *wept*, incredulous that so great a man as his mentor could possibly ever sink to depths of betrayal of the sultan and the kingdom.

"Lisan al-Din ibn al-Khatib, your great-great-great-great-great *jiddo,* was judged guilty of a capital crime, one punishable by beheading."

Danah has tears in her eyes.

"In the end, the sultan could not bring himself to execute his grand vizier, so he instead exiled Baba to the Maghreb, banished forever from his beloved Alhambra. He was given three days to settle his affairs, though all of his wealth and possessions were forfeit by law. He was strictly forbidden from taking anything but the clothes on his back. No books, no letters, no gold, nothing."

"Dear Lord. What happened to Zamrak?"

Tetta Layla smirks. "In retrospect, the obvious, I suppose. He was appointed grand vizier, as Baba's replacement."

"*No.*"

"So goes the evil heart, Danah. Alas, in the end, I foiled Zamrak's plan." A sad smile. "He came to me just after the conviction, not to gloat, exactly, though he was clearly pleased with his triumph over Baba. No, he once again professed his love and implored me to agree to marry him. This time to save myself and my son from shame and exile. His plan all along, no doubt. What nerve the devil had! As if I did not know the truth of his scheming!"

"But you left with your father for the Maghreb."

"Of course I did. Shahab and I departed with Baba for the Maghreb, with absolutely nothing to our name, not even a letter of introduction. There we settled. Exile. Before I left, I gathered my prized possessions together. The *Ambrosian Iliad,* the mahr given by our Umayyad ancestor Zafir to his Great Love, Rayhana. They were the first al-Khatibs, you know—I was the last. The silver plate of their portraits, a lock of Shahab's hair, the Quran given to us by Salamun on our wedding day. William's last letter to me. I put them in my treasure box and hid them all in the Atfal so that they might one day be discovered and hopefully preserved."

"The box Ezar gave me."

"The one."

"You left it for me to discover, Tetta. So that I would seek out your story."

The old woman does not answer, she just smiles and closes her eyes as she recites the poem of Rumi from so long ago.

> *"Face that lights my face, you spin*
> *Intelligence into these particles*
> *I am. Your wind shivers my tree.*
> *My mouth tastes sweet with your name*
> *In it. You make my dance daring enough*
> *To finish. No more timidity! Let*
> *Fruit fall and wind turn my roots up*
> *In the air, done with patient waiting."*

She continues to smile with the memory. "Dear Lord, I loved that man so. Even after all these years I miss him terribly." Her smile fades. "I will never forget the pained look on Zamrak's face the day we left the Alhambra. He got the revenge he desired, Baba's fall from grace, but he did not get the one thing he wanted most—me. It was a sad, sad journey to Africa. We both wept the entire way. The Marinids offered us sanctuary in Fez. They valued Baba, after all, why would they not? He was a famous man. And I suppose it was a way to stick their thumb in the eye of the Nasrids. But Baba's spirit was broken for the rest of his days, brief as they ended up being."

"How sad, Tetta."

"Alas, child, it got worse still. But know, dear girl, deep in your heart, that your jiddo, my Baba, was never a traitor. Never. It was all a carefully crafted lie. Sadly, one concocted because I rejected Zamrak's advances. If only William had lived. If only . . ."

"Tell me the rest of the story, Tetta."

The old woman takes a deep breath and attempts to exhale her pain. Resurrecting these ancient memories is not easy. "Well, as Baba's stature predictably grew at the Marinid court, Zamrak resented it all the more, even if from afar. In the end, barely a year later, he used his influence as grand vizier to secretly recruit an assassin from Persia, whom he sent to Fez. One fine spring morning I came into Baba's room with his hot tea and sweetmeats. He had been strangled. The purpling on his neck left by his murderer was plain enough to see. A letter had been daggered to his chest. It was addressed to me." The old woman's eyes well up, then spill. "His blood is upon your hands, green-eyed devil. Can you guess what comes next? Z."

Danah is crying with her. "I am so sorry, so very sorry."

Tetta Layla sniffs back her tears. "His intended next move was obvious enough. The assassin would be returning for Shahab, my only remaining link to William. Why he chose not to kill my boy when he murdered Baba, I will never know. To stretch out the pain and fear, perhaps. I did what I had to do, the only option remaining to me. I ran. Late that night I gathered little Shahab and I vanished into the desert." She dabs at her eyes.

"Dear Lord, Tetta, to where?"

"Half the villages in the Maghreb, or so it seemed. I had what little gold Baba had acquired in Fez, so we had some means to secure temporary lodging and food for our table, at least for a time. First, we disappeared into the Tazekka Mountains to give the assassin the slip, and then on to Taza. As you might imagine, traveling as a single woman with a young child attracted some attention. And scorn. I told those who insisted on knowing that I was traveling to see my husband's sister on the coast. We moved on to Oujda for a time, then a small village outside Tlemcen, and several months in and around Relizane. But I never felt safe. I was always looking over my shoulder to see who was following me down the street, surprised each morning when I awoke that little Shahab had not been strangled in his sleep. It was an awful time, I can tell you. This living hell continued for almost half a year, seldom more than a week, sometimes two, in any one place. Finally, I decided I needed the safety of a big city. So, I left Relizane for Algiers."

Danah grows wide-eyed. She whispers, "Tetta. The Abencerrajes emigrated to Granada from Algiers."

The old woman smiles. "Well of course they did, my dear. After a few months of getting to know the place, I found what I was looking for. At that time, the Abencerrajes were a relatively small and unimportant clan. Respected, yes, but not yet powerful enough to attract the attention of jealous enemies. And they were no friends of the Marinids." She marvels at the recollection. "It was a perfect place to hide. Most important, though, they were devoted followers of Sufism. Unusual for the Maghreb, at least at that time. Back then, all the Abencerraje imams were Sufi-trained.

"They had settled in and around a hamlet in Algiers called Bachdjerrah, and their Sheikh was a man named Abu l-Fadl. A wise and good man, loved by his people. Shahab and I stayed nearby, and I made myself known to the community as best I could. Eventually I approached one of the Sufi imams, a man named Fulayh ibn al-Awra, and offered my services as a calligrapher. It was a skill I picked up in my own Sufi training. Once he saw examples of my work he took me on as calligrapher for the madrasa he founded, and which served the clan. As it turns out, he knew of my Sufi master, Mansur al-Mussib, if only by reputation. So far so good.

"Of course, the Abencerrajes were naturally skeptical of me as an outsider, but slowly I began to gain acceptance. It took time, and energy. Imam al-Awra helped me continue my training in the Sufi Way, and eventually I was able to talk him into allowing me to teach the young girls whose brothers were students of his at the madrasa. No small feat of convincing, I can tell you! The work I began at the Atfal continued on in the Maghreb."

"How wonderful."

"When the time was right I took a serious gamble with Imam al-Awra, because I had to. I shared my story with him, all of it, and told him of my desire. He knew of my father, of course, and the rumors surrounding his exile. Everyone did, even in the Maghreb. He was kind enough to arrange an audience with Sheikh Abu l-Fadl for me to present my case.

"He brought me to the sheikh and introduced me and stated my request. The sheikh was a serious man, but fair and pious. He wanted to hear my story for himself before rendering judgment. So, I shared it all once more. He listened without offering a single word, though I could tell he was impressed to learn of my Sufi training and what I had done at the Atfal. My heart was pounding as I waited for his decision. He started by asking what I most desired in my heart. I told him. He fingered his beard and nodded for what seemed like hours before he said, 'As Sheikh of the Abencerrajes, I, Abu l-Fadl, proclaim the following: Layla al-Khatib, former Sufi princess of the Nasrid clan, wife of Shahab Chandon, may peace be upon his soul, from this day hence you will live among us as blood-kin, and enjoy the protection of the clan. We will defend you and your son, Shahab, with our lives. You are now Abencerraje.' Well, imagine my reaction, dear girl. I burst into tears and threw myself at his feet and kissed them." She laughs. "Then he said, 'The name al-Khatib is from this day hence unknown to us. You and all your offspring for all time will be called . . . Amiriya.'"

Danah gasps.

She stops to let Danah absorb this. "He then said, 'So that his memory and good name may endure, your son, Shahab, shall know the truth about his jiddo Ibn al-Khatib, may peace be upon his soul. When Shahab marries, his wife shall know the truth, as will his firstborn child. And when that child marries, his spouse shall know the truth, and their firstborn child, and so on for all time. But no others beyond this.'"

"Oh, dear Lord . . ."

"When Shahab came of age I told him, of course, and swore him to secrecy. And when he married Amina, she knew, and then my grandson, Ali Amiriya, and his wife Hawa, and their daughter Nuzha."

"Oh Lord . . ."

"I got to hold Ali in my arms, that beautiful, emerald-eyed little boy, but alas, no Amiriya beyond him. It was one of the reasons I came to you, dear Danah." She hesitates, then continues, "Do you know why the Abencerrajes emigrated from Algiers to Granada a hundred years ago?"

"Baba told me that the Wattasids came to power when they murdered the Marinid royal family in Fez and drove them out of Algiers."

"That is correct. The Wattasids were cruel and intolerant, and they hated the Abencerrajes for their devotion to the Sufis, whom they considered heretics, if you can imagine. Within a short time, it became clear to all that the clan was no longer welcome in the Maghreb."

"And so, the Abencerrajes left for al-Andalus."

"Yes."

"But not you."

The old woman's brilliant emeralds well up once more as she shakes her head. "Because of Zamrak, it was impossible for me to return to Granada. Shahab and Amina were adamant that they would not leave me behind, that they would find some way to remain in the Maghreb. But I could not allow that, of course; it was far too dangerous. And so once more, I ran. Late at night I kissed dear Ali for the last time . . . and I disappeared into the desert. It broke my heart not to say goodbye to my son, all that

462

was left of the Great Love William and I shared." She stops to compose herself.

Danah is weeping.

The silence stretches out. The old woman looks as if she has aged a decade in an hour.

"Then my father knows the history of our family."

"He does. And your mother."

"But they never told me, Tetta."

"No. Another of the reasons I came to you, dear girl. Do appreciate, Danah, that a blood connection to the Nasrids, even a distant one, would be deeply problematic for your father given his status as Abencerraje elder. As you know, the Nasrids are now blood-enemies of the Abencerrajes. And any connection to me and Baba, with the sordid history attached to it, false though it is, would be deeply damaging to your parents within the community. Perhaps even tragic. Still . . . they broke the oath by not telling you. I had to set things right."

Danah mulls this over. "Yusef must know."

"Yes, your beloved must know . . . as well as your son." Tetta Layla smiles.

It takes a moment for this to sink in. Danah lifts her eyebrows in surprise. "My son?"

The old woman continues to smile but says no more.

"Tetta, dear Tetta."

"I love you, child. Now you know the story of how we both came to share these marvelous emeralds of ours."

Danah is beaming. "Thank you for telling me the story, Tetta."

The old woman suddenly looks pained. Her eyes close as a shuddering sigh consumes her. She reopens her eyes. "I am weary now, so weary. My time is short, dear girl, very short. Soon I must rejoin my beloved. William is waiting for me."

"But, Tetta, I need you."

Sparkles of gold begin to dance around the old woman.

"I must rest, child."

"Tetta, no." Danah reaches for her, but there is nothing to grab but air. She is gone.

"Tetta . . . Tetta . . ."

Lucena

"How many made it back?" Terse, and to the point.

The king cannot bring himself to answer. A rider from Antequera arrived just an hour ago. Fernando and the Great Captain were stunned by the terrible news but knew the queen needed to be immediately informed about the crushing defeat in the Ajarquía Mountains.

She feels nothing but disdain for her husband's silence. Her withering glare remains unanswered. She turns. "How many, Gonzalo?" Her tone tightens dangerously.

"A little over eight hundred, all told, majesty."

Queen Isabel's head sinks forward under the weight of this shocking news. "Out of how many?"

"Twenty-seven hundred, majesty."

"Dear God . . . so many. The lion's share of Castile and Aragon's finest men-at-arms. Are we to lose this war before it even begins?" Without warning, her eyes well up. She gave birth only two weeks back. Another girl, Catherine; her fifth child. She has yet to be seen in public. She stands with her arms crossed over her aching breasts, which, though tightly wrapped, still leak milk when her baby cries. Nursing a child is beneath a queen, of course—little Catherine gets her nourishment from a royal wet nurse. Isabel's emotions rise and fall as if some monstrous rogue wave suddenly crests and sweeps over her, only to leave a tranquil sea behind in its wake. The queen's attendants tread upon eggshells when they enter her chambers, not sure whether she will be kind and weepy or furious and caustic, her state each moment seemingly dictated by the random flip of a coin.

She stifles her tears and asks, "Do we know what happened?"

"Only a little, majesty. Somehow the Moors knew that we were coming. By the time the army arrived at the walls of Málaga, Sultan Muley Hacén's army was waiting for us. They fired cannons upon us, majesty—something we did not expect. Ponce de León wisely ordered a retreat, since there was no hope of victory without surprise, but al-Zaghal and the Berbers were waiting in the mountain passes with their cavalry and ambushed us at every turn. There was no easy escape to be had."

"How horrible. Don Alfonso and Ponce de León and the duke?"

"They are safe, majesty."

"Don Pedro Henriquez?"

The Great Captain shakes his head. "He did not return, majesty."

"The Count of Cifuentes?"

The Great Captain again shakes his head.

She releases an anguished sigh. "Don Alonso de Aguilar?" Her voice is developing an uncharacteristic frantic edge.

"Unknown, majesty. I am afraid we have very little information as yet on the dead and wounded."

Fernando recovers his voice. "You can be sure that not all are dead, Isabel. A large number were evidently captured. The men of rank will be ransomed, God willing."

She turns on her husband and sneers. "With what gold, Fernando, tell me please? What gold?" Even with what they have garnered so far from the Inquisition, Castile's treasury remains bare. Fielding an army is no small expense.

The king has no answer.

The queen's expression softens. "Thanks to your wisdom, Gonzalo, at least little Catherine still has a father."

Neither man responds. It indeed proved judicious to insist upon the king's return to Córdoba.

"Isabel, we will push harder now to complete the outfitting of the army. I will make the Moors pay dearly for their treachery. This time we will return with a dozen heavy cannons in tow, so we can lay siege to their castles."

"Mm." She seems unimpressed, distant.

The Great Captain does his best to try to boost the queen's spirits. "Even the mighty castles of the Moors will not be able to resist the French cannons, majesty. Their cities will soon fall one by one as we tighten the noose around Granada and strangle her."

Fernando adds, "I aim to put the Vega to the torch, Isabel, to starve them out. And I will march the army to the gates of Málaga and lay siege to that cursed city. They will pay for their deeds, you may depend upon it."

She nods. "Let us hope. With these losses we must have more men-at-arms if we are to win this war. I will issue letters to all the kings of Europe. A call for cavaliers to join my crusade against the Moors. Pope Sixtus IV will be happy to offer indulgences to all who take up their swords to fight the Moors. Perhaps even gold for wages and arms." Her expression hardens. "We shall have our revenge upon Muley Hacén; we *shall* have it. See that my army is ready to march within the month."

The Great Captain bows.

Fernando says, "You shall have your triumph over the Moors, Isabel. Be patient." An unwise choice of words.

She glowers at her husband. "Patient? *Patient?!* I need a victory, Fernando. See to it."

A sober nod from the king. As the two men turn and leave, a pair of bodyguards enter and take up their stations beside the door.

The queen walks to the window and stares out upon the bustling courtyard. She brings her hands together in prayer. "Grant me, O God, victory in thy Holy Name, that your Son, Christ Jesus, may rejoice in my deeds. Aid thy humble servant, O God, purify my heart, that I may smite the Moors and rid this land of them. Amen." She genuflects, then turns to her bodyguard. "Send for Talavera; I have need of his services."

A brisk knock.

"Enter."

The adjutant bows. "My lord. Signal fires have been sighted."

Diego Fernandez de Córdoba, Count of Cabra, rises from his desk. "Where?" The count is pudgy with middle-age, his best fighting days behind him. Still, he has an abundance of experience in frontier skirmishes, often a game of cat and mouse, incursions by small raiding parties that strike quickly and retreat to the safety of the Moorish kingdom. He is fiercely loyal to the queen, and takes chivalry quite seriously, even with one's sworn enemy.

"The beacon east of Rute, my lord."

"The number?" The frontier signal system consists of carefully placed mountaintop signal fires. One bonfire means a band of Moor riders on the move; two bonfires means a full-fledged Moor raiding party making for Castilian territory; three bonfires means an attacking battalion of Moor cavalry; four bonfires means an attacking Moor force one thousand strong, with cavalry and infantry; and five bonfires, clearly cause for alarm, means an attacking Moor army larger than five thousand men is approaching.

"Five, my lord."

The count muses. "Dear God, what now?" His jaw juts out. "The Rute beacon, you say?"

"Yes, my lord."

He considers the possibilities. "The Moors make for Lucena, then, just as Don Gonzalo de Córdoba said. Sound the alarm and spread the word. Send a rider to alert the commander of the garrison at Lucena to what is coming his way, and tell him we are assembling to aid in his defense and will be there as quickly as possible. Send riders to Zuheros, Doña Mencia, Llanos Espinar, Vereda de Cerro Macho, and Monturque. Oh, and Gaena-Casas Gallegas. I want every man-at-arms my vassals possess." He widens his eyes to make himself clear. "*Every. Single. Man.* Understood?"

"Yes, my lord."

"We will rally at Cabra castle. I intend to be at Lucena by first light. Oh, and send word to La Rambla, Santaella, and Montilla. The marquess has pledged fealty to ride with me against the Moors in times of need. I am afraid that time has arrived."

"My lord, they will not reach us until mid-morning."

He muses. "No, I suppose not. Send word anyway. And go ahead and send word to Córdoba. The king and queen must know what is unfolding. Tell them . . . tell them the Count of Cabra and every able-bodied man in his realm is riding to the defense of the queen and Castile. Godspeed, man!"

The Count of Cabra moves to the window and stares into the blackness of the mountains. "So it comes to this . . ." His voice hardens. "I will have my vengeance on the Moors for Loja. That, or die trying, so help me God."

The first alarm bell on Cabra castle sounds. "*Clang-clang-clang. Clang-clang-clang. Clang-clang-clang.*" Other bells begin to follow suit as the castle springs to life.

The march of Boabdil's army began as planned, slipping out of Granada without detection and traveling only under cover of night. Still, by the third day of cold food, the infantry was grumbling, and cooking fires began to sprout up here and there when they stopped to camp just past dawn. Wood smoke is not something that can be easily disguised. Aben Comixa cautioned Boabdil about this, to no avail. "Relax. We are past Loja now, and only a half-day from Lucena. Even if the Christians do manage to catch sight of the army they will not have time to sound the alarm."

The grand vizier frowned his response. Aben Comixa has zero experience as a battlefield commander, but some things are obvious. The value of surprise, for one. He was ordered by Abu al-Haytham to accompany the young sultan-in-waiting, to offer advice and hopefully keep things on track for a victory.

Boabdil, despite his bravado, has only fought in one real battle, at Zahara. Since that minor victory emboldened him, he lives for the allure of conquering hero and savior of the realm. A childhood fantasy writ large. His mother has ensured he looks the part at least. Over his trousers and quilted tunic, a long, crimson velvet marlûta overcoat, embroidered with elaborate swirls and designs using pure-gold thread; turban cloth of the finest white cotton and long tassels of Granadine blue; tan calf-leather slippers and overboots. Embossed steel chest armor studded with gold nails and lined with crimson velvet. A finely tooled steel helmet with inlaid rubies; priceless broadsword of tempered Damascus steel; bejeweled Granadine ear-dagger. A heart-shaped leather shield engraved with Quranic verses and Granada's insignia. He rides a beautiful, solid-white charger, big for an Andalusian stallion, a regal beast that struts among lesser horses. The animal's elegant, arched neck is draped in Granadine blue and white silk, a finely hewn wooden saddle, and tack of the most expensive oiled leather, with a polished silver bit and fittings. If only appearances defined leadership skill in battle.

Early morning on the fifth day, Aben Comixa storms into Boabdil's lavish tent. "We have been sighted, sire!"

"How do you know?"

"Signal fires on the mountains east of us."

Boabdil waves him off. "So what?"

"The Christians will know our strength, sire, and our target will be obvious."

Boabdil stops to consider this. "Fine." He stands. "Spread the word. We will quicken our march for Lucena. When I arrive at their gates I will issue an ultimatum to the castle commander to either surrender, or I will put the entire town to the sword."

The grand vizier just blankly stares. "And if he refuses, sire?"

Boabdil frowns. He has apparently not considered this possibility. "Then we will lay siege to the city, of course, and he shall pay the price."

"But what about—"

"Leave me."

"*But, sire?*"

"Leave me!"

"You *cannot* be serious?" Ali al-Attar scowls at his nephew.

"I am afraid I am, Uncle. It is Boabdil all right. My men said his standard was easy enough to see. He was riding that white charger of his, bedecked in all his court finery and frills, as if those made him a real knight-commander. He will find battling the well-armed Christian army a little different than tournament jousting, I am afraid."

"Where?"

"Just this side of Rute. The smoke from cooking fires gave them away, if you can believe that. My men were astounded."

Ali al-Attar curses. "A lack of field discipline tends to get good knights killed, Umar."

"Yes. Once they resumed their march, my men moved closer to assess their strength."

"And?"

"Surprising. Almost ten thousand—nine thousand infantry and seven hundred cavalry. Boabdil clearly intends to lay siege. My guess is Lucena."

The old warrior considers this. "Agreed. Then he clearly does not know that Fernando already took most of his army back to Córdoba."

"It would appear not."

Ali al-Attar shakes his head. "Hard to believe that stupid boy has the sultan's blood flowing in his veins."

"Mm. Not an easy person to respect, despite his bloodline."

"Well, if your men spotted his army so easily, the Christians will soon be aware of his presence too."

"I am afraid they already are. The signal fires at Rute were sighted an hour ago."

"I see. I wonder if the fool has ever seen someone strike a hornet's nest with a stick? He soon will. Half of the borderlands will already be mustering to ride to the aid of Lucena."

"Yes. What should we do?"

The old man grumbles as he strokes his beard. "My *desire* is to let him make his own bed and lie in it." He frowns. "But then I think of all the mothers in Granada who will never see their boys again. We must ride in support, Umar. I will never join with his army in a fight. Instead, we will stand in the wings in case he does something foolish enough to put his entire army at risk. Then we will move, but only to alleviate the danger."

"That will require some nuance, Uncle." Umar smiles.

Ali al-Attar smiles warmly at his nephew. "Nuance is my middle name, boy. Your cavalry will flank him to the west; mine to the east. But stay out of sight, no closer than a mile. Use scouts to track his march and reconnoiter the enemy position as they close on him. Remember. We will not engage unless disaster looms."

"Should we bring Yusef's cannons?"

The old warrior shakes his head. "No. They would only slow us down. Assuming Boabdil makes it to Lucena unscathed, that battle is his to lose. I will not get sucked into a futile siege of an empty castle."

Umar nods, "Understood."

A soft knock and the door cracks open. "Sultana? High Elder Abu al-Haytham is here to see you." Her eunuch bodyguard.

"Show him in, Muflit."

The white-bearded wizard dressed in all black rudely pushes past the bodyguard. "I assume you heard the news?" His voice betrays an uncharacteristic touch of panic.

She calmly looks up. "I have." Her tone is even, smooth as silk.

"As you know, Fatima, another Nasrid victory is something we can ill afford. Our cause is teetering."

Fatima stares at the old wizard. "What would you have me do, Abu al-Haytham? Weep?"

He ignores this. "My sources are telling me the sultan and al-Zaghal somehow managed to annihilate the entire Christian army in the Ajarquía Mountains. And they lost only a hundred men doing it."

"Even *I* would admit that my husband has some skill on the battlefield, Abu al-Haytham. His brother is even more gifted in such matters. I certainly would not want to fight them."

"Twelve-hundred prisoners, many of them famous men-at-arms. A complete rout. *Worse* than Loja."

"Ninety-seven killed, to be precise. And twelve-hundred thirty-four prisoners, including six counts and eleven minor dukes, three high-ranking officers in the Order of Santiago, two from the Order of Calatrava, and four from the Order of Alcantara. They even captured the Order of Santiago's battle standard." She cannot resist demonstrating the superiority of her spy network.

He opens his mouth to speak, then closes it. Point taken. "Any word from Boabdil?"

She answers, "He should have reached Lucena by now, I should think, and hopefully is beginning his siege of Fernando's army. That is, of course, unless Fernando had advance warning of our army's approach and decided to leave the safety of Lucena's walls and challenge my son to a fight on open ground. Unlikely, I would say, but always a possibility."

"Let us pray that Boabdil enjoys success. We need our own victory, and very soon."

A condescending sniff. "You must trust in the providence of Allah to support our worthy cause, Abu al-Haytham." She chases this with her best cunning smile.

The bite of the sultana's sarcasm does not escape the old man. He mutters something unintelligible, but the gist is obvious.

"Abu al-Haytham, we must preemptively announce to all of Granada that Boabdil has taken up arms and is marching to defeat King Fernando at Lucena, and carefully paint a picture of my son's unselfish quest to rescue the kingdom from the Christians." She muses. "Call it jihad against the infidels. This must be done before word spreads about Málaga. It will take some time for my husband to return to celebrate his triumph. Trust me, he will relish the moment and milk it for all it is worth, first on the streets of Málaga, then in every town he passes on the journey back. It is vital that we make the most of what time we have left until he arrives. When he finally rides into the city, Boabdil must already be trumpeting his own victory, hopefully with a captive king in tow."

This time, the wizard grumbles. The man clearly has his doubts about Boabdil's chances.

"You must be a true believer, Abu al-Haytham." That cunning smile returns.

The wizard scowls at her, but he knows she is right about the importance of a well-placed propaganda campaign. He finally says, "I will set things in motion today." Without another word he turns and vanishes.

Fatima's smile slowly fades. She realizes better than anyone what is at stake at Lucena.

"But, sire, I am duty-bound to tell you—splitting our forces is unwise." Almost a whine.

Remarkably, Boabdil's army, discreetly dogged by a thousand of Loja's cavalry, makes it to Lucena by early afternoon. The countryside is completely devoid of any human presence, a fact Boabdil naively assumes means the populace had taken sight of the approaching army and retreated to the safety of the city walls for refuge. His undisciplined army constantly breaks ranks as they approach Lucena to raid and take booty from the farms and villages—livestock, grain, cured hams, jewelry, gold, anything of value. When the army arrives at the city gates, the town is locked up tight and unnaturally quiet. Boabdil rides forward with his officers and bannermen to great fanfare and offers his ultimatum. To no answer. Boabdil gives the command to lay siege.

"Aben Comixa, all is well. Siege is a simple matter. We dig in and cut off all paths for food and water into the city. There is nothing to worry about."

"And if we are attacked from the surrounding countryside before our defenses are ready? With no cavalry to support the infantry? We still have no sight of King Fernando's army, you know. None at all. For all we know, he is rallying his men to attack right now." A spineless, cowardly taint clings to Aben Comixa like glue. The man has no business being second-in-command on the field of battle.

A condescending smirk from Boabdil. "Trust me, Fernando's pathetic army, what is left of it, is presently cowering behind the safety of Lucena's walls. They will soon suffer the consequences for defying me. If it makes you happy, I promise not to go farther than Aguilar de la Frontera. I must strike fear into the heart of Queen Isabel. Think of it, Aben Comixa. The bitch will tremble when she hears that my cavalry is riding for Córdoba. I will gather booty and prisoners to parade through the streets of Granada."

"But, sire?"

"Aben Comixa. All is well. I will be back to Lucena by morning."

The grand vizier looks terrified.

Lightning flashes in the sky to the east, the golden zig-zag throwing a bronze glint against the menacing dark cloud that gave birth to it. Then, nothing but darkness. Another strike off to the right; a third farther south. Then, a horizontal strike between clouds to the north of the others that snakes in a dozen directions and just hangs in the sky before vanishing. Still too far away to hear thunder. A line of storms is approaching.

The Count of Cabra manages to muster two hundred and fifty mounted men-at-arms and twelve-hundred footmen, a seven-to-one disadvantage against the Moors. Riders brought word of an additional force of six hundred mounted men-at-arms and eleven hundred footmen coming from the towns of La Rambla, Santaella, and Montilla to the north, but alas, even at double time they will not arrive until mid-morning. A slow, sober nod as the count reads the letter from the Marquess of La Rambla. He turns to his second. "Help is on the way, but we must be in Lucena by first light. Pass the word. We march!"

"Yes, my lord."

Boabdil's cavalry fans out and raids the unsuspecting countryside along the road linking Lucena and Córdoba. Even with the advanced warning of the signal fires, there is virtually no organized resistance, and what little is offered is swiftly cut down. His raiders burn village after village and pillage as they go, seemingly unaware that the plumes of smoke marking their passage are visible for many miles.

As promised, he halts at Aguilar de la Frontera, where resistance is beginning to stiffen. His men manage to force the gate, round up prisoners, then they put the town to the torch. He begins to retrace his steps toward Lucena, only now with a hundred pack-mules loaded down with booty, and four hundred prisoners on foot crudely roped together. His newly accumulated wealth slows his cavalry to a crawl.

The Moorish siege works are not even close to complete when the count's attack commences just before sunrise. Much of the Moorish infantry is still sleeping. Boabdil's cavalry is still four miles to the north, lumbering toward Lucena.

With so few men at his disposal, the Count of Cabra wisely opts to use his cavalry as a battering ram, with infantry following in close support, to first puncture the enemy siege encirclement and then strike for the main gate from within the circle. The garrison commander, who can easily see what is coming from atop the castle tower, musters his troops and throws open the main gate to lead his six hundred footmen out to link up with the count's forces, sowing mayhem through the unsuspecting ranks of the Moor infantry. A wide swath of the siege ring collapses, and panic among the Moors quickly ensues.

The sounds of battle on the opposite side of the city first raise puzzled looks in the command tent, then concern, then a frantic call to arms. Trumpets blare. Aben Comixa scurries about, shouting conflicting orders at his confused officers as he tries to learn what is actually happening. The knight-commanders desperately struggle to rouse the men and establish order in the ranks to organize lines of defense for the presumed assault that is coming. All assume that King Fernando and his army are upon them.

As the battle continues to unfold, some of the dazed Moor infantry in the path of the onslaught predictably drop their weapons and run, and within minutes, word races through the ranks, wild and conflicting reports of enemy strength and tactics. "Five thousand cavalry from Córdoba have broken through our lines. King Fernando and his army are spilling out of Lucena like ants. Thousands." On and on it goes. The veteran knights attempt to shout this nonsense down, but such wild-eyed proclamations soon gain a life of their own.

Despite the fact that no one has yet to see any real evidence of King Fernando and his massive Christian army at their doorstep, Aben Comixa, heart pounding and growing increasingly agitated, rashly gives the order to immediately lift the siege and retreat southward to safer ground that can be defended. Despite scornful glares from his officers, no one dares question his judgement. Riders race to deliver orders to the Moor knight-commanders encircling the city. A disorganized retreat commences, to the wild cheers of the Count of Cabra's and Lucena's men. So go the unpredictable fortunes of war.

On a bluff a half-mile to the east, and with the rising sun at his back, Ali al-Attar watches this unfold with a chiseled scowl and a storm of curses. He refuses, however, to enter the fray. He summons his adjutant, asks for writing materials, and scribbles a note.

> *Siege lifted. Unclear who is attacking. My guess is Cabra. Army now in retreat toward Rute. Do NOT engage. Follow Boabdil until he returns. I shall remain on the east flank of the retreat. You stay west. Send word when you arrive. Uncle.*

He folds the communique, hands it to the man. "For Prince al-Makki's eyes only. Quickly."

"Yes, my lord."

"By God, Juan, I aim to give chase!" The count is flushed with the thrill of victory. "Dear God, man, the cowards are running from us. Running! And my scouts say the fools are marching along the road back through Rute, not cross-country. Easy prey. They are beaten, Juan, I can feel it in my bones. They are racing for the safety of home. We cannot let them escape across the River Genil. Now is the time to strike some fear in the Moors; chase them all the way back to the Kingdom of Granada with their tails between their legs! Loja, man, I will have my revenge for Loja!" His face is alive with bloodlust.

The garrison commander, himself a seasoned veteran of border skirmishes, replies, "I agree with pressing the attack, Diego, but not without reinforcements from the marquess. Even if beaten, the Moors still greatly outnumber us." A logical argument.

The count grumbles his displeasure but concedes. "Fine. The marquess will be here by mid-morning latest. We march the instant he arrives."

"Very well. You shall have half of my garrison."

"Good." The Count of Cabra turns to his second. "Get the men ready. As soon as the marquess arrives we march for battle!"

"With pleasure, my lord."

As the Moor army approaches the village of Llanos de Don Juan, the storm line finally spills out of the mountains, bearing down upon them like a charging bull. The lightning has thankfully vanished, having been wagered upon the high peaks, but the clouds are swollen tight with rain, dark and menacing things. The smell of rain hangs heavy upon the wind, whipping and snapping the army's banners. A translucent wall stretching from cloud to ground marks the edge of the coming onslaught. Closing rapidly.

Aben Comixa's adjutant touches his shoulder and points. The dejected grand vizier raises his eyes and winces just as the first drops begin to fall. Within thirty seconds a giant stopcock is turned, and thick sheets of rain sweep across the Moors with a heavy, dull "*SHHHHHHH*," erasing the landscape. Heads down and sullen, the army trudges onward in the deluge.

An hour later, at Zambra, four miles shy of Rute, the army finds some cleared farmland with high ground that at least passes for defensible, and after desperate pleas by the knight-commanders, Aben Comixa gives the word to halt and wait out the storm. Scouts are sent to inform Boabdil of their location and to make sure he knows to bypass the trouble at Lucena.

"How dare you lift the siege and order retreat without consulting me? You fool! We had Fernando surrounded and in our grasp. HOW DARE YOU?!" Boabdil is livid.

Aben Comixa cowers. The man raises his hands as if to fend off a blow. "They were upon us, sire. Many thousands of them. King Fernando's entire army, sire."

Nearly two hours elapsed before Boabdil's cavalry, mules, and prisoners managed to link up with the rest of the army. The scouts had them swing wide around Lucena and cut across the countryside to Zambra. As if by magic, the storm has passed, and now there is blue sky and sun, though a dense shroud of mist has swallowed the entire landscape, cutting sightlines to nothing.

The young sultan-to-be continues to fume. "So *you* say, Aben Comixa. My knight-commanders saw no such army. A few hundred cavalry and some infantry. You were duped into retreating." He turns on his officers and glowers, challenging any one of them to contradict him. The men remain silent.

The grand vizier has nothing to offer in his defense.

Boabdil begins to pace as he tries to decide what to do. He stops and turns on them. "I aim to march back to Lucena to finish what we came for. The booty and prisoners will be sent home as evidence of our great campaign. With more to come." The young man brightens with his decision, rash though it may be. His officers seem troubled by this intended course of action, but keep their mouths closed. "And if King Fernando dares challenge us on open ground, I will crush him and bring him back to Granada in chains! Understood? Well?!"

The men offer their reluctant concurrence.

"Now, make your preparations and—"

Eyes turn as a scout gallops up and dismounts, races forward, and bows. "Sire. News."

"Out with it!"

"Enemy cavalry sighted, sire. Closing quickly from the west."

Unease circles the gathering.

"How far?"

"A half-mile, sire."

"How many?"

"Impossible to tell, sire, the mist is too thick. It appears to be a large force, though. Multiple battalions of armored knights."

Boabdil suddenly looks uncertain about what to do.

The knight-commander standing beside him says, "Sire, we must sound alarm and make ready for battle."

Boabdil recovers himself, "Yes. Of course. Sound alarm. All is well, gentlemen. After all, we have the high ground." The young man suddenly sounds tentative.

Aben Comixa's face is beaded with sweat, and he looks as if he might faint.

The Count of Cabra and the Marquess of La Rambla have split their forces, the former attacking from the woods to the west, the latter from the north, down the road leading to Rute. Their scouts have already informed them of the location of the Moor army, and they have laid their plans for a coordinated assault. By stroke of luck, their modest strength, still nearly a five-to-one disadvantage in numbers, is obscured by the thick mist, and they know how to take full advantage of such good fortune.

Boabdil, Aben Comixa, and the cavalry sit atop their mounts in formation behind the first line of infantry, who are arrayed in close ranks, staggered battalions of crossbowmen and pikemen. They do not possess enough cavalry for standard Moorish battle tactics, which typically enjoy the advantage of superior mobility. The officers feel vulnerable to a direct assault by fully-plated men-at-arms, and they are. This is an army designed for siege, after all, not close-quarter combat.

The sun is struggling mightily against the eerie, mist-shrouded landscape, with little progress. The air stills with the anticipation of violent battle and death.

As the Count of Cabra approaches the rise where he knows the Moors lie in wait, his men spread out into a wide arc, then halt. He can see nothing to his front but opaque, steamy-white mist. He gives the word, and on command, every single man in the count's force breaks into blood-curdling screams and begins banging his broadsword hilt again his chest armor, making as much noise as he is able. Strategically-placed battle trumpets begin to sound, giving the impression of a large army a quarter-mile wide preparing to attack.

Aben Comixa's eyes grow monstrous. "Dear Lord, have mercy on us." He wets himself, causing his indignant mount to rear and whinny, bucking him off. His stallion tramples him as it dashes for safety, breaking both leg bones just below the knee, then crushing his skull with a hoof to the head. A quick, terrified scream, and it is over. The pathetic little man's demise is barely noticed.

Boabdil spurs his mount among his troops, shouting, "The enemy army is upon us, men! We fight for the honor of Granada!" His words are the correct ones, but the bravado in his voice is beginning to wear thin. "Prepare for attack!"

Weapons are readied, and the infantry braces for the coming assault of armored Christian horsemen.

The screams and trumpets down the hill in front of them suddenly cease. The silence is deafening. Now the sounds of galloping horses to their front, growing louder. Heavy cavalry charging. Ominous. Those in the front ranks exchange uneasy looks, shift their stances, then tighten their grips on their weapons. The devout begin to mutter prayers.

A rider gallops up to Boabdil. "Sire! We are also being attacked from the north. The north, sire! Along the road. Armored cavalry sighted, sire! Thousands, sire!" Even the scout is rattled.

Boabdil looks stunned. "*What?*" His head snaps back to the thunder growing in front of him. "But that is not possible." Distant screams and banging on armor and dozens of battle trumpets now begin to sound to the north. Uncomfortably close. A pincher movement upon his position. Boabdil is paralyzed in his saddle, each of his prized stallion's ears cocked at sharp angles toward the violence that is coming for them.

One of his officers rides alongside and barks, "Sire, we must retreat! We cannot stand against thousands of armored cavalry—we will be annihilated. The king's army is upon us. We must retreat, sire, and quickly. Sire! SIRE!"

Boabdil recovers, "Sound retreat. We make for the road to Rute." He screams, "See to it! Now, before it is too late. I want a fighting retreat! Call the cavalry up to protect the rearguard as we withdraw."

Trumpets sound retreat, and the Moor army begins to withdraw down the rise toward the road. To their credit, this retreat is better organized than the one at Lucena, and the cavalry does, in fact, secure the rearguard. The count and marquess each emerge from the swirling mist and engage the Moor cavalry, but only briefly before they break off their pursuit, content to let the Moor army retire from the high ground where they had an advantage. The Count of Cabra's aim is to confuse and demoralize the Moors, then launch quick cavalry thrusts at the retiring flanks to harass and further disorganize the enemy. Then, when the time and place is right, move in for the kill.

The mist slowly begins to lift under the hot stare of the late-morning sun.

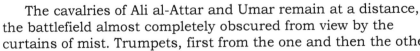

The cavalries of Ali al-Attar and Umar remain at a distance, the battlefield almost completely obscured from view by the curtains of mist. Trumpets, first from the one and then the other of the Christian battalions, then from the sounding of retreat by the Moors. It takes little time for the old man to deduce the calamitous flow of events. He sends for information from his scouts, and ten minutes later one arrives with news.

"Which direction are they retreating?"

"South, my lord. Toward Rute."

The old man curses. "Too predictable. They will be nipping at his heels all the way to the river." He takes paper and quill from his tunic.

> *Fool is retreating with five-to-one numbers. Road to Rute. I will ride in advance to ensure the Count of Rute does not challenge the retreat. You see that the Christians break off their assault of the rearguard. Do NOT engage more than necessary. Uncle.*

He summons a rider. "For Prince al-Makki's eyes only. Quickly, man!"

As predicted, the Count of Cabra and the Marquess of La Rambla harry the retreating army every step of the way. Unwisely, Boabdil refuses to part with his booty and prisoners, further slowing the progress of the retiring army. Hundreds of Moors in the rearguard are cut down between Rute and La Celada during the series of quick-hitting skirmishes, and the inevitable clots of stragglers are easily separated from the main force, rounded up and captured.

Ali al-Attar and Umar hold their distance on the east and west of the road back to the kingdom, holding at a half-mile, protecting the army's flanks, but otherwise not engaging. Boabdil is not even aware of their presence. The Christian commanders are well aware, of course, and while they remain puzzled that the Moor cavalries do not choose to engage, they seem satisfied to keep a wary eye peeled and let them be.

The Moor army makes for the safety of the border. The army pauses to regroup for the final push when it reaches Iznájar, a quiet little town on a bluff overlooking the River Genil, which marks the uneasy dividing line between Castile and the Kingdom of Granada. The plan is to ford the river to safety, then make their way east, bypassing Loja, then on to Granada. The Christians would not dare cross the river in pursuit, or so they hope. If they do, Boabdil will stop and solicit the aid of Loja, which, while controlled by the Nasrids, has the most formidable castle-garrison in these parts.

Boabdil and several of his officers kick their mounts to the edge of the bluff to survey their intended escape route. Eyes widen as the panorama spreads before them. The River Genil, typically shallow enough to wade across, and at best fifty feet wide, is now a swollen and angry torrent, a fast-moving, head-high muddy mess quadruple its normal breadth. The River Genil is known to be prone to flooding, especially during the rainy season, but this is completely unexpected by everyone.

The officers just stare, dumbfounded.

Boabdil curses. "Dear Lord, what now?"

One of the officers says, "The violent rains, sire. They must have passed this way."

Another states the obvious. "Impassable, sire."

Boabdil stares the man down. He turns in his saddle. "How long before we can cross?"

"In my experience, sire, two days, perhaps three."

Boabdil screams, "We do not have days, man! Can you not see what is following us, you fool! The Christians are cutting down or capturing hundreds of our rearguard with every mile we cover. If we turn and fight, our backs will be against the wall, and soon there will be nothing left of us!" That unseemly frantic edge has returned to the young man's voice.

A third officer chimes in, "Sire, the ford due south of Fuentes de Cesna might work."

"*Where?*"

"Fuentes de Cesna, sire. A three-hour march along the river. There is a place where the valley widens out. It should spread the river out, slow it down some, and hopefully make it shallow enough to ford."

Boabdil seems skeptical. "You have been there?"

"Yes, sire. I grew up in Ventorros de la Laguna, a mile south of the ford. Challenging to cross, but still passable during rainy season. I have made the crossing myself."

Boabdil weighs this. There are no good options. "Very well. We turn east and follow the Genil valley until we can ford. The Christians will surely follow. Spread the word, and make haste." A grim, uneasy smile settles on the young man's face. "Oh, and have the men round up some prisoners and put Iznájar to the torch. It is the least we can do for Castile's hospitality. Make it so!"

"Of course, sire."

"What is Boabdil thinking? Stupid fool." Ali al-Attar and his second are at the edge of a cliff on a high bluff a quarter-mile due east of the army, overlooking the ford at Fuentes de Cesna. Umar's cavalry is clearly visible in the distance, close to the river's edge a half-mile west of the crossing. Unlike Umar, Ali al-Attar has a perfect sightline of the advancing Christian army, which has divided into a three-pronged assault and is closing rapidly on

Boabdil's precarious position, which has devolved into a disorganized crush of thousands of troops bunched at the river's edge trying desperately to ford the chest-deep, swiftly moving muddy water.

The Moor infantry massed at the river's edge easily spans five hundred paces. No formations, no order, no discipline, no nothing. One by one the men tentatively begin to wade in, but many only make it halfway across before losing their footing and being carried with the muddy current quickly downstream. To save themselves they are forced to ditch their weapons, gear, and what booty they still carry, and try their best to swim for the safety of the opposite bank. Some never mastered that art, or else refuse to drop their belongings, and drown in the torrent, predictably inducing panic in those about to attempt their own crossings. The ones who make it to the other side are safe, for the time being at least, but largely unarmed.

The booty-loaded mules and the hundreds of roped prisoners cower in a tight circle near the water's edge. Thinking only of their own escape, the Moors seem to have forgotten they are even there.

The cavalry gathered on the flanks has an easier time with the ford, but now half of Boabdil's cavalry is across the Genil, exposing the army to attack, which is quickly coming.

The old man turns to his adjutant. "Hasan, I am afraid the time has come for us to act. If we do not give them time to cross the Genil, the army will perish. Abencerraje or not, I cannot watch that happen. He takes out paper and begins to scribble a note.

> *Disaster looming. Three-pronged assault imminent. I will attempt to stave off the east prong. You try for the west. Hopefully Boabdil can handle the middle. We will join forces when we are able. Uncle.*

"See that this gets to Prince al-Makki. You will have to circle wide, so it will take some time. Hopefully he can see what is happening from where he is. Tell the men to ready their weapons. We ride."

By the time Ali al-Attar joins the fight, the Christian cavalry attacking the two flanks of Boabdil's army have already begun methodically slicing through the dissolving Moor lines like a sharpened sickle cutting through ripe wheat. After all, this is what mounted knights in full body armor do best: close-quarter combat against footmen. Limbs are cleaved, skulls are crushed, thick splatters of blood and ropey gore arc high and wide. The crush and tangle of hundreds of troops crammed into a tight space; screams and anguished pleas and curses and shouts, even begging; the desperate barking of frantic commands to form ranks and hold the line; the *ping, ping-ping* of blade upon blade; the sickening, heavy thud of mace against bone. The bolts of the Moor crossbowmen are useless here, and except for a few lucky shots their bolts simply dent the tempered plate and fall harmlessly to the dirt. The smarter of the crossbowmen aim instead for the exposed haunches of the horses and are able to bring down some of the knights to the ground for a fairer fight. The Christian footmen follow closely behind their own cavalry, their wicked, eight-foot-long ax-head pikes stabbing and cleaving at will.

Those Moors gathered at the river's edge in the center of the army grow understandably anxious as their lines begin to dissolve, and throngs of infantry clot together and begin to frantically push their way into the muddy water in one mass, exactly what one would *not* want to do to ensure a safe crossing. Hundreds drown before they make it across.

The Moor cavalry are now mid-river, their mounts swimming their way back to the fight. Boabdil, on the beautiful white charger, leads the defense against the center prong of the Christian attack, but his cavalry is low in numbers, and not intended for this type of fight. Amazingly enough, though their odds are long, the young sultan-in-waiting fights valiantly, and almost to his surprise manages to score his first kill, the Damascus steel of his broadsword neatly slicing through the chain mail of a knight from La Rambla at the crease between the man's visored helmet and shoulder guard. Blood geysers from the severed artery, spraying the young sultan square in the face. But this seems to energize him, and with a shout he kicks his mount to lock broadswords with another of the enemy men-at-arms.

Umar is late to the fight. He finally tops a rise with a clear view of the unfolding carnage and halts to assess. The Christian cavalry on his side are raking through the Moor lines almost unopposed. He sees that Boabdil and his cavalry in the center are undermanned and will soon begin to give way. His uncle is having much better luck, and at least on the eastern edge where there is more space, the army is beginning to organize itself enough to cross the torrent with some modest assurance of success. The Christians are pressing the fight, however, determined to inflict maximal damage before the Moors can manage an escape.

Umar issues his commands, and his cavalry charges. "ALLAHU ACKBAR! ALLAHU ACKBAR! THERE IS NO VICTOR

BUT ALLAH!" His arrival is unanticipated, and he quickly cuts the attacking Christian force to his front in half. He takes the fight to them, and now with almost even numbers of the western flank, manages to begin pressing them back from the river, giving the infantry room to spread out and cross in large numbers.

By this point, the Count of Cabra, who is leading the cavalry on the east edge of the battle, realizes the identity of the Moor commander he has locked horns with. The grizzled old Moor swordsman is dressed in a bright red cloak with a flowing white, gold-trimmed turban, and is creating havoc in the count's attack as he cuts and turns his black Andalusian through the advancing Christians. Ali al-Attar is a living legend in the borderlands, after all, both respected and feared by the Christians. Though the Count of Cabra has faced him several times over the years, he has never succeeded in besting the Moor on the field of battle. On this day the count has grown fearless, however, and he gathers a dozen of his best knights and ten pikemen and begins to fight his way straight for the old warrior, determined to settle the score.

Ali al-Attar's back is turned as he fights on, and he does not see them coming until it is too late. Two of his men turn to defend him at the last minute but are slammed to the ground by mace blows. The old warrior is quickly cut off and surrounded. His ebony eyes circle his captors one by one, and then he nods his understanding and sheathes his broadsword.

The Count of Cabra is beaming with his victory over his old adversary. He raises up in his stirrups. "I finally have you, Ali al-Attar, you old scoundrel. God has willed this to be my day, not yours." He studies the old man, pleased with himself. Never did he expect such a great catch in this fight. But the count is a chivalrous man and knows this famous Moorish commander deserves his respect. "I offer you quarter for a fine gold ransom. You will live to fight again another day, you devil. What say you, sir?"

The old warrior's Castilian is weak, but he gets the gist. He scans the battlefield for Umar, but his nephew is too far away to help. He frowns his disappointment at this sad turn of events, as if he has just been informed of an unexpected change of plans that does not suit his liking. He nods once more, then offers a wicked smile to his adversary. In his broken Castilian, he says, "Cabra. I will rot in hell before giving you the satisfaction." He whispers in the ear of his stallion, who rears and whinnies in reply, then he draws his broadsword and raises it high above him, shouting the Nasrid battle cry, "There is no victor but Allah!", and charges directly for the count. Two pikemen jump into his path and jab their blades at the old knight, one puncturing his chain mail and plunging deep into his organs, the other striking a glancing blow that destroys the shoulder joint of his sword arm. The horse seems to sense its master's distress and stops in its tracks, nostrils angrily flaring. The old warrior grimaces, then spits blood and curses. He attempts to raise his broadsword but cannot—his beloved ancient blade slips from his hand. His eyes grow wide with surprise, and with a grunt he helplessly slides from his mount and crumples to the earth.

Surrounded by the terrifying soundscape of vicious, close-quarter battle, a cone of silence settles over the legendary Moor. An odd peacefulness descends as time slows then stops.

Ali al-Attar's eyes remain bright and defiant even though he cannot move. The Count of Cabra dismounts and approaches, kneels down beside the fallen warrior. "Rest easy, sir. You have always fought bravely, and with honor." The Christian bows his head and genuflects as the light begins to fade from the grizzled old knight. Ali al-Attar hisses his final words, "I would have much preferred to die by sword." He inhales sharply and shudders, then his eyes close for good.

The battle rages on. By now, most of what remains of the Moor army has made it across the River Genil, and line after line of the final elements of the infantry are moving into the water's edge to cross. Umar has turned back the marquess' attack on the western flank. He reforms ranks and orders his men to move to join up with Ali al-Attar's cavalry so together they can retire from the battlefield.

Umar arrives on the east flank, and their combined forces begin to turn the Count of Cabra's men back from the river. Satisfied that he has bought Boabdil's army sufficient time to escape, he begins to search for his uncle, to no avail. He summons one of the officers, "Where is Prince Ali al-Attar?" He sees the answer before he hears it. There are tears in the officer's eyes. "He has fallen, my lord; he has fallen." He turns and points. Umar kicks his stallion to a gallop and is instantly at the old warrior's side. He cradles his uncle's broken body in his arms, then looks at the sky, furious at the injustice of it all. He shakes his fist and screams, "NO! NOOOOOO!"

Consumed as he is with his newfound prowess in battle, Boabdil the Valiant is not even aware that Ali al-Attar and Umar's cavalries rushed in to save his army from a complete rout. When he sees that his remaining infantry are now crossing, he gives the order to his cavalry to commence a fighting retreat to the ford, and then, in a fit of storybook heroism, insists he will be the last to leave the field of battle. It is said that foolishness will always find the light of day.

As he is giving this command, a mounted Christian knight pulls beside him and swings his studded heavy mace at his head. Boabdil manages to bend away from the peril at the last instant, but the evil weapon instead catches his beautiful white stallion square in the side of the head, splattering the poor thing's brains. The beast does not even move a muscle; it simply keels over like a felled oak. Remarkably, Boabdil is pinned only by his boot and he is able to pull free and stand. He does not even bother to look for his sword, he simply sprints for a thicket of brush a stone's throw away. He watches, aghast, as his remaining cavalry begin the swim for the other side.

The maelstrom still swirling through the battlefield slowly begins to settle. The carnage spread along the river's edge is shocking. A dense tangle of dead and wounded, and downstream the banks of the swollen Genil are lined with the hundreds of dead bodies of the drowned, inevitably beginning to wash up. The Christian infantry and cavalry start to round up Moor prisoners and care for their wounded.

Boabdil crouches, debating whether to make a run for the river, when from behind him he hears, "You there. Raise your hands. You are my prisoner, sir."

Boabdil slowly turns. The man's pike is pointed at his chest. Alas, not something easily argued with. Boabdil reaches for his dagger, but it is gone. The man repeats, "I say, sir, I am Martin Hurtado, cavalier of Lucena, and you are my prisoner."

Boabdil slowly raises his hands and spouts in passable Castilian, "I demand quarter. I am a man of noble birth and possess much gold. Quarter, I say, I demand quarter."

"Out with you." The man menacingly jabs with his pike, pushing Boabdil into the open. He waves to his comrades. "Hey, over here. Juan, Miquel, over here! Look what I found. A Moorish prince!"

As soon as they are safely across the river, Boabdil's officers turn and silently watch this exchange transpire. There is no move to re-cross the torrent and attempt a rescue. Perhaps they are relieved that he is lost. Perhaps the harrowing day has simply taken its toll on their will. They stare across at the sprawl of dead and dying and watch their commander thrust his hands high in the air and surrender. To their relief, they see that the Christians have made no move to cross the River Genil and press their attack. Understandable, of course, since the count and the marquess have endured their own fair share of dead and wounded this day, largely at the hands of Umar and Ali al-Attar. Crossing into enemy territory would be a risky venture indeed.

Remarkably, the circle of Boabdil's prisoners and his booty-laden mules remain more or less unscathed at the river's edge where they were originally sequestered. Their ropes are now cut, and they are cared for with water and kind words to soothe the misery of what they have endured.

A few soft words are spoken among the Moor officers, and the army begins to gather up its disheveled ranks and limp its way back to Granada.

"Your orders, my lord?" Hashim, Umar's second-in-command, offers the very gentlest of queries. He idolized Prince Ali al-Attar. They all did.

Umar does not appear to hear the man.

Hashim sees the confusion and helpfully adds, "Should we cross the Genil, my lord?"

Umar's heartbroken eyes finally rise. "Cross the Genil?"

The officer presses on. "Should we cross the Genil to pursue Boabdil's army? Even with their numbers they are no match for us, my lord. We may be able to end this Abencerraje revolt here."

Umar forces himself to focus. He sees the logic but just does not have the stomach for it, at least not today. He shakes his head. "There has been enough Granadine blood spilled for one day, Hashim. Gather our wounded and dead and let us make for Loja. Stay on this side of the Genil. We will easily outpace their retreat, and can deal with them when they pass Loja on the way back to Granada."

His second nods, "Of course, my lord."

Within a few minutes, the Count of Cabra arrives and sizes up the battle-bloodied Moor. Boabdil is clearly a person of high rank. "Who are you?"

"I am Boabdil, the only son and heir of Sultan Abu l-Hasan, twenty-first sultan of Granada. I commanded this army, and I demand quarter."

"Ali al-Attar I know, God rest his soul. You, sir, I do not. However, quarter you shall have." He turns to an officer. "See that this man is treated well. If anything should happen to him it is upon your head, understood?"

"Yes, my lord."

"My family will pay a large ransom for my safe return."

"Mm. Let us hope that they value your life, sir." He turns back to the officer. "This man will be sent under armed escort to the king and queen in Córdoba. They can figure out who he is and what to do with him."

"Yes, my lord."

He calls to Boabdil's captor, who is still holding his pike on his prisoner. "Your name?"

"I am Martin Hurtado, my lord. Pikeman of Lucena."

"You have done well, Martin. Should this man's ransom be paid, you will be rewarded."

"Thank you, sir!"

Remarkably enough, Boabdil's officers manage to recover some semblance of actual battlefield instinct and steer their retreating army well south of Loja to avoid Umar's scouting parties. What is left of Boabdil's army makes it back into the Albayzín, stunned and frightfully mauled, but mostly intact. They slowly begin to fill in the threadbare defensive positions along the walls of the Albayzín in case the sultan feels emboldened to attack the Abencerraje positions.

Sorrow and Scorn

A quiet knock and the door opens. "Hakim Amiriya? Prince Umar al-Makki is here."

She looks up from her paperwork with a spontaneous smile as he walks in. "Umar! How wonderful! We did not expect to see you again for some time."

He just stares at her with full eyes and a quivering chin.

Danah's bright smile vanishes. "Umar?"

"I must . . . see Yusef." His voice is quavering, the words weighed down by lead, as if all the burdens of the world have been suddenly placed upon his shoulders.

"Umar, what has happened?" She rises and moves to him.

Umar chokes back a sob. "Uncle . . ." He wipes at his eyes with his sleeve, but tears are flowing now.

"Umar, tell me."

"Uncle is gone, Danah."

"No. Please, no . . ."

"He was killed at Fuentes de Cesna. On the banks of the Genil. He was . . . we were trying to save Boabdil's army from disaster."

Danah is weeping now. She embraces him, and they cry together.

Umar sniffs, "I came straight here. Yusef must know."

"Yes. This will wound him terribly, Umar."

"I know. Where is he?"

"Come, I will show you." She takes his hand and leads him out of the room and down the hallway.

Yusef sits ashen-faced, still as a stone as he numbly listens. He has yet to shed a tear, or even to show anything more than shock at the terrible news. He insisted upon hearing every single word of it, of course, from the sighting of Boabdil's army, to Lucena, to the river, as if he aims to dissect an intricate tactical problem and grasp what could have happened differently to prevent this tragedy; what *should* have happened differently. Umar has to fight back his tears as he tells the whole painful story.

Danah stares at her betrothed, her eyes red and puffy, her face a portrait of deep concern. She knows why he does not give in to the grief. To do so would be to claim the reality of the awful truth of it all, that the man who was for all intents and purposes their father, has been violently subtracted from this world . . . and that the two of them are now alone. Orphans.

Yusef stops him for clarification several times, and when Umar begins to tell him what transpired at the river leading up to the end, Yusef violently curses. Danah gasps. His jaw clenched tight, he hisses, "If I had my sight and I had been at his side—"

Umar angrily stops him. "No! No, Yusef! If you had your sight you would have been with me. We would have ridden together. You know this is so. Yusef, he would have died anyway, even if you were there."

Yusef opens his mouth to challenge this assertion but remains silent. He knows Umar is right.

Umar reaches for his brother's hand. "Yusef, one of Uncle's men told me what happened at the end. The Count of Cabra must have recognized him. Cabra cut him off and was able to surround him with mounted men-at-arms and pikemen. But, Yusef, Cabra offered him quarter. Uncle refused. He raised his broadsword and shouted, 'There is no victor but Allah!' and then he tried to run Cabra down. He was mortally wounded by pikemen before he could get to him."

The brothers are silent. Umar smiles through his tears and says, "The old goat was stubborn to the very end. He always said he would die in battle."

Yusef's eyes are swimming now, but he manages a smile. "Yes. The old goat was always stubborn. He got his wish." He chokes back a sob. Danah moves to his side and holds him. "Yusef . . . let it come. Let it come, darling."

He leans his head against her in despair. "Oh, Danah. Uncle will never get the chance to know you. Or our children. Oh, Danah, he is gone . . . Uncle is gone." Tears slide down his cheeks.

"I know . . . I know . . . I am here. Let it come. I am here . . ."

Yusef begins to sob. The three of them hold each other and let the terrible waves of sorrow crash down upon them.

"Go ahead. Say it." Fatima is staring out the window across the Darro valley at the angled silhouette of the Alhambra as it is lovingly kissed by the morning's first light. The sultana has the look of a checkmated queen after a long and grueling match. She has an unhealthy pallor, her face drawn and haggard, bags weighing down her eyes. Rare for her to show her age like this. She learned of her son's fate just before midnight and has not slept since. She has spent the night sifting their options now that the worst has come to pass, trying desperately to find a viable path forward—some thread that can be grasped and held on to. She has found nothing, not a single thing. After Boabdil's debacle at Lucena and his capture, the tempting conclusion is that her husband has already won the match. She can sense defeat creeping toward her, step by inevitable step, like a sleek, prowling lynx moving in for the kill.

Abu al-Haytham looks as if he has not slept either. "Your son's defeat is no real surprise. At least to me. That he managed to get himself taken prisoner? Even I did not anticipate that level of incompetence."

She turns to face him and opens her mouth to dispute this, but what is there to say?

He continues, "I was foolish to believe that Aben Comixa could provide him useful counsel." The wizard sadly shakes his head. "Trampled to death by his own horse. The man deserved better than he got."

"Yes." The sultana is uncharacteristically contrite, though she had no love for the grand vizier.

"More news has just arrived."

All she can manage is a resigned sigh. "There is more?"

The High Elder of the Abencerrajes is genuinely surprised that he possesses information that she does not. "Yes. About your husband."

Her eyes narrow. "Well?"

"I am afraid he has been stricken again by his brain malady."

"No . . ." Perhaps because of her exhaustion, she is helpless to prevent the wave of concern from washing over her face, concern for the man she once loved more than life itself, though it seems like an ancient memory. Her eyes fill without warning, and she looks away.

He studies her reaction, sees the rare display of vulnerability before she can hide it. *So, she is a woman with a heart after all.* His tone softens. "It happened on the journey home. He is evidently close to death, Fatima." He has never once used her given name. Does this scheming man possess a modicum of compassion? "Al-Zaghal arrived late in the night. Their army will be here in two days."

"I see. Is my husband already back in the Alhambra?" Her informants must have wanted to spare her the added pain until morning. She makes a mental note to chastise them for this inexcusable failure. By now she has successfully erased all

490

emotion from her face, her feelings for her ailing husband safely buried.

"I would think so, yes."

This means it is impossible for her to see him. They fall silent as both ponder this unexpected development.

He says, "I expect al-Zaghal to assume leadership, like before."

She weighs this. "Agreed. Unless the Christian whore has her way." She frowns. "I underestimated her once before, Abu al-Haytham, I do not intend to make the same mistake twice."

The high elder replies, "No, nor I. What if she is again with child?"

"Then we will have an even larger problem to face. But, believe me, if she were with child, we would already know." Fatima muses. "Without a potential heir, Boabdil and al-Zaghal have the only legitimate claims to the throne."

The wizard grumbles. "Sultana, let me remind you that Boabdil is by now already sequestered in a prison in Córdoba."

She chews her cheek. "For now. Fernando and Isabel are not fools, Abu al-Haytham. They need gold. We have it. They will be amenable to a ransom . . . given the proper inducements."

He considers this. "Perhaps. But I can easily imagine that the price they ask will be too high to pay."

She turns on him and sharpens her tone. "Too high for the Abencerrajes, Abu al-Haytham? With the Alhambra finally within reach? You people have been saving for decades to reclaim what you lost." She scoffs. "You surprise me. You and I both know that the Abencerrajes possess mountains of gold."

All he will give her is an acknowledging grunt. She is right, of course; but gold is never easy to come by, and even harder to part with. He decides to change the subject. "What about al-Zaghal?"

She frowns. "Yes. Al-Zaghal. Admittedly, a problem that must be faced." She begins to pace as her astute mind races down a slew of parallel paths toward their logical conclusions. She stops and turns, face brightening. "With their victory at Lucena, the Christians will be anxious to quickly resume their campaign against us. Trust me, they will not rest until they secure revenge for the disaster in the Ajarquía Mountains. They will return to Málaga." She smiles and nods as the answer to their problems crystallizes. "Yes, they will return. Soon. Count on it. That path remains their best means to strangle and defeat Granada. We know this. They know this. But this time they will bring a massive army and heavy cannons and lay siege to the city."

"And?"

I should not have to explain such things to him. "And without my husband and without Ali al-Attar, al-Zaghal will have no choice but to leave the Alhambra with his army and challenge the Christian invasion. Málaga is a long way from here, Abu al-Haytham. His absence gives us plenty of room to maneuver."

"There is still the one Falcon."

She smirks her displeasure. *So slow.* "Yes, but he will be forced to remain in Loja to defend against an attack from the north. If not, the Christians will march right into the Vega and put the kingdom's breadbasket to the torch. I would. And let us not forget that the Christians still hold Alhama. A conveniently placed stronghold that can easily support a northern assault. No, the Falcon and his cavalry will remain in Loja; they have no choice. When al-Zaghal leaves the city for Málaga with the main army, we will make our move. By then, we will have paid Boabdil's ransom, and he will be safely back in the city. Secretly, of course—that will have to be part of the deal with Castile."

He questions this with his eyebrows but does not speak.

"Then we will storm the Alhambra and capture it once and for all."

He frowns. "We tried that once before, or did you forget?" His sarcasm is biting.

An exasperated exhale. "We will *not* approach it like last time, Abu al-Haytham. That idea belonged to you and Aben Comixa. This time there will be no bribes and clandestine maneuvering to slip in and open a gate in the dead of night. We will launch a surprise attack, a full-scale assault with everything we have." She is pleased with her logic. Her smile subtracts from her age. "Trust me, Venegas will never destroy the Alhambra to keep it from us. No, when all is said and done, he will surrender the prize intact. Victory will be ours, and you and I will move back into our proper lodgings in the Lion Palace, Abu-al-Hasan."

The wizard weighs this. "You are forgetting the condition of the army that returned from the debacle at Lucena, Sultana. If you can still call it an army. I have seen them first-hand. Not just beaten. Broken. Demoralized to a man, and half of them without weapons."

"I know."

"It remains a minor miracle that they managed to slip past Loja undetected and make it back to Granada at all. Uncharacteristic generosity for a Falcon prince with the opportunity to punish us for our ineptitude."

She does not respond even though she agrees. *Perhaps more than a minor miracle.* "He will come to regret his miscalculation."

"Perhaps. But as we both know, Sultana, even if we enjoy an advantage in numbers, in their current state our army would have a difficult time capturing even a lightly-garrisoned Alhambra."

"Then we must rearm them and retrain them into an effective fighting force. Quickly, before the opportunity passes us by."

"That is impossible, Sultana. Granada's forges are not within the Albayzín. We have no means to produce the steel needed to refit an army."

She ticks her head to concede his point, then offers a cunning smile. "Abu al-Haytham, *surely* the Abencerrajes still maintain connections back to the Maghreb. After all, it is your ancestral homeland."

An unintelligible grunt from the wizard.

"Given enough gold I am sure we could purchase what we require to refit our army. As we both know, the Maghreb has no love for the Nasrids. We would need to do this without attracting notice, of course. Perhaps using armorers that are used to, shall we say, making deals that can stand up to scrutiny. Those who work with the mercenary trade, for instance. As you know, my husband had no great difficulty hiring a Berber army to defend Málaga."

He scowls. "You are remarkably generous with other people's gold, Sultana. From what my sources tell me, your husband's hiring of the Berber mercenaries nearly emptied his treasury."

She answers with a sweet smile. "Wealth is fleeting, Abu al-Haytham. The Alhambra, however, is timeless." Her expression hardens. "There is only one goal here: to take back the Alhambra and seize what is rightfully ours. If gold is required, then gold must be provided."

He glares at her for a long moment. "Such an arrangement is possible." He raises a finger. "With a condition." He waits for an objection, but it does not come. "In addition to securing arms, we will hire *competent* Berber officers for this new army of ours. Boabdil will lead the army in name only. The planning of the attack and its execution will be left to the Berber mercenaries. They are experts in such matters."

She weighs this and concedes the point with a nod. "Done." She is beaming like a young bride on her wedding day.

"Of course, I cannot make decisions on the Abencerraje treasury on my own, Sultana."

"Of course. But you will find a way to convince them of the wisdom of our plan, Abu al-Haytham." Her laugh is pure confidence.

His somber expression remains set in stone. The man has not laughed in years. He cannot resist the temptation to probe her once more for a latent weakness. "It seems that the demise of your husband has been a great gift to our cause, Sultana." He waits to scrutinize her response.

She answers instantly. "Indeed, Abu al-Haytham. The curse of his malady is our good fortune." The woman looks a decade younger than when he first arrived, and not even a hint of the vulnerability he earlier glimpsed.

The wizard continues to study her. *I was mistaken. She has no heart.* He adds this cautionary reminder to his mental dossier of this formidable woman who is his unlikely co-conspirator. "I will consult this evening with the Council of Elders."

"And I have letters to write."

It is Venegas who wakes her. No one else would dare disturb her sleep. "I am afraid it is urgent, Sultana. Please."

Zoraya cracks the door to find out the meaning of his rude interruption, ready to chastise.

Venegas holds a small oil lamp, his expression predictably unreadable. "Sultana. I am afraid the sultan relapsed on the journey back from Málaga. His condition is grave."

Her mouth helplessly slides open as color drains from her face. She opens the door and steps into the hallway just in time to see two stretcher bearers turn the corner and come down the hall carrying her husband. She stares in disbelief.

The two officers stop in front of her.

She gasps. Her husband's face looks like death warmed over. Zoraya is dressed still in her bed clothes, a thin wisp of a thing that barely covers her body and does nothing but accentuate her lovely curves. Her marvelous blond curls hang full and loose down her back. Seemingly with a mind of their own, her nipples strain mightily against the sheer white silk, begging for attention. Which they get. Venegas frowns his disapproval. The eyes of the two officers widen as they try to avert their gazes. Unsuccessfully. Scantily clad, the woman is something extraordinary to behold, even in the dead of night, even though unnaturally pale and without makeup or adornment.

Acutely aware of their wandering eyes, she makes no move to conceal her breasts. She knows these two will retell the story a thousand times, a lurid tale that will simply add to her legend—and allure. She turns to the two of them. "Bring him into my quarters. And send for the royal physician immediately." The officers' eyes are transfixed, and they do not move fast enough for her liking. Her demeanor shifts as quickly as a viper strikes. Instantly livid, she barks, *"I said bring him into my quarters!"* Then she screams, *"*NOW, YOU FOOLS!*"* This has the intended effect. She looks at her comatose husband, distraught, then up to Venegas, who is pleased to see in her that the alarm bells of panic have begun to sound as the cascade of implications crash down upon her.

He says, "I have already sent word to the royal physician, Sultana. He should be here shortly." He clears his throat. "Perhaps you might wish to find a robe?" His eyes retreat, fearing an explosion.

She scowls but remains silent. "Where is al-Zaghal?"

Venegas looks up, sees that the gears are already turning. "He went to inform the Supreme Council, Sultana."

She mulls this over with a worried frown. "When he returns, send him to me immediately."

Venegas nods. "I will convey your request as soon as he arrives, Sultana."

"You wished to see me?" Al-Zaghal has not slept in days. He looks haggard.

"I did, yes." Zoraya's appearance is a definition of regal. The room's lamps have been arranged to cast flattering tones upon her face. She is freshly made up, dabbed with priceless royal scent, and dressed for the part in a lavish silk gown. Her glorious hair is down and fully exposed. Social mores with this one went out long ago. She studies him for clues. "Sit, Muhammad." Her tone is gentle, kind even. She has never before used his first name, not once. "Please."

"I prefer to stand." All business.

She continues to sift his expression. "Very well." *The man looks positively exhausted. More the better.* "I wanted to know the details of what happened to my husband. Venegas said he did not know."

A lie. The tense moment stretches out.

He clears his throat. "There is little to tell, really. The journey back from Málaga was uneventful. It happened just this side of Agrón. We were side by side as we rode, talking about the plans for a triumphal march in the city. He stopped mid-sentence with a worrisome look as that odd twitch began to take over his cheek. He shuddered, then grunted. He winced and then fell from his horse. He has not woken since."

495

"I see. So he never spoke?"

"No."

"Thank you, Muhammad." She falls silent as she studies him. "The royal physician says it is highly unlikely that he will ever wake from this relapse. Evidently it was much more severe than last time. Without food or water, he will fade, then die. A week, maybe two." So matter of fact.

Al-Zaghal nods. He assumed as much. "Yes." When all is said and done, he loves his ailing brother and will miss him, despite his many flaws. His eyes drift to the floor. It seems he cannot bear to look at her face.

His apparent retreat emboldens her. "There is something important you must know, Muhammad. Before my husband left for Málaga, I had the pleasure of informing him that I was again with child. Surely a son this time, inshallah." Her warm smile and soft glow is a perfect caricature of a beautiful young woman who has just learned that she is carrying her lover's child within her body. In fairness, a snare has already been set for achieving her goal—a late night meeting with the more handsome of the two officers who carried her husband has already been arranged. Wandering eyes make for easy pickings.

Al-Zaghal's gaze rises.

"He told me that if anything should happen to him in battle that I should serve as regent until his heir comes of age and assumes the throne." She studies al-Zaghal for a reaction. The man remains stone-faced. "I assured him that no such plan was needed, of course. But he was insistent." She hastens to add, "Obviously, if Allah sees fit to work a miracle and he recovers, then my service as regent would not be needed."

Al-Zaghal simply stares.

"I thought you should know his wishes. Of course, as my husband's designated regent for his heir, I would insist that you serve as military vizier . . . now that Ali al-Attar is gone."

"I see." He muses. "I assume my brother put his wishes in writing?"

A wisp of doubt, just for an instant, then it is gone. "Well, no, not exactly. But my husband's word is surely good enough for you, his brother." Almost a challenge.

"Congratulations on the conception of your child, Zoraya."

Her face hardens. "Sultana." It is not in her nature to entertain insults.

He ignores this. "What wonderful news. I assume you would have no objection to Hakim al-Adani examining you to confirm this assertion. I am afraid he will need to spread your legs and open your womb to see what monster lurks within. I plan to be in attendance, so I can witness the fruits of the miraculous conception."

She flushes dark. "How dare you!"

"You see, Zoraya, my brother spoke to me about you while we were journeying home. He confessed that even in his time of illness you were constantly on him . . . extracting his seed. Even when he begged you for rest. And yet somehow . . ." He stops to offer a wicked smile. "Somehow, you still could not manage to conceive an heir. Remarkable. Perhaps you are infertile."

Her eyes are smoldering with raw hate now. "That is a lie! He knew I was with child. *I told him before he left!*" There is a desperate edge to her tone now.

Al-Zaghal reaches into his cloak and retrieves a folded piece of parchment. "While my brother was being brought into the palace, I took the liberty of calling on Supreme Mullah Abd Allah. Venegas arranged it."

The paralysis of uncertainty sets in. "*What?*"

"Yes. You see, I explained to the Supreme Mullah the situation of my brother's collapse. And that he was near death. As you might imagine, he has no great love for you and your cunning ways. He quickly convened the Supreme Council and issued a proclamation attesting to my brother's true wishes, which, fortunately, he *did* convey in written form before we marched, and signed, and embossed with his signet. Not only does the proclamation condemn Boabdil as a traitor to the realm, it says that in the event of his demise that I, Muhammad al-Zaghal, should succeed him as the twenty-second sultan of Granada." He smiles. "You are welcome to examine its contents."

She is speechless.

"No? Well, rest assured that unlike yours, Zoraya, my document is quite legitimate and will withstand scrutiny in court."

Remarkably, Zoraya's eyes spontaneously fill and she begins to blubber. "I am so sorry. Forgive me. I never intended any harm, surely you know that, Muhammad. I loved your brother, and now he has been taken from me. I am the mother of your niece, Muhammad, an innocent baby girl. You must protect us." Heaving sobs commence, and a moment later, by some conjured magic, she ends up against him, her head pressed to his chest, clutching him for dear life, a devastated young woman in serious need of comforting. The top of her freshly-washed blond curls lie just beneath his chin, and her alluring perfume seems somehow to have filled the room.

He stands planted like a mighty oak, arms at his side, and does not offer a single word of consolation or make a move to touch her. Her crying jag finally begins to ebb, and soon only sniffles remain. Without looking up she says, "I can hear your heartbeat." The woman is smiling through her tears. "Surely you do not find me unattractive, Muhammad. I have seen how you look at me." Now coy. "As sultan you will need a wife, you know." She holds for a response, and getting none, she adds in her most seductive voice, "I have always thought that you were far more handsome than your brother. And though I probably should not be telling you this, his lack of skill in bed . . . well, let us just say that he left me unsatisfied many a night." She chases this with a cute girlish giggle.

His left hand slowly rises. He grabs a handful of hair just behind her neck and violently yanks her head back, exposing her throat. She yelps. With his right hand he grabs the top of her gown and rips it open, exposing her breasts. She tries to twist away from him but cannot. The unexpected malice of the act startles her into silence. Her eyes are wide with fear, her lower lip quivering, a rare state indeed for this one. His head bends forward until his lips are an inch from the soft, luscious skin of her neck. He breathes in her scent and hisses, "I should have kept you for myself, you bitch. I could have enjoyed your body, and when I was done with you, I could have pulled your claws one by one and rendered you harmless."

Her voice is quavering, "Please do not hurt me."

"May Allah curse me for giving you to my weak brother. His fall from grace was my doing. *Mine*. Forgive me, Ali, forgive me." He releases her hair and roughly pushes her backward. "Your days in the Alhambra are done, Zoraya."

The tears are flowing again, this time for real. "Muhammad, please. Forgive me. If you will not protect me, at least protect your niece. Muhammad. *Muhammad! Please!*"

"You will not leave the guest room in the Comares Palace until my brother dies. You will be escorted to his funeral to pay your respects, but you will speak to no one; not a single person. If you do, I will have your tongue cut out. After the funeral, you will leave the city with your unholy child, never to be seen again. I care not where you go, but should you ever try to return to Granada, or ever attempt to meddle in court politics, you will be arrested on sight and turned over to the Supreme Council for trial on charges of conspiracy, treason, and blasphemy."

She is quietly sobbing, numb with shock.

"Now get out of my palace before the sun sets, you whore."

She opens the door. The sunlight shimmers on the reflecting pool in the Courtyard of the Myrtles, the reflection of the Hall of the Ambassadors playfully swaying and dancing upon the water. She looks up into the crystalline blue. The palace swallows flit about through the pristine air, twisting and darting at ridiculous speeds, their playful squeaks of delight echoing off the stucco walls. A beautiful day.

"A letter for you, madam. From the Albayzín." The courier extends the scroll.

She drifts back to reality. "The Albayzín? From whom?" Her words are dead.

"The messenger would not say. Only that it was for your eyes only."

Zoraya takes it without a word. She closes the door and sits to examine the thing. How odd. Sealed with red wax, but no imprint by the author. Curious now, she opens the letter with her fingernail, unrolls it, and begins to read.

Her eyes briefly furrow with confusion then relax in resignation with the awful truth. Her face begins to wilt as her eyes swim. When she finishes, her shaking hands helplessly fold back to her lap.

The time of your reckoning has come. The day he passes from this world is the day your hell begins. Rest assured, a slow and excruciating death awaits you. I have procured a special potion for you, my dear, one crafted to ravage that lovely face and disfigure that beautiful body as it worms its way into your brain to destroy your scheming mind. I am afraid it will keep you alive until the very end as it has its ugly way with you, so that you might enjoy the time to properly reflect on your evil schemes and your self-inflicted fate . . . and me. You crossed swords with the wrong woman, my dear. Alas, you will not know the day or the hour or the minute when the devil comes to call your name and deliver my gift. You will live in dread of your horrible end. Every bite you eat, every sip you drink, every doorway you step through, every night you close your eyes, every person you pass on the street. One of these will mark your demise, the beginning of your eternal suffering, you Christian whore. Please, take every precaution possible to believe that you are safe. Alas, they will be useless against me. Time to pay the devil for the evil you have done.

Habib Albi—Love of My Heart

This is the fifth consecutive night Yusef has had the same dream. Identical in every detail each time. Not a nightmare, no. Perhaps unsettling would be the right word, at least in the beginning. By now, however, he finds them fascinating, comforting even, and is almost sad when they end and he wakes. Still, the whole thing remains a mystery to him, especially its odd repetition. The dreams are vivid, so incredibly real. He thinks about Danah's dreams and imagines it must be like those of her tetta—real enough to reach out and touch.

In his, he is at the al-Adani home, meeting Ummah for the first time. Everything is consistent with what he recalls happening on that memorable visit—all but the ending, which differs wildly.

Nervousness. That is what he feels while standing in the room. Extremely nervous, unsure of what to expect. The dream begins with Miriam saying, 'Come children. I would like to introduce Prince al-Makki of the Alhambra.' And then not a word, not a sound—nothing. And he, a grown man, is suddenly terrified. His heart begins to race. He, a knight of the realm, is scared of these little creatures, these children he cannot see but knows are standing right in front of him. All he can think to say is, 'I am pleased to meet you.' Then nothing, for what seems like hours. His fear grows, unbounded. He is ready to turn and run, blind though he is. And then he hears her little voice, Ummah, standing right in front of him. 'You cannot see.' Miriam scolds her, but then, for some odd reason, he finds her impolitic statement funny, and he laughs. 'That is right, Ummah, I cannot see.' She reaches up and takes his hand. 'How did it happen?' Disarmed by her boldness, all he can think to do is tell the truth. 'I was wounded in battle.' The little girl answers this oddly. 'I will make you better.' He thinks to himself: *If only it were that simple, little girl.* He feels her hand tugging him down, and so he kneels. And then her arms wrap themselves around his neck, and the young girl hugs herself to him, tightly, so tightly. Almost against his will he is drawn to hug the little girl back, and he does. Her whisper, 'Mercy,' and he feels his world melt into an incredible fluid warmth, a healing tranquility that brings inexplicable peacefulness.

This much is consistent with what he recalls of that day. But then the incredible difference. Suddenly he is bathed in a brilliant light, a million suns focused on him, surrounding him, enveloping him. He cannot see the light, of course, but by some miracle he *feels* its presence trying to burn its way into his world of blackness. It feels hot on his skin, scalding. He squeezes his blind eyes shut as tightly as he can to try and hold off the incredible brightness, but he feels it burrowing through his closed lids. With his eyes squeezed shut Ummah softly kisses one blind eye, and the other, then whispers, 'You are forgiven.' *Forgiven! How did she know that that is what he most needed to hear? How? How?!* He is overwhelmed by emotion and chokes back a sob. And then he wakes. Not with a start, as unsettling dreams can do, but with a deep sense of peace. He simply wakes up, refreshed, as if from a full night's rest, amazed once more that the dream has visited him. He cocks his ear and listens. Birdsong. Sunrise. He always wakes from the dream at sunrise. He thinks to himself—*the light. Why the light?*

He has yet to tell Danah of his unusual dreams. He is not sure what to say exactly. She was there; she knows what happened with Ummah. They have talked about it many times, futilely teasing it apart as they search in vain for some hint of meaning. And besides, with her latest dream of her family history, his dreams, odd though they may be, seem of little consequence next to hers. That night she dreamed of her tetta and was told the truth of who she really is, she came to his room and woke him, and with great excitement told him everything. They lay in each other's arms until first light talking about it, and then she slipped back to her room. Later that day they talked again about it. At one point he laughed, said he could not wait to tell Umar that she was the direct descendent of the legendary knight, Shahab Chandon. He made her promise to tell her mother what she now knew to be true. She said she would, and yet a week has gone by and still she has not. Predictable Danah.

This fifth dream is exactly the same. The fear, the hug, the 'Mercy,' the bright light, the 'You are forgiven.' He chokes back a sob and wakes . . . to vermillion. He frowns, confused. *What now?* He sits up, turns his head in different directions. All he sees is a vermillion fog, a vermillioned nothingness. He cocks his ear for the birdsong and hears it. *Sunrise.* He flattens his hand and brings it to his face to cover his right eye. The vermillion dims perceptibly. His mouth folds open, incredulous. He does the same thing with his other eye, with the same result. *Dear Lord.* His heart begins to race. *Dear Lord!* He jumps up and feels for his clothes and wrestles on a shirt, fumbles for his cane, trips over his mattress, and falls flat. He gets back up and opens the door, begins to move as quickly as he can down the hallway to Danah's room, his cane quickly flicking side to side to follow the walls— *tap-tap, tap-tap, tap-tap.* When he arrives, he does not even think to knock; he just opens the door. "Danah! *Danah!*" No answer. He curses, turns, and starts in the opposite direction for the night attendant's station. *Tap-tap, tap-tap, tap-tap.* He grows more frantic with each passing step, and twice nearly trips in his haste. The light behind the vermillion fog has perceptively brightened, as if the sun is struggling to shine through. He can see ghostly shadows. "Juan? Juan?!"

"Yes, my lord." The night attendant rises from his desk.

"Danah. Where is she?"

"She is not here, my lord. She left late last night for the al-Adani's home. She said she was going to stay the night and return today."

Yusef curses again.

"Prince al-Makki, is something wrong?" The attendant looks concerned.

"Yes! No! I mean—" He is breathing heavily, his heart pounding. "Has Hakim al-Adani arrived yet?"

"He just got here, my lord. He should be in his office by now. Would you like me to take you to him?"

Yusef has already turned and is tapping down the hallway. "I can manage."

Juan watches Yusef race away, hastily tapping down the hallway. He has never seen a Falcon so flustered.

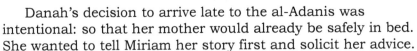

Danah's decision to arrive late to the al-Adanis was intentional: so that her mother would already be safely in bed. She wanted to tell Miriam her story first and solicit her advice. Danah feels considerable guilt over letting her promise to Yusef drag out, and thus she opted not to inform him of her plans, preferring instead to surprise him the next day with the news that the deed was already done.

Miriam was amazed at the tale—Who would not be? "Dear Lord, what a remarkable story." She considers all that she has heard, then offers only this. "Danah, your mother has grown a great deal these past few weeks, and the beginnings of a real relationship now exist between you two. Do not destroy that. You must tell her the truth, of course, and how she hurt you. And then you must forgive her. Your new life with Yusef will be so much richer with your parents a part of it. Do not build walls, Danah; work to tear them down. It is the Sufi Way."

As is her practice, Danah was up at first light, and is now nervously waiting at the dining room table with a cup of hot tea. She hears her mother step softly down the stairs, with at least an hour still before the children will require attention. Miriam has said she will ensure they remain upstairs as long as needed.

When she catches sight of her daughter, Mayya stops and instantly brightens. "Danah! I did not expect to see you until Saturday. How wonderful! You are here early."

Danah forces a smile. "Hello, Mama. I wanted to surprise you."

"You *have*, my dear, and what a lovely surprise it is." Mayya is beaming. "And I have a surprise for you too, darling! A letter from Abd al-Salam arrived late yesterday. Danah, he says he thinks he has found a way to get your father here for the marriage ceremony. It will take a few weeks still to arrange, but there seems to be a way now. Is that not wonderful news, darling? Baba will get to join the celebration."

"Of course it is, Mama." Not quite enough energy.

As mother studies daughter, Mayya's countenance changes, grows serious. "Danah, what is wrong?"

"Come, Mama, we must talk." Her heart is pounding.

Mayya freezes where she is.

"Please, Mama, come sit. We must talk."

Mayya warily approaches but sits down beside her daughter without another word. "Something happened between you and Yusef."

"No, Mama. Yusef and I are fine."

Relief. "What then?"

There is a long, tense moment before she says anything. "I had another dream, Mama."

Mayya instantly frowns. "Not *her* again?"

"Yes, Mama. Tetta Layla came to me again. This time she told me my story. All of it. I finally know who I really am, Mama. Who *we* are."

Mayya gasps and blanches. "But that is not possible, Danah."

"No, Mama, it *is* possible. I know who I am. I know everything now. Tetta Layla told me. I have Nasrid blood flowing in my veins. I have Layla al-Khatib's emerald eyes. I am descended from Shahab Chandon."

Mayya just blankly stares at Danah, aghast.

"I am going to tell you everything I know, Mama. You listen; I will talk. Do *not* interrupt me. Listen." As Danah begins to tell the story from the beginning, Mayya first fades like a late summer blossom then begins to shrivel like a discarded apple. Soon her eyes fold closed and her head and shoulders droop. At the point in the story when Sheikh Abu l-Fadl of the Abencerrajes says, 'The name al-Khatib is from this day hence unknown to us. You and all your offspring for all time will be called Amiriya,' Mayya's eyes squeeze tight and tears begin to course down her cheeks.

Danah recounts everything the sheikh said, word for word. 'So that his memory and good name may endure, your son Shahab shall know the truth about his jiddo, Lisan al-Din ibn al-Khatib, may peace be upon his soul. When Shahab marries, his wife shall know the truth, as will his firstborn child. And when that child marries his spouse shall know the truth, and their firstborn child, and so on for all time.' On Danah goes until the bitter end. Then she stops, and voice quavering, she hisses, "Why Mama? *Why* would you and Baba deny me the truth? *Why*, Mama? Why? *Why*?"

Through her tears, Mayya begins to stammer, "We intended to tell you, Danah, truly we did. We wanted to . . . I mean . . . but when Baba was appointed elder . . . and, well, it was just too dangerous, Danah. Our place in Abencerraje society would have been in jeopardy if ever you let it slip, even a word . . . surely you can . . ." Mayya falls silent.

Danah is crying now. "You robbed me, Mama. You robbed me of my history, of who I really am. You hurt me, Mama. You hurt me deeply, Mama. How could you? *How could you?!*"

"Blame me, Danah. Battal wanted to tell you in spite of the risk . . . but I forbade him. He wanted to, he did . . . you must forgive me, Danah. Forgive us both. Dear Allah, I have done wrong by you, you must forgive me . . . please forgive me." Mayya begins to sob uncontrollably.

Danah hesitates . . . then reaches for her mother's hands.

Tears are streaming down his face when he arrives at David's office. His cane is on the floor back at the last turn in the hallway. He can see well enough to make out the walls and doors. He does not bother to knock; he just barges right in.

David is standing in the back of the room, in the middle of his morning prayers. His eyes fly open as he pivots. "Dear Lord! *Yusef?*" He removes his prayer shawl and rushes to the young man. "What has happened, Yusef? Did something happen to Danah? Yusef, *what*? Yusef?!"

"David!" Yusef is unhinged. "David! I can . . . I can . . . I can see. David, I can see!" He grows weak-kneed and faint and begins to teeter. David grasps his arm to steady him as Yusef continues: "I can see! David, I can see!"

"Oh, dear Lord! Dear Lord! Come, sit over here, let me take a look. Come, sit!" He walks Yusef to the chair and settles him. "Relax, Yusef. Please, you must relax. Let me get my instruments."

It takes David several minutes to calm Yusef down enough to examine him. He holds a magnifying glass and a long tapered candle.

"I am fine now. Forgive me."

"Dear Lord, man, there is nothing to forgive. This is amazing! Now tell me *exactly* what happened."

Yusef takes a deep breath, exhales. "I have had the same dream each night for five nights, David. Incredibly vivid. About my first visit to your home, and Ummah. There was this light, a burning light . . ."

David frowns his confusion.

"This morning when I woke from the clutches of the dream, all I could see was a vermillion fog. Color, not blackness! Vermillion. I was not sure what was happening."

"Mm. The same hue you saw after the explosion?"

"Yes, identical. I could tell from the birdsong that it was sunrise, and when I brought my hand to my eye the fog darkened."

"I see. How quickly did your vision begin to return?"

"Very quickly. I rushed to tell Danah, but she was not there."

"No. She stayed with us last night. She and Miriam were up late."

"By the time I got to Juan's station I could see some dull shadows. He told me you had just gotten in, so I rushed here. By the time I was halfway down the hall I could see well enough to walk without my cane."

"And now?"

Yusef looks across the room. "I have almost all of my vision back. Still a little blurry, and the colors seem too brilliant somehow. But I can see. I can see, David."

David nods. "Remarkable." He lifts his eyeglass. "Let us have a look. Can you hold the candle for me?"

"Yes."

David lights the taper from the lamp and hands it to Yusef. "Be careful. I need it held steady, right here." He moves it to aid an oblique view into the interior of the eyeball. "Got it?"

"Yes."

David leans in. "Steady now. Open wide." He parts the lids with thumb and finger and leans close to scrutinize his eye, first the iris and the lens and then within the eyeball itself.

"Completely normal, just like before. Now the other." When he is done he takes the taper and blows it out.

He holds up a large white card. "Stare at the center of the card. Do you see any black objects or lines out on the edges?"

"No. Just white."

"Good." He takes a step back. "Now look straight ahead and tell me when you see my fingers move. He lowers his hand downward and begins to wiggle his fingers as it moves slowly upward, checking the young man's peripheral vision.

"Now."

He moves his hand to his right.

"Now."

Left.

"Now."

Above him. "How about now?"

"Yes."

"Excellent." He lifts another card, this one with lettering on it. "I am going to hold this up and slowly back away. Tell me when you can no longer read it." He begins to step backward.

"There."

David smiles. "My, my. Your vision is almost as good as mine, Yusef. I expect the fog to lift and the colors to return to normal within a few hours. However, you must rest. Some sort of incredible healing process has begun, and you must let it run its course." A mock frown. "So rest. Do you hear me?"

"Yes."

"I want to examine you daily for a while to make sure all is well."

"But how, David? How did my vision suddenly return? You said—"

"What I said is that the longer the blindness drags on the less likely it was for you to recover your sight." A warm smile. "I never said it was impossible, Yusef." His smile fades. "Though, to be honest, I had long since given up hope."

"Yes, me too. Have you ever seen this happen before? A recovery of sight like this?"

David shrugs. "Actually, no, never after so much time has passed. But I have lived long enough to have witnessed the body heal in ways that I never would have imagined possible. Many times. The human body is a divine miracle, Yusef, capable of remarkable feats."

"But the dreams. It seemed tied somehow to my dreams."

"Yes. That, I cannot explain." He smiles. "Perhaps it is a question you can pose to Abd al-Salam. A Sufi mystic may be able to shed some understanding on the unexplainable."

"I will." Yusef falls into silent thought. "David?"

"Yes, Yusef?"

"I want to tell Danah myself. Please."

"Well, of course you do. I will not breathe a word." He chuckles. "You should be prepared for tears."

Yusef smiles. "I will. And, David?"

"Yes?"

"Thank you for everything you have done. For the both of us."

A loving, fatherly smile. "You two belong together, Yusef. Everyone can see that. The day you two marry will bring such joy to me and Miriam."

Late that night, the lamp in Danah's room is lit, the door latch locked. Since their betrothal these two have grown considerably bolder. How could they not? Aside from the one night attendant and the four remaining patients, they are the only two who sleep in the Bermejas.

Not surprisingly, Mayya made sure to let slip the mandates of protocol—even if betrothed, Danah should stay with the al-Adanis until the wedding. Danah demurred, of course, insisting that her work as hakim required her presence at the hospital at night. Mayya briefly considered pointing out that the royal physician himself felt no such need, but in the end, she chose to let the matter rest, no doubt because of the recent revelation, which, though it ended with forgiveness and reconciliation, still weighs on her conscience. Miriam watched this exchange transpire with an amused smile, surprised neither by the mother's reminder nor the daughter's response.

The young couple's rooms at the Bermejas are conveniently located on the wing farthest from the ward and the length of a long hallway from the night attendant's desk. Privacy is a beautiful thing to young love.

And thus, their habit is to spend time alone each evening before they head off to bed. They use her room, since it is larger and more comfortable. At first it was every third night, then every two, and now . . . well, yes, every night. They carefully avoid her mattress, instead either standing or sitting. Their desires for each other are wound far too tightly to dare lie together, even fully clothed. One must not tempt fate in such matters.

So, after night prayers, which they have begun saying together, they retreat to her room to talk and kiss and torture each other with light touches over clothing, not necessarily in that order. They have remained chaste. Mostly. Enduring the sweet agonies of pent-up desire has become something of a game for the two of them; a delicious torture.

And so, they stand together in their usual places, face to face, their bodies almost touching, her head scarf off, hair unpinned and down in all its glory. Her arms are at her sides, her eyes are closed. Both of his hands are lovingly exploring her face, feathering over her nose, her forehead, her chin, her eyes, her ears, her lips. Each night he tells her he must memorize every inch of her face. With a smile she indulges his request. By tradition, he speaks no words for quite some time, and then only four, the same four each night. "You are so beautiful." And then on he goes, just gentle, loving caresses as his fingers lightly dance upon her lovely features. This has become something of a ritual for the two of them, one that fills her with so much desire she can barely manage to stand straight.

As with most nights, this stretches on for many minutes. He has already whispered the four magic words. His fingers trace the soft curve of her jaw, then slip down between her moistened lips, exciting a tortured sigh from her, a rush of damp heat, an involuntary bending of knees. And then his hands lift from her face.

She licks her lips and smiles, slowly opens her eyes. Instant concern. "Yusef? Why are you crying?"

His cheeks are wet, his chin aquiver.

"Yusef, what is wrong?" Something about his appearance has changed.

"You are the most beautiful woman I have ever seen."

She smiles. "*Yusef.*" Puzzlement takes hold of her features. Something is different about him. Something.

His eyes are boring into her, plumbing the depths of her sparkling emeralds. He smiles through his tears as he whispers, "I have so longed to see those magical emeralds once again."

"Yusef."

"I love you."

"And I love you."

"Danah—"

"Yes, my love? What is the matter? What is it, Yusef? Tell me." Her eyebrows furl. "What did you mean by 'once again'?"

"I can see you, Danah. I can see you. *I can see you!*" He is beaming through his tears.

"What?" She is bewildered. "What do you mean you can see me? Yusef? *What?*"

"My sight has returned, Danah. I can see again." He points to his eyes. "I can see again. *Danah, I can see again.*"

It takes a moment for this to sink in, and then she spontaneously combusts. A cascade of raw emotion sweeps over her like a tidal wave. She gasps, then cries out, then tries to smile, only to gasp again; then she mewls, then begins to wail, then she bursts into a convulsive jag of heaving sobs she is absolutely powerless to resist. He wraps her in his arms and pulls her tight against him. "Shhh, Danah . . . shhh, darling . . . shhh. Allah the Merciful has cast His Grace upon me. Upon us." Her sobbing intensifies, and he pulls her tighter still. "Shhh . . . Danah . . . shhh . . . I love you . . . I love you, shhh . . ."

Within a few minutes the storm has passed, and they are again kissing and touching, searching each other's eyes now, beaming at the wonderment of it all, then breaking into shared giggles as their giddiness consumes them, then kissing some more, just basking in the miracle of love and the gift of Allah's Grace.

"Tell me everything, Yusef, everything." He does—the dreams, the strange light, the vermillion fog, the rushing to her room only to find it empty, David's examination, all of it. She chortles. "How did you manage not to give it away? All afternoon and all evening, you never once let on that you could see." She smirks. "Wait, David, knew? He and I talked at length, and he never said a word."

Yusef laughs. "Alas, sworn to secrecy."

She chides him. "And you held out for half a day! Through my story about Mama, through dinner, through night prayers. "Youuuu . . ." She hits him in the shoulder, eliciting his bright laugh.

"I wanted to surprise you, Danah. I figured you would never let me just slowly caress your face if you knew that I could see again. I wanted to absorb you inch by inch, feature by feature. Slowly, like seeing you for the very first time."

"That ritual of ours . . . well, I certainly never intend to deny my husband his pleasure." She smiles. "Your willpower is remarkable, sir." A girlish cackle. "I am glad you waited to tell me." Another kiss, deeper now. They part with satisfied sighs, then he cradles her head against his chest. "Danah, I cannot wait to tell Umar. Dear Lord, he will be surprised."

"Yes, he will. He will be so happy for you, and for us. And Faynan." She beams. "And Mama. And Baba. And Miriam. And Samra. And little Ummah. All the children. Dear Lord, they will all be so happy, so very happy."

"Yes . . ." Then a wistful, "If only Uncle were still with us."

Softly, she says, "He knows, Yusef, he does. From his new home, he knew before anyone else did. He knows."

"Yes, I guess he does. Yes." He brightens. "We can go riding together, now, Danah, just you and me. Think of all we can do together, my love. We can ride out into the Vega, anywhere we want to go." They both laugh. He grows animated. "And I can walk about the city with my beautiful wife on my arm. Hakim Amiriya. *The* Hakim Amiriya." She laughs. "And when we are married, we can move into my suite in the Lion Palace. And I can pamper you in any way you like. Jewels, perfumes, silks. I will again be a Prince of the Alhambra. Imagine what that means, Danah." He is glowing with excitement.

Danah lifts her head from chest, her face suddenly troubled. She pulls away from him.

When he sees her expression he is first confused, then concerned. "Danah. What? What is the matter, darling? *Danah?*"

Her eyes have filled once more, and her chin is trembling. She quavers, "Yusef . . . what about our plans? The hospital . . . the Sufi Way. Yusef, what about the Sufi Way?"

"Danah . . ."

A neat tear rolls down each cheek.

He reaches for her, but she takes a step backward. She whispers, "They will put a sword in your hand again."

"*Danah . . .*"

"They will put a sword in your hand again, and you will ride off to battle. Yusef, you will leave me to go fight." She starts to cry.

He steps to her and grasps her shoulders, locks his eyes on hers. "Danah, nothing will separate us. Nothing. *Nothing.*"

Her words are listless. "Do not be a fool, Yusef. When the Christians invade again, and you *know* they will, al-Zaghal will come calling. He will demand your allegiance *and* your sword, Yusef. He *will.* And so will Umar. Your brother will insist that the Falcons ride together as they always have. Oh, Yusef. Yusef, you know they will come calling. They will. What will become of our love, of our children? What?"

"Danah . . ."

She begins to gasp and heave.

She allows him to pull her against him. He wraps his arms around her to calm her, hugs her tightly to him. "Danah, no matter what happens, I will always love you. You know this. Danah, I will always love you. Always."

Her crying ebbs. "Make love to me." Barely a whisper. "Make love to me, Yusef." Her voice is steady now, determined.

"What? Danah, what did you say?"

"I said, *make love to me.* Please."

"Danah."

"Make love to me, Yusef. Please."

"We said we would wait, Danah. Only a few more weeks, my love, and then we will be married."

"No. Tonight. Now. In this room. Make love to me."

He does not respond.

"Yusef. I need you. Make love to me." She slips from his arms, looks up at him. "Kiss me." Her eyes fold closed.

He looks at her, suddenly unsure of his willpower. Then he does kiss her. Slowly at first; a simple brush of his lips upon hers. Then harder, deeper. She pulls him to her. Love murmurs escape from her as somehow the room grows closer, warmer. Their hearts are racing, the sizzle of their passion compressing their chests, making it difficult to breathe.

Their lips part, their eyes now lock together, each pressing their desire upon the other. She begins to tug inexpertly at the buttons on his shirt. He lays his hands upon hers to stop her. Their eyes meet, words are silently spoken, and then he helps her work her way down his chest until his shirt folds open. She eases the shirt off his shoulders, then slides her arms around his bare waist and kisses his chest.

He turns her around so that her back is now facing him. He runs his fingers through her hair, then pulls it to the side, exposing the dark, downy nape of her neck. When his lips touch her skin she softly moans, tilts her neck to expose it more. His kisses roam to her shoulders, releasing a cascade of shivers. She begins to unbutton her physician's robe, one by one. He is nibbling on her ear now, her fingers fumbling as if they are drunk. He pulls back to allow her to finish, then he lifts the robe from her shoulders, allowing it to slide to the floor. She steps forward out of the robe, and he follows, her silk undergarment all that she has left. She unbuttons this, and it slips to the floor. She unpins her bosom wrap and drops it. He reaches around her and pulls her against him. They are both so excited their knees are trembling. His hands rise to slowly trace the sweet curves of her breasts. He steps back to unfasten his trousers and lets them fall to the floor, then he returns to kissing her neck and shoulders.

He stops and turns her, his eyes widening. She guides him to her breasts and has to hiss the pleasure between clenched teeth to avoid crying out. He sweeps her into his arms and carries her to the mattress. Their pupils are dilated into oceans of black, their faces flushed with longing. They lock eyes once more as he pours himself into her emeralds and whispers, "I love you."

511

"And I love you."

"You are a goddess."

She tries to smile but does not quite make it. "Take me. Please." He lays her down. Both of them lie on their sides, facing each other, as they once did that first night together.

"I want you, Danah."

"And I want you, Yusef."

She rolls onto her back, and he follows. A light touch of their lips and they begin to kiss, softly, lovingly, then harder, deeper, as desire consumes them. As he begins to ease himself inside her, he pauses, not wanting to hurt her. She lifts her knees, and with her hands presses his face to hers, kissing him harder, and with a shared gasp he completes their union.

What has been for many months a lidded pot placed upon a bonfire and sealed tight, threatening to explode at any instant, becomes instead a delicious rolling boil. Being joined as one flesh feels so good, so right, that the two of them are afraid to move, wanting the moment to stretch to eternity. He finally can stand it no longer and begins to move within her liquid silk, but slowly, so slowly. A deluge of intense pleasure overwhelms her senses, engulfing her in ways that she never imagined possible. Their lips part to allow her to gasp each time he pushes. She arches her back with each thrust, her hands gripping him, pulling him harder against herself, deeper.

"Look at me. Danah, look at me. Danah."

Brilliant emeralds answer him.

"I will always love you, Danah. Always."

"I love you, Yusef. I will always love you. Always."

She senses the giant wave rise high above them before she begins to feel it, building, cresting, higher, higher still.

He whispers, "I will always love you, Danah. Danah, I will *always* love you. *Always.*"

The wave begins to crash down upon them, the flood of pleasure reverberating like a giant bell struck with a hammer, overwhelming their senses. They both cry out under the desperate crush. Tears immediately come, from both of them, the only imaginable response to the sheer intensity of what they have just experienced. They rest in the sacred stillness for a long while, then finally he eases from her and lies back, pulls her over against him. "I will always love you."

"And I will always love you." She shyly whispers, "Dear Lord, that was intense."

He smiles. "Yes, it was. And beautiful."

"Yes. It was everything I imagined, Yusef, and more. Thank you."

They lie in silence, luxuriating.

She whispers, "Tawhid."

"What?"

"Tawhid. The mystical union sought by all Sufis. It is when the individual is extinguished and union of the human soul with Allah is finally achieved. Abd al-Salam says that the easiest path to tawhid is through the sacred love of another. I never quite understood what he meant by that. But then when Tetta Layla first appeared to me, she told me that she had experienced tawhid when William—Shahab—made love to her. She said that those who experience Great Love can experience tawhid with their beloved." She muses. "In the *Ambrosian Iliad*, the ancient codex that was one of Tetta Layla's most cherished possessions, it says inside the cover, 'Zafir Saffar gives this mahr to his beloved, Rayhana Abi Amir, in the royal gardens of Madinat al-Zahra, the glorious evening of Eid, 29 September 976. Let the Great Love begin.' Tetta Layla said my emerald eyes trace back to Zafir."

He is incredulous. "Madinat al-Zahra? In 976? The Umayyads? *That* is your lineage?"

"It is. And it will be our children's lineage, Yusef. Below that entry, later in the list of al-Khatib marriages, it says, 'Layla al-Khatib of Granada married William Chandon of Brittany, 26 September 1368. The Great Love continues.' Tetta Layla told me that when she experienced tawhid with her William, it was like this: 'No Layla, no William, only Layla *and* William. One body, one heart, one soul.' And now I, too, know what Great Love is. I, too, have experienced tawhid."

"Then both of us have experienced it, Danah. That is exactly what I felt. Allah has cast a great blessing upon us and our love. *Alhamdulillah*." Praise be to Allah.

"Alhamdulillah."

They kiss.

"Stay with me tonight, Yusef."

"Of course, my love."

He rises to turn the lamp flame down to a nub, then gets a blanket to cover them. He spoons her, and they continue to talk for some time before falling asleep; not about the looming war, but about their many blessings, Allah's Grace, forgiveness, Great Love, tawhid, their coming wedding day, the hopes for their children. Finally, they drift off to sleep, she still lovingly cradled in his arms.

The room is still, peaceful, their breathing even and relaxed. The jinn's hour approaches. Danah's pupils begin to flick back and forth in tandem beneath her lids. The lamp flame sputters and pops, rises in height as if by magic, then settles. Brilliant gold sparks alight in the still air like magical fireflies and begin to shimmer and dance.

Danah opens her eyes. Tetta Layla looks up from the letter she is writing. Danah does not want to wake Yusef, so she lies still and speaks quietly.

"I have found Great Love, Tetta Layla."

The old woman smiles. "Yes, you have, dear girl."

"And tawhid."

"Something remarkable to experience, is it not?"

"It is. Beyond words, but impossible to deny."

"Precisely. You have come so far, my cherished girl. A woman now, who knows her history, and is soon to be married to her beloved."

"Tetta, did you know Yusef's sight would return to him?"

The old woman does not answer. "You must make an entry in the *Ambrosian Iliad* I left you, Danah. You can write . . . 'Great Love has returned to the al-Khatibs.' Your son will cherish it."

Danah's turn to smile. *A son.* "I will, Tetta. You *knew* that Yusef would regain his sight." No longer a question.

A coy smile from the old woman. "The Sufis say that if one wishes to be sure of the road they tread on, they must close their eyes and walk in the dark. My dear, there were things that both you and Yusef needed to learn, both about yourselves and about each other, if Great Love was to come to be. That is all."

Danah nods her understanding. "You look tired, Tetta."

The old woman's smile fades. "My time with you has come to an end, cherished one."

Danah replies, "I know," and somehow, she is certain of this in the depths of her heart. "The future terrifies me, Tetta. Yusef will ride to war. Is he to die like William, Tetta? Is he? Tell me, Tetta. Please."

"Danah, you must remember your roots; the blood that flows in your veins. And you must trust your heart and embrace Great Love. Live it, Danah. Nothing else matters in the end."

"But Tetta, what about—"

"Remember your roots, Danah. Trust your heart. Embrace Great Love, and live it. Nothing else matters in the end. I must go now, cherished one. I will miss you so."

"And I will miss you, Tetta. Thank you for all that you have done for us."

"Rejoice for me, Danah. My William waits for me even now. A lifetime is nothing but the blink of an eye to Allah." Her brilliant emeralds stare out into the distance as she smiles. Brilliant gold sparks begin to twinkle in the air around her face. "William, I am coming. William!" She turns to look at Danah one last time. "Rejoice for me, Danah. Rejoice . . ." And then she is gone.

Danah wakes with a deep sense of peacefulness. She manages to turn within his arms without disturbing him. She whispers, "I will remember my roots. I will trust my heart. I will embrace Great Love and live it. Nothing else matters in the end." She kisses him. "*Habib albi.*" Love of my heart.

Yusef's eyes blink open, and he smiles.

To Be Continued

Night of Love

When the sun bowed low before leaving us
I made her promise to visit me
Like another sun the moment the moon
Started its nocturnal voyage.

And she came like bright dawn
Opening a path through the night
Or like the wind
Skimming the surface of the river.

The horizon all around me
Breathed out her perfume
Announcing her arrival
As the fragrance precedes a flower.

I went over the traces
Of her steps with my kisses
As the reader goes over
The letters of a line.

While night slept,
Love was kept awake
By her reed-waist, dune-hips
And face beautiful as the moon.

Part of the night I spent embracing her
And part kissing her
Until the banner of dawn summoned us to leave
And our circle of embraces was broken.

Oh, fateful night!
Hold back the hour of sundering!

Ibn Safr al-Marīnī
(d. 1170 C.E. — Almería)

The Path to Conscious Love

Love is the participation of the human heart in the Creator's Divine Dance. When by Grace two individuals find their intended beloved, love manifests itself in five unique ways: *philia* (their friendship), *eros* (the consuming fire of longing and desire to find completion in each other), *storge* (their sacrificial love for the children they create), *agape* (the emptying love that moves from the wellspring of their hearts outward into selfless service of each other and their world), and *bliss* (the embracing and living out of the vocations to which they have each been uniquely called—their Original Purpose). Loving deeply in this way necessitates an element of suffering for the beloved, so that the Creator's refining fire may purify and strengthen their hearts to prepare them for their Path to Conscious Love.

Great Love—Conscious Love—Unitive Love becomes possible when the Creator's Point of Pure Light and Truth residing within each partner resonates, and their love for each other grows unbounded. Through transforming Grace, as each freely give themselves to their beloved and they become one flesh, each is extinguished in their separateness to join with the other in Oneness, producing a single transformed Heart in union with the Creator. This is Conscious Love, the human embodiment of Divine Love. This new state of transformed being allows the Creator, the perfection of Love, to flow without limit into the now conjoined beloved, so that when their earthly life ends their Conscious Love can be absorbed back into the Creator's Divine Dance to endure for all eternity.

Glossary

Abencerraje *(Banu Surraj)* - Influential Granadine clan of
Maghrebi Berber ancestry; fierce rivals of the Nasrids.

Ablution - Ritual purification with water for Muslims before
beginning prayer or entering a mosque.

Adhan - Muslim call to prayer.

al-Andalus - Lands of Iberia under Muslim rule.

Albayzín - Dense, maze-like Muslim quarter of Granada.

Alcaiceria - Silk market of Granada.

Alcazaba - Walled fortification within an Islamic town. The
castle-garrison, typically in the center of the town on a rise.

Alcázar - Fortified royal palace in an Islamic city.

Arabesque - Form of artistic decoration consisting of surface
decorations based on rhythmic linear patterns of scrolling and
interlacing foliage, tendrils, and lines, often combined with
other elements. Arabesque usually consists of a single design,
which can then be tiled as many times as needed to cover a
wall.

Arab mile - Unit of length between 1.8 and 2.0 *km* (about 1.2
English miles). The Arab mile, the predecessor of the modern
nautical mile, was used by Muslim geographers and
astronomers and was defined as the length of one minute of
an arc of latitude measured along a north-south meridian.

Arquebus - Early muzzle-loaded smoothbore firearm, a precursor
to the musket.

Auto-da-fé - Literally "act of faith," the ritual of public penance of
condemned heretics that took place during the Spanish
Inquisition.

Ave Maria - Literally, "Hail Mary," a Christian prayer.

Baba - Arabic for "Daddy."

Baptism - Christian Rite of Initiation, culminating in the
forgiveness of Original Sin.

Barbican - Fortified tower attached to a castle, but situated
outside the main defensive walls.

Caravel - Small, highly maneuverable sailing ship developed by
the Portuguese for oceanic exploration. A lateen (triangular
sail) allowed it to tack (sail into the wind).

Carmen - Traditional multi-storied home of the Muslim upper
middle class found in the Albayzín (Muslim quarter) in

Granada, typically containing an outer wall, a peristyle courtyard with an interior garden and water features, and often a tower.

Cathay - China.

Cipangu - Japan.

Confession - Christian rite in which a person confesses sins to a priest and is absolved and given penance. Sins can be either venial (minor transgressions) or mortal (soul threatening).

Converso - Literally, "convert" to Christianity.

Coracha - Defensive wall linking a castle with another fortification.

Dhikr - Islamic prayer in which the ninety-nine names of Allah are chanted as a "remembrance" or "invocation."

Dinar - Islamic gold coin.

Dirham - Islamic silver coin.

Dobla - Castilian gold coin.

Edict of Grace - When the Inquisition entered a city, the Edict of Grace was read after Sunday Mass to indicate the types of heresies that would be rooted out, and the consequent punishments. Those who turned themselves in within the Period of Grace (typically 30-40 days), were offered the possibility of reconciliation with the Church without severe punishment.

Emir - Title for local governors within the sultanate.

Eucharist - During Mass, the priest transforms the bread and wine into the real presence (body and blood) of Jesus Christ.

Hadith - Literally, "tradition" in Islam. The collection of the deeds and sayings of the Prophet Muhammad.

Hakim - Honorific for a physician.

Hammam - Muslim bath house.

Harem - Literally, "forbidden." The collection of the sultan's wives, children, and concubines, housed in a section of the palace off limits to all but royal eunuchs.

Hijab - Veil worn by females in certain Islamic traditions to cover their hair.

Jiddo - Arabic for "Grandpa."

Jihad - Literally, "struggle." The word jihad can be used to represent a personal struggle, but more commonly stands for a Muslim holy war.

Jinn - Jinn (or genies) are spiritual creatures. They are mentioned in the Quran and inhabit the unseen world beyond the bounds of the universe visible to humans.

Jizya - Tax paid by foreigners living in Muslim principalities.

Kippah - Jewish yarmulke.

Kufic - Oldest calligraphic form of the various Arabic scripts, developed around the end of the seventh century in Kufa, Iraq.

Lateen - Triangular sail used on a caravel.

Latitude - Lines of latitude run east to west.

Limber - Two-wheeled cart designed to enable the towing of a cannon.

Longitude - Lines of longitude run north to south.

Madrasa - Islamic school.

Maghreb - Western North Africa. Literally, "Berber world," known to Europeans as "Barbary" (as in, 'pirates of the Barbary Coast'). The traditional definition includes the Atlas Mountains and the coastal plains of modern Morocco, Algeria, Tunisia, and Libya.

Mahr - Wedding gift presented by the husband to the bride.

Mama - Arabic for "Mommy."

Mamluks - Military caste in Egypt, which developed from the ranks of slave soldiers.

Maravedis - Castilian copper coin.

Marrano - Literally, "swine." A Jew who has publicly converted to Christianity but continues to practice Judaism privately.

Matula - Glass urine flask used by a physician for diagnosing disease.

Medina - Maze-like center of an Islamic city.

Mihrab - Semicircular niche in the wall of a mosque that indicates the direction of the Kaaba in Mecca, and hence the direction that Muslims should face when praying.

Mocárabes - Honeycomb-like architectural ceiling ornamentation reminiscent of stalactites, which was used to manipulate both sound and light.

Moor - The catch-all, monolithic term used by medieval Europeans to refer to the ethnically and culturally diverse Muslim inhabitants of al-Andalus and the Maghreb, regardless of ancestry. It should be noted that while historical, the word "Moor" or "Moorish," in its modern usage, carries significant baggage, with undesirable racial, ethnic, and religious overtones. Still, it is word that fifteenth-century Christians would have used, and hence is spoken by my characters.

Morion - Iconic iron helmet worn by Castilian troops, usually having a flat brim and a curved comb crest from front to back.

Morisco - Muslim who has converted from Islam to Christianity.

Muezzin - Man who calls Muslims to prayer from the minaret of a mosque.

Mullah - Islamic cleric, educated in both theology and sacred law.

Muraqaba - Literally, "to watch over," in Arabic, and the word used to describe the various Sufi meditation practices. It implies that with meditation a person watches over or takes care of his spiritual heart (his soul), and acquires knowledge about it, its surroundings, and its creator.

Nasrid *(Banu Nasr)* - Ruling clan of Granada. The Nasrid dynasty began with Muhammad ibn Nasr (1232 - 1278 C.E.) and continued until its fall in 1492 C.E. Fierce rivals of the Abencerraje clan of Granada.

Novice - Person who has entered a Christian religious order and is under probation, before taking his vows.

Order of Santiago - Founded in the twelfth century and named for the national patron of Galicia and Spain, Santiago (Saint James), the order consisted of knights of noble descent who had committed themselves to the armed defense of the crown and Christendom.

Portcullis - Strong, heavy iron grating sliding up and down in vertical grooves, lowered to block a gate to a fortress.

Prior - Superior of a monastery.

Qadi - Judge who rules in cases of Sharia Law.

Quran - Literally, "the recitation" (of holy instructions from God, Allah, to the Prophet Muhammad). The Quran is the sacred text of Islam, which Muslims believe to be the revelation of God.

Salah - Muslim ritual prayer, conducted five times a day.

Santa Hermandad - Religious brotherhood of vigilantes, who answered to the crown and served as a local peace-keeping force throughout Castile.

Shabbat - Ritual meal in Judaism marking the beginning of the Sabbath.

Staff of Asclepius - Serpent-entwined staff wielded by the Greek god Asclepius, a deity associated with healing and medicine. The symbol of a physician.

Shofar - Hollowed-out ram's horn that is blown during the Jewish High Holiday period, including on Rosh Hashanah, the Jewish New Year.

Sufi - Sufism is the "mystical" tradition of Islam and focuses on the purification of the inner self as a means for achieving direct and intimate union with Allah.

Tawhid - Literally, the "Oneness of Allah," which is fundamental to the monotheism of Islam. In Sufism, tawhid is not only this affirmation of the indivisible Oneness of Allah, but also an existential *experience* of that unity, when the self is extinguished, and Mystical Union with Allah is achieved.

Tetta - Arabic for "Grandma."

Tikkun Olam - Hebrew phrase meaning "healing the world," suggesting humanity's shared responsibility to heal, repair, and transform the world.

Vega de Granada - Granada's breadbasket. The extensive and exceptionally fertile alluvial plains to the west and south of Granada, converted to irrigated cropland, grazing fields, and orchards. Vast and lush.

Vespers - Evening prayers, generally at six o'clock p.m.; a part of the Christian Liturgy of the Hours.

Vizier - High-ranking advisor to the sultan.

Wali - Formal legal representative of the bride at a Muslim wedding, typically a parent or relative.

Westerlies - Trade winds running east to west across the Atlantic Ocean.

My Reflections

Like both *Emeralds* and *Shadows*, *Fortune's Lament* is a true story, at least in its broad brushstrokes. Unlike for the first two, this territory may be a tad more familiar to American readers, though I suspect most folks remain oblivious to much of this fascinating, nuanced history, beyond perhaps a simple, "In 1492, Isabella and Ferdinand conquered Granada and expelled both the Muslims and the Jews from Spain."

As with all history, there were extraordinary people pulling the levers on both sides, and turns of luck, both good and bad, often sealed the fate of those involved. Women played an exceptionally important role in this history, on both the Christian and the Muslim sides, and I have tried to bring that to light. The iconic Columbus and his consequential discovery of the Americas in 1492 is firmly anchored to this history. The Spanish Inquisition rears its ugly head during this period, which will culminate not only in the expulsion (or forced conversion) of Spain's Muslims, but also in the great diaspora of the Sephardic Jews; two of history's great tragedies. This is rich history indeed, and worth knowing. You would be hard-pressed to identify a ten-year period of time of more consequence to present-day world events.

As I have for each of my novels, I traveled to Spain in May of 2015 to joyfully immerse myself once again in the places I needed to write about—Málaga, Gibralfaro Castle, the Ajarquía Mountains, Vélez-Málaga, the Zafarraya Pass, the Vega de Granada, Alhama, Moclín, Loja, Montefrío, Íllora, Pinos Puente, Santa Fe, the Alpujarras Mountains, Lanjarón, Juviles, Pampaneira, Trevélez, Órgiva, the Ermita de San Sebastián, the Suspiro del Moro, and, of course the Albayzín and my treasured Alhambra. I write these words one day before I take my beloved wife, Maria, to see Granada for the very first time, to celebrate our thirty-fifth wedding anniversary—in style. Yes, a night tour of the Alhambra by full moon is most definitely in store!

A word about 'Great Love.' On one level, my fiction is a warm and loving remembrance of a largely forgotten, though still highly relevant, time and place—al-Andalus. There are many important lessons from Islamic Spain that can (and must!) be gleaned if we desire as peoples of this planet to overcome the brokenness and disharmony that so defines our twenty-first-century milieu. At a deeper level, however, my novels embody my own exploration of the sacred depths of *love*, that simple word with a thousand different nuanced meanings. I have been profoundly blessed in my own life to experience with my beloved, Maria, the Great Love about which I write. Great Love touches everything I think and do . . . and who I am as a writer. After finishing *Fortune's Lament*, I went on my biannual Ignatian silent retreat—eight glorious days this year! In a powerful mystical encounter, I was called to define what exactly I mean by Great Love . . . and did so. I have included my definition at the end of the story for your further reflection. It goes without saying that this is *my* understanding of Great Love. Your definition may well be different. It is important to appreciate, however, that the basic concept of Great Love can be found (by different names) in the mystical traditions of all three Abrahamic faiths. For insights on the topic of love relationships as the pathway to spiritual awakening, I am indebted to John Welwood's *Journey of the Heart: The Path to Conscious Love* (1990) and Cynthia Bourgeault's *The Meaning of Mary Magdalene* (2010).

I originally intended to cover Isabel and Fernando's ten-year campaign of conquest (1482-1492) in one book, but by halfway through it became obvious that this was an impossible goal. This is a big story with many parallel plot threads, and to try to cram it all into one book would have done a disservice to both you and the characters. On the bright side, Danah and Yusef have miles to go before they sleep! In addition, since the next book will begin where this one left off, I will be able to finish it much quicker. Promise! So, hang on tight; there is a remarkable series of events yet to transpire for these two young lovers!

Once again, I humbly lay my heartfelt words at your feet, and hope that you will pick this book up and read it, and in the end, both laugh and cry over this important history, and the story of Great Love that it tells. Enjoy!

Salaam
Shalom
Peace

Language and Pronunciation

To make the book more accessible to readers, diacritics and other accent marks, which abound in both Arabic and Hebrew, have for the most part been omitted. For instance, I use *Quran* instead of *Qur'ān*.

The place names used follow their contemporary (Spanish) spellings. Within the Alhambra, the names of the various points of interest (Court of the Myrtles, Generalife, etc.) follow current usage, since most of the original Arabic names have been lost to history. For the Christian characters, I use their Spanish names (e.g., Isabel and Fernando instead of Isabella and Ferdinand, Colón instead of Columbus). If the characters are not historical (e.g., Danah and Yusef), their names and spellings have an historical basis; meaning, these names were in common usage in late fifteenth-century al-Andalus. Often the Castilians had nicknames for many of the important Muslim characters. For example, Fernando and Isabel would have used the name Muley Hacén for Sultan Abu l-Hasan. This practice was presumably for ease of pronunciation, though it is also likely an indication of the eroding mastery of Arabic by Christians of that era. For clarity, the list of characters shows both names.

I have chosen to have my Muslim characters use the Arabic word *Allah* for 'God' when they speak, but it is important to emphasize that a Muslim uses 'Allah' in a manner that is identical to how a Christian uses 'God' and a Jew uses 'YHWH' (Yehovah, Adonai). That is, the words 'God,' 'Allah,' and 'YHWH' are simply the English, Arabic, and Hebrew words for the Supreme Being shared by the three Abrahamic faith traditions.

Muslim and Jewish words with no conventional English equivalents, as well as Christian words that may be unfamiliar to readers, appear in italics the first time they are used, but not afterward. They are included with explanation in the glossary.

There are times when my characters are speaking Arabic and Hebrew that I use a Romanized phonetic pronunciation to lend dramatic effect. Such phonetic choices are obviously subject to interpretational latitude. It goes without saying that the languages spoken in the late fifteenth century clearly had some significant differences from their modern counterparts, and no attempt has been made to account for these nuances.

Some preferred pronunciations of names and places:

Abd al-Salam (abb-duh ahl-sah-lom)
Abencerrajes (ah-been-cer-rah-hays)
Abu al-Haytham (aboo ahl-hey-thum)
al-Andalus (ahl-on-duh-luze)
Albayzín (ahl-by-zin)
Alhama (ahl-om-uh)
Alhambra (ahl-om-bruh)
Ali al-Attar (ah-lee ahl-ah-tar)
al-Zaghal (ahl-zuh-gall) – rhymes!
Antequera (an-tey-queer-uh)
Atfal (at-fall)
Battal (bah-tall)
Bermejas (bear-may-hass)
Boabdil (boh-abb-dill)
Colón (co-LAHN) – accent on the second syllable
Córdoba (CORE-doe-bah) – accent on the first syllable
Danah (day-nuh)
David (dah-veed)
Ezar (eh-zahr)
Fatima (fah-tea-muh)
Granada (gruh-nah-duh)
Layla (lay-luh)
Loja (low-hah)
Lucena (loo-cen-uh)
Málaga (MAH-la-guh) – accent on the first syllable
Malik (mah-leek)
Umar (ooh-marr)
Venegas (venn-eh-gahs)
Yusef (you-seff)
Zoraya (zor-ray-uh)

The Nasrid Palaces in the Alhambra

The following views of the fifteenth-century Nasrid palace complex within the Alhambra were made from photographs taken of the scaled model found in the Calahorra Tower Museum in Córdoba.

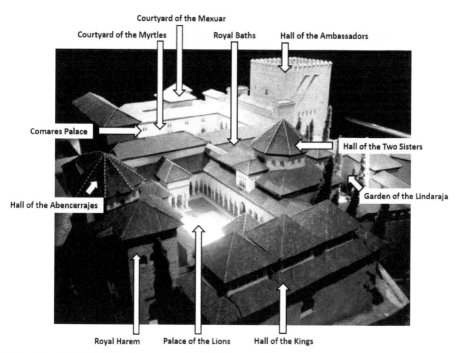

View 1. The Nasrid palace complex looking to the west. The Comares Palace is in the background, and the Palace of the Lions is in the foreground.

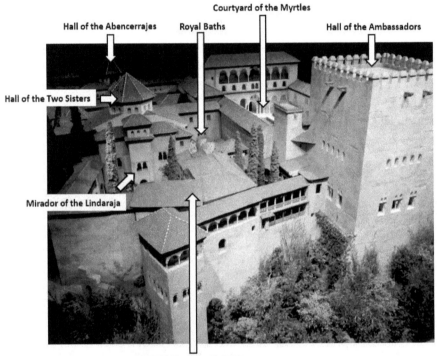

Hall of the Abencerrajes

Courtyard of the Myrtles

Royal Baths

Hall of the Ambassadors

Hall of the Two Sisters

Mirador of the Lindaraja

Apartments of the Lindaraja

View 2. The Nasrid palace complex looking to the south. The Comares Palace is to the right, and the Palace of the Lions is to the left.

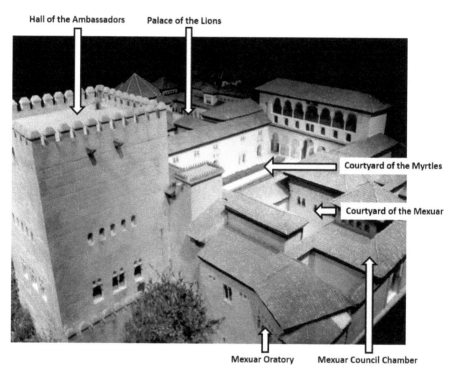

View 3. The Nasrid palace complex looking to the east. The Comares Palace is in the mid-ground, the Palace of the Lions is in the background, and the Mexuar Palace is to the right.

Photographs

Included below are photographs taken on my visit to Spain during May of 2015 when I was researching *Fortune's Lament*. Photographs of the weaponry and armor were made at the Musée de l'Armée in Paris in 2014. Color versions may be found on my website: *http://johndcressler.com.*

Photograph 1. The outer walls of the Alcazaba in Málaga.

Photograph 2. View from the Gibralfaro Castle down the ramparts to Málaga's harbor.

Photograph 3. Entry into the Alcazaba in Málaga. Note the flowing water, reminiscent of the Alhambra.

Photograph 4. View back toward the sea and Málaga from the Zafarraya Pass leading to Alhama and the Vega de Granada.

Photograph 5. View of the gorge at Alhama.

Photograph 6. Looking eastward in the Vega de Granada toward Alhama. The Sierra Nevada Mountains are in the distance.

Photograph 7. Ubiquitous red poppies in the Vega de Granada near Alhama.

Photograph 8. View of the Alhambra from the top of the ridge in the Albayzín.

Photograph 9. View of the Alhambra from the Dar al-Horra, Fatima's carmen in the Albayzín.

Photograph 10. Looking westward at the Nasrid palace complex in the Alhambra.

Photograph 11. View of the Albayzín looking toward the northwest from the walls of the Alcazaba in the Alhambra.

Photograph 12. View toward the south of the Alhambra from the River Darro in the Albayzín.

Photograph 13. View from the River Darro in the Albayzín back toward the east. Note the original city walls of Granada running over the ridge.

Photograph 14. The Justice Gate of the Alhambra, the main entrance to the Nasrid palace complex.

Photograph 15. View of the Hall of the Ambassadors from the Courtyard of the Myrtles within the Comares Palace of the Alhambra.

Photograph 16. Interior view of the Hall of the Ambassadors within the Comares Palace of the Alhambra.

Photograph 17. Courtyard and fountain in the Palace of the Lions of the Alhambra.

Photograph 18. Interior view of the Hall of the Two Sisters in the Palace of the Lions of the Alhambra.

Photograph 19. View in the courtyard of the Palace of the Lions of the Alhambra. The running Arabic header reads, "There is no victor but Allah," the Nasrid motto.

Photograph 20. Example of the original colors used in the elaborate stucco designs of the Alhambra. This well-preserved example comes from the madrasa down in the city proper.

Photograph 21. Example of the remarkable tilework within the Alhambra.

Photograph 22. Original dedication plaque of the Maristan Hospital, a gift from Sultan Muhammad V to the people of Granada.

Photograph 23. An example of a late fifteenth-century "bombard" (cannon). (Courtesy of the Musée de l'Armée in Paris.)

Photograph 24. Example of a bronze French "heavy cannon" dating to the late fifteenth century. This would have been similar to what King Fernando's siege army would have used against the sultan. (Courtesy of the Musée de l'Armée in Paris.)

Photograph 25. Other examples of late fifteenth-century cannons. (Courtesy of the Musée de l'Armée in Paris.)

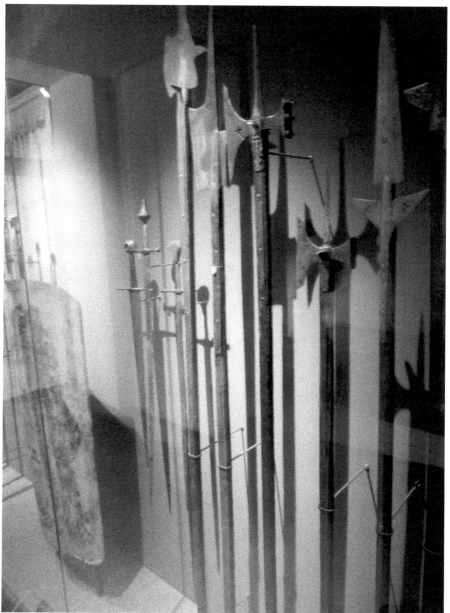

Photograph 26. Examples of late fifteenth-century pikes, battleaxes, and swords. (Courtesy of the Musée de l'Armée in Paris.)

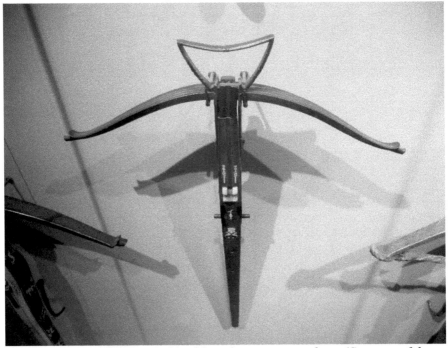

Photograph 27. Example of a late fifteenth-century crossbow. (Courtesy of the Musée de l'Armée in Paris.)

Photograph 28. Examples of late fifteenth-century armor worn by Christian men-at-arms. (Courtesy of the Musée de l'Armée in Paris.)

Photograph 29. Example of a late fifteenth-century mounted Christian knight in full armor. (Courtesy of the Musée de l'Armée in Paris.)

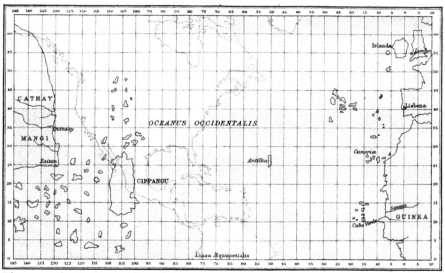

Photograph 30. Toscanelli's 1474 map, which deeply influenced Columbus. Here, Toscanelli's map is overlaid with North America's correct location. (Courtesy of Florida Center for Instructional Technology—from the private collection of Roy Winkelman.)

A Few Historical Footnotes

Historical background of medieval Islamic Spain is included in both *Emeralds* and *Shadows*, and the interested reader is referred to those books for a more general treatment of the 791-year history of al-Andalus. Given that *Fortune's Lament* (and the book that follows) deals with the final collapse of Islamic Spain, there are a few interesting tidbits I'd like to share.

When Queen Isabel set out on her final conquest of Granada in 1482, she appointed Hernando del Pulgar to make an official record of everything that happened. She was well aware of the significance of these looming events on the world stage and wanted to claim them for posterity. Needless to say, this recorded history is told from a Christian perspective, and it predictably focuses on people and events, not personalities and motivations and secret deals. Pulgar's *Crónica de los Reyes Católicos* (1545) laid down in significant detail the happenings of the campaign of conquest, typically in tones flattering to the king and queen (duh!). Still, much of the factual content is, in all probability, correct, at least to the extent that it was known at the time. Like many self-authored accounts of wartime victories, however, exaggeration clearly creeps in from time to time.

Washington Irving made great use of Pulgar in his well-known book, *Chronicle of the Conquest of Granada* (1829), which I employed many a day while writing to check names, places, dates, army strengths, battlefield decisions, and also had constantly in my hands in Spain while on the battlefields, trying to visualize what actually transpired (more on some of those insights in the next book). Unlike with his often-fanciful *Tales of the Alhambra*, when read with a healthy degree of skepticism, I found Irving's *Chronicle* to be an excellent resource for delineating the chain of events leading up to the surrender of the Alhambra in 1492.

Remarkably enough, it takes Isabel and Fernando ten years to complete their conquest of Granada, and I have intentionally altered some events in time (see discussion below). In actuality, the faux-truce between Castile and Granada occurred in 1478, and the battle of Zahara, which to my mind marks the beginning of the war, unfolded on 26 December 1481. Ponce de León's surprise attack on Alhama, which was in direct response to Zahara, happened on 28 February 1482. The Battle of Loja began on 1 July 1482, the Battle of the Ajarquía Mountains on 19 March 1483, and the Battle of Lucena on 20 April 1483. The war would not end until 2 January 1492, when the Alhambra was surrendered to Isabel and Fernando by Boabdil. (The major events from 1483 to 1492 will be told in the next book, which will begin where *Fortune's Lament* ends.)

At the conclusion of all of my research I was left with a nagging question: If Granada had not been so divided between the ruling Nasrids and the aspiring Abencerrajes, between sultan and son, between concubine and wife, would Isabel and Fernando ever have won the war? A great question, and one that we will never be able to answer, of course. As for myself, I tend to believe the answer would have been 'no,' at least for the short term, and certainly not in the early 1490s. At the beginning of the war, Granada arguably had the more formidable army, one that was ably led by highly experienced commanders. She had ample wealth, the vast resources of the Vega and the rest of the kingdom at her disposal, and the vibrant port of Málaga, with its well-established trade routes to furnish needed supplies. In contrast, Castile and Aragon were only recently united, the queen was still limping under the crippling payment to Portugal, and Castile's entrenched noble families often had divergent ambitions not always allied with the court. In the end, internal strife doomed Granada. The final devastating blow was that no one in the Muslim world came to Granada's aid in their time of dire need. At the eleventh hour, she was simply hung out to dry and had no real choice but to surrender.

Fact and Fiction

I think about historical fiction the way impressionist painters think about landscapes—worry less about the specific details of the subject matter, and worry more about capturing its true essence. With my novels, I am attempting to convey the spirit of the people and the time in which they lived, the backstory underlying key events, and the decisions made. I strive to give the reader a sense of what it must have been like to have participated in this momentous historical unfolding.

I am not a trained historian, and I would not claim to be an expert in the many complexities of the nearly 800-year history of Islamic Spain. I have read a lot, yes; and I have reflected a lot, yes; and I have visited the places I write about and absorbed them as an artist might, yes. With that backdrop I then freed my imagination to roam about the time and the places and the people that I write about, which are endlessly fascinating to me. For any specialists I might offend along the way, either with a too-casual use of term A or B, or some unintended distortion of historical fact C or D, or some lack of nuance in matter E or F, all I can say in my defense is . . . forgive me, please! I love medieval Islamic Spain, with all of its quirks and contradictions, with all of its toe-stubbing stupidity and breathtaking sophistication. My central aim with my fiction is quite simply stated—to break open the magic of al-Andalus for a modern audience in a compelling way.

My litmus test for creative license remains the same: Given what we *do* know today from the historical record, is this person's personality, or that person's actions, or a given sequence of events, or a particular plot twist, historically plausible? There are times, as a novelist, when I deliberately choose to bend history in service of the story. After all, telling a good yarn is my first goal. That said, I do believe strongly in full disclosure, and I attempt here to differentiate between what is historical and what is fictional in *Fortune's Lament*.

- As with *Shadows*, my main deviation from history lies in the distortion of time between events in the story. *Fortune's Lament* begins on 6 January 1488, which is very late in the game when laid against the history. I did this to end the next book with the fall of Granada on 2 January 1492, where history places it. Unlike with *Shadows,* I deliberately chose not to use specific dates as the story evolves, but clearly not much more than a year transpires in *Fortune's Lament.* As with *Shadows,* I opted to compress my timeline in places and expand it in others to enhance the pacing and the dramatic weight of events, especially given the urgency of the parallel love story of Yusef and Danah. That said, the key events depicted are all historical.

- Quite a few of the characters in the book are historical, including (in alphabetical order): Aben Comixa, Abrabanel, Ali al-Attar, al-Zaghal, Boabdil, Cárdenas, Colón, the Duke of Medina-Sidonia, Fatima, Fernando, the Great Captain, Isabel, Mendoza, Ponce de León, Santangel, Seneor, Sultan Muley Hacén, Talavera, Torquemada, Venegas, and last but not least, Zoraya herself. Many of these people we know a decent amount about; others very little. For many (most) of the characters, I have fleshed out their personalities in ways that made sense to me and were consistent with their actions, though clearly significant latitude was involved for the lesser-known characters.

- Fernando and Isabel (King Ferdinand and Queen Isabella to American readers) are fascinating characters. I discovered in my research that Isabel was an extraordinarily complicated woman. She was adept at making the ruthless power plays (many on questionable moral grounds) required to take the throne of Castile and secure it, but she was also a woman who insisted she would only marry for love. And she did fall in love with Fernando. She loved her children, while using them as pawns to garner power for Spain on the world stage by marrying them off to help fashion alliances. She was ruthless in prosecuting the defeat of Granada, and it seems to me that she believed that it was her destiny to drive the Muslims out of Iberia once and for all and unite Spain under her rule. Her decision to expel the Jews came later (more on this in the next book). She possessed the respect and deep loyalty of those who fought and died for Castile, and she did not hesitate to ride into the battle lines to spur her troops onward when they were demoralized. She was by all accounts devout in her religious convictions and practice. Regarding my plot thread involving the Great Captain, there is, in fact, a single letter from Fernando that at least obliquely supports this contention, though there is no evidence that I am aware of that she ever consummated that relationship. Fernando, in contrast, is well known to have possessed a wandering eye and had numerous affairs during their marriage, as depicted. Isabel clearly resented this lack of fidelity. I was fascinated to learn that their marriage contract guaranteed that Isabel retain all power over Castile, not to be shared with her husband, and in a great many instances she, not he, was the driver of many pivotal decisions throughout the war. History books seem intent to conveniently omit the fact that she was very often the dominant voice of the two in decision making. For example, she was the one who instructed her army to march to the rescue of Ponce de León at Alhama and to hold it at all costs. Despite her early misgivings, both Isabel and Fernando embraced the Inquisition and used it as a weapon of terror for control of the people of Spain, as well as to fund their incredibly expensive campaign against Granada. It should be said, however, that Fernando was far more enthusiastic than Isabel about the rich possibilities offered by the Inquisition for helping to unify Spain. That said, there have been a great many books that paint Isabel in an overly positive light (my view). As stated above, she was a complicated woman. For a contemporary, more nuanced discussion of this remarkable person, I would refer the interested reader to Downey's *Isabella, the Warrior Queen* (2014), which I found quite insightful.

- Columbus (Cólon) is another fascinating character, and like Isabel, he remains a controversial figure on multiple levels. (This will be explored more fully in the next book.) My depiction of him is historically accurate, even down to his looks and personality. He was by all accounts arrogant and a curmudgeon. It remains contentious as to whether Columbus actually had Jewish ancestry. To my mind, the evidence, while only circumstantial, is compelling, and it certainly lent itself well to the drama of the story, so I went with it. Interested readers are referred to Gerber's *The Jews of Spain* (1992), which lays out the case in detail.

- The storm that ravaged Granada during the celebration after Zahara is historical, as is the sultan's collapse during it (likely from a stroke). The hermit of the Sacromonte's prophesy about the doom of Granada is also historical.

- Fatima was a fascinating woman. She reminds me a bit of Subh in *Shadows*. She was known to be a woman of both beauty and cunning. She was in fact duped by Zoraya and banished to a carmen in the Albayzín, as depicted (Dar al-Horra, which still exists, and is worth a visit). Boabdil was a complicated young man. Needless to say, his role in the following book will be larger. Based upon his actions, I think I have painted a fair portrait of him, as unflattering as it can be at times. Mother and son's relationship with the High Elder of the Abencerrajes is speculative. Here is what we do know: The Abencerrajes did hail from the Maghreb; their leadership was, in fact, wiped out in a dastardly fashion (hence the animus between the two clans); and they were suppressed and went underground to survive, only to join forces with Fatima and Boabdil against the Nasrids. More of their story will be told in the next book.

- The portrayal of the auto-da-fé, the looming Inquisition, and Torquemada (all of which will be treated much more exhaustively in the next book) are all historical. I am indebted to Steven Nightingale's *Granada, Pomegranate in the Hand of God* (2015), for the letter describing an early auto-da-fé in Toledo. I changed some of the wording to make the language flow a little better for a modern reader, but not the facts. The contents are shocking, even today. The Spanish Inquisition was a horrible thing, indeed. The exact number of "heretics" actually burned at the stake is still hotly debated. Thousands, certainly; possibly more. Torquemada was not a nice guy.

- Danah is fictional, though female physicians do have historical precedence in the history of al-Andalus. Yusef and Umar are fictional, although dashing, well-educated, chivalrous knights were clearly commonplace in fifteenth-century Granada. David and Miriam are also fictional, but it should be appreciated that Jews were held in high esteem at Granada's court during this period, particularly in the medical profession. It certainly is plausible that a Jew served as royal physician in late fifteenth-century Granada. Medicine, and medical practice in general, in al-Andalus was far more advanced than that of the rest of Europe, as depicted. Granada led Europe in its use of hospitals to care for their wounded. The Maristan Hospital is historical, and we know Granada had many hospitals at this time, though the Bermejas and Atfal Hospitals are my inventions.

- Granada was celebrated for the beauty of her women, and like the Umayyad princes 500 years earlier, the Nasrid royalty were known to fancy beautiful blonds, presumably because of their uniqueness. They were commonly brought into the royal harem as concubines, later transitioning to wives of the ruling elite. Zoraya is a prominent historical example. Her beauty and skill in the arts of seduction are legendary, as depicted. She was both cunning and ruthless in worming her way into power. That she outmaneuvered Fatima and used her new position to influence both the sultan and court politics is historical. Although we know relatively little about her, she had to have been quite a woman. Her fall from grace is historical, and when she was exiled, she left for Castile, and interestingly enough, converted back to Christianity. The letter from Fatima at the end of the book was added for dramatic impact and is fictional, but seems plausible to me given their relationship. I have not seen any information as to whether Zoraya died of natural causes or not. Perhaps.

- The foods I have served at the Jewish Rosh Hashanah feast are historical. Given the proximity of the Vega, the people of Granada, in particular, ate very well—far better than the rest of Europe.

- As always, I have tried throughout the book to be respectful of all three of the religious traditions represented. The Jews in Granada at this time were reasonably well-accepted members of society and enjoyed many benefits, although they were only permitted to live in the Jewish Quarter of the city and had to pay the jizya tax. Needless to say, this is *not* the period of *convivencia* (coexistence), and the only Christians to be found in Granada in the late fifteenth century were slaves or prisoners. However, converts from Christianity to Islam were accepted in Nasrid society and could rise to high rank. Grand Vizier Venegas is a prominent example. It should be said, as well, that from today's perspective at least, this period does not cast an especially favorable light on Catholicism and Christianity in general. (Martin Luther and the Reformation will not come until 1517.) Sad to say, it will get worse in the next book as the Inquisition takes hold of Spain.

- The battles in *Fortune's Lament* are accurately represented, with a few exceptions. The description of the surprise attack on Alhama is historical, though the presence and importance of the cannons in that battle is fictional, as far as I know. However, the development of pelleted black powder is historical. Its use in creating mobile, small-bore cannons as a tactical battlefield advantage is fictional (though certainly plausible). It is impossible to overemphasize the role that heavy cannons (French bronze cannons, in particular) will play in the ten-year war of conquest. (More on this in the next book.) In fact, heavy cannons profoundly alter the character of battle, and Islamic castles—which were for centuries considered impervious to attack—became instantly vulnerable. After the Ajarquía disaster, Fernando did not engage in any substantive battles without his heavy cannons in tow. The lightly armored Muslim cavalry, in particular, was rightly feared by the Christians for their mobility and quick-strike capability, and man-for-man, the general perception of the times was that the Muslims were better fighters than the Christians. As depicted, armor-plate was standard for Christian men-at-arms, but not for their Muslim adversaries. The Muslims were known for the skill of their crossbowmen, while the Christians tended to prefer traditional archers. Ali al-Attar and al-Zaghal were both seasoned and formidable battlefield commanders, as depicted. Chivalry was very much in action during this period, on both sides, though battles were bloody and brutal, and often merciless, as depicted.

Bibliography

Included below is a selected list of references that I found particularly helpful while writing *Fortune's Lament*. Starred books were especially useful. Additional references on al-Andalus can be found in *Emeralds* and *Shadows*.

[1] J.F. O'Callaghan, *The Last Crusade in the West, Castile and the Conquest of Granada*: University of Pennsylvania, Philadelphia, 2014.

[2] K. Downey, *Isabella, the Warrior Queen*: Doubleday, New York, 2014. ***

[3] R. Fletcher, *Moorish Spain*: University of California Press, Berkeley, 1992. ***

[4] C. Franzen, *Poems of Arab Andalusia*: City Lights Books, San Francisco, 1989. ***

[5] J.S. Gerber, *The Jews of Spain, A History of the Sephardic Experience*: The Free Press, New York, 1992. ***

[6] W. Irving, *Chronicle of the Conquest of Granada*: G.P. Putnam, New York, 1863. ***

[7] M. Jacobs, *Alhambra*: Frances Lincoln, Ltd., London, 2000.

[8] S.K. Jayyusi, *The Legacy of Muslim Spain, Volume 1*: Brill, Leiden, 1992. ***

[9] S.K. Jayyusi, *The Legacy of Muslim Spain, Volume 2*: Brill, Leiden, 1993. ***

[10] H. Kennedy, *Muslim Spain and Portugal - A Political History of al-Andalus*: Addison Wesley Longman, Essex, 1996. ***

[11] J.C. Murphy, *The Arabian Antiquities of Spain—the Alhambra*: Editorial PROCYTA, Granada, 1812.

[12] B. Netanyahu, *The Origins of the Inquisition in Fifteenth Century Spain, 2nd Edition*: New York Review of Books, New York, 1995.

[13] D. Nicolle, *Granada 1492, Twilight of Moorish Spain*: Praeger Illustrated Military History Series, Osprey Publishing, Oxford, 2005. ***

[14] D. Nicolle, *The Moors - the Islamic West, 7th - 15th Centuries AD*: Osprey Publishing, Oxford, 2001.

[15] D. Nicolle, *El Cid and the Reconquista, 1050-1492*: Osprey Publishing, Oxford, 1988.

[16] S. Nightingale, *Granada, Pomegranate in the Hand of God*: Counterpoint, Berkeley, 2015. ***

[17] J. Augustín Núñez (Editor), *The Alhambra and Generalife, in Focus*: Edilux S.L., Madrid, 2000. (Translated by J. Trout.) ***

[18] J. Pérez, *The Spanish Inquisition, A History*: Yale University Press, New Haven, 2005. ***

[19] W.D. Phillips, Jr., and C.R. Phillips, *The Worlds of Christopher Columbus*: Cambridge University Press, Cambridge, 1992.

[20] J.M.D. Pohl, *Armies of Castile and Aragon, 1370-1516*: Osprey Publishing, Oxford, 2015.

[21] W.T. Walsh, *Isabella of Spain, the Last Crusader*: McBride and Company, New York, 1930.

[22] J.N. Wilford, *The Mysterious History of Columbus*: Vintage Books, New York, 1992.

Acknowledgments

My heartfelt thanks to Lawrence Knorr of Sunbury Press (I am now under Sunbury's new fiction imprint, Milford House Press) for opening the door for my fiction. What a wonderful ride it continues to be! I am grateful for the wordsmithery and insights of my amazing editor, Jen Cappello, would like to thank Crystal Devine for typesetting and e-Book generation, and Tammi Knorr for her assistance with all things book-related.

While writing *Fortune's Lament* I fell in love (once again) with contemporary poetry and could not resist the temptation to work into my prose a few special phrases from a few special poets—an homage of sorts. As examples, "vermillioned nothingness" and "green's green apogee" come from Wallace Stevens, and the lurid description of the dead after Loja belongs to Mary Oliver (though she was referring to the sad demise of the buffaloes of the Great Plains). There are others. I will leave it to interested readers to sniff these out.

I am grateful to Cola Franzen and City Lights Books for use of the poems: "Qasida in the Rhyme of Nūn," "Absence," "The Sun," and "Night of Love." Her *Poems of Arab Andalusia* (1989) offers a magical glimpse into the inhabitants of medieval al-Andalus. As beautifully stated in the introduction by García Gómez, the great Arabist and original discoverer and translator into Spanish (1928) of Ibn Sa'īd's lost volume of poetry, *Rāyāt al-Mubarrizin wa-ghāyāt al-mumayyizīn* (The Banners of the Champions and the Standards of the Select Ones—1243), ". . . a few verses can reveal the soul of a people better than long pages of history."

I would like to thank Julia Baumgardt for reminding me of a few things with respect to the use of the words "Moor" and "Reconquista."

I am deeply indebted, as always, to my early readers, that faithful and steadfast test audience who waited so patiently for me to finish: Denise Black, Trish Byers, Angela Como, Doug Davis, Dennis Day, Howard Holden, Tom Jablonski, Roger Meyer, Barbara Nalbone, Acar Nazli, Joanna Ramsey, Patty Smith, Bud Treanor, Lara Tucci, and George Tzintzarov.

Of this list of early readers, several folks deserve special mention because their feedback prompted me to make some important changes to the manuscript. Doug Davis reminded me of when a full moon actually rises, wondered why Yusef's mobile cannons were not used at Loja, and was puzzled about how Boabdil's defeated army got back to Granada after Lucena. Tom Jablonski identified an inconsistency in my chapter ordering. Roger Meyer thought I should enhance the sense of foreboding about Torquemada and the coming Inquisition. Patty Smith found the most typos. Lara Tucci made me rethink my original inclusion of a prologue.

And, of course, my Maria. Needless to say, she inhabits everything I do, as anyone who has shared a joy-filled life with their soul mate can attest. Even more so, however, with my fiction. When I write about love, I necessarily write about Great Love as I have experienced it with her, for thirty-five years now and counting. As with *Emeralds* and *Shadows,* Maria had some strong opinions to offer. Her critique of the first draft of my first chapter forced me to step back a bit (after some serious grumbling on my part—hey, we authors are sensitive creatures!) and see Danah a little differently. She also wondered (euphemism alert!) whether Yusef would have ever written his letter to Danah if there had not been more going on behind the scenes in his psyche (hint: there was!). Maria's advice with my characters, especially the females, is always spot on. No, we didn't agree on everything, my love, but thank you, as always, for helping to make this a better book.

About the Author

John D. Cressler is the Schlumberger Chair Professor in Electronics, and the Ken Byers Teaching Fellow in Science and Religion, in the School of Electrical and Computer Engineering at Georgia Tech, Atlanta, GA, USA. He received his PhD from Columbia University, New York, in 1990. His academic research interests center on the creative use of nanoscale-engineering techniques to enable new approaches to electronic devices, circuits, and systems. Cressler and his students have published over 700 scientific papers in this field, and he has received a number of awards for both his teaching and his research, including the 2010 Class of 1940 W. Howard Ector Outstanding Teacher Award (Georgia Tech's highest teaching honor) and the 2013 Class of 1934 Distinguished Professor Award (the highest honor that can be bestowed on a faculty member at Georgia Tech). He has graduated 52 PhD students in his twenty-five-plus-year academic career.

His previous books include: *Silicon-Germanium Heterojunction Bipolar Transistors* (2003), *Reinventing Teenagers: the Gentle Art of Instilling Character in Our Young People* (2004, for general audiences), *Silicon Heterostructure Handbook: Materials, Fabrication, Devices, Circuits and Applications of SiGe and Si Strained Layer Epitaxy* (2006), *Silicon Earth: Introduction to the Microelectronics and Nanotechnology Revolution* (2009, for general audiences), *Extreme Environment Electronics* (2012), *Emeralds of the Alhambra* (2013, his debut historical novel), *Shadows in the Shining City* (2014, the second release in the Anthems of al-Andalus Series), and *Silicon Earth: Introduction to the Microelectronics and Nanotechnology, 2nd Edition* (2016, for general audiences). *Fortune's Lament* (2018) is the third release in the Anthems of al-Andalus Series, and he is already hard at work on the fourth!

One of Cressler's passions is speaking on technical topics to non-technical audiences, and on non-technical topics to technical audiences, both of which he does quite a bit. The former began in earnest with the release of his book *Silicon Earth* (now in its 2nd Edition), which introduces microelectronics and nanotechnology and their societal impact to general audiences. He also teaches a course on the topic, which is open to undergraduates of all majors and years, and which is required for business majors in the Georgia Tech's Technology and Management Program. Cressler is also deeply interested in the interaction between science and religion, as well as interfaith dynamics, and he recently introduced a new course at Georgia Tech, a first of its kind, titled, "Science, Engineering, and Religion: An Interfaith Dialogue," which is also open to undergraduate students of all majors and years.

He and his soulmate Maria have been married for thirty-five years and are the proud parents of: Matthew (and now Mary Ellen), Christina (and now Michael) and Joanna (and now Eric). They are the doting grandparents of seven little angels: Elena Cressler, Owen Gawrys, Moira Cressler, Amelia Gawrys, Lucy Gawrys, Jane Cressler, and Keira Ramsey. Yup, six little girls and one little boy. Yikes!

Dr. Cressler's hobbies include: hiking in the mountains, mushroom foraging, vegetable gardening, collecting (and drinking!) fine wines, history, cooking, the evolving dialogue between science and religion, IPAs, food as art, and carving walking sticks, not necessarily in that order. He strives for an intentional life filled with social justice ministry, interfaith dialogue, and Ignatian silent retreats. He considers the teaching and mentoring of young people to be his life's work, with his writing a close second.

He can be reached at:

School of Electrical and Computer Engineering
777 Atlantic Drive, N.W.
Georgia Tech, Atlanta, GA 30332-0250 USA

E-mail: cressler@ece.gatech.edu
URL (books): http://johndcressler.com/
URL (research/teaching): http://cressler.ece.gatech.edu/
FB: https://www.facebook.com/BooksByJohnDCressler/

Questions for Discussion Groups

- Were you aware of the events leading up to the final collapse of the Kingdom of Granada, including the role of Isabel and Fernando and the Spanish Inquisition? If not, why not? If so, was your understanding different from what is portrayed here? How?

- For Christian readers, how do you feel about the portrayal of Christianity, especially as it relates to the coming Inquisition? Was Isabel's quest to rid Spain of Muslims justified? Why or why not?

- For Muslim readers, what differences between medieval Islam and modern Islam struck you as interesting? Were you aware of the underlying tensions between the Nasrids and the Abencerrajes in late fifteenth-century Granada?

- I assume that many/most Jewish readers are familiar with the Spanish Inquisition and the coming Sephardic diaspora (a subject of the next book). What wells up within you when you think about his period of Jewish history, especially knowing that the Golden Age of Judaism occurred in tenth- and eleventh-century Islamic Spain (the subject of *Shadows*)?

- Did you know that Columbus was intimately wrapped up in this history? Were you aware that he ran slavers for the Portuguese? How does it strike you that Columbus may have had a Jewish ancestry? Does it matter one way or the other? Would it have mattered to Isabel and Fernando? Why? Why not?

- How would world history have played out if Columbus had not discovered the new world under the Spanish flag? What if he had been sponsored by Portugal? Or Italy? Or England? Would it have made a difference?

- What did you like most about Danah? Least? What did you like most about Yusef? Least? How did Danah and her mother's relationship evolve over time? Did Danah's experience of love play in that change? How?

- Dreams play a significant role in *Fortune's Lament*. Do they in your own life? Have you ever had an incredibly vivid dream experience that seemed real? What?

- How we see things, or fail to, also plays an important role in the book. Can you give some examples? Can you relate to any of them?

- The sultan is manipulated by the women around him. They use their sexuality, among other things, as a tool of control. Is this a valid means for securing a place at the table of power when it would be otherwise denied to them? Why? Why not?

- How does medieval battle differ from modern warfare? Are their similarities? Is there a place for chivalry in warfare? Honor? Why? Why not?

- Were you aware that in the late fifteenth century, cannons were about to change the nature of warfare? Was it for better? For worse?

- Was the use of armor by Christian knights a good thing? A bad thing? Did vanity play a role? How?

- Was ransom by captured knights a good practice? Why or why not? Are there permissible reasons for denying ransom?

- What did you know about the Spanish Inquisition before reading this book? Has your impression changed? If so, how? Did anything about it surprise you? What?

- Why do you think Sultan Muley Hacén rejected Boabdil as his heir? What would the consequences have been for Granada if he had been treated as the rightful successor?

- What are your impressions of 'The Path to Conscious Love' shared at the end of the book? Have you known 'Great Love' in your own life? When? With whom? How did it differ from what Danah and Yusef experienced? How was it the same?

Author's Note:

Ten percent of the author's proceeds generated by sales of this book will be donated to organizations committed to opening dialogue and fostering mutual understanding, respect and tolerance between Christians, Muslims, and Jews.

Lightning Source UK Ltd.
Milton Keynes UK
UKHW021827280920
370666UK00009B/2062